Locked Room Murders
Second Edition, Revised

Paul Halter books from Locked Room International:
The Lord of Misrule (2010)
The Fourth Door (2011)
The Seven Wonders of Crime (2011)
The Demon of Dartmoor (2012)
The Seventh Hypothesis (2012)
The Tiger's Head (2013)
The Crimson Fog (2013)
(Publisher's Weekly Top Mystery 2013 List)
The Night of the Wolf (2013)*
The Invisible Circle (2014)
The Picture from the Past (2014)
The Phantom Passage (2015)
Death Invites You (2016)
The Vampire Tree (2016)
(Publisher's Weekly Top Mystery 2016 List)
The Madman's Room (2017)
**Original short story collection published by Wildside Press (2006)*

Other impossible crime books from Locked Room International:
The Riddle of Monte Verita (Jean-Paul Torok) 2012
The Killing Needle (Henry Cauvin) 2014
The Derek Smith Omnibus (Derek Smith) 2014
(Washington Post Top Fiction Books 2014)
The House That Kills (Noel Vindry) 2015
The Decagon House Murders (Yukito Ayatsuji) 2015
(Publisher's Weekly Top Mystery 2015 List)
Hard Cheese (Ulf Durling) 2015
(Crime Fiction Lovers Top 10 Nordic Noir 2016 List)
The Moai Island Puzzle (Alice Arisugawa) 2016
(Washington Post Summer Book List 2016)
The Howling Beast (Noel Vindry) 2016
Death in the Dark (Stacey Bishop) 2017
The Ginza Ghost (Keikichi Osaka) 2017
The Realm of the Impossible (Anthology) 2017
Death in the House of Rain (Szu-Yen Lin) 2017
The Double Alibi (Noel Vindry) 2018
The 8 Mansion Murders (Takemaru Abiko) 2018

Visit our website at: www.mylri.com or
www.lockedroominternational.com

Locked Room Murders
Second Edition, Revised

By Robert Adey
Edited by Brian Skupin

Locked Room Murders

SECOND EDITION, REVISED
Library of Congress Cataloguing-in-Publication Data
Adey, Robert C.S. ; Skupin, Brian, editor
Locked Room Murders, Second Edition, Revised

For information write Locked Room International at:
pugmire1@yahoo.com
Or go to:
www.lockedroominternational.com
www.mylri.com

Contents

Dedicated to Sue Adey with grateful appreciation for her permission to publish this Revised Edition.

Editor's Preface to the Second Edition—Revised

Locked Room Murders by Robert C.S. Adey was originally published in 1978 by Ferret Fantasy. An updated and enlarged second edition was printed by Crossover Press in 1991. Both of these editions had small print runs and are difficult to obtain.
This volume is a new version of the 1991 second edition. It contains the same material as that edition, with corrections to typographical and other errors, and the addition of new sources for many items. It does not contain any new entries.
A Supplemental Edition of *Locked Room Murders*, with all-new entries, will be published by Locked Room International in 2019. To have a complete Locked Room reference, you will require the original Crossover Press edition from 1991 (or this edition), plus the new Supplemental Edition. The Supplemental Edition will have many new entries, and for the first time will add items from film, television, comic books, and other media.

The categories of changes included in this Revised Edition are:

- The inclusion of new editions of novels or short story collections that were previously difficult to obtain at a reasonable price, such as Stacey Bishop's *Death in the Dark*, now reprinted by Locked Room International, or *The Complete Curious Mr. Tarrant*, now available from Crippen & Landru. For easily available works, such as those by Agatha Christie, I've followed Adey's original guidelines by not attempting to list all editions.
- Correction of typographical errors
- Correction of errors of fact
- Addition of details where information was clearly missing
- Removal of unnecessary spoilers (plot giveaways)
- Inclusion of real author names in some cases of pseudonyms or house names
- Identification of some items as non-impossible despite being listed here. See for example #263.
- Additional magazine and anthology reprints of short stories. As opposed to new editions of novels (see above), I felt it worthwhile to list these. In the first and second editions,

Adey specified that with respect to short stories "the older and more obscure magazine publications have, of necessity, been omitted, and where many reprints have taken place, only those considered important or readily accessible have been included." In this edition I have added more magazine publications, even the "older and more obscure," because, thanks to the Internet, many are now more easily obtainable. In addition, I've frequently found stories lurking in my collection that I didn't realize I had, since the magazine or anthology appearance wasn't listed in Adey. I hope these additional listings will be of benefit to other readers who may find buried treasure on their own bookshelves.

There are over 200 changes herein, ranging from the typographical (there was a spelling error in the title of *Murder in Millennium VI*, by Curme Gray) to the minor (the entry for the detective's name was missing in James Hadley Chase's *This Way for a Shroud*) to the critical (errors in the solutions to Leroux's *The Mystery of the Yellow Room* and Sladek's *Invisible Green*; see below for details). Here is a sample list of some of the more notable corrections or additions:

- New editions of previously rare and scarce novels and short stories that have been issued in book form by specialty publishers such as Crippen & Landru, Locked Room International, and Ramble House. Note these are new *editions or appearances* of works already appearing in the 1991 edition, not new *entries*.
- Inclusion of short story appearances in anthologies published since 1991, such as *The Realm of the Impossible* (Pugmire and Skupin, Locked Room International, 2017) and *The Big Book of Locked-Room Mysteries* (Penzler, Black Lizard, 2014). (These are the only "updates" included in this corrected edition. Although this is contrary to the idea of this being only a corrected edition as of 1991 without updates, these were included to avoid the need to add duplicate entries in the forthcoming Supplemental Edition.)
- Correction to T*he Mystery of the Yellow Room*, by Gaston Leroux. The original solution to the locked room problem was incorrect, and the problem of the impossible disappearance, which was missing, has been added.
- Correction of the solution to the first problem in John Sladek's *Invisible Green*, and the inclusion of the other two

problems and solutions, which were missing.

- Clarification to the solution of the classic "The Mystery of the Fabulous Laundryman" by Ben Hecht.
- Correction to the solution to the second problem in *The Hollow Man (The Three Coffins)* and the solution to *A Graveyard to Let,* both by John Dickson Carr.
- Identification of the writers of five of the short stories originally listed as by "Anonymous". To avoid renumbering the entries, these entries remain in the Anonymous section, with the author's name added, and the author's name has been added to the alphabetical listing with a reference to the numerical story entry.
- "The Pawns of Death", as by the house name Robert Hart Davis, was written by Bill Pronzini and Jeffrey M. Wallman.
- Correction of the spelling of Anthony Lejeune's book *Mr. Diabolo*. (To any who have wasted time searching for this book based on the misspelled title ("Mr. Diablo") I assure you this fine book is readily available at online used booksellers.)
- Change in Adey's original Introduction to clarify the paragraphs about Anthony Abbott.
- Change in Adey's original introduction to distinguish *The Woman in the Wardrobe* as being the work of Peter Shaffer alone (as noted in Anthony Shaffer's autobiography: *So What Did You Expect?*, Picador, 2001).

There were some categories of errors found that I chose not to fix, because to do so would have required re-numbering the Problems. I prefer that the numbering in the original edition and this edition rename the same. Examples of this type of error include cases where the alphabetical listing of titles was incorrect, or where a story written by Carter Dickson was listed under John Dickson Carr.

The publisher of Locked Room International, John Pugmire, and I both had the opportunity to meet and work with Bob Adey on various projects. Bob was kind, generous with his time and correspondence, and extremely learned. John and I are pleased to be able to make this seminal work of his available again.

Brian Skupin, New York, July 2018

Preface to the Second Edition

I MUST TURN the clock back thirty years for my first venture into detective fiction and the origins of this book. In 1958, on a school holiday abroad and temporarily out of reading material, I reluctantly borrowed a couple of detective novels from a well-meaning friend. I discovered that they were no ordinary detective novels, but two first-class locked-room mysteries written by John Dickson Carr, the maestro of the form. One, *The Judas Window,* is perhaps the best locked-room mystery ever written. It was not surprising that by the time I'd finished the two books—and that took no time at all!—I had developed an addiction that has lasted thirty years and shows no sign whatsoever of abating.

A small paperback library quickly grew. Carr and his contemporaries were well represented, and I found to my delight that there were many other writers who had written impossible-crime stories. As time passed, my book collection grew enormously. The paperbacks with which I had started were gradually replaced by ranks of hardbacks, and piles of books and magazines filled every available space.

My first love remained, however, the locked-room problem, and in 1972 I hit upon the idea of listing all the impossible-crime novels and short stories known to me. The list was published in fan magazines on both sides of the Atlantic, and the response was absolutely staggering. I received letters from readers and collectors all over the world, containing all manner of new information. I was not alone in my addiction.

Sixteen years have passed since that original list was published, and the flow of information has never really stopped. It has been sifted and sorted, annotated and indexed. I have spent more hours on it than I care to remember, and must offer in advance a warning that the length of time over which the book has been written has inevitably led to inconsistencies in style as it evolved.

A book of this kind is never complete, so if your favourite locked-room story is not to be found among these pages—or, for that matter, one that is not your favourite—then please write and tell me about it. I hope in the meantime you will be enlightened . . . and enlivened.

Bibliographical details

For each item I have tried to record the first British and United States book publications and/or recent magazine appearances. The object is to give the readers sufficient sources for them to be able to locate and read those items in which they are interested. Some of the older and more obscure magazine publications have, of necessity, been omitted, and where many reprints have taken place, only those considered important or readily accessible have been included. It should also be noted that when a book has been published in both the United States and in Britain in the same year, I have listed the British details first, followed by the U.S. details. This should not be taken to indicate the correct chronology of publication.

New titles

Titles new to this edition—over 700—are designated with a ✓.

The facts

The complexity of some of the plots is such that no brief synopsis can do full justice to them. In such cases, the reader has been recommended to go to the source itself.

The sources

There are sure to be many items I have omitted. If you know of any that should have been included, I would be pleased to hear about them.

Abbreviations

Certain abbreviations have been used in this bibliography: AHMM = Alfred Hitchcock's Mystery Magazine; EQMM = Ellery Queen's Mystery Magazine; F&SF = The Magazine of Fantasy and Science Fiction; MSMM = Mike Shayne Mystery Magazine; SBL = Sexton Blake Library.

Publishers' names

Many publishers' names have been shortened. For example, Bobbs-Merrill = Bobbs; Chapman & Hall = Chapman; Carroll & Graf = Carroll; Chatto & Windus = Chatto; Herbert Jenkins = Jenkins; New American Library = N.A.L.; New English Library = N.E.L.; etc.

Acknowledgments

No book of this type is ever written single-handed. My thanks go to those friends and fellow enthusiasts who have provided so much in the way of information and encouragement. Among those on the international list—and strictly in alphabetical order—are:

The British Isles: Jack Adrian, Russell Aitken, Bill Berry, John Boyles, Geoff Bradley, Miss A. Clarke, Ken Cowley, Richard Dalby, Phil Harbottle, Robert Hoffman, Don Ireland, Nick Kimber, the late Vernon Lay, Steve Leadbeatter, Tony Medawar, Barry Pike, Robin and Marion Richmond, Don Rudd, Ralph Spurrier, Andrew Stephens, Peter Tyas, and Neville Wood.
Canada: Ed Demchko and John Dobson.
Eire: John Curran.
France: Jacques Baudou, Roland and Danièle Lacourbe, and Jean-Jacques Schleret.
Philippines: Alan L. Mescallado.
Sweden: Jan Broberg.
The United States of America: The late Bob Aucott, Bernard Beauchesne, Jon Breen, Bob Briney, Mark Brosche, Barbara Buhrer, George Cloos, Joe Commings, Ted Dukeshire, Bill Dunn, Chris Fredericks, David L. Godwin, Greg Goode, Doug Greene, the late R. W. Hays, Paul Herbert, Ed Hoch, Al Hubin, Henry Jewell, Jr., Amnon Kabatchnik, Ed Kessel, Richard Lackritz, Steve Lewis, Frank McSherry, Jeff Meyerson, Mike Nevins, Bill Pronzini, Lee Sheldon, Chet Skinder, Peter Stem, Jean Stilwell, the late Howard Waterhouse, Dan Webb (of Old Sleuth Books), and Don Yates.
Finally, particular thanks go to:
George Locke, without whose invaluable contribution this stage would never have been reached;
Chris Lowder, who has prodded and chivvied, encouraged and enthused;
David Smith, who first introduced me to locked-room mysteries;
Derek Smith, who has been a veritable mine of information;
and my three partners in crime in this collaborative publishing enterprise (surely the furthest flung foursome ever): Bill Deeck, Steve Stilwell, and Bruce Taylor.

Additional acknowledgments for the Second Edition, Corrected:

Michael L. Cook and Stephen T. Miller for their **Mystery, Detective, and Espionage Fiction Index**, Garland, 1988
William G. Contento and Martin Harry Greenberg for the **Index to Crime and Mystery Anthologies**, G.K. Hall, 1991

Phil Stephensen-Payne, for his excellent online resource **Philsp.com**, incorporating the above two works with corrections and additions.

Introduction

1 The Victorians 1838—1889

The first fully fledged detective story was published in Philadelphia in 1841. The April issue of *Graham's Magazine* contained "The Murders in the Rue Morgue" by Edgar Allan Poe. It was reprinted in 1843 in *The Prose Romances of Edgar A Poe,* the first and only number of a projected pamphlet series, again published by Graham; in 1845 in *Tales;* and on many subsequent occasions.

"The Murders in the Rue Morgue" was not, however, just the first detective story—complete with sleuth, faithful confidant, and solution by ratiocination. It was also the first impossible-crime "locked room" detective story. The mystery concerned the murder of a woman in a room from which there was no apparent means by which the murderer could have escaped after committing the deed. All the doors and windows were locked or secured on the inside, and the keys were in position on the inside of the doors. The chimney offered no means of escape and was in any case blocked by the victim's body. The crime seemed impossible—yet it had happened, and detective Chevalier Dupin was able to work out the solution.[1]

In an essay entitled "A Ghost Haunting America" from that excellent miscellany *In the Queen's Parlor,* Ellery Queen listed no fewer than six major innovations that Poe had made in "The Murders in the Rue Morgue." One, he said, was the introduction of "the motif of the hermetically sealed room." For once, however, Queen was wrong, because, contrary to popular opinion, Poe did not invent the locked-room mystery.

That honour goes instead to J. Sheridan Le Fanu, the famous Irish novelist.[2] In the November 1838 issue of the *Dublin University Magazine,* which he was later to own and edit, he offered anonymously

---

1. Many years later a detailed criticism of Dupin's solution was made by Laura Riding in which she demonstrated the impractability of it. This must, however, be considered a mere quibble that in no way detracts from the high quality of the theory behind the solution.
2. It should not be overlooked that the literary ancestor of the detective story was the Gothic novel, and that ghostly visitants and inexplicable disappearances were part of their stock in trade. I do not consider that they are relevant to this study, nor would it be practicable for me to cover what is essentially a different subject. However, it should be borne in mind that many of them contain similar problems, if sometimes imprecisely stated and often solved via a secret passage. Several of the better-known items—see, for instance, Hoffman and Radcliffe—are covered in this book.

"A Passage in the Secret History of an Irish Countess." This eerie tale, which was later reprinted in *The Purcell Papers,* opens with a description of an unsolved locked-room murder of years before, and during its telling the heroine almost succumbs to the same fate. She survives, however, to reveal the secret, and it was certainly not the same solution as Dupin was to propound three years later.

Le Fanu was not the man to waste a good idea on one short story, and it is therefore no surprise to find the same locked-room problem, with fresh characters, in "The Murdered Cousin" in *Ghost Stories and Tales of Mystery* (Dublin, 1851), a volume of great rarity. Even then he had not finished with the gimmick, for in 1864 he wove the same locked-room situation into *Uncle Silas,* his fifth novel. *Uncle Silas* is, in the judgment of most of his followers, the best or one of the two best novels that he ever wrote—the other being *The House by the Churchyard.* It features, aside from the locked-room mystery, one of the most memorable villains of any book, the hideous and sinister Madame de la Rougierre, and is the one mystery novel from the Victorian era that I can recommend without any reservation whatsoever.

Le Fanu, something of a recluse, continued to write mystery novels until his death in 1873, but only one other involved a locked room and then in not so direct and clear a manner as *Uncle Silas.* This second book *is A Lost Name* (three volumes, 1868), and in true Le Fanu style was preceded by two embryonic short-story forms. Not at all a bad novel, but nowhere near the standard of *Uncle Silas.*

We do not know whether Poe stumbled across Le Fanu's first locked-room story and saw where it could be improved by the introduction of Dupin, or whether those two fertile minds hit upon the idea independently. The locked-room theme was here to stay, however, and in the years that immediately followed there was no shortage of writers to try their hands at the new plot. Many are as obscure as the magazines in which their stories saw print, but three at least between 1852 and 1862 were literary figures of some stature.

The February 1852 issue of Dickens's magazine *Household Words* contained Wilkie Collins's story "A Terribly Strange Bed," in which the hero escaped a dreadful fate in a locked room and led the gendarmerie to the diabolus ex machina that almost cost him his life. The story was collected in *After Dark* (1856), is much anthologised, and has been the subject of at least two plagiarisms. The first, H. Barton Baker's "An Odd Tale," appeared in what today must be regarded as a fairly obscure periodical, the Christmas Annual for 1883 of the *Belgravia Magazine,* although it was popular enough in its heyday. The second, as Michael Innes has pointed out, was "The Inn of the Two Witches" by none other than Joseph Conrad.

"The Diamond Lens" by Fitz-James O'Brien was first published in the January 1858 issue of the American magazine, *The Atlantic Monthly.* The author, born in Ireland but settled in America, devised a clever new way of leaving the locked room intact but incorporated it into a tale that has become a science-fiction classic. Although O'Brien did not employ a detective, his great friend Thomas Bailey Aldrich did so in 1862—the year in which O'Brien was killed while serving with the Unionist forces. Aldrich's *Out of His Head* is a fine episodic novel featuring perhaps the first of the truly eccentric detectives, Paul Lynde—although not the first American variation on the locked-room theme, as Ellery Queen would have it.

The locked-room mystery had thus got off to a tremendous start. It was inevitable that there would be a hiatus. It came in fact after Aldrich's book. For a number of years the combined literary imaginations of Britain and America could make no further contributions of real merit. The picture was different in Europe, however.

A little earlier, in Germany of 1858, a strange book entitled *Nena Sahib* was published. The author was a native German named Hermann O. F. Goedsche, who used the pen name Sir John Retcliffe. The book is long and rambling, displays a strong bias against the British Raj, and the mystery content is slight. There is, however, a well-documented locked-room murder, with a solution so simple and appealing that a real murderer adopted it in 1881. (He was caught, nonetheless.) *Nena Sahib* has never been translated into English, but a brief synopsis can be found in the May 1973 issue of *The Armchair Detective.*

France has always produced writers with a liking and flair for tales of impossible crime. In those early days it was left to two French authors to set the pattern. The first was Eugène Chavette with a novel entitled *La Chambre du Crime (The Bedroom of the Crime)* (1875). A long, wordy novel of typical Victorian complexity, it does not rate as a masterpiece but surely deserved the English translation it never received.

Later, in 1888, there was "The Black Pearl," a short story by Victorien Sardou, the famous farceur. In this, the detective is faced with a theft from a locked room instead of the almost obligatory murder. The solution provided is scarcely credible but lacks nothing in ingenuity, and the story moves along nicely under the charge of detective Cornelius Pump. It can be found in translation in *Three Romances* (Brentanos, 1888) and in *The Lion's Skin* (Vizetelly, 1889).

2 The Victorians 1890—1901

The nineties arrived, to witness the locked-room mystery develop from the sensational story that it had been for thirty years into something sharper and more sophisticated. During those years the fiction magazines had been sprinkled with a strange array of diabolical death traps, weird poisons, and fiendish machines. But the year 1892 saw new stars emerge, glowing bright with new ideas.

Israel Zangwill had for some time been fascinated by the locked-room problem and concocted a new way of solving it with a subtlety that had been lacking in most of the earlier writers. The book that Zangwill produced was *The Big Bow Mystery.* The action was set in the East End of the London that the author knew so well. The "Bow" of the title is a district in London and has nothing at all to do with archery. The book was a marked success on all counts, but Zangwill thereafter concentrated on the novels of Jewish life that made his reputation.

The other major piece for 1892 was written by Arthur Conan Doyle and featured the maestro, Sherlock Holmes, in "The Adventure of the Speckled Band." The Holmes stories were at the height of their popularity and Doyle was at the height of his powers when the story appeared in *The Strand Magazine.* It is an ingenious tale in which the great detective faces a locked-room problem and, in Dr. Grimesby Roylott, one of his most evil and dangerous adversaries.

In later years Holmes again faced impossible crimes, and not only in the unrecorded but often-reported disappearance of a certain Mr. Phillimore. Doyle also made other notable contributions and innovations to the saga of the apparently inexplicable without calling on the services of the great detective. "J. Habakuk Jephson's Statement" preceded "Speckled Band" by four years and was Doyle's attempt to provide a rational explanation of the most famous sea mystery of all time, the *Marie Celeste.* The ship had been found abandoned in the year 1872, and ever since men have taxed their brains to explain the sudden disappearance of her crew. Doyle's story was the earliest of a number of yams attempting to do the same thing. The most interesting and successful of those that followed were "The Yellow Cat" by Wilbur

Daniel Steele (1918) and "The Episode of Torment IV" in C. Daly King's *The Curious Mr. Tarrant.*

Doyle's "The Story of the Lost Special" appeared in the August 1898 issue of *The Strand Magazine.* The mystery concerned the disappearance of a train from a restricted stretch of railway line. Although there was no detective directly involved, the case excited sufficient interest for "an amateur reasoner of some celebrity" to make one of his most famous remarks: "It is one of the elementary principles of practical reasoning, that when the impossible has been eliminated the residuum, however improbable, most contain the truth." Since then, trains have been disappearing at regular intervals, under the skilful hands of such engineers as Leslie Lynwood, Melville Davisson Post, August Derleth, and Ellery Queen. For what appears to be a fairly limited area in which to work, it is amazing how many authors have successfully handled the vanishing-train problem.

The Victorian era also saw the publication of stories illustrating other forms of impossible crime. W. H. Stacpoole's "The Manufacturer" (1897) and L. T. Meade and Robert Eustace's "Mystery of the Strong Room" (1899) involved thefts under impossible conditions. Meade, usually with Eustace, was in fact responsible for a number of short stories of impossible crime, and they can perhaps be seen at their best in the adventures of John Bell, a man of private means, for whom the weird and the mysterious had an irresistible fascination. Bell's cases were collected *in A Master of Mysteries* (1898), with a final investigation charted in *The Oracle of Maddox Street* (1904). Eighteen ninety-eight also saw the publication of *The Adventures of an Engineer* by Weatherby Chesney—in fact Cutcliffe Hyne—containing "The Horror of the Folding Bed," concerning the inexplicable disappearance of an inventor and its gruesome denouement. Equally gruesome was the explanation offered by Ada Cambridge in her tale of disappearance, "At Midnight" (1897), further proof, if it were needed, that Victorian ladies had a rather macabre side to their nature.

The Victorian era closes with a look at three novels, each a little out of the ordinary.

Frank Barrett was one of the many writers of the time who produced sensational literature that incorporated mystery, drama, detection, and even science fiction in heady brews with titles like *The Woman of the Iron Bracelets* and *The Strange Mark.* One book that managed to combine all those elements was *The Justification of Andrew Lebrun.*

Published in 1894, it is one of the earliest examples of an impossible disappearance of a person from a locked or guarded room— in this case a laboratory—and the victim was the beautiful daughter of the strange scientist who used the laboratory. The solution is quite fair. Altogether an unusual and interesting book.

The impossible problem in Louis Zangwill's *A Nineteenth Century Miracle* (1897) was also unusual. Zangwill wrote under the name of "Z.Z.," and in this, his only mystery, he set his detective—Mr. Warlock-Jones—the task of discovering how it was possible for a man to have been swept overboard from a channel packet yet, simultaneously, to have fallen through the skylight of a London studio as a drowned corpse. The book falters at points, and the detective enters into a somewhat unnecessary romantic intrigue. The solution, almost inevitably, is disappointing, but the ingenuity of the problem has never been bettered.

If Zangwill's detective bore a name similar to that of the most famous sleuth ever—and the Holmes fraternity seems unaware of this fact—then there is surely a strange sense of precognition about Fred M. White's "Who Killed James Trent?" *(Pearson's Weekly*, 1901). There is nothing special about the story itself or its impossible crime, and I have so far failed to trace a book version of this magazine serial. What singles it out, however, is that the prolific Mr. White named his detective Jasper Carr and described him as a rising young novelist. An amazing coincidence and an unconscious pointer to an author yet to come.

And so the Victorian era, which had begun so well with Le Fanu and Poe, closed equally well with Israel Zangwill and Doyle. The locked-room theme had regained its early stature because once again it was patronised by authors of real literary talent, writers who knew how to write.

3 The Second Phase 1902—1929

The Strand Magazine, which had already contained so many good stories and was to publish many more, presented in the March and April issues of 1903 a story that was in its way something of a milestone. Locked-room mysteries had previously tended to take place, not unnaturally, in locked rooms. Samuel Hopkins Adams, however, was an author who saw that locks, keys, fastened windows and doors were not essential to the problem. Thus, he set the scene of "The Flying

Death" on a sandy Long Island beach and created the locked-room effect by having the victim's body found in an area of sand unmarked by any prints except the victim's. The problem was not how the locked room was left intact but how the murderer escaped from the sandy area without leaving tracks. Adams was certainly not the first to use the device—Maxwell Scott had used it ten years earlier in a story written for the juvenile market—but he was the first to use it in a formal adult detective story. Furthermore—shades of Le Fanu!—he later expanded it into a full-length novel of the same title onto which he grafted a finishing touch of fantasy.

Other writers soon followed Adams's lead. By strange coincidence, 1906 produced Alfred Henry Lewis's "The Man Who Flew" (U.S.) and Oswald Crawfurd's "The Flying Man" (English), both concerning murder in or disappearance from snow-covered areas. Crawfurd's tale, incidentally, is the only one to make use of the English legend about a mysterious figure, Spring-Heeled Jack, endowed with the ability to leap prodigious distances.

A year earlier, in 1905, a series of six stories appeared in *The Penny Pictorial Magazine,* a very poor relation of the better-known and more expensive publications then available such as *The Strand* and *Pearson's.* These stories, although sadly of a quality commensurate with the magazine that featured them, are noteworthy as the earliest endeavour to write a series of stories where the link is the impossible nature of the problems stated. Truth to tell, the problems are generally a great deal more ingenious than the solutions provided, but they have a definite historical importance and were well worth the book publication they eventually received in 1980 from the adventurous British publisher Ferret Fantasy. The authors, incidentally, named Mansfield, wrote under the strange pseudonym of Huan Mee, and had other, and better, stories to their credit.

A major figure to take the stage at this time was an American journalist bearing a French name and, like Le Fanu, of Huguenot stock. Jacques Futrelle was the first major prolific exponent of the impossible-crime story. He began in 1905 by facing his omniscient detective, Professor S.F.X. Van Dusen—the "Thinking Machine"—with "The Problem of Cell 13," reputedly the most anthologised story of all time. The Thinking Machine solved the mystery of how a man could escape from a guarded prison cell by the simple expedient of performing the miracle himself.

This brilliant tour de force was followed by many other stories in which Futrelle displayed in full his talent for inventing new types of impossible crimes or putting ingenious fresh twists on the old ones. He killed his victims by sucking all the air from their bodies ("The Case of the Mysterious Weapon"), made roads and houses disappear ("The House That Was"), removed a child from unmarked snow ("Kidnapped Baby Blake, Millionaire"), made various other objects and people vanish, and in one of the very best of the tales, "The Phantom Motor," succeeded in spiriting away a car by the most plausible of means. Futrelle perished, alas, with *The Titanic* in 1912, and we can only speculate on what further leaps he might have induced the detective story to take had he lived.

The novelists of the period were also busy. Melvin L. Severy produced in *The Darrow Enigma* (1904) the earliest example of death by an invisible agent in full view of an audience. Then, in 1905, a young journalist named Edgar Wallace founded his own publishing firm, The Tallis Press, and published his first novel, *The Four Just Men.* The story was left deliberately incomplete, and readers were invited to guess at the correct solution, a prize of £500 being offered to anyone who got it right. The mystery to be solved was the murder of the British Foreign Secretary behind locked doors, and it is perhaps a reflection on the British reading public of the day that so many guessed correctly that the publishing house got into severe financial difficulties. Wallace was, however, a very resilient man and survived to write many more books, including several impossible-crime stories.

The Mystery of the Yellow Room, one of the classic locked-room novels, appeared in 1907 in France and was translated into English in 1908. It was written by a French journalist, Gaston Leroux, who created in Joseph Rouletabille a durable detective of his own profession. The locked-room method was a new one, but what really distinguished Leroux's book was the author's journalistic flair for the dramatic. Leroux took every opportunity to break up the text by such gimmicks as reported passages from newspapers and question-and-answer sessions. Chapter headings such as "In which we begin not to understand" and "A man has passed like a shadow through the shutters" point the way to the sharp exclamatory dialogue and the rapidly moving plot that were his stock in trade. John Dickson Carr considered *Yellow Room* to be the best locked-room mystery ever written. However true that may be, there is no denying Leroux's influence on his American follower.

Rouletabille starred in several other novels. None was so successful as *Yellow Room,* although *The Perfume of the Lady in Black* (1909) is a better book than some reviewers have allowed.

Nineteen ten saw the emergence of another of Carr's favourite detectives, the ubiquitous Hamilton Cleek, the "Man of the Forty Faces," created by Thomas Hanshew. Cleek's adventures were collected in several volumes of short stories. Although they have no great literary merit, there is enough pace and drama to carry them through. The later novels, under the byline of Mary E. and Thomas Hanshew, should be avoided.

Ellery Queen has referred to the following year, 1911, as that of the miracle book. The volume that was the object of Queen's adulation was *The Innocence of Father Brown* by G. K. Chesterton, already a famous literary figure with such fine books as *The Club of Queer Trades* to his name. Father Brown, whose adventures were first published in *Cassell's Magazine,* ultimately appeared in five volumes of short stories. It was tempting to include them all in this survey. There is a degree of strangeness, if not quite impossibility, about most of the cases undertaken by the unassuming, often intuitive, priest. It has, however, been possible to isolate twenty-one of the tales—plus two or three about detective Horne Fisher—to illustrate the sheer ingenuity of Chesterton's mind: ingenuity that found several different angles for the locked-room problem, spirited people away with consummate ease, and, in "The Dagger with Wings" from *The Incredulity of Father Brown* (1926), provided the most satisfying environment and solution to the tracks-in- the-snow problem.

The next author to claim our attention had none of Chesterton's brilliance but was very prolific. Carolyn Wells's first detective novel, *The Clue,* had been published in 1909 and had marked the debut of her private investigator Fleming Stone. It was in her third book, *The White Alley* (1912), that she first tried her hand at a locked-room novel, and the exercise obviously appealed to her. Over the next thirty years she wrote more than twenty impossible-crime novels, most of them concerning murders behind locked doors. Sad to say, the plotting was no more imaginative or original than the detectives she employed, but Miss Wells has her place as the first novelist who made a specialty of locked-room problems.

The Great War then intervened, and there was a temporary stemming of the flow. But the war years were not entirely barren; two novels in particular are noteworthy, although both are quite obscure. The first was C. Guise Mitford's *The Hidden Mask* (1914), published by the failing house of Greening. In addition to a locked-room problem, the book was distinguished by the presence of a monstrously evil criminal who eventually got his long-overdue deserts.

W. A. Mackenzie's *Flower o' the Peach* (1916) is memorable for its odd detective, the rather common, aitch-dropping "Slow and Sure" Jackson. An additional point of interest is that Jackson solved the locked-room mystery because of his knowledge of a nineteenth-century French short story "Le Verrou" ("The Bolt") by Armand Sylvestre. No English edition exists of this early locked-room story.

During those war years there also appeared a new type of impossible crime that marked man's growing involvement with the motor car. The problem concerned a car that was driven by a man who was then discovered to have been dead for some little time, and was investigated by Mason Brant in "The Moyett Case" from *The Strange Cases of Mason Brant* by Nevil Monroe Hopkins (1916). The trick has been repeated at least five times—but not necessarily with the same explanation—by John Dickson Carr, Nigel Morland, J. E. Gurdon, Arthur Upfield, and Ed Hoch.

The war ended in 1918, the same year in which Melville Davisson Post's *Uncle Abner* was published in the U.S. Uncle Abner, as a detective, is quite rightly regarded as one of the Big Four, together with Dupin, Holmes, and Father Brown. Abner's most famous case was "The Doomdorf Mystery," a locked-room story handled with considerable ingenuity and available in a host of anthologies. Post had once before written a locked-room murder story, in *The Nameless Thing* (1912), and was to do so again in "The Broadmoor Murder" (1929), but "The Doomdorf Mystery" is the one that is most remembered.

For a number of years after Uncle Abner there were no major impossible-crime innovations, although many meritorious tales were written. In 1921 Eden Philpotts, the Devonian writer, produced *The Grey Room,* the best known of his detective novels and certainly the best locked-room mystery that he wrote. By comparison, *The Marylebone Miser* (1926) is an awful affair. Will Scott also wrote a number of creditable stories, of which "The Vanishing House" from *Giglamps* (1924) is a personal favourite and only the second—after Futrelle—to deal with a particularly fascinating problem.

The Layton Court Mystery, published anonymously in 1925, introduced the world to that affected young gentleman, Roger Sheringham, in the author's earliest essay into impossible crime—if you overlook the unfortunate *Death in the House* (1939). The author was, of course, A. B. Cox (Anthony Berkeley; Francis Iles).

An unusual publishing history attends the two books of Charles Chadwick, an American. The earlier, *The Cactus* (1925), a locked-room mystery, was published only in America; the second book, *The Moving House of Foscaldo* (1926), was published only in Britain. Both are well worth reading.

It was also in 1926 that a strange publishing coincidence occurred. Two books were published, both independently, with titles so similar and plots not so dissimilar, that one of the authors, Douglas Timins, felt it necessary to include a special note about the matter at the front of his book. His novel was *The Phantom Train,* while the other book, by Ruth Alexander and Arnold Ridley, was *The Ghost Train,* founded on a play of the same name that has remained famous far longer than either of the books. Indeed, it had a further London revival in the 1970s.

Walter S. Masterman, now largely forgotten, wrote several successful impossible-crime novels. *The Wrong Letter* (1926) and *The Curse (Crime) of the Reckaviles* (1927) were both locked-room mysteries, but Masterman then moved on to the more sinister world of giant toads and other misshapen monsters. The nastiest story of those was undoubtedly *The Border Line* (1936), although strangely enough *The Baddington Horror* is a straight detective novel with no impossible overtones at all.

Strange also is *Werewolf* (1928), the only book by Charles Lee Swem and an attempt to rationalise the age-old man-into-wolf legend. Later examples of the same theme include Norman Berrow's *It Howls at Night* (1937) and Max Dalman's *Vampire Abroad* (1938).

The major detective novelist that America had long awaited finally arrived in 1926. Writing as S. S. Van Dine, Willard Huntington Wright's first book, *The Benson Murder Case,* was immediately acclaimed as a masterpiece. Van Dine peopled his books with characters who were the archetypes for so many more to come: Philo Vance, the drawling dilettante amateur detective; S. S. Van Dine, the virtually invisible Watson; John F.-X. Markham, the intelligent but quite unsuccessful—in terms of solving the crimes—district attorney; and Sergeant Heath, the dumb, almost comically dumb, cop. Their second case, *The "Canary" Murder Case* (1927), was almost as good as the first, and in some respects it might be said to be better since it involved an ingenious locked-room problem. Van Dine repeated the locked-room mixture in *The Kennel Murder Case* (1933) and hit upon an original impossible-crime idea in *The Dragon Murder Case* (1934) in which he had a man disappear from a swimming pool under constant observation. In neither of those later books, however, did Van Dine approach the form that he had shown in the Canary case.

Two other novels that are highly recommended were published about this time, each from the pen of an unprolific author. *The Medbury Fort Murder* (1929) by George Limnelius is a straight locked-room novel that rises above most of its many contemporaries by virtue of the excellent writing and characterisation. Excellent also, but for rather different reasons, is *Into Thin Air* (1928) by Horatio Winslow and Leslie Quirk. Who was the Salem Spook and how did he pull off his amazing disappearing tricks? How did he manage to walk right out of gaol? And were those his charred remains that were eventually buried in a remote graveyard? This, believe it or not, is just the prologue, and throughout the book the Salem Spook continues to put in his impossible appearances. Add to this a magnificent detective named Dr. Klotz and another calling himself The Great Galeoto, and you will understand the reason for my recommendation.

While I'm in the mood to allot praise, I must also mention two short stories that appeared in 1928. "The Tea Leaf" by Edgar Jepson and Robert Eustace had originally been published in 1925 in *The Strand Magazine,* and was included in the Sayers-edited *Great Short Stories of Detection, Mystery and Horror.* It is a particularly ingenious and original locked-room problem investigated by a woman detective. Equally ingenious is Nicholas Olde's "The Invisible Weapon." The volume in which it appeared, *The Incredible Adventures of Rowland Hem,* is the most surprising omission from *Queen's Quorum.*

The decade closed with the first of a series of impossible-crime novels written by Anthony Wynne about detective Dr. Eustace Hailey. This first book, *The Room with the Iron Shutters* (1929), was a fairly standard locked-room mystery, but Wynne soon established himself as the champion of another form of impossible crime: death by invisible agent. Time after time he confronted his able, if plodding, detective with situations in which the victim was killed, quite on his own, in plain view of witnesses who were unable to explain how a close-quarters blow could have been struck. Wynne also wrote several competent "tracks in the snow" novels.

4 The Maestro

The book began: "—and not least foul among these night-monsters (which may be found even in our pleasant land of France) is a certain shape of evil hue which by day may not be recognised, inasmuch as it may be a man of favoured looks, or a fair and smiling woman, but by night becomes a misshapen beast with blood-bedabbled claws." Capturing the reader's attention with those first lines, the author went on to relate the tale of a macabre impossible murder in which the victim's head had been completely severed from his body in a room that, witnesses swore, he alone had occupied. The year was 1930, the author was John Dickson Carr, and the book was *It Walks by Night.* The maestro of the impossible crime had arrived.

Carr's last book was published in 1972, and for most of the intervening years he was the foremost exponent of the impossible-crime novel. He invented scores of ingenious new ways of working the old tricks as well as several brand-new problems of his own. But it is not just this virtuosity that places Carr head and shoulders above the rest. There are his sense of the dramatic and his ability to create atmosphere, his flair for humour coupled with his flair for the macabre, his ability to write. Dorothy L. Sayers has said, "He can create atmosphere with an adjective (and) alarm with an allusion. In short he can write." A perfect summing up.

I have no intention of including a biography of John Dickson Carr in this history as Doug Greene's new book covers that ground in exemplary fashion. It is sufficient for my purposes to note that Carr was born in America, spent a formative year or two in Paris, and then settled for a time with his English wife in her native land: a cosmopolitan life upon which to draw.

It is the Paris interlude that was responsible for the setting of that germinal *It Walks by Night.* Most of the action took place in the gaming rooms above a popular restaurant, Fenelli's, and the detective was juge d'instruction Henri Bencolin. With his small moustache and black beard, Bencolin has often been described as saturnine. He has always seemed a sinister character and somehow too vague to make the same impact as Carr's later detectives. Moreover, the impossible crime in *It Walks by Night* was not of the top flight. It depended too much upon the second-floor plan given in the front of the book—which in all fairness is marked "very important"—and a measure of coincidence. Despite those minor flaws, however, it was an excellent debut, and there was much better to come.

Bencolin remained Carr's detective for the next three books. The last of them, *The Waxworks Murder* (U.S. title *The Corpse in the Waxworks)* (1932), had no impossible crime at all but did have the atmospheric setting of the Gallery of Horrors in a wax museum. Carr's liking for waxworks and dummies was demonstrated in several later stories. Of the two other books, *Castle Skull* (1932) was a very odd affair set in Germany and a direct throwback to the Gothic school of more than a hundred years before. The remaining book, *The Lost Gallows* (1931), is probably the best of the bunch, involving strange events at the Brimstone Club and clever variations to both the locked- room theme and the problem that Hopkins had first propounded nearly twenty years before: How can a dead man drive a car?

In the same year as *The Waxworks Murder,* Bencolin's sidekick, Jeff Marle, returned to his native Pennsylvania, which was also Carr's own state. Many reviewers have commented on how often Carr has placed himself in his books in the role of naive young American observer. Marle (or Carr) found himself embroiled in a most unpleasant poisoning case, *Poison in Jest.* A minor impossible conundrum was posed, and very quickly solved, but the book is chiefly memorable because it is the first time that Carr introduced a generous measure of comic relief, on this occasion in the person of Pat Rossiter, a clumsy amateur detective.

Rossiter proved nevertheless to be an extremely capable investigator, and there are those who regret that he was never heard of again.

In 1933 under the pseudonym of Carter—or Carr—Dickson, the young maestro created another detective who survived only a single book: John Gaunt in *The Bowstring Murders.* The locked-room problem was the soundest so far, but the detective was unremarkable and was overshadowed by the peevish old man who was one of the victims and who surely provided the basis of the character of one of Carr's two main detectives.

Carr had tried out three different detectives in his first six books, but had not been completely satisfied with any of them. However, in the same year that Gaunt solved his only recorded case, Carr produced under his own name the detective who was to stay with him for almost thirty years.

"The old lexicographer's study ran the length of his small house." The old lexicographer in question was Dr. Gideon Fell, whom Carr described as "very stout and (walking), as a rule, with two canes. (A) big mop of dark hair streaked with a white plume and a large, round, ruddy face and a (bandit's) moustache somewhere above several chins. He wore eyeglasses on a broad black ribbon, a slouch (or shovel) hat and a plaid shawl (or cape)." Most of these particulars of Fell, "the great goblin figure," are taken from his first adventure, *Hag's Nook.* Fell, whom Carr had modelled on G. K. Chesterton, started his career on a high spot. Hag's Nook was a location in Lincolnshire where witches used to be hanged. Later it had become the site of a prison of extremely bad repute. It was this disused and crumbling prison that served as a most effective setting for a gruesome murder carried out under the steady gaze of witnesses. The book is the first in which Carr found his touch in all respects, and Dr. Fell caught the murderer in a magnificent debut.

Dr. Fell's next two adventures, *The Mad Hatter Mystery* (1933) and *The Blind Barber* (1934) were perhaps a little inferior to the first. The impossible-crime element was slight in the former and totally absent from the latter. The settings, however—the Tower of London and a transatlantic liner—were well chosen and ideal vehicles for Carr's talents.

Carr's second major detective made his bow in 1934 under the Carter Dickson pseudonym. Sir Henry Merrivale (H.M.) had, according to Carr, a little of Winston Churchill in his character. He was, if anything, even more eccentric than Fell, with his large bald dome, his odd expressions, and his delight in dressing up. Officially he was attached to the War Office but somehow managed to involve himself in a succession of weird cases, the first of which was *The Plague Court Murders.* Plague Court was an old house in London with evil associations, and the action began with a ghost-laying session that became something else when the priest was found shot to death in a locked room. The sense of the macabre in this book is as strong as Carr ever achieved. Not least among the contributory factors were extracts from contemporary journals written at the time that Plague Court had earned its reputation. (The same device had been used, less effectively, in *Hag's Nook,* and would be used by Carr again.) The solution was, of course, eventually discovered by the "old man," as Sir Henry frequently referred to himself, but he was in this book in a more sombre mood than in many of the later ones. *The Plague Court Murders* is probably the strongest first book about any series detective, and it is small wonder that such critics as Torquemada and Howard Haycraft have named H.M. as their favourite detective.

For a number of years Carr produced two or more books per annum, and the majority of them featured either Fell or Sir Henry. At first there is no doubt that Sir Henry had the upper hand. After *The Plague Court Murders* came a run of five books, each of excellent standard: *The White Priory Murders* (1934), *The Red Widow Murders* (1935), *The Unicorn Murders* (1935), *The Punch and Judy* (or *Magic Lantern) Murders* (1936), and *The Peacock Feather Murders* (or *The Ten Teacups)* (1937). They have magical titles—something Carr never failed to provide—a selection of two locked-room murders, a death by invisible agent, and death in a pavilion surrounded by unmarked snow. If I had to pick out a favourite, it would be *The Unicorn Murders* where H.M. tangled with a master thief who would have been quite at home in one of Chesterton's tales.

On the other hand, Fell, after three good opening books, found himself in *The Eight of Swords* (1934), which was not nearly so good, and in *Death-Watch* (1935), which has so complex a plot that it has to be read just a little too closely for comfort. However, with Fell's next case Carr produced what is, in my opinion, one of the best books that he wrote.

The Three Coffins (1935), or *The Hollow Man,* as it was more imaginatively called in Britain, was set in London. Its background, however, was that part of Central Europe that still believed in vampires and werewolves, for vampires were being mentioned in connection with an impossible crime that was committed in snow-covered streets by a killer who left no tracks. Fell was, of course, called in but could not prevent a second impossible death that occurred in a locked and guarded room. It was fortunate for us that he could not prevent it, because his subsequent investigation led him to discourse at length on the subject of locked-room murders, in a chapter that has often since been reprinted as a separate essay in itself—the first, and most interesting, essay on the subject. The book concludes with a stunning revelation in which Fell neatly dovetails all the pieces.

Fell's next two cases were hardly likely to match the previous one. The earlier of them, however, *The Arabian Nights Murder* (1936), is distinguished by being Carr's most able demonstration of how to start off a book with a series of inexplicable and apparently unconnected incidents that are eventually shown to be constituent parts of the same whole. The other book, *To Wake the Dead* (1937), was not above average.

Nineteen thirty-seven also saw the publication of two novels in which neither Fell nor Merrivale appeared. *The Four False Weapons* was Bencolin's last adventure and a rather complicated affair. *The Burning Court,* however, was far more interesting. There were two impossible crimes—one in a sealed crypt—and at the end of the book a hint of the supernatural as we are left to wonder whether Edward Stevens' young wife was in fact a reincarnation of Marie de Brinvilliers, the famous poisoner.

These two books show Carr merely warming up for his next, a novel that is regarded by many as the best locked-room mystery of all times, *The Judas Window* (1938). Jimmy Answell visits Mr. Avory Hume to ask for his daughter's hand in marriage. He is received in Hume's study-cum-trophy room—Hume was a toxophylite—but blacks out. When he comes to, he finds himself locked in with Mr. Hume, who has been shot dead with an arrow. This is the opening gambit, and the bulk of what follows is taken up with a thrilling courtroom scene in which Answell is defended by none other than Sir Henry Merrivale. H.M. and Carr display tremendous form and rescue the defendant from what seems an almost indefensible position.

The prewar period continued with Fell investigating *The Crooked Hinge* (1938) and *The Problem of the Wire Cage* (1939) and Sir Henry *Death in Five Boxes* (1938) and *The Reader Is Warned* (1939). Not a weak book among them, but all eclipsed by Fell's handling of *The Problem of the Green Capsule* (1939)—again I find the British title *The Black Spectacles* more enticing. In this a man is killed by a substituted poisoned chocolate, but even though the event had been filmed none of the witnesses could say precisely what happened. A tour de force, although there is no impossible crime as such, and aptly subtitled "The Psychologists' Murder Case."

In 1939 also, Carr collaborated with John Rhode in *Fatal Descent* (British title *Drop to His Death),* in which murder took place in a closed lift. Several authors had already attempted this problem—Alan Thomas in *The Death of Laurence Vining* (1929) had been the most successful— and the Carr/Rhode version lacked the pace that Carr would surely have employed on his own. Rhode had already written a number of impossible-crime novels under two names, but only *Invisible Weapons* (1938) rose above the pedestrian.

One final book has to be mentioned at this point, although not published until 1940, and that is Carr's first short-story collection, the Carter Dickson *The Department of Queer Complaints.* Most of the stories feature Colonel March of Scotland Yard and originally appeared in *The Strand Magazine* in 1938 and 1939. Several are classics that have been anthologised over and over again.

In his first ten years the amazing Mr. Carr had written twenty-eight solo novels and a volume of short stories, plus a long study of the Sir Edmund Godfrey mystery. Each book involved closely detailed plotting, filled out to almost 300 pages per book with the other ingredients that Carr had at his command. Even more amazing is the fact that there wasn't a totally bad book among them, while two were all-time greats and several others came very near to that status.

During the war Carr was involved in other, vital, work and wrote a great many broadcast plays. Inevitably his book-production rate suffered, but even so he managed to write five under his own name—including four Fells—and seven more adventures of Sir Henry Merrivale. Once more the H.M. tales call for special mention: *Nine—and Death Makes Ten* (1940) *(Murder in the Submarine Zone),* a very good atmospheric piece about a blacked-out wartime transatlantic sea crossing; *Seeing Is Believing* (1941), in which the victim is stabbed to death by a woman in a hypnotic trance; *He Wouldn't Kill Patience* (1944), a hermetically-sealed-room problem that was a more than effective answer to a challenge laid down by Clayton Rawson, and *The Curse of the Bronze Lamp* (1945) (originally in Britain as *The Lord of the Sorcerers),* a vanishing-lady problem resolved most satisfyingly.

After the war Carr continued to write, but not as prolifically, and rarely with quite the flair of the prewar days. There were eight more Fell books, of which *He Who Whispers* (1946), *The Sleeping Sphinx* (1947), and *The House at Satan's Elbow* (1965) are good examples of the later Carr period, and six more H.M. novels. One of the latter stands out and is in my view the best thing Carr did after the war. The book is *A Graveyard To Let* (1949), and the main problem, superbly handled, was the same one that Van Dine had posed many years before: How can a man vanish from a small swimming pool into which he has just been seen, by many witnesses, to dive. Sir Henry, in America for the first time, is magnificent, and Carr's solution far more ingenious than that provided by Van Dine.

Three more volumes of short stories also appeared, one of which, *The Third Bullet* (1954), contained the title novelette and several shorts collected from prewar magazines. The best story by far was, however, a postwar offering that had won a special award of merit in EQMM's second annual contest. Queen predicted, quite rightly, that "The House in Goblin Wood" (1947), an eerie story in which H.M. investigated a disappearing girl, would become an anthologisers' favourite. He described it as "almost the complete manual of detective story theory and practice."

Nineteen fifty saw Carr embark on a new course. *The Bride of Newgate* was a mystery set in Regency London and was the first of twelve historical mysteries that he went on to write. The first and the second, *The Devil in Velvet* (1951), were by far the best, although the second contained no impossible crime at all, and indeed in most of the later examples the impossible-crime element was slight.[3]

In his postwar period Carr wrote twenty-nine novels. They and the wartime output were generally not up to the standard of his best prewar books, but a large number were nevertheless very good indeed and far better than most of the books that other authors were writing. It was only after Sir Henry bowed out (1954) and Dr. Fell was on his last case (1967) that the words began to outweigh the action and the plots became unnecessarily tedious and tortuous. Nevertheless we have a legacy of excellent mysteries for which to thank Mr. Carr.

5 Other Golden-Age Contributors

The decade preceding the Second World War is often referred to as the Golden Age of detective fiction. It was also the Golden Age of the impossible crime. Carr was, of course, the dominant figure, but there were many other authors who devised murders in impossible circumstances, and some of them did so very successfully.

The American cousins who wrote as Ellery Queen had begun their career in 1929. Their sixth book was *The American Gun Mystery* (1933), in which a gun was mysteriously spirited away from a sportsdome.[4] The impossible-crime element in the Queen book was fairly tenuous, but

---

3. In 1934, under the name of Roger Fairbairn, Carr wrote a historical novel, *Devil Kinsmere.* In fact, *Most Secret* (1964) is a virtual rewrite of the 1934 book.
4. For another impossible crime involving a rodeo, see Hal Pink's *The Rodeo Murder Mystery* of 1941.

two books later, in *The Chinese Orange Mystery* (1943), Queen presented the public with a fully fledged locked-room mystery. Queen's critics have pointed to flaws in the construction of this book, but, however that may be, the locked-room problem is a very clever one and so, too, was the book's major clue of everything in the murder room being turned back to front.

But no criticism should be levelled at Queen's next excursion into the impossible, *The Door Between* (1937). A better novel than *The Chinese Orange Mystery,* it had a locked-room problem with a solution just as ingenious and rather more plausible and comprehensible. The characterisations were also stronger and the book generally better written.

High praise, too, for Queen's novelette "The Lamp of God," from *The New Adventures of Ellery Queen* (1940), a most satisfying treatment of the vanishing-house problem and further proof—together with later books and stories—that Queen could handle the impossible-crime problem very well, when he chose.

Jonathan Latimer is not nearly as well known as he ought to be. Starting in 1934 with *Murder in the Madhouse,* he produced a number of cheerful detective novels, full of the wisecracking wit that is normally associated with Chandler and Hammett. Three of them—*Murder in the Madhouse, Headed for a Hearse* (1935), and *The Dead Don't Care* (1938) —starred investigator William Crane in impossible-murder cases, two of them in locked rooms. A much later novel, *Black Is the Fashion for Dying (The Mink-Lined Coffin)* (1959) is equally good, but in a more serious vein.

Two more authors from the thirties who are unjustly shrouded in obscurity are American Clyde Clason and Australian Max Afford, both of whom wrote their fair share of impossible-crime novels and both of whom first saw print in 1936. Indeed, Max Afford's detectives, Jeffery Blackburn and Chief Inspector Read, tackled virtually nothing but impossible crimes. The best of them is the carefully plotted, cleverly explained *The Dead Are Blind* (1937). Only the unremarkable qualities of the detectives prevent the series from being top flight. Far more memorable is Clyde Clason's mild-mannered little professor, Theocritus Lucius Westborough, whose adventures began in 1936 with *The Fifth Tumbler.* Seven of Clason's books qualify for inclusion, and all of them display the impossible crime in an unusual light and often with an Oriental setting.

Agatha Christie is not generally linked with locked-room murders. The 1936 *Murder in Mesopotamia,* however, contained just such a problem—or, at least, murder in a room under constant observation—and this was shortly followed, in 1939, by *Murder for Christmas (Hercule Poirot's Christmas)* in which a locked-room murder occurred, and *Ten Little Niggers (And Then There Were None),* a work far too renowned to require any description of mine. The books are all extremely competent, and it is particularly illuminating to draw a comparison between Christie's almost off-hand treatment of the locked-room gimmick in *Murder for Christmas*—and a fairly complicated gimmick it was, too— and Carr's handling of the same situation in his books of that period. There's a world of difference.

Nineteen thirty-six, which was a very good year, also brought the best pastiche ever written of a locked-room mystery: *Case for Three Detectives* by Leo Bruce. In fact, like the Musketeers, there were really four of them, but the parodied trio of the title were Monsignor Smith, Amer Picon, and Lord Simon Plimsoll ("another of these locked room cases, I was hoping it might be something new, what"). It is not difficult to guess the names of the detectives on whom the trio was based. The star of the book—the fourth Musketeer—was, however, the red-faced, beer-drinking village police sergeant Beef whose stolid "I know who done it" proved at the end to be quite true. Beef's solution was a fairly well tried one, though neatly handled, but we have as a bonus three alternative and incorrect solutions from the famous trio.

If Theodore Roscoe is remembered at all today, it must surely be for the adventure stories that he regularly contributed to the American magazine *Argosy* between 1929 and 1943. His most popular story spinner was the retired French legionnaire Thibaut Corday, with his tall tales of strange desert happenings, but only a handful of Corday's yams have ever found book publication.

What are often overlooked are two detective novels of Roscoe's that were published in the mid thirties. *Murder on the Way!* (1935) is an astonishing tale of murder and mayhem set in Haiti and featuring, as well as the hero and heroine, as strange a bunch of characters as you could wish not to meet, and all thrown together in a decaying chateau where death strikes again and again, to leave the last survivor as heir to an immense fortune. There are impossible killings and disappearances, voodoo ceremonies, and reincarnations, and everything carried along at a truly fearsome pace. *I'll Grind Their Bones* (1936) moves just as quickly and is a future-war tale in which the antagonists are a thinly disguised Germany (Teutony) and France (Esperance). The cause of hostilities is the death—behind locked doors—of Teutony's Iron Premier and Esperance's Foreign Minister, who were assumed to have shot one another. But American newsman John Keats eventually unmasks the real culprit and reveals the solution to a diabolically clever locked-room crime.

Nineteen thirty-seven was a fairly quiet year. It was only the lull before the storm that introduced in 1938 one of the major figures of the impossible crime. He was a semiprofessional magician, to quote the dust-wrapper blurb from his first book. He created the Great Merlini, a magician, as his detective, and had a conjuror's flair for locking murder rooms and making victims disappear. Clayton Rawson, with only four novels, was nowhere as prolific as Carr, nor did he write quite as well. But like Carr's, his settings were impeccable, his impossible crimes brilliant and devious, and his total output was dedicated to crimes of the impossible.

His first book, *Death from a Top Hat* (1938), involved two locked-room murders and a disappearance trick and called for quite a performance from Merlini. It also contained a most informative piece on the general subject of locked-room murders. His second, *The Footprints on the Ceiling* (1939), contained two problems far more original and the classic setting of a group of people marooned—for a time—on an island. His last two novels were less interesting from an impossible-crime point of view but are still well worth reading. A word of warning about Rawson: Don't, as I first did, race through the books at breakneck speed and consequently find them too complicated for such treatment. They repay careful reading.

"In for a penny—in for a puzzle," said his publishers—but Rupert Penny is now largely forgotten. Yet between 1936 and 1941 he produced a series of eight excellent light humorous novels about Chief Inspector Beale. The last of them, *Sealed Room Murder* (1941), contained a particularly ingenious murder device, but an even better book is *Policeman's Evidence* (1938), with a far more believable plot and locked-room-murder method.

It is worth noting that 1938 also saw the publication of the first book by Helen McCloy, of whom I shall have more to say. This first effort, *The Dance of Death* (British title *Design for Dying),* introduced Dr. Basil Willing and left him to solve a most unusual murder mystery.

Anthony Boucher is best known for his penetrating criticism. In 1940, writing as H. H. Holmes, he contributed a novel to the locked-room theme he loved so well, *Nine Times Nine.* It was excellent and contained a locked-room method that no one had previously thought of, no mean feat by 1940. In 1942 his detective, Sister Ursula, investigated a further locked-room crime in *Rocket to the Morgue,* while squeezed in between those two books was a third, under his own name, *The Case of the Solid Key.*

The last major figure of the Golden Age was Hake Talbot, who in *The Hangman's Handyman* (1942) and *Rim of the Pit* (1944) produced the only books that challenged Carr on his own terms and earned a draw. The plots of both books were amazingly complex, and the impossibilities piled up rapidly. The first concerned a man, struck dead by an ancient curse, who was then discovered—by the condition of the corpse—to have been dead for some time.[5] The second, even better, involved séances, murder in a closed room, flying creatures, wendigos, and snow tracks that suddenly stopped. Rogan Kincaid was an able, if not very memorable, detective, and it is a great pity that those two novels, plus two short stories, were his creator's total.

6 More Golden-Age Contributors

I cannot leave the Golden Age without a quick word about a few other authors of interest and not without merit.

Stacey Bishop's *Death in the Dark* (1930) is an odd book packed with impossible murders. It is badly written, but not so bad as to deter one from trying to track down his second mystery. Julian Symons refers to that book in *Bloody Murder (Mortal Consequences),* but, alas, I have not been able to trace it and must, after all these years, doubt its very existence.

Philip MacDonald wrote several competent but undistinguished impossible-crime novels under his own name, but his best effort was *Mystery at Friar's Pardon* (1931)—as by Martin Porlock—mainly because, by succeeding in drowning a victim in a locked, waterless room, he had hit upon something new.

In 1932 *(About) the Murder of the Circus Queen* by Anthony Abbott (pseudonym of Fulton Oursler) appeared, the first of four solid impossible-crime chronicles of Police Commissioner Thatcher Colt.

---

5. There are similar, but less effective, ideas in R.T.M. Scott's *The Black Magician* (1925) and Lou Cameron's *Behind the Scarlet Door* (1971).

The other three are *(About) the Murder of the Night Club Lady* (1931), *(About) the Murder of a Startled Lady* (1935), and *The Shudders* (British title *Deadly Secret)* (1943).

Virgil Markham wrote a number of detective novels starting in 1928 with *Death in the Dusk,* set in Wales. Several of them involved impossible crimes, but the writing and plotting were so patchy that while I give a hearty recommendation to *The Devil Drives* (1932), I must also issue the direst warning about the awful *The Dead Are Prowling* (1934).

Alex Barber's only detective novel, *The Room with No Escape* (1932), with its cat-napping detective Urban Dormer, might well have achieved classic status had it been just a little more original. But originality there certainly was in John V. Turner's 1932 *Death Must Have Laughed* (U.S. title, *First Round Murder),* in which a knocked-out boxer is found to have been, impossibly, poisoned. John Bentley used a similar plot line in *The Whitney Case* (1937).

Freeman Wills Crofts, the "alibi" man, also contributed a couple of his plodding stories to the genre. *Sudden Death* (1932) is the more obvious locked-room problem, but *The End of Andrew Harrison* (1938) is a rather better book on all counts.

I suspect that French detective fiction of this period is rich in impossible-crime novels. The problem, of course, is that so many of them were never translated into English. However, two authors who did find translators were Stanislas-André Steeman, whose *Six Dead Men* won him the Prix du Roman d'Aventures for 1931, and Jean Toussaint-Samat, whose *Shoes That Had Walked Twice* won it the following year. Steeman's *Night of the 12th-13th* (1933) has also been translated.

Hugh Austin is another of the brigade who have several impossible-crime novels to their name. He in fact wrote four, all competent, and his chief claim to fame may be that he was the first author to raise the possibilities of substituting toe prints for finger prints. His detective was Lt. Peter Quint.

Scobie Mackenzie is a two-book man, the earlier of which, *Doctor Fram,* I have yet to find. His second book, the rather unimaginatively titled *Three Dead, One Hurt* (1934), is an almost Buchanesque tale of an oddly assorted group of people marooned on a Scottish island. Most of them appear to have dubious backgrounds, and it is no surprise when one of the less pleasant characters is struck down. Perhaps more surprising are the clever locked-room situation that attends the murder and the direction the book takes thereafter, marking it out as something a little different.

Wallace Irwin, on the other hand, wrote only one detective novel, but a very odd one it is. *The Julius Caesar Murder Case* (1935) was set in Roman times and had as its detective Publius Manlius Scribo, a reporter—and therefore, in a manner of speaking, the earliest example of a journalist-detective. The book is excellent fun, and the impossible crime, a stabbing by invisible agency, is well handled.

The Marceau Case and *X. Jones (of Scotland Yard)* (1936) by Harry Stephen Keeler are typical products of that author's peculiar, convoluted mind. They deal with the same murder case as investigated and solved by two different detectives, Alec Snide (Alex Nide!) and Xenius Jones. The murder was the garrotting of a man in an unmarked area of rolled loam. Just before his death he was heard to exclaim, "The Babe from Hell," which led to all sorts of conjectures involving midgets and helicopters and goodness knows what else. Keeler has his faithful band of followers, but equally there are those who can make nothing of him at all. My own position is as equivocal as Keeler's books, but, whatever else, I would not deny that he produced something unique.

The Lady Vanishes was one of the most successful prewar mystery films (1938). It had been adapted from Ethel Lina White's *The Wheel Spins* (1936) and concerned the disappearance of an old woman from an express train. Miss White used the vanishing-person motif again in *She Faded into Air* (1941).

Three British authors who, among them, wrote a dozen or so impossible-crime novels were Edwy Searles Brooks (Victor Gunn and Berkeley Gray), Gerald Verner (Donald Stuart), and Gwyn Evans. The books were good enough in themselves—and were sometimes very good—but the interesting fact is that most of them were adaptations of earlier Sexton Blake stories. Blake's adventures—and those of contemporaries Nelson Lee and Dixon Hawke—were written by a host of different authors for the boys' papers, and it was inevitable that there would be a sprinkling of locked-room cases among them. I refer the reader also to Rex Hardinge, Pierre Quiroule, and Desmond Reid, the latter being a house name.

In the same way, the American pulp magazines of the twenties and thirties recounted the adventures of literally hundreds of detectives and superheroes. Alas, they now command such astronomical prices that it has been impossible for me to examine more than a handful of them. It took me years, for instance, to track down for a reasonable sum a copy of The Shadow adventure entitled "The House That Vanished" (Oct. 15, 1935). Some of the pulp stories have recently been reprinted, and in the case of Doc Savage and The Phantom I am happy to say that availability is no longer an insuperable problem. The books themselves have no pretensions to literary merit, and the impossible crimes, sometimes ingenious, were often just as crudely described. However, they had a sheer life and pace that are enviable and that should still commend them to the modern reader.

The thirties had produced the best of the novels, but magazine fiction had been slowly declining. The result was that there are far fewer stories to recommend. Despite that, 1935 produced probably the best collection of impossible-crime stories about one detective.

C. Daly King was an American scientist whose output of mystery novels was only published complete in Britain. Also unavailable to the American public was a collection of eight tales of *The Curious Mr. Tarrant* (1935). Amazingly, seven of those first-rate stories qualify for inclusion as impossible-crime stories—as does an eighth tale that the author wrote later for EQMM. The book is now extremely scarce in its original published form, although, happily, there has been an American paperback reprint.

The thirties also saw the publication of three other classic locked-room short stories: "The Mystery of the Fabulous Laundryman" (1933) by Ben Hecht, based on a real case; "Solved by Inspection" (1931) by Ronald Knox, a grim little mystery investigated by insurance man Miles Bredon; and "The Case of Dr. Ceccioni" (1935) by Georges Simenon, showing that he knew all about the puzzle type of story.

There was also the first publication of the famous, gruesome impossible disappearance story "The Two Bottles of Relish" (1934) featuring Lord Dunsany's Detective Linley, and a few good-natured capers by Leslie Charteris. Christie and Boucher—mainly as H. H. Holmes—also wrote several good short stories, but the catalogue is very short by comparison with the novels.

7 More Moderns

During and after the war, the one writer who continued to concentrate his powers almost exclusively on impossible-crime novels was John Dickson Carr. The only other author who produced them in any quantity was John Russell Fearn, and he used half a dozen different pen names and as many publishers. Other authors had far less to contribute, but some of their efforts were nevertheless excellent.

Starting in 1943 Francis Leslie produced a short series of traditional detective stories starring crime reporter the Hon. Jimmy Langtry. Rather better than average fare, the first book, *Study of Death* (1943), is distinguished by a genuinely clever and original locked-room gimmick.

Edmund Crispin began writing in 1944, and his first book, *The Case of the Gilded Fly (Obsequies at Oxford),* was a sheer delight, with a very neat "observed" room problem. His detective, Professor Fen, investigated seven more cases in the same number of years, and two of those featured impossible happenings. *Swan Song* (1947) (U.S. title *Dead and Dumb)* contained a locked-room murder devised with the same type of fiendish ingenuity that Queen had employed in *The Chinese Orange Mystery.* The best, however, was probably *The Moving Toyshop* (1946). The title clearly states the nature of the problem, and Crispin deals with it extremely well. A volume of short stories, *Beware of the Trains* (1953), contained two further examples of Crispin's ability with impossible crimes.

Joel Townsley Rogers's *The Red Right Hand* (1945) is quite unique. It is an involved tale of murders and disappearances, with a crazy murderer named Corkscrew on the loose and the vital intercession of a retired criminologist. The unravelling at the end has to be read to be believed, but it is all quite fair and "tour de force" is not too generous a description. Rogers's novelette "The Hanging Rope" is almost equally as rich and complicated a mixture.

The novels of Christianna Brand, a British author born in Malaya, are as sharp, witty, and ingenious as any that have been written, and her detectives, Inspector Cockrill and Detective Inspector Charlesworth, are delightful. In *The Crooked Wreath* (1946) (British title *Suddenly at His Residence)* Cockrill was in charge and with all the equanimity he could muster met the challenge of two murders in which the killer had—impossibly—left no prints. Having solved that one, he then found himself in *Death of Jezebel* (1948) having not only to solve a type of locked-room murder—by decapitation, no less—but also to contend with the sallies and attentions of the younger Charlesworth. Equally good are Brand's two books of short stories, *What Dread Hand* (1968) and *Brand X* (1974), each of which includes a typical Brand impossible-crime mystery.

Also worthy of mention is the obscure *Pray for the Dawn* (1946) by the equally obscure Eric Harding, who wrote only one other mystery. Taking the conventional "cut off on an island" scenario, the author invests it with a degree of novelty by the introduction of an encoffined dwarf, apparently dead, yet seeming to breathe and be instrumental in a series of unexplained deaths. A thriller rather than a detective novel, as the author's note frankly states, but well worth seeking out.

New Zealander Norman Berrow had been writing before the war, but after it he introduced a new detective, Lancelot Carolus Smith, in a series of rather weird mysteries, four of which involved impossible crimes. The earliest, *The Three Tiers of Fantasy* (1947), was a very ambitious affair involving vanishing people, rooms, and even streets. *The Bishop's Sword* (1948) and *The Spaniard's Thumb* (1949) were a little more down to earth, while the last, *The Footprints of Satan* (1951), is worthy of note as one of the surprisingly few stories to make use of the devil's-hoofprints case of early-nineteenth-century Devon. Unfortunately, Berrow was better at stating mysteries than explaining them, and his attempts at English dialects are painful. In fact, probably his best book—another "vanisher" novel—was *Don't Jump, Mr. Boland!* (1954), which he set more happily in the Antipodes and from which he excluded the colourless Mr. Smith.

About this time (1946-1948) three writers each wrote their first book and in so doing made a foray into the world of impossible crimes. Michael Gilbert in *Close Quarters* (1947) used a cathedral close as the restricted area in which the murder could not have been carried out—but was! David Duncan, better known as a writer of science fiction, set his first book *The Shade of Time* (1946) among a group of scientists, one of whose number had been impossibly killed with an arrow years before. Another member had been found guilty of the crime, but he was now returning to the scene after his release and was intent on proving that he had not done it. Herbert Brean's *Wilders Walk Away* (1948) contained a whole list of impossible disappearances that newsman Reynold Frame was eager to rationalise on account of his interest in another, female, member of the Wilder family. There were no great surprises in the solution, but the book was very well written and portrayed the New England scene vividly. Both Gilbert and Brean have made other contributions to the impossible genre.

Humorous detective novels are among the most difficult to write, but Alan Green succeeded very well with *What a Body!* (1949) and *They Died Laughing* (1952). They both involved locked-room murders, and the earlier book was particularly ingenious in that it contained a fair answer to the question: "How can a man be shot dead in a locked room, with the wound in his chest but not in the clothing that covered it?"

I have already mentioned Helen McCloy's first, prewar, impossible-crime mystery. She had continued to write, and in 1950 there appeared what she herself and many critics regard as her best book. *Through a Glass, Darkly* had as its main theme a different type of impossible problem, the doppelganger. Dr. Basil Willing, a most capable detective, was faced with discovering how it was possible for schoolmistress Faustina Crayle to be—apparently—in two places at once. A rational answer was eventually provided and a very clever one, too, but just as Carr had done some years earlier in *The Burning Court,* so did Miss McCloy skilfully leave her readers with doubts as to whether, perhaps, there really had been a doppelganger. She has written three more novels of impossible crime, as well as a short story or two. *Mr. Splitfoot* (1968) is a particularly good locked-room problem with lots of macabre overtones, but even it doesn't quite measure up to *Through a Glass, Darkly.*

Nineteen fifty-one turned out to be one of the best of the postwar years. One book may well be described as the best postwar locked-room mystery. It had a brilliant new solution—and by then they were as impossible (to find) as some of the crimes—a most memorable detective in Mr. Verity, and a droll, tongue-in-cheek style that was extremely apposite. Add to this delightful illustrations by Nicholas Bentley and you will see why I think so highly of *The Woman in the Wardrobe* by Peter Antony (Peter Shaffer). He went on to write, with his brother Anthony under the name A. and P. Shaffer, another impossible-crime novel about Verity—although, strangely, he was called Fathom—called *Withered Murder* (1955), and years later Anthony Shaffer was to poke gentle fun at the genre in the opening lines of his very successful play, *Sleuth.*

Next we turn to *The Sleeping Bacchus* by Hilary St. G. Saunders. The author explained in the introduction that he had, with permission, taken the book from *Le Repos de Bacchus* by French author Pierre Boileau. I am not sure, therefore, how much of the material is Saunders's own, but the resulting book is a very good one dealing with vanishing men, canvasses, and even a disappearing black maria. Curme Gray's *Murder in Millennium VI* must also be mentioned not only as a most unusual serious modern science-fiction novel but also as the first in which an impossible crime occurs. Finally, Nigel Morland entered into his most satisfying phase of impossible-crime writing with *The Lady Had a Gun, Death When She Wakes,* and, in 1952, *A Girl Died Singing.*

Nineteen fifty-three saw publication of *Whistle Up the Devil* by Derek Smith. The author is one of the foremost students of the locked-room crime, and this comes over clearly in his book, which contains some nice little tidbits of locked-room lore as well as a couple of very competent locked-room puzzles. It is his only published work, but I do know that he has two more in draft form that ought to be published.

Another science-fiction writer to turn his attention to crime fiction was Isaac Asimov, who in 1954 in *The Caves of Steel* and in 1957 in *The Naked Sun* gave his public two excellent mysteries set in a future where huge conglomerate cities existed inhabited by people who had become agoraphobes. One of those was policeman Lije Baley, who, with the assistance of R(obot) Daneel Olivaw, solved impossible crimes in one of those cities and—in the second book—on Solaria, "an outer planet." Asimov intelligently took his impossible crimes away from the traditional forms and made them impossible in relation to the futuristic environs in which they were set.

Thin Air (1954) by Howard Browne is a taut mystery of an impossible disappearance that was later developed for television's *The Rockford Files.*

The years that followed *Thin Air* were themselves thin, as far as the impossible-crime novel was concerned. A nice little book from Nieves Mathews *(She Died Without Light)* was issued in 1956. Anthony Lejeune's imaginative *Mr. Diabolo* in 1960 and a couple of the Carter Brown thrillers qualify. But we had to wait until 1968 for a minor renaissance.

The book that started it off was Randall Garrett's *Too Many Magicians,* a locked-room story set in an alternate universe where an Anglo-French empire flourished that included Britain, France, and both continents of the New World. The detective was Lord Darcy, Chief Criminal Investigator for His Royal Highness, Richard, Duke of Normandy. Although the book creaked a little in places, the over-all effect was quite good. Darcy had also investigated a series of impossible crimes in short-story form, to which the setting seems better fitted and which have been published as the collections *Murder and Magic* (1979) and *Lord Darcy Investigates* (1981).

Douglas Clark's *Death After Evensong* (1969) is the next interesting book, involving as it does an impossible murder with a vanishing bullet. Following that is Tony Kenrick's well-named *A Tough One To Lose* (1972), a pacey, often humorous novel in which the author successfully de- and re-materialized a Jumbo Jet full of passengers.

In 1973 Jeremy Sturrock published his second historical mystery, *A Wicked Way To Die,* and included in it a locked-room murder, while in the same year Catherine Aird incorporated an impossible killing into one of her Calleshire novels, *His Burial Too.* But the year's most unusual mystery was Roland Puccetti's *The Trial of John and Henry Norton,* on the blurb of which is written, "Ellery Queen might well have turned (this case) into a locked room mystery." Puccetti doesn't quite do that, but it's a spellbinding mystery. The author is an American Professor of Philosophy.

The end of this minor renaissance came in 1974 with two books. The first was Peter Dickinson's *The Poison Oracle.* Dickinson is one of the most interesting of the current writers and specialises in unusual settings for his books. In *The Poison Oracle* he set the scene in the private zoo of the Sultan of Q'Kut, an Arab oil state where Wesley Morris, a behaviourist, was engaged in conducting experiments with intelligent chimpanzees. But the sultan was murdered, apparently when he was by himself, and it was left to Morris to sort out the truth.

Equally excellent was *Black Aura* by yet another refugee from science fiction, American John Sladek. Sladek had won the 1972 Times Detective Story Competition with a clever locked-room-murder short story, "By an Unknown Hand," and part of his prize was a contract for a full-length novel. *Black Aura* was the result and Thackeray Phin the detective in both cases. Sladek's novel was very good in all respects and dealt, among other things, with an impossible disappearance and an even more incredible levitation. In 1977 Sladek produced a second, even better, impossible-crime novel, *Invisible Green,* and there were high hopes of a major series. Unfortunately Sladek decided differently and returned to his science-fiction origins. Phin seems to have taken a permanent and premature retirement.

Indeed, in the years since *Invisible Green* there have been few developments in the impossible-crime novel from which to derive much comfort. Not that there has been any shortage of writers prepared to try their hand at the impossible-crime format—or sometimes a blurb written to suggest that they have. Of writers new to the field only one, Herbert Resnicow, has created an impossible-crime dynasty. His novels feature his witty husband-and-wife team, Norma and Alexander Gold, and a series of complex and involved murder cases with equally detailed solutions.

For the rest I can commend Robert Gillespie for his dry and unusual *The Crossword Mystery* (1979), Orania Papazoglou's *Sweet, Savage Death* (1984)—set at an annual conference of the American Writers of Romance—and Lucille Kallen's *The Tanglewood Murder* (1980), one of five books starring C. B. Greenfield and his female Archie Goodwin, Maggie Rome. All of Miss Kallen's books are to be recommended.

Of the older hands, Richard Forrest continues to entertain with his delightful couple Bea and Lyon Wentworth. Their most recent adventure—and third impossible-crime investigation—is *Death on the Mississippi* (1989), in which a large houseboat performs a vanishing act. Francis Selwyn also added a final Sergeant Verity romp of the impossible variety in 1979 with *Sergeant Verity and the Blood Royal* but now seems to have bowed out.

But one author who has by no means taken the curtain from the impossible-crime stage is Bill Pronzini. In 1979 I reported four short stories of impossible crime in which Bill had been involved. The count in the intervening period has risen to three novels and 19 short stories, many of them featuring Pronzini's nameless gumshoe, and all of them with impossible situations of flair and originality. The hardboiled-detective story is by no means the easiest milieu in which to set a puzzle of the locked-room variety, but Pronzini does this time and time again as well as it's ever likely to be done. A student of the impossible genre, he is also responsible for uncovering several forgotten tales of the impossible, most notably the magnificent "The Day Nobody Died" by pulp writer D. L. Champion.

So where is the white knight of the impossible, in which role I fatally cast Sladek when I wrote twelve years ago? Only Pronzini and Resnicow, in terms of output, could have the slightest claim, but neither of them in my view is assuming or trying to assume the mantle laid down by the maestro, John Dickson Carr.

And yet I am able to reveal that there is just such a man. He is thirty-five years old, a fervent admirer of Carr, and a disciple of the traditional impossible-crime school. He has six books published and a seventh due out soon. Those published are *The Fourth Door* (1987), *The Red Mist*

(1988), *Death Invites You* (1988), *Death Behind the* Curtains *(1989),* Madman's Room *(1990), and* The Head of the Tiger *(1991).*

Take *Death Invites You,* for instance, in which we do not find simply a locked-room murder but one where the victim is himself a writer of locked-room murders, and Vickers, the Scotland Yard detective, is faced with an intriguing range of complications, including a disfigured corpse, twin brothers, an illusionist and a madwoman, and a ghost in a neighbouring cemetery.

This author's first two books were prize winners against stiff competition and are highly regarded by those devotees in a position to compare them with the traditional qualities of Carr. But there is a problem, if he will forgive me for putting it that way. The author, Paul Halter, is a Frenchman, and thus far his books have not been translated into English. I can only hope that this omission is soon remedied.

8 More Golden-Age Contributors

If the postwar impossible-crime novel has been in something of a decline, the same cannot be said of the short story. The fiction magazine, in pulp and slick format, had begun to wane as America became involved in World War Two, but in 1943 the Ellery Queen team made their second foray into the detective-fiction magazine market—their first had been the pulp-size *Mystery League,* which had folded after only four issues—and *Ellery Queen's Mystery Magazine* (EQMM) was born and changed the situation entirely.

The Queens' new magazine was in small "digest size" format, and from the very beginning it concentrated on bringing together "lost" stories by famous authors, a few old favourites, and new stories by unknown writers. This last feature of its policy has produced a host of excellent authors, many of whom have contributed generously to the impossible-crime saga.

The first two authors to achieve some degree of prominence through the medium of EQMM were what might be termed "boy wonders." James Yaffe sold his first Department of Impossible Crimes story to the Queens in 1943, and the editors in ensuing correspondence with the author learnt to their amazement that he was only fifteen years old. Yaffe continued to write for the magazine for many years, and his first six stories featured detective Paul Dawn. They all involved impossible crimes.

The second prodigy was Leonard Thompson. In 1946, at the age of sixteen, he contributed two locked-room problems investigated by lawyer William S. Gray. In retrospect, it must be said that this early work of both Yaffe and Thompson was as immature as one would expect. Thereafter, Thompson seems to have disappeared from the scene altogether, while Yaffe turned to writing stories that had no impossible-crime element.

But if the youngsters never quite fulfilled their early promise, the June 1948 issue of EQMM contained more than adequate compensation in the form of the first short story by Clayton Rawson about the Great Merlini. Some years earlier, Rawson had written four novelettes under the name of Stuart Towne for *Red Star Mystery Magazine.* They were later collected in two books, *Death Out of Thin Air* and the extremely rare *Death from Nowhere.* Good as they were, they were eclipsed by the scintillating first Merlini short, "From Another World," which dealt with that most difficult of problems, death in a locked room where all exits were sealed with tape. Carr had first solved the problem in *He Wouldn't Kill Patience* (1944)—and dedicated the book to Rawson!—but Rawson's solution was different. The second Merlini short, "Off the Face of the Earth" (1949), was almost as good and dealt with another classic situation, disappearance from a telephone booth. Other Merlini stories followed at irregular intervals, the last in 1971 just before Rawson's death. They were eventually collected in *The Great Merlini* (1979), an essential addition to any mystery library.

While the Rawson stories have at long last been collected, the stories of my next author have not been so fortunate. Starting with "Murder Under Glass" in the late pulp *10 Story Detective Magazine* in March 1947, Joseph Commings contributed a whole host of inventive tales to the pulps and, succeeding them, to an avant-garde digest publication entitled, quite reasonably, *Mystery Digest.* This oddball magazine, which viewed mystery from an unusual and often provocative angle, began publication in May 1957 and lasted just six years. During the last two years of its life its editor was Joseph Commings, and Commings was also its most regular contributor. Almost every issue contained a story by him under his own name or that of Monte Craven, and most of the stories were about detective Brooks U. Banner.

In all, Banner appeared in over thirty stories—in one case the editor perversely insisted that he be called Mayor Landin—and was a larger-than-life United States Senator of whom John Dickson Carr would have been proud. The bulk of Banner's cases involved impossible crime, and not only is most of the writing up to Carr at his best, the plotting is also of the highest level and the impossible-crime element is original and ingenious. Banner—or Landin—appeared in no fewer than twenty-six impossible-crime stories, and it is only necessary to detail one of them, "The X Street Murders," to see the kind of murderer he was usually up against. In this tale, which appeared in the March/April 1962 issue of *Mystery Digest* and which has recently been anthologized, a man is shot in a closed room by a gun that is produced only seconds later from a sealed envelope opened in another room. Needless to say, Banner solved it. Recently far more Banner adventures have been finding their way into anthologies, but publishers are certainly missing out on a volume for which many catchy titles suggest themselves: "Banner Headlines," or even, dare I say, "Star Spangled Banner."

All my searches have failed to turn up the texts of three of Commings's impossible-crime stories—"The Devil's Elbow" from *Ten Detective Aces,* November 1947; "Satan Forks a White Horse" from *Western Trails,* December 1948; and "The Riddle of Hangtree County" from *Western Trails,* April 1949—so they are not covered in this bibliography. I hope that some day I shall be able to rectify this omission.

The forties and fifties saw the publication of many other impossible-crime stories in EQMM and similar magazines such as *Double Action, Alfred Hitchcock's Mystery Magazine, Mike Shayne Mystery Magazine,* and *Mystery Book.* The authors included Lillian de la Torre with two adventures of Dr. Sam: Johnson; August Derleth and his Solar Pons in, among others, a version of the devil's-footprints problem; Robert Arthur with several highly original tales such as "The 51st Sealed Room"; Anthony Boucher; Thomas Flanagan; and South African Peter Godfrey, who wrote about detective Rolf le Roux.

There were Margery Allingham and her detective Albert Campion; Leonard Pruyn with his very unusual "Dinner at Garibaldi's," in which a gourmet died, inexplicably, of starvation; William March with his classic locked-room tale "The Bird House"; John F. Suter; Hazel Hills; the Lipmans, and so on.

It was also still a time for prolific authors to flourish, and two deserve special mention. Arthur Porges seems to have contributed to every mystery-fiction digest that has appeared, and his stories range widely in the telling. The impossible-crime theme is one that he has given a lot of attention to, and I have been able without too much difficulty to identify almost thirty that are relevant to this bibliography. It must be said at once that the characterisations are on the sketchy side, but there is still plenty of meat in the trim little stories, and the plotting is excellent. There are two Holmes pastiches worth remembering (other authors such as Robert Arthur and Jon Breen have also contributed Holmes pastiches to the impossible-crime saga). Another story, "Coffee Break," is a perfect example of how to put a new shine on the old locked-room technique.

Equally prolific is Edward D. Hoch, and a more than generous correspondent. Again it seems to be almost impossible to pick up a modern mystery digest without finding his name on the contents page. He has many series detectives to his name, but the one for which he is probably most famous is Simon Ark. Ark is, to quote Hans Stefan Santesson's introduction to *The Judges of Hades and Other Stories* (1971): "a Copt, almost certainly a one time priest, who has been denied the grace of dying but has instead been condemned to hunt down the forces of Evil." A number of adventures of this strange detective are concerned with crimes of the impossible, and one of them, "The Hoofs of Satan," is a personal favourite. Ark has, after a long absence, reappeared on the scene, and some of Hoch's other detectives—Captain Leopold, Rand, and Nick Velvet, a professional thief—continue to pit their wits against the impossible. Furthermore, in 1974 Hoch introduced a brand-new series detective, old toper Dr. Sam Hawthorne, who reminisces about impossible crimes he solved in the old days. Thus far the old doctor has featured in an amazing count of thirty-eight impossible-crime stories.

In 1959 a book appeared entitled 77 *Sunset Strip* that contained the adventures of television private investigator Stuart Bailey. The television series was very popular and the book a by-product of it. However, unlike so many of the "you saw the film, now read the book" publications, this book had merits of its own. In fact, it contained three separate short stories that had originally appeared in *The Saturday Evening Post* and *Esquire* and that author Roy Huggins had reworked for the television detective. Each of the three stories is an excellent impossible-crime problem.

77 *Sunset Strip* is not, of course, the only television link-up. When mystery series replaced Westerns on television, many of the episodes of *McCloud, MacMillan and Wife, Columbo, The Rockford Files,* etc.,

had their origins in novels and short stories of impossible crime. Detective Banacek, indeed, investigated nothing but impossible crimes, and many of them were old friends in slightly altered garb. Deane Romano turned one of them, "Let's Hear It for a Living Legend," into the novel *Banacek.*

The locked-room mystery has, of course, always had its critics. Most experts, including Howard Haycraft, have advised budding authors to steer clear of it, and others have been openly hostile. Julian Symons is a strong advocate of the modern crime novel, and it was therefore inevitable that his dislike of the pure detective novel would be crystallised in, among other places, a short satirical essay called "Take That Body Out of the Library," which appeared in *Suspense* (British version) in July 1960. Symons poked fun at the locked-room problem with detectives Monty Languid and Inspector Numbskull, and repeated the dose some years later in a television arts programme. Strangely—and perhaps there is hope after all for Mr. Symons!—I have found that two of his Francis Quarles short stories qualify for inclusion in this bibliography.

The locked-room story was honoured in 1968 by the first anthology on the subject. *The Locked Room Reader* is an excellent collection edited by Hans Stefan Santesson and containing some very fine examples of the impossible-crime story. Shorter versions appeared in 1970 in paperback as *8 Keys to Murder* and *8 Doors to Death.* A much earlier book, *The Saint's Choice of Impossible Crimes,* deals only with science-fictional crimes. Further impossible-crime anthologies have been published in the last ten years. In 1981 Ed Hoch edited *All But Impossible!* where, apart from the excellence of the contents, much interest is to be found in the introduction, wherein is given the result of a poll of experts as to the choice of the best locked-room novel. No surprise, incidentally, that Carr came first, fourth, fifth, and tenth. In 1982 there followed *Tantalizing Locked Room Mysteries,* an excellent compendium edited by Asimov, Waugh, and Greenberg.

Then in 1987 Douglas G. Greene and I collaborated over *Death Locked In*—with Doug doing the lion's share of the work, I should add—a collection that featured a lot of unfamiliar, yet creditable, material. Finally, and even more recently, Jack Adrian and I have jointly edited a further collection of impossible mysteries, *The Art of the Impossible (Murder Impossible* in the U.S.), featuring previously uncollected stories by such luminaries as Hake Talbot, Joel Townsley

Rogers, and William Hope Hodgson.

In 1973 Gollancz published a book by Czechoslovakian Josef Skvorecky with the unlikely title of *The Mournful Demeanour of Lieutenant Boruvka.* Boruvka is an intelligent, sympathetic policeman, and the book is in fact a series of his adventures. Among them are several with the theme of impossible crime, and Skvorecky's skilful handling of both the techniques and his characters makes them well worth reading. It is comforting to know that locked-room murders cross international and political barriers. Further adventures of Boruvka have appeared more recently in *Sins for Father Knox* (1989) and *The End of Lieutenant Boruvka* (1989).

All of which brings us finally full circle to John Dickson Carr himself, the maestro, and to possibly the most important books to have appeared in the last decade. I refer to *The Door to Doom* (1980) and *The Dead Sleep Lightly* (1983), collections of previously unpublished stories and plays, many of which date from Carr's college days and show— "The Shadow of the Goat," for instance—the master at his full powers even at the very beginning of his writings, and before *It Walks by Night.* A great debt is owed to Doug Greene, without whose scholarship and sheer persistence it is unlikely that most of these stories would ever have found the wide audience they so richly deserved. Material for a third volume has been assembled and would make a very worthwhile addition to the canon if only an enterprising publisher can be found.

So there we have it. The short story still safely in the hands of a number of tried and tested practitioners, and the novel still awaiting a major new force that may just be across the channel in France. Time alone will tell.

Publication Data and the Problems

A

Aanrooy, Jacques

1. ✓ OFF THE TRACK *novel* U.K.: Walker Bros., 1895; South Africa: J. C. Juta & Co., 1895 *Detective:* Donald Fraser.
   Problem: Death by stabbing in a locked surgery.
   Comment: Compare this book with that of the same title by Sir Henry Juta (Item 1098). Even the detectives have the same surname. One of those simply amazing coincidences, or can one derive some significance from the shared name of the Victorian South African publisher and the much later author?

Abbot, Anthony

2. ABOUT THE MURDER OF THE CIRCUS QUEEN *novel* U.S.: Covici, 1932; U.K. (as "The Murder of the Circus Queen"): Collins, 1933
   Detective: Thatcher Colt, police commissioner.
   Problems: (1) Death of a trapeze artist during her act.
   (2) Death by throat cutting in a locked room.
3. ✓ ABOUT THE MURDER OF THE NIGHT CLUB LADY *novel* U.S.: Covici, 1931; U.K. (as "The Murder of the Night Club Lady"): Collins, 1932
   Detective: Colt.
   Problem: Death by poison in a room under guard.
4. ABOUT THE MURDER OF A STARTLED LADY *novel* U.S.: Farrar,1935; U.K. (as "The Murder of a Startled Lady"): Collins, 1937
   Detective: Colt.
   Problem: A medium states that she has received a spirit message giving the location of a corpse, which proves to be there.
5. THE SHUDDERS *novel* U.S.: Farrar, 1943; U.K. (as "Deadly Secret"): Collins, 1943
   Detective: Colt.
   Problem: Series of deaths of an inexplicable nature engineered

by one man.

6. ✓ "About the Disappearance of Agatha King" *short story* in "The Mystery Book" U.S.: Farrar, 1939
Detective: Colt.
Problem: Disappearance, on her wedding day, of a bride-to-be from a guarded suite of rooms.

Abshire, Richard K., and William R. Clair

7. ✓ GANTS *novel* U.S.: Dell, 1987
Detective: Charlie Gants, homicide detective.
Problem: Death by shooting in a room from which no one apparently had time to leave.

Adair, Gilbert

8. ✓ "The Giant Rat of Sumatra" *short story* in The Independent, Aug. 29 and 30, 1988
Detective: Sherlock Holmes.
Problem: Death by the hideous fangs of a giant rat in a locked room.

Adams, Harold

9. ✓ THE MAN WHO MISSED THE PARTY *novel* U.S.: Mysterious, 1989
Detective: Carl Wilcox.
Problem: Death by shooting in a locked shower stall.

Adams, Herbert

10. BLACK DEATH *novel* U.K.: Collins, 1939
Detective: Roger Bennion.
Problem: Death by stabbing in a locked room.

11. Death OFF the Fairway *novel* U.K.: Collins, 1936
Detective: Bennion.
Problem: Death by drowning and only the victim's footprints on the surrounding ground.

12. ✓ FOUR WINDS *novel* U.K.: Collins, 1944
Detective: Bennion.
Problem: Information in secret meetings in a special room is being obtained by the enemy, but all those taking part in the meetings are above suspicion.

13. ✓ THE JUDAS KISS *novel* U.K.: Macdonald, 1955
Detective: Bennion.
Problem: Death by poison in a locked room.

14. ✓ THE QUEEN'S GATE MYSTERY *novel* U.K.: Methuen, 1927;

U.S.: Lippincott, 1927
Detective: Jimmie Haswell.
Problem: Appearance of various persons inside a locked house.

15. ✓ ROGUES FALL OUT *novel* U.K.: Methuen, 1928; U.S.: Lippincott, 1928
Detective: Haswell.
Problem: Death by shooting in a locked, upper-storey room of an inn.

16. ✓ THE SPECTRE IN BROWN *novel* U.K.: Macdonald, 1953
Detective: Roger Bennion.
Problem: Murder by strangulation carried out by a cowled figure identified as Father Savrola, although he claimed to be well away from the scene of the crime.

Adams, Samuel Hopkins

17. THE FLYING DEATH *novel* U.S.: McClure, 1908; "Big Book of Locked-Room Mysteries", Black Lizard, 2014
Detectives: Prof. Willis Ravenden and Stanford Colton.
Problem: Two murders on sand unmarked apart from the prints of a gigantic prehistoric bird.

18. "Aunt Minnie and the Accessory After the Fact" *short story* in "Murder for the Millions" U.S.: Fell, 1946; Liberty Magazine, 6-Oct-1945; "Stories of Crime and Detection" U.S. McGraw, 1974; (as "Accessory After the Fact") in EQMM, October 1949
Detective: Aunt Minnie.
Problem: Disappearance of a murder knife from a guarded room in which victim and killer were under constant observation.

19. "The Flying Death" *short story* in The Strand Magazine, March-April 1903; McClure's Magazine January 1903; EQMM, January 1944; "Ellery Queen's Anthology, 1964 Mid-Year Edition" U.S.: Davis, 1964
Detectives: Prof. Willis Ravenden and Stanford Colton.
Problem: Two deaths on sand unmarked apart from the prints of a gigantic prehistoric bird.

Adrian, Jack

20. ✓ "The Absolute and Utter Impossibility of the Facts in the Case of the Vanishing of Henning Vok (a.k.a. The Amazing Blitzen) (r.n. Jack Ralph Cole)" *short story* in "New Crimes 3" U.K.: Robinson, 1991

Detectives: Prof. Stanislaus Befz and Patrolman O'Mahoney.
Problem: Disappearance from a locked and guarded bathroom of a murderer who, in front of police witnesses, had calmly stabbed his victim to death while they were both just inside the bathroom, then pulled the door to and locked it before the stunned witnesses could react.

21. ✓ "The Phantom Pistol" *short story* in "Felonious Assaults" U.S.: Ivy Books, 1989; "The Year's Best Mystery & Suspense Stories" U.S.: Walker, 1990
Detectives: Mr. H. and Superintendent Stanley Hopkins.
Problem: Death by shooting on stage by an apparently empty gun.

Afford, Max

22. BLOOD ON HIS HANDS! *novel* U.K.: Long, 1936; U.S.: Ramble House 2005
Detectives: Jeffery Blackburn and Chief Inspector Read.
Problems: (1) Death by stabbing in a locked room.
(2) Death by stabbing within a guarded area of a shop.

23. THE DEAD ARE BLIND *novel* U.K.: Long, 1937; U.S.: Ramble House 2005
Detectives: Blackburn and Read.
Problem: Death by stabbing in a locked room.

24. DEATH'S MANNIKINS *novel* U.K.: Long, 1937; U.S.: Appleton, 1937; U.S.: Ramble House 2005
Detectives: Blackburn and Read.
Problem: Death by stabbing by invisible agency in a chapel.

25. FLY BY NIGHT *novel* U.K.: Long, 1942; Australia (as "The Owl of Darkness"): Angus, 1942; U.S. (as "The Owl of Darkness"): Ramble House 2005
Detectives: Blackburn and Read.
Problem: Disappearance of master-criminal "The Owl" with victim from a locked, inaccessible room.

Aird, Catherine (Kinn Hamilton McIntosh)

26. HIS BURIAL TOO *novel* U.K.: Collins, 1973; U.S.: Doubleday, 1973
Detective: Inspector C. D. Sloan.
Problem: Death within a church, one exit locked, the other blocked by a huge stone monument that had crushed the victim.

27. ✓ "Cause and Effect" *short story* in "A Classic English Crime"

U.K.: Pavilion, 1990

Detective: Henry Tyler of the Foreign Office.

Problem: Death by poisoning during a meal at which other guests ate the same food as the victim and were unaffected.

Aldous, Allan

28. IT'S MURDER IF YOU SAY SO! *novel* U.K.: Skeffington, 1952
Detective: Galahad Urban Browne ("Gub"), a strip cartoonist.
Problem: Death by shooting in a locked room.

Aldrich, Thomas Bailey

29. OUT OF HIS HEAD *novel* U.S.: Carleton, 1862; in part in EQMM July 1949; "Death Locked In" U.S.: IPL, 1987; "The Mammoth Book of Locked-Room Mysteries and Impossible Crimes", UK: Constable and Robinson, 2000, US: Carroll and Graf
Detective: Paul Lynde.
Problem: Death by stabbing in a locked room.

Alexander, David

30. ✓ THE DEATH OF HUMPTY-DUMPTY *novel* U.S.: Random, 1957; U.K.: Boardman, 1959
Detective: Bart Hardin, newspaperman.
Problem: A man in a Humpty-Dumpty outfit is seen to fall from an upper-storey window but doesn't land on the pavement below.

Alexander, Ruth, and Arnold Ridley

31. THE GHOST TRAIN *novel* U.K.: Readers Library, (1926), and Arrowsmith, 1927; U.S.: Small, 1926
Detective: Capt. Edward Gascoyne Morrison.
Problem: Appearance of a mysterious train, reputedly a "ghost train."

Allan, Luke

32. BEYOND THE LOCKED DOOR *novel* U.K.: Jenkins, 1938
Detective: Gordon Muldrew.
Problem: Death by shooting in a locked room.
33. THE FOURTH DAGGER *novel* U.K.: Arrowsmith, 1932.
Detective: *Muldrew.*
Problem: Death by stabbing in a locked room.

Allen, Clifford

34. "A Lecture on Detection" *short story* in London Mystery Magazine No. 98
Detective: Detective Chief Superintendent J. V. Strutt.
Problem: Death by drowning in a locked bathroom.

Allen, Steve

35. "Everybody Hates David Starbuck" *short story* in Playboy, December 1958; (as "Murder à la Hollywood") in EQMM, September 1959, and "Ellery Queen's Minimysteries" U.S.: World, 1969
Detective: None.
Problem: Death by wrist slashing in a locked bathroom.

Allen, Warner

36. THE DEVIL THAT SLUMBERS *novel* U.K.: J. Hamilton, (1925)
Detectives: George B. Edgehill ("Puck") and Aristide Govin, chief of the Anti-Bolshevist Bureau.
Problems: (1) Theft from a locked jewel case.
(2) Voices heard inside a guarded room. Later, its—supposedly—only inhabitant is found dead in a well with the top cover still on.
(3) Poisoning in a locked room.
(4) Disappearance of two men each under separate guard.

37. THE UNCOUNTED HOUR *novel* U.K.: Constable, 1936
Detectives: Philip Gaymore and Inspector Wake.
Problem: Death by gassing in a locked room.

Allingham, Margery

38. FLOWERS FOR THE JUDGE *novel* U.K: Heinemann, 1936; U.S.: Doubleday, 1936
Detective: Albert Campion.
Problem: Disappearance of a man under constant observation walking along a walled road.

39. "The Border-Line Case" *short story* in U.S.: "Mr. Campion: Criminologist" Doubleday, 1937; "Challenge to the Reader" Stokes, 1938; "101 Years' Entertainment" Little, 1941; Rex Stout Mystery Quarterly August 1945; MacKill's Mystery Magazine September 1953; MacKill's Mystery Magazine (US) November 1953; "The Allingham Case-Book" Morrow, 1969; U.K.: "Mr. Campion and Others" Heinemann, 1939; "The Allingham Case-Book" Chatto, 1969; "Big Book of Locked-Room Mysteries", Black Lizard, 2014
Detective: Campion.
Problem: Victim found at a point where no shot could have been fired.

40. "Family Affair" *short story* in EQMM, October 1960; "16th

Mystery Annual" U.S.: Random, 1961, and U.K. Gollancz, 1962; (as "Villa Marie Celeste") in "The Allingham Case-Book"
Detective: Campion.
Problem: House vacated suddenly in "Marie Celeste" condition—i.e., breakfast half-eaten, etc.

41. "The Neatest Trick of the Month" *short story* in EQMM, March 1959; "Ellery Queen's 14th Mystery Annual" U.S.: Random, 1959; (as "Little Miss Know It All") in "The Allingham Case-Book"
Detective: Campion.
Problem: Fur coat disappeared from hotel apartment. Suspect owner apparently under surveillance throughout.

42. "Tall Story" *short story* in EQMM, April 1954; "The Queen's Awards 9th Series" U.S.: Little, 1954, and U.K.: Collins, 1956; "The Quintessence of Queen" U.S.: Random, 1962, and U.K.: (as "A Magnum of Mysteries") Gollancz, 1963; "The Allingham Case-Book"
Detective: Campion.
Problem: Disappearance of loot and murder gun from within an alley guarded by police at either end.

Allison, William

43. A SECRET OF THE SEA *novel* U.S.: Doubleday, 1920
Detective: Peter Knight.
Problem: The finding of a derelict yacht abandoned for no apparent reason.

Alner, James Z.

44. THE CAPITAL MURDER *novel* U.S.: Knopf, 1932, U.K.: Hurst, (1933)
Detective: Trevor Stoke.
Problem: Death by poison in a locked room.

Ames, Mel D.

45. ✓ "The Christmas Eve Ghost" *short story* in MSMM, December 1983; "Amazon: The Complete Adventures of Cathy Carruthers, Mosaic, US 1999
Detective: Detective-Lieutenant Cathy Carruthers.
Problem: Attempted murder by poison in a room under guard.

46. ✓ "A Matter of Observation" *short story* in MSMM, November 1980; "Amazon"
Detective: Carruthers.

Problem: Death by strangulation in a locked hotel room.

Anderson, Frederick Irving

47. "The Fifth Tube" *short story* in "The Adventures of the Infallible Godahl" U.S. Crowell, 1914; "Big Book of Locked-Room Mysteries", Black Lizard, 2014

    Detective: Infallible Godahl.

    Problem: Disappearance of 40 gallons of gold from a tank.

48. "The Half-Way House" *short story* in The American Magazine, May 1922; EQMM, February 1948; EQMM Australia February 1949; "EQMM Anthology, 1963 Mid-Year Edition" U.S.: Davis, 1963; AHMM October 2003

    Detective: Oliver Armiston.

    Problem: Death by poisoning in the bedroom of a locked house.

Anderson, Poul

49. "The Martian Crown Jewels" *short story* in EQMM, February 1958; "The Science-Fictional Sherlock Holmes" U.S.: Council of Four, 1960; "Ellery Queen's Anthology #12 1967"; "All But Impossible!" U.S.: Ticknor, 1981; "The Misadventures of Sherlock Holmes" U.K.: Xanadu, 1989; "The Realm of the Impossible", Locked Room International, 2017

    Detective: Syaloch, a Martian.

    Problem: Crown jewels disappear from inside an unmanned spaceship journeying from Earth to Phobos Station (on a satellite of Mars).

Andrews, Charlton

50. THE BUTTERFLY MURDER *novel* U.S.: Sears, 1932; U.K.: Allan, 1934

    Detective: Derek Whitby.

    Problem: Set up as a locked-room mystery but not really genuine; see solution.

Andrews, V., and H. Penn

51. ✓ "The Mystery of the Sealed Room" *short story* in U.S. Magico Magazine, 1980

    Detective: Sherlock Holmes.

    Problem: Death by stabbing in a locked bathroom.

Annesley, Maude

52. ✓ "A Lost Identity" *short story* in "Nights and Days" U.K.: Mills, 1915

    Detective: None.

Problem: Death by shooting from a room under constant watch and which proved to be empty when broken into.

Anonymous

53. ✓ "The Banshee's Cry" *short story* in Cheer Boys Cheer, Dec. 21, 1912
Detective: Lester Griffith, the Ghost-Layer.
Problem: The sound of a banshee outside a remote Irish mansion.

54. ✓ "The Case of the Locked Door" *short story* in The Boy's Journal, March 23, 1914
Detective: Dr. Randall Keen.
Problem: A blow struck by an invisible assailant on unlocking the door of a forbidden room.

55. ✓ "The Case of Mrs. Peters" *short story* in Pearson's Weekly, Oct. 24, 1896
Detective: None.
Problem: Disappearance of a thief from a locked railway carriage.

56. ✓ "Death at Midnight" *short story* in The Crime-Book Magazine, June & September 1937
Detective: Inspector Cornell.
Problem: Death by shooting in a locked room.

57. ✓ "Death in the Sealed Room" *short story* in The Crime-Book Magazine, January & March 1937
Detective: Inspector Cornell.
Problem: Death by shooting in a locked room.

58. ✓ "The Diamond Widow", by **Julian Hawthorne**, **q.v.**, *short story* in The New-York Ledger, December 15, 1888; U.K.: Pearson's Weekly, Oct. 4, 1890
Detective: Not known.
Problem: Disappearance of a diamond necklace from a locked room guarded inside by a poodle.

59. ✓ "An End to Life", by **Amy Carroll**, **q.v.**, *problem story* in "Scotland Yard Photo Crimes" U.K.: Kindersley, 1983
Detective: Inspector Black.
Problem: Death by gassing in a room with a sealed door.

60. ✓ "The Flaming Owl" *short story* in Cheer Boys Cheer, Dec. 14, 1912
Detective: Lester Griffith, the Ghost-Layer.

Problem: Appearance of a ghostly owl in a haunted house.

61. ✓ "Going for Broke", by **Amy Carroll, q.v.,** *problem story* in "Scotland Yard Photo Crimes"
Detective: Inspector Black.
Problem: Death by shooting in an office in which the victim was alone.

62. ✓ "Locked Room Mystery", by **Amy Carroll, q.v.**, *problem story* in "Scotland Yard Photo Crimes"
Detective: Inspector Black.
Problem: Death by poisoning in a locked room.

63. "A Mysterious Case" *short story* in Winter's Magazine, March 24, 1894.
Detective: Unnamed.
Problem: Death by shooting in a locked room.

64. ✓ "The Secret of the Ockfield Attic" *short story* in The Penny Pictorial Magazine, April 16, 1921
Detective: Peter Tenway, super-detective.
Problem: Various deaths in a locked bedroom.

65. ✓ "The Strange Death of Anna Maria Sonde" *short story* in Pearson's Weekly, Feb. 10, 1894
Detective: Not known.
Problem: Death within a locked room.

66. ✓ "Theft at a Séance", by **Amy Carroll, q.v.,** *problem story* in "Scotland Yard Photo Crimes"
Detective: Inspector Black.
Problem: Disappearance of some pearls stolen during a séance.

Anonymous (Dixon Hawke stories)

67. ✓ "The Case of the Broken Door" *short story* in Dixon Hawke's Case Book No. 8 U.K.: Thomson, 1942
Detective: Dixon Hawke.
Problem: Death by hanging in a locked and bolted hotel room.

68. ✓ "The Case of the Double Opening" *short story* in Dixon Hawke's Case Book No. 2 U.K.: Thomson, 1939
Detective: Hawke.
Problem: Disappearance of a murder suspect from a locked and bolted attic room at the time of the murder.

69. ✓ "The Case of the Dusty Floor" *short story* in Dixon Hawke's Case Book No. 5 U.K.: Thomson, 1940
Detective: Hawke.

Problem: Death by stabbing of a man found in the middle of a room when the dust on the floor was undisturbed by any prints.

70. ✓ "The Case of the Eucalyptus Bottle" *short story* in Dixon Hawke's Case Book No. 16 U.K.: Thomson, 1949
Detective: Hawke.
Problem: The concealment of a valuable picture within a locked room that was searched from top to bottom.

71. ✓ "The Case of the Giant's Footprints" *short story* in Dixon Hawke's Case Book No. 6 U.K.: Thomson, 1941
Detective: Hawke.
Problem: Disappearance of a murderer from a house surrounded by snow with no footprints to explain his escape.

72. ✓ "The Case of the Hollow Spoon" *short story* in Dixon Hawke's Case Book No. 10 U.K.: Thomson, 1944
Detective: Hawke.
Problem: Death by strychnine poisoning, effective within seconds, when the poison was not apparently contained in anything the victim had swallowed.

73. ✓ "The Case of the Kandahar Ruby" *short story* in Dixon Hawke's Case Book No. 14 U.K.: Thomson, 1947
Detective: Hawke.
Problem: Disappearance of a valuable ruby stolen during a brief blackout but not removed from the room in question.

74. ✓ "The Case of the Missing Bishop" *short story* in Dixon Hawke's Case Book No. 13 U.K.: Thomson, 1947
Detective: Hawke.
Problem: Death by shooting inside a locked room.

75. "The Case of the Missing Footprints" *short story* in Dixon Hawke's Case Book No. 15 U.K.: Thomson, 1948
Detective: Hawke.
Problem: Victim killed at close range by gunshot in open field while no one was near to him.

76. ✓ "The Case of the Road of No Return" *short story* in Dixon Hawke's Case Book No. 8 U.K.: Thomson, 1942
Detective: Hawke.
Problem: Death by shooting of a man lying in snow and at a point to which only his own tracks led.

77. ✓ "The Case of the Vanishing Tank" *short story* in Dixon Hawke's Case Book No. 6 U.K.: Thomson, 1941

Detective: Hawke.
Problem: Theft of a World War I tank from a rolled and fenced enclosure in a public park, with no tracks to explain the tank's disappearance.

78. "Death Was Locked In" *short story* in Dixon Hawke's Case Book No. 20 U.K.: Thomson, 1953
Detective: Hawke.
Problem: Death by shooting in a locked room.

79. "The Iron-Studded Door" *short story* in Dixon Hawke's Case Book No. 15 U.K.: Thomson, 1948
Detective: *Hawke.*
Problem: Death by shooting in a locked room.

80. "The Knife from Nowhere" *short story* in Dixon Hawke's Case Book No. 20 U.K.: Thomson, 1953
Detective: Hawke.
Problem: Victim killed by stiletto that seemed to come from nowhere.

81. "A Lesson for a Lady" *short story* in Dixon Hawke's Case Book No. 20 U.K.: Thomson, 1953
Detective: Hawke.
Problem: Disappearance of diamonds during a club meeting, all exits blocked.

82. "Paper and Pencil Solved the Case" *short story* in Dixon Hawke's Case Book No. 20 U.K.: Thomson, 1953
Detective: Hawke.
Problem: Death by gassing in a locked room.

Anthony, Wilder

83. DEEP VALLEY *novel* U.S.: Dorrance, 1940
Detective: Dr. Norton, coroner.
Problem: Death by blunt instrument in a locked study.

Antony, Peter (Peter Shaffer; see also Shaffer, A. and P.)

84. THE WOMAN IN THE WARDROBE *novel* U.K.: Evans, 1951
Detective: Mr. Verity.
Problem: Death by shooting in a locked room.

85. "Before and After" *short story* in London Mystery Magazine No. 16 1953
Detectives: Mr. Verity and Inspector Rambler.
Problem: Murder in a room under constant guard.

Anvil, Christopher

86. "The Drop of a Pin" *short story* in MSMM, April 1974
Detective: Richard Verner, heuristician (problem solver).
Problem: Death by stabbing in a locked room.

87. "The Murder Trap" *short story* in The Man from U.N.C.L.E. Magazine, January 1967
Detective: Verner.
Problem: Death by stabbing in a locked room.

Applin, Arthur

88. ✓ THE ACTRESS *novel* U.K.: Hurst, (1927); U.S.: Duffield, 1930
Detective: Andrew Mordent.
Problem: Death by shooting in a locked library.

Archer, Robert

89. ✓ DEATH ON THE WATERFRONT *novel* U.S.: Doubleday, 1941; U.K.: Swan, 1948
Detective: Joel Stem, attorney.
Problem: Death by gassing in a locked room.

Arden, William (Dennis Lynds, q.v.)

90. "The Bizarre Case Expert" *short story* in EQMM, June 1970; "Ellery Queen's Anthology #30 1975; "Ellery Queen Masters of Mystery" U.S. Galahad, 1987
Detective: Sgt. Joseph Marx.
Problem: Death by blunt instrument of a woman in a room under constant observation. The only other person in the room was her ex-husband, who had been knocked unconscious. The blunt instrument was an antique telephone that was found standing upright on the floor, thus apparently alibiing the husband, who could not have struck the fatal blow, been knocked out by the victim, and still managed to leave the phone in that position.

Armstrong, Anthony

91. ✓ THE POISON TRAIL *novel* U.K.: Benn, 1932
Detective: Jimmy Rezaire.
Problem: Death by poison in a room under constant view.

Armstrong, Charlotte

92. ✓ THE DREAM WALKER *novel* U.K.: Davies, 1955, and U.S.: Coward, 1955; U.S. (as "Alibi for Murder"): Pocket, 1956
Detectives: Charley Ives, Olivia Hudson, and others.

Problem: Appearance of a woman's doppelganger in various places.

Arthur, Robert

93. "The Adventure of the Single Footprint" *short story* in EQMM, July 1948; EQMM Australia, January 1950; "Queen's Awards 3rd Series" U.S.: Little, 1948; U.K.: Gollancz, 1950; EQMM, February 2016
Detectives: John S. (Sherlock) Holmes and Lt. Oliver Baynes.
Problem: Death by shooting in the grounds of a fenced-in, inaccessible shooting lodge.

94. "The Case of the Murderous Mice" *short story* in Tower Magazines, 1933; The Mysterious Traveller, June 1953
Detective: Max Million.
Problem: Death by shooting in an upper-storey room locked on the outside and with one window open and in line of fire from another building where all inhabitants were alibied.

95. "The 51st Sealed Room, or, The MWA Murder" *short story* in EQMM, October 1951; "Tantalizing Locked Room Mysteries" U.S.: Walker, 1982
Detective: Harrison Mannix.
Problem: Death by decapitation in a locked room.

96. "The Glass Bridge" *short story* in AHMM, July 1957; "A Choice of Murders" U.S.: Scribners, 1958; "Alfred Hitchcock's Anthology # 5", Davis, 1979; U.K.: Macdonald, 1960
Detective: Baron de Hirsch.
Problem: Disappearance of a girl from a guarded, snow-surrounded house.

97. "The Mystery of the Man Who Evaporated" *short story* in "Alfred Hitchcock's Solve-Them-Yourself Mysteries" U.S.: Random, 1963; U.K.: Reinhardt, 1965
Detectives: Jeff Landrum and Howard Matthews.
Problem: Disappearance from a locked room.

Ashton, Charles

98. DANCE FOR A DEAD UNCLE *novel* U.K.: Museum, 1948
Detective: Inspector Merton.
Problem: Death by stabbing in a locked library.

99. DEATH GREETS A GUEST *novel* U.K.: Nicholson, 1936
Detective: Maj. Jack Atherley.
Problem: Death by shooting of a man sheltering in a summer

house during a rainstorm and under constant observation.

100. HERE'S MURDER DONE *novel* U.K.: Hale, 1943
Detective: Dick Sangster.
Problem: Murder in a locked, guarded house.

Ashton, Herbert (Jr.)

101. "The Locked Room: A Comedy Mystery in Three Acts" *play* U.K. and U.S.: French, 1934
Detectives: Det. Sgt. Dan Ryan and insurance investigator Ned Parker.
Problem: Death by shooting or stabbing in a locked study.

Ashton, Mark

102. ✓ A SILENCE OF BIRDS *novel* U.K.: Hale, 1979
Detective: John Radmell, journalist.
Problem: Death by unknown means of a man alone on a path near the coast.

Ashton-Wolfe, H.

103. "The Scented Death" *short story* in "Warped in the Making" U.K.: Hurst, (1928); U.S.: Houghton, 1928
Detective: Dr. Bertillon.
Problem: Death by poisoning in a locked room.

104. "The Suicide Room" *short story* in "Warped in the Making"
Detective: Bertillon.
Problem: Death by strangulation in a locked room.

Asimov, Isaac

105. THE CAVES OF STEEL *novel* U.S.: Doubleday, 1954; U.K.: Boardman, 1954
Detectives: Lije Baley and R(obot) Daneel Olivaw.
Problem: A spaceman is killed with a blaster inside a restricted area where blasters are not allowed. The only ways in are via normal entry points where a thorough check is made and via the open countryside that human beings can no longer tolerate; set in the future.

106. THE NAKED SUN *novel* U.S.: Doubleday, 1957; U.K.: Joseph, 1958
Detectives: Baley and Olivaw.
Problem: Murder with blunt instrument but no weapon at scene of crime; set on Solaria, "an outer planet."

107. "The Brazen Locked Room" *short story* in The Magazine of Fantasy & Science Fiction, November 1956; "Earth Is Room

Enough" U.S.: Doubleday, 1957, and U.K.: Faber, 1959; "All But Impossible!" U.S.: Ticknor, 1981

Problem: How to escape from a solid-bronze locked room. Success would mean a good position in Hell, failure relegation to that of an ordinary damned soul.

Asterley, H. C.

108. TALE OF TWO MURDERS *novel* U.K.: Readers Library, (1925-1935), and Jarrolds, 1932; U.S. (as "Mortmain"): Sears, 1932
Detective: None.
Problem: Death by defenestration from within a locked room.

Atholl, Justin

109. ✓ THE TRACKLESS THING *novel* U.K.: Everybody's, c. 1945
Detective: Superintendent Lakin.
Problems: (1) Various deaths by shooting in inaccessible upper-storey rooms or on a lawn with no footprints to account for the killer.
(2) The use of a gun as murder weapon that had remained locked in a drawer throughout the whole period.

Austin, Hugh

110. IT COULDN'T BE MURDER *novel* U.S.: Doubleday, 1935; U.K.: Heinemann, 1936
Detective: Peter Quint.
Problem: Death by gassing in a locked room.

111. MURDER IN TRIPLICATE *novel* U.S.: Doubleday, 1935; U.K.: Heinemann, 1936
Detective: Peter Quint.
Problem: Death by stabbing in a bathroom letting off a barricaded bedroom.

112. MURDER OF A MATRIARCH *novel* U.S.: Doubleday, 1936; U.K.: Heinemann, 1937
Detective: Peter Quint.
Problem: Death by poison in a guarded kitchen.

113. THE UPSIDE DOWN MURDERS *novel* U.S.: Doubleday, 1937; U.K.: Heinemann, 1938
Detective: Peter Quint.
Problem: Fingerprints of murderer do not match up to any of the suspects in a guarded area.

Aveline, Claude

114. THE DOUBLE DEATH OF FREDERIC BELOT *novel* U.S.: Holt,

1940; U.K.: Dobson, 1949

Detective: Simon Riviere.

Problem: (non-impossible) Chief of detectives found murdered and in the same room his murdered double.

Ayre, Thornton (John Russell Fearn, q.v.)

115. "The Crimson Rambler" *complete novel* in Toronto Star Weekly (Canada), May 31, 1947

Detective: Chief Inspector Douglas Gossage.

Problem: Death by shooting in a locked library.

B

Bailey, Seth

116. "The Hand in the Cobbler's Safe" *short story, true crime* in "The Hand in the Cobbler's Safe" U.S.: Bart, 1944

Detectives: Lieutenant Hass and others.

Problem: The finding of a severed hand in a safe locked and lockable only by its owner.

Baird, Edwin

117. "The Mystery of the Locked Door" *short story* in Sales Tales, 1928; "The World's Best One Hundred Detective Stories" (Volume 2) U.S.: Funk, 1929

Detective: Herbert Barry.

Problem: Death by cocaine poisoning in a locked room.

Baker, Douglas

118. "Lesson of History" *short story* in The Evening News, an issue for 1978

Comment: A nice little story about a time machine and providing, incidentally, an unusual solution to the "Marie Celeste" conundrum. When the time machine landed on the ship's deck, the whole crew in fear jumped overboard!

Baker, H. Barton

119. "An Odd Tale" *short story* in Belgravia Christmas Annual, 1883

Detective: The narrator, unnamed.

Problem: Attempted murder in a locked room in an inn.

Baker, Hugh

120. ✓ CARTWRIGHT IS DEAD, SIR! *novel* U.S.: Houghton, 1936

Detective: Richard Lind.
Problem: Death by unknown means aboard an ocean liner.

Ball, John

121. ✓ "Virgil Tibbs and the Fallen Body" *short story* in EQMM, September 1978; "Detectives A to Z" U.S.: "Ellery Queen's Anthology #45" Davis, 1983; Bonanza, 1985
Detective: Virgil Tibbs.
Problem: Death by defenestration from a building where it is found that no windows are broken, no one could have squeezed out of a window, and the dust on the inaccessible roof is undisturbed.

Ballinger, Bill

122. ✓ THE BODY BEAUTIFUL *novel* U.S.: Harper, 1949; U.K.: World, 1960
Detective: Barr Breed.
Problem: Death by stabbing of a showgirl sitting in a gilded seat hanging above the stage and not therefore accessible.

Balmer, Edwin, and Philip Wylie (q.v.)

123. FIVE FATAL WORDS *novel* U.S.: Smith, 1932; U.K.: Paul, (1933)
Detective: Donald Cornwall.
Problem: Death by electrocution in a locked bathroom.

Bankier, William

124. ✓ "The Locked Roomette" *short story* in EQMM, November 1990
Detective: Penni Dandridge, account executive.
Problem: Death by poison in a locked roomette on a moving train.

Barber, Alex

125. THE ROOM WITH NO ESCAPE *novel* U.K.: Hutchinson, (1932)
Detective: Urban Dormer.
Problem: Death by stabbing in a locked room.

Barker, Elsa

126. THE COBRA CANDLESTICK *novel* U.S.: Sears, 1928; U.K.: J. Hamilton, (1930)
Detective: Dexter Drake.
Problem: Death by blunt instrument in a room guarded at all exits.

Barker, Ronald

127. ✓ CLUE FOR MURDER *novel* U.K. & U.S.: Abelard, 1962

Detective: Inspector Harris.
Problem: Death by blunt instrument in a locked apartment in which the other people present claimed to be innocent.

Barlow, Vernon

128. THE GREEN MURDER *novel* U.K.: Cranton, 1931
Detective: Capt. Mark Fanning.
Problems: (1) Death by shooting in a locked room.
(2) Subsequent disappearance of the body from the locked, sealed room.

Barr, Mike W.

129. ✓ "Double Edge" *comic* in "The Maze Agency No. 6" U.S.: Comico, 1989
Detectives: Jennifer Mays and Gabriel Webb.
Problem: Death by stabbing in a room to which one door was barred and the other under surveillance.

130. ✓ "The English Channel Mystery" *short story* in "The Maze Agency No. 9" U.S.: Comico, 1990
Detectives: Mays, Webb, and Ellery Queen.
Problem: Death by shooting in a tent surrounded by unmarked sand.

Barr, Stephen

131. "The Locked House" *short story* in (as "The Locked Room to End Locked Rooms") EQMM, August 1965; "Best American Detective Stories of the Year 16th Annual Collection" U.K.: Boardman, 1967; "Best of the Best Detective Stories" U.S.: Dutton, 1971; "Big Book of Locked-Room Mysteries", Black Lizard, 2014
Detective: Dr. Sylvan Moore.
Problem: Death by decapitation in a locked house, with no one inside.

132. "The Procurator of Justice" *short story* in EQMM, February 1950
Detective: Fielding.
Problem: Disappearance of a man from a house under observation.

Barrett, Frank

133. THE JUSTIFICATION OF ANDREW LEBRUN *novel* U.K.: Heinemann, 1894; U.S.: Appleton, (1894)
Detective: David Leigh.

Problem: Disappearance of a girl's body within a guarded laboratory.

134. LADY JUDAS *play* U.K.: Chatto, 1903
Detective: Dr. Sturgess.
Problem: Death by poisoning in a locked room.

Barrett, Monte

135. ✓ THE PELHAM MURDER CASE *novel* U.S.: White House, 1930
Detective: Peter Cardigan, mystery novelist.
Problem: Death by shooting in a locked room.

Barry, Charles

136. ✓ THE SHOT FROM THE DOOR *novel* U.K.: Hurst, (1934); U.S.: Dutton, 1934
Detective: Retired Detective Superintendent Laurence Gilmartin.
Problem: Death by shooting in a room in which there were only the victim and one other innocent person.

Bartlett, E. G.

137. THE CASE OF THE THIRTEENTH COACH *novel* U.K.: Staples,1958
Detective: David Leigh.
Problem: Disappearance of a bullion coach from a moving train.

Barton, George

138. "The Adventure of the Bolted Door" *short story* in "The Strange Adventures of Bromley Barnes" U.S.: Page, 1918
Detective: Bromley Barnes.
Problem: Death by shooting in a locked room.

Baum, L. Frank

139. "The Suicide of Kiaros" *short story* in "The White Elephant," September 1897; Mystery Magazine February 15, 1918; EQMM, November 1954; EQMM UK January 1955; EQMM Australia March 1955; "Death Locked In" U.S.: IPL, 1987
Detective: The narrator, unnamed.
Problem: Death by stabbing in a locked room.

Bayly, A. Eric

140. ✓ THE HOUSE OF STRANGE SECRETS *novel* U.K.: Sands, 1899; U.S.: Dutton, 1899
Detective: Laurence Carrington.
Problem: Murderous attacks in a bedroom under guard.

Beck, Henry C.

141. ✓ DEATH BY CLUE *novel* U.S.: Dutton, 1933
Detectives: Father Mickle and Hilary Meredith, reporter.
Problem: Death by poison in a locked library.

Beck, K. K.

142. ✓ DEATH IN A DECK CHAIR *novel* U.S.: Walker, 1984
Detective: Iris Cooper.
Problem: Death by stabbing on the deck of a ship with all movements of other passengers apparently accounted for.

Bellem, Robert Leslie

143. ✓ "Homicide Spike" *short story* in Hollywood Detective, 1948; "Dan Turner, Hollywood Detective" U.S.: Bowling Green, 1983
Detective: Dan Turner.
Problem: Death by stabbing in a dummy iron maiden with fake rubber spikes.

Benedict, Gerald

144. ✓ THE CASE OF THE DEADLY DROPS *novel* U.S.: Phoenix, 1941
Detective: Nigel Mayne.
Problems: (1) Deaths by shooting in locked or watched apartments.
(2) Death by bludgeoning in an upper-storey area in which the victim was alone.

Bendel, Christopher

145. ✓ "Golconda's Magic Death" *short story* in "Amazing Stories from the World of Crime" U.K.: Hamlyn, 1983
Detectives: Mr. H. and Superintendent Stanley Hopkins.
Problem: Death by shooting on stage by an apparently empty gun.

Benét, Stephen Vincent

146. "The Amateur of Crime" *short story* in The American Magazine, April 1927; EQMM, December 1947; "Masterpieces of Mystery: The Prizewinners" U.S.: Davis, 1976
Detective: Peter Scarlet.
Problem: Death by stabbing in a locked room.

Bennett, Kem

147. ✓ THE WINK *novel* U.K.: Hart, 1951; U.S. (as "The Fabulous Wink"): Pellegrini, 1951
Detective: Inspector Robinet.

Problem: Disappearance of a small plaster statue from a locked and sealed church.

Bennett, Rolf

148. ✓ THE WEB *novel* U.K.: Hodder, 1917
Detective: James Turner, journalist.
Problem: Death by snake bite in a locked room under guard and where a second man in the room had mysteriously disappeared.

Benson, E. F.

149. ✓ "The Disappearance of Jacob Conifer" *short story* in The Windsor Magazine, October 1927; "Desirable Residences & Other Stories" U.K.: Oxford, 1991
Detective: None.
Problem: Disappearance of a millionaire from a workhouse bed leaving only pyjamas behind, and witnesses who swore that he never left.

Bentley, E. C.

150. "The Ordinary Hairpins" *short story* in "Great Short Stories of Detection, Mystery and Horror" U.K.: Gollancz, 1931; "Second Omnibus of Crime" U.S.: Coward, 1932; "Trent Intervenes" U.K.: Nelson, 1938; U.S.: Knopf, 1938; "Big Book of Locked-Room Mysteries", Black Lizard, 2014
Detective: Philip Trent.
Problem: Disappearance and assumed suicide of an operatic star.

151. "The Sweet Shot" *short story* in "Trent Intervenes"; "Detection Medley" U.K.: Hutchinson, (1939); "Line-Up" U.S.: Dodd, 1940; "101 Years' Entertainment" U.S.: Little, 1942; "Sporting Detective Stories" U.K.: Faber, 1946; EQMM Australia November 1952; AHMM March 2003
Detective: Trent.
Problem: Death of a man playing a solitary round of golf; no one else in his vicinity.

152. "The Unknown Peer" *short story* in "Trent Intervenes"; "Second Century of Detective Stories" U.K.: Hutchinson, (1938); "The Delights of Detection" U.S.: Criterion, 1961
Detective: Trent.
Problem: Disappearance of a peer while on a sketching trip.

153. "The Vanishing Lawyer" *short story* in "Trent Intervenes"
Detective: Trent.

Problem: Vanishing of a lawyer.

Bentley, John

154. BULLETS MAKE HOLES *novel* U.K.: Hutchinson, (1944)
Detective: Glen Gibson, attorney.
Problem: Death by hanging in a locked room.

155. THE LANDOR CASE *novel* U.K.: Chapman, 1937
Detective: Sir Richard Herrivell.
Problem: Death by hanging in a locked office.

156. THE L'ESTRANGE CASE *novel* U.K.: Eldon, 1935
Detective: Herrivell.
Problem: Death by strangulation of a medium in a séance room where the other occupants could not have committed the crime.

157. THE WHITNEY CASE *novel* U.K.: Chapman, 1937
Detective: Herrivell.
Problem: Death of a boxer by an invisible agent during a fight.

Berkeley, Anthony (see also Platts, A. Monmouth)

158. DEATH IN THE HOUSE *novel* U.K.: Hodder, 1939; U.S.: Doubleday, 1939
Detective: Lord Arthur Linton.
Problem: Death by poisoning in the House of Commons in full view of the whole assembly.

159. THE LAYTON COURT MYSTERY *novel* U.K.: (first published anonymously) Jenkins, 1925; U.S.: Doubleday, 1929
Detective: Roger Sheringham.
Problem: Death by shooting in a locked room.

Bernede, Arthur

160. THE HAUNTED HOUSE *novel* U.K.: Readers Library, (1930)
Detective: Chantecoq.
Problem: Various phenomena such as knockings and fireballs occurring inside and outside of locked doors and houses.

161. THE MYSTERY OF THE LOUVRE *novel* U.K.: Readers Library, (1929)
Detective: Chantecoq.
Problem: Various deaths, attacks, etc., in the locked, guarded room of the barbarous gods in the Louvre.

Berrow, Norman

162. THE BISHOP'S SWORD *novel* U.K.: Ward, 1948; U.S. Ramble House 2005
Detective: Detective Inspector Lancelot Carolus Smith.

Problems: (1) Disappearance of a sword from a hermetically sealed cabinet.

(2) Appearance of a jailed man's "psychic body" in the chief constable's bedroom.

(3) Disappearance of a man from a cave while the only exit was under observation.

163. DON'T JUMP, MR. BOLAND! *novel* U.K.: Ward, 1954; U.S.: Ramble House 2005

Detective: J. Montague Belmore, actor.

Problem: Disappearance of a man who jumped from a sheer cliff and was not to be found at the bottom of it.

164. THE FOOTPRINTS OF SATAN *novel* U.K.: Ward, 1950; U.S.: Ramble House 2005

Detective: Detective Inspector Smith.

Problem: Two deaths in open snow. The only footprints about are those of the victim and Satan.

165. GHOST HOUSE *novel* U.K.: Ward, 1940; Hale, (1979); U.S.: St. Martin's, 1980; U.S.: Ramble House 2005

Detective: Captain Matthews.

Problem: Death of a man in a section of an old house while the only other occupants were gathered elsewhere.

Comment: The St. Martin's edition is a re-written version of the 1940 original. Ramble House sells both the original text and the updated text.

166. IT HOWLS AT NIGHT *novel* U.K.: Ward, 1937; U.S.: Ramble House 2005

Detectives: Lt. Geoff Martin and his three "silly ass" assistants.

Problem: Deaths of several people by having their throats torn out by a supposed werewolf.

167. THE SPANIARD'S THUMB *novel* U.K.: Ward, 1949; U.S.: Ramble House 2005

Detective: Detective Inspector Smith.

Problem: Death by blunt instrument in a locked cellar.

168. THE THREE TIERS OF FANTASY *novel* U.K.: Ward, 1947; U.S.: Ramble House 2005

Detective: Smith.

Problems: (1) Disappearance of a man from a house where he was heard to go upstairs. The man had supposedly been dead for seven years and was not visible to anyone but his lady friend.

(2) Disappearance of a room from an inn and on the floor in which it existed.

(3) Disappearance of a street.

Bestor, George Clinton

169. THE POSTAGE STAMP MURDER *novel* U.S.: Dial, 1935; U.K.: Low, 1936

Detective: Gwaylor.

Problem: Death by electrocution in a locked bathroom.

Betteridge, Don

170. CAST IRON ALIBI *novel* U.K.: Jenkins, 1939

Detectives: Inspector Duncan and Capt. Peter Darrell.

Problem: Death by shooting in a room under observation and containing, apart from the victim, one person who did not commit the murder.

Bishop, Stacey

171. DEATH IN THE DARK *novel* U.K.: Faber, 1930; U.S.: Locked Room International, 2017

Detective: Stephen Bayard.

Problems: (1) Death by shooting in a pitch-black room where no one but the victim was apparently present.

(2) Death by shooting in a room full of people, without trace of the weapon.

(3) Death by shooting in a locked room.

Black, Lionel

172. ✓ THE PENNY MURDERS *novel* U.K.: Collins, 1979; U.S.: Avon, 1980

Detectives: Kate and Henry Theobald.

Problem: Death by shooting in a house in which the alarms had not been activated and yet the only key to them was found on the person of the deceased.

Blackmon, Anita

173. THERE IS NO RETURN *novel* U.S.: Doubleday, 1938; U.K. (as "The Riddle of the Dead Cats"): Butterworth, 1939

Detective: Adelaide Evans.

Problem: Attempted murder in a locked room.

Blake, Nicholas

174. ✓THE CASE OF THE ABOMINABLE SNOWMAN *novel* U.K.: Collins, 1941; U.S. (as "The Corpse in the Snowman"): Harper, 1941

Detective: Nigel Strangeways.
Problem: Death by hanging in a locked bedroom.

Blassingame, Wyatt

175. "The Murder Master" *short story* in Detective Tales 1940; "John Smith Hears Death Walking" U.S.: Bartholomew, 1944
Detective: John Smith.
Problem: Death by poisoning by invisible agency.

Blayn, Hugo (John Russell Fearn, q.v.)

176. THE FIVE MATCHBOXES *novel* U.K.: Paul, (1948)
Detectives: Inspector Garth and Sergeant Whittaker.
Problem: Death by shooting in a locked room.
177. FLASHPOINT *novel* U.K.: Paul, (1950)
Detective: Dr. Carruthers.
Problem: Arson by remote control involving the destruction of a fishmonger's shop.
178. THE SILVERED CAGE *novel* U.K.: Dragon, 1955
Detectives: Inspector Garth and Sergeant Whittaker.
Problems: (1) Disappearance of a woman from within a silvered cage.
(2) Murder in a locked room.
179. ✓ WHAT HAPPENED TO HAMMOND? *novel* U.K.: Paul, 1951
Detectives: Dr. Carruthers and Inspector Garth.
Problem: Disappearance of a man from a house that he is seen to enter but that contains an undisturbed covering of dust, and his subsequent, almost immediate, reappearance as a corpse some miles away.

Bliss, Adam

180. THE CAMPDEN RUBY MURDER *novel* U.S.: Barse, 1931; U.K.: Rich, 1934
Detective: Captain Keyes.
Problem: Victim killed in the presence of witnesses but no one close enough to touch her.

Blochman, Lawrence G.

181. "Dr. Coffee and the Pardell Case" *short story* in EQMM, June 1972
Detective: Dr. Daniel Coffee.
Problem: Death by shooting in a locked room.
182. "Murder Behind Schedule" *short story* in "Clues for Doctor Coffee" U.S.: Lippincott, 1964; formerly "Young Wife" in This

Week Magazine
Detective: Coffee.
Problem: Murder in a locked room.

183. "Reprieve" *short story* in Private Detective Stories, December 1943; The Saint Mystery Magazine (UK), December 1962; The Saint Mystery Magazine, April 1963; "The Locked Room Reader" U.S.: Random, 1968; "8 Doors to Death" U.S.: Dell, 1970
Detective: Roderick Poplar of the Abraxas Detective Agency.
Problem: Death by gassing in a locked room.

184. "Wrong-Way Tosca" *short story* in "Clues for Doctor Coffee"; (as "The Killer with No Fingerprints") in EQMM, June 1964
Detectives: Coffee and Dr. Mookerji.
Problem: Murderer left bloody fingerprints but prints had no identifying marks.

Block, Lawrence

185. BURGLARS CAN'T BE CHOOSERS *novel* U.S.: Random, 1977; U.K.: Hale, 1978
Detective: Bernard Grimes Rhodenbarr, burglar.
Problem: Death by blunt instrument in a locked apartment in which an innocent, nonhomicidal burglar was supposedly working alone.

Blow, Lynton

186. THE BOURNEWICK MURDERS *novel* U.K.: Butterworth, 1935
Detective: Police Constable Murdoch.
Problem: Death by close-range pistol shot with no footprints in the surrounding sand.

Blyth, Harry

187. ✓ SEXTON BLAKE'S TRIUMPH *novel* in The Union Jack No. 15, Aug. 18, 1894
Detective: Sexton Blake.
Problem: Disappearance of a man from a locked house under surveillance.

Bobin, J. W.

188. "The Secret of the Sarcophagus" *novelette* in The Union Jack, April 5, 1924
Detective: Sexton Blake.
Problems: (1) Disappearance of a killer whose scent suddenly stops (makes a change from footprints!).

(2) Appearance of a ghostly figure within a guarded room.

Bodkin, M. McDonnell

189. "Murder by Proxy" *short story* in "Paul Beck, the Rule of Thumb Detective" U.K.: Pearson, 1898; U.S.: Short Stories, Doubleday Page, January 1918; "Death Locked In"; IPL, 1987
Detective: Paul Beck.
Problem: Death by shooting in a room in which the victim was alone.

190. "The Unseen Hand" *short story* in "The Quests of Paul Beck" U.K.: Unwin, 1908; U.S.: Little, 1910
Detective: Beck.
Problem: Death by blunt instrument in a train compartment of which the victim was the only occupant.

191. "The Vanishing Diamonds" *short story* in Pearson's Weekly, Jan. 23,1897; EQMM, August 1949; EQMM Australia, June 1950; "Paul Beck, the Rule of Thumb Detective"; MSMM, October 1973
Detective: Alfred Juggins/Paul Beck.
Problem: Disappearance of diamonds from a sealed jewellery case.
Note: In the original magazine appearances of the first series of "Paul Beck" stories, the detective was given the name of Alfred Juggins, the name being changed to Paul Beck for book publication. Juggins was retained for the 1973 magazine publication, which was accompanied by an article by Sam Moskowitz describing the history of the change.

Bohle, Edgar

192. THE MAN WHO DISAPPEARED *novel* U.S.: Random, 1958; U.K.: Boardman, 1960
Detective: Dick Stoddart.
Problem: Disappearance of a man from a guarded area.

Boileau, Pierre, and Thomas Narcejac

193. THE TUBE *novel* U.K.: H. Hamilton, 1960
Detective: Superintendent Mareuil.
Problems: (1) Death by shooting in a guarded laboratory.
(2) Death by shooting in a guarded house.

194. "The Sleeping Beauty" *short story* in "The Evil Eye": U.K.: Hutchinson, 1959
Detective: Alain de Muzillac.

Problem: Return from death of a nobleman and his family.
Bonnamy, Francis

195. "The Loaded House" *short story* in EQMM, December 1950
Detective: Peter Utley Shane.
Problem: Death by shooting of a man trying on his own to open the front door of a house.

Bonney, Joseph

196. NO MAN'S HAND *novel* U.K.: Heinemann, 1940; U.S.: (as "Murder Without Clues"): Carrick, 1940
Detective: Simon Rolfe, crime analyst.
Problem: Death by stabbing in a locked room.

Booth, Charles

197. ✓ SINISTER HOUSE *novel* U.S.: Morrow, 1926; U.K.: Hodder, 1927
Detectives: Kerry O'Neil and Gail Hollister.
Problem: Death by strangulation in a locked house.

Booth, Christopher

198. ✓ DECEIVER'S DOOR *novel* U.S.: Chelsea, 1929
Detectives: Bob Fetherston and Sergeant Quinn.
Problems: (1) Disappearance of a man from a house under constant observation.
(2) A figure which is impervious to bullets and which crumples before a hand-to-hand attack.

Boucher, Anthony (see also Holmes, H. H.)

199. THE CASE OF THE SOLID KEY *novel* U.S.: Simon, 1941
Detective: Fergus O'Breen.
Problem: Death by blunt instrument in a locked room.

200. "The Anomaly of the Empty Man" *short story* in F&SF April, 1952; "Crooks Tour" U.S.: Dodd, 1953, and U.K.: Macdonald, 1954; "Cream of the Crime" U.S. Holt, 1962; U.K.: Harrap, 1964
Detective: Inspector Abrahams.
Problem: Disappearance of a man from a complete outfit of clothes.

201. "Elsewhen" *short story* in "Murder: Plain and Fanciful" U.S.: Sheridan, 1948; "Death Locked In" U.S.: IPL, 1987
Detective: Fergus O'Breen.
Problem: Death by stabbing in a locked library in the presence of one innocent witness.

202. "Gandolphus" *short story* in "A Decade of Fantasy & Science Fiction" U.S.: Doubleday, 1960
Detective: O'Breen.
Problem: Murder in a locked room under observation.

203. "The Smoke-Filled Locked Room" *short story* in "The Locked Room Reader" U.S.: Random, 1968; "8 Doors to Death" U.S.: Dell, 1970
Detective: Lieutenant Liebermann.
Problem: Death by throat cutting in a bathroom, without trace of weapon.

Bowen, Joseph

204. THE MAN WITHOUT A HEAD *novel* U.S.: Covici, 1936; U.K.: Butterworth, 1937
Detective: Manuel Cortina.
Problem: Death by decapitation in a locked room.

Bowen, Marjorie

205. ✓ "The Orford Mystery; Covent Garden 1734" *short story* in "Old Patch's Medley" U.K.: Selwyn, 1930
Detective: Captain Hoare.
Problem: Death by stabbing in a locked room.

Bowen, Michael

206. ✓ WASHINGTON DECEASED *novel* U.S.: St. Martin's, 1990
Detective: Richard Michaelson.
Problem: Death by shooting, as recorded on videotape, inside a locked supply room.

Bowen, Wilfred J. L.

207. "The Bungalow Mystery" *short story* in "Contemporary Short Stories" U.K.: Mitre, 1929
Detective: Centenier Pinot.
Problem: Disappearance of a briefcase from a locked room.

Brady, Nicholas (see also Turner, John V.)

208. THE HOUSE OF STRANGE GUESTS *novel* U.K.: Bles, 1932; U.S.: Holt, 1932
Detective: The Rev. Ebenezer Buckle.
Problem: Death by gassing in a locked bathroom.

Braly, David

209. ✓ "The Gallowglass" *short story* in AHMM, August 1986
Detective: Gardai Detective Chief Inspector Phelim Kane.
Problem: Death by blunt instrument in a locked library.

Bramah, Ernest

210. "The Ghost at Massingham Mansions" *short story* in "The Eyes of Max Carrados" U.K.: Richards, 1923, and U.S.: Doran, 1924; "Great Short Stories of Detection, Mystery and Horror" (first series) U.K.: Gollancz, 1928, and U.S.: Payson, 1929; 'Tales of Detection" U.K.: Dent, 1936; "Best Max Carrados Detective Stories" U.S.: Dover, 1972

Detective: Max Carrados.

Problem: The gas is lit and a bath filled with water—regularly— in a locked, uninhabited flat.

211. "The Tragedy at Brookbend Cottage" *short story* in "Max Carrados" U.K.: Methuen, 1914; "101 Years' Entertainment" U.S.: Little, 1941; EQMM August 1951; AHMM March 1997; "Best Max Carrados Detective Stories" U.S.: Dover, 1972

Detective: Carrados.

Problem: Death by electrocution in an isolated room.

Brand, Christianna

212. THE CROOKED WREATH *novel* U.S.: Dodd, 1946; U.K. (as "Suddenly at His Residence"): Bodley, 1947

Detective: Inspector Cockrill.

Problems: (1) Death by poison in a lodge only approached by a sanded path, unmarked but for one set of apparently innocent tracks.

(2) Death by poison in a room covered with dust and with only the victim's footprints in the room.

213. DEATH OF JEZEBEL *novel* U.S.: Dodd, 1948; U.K.: Bodley, 1949

Detectives: Cockrill and Detective Inspector Charlesworth.

Problem: Murder in a sealed, guarded section of a stage.

214. "Murder Game" *short story* in "What Dread Hand" U.K.: Joseph, 1968; (as "The Gemminy Crickets Case") in EQMM, August 1968; "Buffet for Unwelcome Guests", Southern Illinois University Press, 1983

Detective: The old man.

Problem: Death by strangulation in a sealed office.

215. "The Scapegoat" *short story* in "Brand X" U.K.: Joseph, 1974; EQMM, August 1970; "Buffet for Unwelcome Guests", Southern Illinois University Press, 1983; "The Mammoth Book of Great Detective Stories" U.K.: Robinson, 1985

Detective: Inspector Block.
Problem: Gunshot fired from a guarded roof where no murderer can be found.

216. ✓ "Upon Reflection" *short story* in EQMM, August 1977; "Buffet for Unwelcome Guests" U.S.: Southern Illinois University, 1983
Detective: Mrs. Dorinda Jones.
Problem: Disappearance from a Rolls-Royce limousine of a man who had apparently stabbed to death the other occupant, an evil but fabulously wealthy sheik.

Brandon, Charles

217. ✓ THE PHANTOM MUSKETEER *novel* U.K.: Jenkins, 1929
Detective: John Fortescue.
Problem: Death by shooting in a locked room.

Brandon, John G.

218. ✓ THE ONE-MINUTE MURDER *novel* U.K.: Methuen, 1934; U.S.: Dial, 1935
Detective: Burman.
Problem: Death of an actress while performing on stage in front of an audience, but no gun can be found in anyone's possession.

Brean, Herbert

219. WILDERS WALK AWAY *novel* U.S.: Morrow, 1948; U.K.: Heinemann, 1949
Detective: Reynold Frame, free-lance journalist/photographer.
Problems: Disappearances (three) from rooms under observation and (two) from a sandy beach.

220. ✓ "The Man Who Talked with Spirits" *short story* in Thrilling Detective, September 1943; Thrilling Detective (U.K.), July 1954
Detectives: Tick Johnson and Fred Murphy, newspapermen.
Problem: Death by shooting in a locked, upper-storey hotel room.

221. "Murder Buys a Ticket" *short story* in Exciting Detective, Winter 1941; (as "Nine Hours Late on Opening Run") in EQMM (U.S.), December 1957
Detective: Marty Malone, bus driver.
Problem: Murder in an isolated bus by a hypodermic syringe that bore the fingerprints of no one on the bus.

Breen, Jon L.

222. "The House of the Shrill Whispers" *short story* in EQMM, August 1972; "Hair of the Sleuthhound" U.S.: Scarecrow, 1982
Detective: Sir Gideon Merrimac ("Old Giddy").
Problem: Death by shooting in a locked, guarded house surrounded by artificial snow.

223. ✓ "The Number 12 Jinx" *short story* in EQMM, May 1978; "All But Impossible!" U.S.: Ticknor, 1981; "Kill the Umpire: The Calls of Ed Gorgon", Crippen & Landru, 2003
Detective: Ed Gorgan, major league baseball umpire.
Problem: Disappearance of a baseball player in the tunnel leading from the playing area to the dressing room.

224. ✓ "The Problem of the Vanishing Town" *short story* in EQMM, November 1979
Detective: Dr. Sid Shoehorn.
Problem: Disappearance of a whole town.

Brenn, George

225. VOICES *novel* U.S.: Century, 1923; U.K.: Jenkins, 1925
Detective: Charlie Fenwick, the phonic criminologist.
Problem: Death by shooting in a locked room.

Brennan, Joseph Payne

226. "The Case of the Uncut Corpse" *short story* in "The Casebook of Lucius Leffing" U.S.: Macabre, 1973
Detective: Lucius Leffing.
Problem: Death by hanging of a man from a tree growing in inaccessible marshland.

227. "Fingers of Steel" *short story* in AHMM, December 1970; "The Casebook of Lucius Leffing"
Detective: Leffing.
Problem: Murder by beating and strangulation in a locked room, where the victim's only companion was his wheelchair-bound sister.

Brennan, Robert

228. THE TOLEDO DAGGER *novel* U.K.: J. Hamilton, (1927)
Detective: Inspector Favart.
Problem: Death by stabbing in a locked room.

Bretnor, Reginald

229. ✓ A KILLING IN SWORDS *novel* U.S.: Pocket, 1978
Detective: Alastair Alexandrovitch Timuroff.

Problem: Various murders in and the disappearance of a life-size mannequin from a locked room in an old house full of secret passages.

Brett, Stephen

230. ✓ SOME DIE HARD *novel U.S.: Manor, 1979*
Detective: Rock Dugan, private eye.
Problem: Death by stabbing while in flight of the only occupant of a light airplane.

Bridgmont, Leslie

231. UNBRIEFED MISSION *novel* U.K.: Falcon, 1953
Detective: Geoffrey Cordell.
Problem: Death by shooting in a locked room.

Brittain, William

232. "The Impossible Footprint" *short story* in AHMM, November 1974; "Death on Arrival" U.S.: Dell, 1979; The Mammoth Book of Perfect Crimes and Impossible Mysteries", UK: Constable and Robinson, 2006, US: Carroll and Graf, 2007
Detective: Joshua Red Wing.
Problem: The print of an amputated foot is found next to the amputee's body, though the foot is in a trap many yards away.

233. "The Man Who Read John Dickson Carr" *short story* in EQMM, December 1965; "Ellery Queen's Crime Carousel" U.S.: N.A.L., 1966, and U.K.: Gollancz, 1967; "The Locked Room Reader" U.S.: Random, 1968; "8 Doors to Death" U.S.: Dell, 1970
Detective: None.
Problem: Death by stabbing in a locked library.

234. "Mr. Strang Finds an Angle" *short story* in EQMM, June 1971
Detective: Mr. Strang.
Problem: Disappearance of a blunt instrument from an area that was under constant guard within seconds of the assault by blunt instrument occurring.

235. "Mr. Strang Pulls a Switch" *short story* in EQMM, June 1969; "Time Bomb and Other Stories of Mystery and Suspense" U.S.: Scholastic, 1971
Detective: Strang.
Problem: Disappearance of a student from his locked bedroom.

236. "Mr. Strang Takes a Field Trip" *short story* in EQMM, December 1968; "All But Impossible!" U.S.: Ticknor, 1981; "The

Mammoth Book of Locked-Room Mysteries and Impossible Crimes", U.K.: Constable and Robinson, 2000, U.S.: Carroll and Graf, 2000

Detective: Strang.

Problem: Disappearance of a solid-gold burial mask from a museum room under guard.

237. ✓ "Mr. Strang Unlocks a Door" *short story* in EQMM, June 17, 1981

Detective: Strang.

Problem: The placing of documents in an envelope already sealed and taped.

Brock, Alan

238. MISS HAMBLETT'S GHOST *novel* U.K.: Macdonald, 1946

Detective: Ex-District Superintendent Beach of the Bengal Police.

Problem: Attempted murder by gassing in a locked room.

Brody, Marc

239. ✓ MURDER IS A MAIDEN'S HANDICAP *novel* Australia: Horwitz, 1958

Detective: Marc Brody, reporter.

Problem: A body that keeps appearing and disappearing from a chair in a room locked on the outside but not on the inside. The detective isn't actually in the room when it disappears, but the number of times it happens and the short intervals between manifestations are little short of surprising.

Brooks, Collin

240. THE GHOST HUNTERS *novel* U.K.: Hutchinson, (1928); Sears, 1928

Detective: Raeburn Steel.

Problem: Death by defenestration from within a locked room.

Brooks, Edwy Searles (see also Gray, Berkeley; Gunn, Victor, and Ross, Carlton)

241. ✓ THE PHANTOM OF TREGELLIS CASTLE *novel* U.K.: Nelson Lee Library, Dec. 1, 1917

Detective: Nelson Lee.

Problem: Disappearance of a phantom cavalier and a kidnap victim from an area of unmarked snow.

242. "The Electric Man" *novelette* in The Union Jack, May 31, 1924

Detective: Sexton Blake.

Problem: Disappearance of a murdered man from a locked library.

Brown, Carter

243. THE CREATIVE MURDERS *novel* U.S.: Signet, 1971
Detective: Al Wheeler.
Problem: Death by shooting in a locked room.

244. THE LADY IS TRANSPARENT *novel* U.S.: Signet, 1962
Detective: Wheeler.
Problem: Death by throat cutting in a locked room.

Brown, Fredric

245. ✓ DEATH HAS MANY DOORS *novel* U.S.: Dutton, 1951; U.K.: Boardman, 1952
Detectives: Ed and Am Hunter.
Problem: (1) Murder by induced heart attack in a room under constant observation. (2) Death by drowning of a man who swam far beyond his known ability to swim back.

246. ✓ "The Case of the Bewildering Bam" *short story* in "The Water-Walker" U.S.: Macmillan, 1990; originally in Feedstuffs magazine
Detective: Ernie, assistant at Feedum and Weap, feed dealers.
Problem: The paint on a freshly painted bam changed colour overnight.

247. ✓ "The Case of the Conjurer's Cat" *short story* in "The Water-Walker"; originally in Feedstuffs magazine
Detective: Ernie.
Problem: The pink paw prints of a cat found on a recently papered ceiling when they had apparently not been present at the time of the papering.

248. ✓ "The Case of the Flying Cow, or How did the Critter Get into the Silo" *short story* in "The Water-Walker"; originally in Feedstuffs magazine
Detective: Ernie.
Problem: Appearance of a cow and two calves inside a metal silo.

249. ✓ "The Case of the Haunted Haystack" *short story* in "The Water-Walker"; originally in Feedstuffs magazine
Detective: Ernie.
Problem: A haystack apparently with the ability to move of its own volition.

250. ✓ “The Case of the Refrigerating Windmill” *short story* in “The Water-Walker”; originally in Feedstuffs magazine
Detective: Ernie.
Problem: Intense cold—bad enough to cause frostbite—coming without reason in the middle of and during a spell of steamy, hot weather.

251. ✓ “The Case of the Uncountable Sheep” *short story* in “The Water-Walker”; originally in Feedstuffs magazine
Detective: Ernie.
Problem: Constantly changing numbers of sheep in a flock as it is counted each night into a large shed.

252. ✓ “The Case of the Wandering Scarecrow” *short story* in “The Water-Walker”; originally in Feedstuffs magazine
Detective: Ernie.
Problem: A scarecrow is apparently seen walking about and is shown to have moved.

253. ✓ “Ernie Catches Up with Wily Willie, or The Case of the Vanishing Duck” *short story* in “The Water-Walker”; originally in Feedstuffs magazine
Detective: Ernie.
Problem: Disappearance of a duck from a pond under constant observation.

254. ✓ “Ernie, Minister of Peace and Goodness, or The Case of the Multiplying Eggs” *short story* in “The Water-Walker”; originally in Feedstuffs magazine
Detective: Ernie.
Problem: Hens apparently laying more eggs than was physically possible.

255. ✓ “Ernie Stops Shivering, or The Case of the Trackless Tractor” *short story* in “The Water-Walker”; originally in Feedstuffs magazine
Detective: Ernie.
Problem: Appearance of a tractor in the middle of a snow-covered field but with no tracks leading to it.

256. “The Laughing Butcher” *short story* in “Mostly Murder” U.S.: Dutton, 1953; U.K.: Boardman, 1954; “Big Book of Locked-Room Mysteries”, Black Lizard, 2014
Detective: Bill.
Problem: A body is found in the middle of a snow-covered field,

with two sets of prints leading to it but none away from it.

257. ✓ "Miracle on Vine Street" *short story* in The Layman's Magazine, January 1941; "The Water-Walker"
Detective: Roger L. Young, Doctor of Divinity.
Problem: Footprints of a cat left in pink paint on a newly papered ceiling.

258. "The Spherical Ghoul" *short story* in The Saint Mystery Magazine (U.K.), December 1961; "Death Locked In" U.S.: IPL, 1987
Detective: Jerry Grant.
Problem: Defacing of a corpse lying in a morgue under constant supervision.

259. "Whistler's Murder" *short story* in Street & Smith's Detective Story Magazine, December 1946, "Street & Smith's Detective Story Annual", 1949; Street & Smith's Detective Story Magazine (UK), September 1950; "The Shaggy Dog and Other Stories" U.S.: Dutton, 1963, and U.K.: Boardman, 1964; (as "Mr. Smith Protects a Client") in EQMM, January 1961
Detective: Henry Smith of the Phalanx Insurance Co.
Problem: Death by stabbing in a guarded house.

Brown, Walter C.

260. MURDER AT MOCKING HOUSE *novel* U.S.: Lippincott, 1933
Detective: Steve Harper.
Problem: Death by shooting in a snow-surrounded house and no footprints to account for the murderer.

Browne, Douglas G.

261. THE STOLEN BOAT-TRAIN *novel* U.K.: Methuen, 1935
Detective: Legarde.
Problem: Disappearance of a boat-train.

262. WHAT BECKONING GHOST *novel* U.K.: Macdonald, 1947
Detective: Harvey Tuke.
Problem: Disappearance of a ghostly figure.

Browne, Howard

263. THIN AIR *novel* U.S.: Simon, 1954; U.K.: Gollancz, 1955
Detective: Ames Coryell.
Problem: (Non-impossible) Disappearance of Coryell's wife from her home after she had returned to it from holiday at 3 a.m.
Skupin Comment: I asked Bob Adey why he listed this when it's not impossible. He said he particularly liked it and wanted to

give it visibility. "Editor's prerogative!" he said.

Bruce, Kennedy

264. ✓ THE POISONED FANG *novel* U.K.: Jenkins, 1930
Detective: Jyotish Babu, the Bengali detective.
Problem: Death by poisoning in a locked and bolted hotel bedroom.

Bruce, Leo

265. CASE FOR THREE DETECTIVES *novel* U.K.: Bles, 1936; U.S.: Stokes, 1937
Detectives: Sergeant Beef, Lord Simon Plimsoll, Amer Picon, and Monsignor Smith.
Problem: Death by throat cutting in a locked room.

266. NOTHING LIKE BLOOD *novel* U.K.: Davies, 1962; U.S.: Academy, 1985
Detective: Carolus Deene, schoolmaster.
Problem: Death by defenestration from a locked room.

Bryant, Lynn S.

267. ✓ "An Inside Job" *short story* in Woman's World, July 3, 1984
Detectives: Detectives Andrews and Holbrook.
Problem: Death by shooting in a locked sitting room.

Buchanan, Madeleine

268. HAUNTED BELLS *novel* U.S.: Chelsea, 1929; U.K.: Skeffington, (1931)
Detective: Ray Bartley.
Problem: Murders in a disused belfry.

Bude, John

269. ✓ DEATH KNOWS NO CALENDAR *novel* U.K.: Cassell, 1942
Detective: Major Boddy.
Problems: (1) Death by shooting in a locked studio.
(2) Disappearance of a car from a stretch of fenced road with no apparent exits.

270. ✓ DEATH ON PAPER *novel* U.K.: Hale, (1940)
Detectives: Sgt. Pembury Green and his father, Superintendent Green.
Problem: Disappearance of an invalid old man, who could only move in a wheelchair, from a house locked and bolted on the inside.

Bull, Albert E.

271. ✓ THE BRAND OF CAIN *novel* in Pearson's Weekly, April 20

and June 1, 1911

Detective: None.

Problem: Murder in a locked room.

Bullivant, Cecil H.

272. "Delgray's Alibi" *short story* in Yes or No, August 1916; "Garnett Bell, Detective" U.K.: Odhams, (1920); Wright, (1935)

Detective: Garnett Bell.

Problem: Death by gunshot in a locked room.

Burmar (Richard Marr)

273. THE SMITH SLAYER *novel* U.K.: Gardner, (1939); (as by Richard Marr) Big Ben, 1940

Detective: Inspector David Reefe.

Problem: Death by poisoning in a watched and guarded house.

Burnaby, Nigel

274. THE CLUE OF THE GREEN-EYED GIRL *novel* U.K.: Ward, 1935

Detective: Sir Timothy Rossiter.

Problem: Death by stabbing in a beach hut, the entrance to which was surrounded by unmarked sand.

Burning, Michael, and Althea Grey

275. ✓ DUSTY DEATH *novel* U.K.: Jenkins, 1949

Detectives: Inspector Hawling and Professor Erskine.

Problem: Death by cyanide poisoning of a lecturer lecturing to a class of students.

Burrage, A. M.

276. DON'T BREAK THE SEAL *novel* U.K.: Swan, 1946

Detective: Nick Rockwell.

Problem: Presence of a sealed room that the hero is not allowed to enter on pain of losing his inheritance.

Burton, Miles (see also Rhode, John)

277. ✓ THE CAT JUMPS *novel* U.K.: Collins, 1946

Detectives: Inspector Arnold and Desmond Merrion.

Problem: Death by stabbing in a locked room.

278. DEATH LEAVES NO CARD *novel* U.K.: Collins, 1939

Detective: Arnold.

Problem: Death by induced heart attack in a locked bathroom.

279. TO CATCH A THIEF *novel* U.K.: Collins, 1934

Detectives: Arnold and Merrion.

Problem: Death by poison in a locked room.

Bush, Geoffrey

280. ✓ "The Last Meeting of the Butlers Club" *short story* in EQMM, March 10, 1980; "Last Laughs" U.S.: Mysterious, 1986
Detective: Lord Peter Wimsey.
Problem: Death by knife wound in a billiard room in which only the victim and his innocent butler were present.

C

Cambridge, Ada

281. "At Midnight" *novelette* in "At Midnight and Other Stories" U.K.: Ward, 1897; also published in the Ward Lock Copyright Editions series
Detectives: Billy and Nettie Wingrave.
Problem: Appearance and disappearance of lights and people inside a locked room.

Cameron, Lou

282. BEHIND THE SCARLET DOOR *novel* U.S.: Fawcett, 1971; U.K.: World, 1972
Detective: Sgt. Morgan Price.
Problems: (1) Deaths of people (three) whose corpses on disinterment show signs of putrefaction further advanced than it should have been.
(2) Assault in a locked room.

Camp, Wadsworth

283. THE ABANDONED ROOM *novel* U.S.: Doubleday, 1917; U.K.: Jarrolds, 1919
Detective: Bobby Blackburn.
Problem: Death by stabbing in a locked room.

284. ✓ THE HOUSE OF FEAR *novel* U.S.: Doubleday, 1916; U.K.: Hodder, 1917; (as "The Last Warning") Readers Library, 1929
Detective: Arthur McHugh.
Problems: (1) Death from induced heart attack in full view of many witnesses.
(2) Disappearance of a ghostlike figure from a passageway under observation inside a locked theatre.
(3) Many other impossible and near impossible happenings, and

even a haunted telephone.

Campbell, Karen

285. SUDDENLY, IN THE AIR *novel* U.K.: Collins, 1969; (as "The Broken Spectre") Fontana, 1972; U.S.: Stein, 1969
Detective: Lisa Massingham.
Problem: Disappearance of an airliner.

"Capstan" (Rex Hardinge, q.v.)

286. ✓ MURDER OF A MUSICIAN *novel* U.K.: Paget, 1949
Comment: The full details are entered under Rex Hardinge and "Murder to Music," Item 904.

Carlson, P. M.

287. ✓ MURDER IN THE DOG DAYS *novel* U.S.: Bantam, 1991
Detective: Maggie Ryan.
Problem: Death by bludgeoning in a locked room.

Carmack, Jesse

288. THE TELL-TALE CLOCK MYSTERY *novel* U.S.: Stokes, 1937
Detective: Stonewall Rountree.
Problem: Death by shooting in a locked room.

Carmichael, Harry

289. POST MORTEM *novel* U.K.: Collins, 1965; U.S.: Doubleday, 1966
Detectives: John Piper, insurance investigator, and Quinn.
Problem: Death by poisoning in a locked room.

290. PUT OUT THAT STAR *novel* U.K.: Collins, 1957; U.S. (as "Into Thin Air"): Doubleday, 1968
Detective: Piper.
Problem: Disappearance of a film star from a hotel under surveillance.

Carnac, Carol (see also Lorac, E.C.R.)

291. THE DOUBLE TURN *novel* U.K.: Collins, 1956; U.S. (as "The Later Miss Trimming"): Doubleday, 1957
Detective: Chief Inspector Rivers.
Problem: Death by broken neck in a locked house.

Carr, John Dickson (see also Dickson, Carter)

292. THE ARABIAN NIGHTS MURDER *novel* U.K.: H. Hamilton, 1936; U.S.: Harper, 1936
Detective: Dr. Gideon Fell.
Problem: There is no impossible crime as such, although at one point the murderer gets to the victim when apparently he

shouldn't be able to. A magnificent story involving Eastern daggers, false moustaches, and a corpse found dead clutching a cookery book.

293. BELOW SUSPICION *novel* U.S.: Harper, 1949; U.K.: H. Hamilton, 1950
Detective: Fell.
Problem: Death by poisoning in a locked house where only two people—including the victim—were present.

294. THE BLACK SPECTACLES *novel* U.K.: H. Hamilton, 1939; U.S. (as "The Problem of the Green Capsule"): Harper, 1939
Detective: Fell.
Problem: (Nonimpossible) Poisoning and death by blunt instrument during the making of a film to illustrate how the poisoning had been perpetrated. One of Carr's best books.

295. THE BLIND BARBER *novel* U.K.: H. Hamilton, 1934; U.S.: Harper, 1934
Detective: Fell, assisted by novelist Henry Morgan.
Problem: (Nonimpossible) Murder and jewellery theft. One of the master's most rapidly paced books, with a complicated plot involving jewel thefts, murders, and general fracas. No impossible crimes but a deliciously tangled tale and a lot of humour. A particularly nasty, demented murderer is revealed at the end.

296. THE BRIDE OF NEWGATE *novel* U.K.: H. Hamilton, 1950; U.S.: Harper, 1950
Detective: Hubert Mulberry.
Problem: Murder by stabbing in a well-kept room that later appeared and proved to have been unentered for over two years.

297. THE BURNING COURT *novel* U.K.: H. Hamilton, 1937; U.S.: Harper, 1937
Detective: Gaudan Cross.
Problems: (1) Disappearance of a woman through a bricked-up doorway.
(2) Disappearance of a body from a coffin in a sealed crypt.

298. CAPTAIN CUT-THROAT *novel* U.K.: H. Hamilton, 1955; U.S.: Harper, 1955
Detective: Minister of Police Fouche.
Problem: Death by stabbing by an invisible agent.

299. THE CASE OF THE CONSTANT SUICIDES *novel* U.K.: H. Hamilton, 1941; U.S.: Harper, 1941
Detective: Dr. Fell.
Problems: (1) Severe injury by defenestration from a locked tower room.
(2) Death by strangulation in a locked hut.

300. CASTLE SKULL *novel* U.S.: Harper, 1931; U.K.: Severn, 1976
Detective: Henri Bencolin.
Problem: Disappearance of a man from a railway compartment under observation.

301. THE CROOKED HINGE *novel* U.K.: H. Hamilton, 1938; U.S.: Harper, 1938
Detective: Dr. Fell.
Problem: Death by throat slashing where the victim stood on sand unmarked by footprints behind a low hedge.

302. DARK OF THE MOON *novel* U.S.: Harper, 1967; U.K.: H. Hamilton, 1968
Detective: Fell.
Problem: Death by blunt instrument on a terrace covered with unmarked sand.

303. DEADLY HALL *novel* U.K.: H. Hamilton, 1971; U.S.: Harper, 1971
Detective: Fell.
Problem: Defenestration from within a locked bedroom.

304. THE DEAD MAN'S KNOCK *novel* U.K.: H. Hamilton, 1958; U.S.: Harper, 1958
Detective: Fell.
Problem: Death by stabbing in a locked room.

305. DEATH TURNS THE TABLES *novel* U.S.: Harper, 1941; U.K. (as "The Seat of the Scornful"): H. Hamilton, 1942
Detective: Fell.
Problem: (Nonimpossible) Death by shooting of an unsuitable suitor. This could well have been an impossible-crime situation. The victim was shot in the head, carried on normal activities, and did not realise that he had been fatally injured.

306. DEATH-WATCH *novel* U.K.: H. Hamilton, 1935; U.S.: Harper, 1935
Detective: Fell.
Problem: Death by stabbing in a darkened house when the only

three witnesses could each vouch for one another.

307. THE DEMONIACS *novel* U.K.: H. Hamilton, 1962; U.S.: Harper, 1962
Detective: Jeffrey Wynne.
Problem: (Nonimpossible) Death by fright in a house on London Bridge.

308. THE DEVIL IN VELVET *novel* U.K.: H. Hamilton, 1951; U.S.: Harper, 1951
Detective: Nicholas Fenton.
Problem: (Nonimpossible) Arsenic poisoning. One of the master's journeys back in time, on this occasion to the late seventeenth century.

309. THE EIGHT OF SWORDS *novel* U.K.: H. Hamilton, 1934; U.S.: Harper, 1934
Detective: Dr. Fell.
Problem: (Nonimpossible) Murder by shooting of an ex-gangland boss.

310. THE EMPEROR'S SNUFF-BOX *novel* U.S.: Harper, 1942; U.K.: H. Hamilton, 1943
Detective: Dr. Dermot Kinross.
Problem: (Nonimpossible) Murder by blunt instrument of a collector of objets d'art.

311. FIRE, BURN! *novel* U.K.: H. Hamilton, 1957; U.S.: Harper, 1957
Detective: Superintendent John Cheviot.
Problem: Death by shooting in a passage when only one person had a gun and she was innocent.

312. THE FOUR FALSE WEAPONS *novel* U.S.: Harper, 1937; U.K.: H. Hamilton, 1938
Detective: Henri Bencolin.
Problem: (Nonimpossible) Death of a woman in a bedroom in which were discovered four potential weapons.

313. THE GHOST'S HIGH NOON *novel* U.S.: Harper, 1969; U.K.: H. Hamilton, 1970
Detectives: Jim Blake and Lieutenant Zack.
Problem: Disappearance of a gun from within a shed under constant observation.

314. HAG'S NOOK *novel* U.K.: H. Hamilton, 1933; U.S.: Harper, 1933
Detective: Dr. Fell.

Problem: Death by broken neck in a disused prison under constant observation.

315. HE WHO WHISPERS *novel* U.K.: H. Hamilton, 1946; U.S.: Harper, 1946
Detective: Fell.
Problem: Death by stabbing in a guarded tower.

316. THE HOLLOW MAN *novel* U.K.: H. Hamilton, 1935; U.S. (as "The Three Coffins"): Harper, 1935
Detective: Fell.
Problems: (1) Death by shooting in a locked, guarded bedroom.
(2) Death by shooting at close range in an empty, snow-covered street; no prints to account for the murderer.

317. THE HOUSE AT SATAN'S ELBOW *novel* U.K.: H. Hamilton, 1965; U.S.: Harper, 1965
Detective: Fell.
Problem: Wounding by shooting in a locked room.

318. THE HUNGRY GOBLIN *novel* U.K.: H. Hamilton, 1972; U.S.: Harper, 1972
Detective: Wilkie Collins.
Problem: Wounding by shooting in a guarded conservatory.

319. IN SPITE OF THUNDER *novel* U.K.: H. Hamilton, 1960; U.S.: Harper, 1960
Detective: Dr. Fell.
Problem: Death by falling from a balcony with no one near enough to have physically engineered the fall.

320. IT WALKS BY NIGHT *novel* U.S. and U.K.: Harper, 1930
Detective: Henri Bencolin.
Problem: Death by beheading in a guarded room.

321. THE LOST GALLOWS *novel* U.S.: Harper, 1930; U.K.: H. Hamilton, 1931
Detective: Bencolin.
Problems: (1) The driving of a limousine by a murdered chauffeur.
(2) The appearance and disappearance of articles inside a locked room.

322. THE MAD HATTER MYSTERY *novel* U.K.: H. Hamilton, 1933; U.S.: Harper, 1933
Detective: Dr. Fell.
Problem: Death by a crossbow shaft from an angle from which

no shot could apparently be fired.

323. THE MAN WHO COULD NOT SHUDDER *novel* U.K.: H. Hamilton, 1940; U.S.: Harper, 1940
Detective: Fell.
Problem: Death by shooting by a gun hanging on a wall.

324. MOST SECRET *novel* U.K.: H. Hamilton, 1964; U.S.: Harper,1964
Comment: Not a detective story but a historical novel set in the time of Charles II. Originally published in 1934 as by Roger Fairbairn under the title "Devil Kinsmere."

325. THE NINE WRONG ANSWERS *novel* U.K.: H. Hamilton, 1952; U.S.: Harper, 1952
Detective: Bill Dawson.
Problem: Poisoning of a man in a bar when no one had been near enough to doctor his drink.

326. PANIC IN BOX C *novel* U.K.: H. Hamilton, 1966; U.S.: Harper, 1966
Detective: Dr. Fell.
Problem: Death from a crossbow bolt in a theatre box, locked from behind and no assailant viewed in the box opposite.

327. PAPA LA-BAS *novel* U.S.: Harper, 1968; U.K.: H. Hamilton, 1969
Detective: Senator Judah P. Benjamin.
Problem: Disappearance of a woman from a moving carriage constantly under observation.

328. PATRICK BUTLER FOR THE DEFENCE *novel* U.K.: H. Hamilton, 1956; U.S.: Harper, 1956
Detective: Patrick Butler.
Problem: Death by stabbing in a room under observation.

329. POISON IN JEST *novel* U.K.: H. Hamilton, 1932; U.S.: Harper, 1932
Detectives: Pat Rossiter and Jeff Marle.
Problem: A number of poisonings, including one in a drink from a sealed bottle of brandy.

330. THE PROBLEM OF THE WIRE CAGE *novel* U.S.: Harper, 1939; U.K.: H. Hamilton, 1940
Detective: Dr. Fell.
Problem: Death by strangulation on a clay-based tennis court where no footprints had been left by the killer.

331. SCANDAL AT HIGH CHIMNEYS *novel* U.K.: H. Hamilton, 1959; U.S.: Harper, 1959
Detective: Jonathan Whicher.
Problem: Death by shooting in a house where all the exits were apparently locked or guarded.

332. THE SLEEPING SPHINX *novel* U.K.: H. Hamilton, 1947; U.S.: Harper, 1947
Detective: Dr. Fell.
Problem: Movement of coffin within a locked vault.

333. TILL DEATH DO US PART *novel* U.K.: H. Hamilton, 1944; U.S.: Harper, 1944
Detective: Fell.
Problem: Death by poisoning in a room with a bullet hole, freshly made, in one of the windows.

334. TO WAKE THE DEAD *novel* U.K.: H. Hamilton, 1937; U.S.: Harper, 1938
Detective: Fell.
Problem: Death by strangulation within a guarded and apparently inaccessible suite of rooms.

335. THE WAXWORKS MURDER *novel* U.K.: H. Hamilton, 1932; U.S. (as "The Corpse in the Waxworks"): Harper, 1932
Detective: Henri Bencolin.
Problem: (Nonimpossible) A good start with a murdered woman found stabbed in the Gallery of Horrors in a waxworks museum. The clueing is of the usual high standard, but the book tends to bog down in the middle and not come alive again until later on when Jeff Marle tangles with the Club of Masks.

336. THE WITCH OF THE LOW TIDE *novel* U.K.: H. Hamilton, 1961; U.S.: Harper, 1961
Detectives: Dr. David Garth and Detective Inspector Twigg.
Problem: Death by strangulation in a beach hut surrounded by sand unmarked by the killer.

337. "The Adventure of the Highgate Miracle" *short story* in "The Exploits of Sherlock Holmes" U.K.: Murray, 1954; U.S.: Random, 1954
Detective: Sherlock Holmes.
Problem: Disappearance of a man from a house under police observation.

338. "All in a Maze" *novelette* in "The Men Who Explained Miracles"

U.S.: Harper, 1963; U.K.: H. Hamilton, 1964; "Merrivale, March and Murder", Crippen & Landru, 1991
Detective: Sir Henry Merrivale.
Problem: Attempted murder by gassing in a locked room.

339. ✓ "As Drink the Dead...." *short story* in The Haverfordian, March 1926; "The Door to Doom" U.S.: Harper, 1980, and U.K.: H. Hamilton, 1981; "Deadly Arts" U.S.: Arbor, 1985
Detective: Von Arnheim.
Problem: Death by poison from a cup then used immediately afterwards without ill effect.

340. "The Black Cabinet" *short story* in "Cream of the Crime" U.S.: Holt, 1962, and U.K.: Harrap, 1964; "The Men Who Explained Miracles"; "The Black Cabinet" U.K.: Xanadu, 1989; "Fell and Foul Play", Crippen & Landru, 1991
Problem: (Nonimpossible) The identity of the man who prevents a woman from assassinating the French emperor.

341. ✓ "The Black Minute" *play* in "The Dead Sleep Lightly" U.S.: Doubleday, 1983; "Fell and Foul Play"
Detective: Dr. Fell.
Problem: Death by stabbing in a locked and darkened séance room with all occupants holding hands.

342. "The Bride Vanishes" *play* in EQMM, September 1950; "The Door to Doom" U.S.: Harper, 1980; U.K.: H. Hamilton, 1981
Detective: Dr. Rutherford Davis, brain specialist.
Problem: Disappearance from a guarded balcony of a woman who had no reason to commit suicide.

343. "Cabin B-13" *play* in EQMM, May 1944; "Twentieth Century Detective Stories" U.S.: World, 1948; Popular, 1964; "The Door to Doom"
Detective: Paul Hardwick.
Problem: Disappearance of a passenger and a cabin from a ship.

344. "The Clue of the Red Wig" *short story* in "The Third Bullet and Other Stories" U.K.: H. Hamilton, 1954, and U.S.: Harper, 1954; "Murder Mixture" U.K.: Elek, 1963; "Ellery Queen's Shoot the Works" U.S.: Pyramid, 1969; "Merrivale, March and Murder"
Detective: Inspector Adam Bell.
Problem: (Nonimpossible) Murder of a woman in her underclothes with her outer clothes neatly folded nearby.

345. "Crime on the Coast" *novelette* serial in the News Chronicle,

August 1954; "Crime on the Coast, and No Flowers by Request" U.K.: Gollancz, 1984; U.S.: Berkley, 1987
Comment: A round-robin spy story to which Carr contributed the first of six chapters. The other contributors, in chronological order, were Valerie White, Laurence Meynell, Joan Fleming, Michael Cronin, and Elizabeth Ferrars.

346. "The Customers Like Murder" *play* in EQMM, April 1952
Detective: Gerald Hawkstone, detective-story writer.
Comment: All about the amateur sleuth and his long-suffering secretary, who are kidnapped by two American gangsters who want them to settle the hash of the Lord Chief Justice of England. But guess whose hash really gets settled. Great fun!

347. ✓ "The Dead Sleep Lightly" *play* in "The Dead Sleep Lightly"
Detective: Dr. Fell.
Problem: A man accidentally rings the number on a gravestone and a dead woman answers him, even though the phone is found not to be connected.

348. ✓ "Death Has Four Faces" *play* in "The Dead Sleep Lightly"
Detective: Jean Goron, prefect of police.
Problem: Death by stabbing in a rain-lashed street under constant observation.

349. "Detective's Day Off" *short story* in Weekend Magazine, December 25/29,1957; "Crime at Christmas" U.K.: Thorsons, 1988; as "Scotland Yard's Christmas" in "Merrivale, March, and Murder"
Detective: Superintendent Robert Pollard.
Problem: Disappearance of a jewel thief and female accomplice from a crowded but guarded department store.

350. "The Devil in the Summerhouse" *play* in EQMM, September 1946; "Dr. Fell, Detective" U.S.: Mercury, 1947
Detective: Captain Burke.
Problem: Death by shooting in a guarded summer house.
Note: Also see Item 2014.

351. ✓ "The Devil's Manuscript" *play* in "The Dead Sleep Lightly"
Detective: Dr. Daniel Shaw.
Problem: Not an impossible crime as such, but a question of how one man could scare another literally to death.

352. ✓ "The Devil's Saint" *play* in "The Dead Sleep Lightly"
Detective: None.

Problem: Death by unknown means in a locked tapestry room.

353. ✓ "The Dragon in the Pool" *play* in "The Dead Sleep Lightly"
Detective: Chief Inspector Fielding.
Problem: Death from stabbing by invisible agent.

354. "The Empty Flat" *short story* in EQMM, May 1945; "The Men Who Explained Miracles"; "Ellery Queen's 12" U.S.: Dell, 1964; as by Carter Dickson in "Merrivale, March and Murder"
Detective: Colonel March.
Problem: Death of a man from fright in an empty flat.

355. ✓ "The Ends of Justice" *short story* in The Haverfordian, May 1927; "The Door to Doom"
Detective: Henri Bencolin.
Problem: Death by stabbing in a room under constant view and surrounded on the outside by unmarked snow.

356. "Flight from Fleet Street" *play* in London Mystery Magazine No. 14, February/March 1952; (as "A Razor in Fleet Street") in "The Art of the Impossible" U.K.: Xanadu, 1990; "Murder Impossible" U.S.: Carroll, 1990
Detective: Chief Inspector Radford.
Problem: Death by throat cutting of a man inside a cupboard under observation.

357. ✓ "The Fourth Suspect" *short story* in The Haverfordian, January 1927; "The Door to Doom"
Detective: Henri Bencolin.
Problem: Death by shooting in a locked room.

358. "The Gentleman from Paris" *short story* in EQMM, April 1950; "The Third Bullet and Other Stories"; EQMM, June 1969; "Manhattan Mysteries" U.S.: Avenel, 1987; "Fell and Foul Play"
Detective: Thaddeus Perley.
Problem: Disappearance of a will in a guarded room.

359. "A Guest in the House" *short story* in "Dr. Fell, Detective"; (as "The Incautious Burglar") EQMM, November 1956; "Ellery Queen's Lethal Black Book" U.S.: Dell, 1965; "Fell and Foul Play"
Detective: Dr. Fell.
Problem: Short-story version of Item 606 with Dr. Fell substituting for H.M.

360. "The Hangman Won't Wait" *play* in EQMM, September 1944; "Dr. Fell, Detective"; "Alfred Hitchcock's Fireside Book of

Suspense" U.S.: Simon, 1947
Detective: Fell.
Problem: (Nonimpossible) Death by shooting of a man with his hands in the air.

361. "The House in Goblin Wood" *short story* in "The Third Bullet and Other Stories"; (as by Carter Dickson) EQMM, November 1947; "The Art of the Impossible" U.K.: Xanadu, 1990; "Murder Impossible" U.S.: Carroll, 1990; "Merrivale, March and Murder"
Detective: Sir Henry Merrivale.
Problem: Disappearance of a girl from a cottage under observation.

362. "Invisible Hands" *short story* in "The Men Who Explained Miracles"; (as by Carter Dickson as "Death by Invisible Hands") EQMM, April 1958; "Death Locked In" U.S.: IPL, 1987; "Fell and Foul Play"
Detective: Dr. Fell.
Problem: Death by strangulation on unmarked sand.

363. "The Locked Door" *short story* in Everybody's, July 13,1957; this is an abridged version of "The Locked Room"
Detective: Fell.
Problem: Assault with a blunt instrument in a room under constant observation.

364. "The Locked Room" *short story* in EQMM, November 1943; "Murder by Experts" U.S.: Ziff, 1947, and U.K.: Low, 1950; "The Third Bullet and Other Stories"; "The Locked Room Reader" U.S.: Random, 1968; "8 Keys to Murder" U.S.: Dell, 1970; "Fell and Foul Play"
Detective: Fell.
Problem: Attempted murder in a locked room.

365. ✓ "The Man Who Was Dead" *short story* in Dime Mystery, May 1935; "Door to Doom"
Detective: None.
Problem: A young man sees his own obituary in the newspaper.

366. ✓ "Menace in Wax" *short story* in Espionage Magazine, November 1985 *Detective:* Bert Rogers, journalist.
Problem: How a German bomber force was able to locate a completely blacked-out Q factory ringed by woodland.

367. ✓ "The Murder in Number Four" *short story* in The Haverfordian, June 1928; "Door to Doom"
Detective: Henri Bencolin.
Problem: Death by strangulation of a man in a train's locked compartment under constant guard.

368. "The Phantom Archer" *play* in EQMM, June 1948; "Door to Doom"
Detective: Professor Ballard.
Problem: Death by arrow in the doorway of a gallery that was empty and had only just been opened.

369. "The Proverbial Murder" *short story* in "Dr. Fell, Detective"; "The Third Bullet and Other Stories"; "The Penguin Classic Crime Omnibus" U.S. and U.K.: Penguin, 1984; "Fell and Foul Play"
Detective: Dr. Fell.
Problem: Murder committed with a gun while locked in a shed.

370. ✓ "The Shadow of the Goat" *short story* in The Haverfordian, November & December, 1926; "Door to Doom"; "All But Impossible!" U.S.: Ticknor, 1981
Detective: Henri Bencolin.
Problems: (1) Disappearance of a man from a locked and guarded room.
(2) Death by stabbing in a locked and guarded house.

371. "Strictly Diplomatic" *short story* in EQMM, January 1946; "Dr. Fell, Detective"; "The Men Who Explained Miracles"; "With Malice Toward All" U.S.: Putnam, 1968; "Merrivale, March and Murder"
Detective: Andrew Dermot.
Problem: Disappearance of a woman from within an arbour.

372. "Terror's Dark Tower" *short story* in Detective Tales, October 1935; "Door to Doom"
Detective: Sir James Fenwick.
Problem: Death by stabbing through the eyes in a locked tower room.

373. "The Third Bullet" *novelette* U.K.: Hodder, 1937 (as a separate book under the Carter Dickson byline); then, in a shorter version, EQMM, January 1948; "The Third Bullet and Other Stories"; "Locked Room Puzzles" U.S.: Academy, 1986; "Merrivale, March and Murder"

Detective: Colonel Marquis.
Problem: Three bullets fired in a locked room, each from a different gun, but the only person present, apart from the victim, did not have the murder weapon.

374. ✓ "Vampire Tower" *play* in "The Dead Sleep Lightly"
Detective: Major Selden, chief constable.
Problem: Death by poison introduced by unknown means.

375. ✓ "The Villa of the Damned" *play* in "The Dead Sleep Lightly"
Detective: Commander Rossi of the Italian Civil Police.
Problem: A young couple leave, then immediately return to a library, only to find that the view outside has changed from suburban buildings to open country.

376. ✓ "White Tiger Passage" *play* in "The Dead Sleep Lightly"
Detective: Bill Stacey of the Daily Record.
Problem: (Nonimpossible) Our hero tangles with and eventually outwits the Slasher of the Boulevard.

377. "Will You Make a Bet with Death?" *play* in EQMM, April 1954
Problem: (Nonimpossible) Young man has to stay alive and escape his stepfather's machinations in order to inherit a small fortune.
Comment: First broadcast in the U.S.A. in 1942.

378. "Will You Walk into My Parlour" *play* in EQMM, September 1945; "Dr. Fell, Detective"
Detective: Major Grant.
Problem: Poisoning by invisible means.

379. "William Wilson's Racket" *short story* in EQMM, November 1944; "To the Queen's Taste" U.S.: Little, 1946, and U.K.: Faber, 1949; "The Men Who Explained Miracles"; "Merrivale, March and Murder"
Detective: Colonel March.
Problem: Disappearance of a man, leaving his complete suit of clothes behind.

380. "The Wrong Problem" *short story* in EQMM, July 1942; "Dr. Fell, Detective"; "Four-&-Twenty Bloodhounds" U.S.: Simon, 1950, and U.K.: Hammond, (1951); "The Third Bullet"; "Thirteen Classic Detective Stories" U.S.: Rosen, 1974; "Fell and Foul Play"; "Big Book of Locked-Room Mysteries", Black Lizard, 2014
Detective: Dr. Fell.

Problem: Death by stabbing in a locked room.

Carr, Joseph B.

381. ✓ THE MAN WITH BATED BREATH *novel* U.S.: Viking, 1934; U.K.: Cassell, 1935
Detective: Oceola Archer.
Problem: Killing and wounding by shooting in a room under constant watch and where afterwards no murder weapon can be found.

Carroll, Amy (q.v. Anonymous; see entries 59, 61, 62, 66)

Carter, Lin

382. ✓ INVISIBLE DEATH *novel* U.S.: Doubleday, 1975
Detective: Prince Zarkon of Novenia.
Problem: Death by invisible agency while the victims were under guard.

Carter, Nick

383. "The Impossible Theft" *novelette* in New York Weekly, October 1895; Nick Carter Magazine, October 1934; "Nick Carter, the 100th Killmaster", U.S.: Award, 1975
Comment: There is certainly an impossible crime in this, but equally impossible is the hiding place of the solution. Despite several readings I have been totally unable to plumb the depths of this badly written story.
Skupin Comment: The writer was Thomas Calvert McCleary.

384. ✓ "The Mystery of Room No. 11" *short story* in "Gideon Drexel's Millions" U.S.: Street, 1899; "Death Locked In" U.S.: IPL, 1987
Detective: Nick Carter.
Problem: Disappearance of a well-dressed woman from a watched and guarded tenement block.

385. ✓ "Northrup's Little Game" *short story* in "Gideon Drexel's Millions"; Espionage Magazine, July 1987
Detective: Carter.
Problem: Disappearance of secret plans from within an office under constant observation.

Casey, Robert J.

386. ✓ THE SECRET OF THE DARK ROOM *novel* U.K.: Mathews, 1932; U.S. (as "News Reel"): Bobbs, 1932
Detective: Jim Sands.

Problem: Death by shooting in a guarded dark room and adjoining printing room.

Castier, Jules

387. "The Footprints on the Ceiling" *short story* in "Rather Like" U.K.: Jenkins, 1920, and U.S.: Lippincott, 1920; "The Misadventures of Sherlock Holmes" U.S.: Little, 1944
Detective: Sherlock Holmes.
Problem: Disappearance of a man (Professor Challenger, no less!) from a room under surveillance.

Cecil, Henry

388. "Chef's Special" *short story* in "Brief Tales from the Bench" U.K.: BBC, 1968; U.S.: Simon, 1968
Detective: The judge.
Problem: The disappearance of the unhelpful staff from a hotel.

Chadwick, Charles

389. THE CACTUS *novel* U.S.: Crowell, 1925
Detective: Bob Ellis, lawyer.
Problem: Death by stabbing in a locked room.

390. THE MOVING HOUSE OF FOSCALDO *novel* U.K.: Cassell, 1926
Detective: Inspector Prontout.
Problem: Disappearance of two men from a windmill tower under surveillance.

Chambers, Whitman

391. ✓ THE CAMPANILE MURDERS *novel* U.S.: Appleton, 1933
Detective: Bill Bartlett, reporter.
Problems: (1) Death by shooting in a locked bell tower in which the victim was shot while bell ringing but no one exited.
(2) Use of a gun as a murder weapon when the gun was locked away during the time of the killing.

392. ✓ DEAD MEN LEAVE NO FINGERPRINTS *novel* U.K.: Cassell, 1935; U.S.: Doubleday, 1935
Detective: Stanton Lake.
Problem: (1) Death by strangulation in a locked room.
(2) Fingerprints found at murder scenes belonging to a man who had been dead for more than a year before the murders took place.

Champion, D. L.

393. ✓ "The Day Nobody Died" *short story* in Dime Detective Magazine, February 1944; "The Arbor House Treasury of

Detective & Mystery Stories from the Great Pulps" U.S.: Arbor, 1983

Detective: Inspector Allhoff.

Problem: Death by shooting of a midget in a locked and guarded room.

Comment: Allhoff is a wonderfully eccentric detective with a vicious tongue, no legs, and a couple of downtrodden, guilt-ridden leg men. The Allhoff stories, if this one is anything to go by, are funny, fair, and extremely clever. The solution here is, as far as I'm aware, original. Bill Pronzini, who edited the Arbor House anthology, is to be congratulated for plucking Allhoff from undeserved obscurity.

394. ✓ "Lock the Death House Door" *short story* in Dime Detective Magazine, December 1938, "The Complete Cases of Inspector Allhof, Volume 1" Altus Press, 2015

Detective: Inspector Allhoff.

Problem: Death by stabbing in a locked cell with a guard present.

Chance, John Newton

395. ✓ THE EYE IN DARKNESS *novel* U.K.: Macdonald, 1946

Detective: David Chance.

Problem: (1) Removal of a bottle of tablets by an invisible hand. (2) Death from a knife thrown with uncanny accuracy in a pitch-black room.

Chancellor, John

396. THE MYSTERY OF NORMAN'S COURT *novel* U.K.: Hutchinson, 1923; U.S.: Small, 1924

Detectives: David Forrester and Superintendent Redarrel.

Problem: Death by stabbing in a locked room.

Chandler, Raymond

397. "Professor Bingo's Snuff" *short story* in Fantastic, Summer 1952

Detective: Lieutenant Waldman.

Problem: Death by shooting in a locked house.

Charteris, Leslie

398. "The Arrow of God" *short story* in EQMM, September 1949; MacKill's Mystery Magazine, October 1952; The Saint Mystery Magazine UK, November 1962, The Saint Mystery Magazine, January 1963; "The Saint on the Spanish Main" U.S.:

Doubleday, 1955, and U.K.: Hodder, 1956; "Homicidal Acts" U.S.: Ivy, 1989

Detective: Simon Templar.

Problem: Death by stabbing with the shaft of an opened beach umbrella, which would apparently have called for superhuman strength.

399. "The Impossible Crime" *short story* in "Alias the Saint" U.K.: Hodder, 1931; The Thriller March 7 1931, as "Bumped Off"; "Wanted for Murder, The Further Adventures of Simon Templar" U.S.: Doubleday, 1931; "The Saint— Wanted for Murder" U.S.: Sun-Dial, 1943; The Saint Mystery Magazine (U.K.), March, 1964 The Saint Mystery Magazine (U.S.), September, 1964

Detective: Templar.

Problem: Death by shooting in a locked room.

400. "The Logical Adventure" *short story* in "Featuring the Saint" U.K.: Hodder, 1931

Detective: Templar.

Problem: Included because the story contains a sequence wherein the Saint himself leaves a door locked on the outside with the key on the inside.

401. "The Mystery of the Child's Toy" *short story* in "Great Stories of Detection, Mystery and Horror" U.K.: Gollancz, 1934; (as "The Man Who Liked Toys") in "Boodle" U.K.: Hodder, 1934; "The Saint Intervenes" U.S.: Doubleday, 1934; "Big Book of Locked-Room Mysteries", Black Lizard, 2014

Detectives: Templar and Andy Herrick.

Problem: Death by shooting in a room under observation.

Chase, James Hadley

402. ✓ THE DOUBLE SHUFFLE *novel* U.K.: Hale, 1952; U.S.: Dutton, 1953

Detective: Steve Harmas.

Problem: Death by wrist cutting on a deserted island under surveillance and apparently without visitors.

403. THIS WAY FOR A SHROUD *novel* U.K.: Hale, 1953

Detective: Paul Conrad, District Attorney special investigator

Problems: Two deaths in guarded rooms.

Chase, Kip

404. MURDER MOST INGENIOUS *novel* U.K.: Hammond, 1962

Detective: Justine Carmichael, retired from the police and now bound to a wheelchair.
Problem: Death by stabbing in a gallery, the exit of which was under constant guard.

Chastain, Thomas, and Bill Adler

405. ✓ THE PICTURE-PERFECT MURDERS *novel* U.S.: Morrow, 1987
Detective: John Lange.
Problem: Death by blunt instrument in a locked cabin.

406. ✓ THE REVENGE OF THE ROBINS FAMILY *novel* U.S.: Morrow, 1984
Detective: Captain Gregory Waltham.
Problem: Death by stabbing while all the other occupants of a snowbound house were locked in another room, apparently by the victim.

407. ✓ WHO KILLED THE ROBINS FAMILY? *novel* U.S.: Morrow, 1983; U.K.: Joseph, 1983
Detective: B. J. Grieg and various police officials.
Problem: Death by stabbing in a locked cruiser cabin.

Chesney, Weatherby (C. J. Cutcliffe Hyne, q.v.)

408. "The Horror of the Folding Bed" *short story* in "The Adventures of an Engineer" U.K.: Bowden, 1898
Detective: Richard Felton, civil engineer.
Problem: Disappearance of an inventor from his suite of rooms.

Chesterton, G. K.

409. "The Absence of Mr. Glass" *short story* in "The Wisdom of Father Brown" U.K.: Cassell, 1914; U.S.: Lane, 1915; EQMM November 1958
Detective: Father Brown.
Problem: Assault and tying up in a locked room.

410. "The Actor and the Alibi" *short story* in "The Secret of Father Brown" U.K.: Cassell, 1927; U.S.: Harper, 1927
Detective: Father Brown.
Problem: Death by stabbing in a room under observation.

411. "The Arrow of Heaven" *short story* in "The Incredulity of Father Brown" U.K.: Cassell, 1926; U.S.: Dodd, 1926
Detective: Father Brown.
Problem: Death by arrow inside a guarded room.

412. "The Blast of the Book" *short story* in "The Scandal of Father Brown" U.K.: Cassell, 1935; U.S.: Dodd, 1935

Detective: Father Brown.

Problem: Five men reputedly vanish on five separate occasions when an ancient book is opened.

413. "The Curse of the Golden Cross" *short story* in "The Incredulity of Father Brown"

Detective: Father Brown.

Problem: A thirteenth-century curse threatens the defilers of an ancient tomb with death.

414. "The Dagger with Wings" *short story* in "The Incredulity of Father Brown"

Detective: Father Brown.

Problem: Death of a vampirelike cloaked figure in unmarked snow.

415. "The Doom of the Darnaways" *short story* in "The Incredulity of Father Brown"

Detective: Father Brown.

Problem: Death by poisoning in a locked room.

416. "The Ghost of Gideon Wise" *short story* in "The Incredulity of Father Brown"

Detective: Father Brown.

Problem: Simultaneous death of three millionaires and later ghostly appearance of one of them.

417. "The Hammer of God" *short story* in "The Innocence of Father Brown" U.K.: Cassell, 1911; U.S.: Lane, 1911

Detective: Father Brown.

Problem: Victim killed by blow with hammer indicating superhuman strength.

418. "The Hole in the Wall" *short story* in "The Man Who Knew Too Much" U.K.: Cassell, 1922; U.S.: Harper, 1922

Detective: Horne Fisher.

Problem: Disappearance of a man recently observed skating on a pond known to be no more than two feet deep.

419. "The Invisible Man" *short story* in "The Innocence of Father Brown"; "Death Locked In" U.S.: IPL, 1987; "Big Book of Locked-Room Mysteries", Black Lizard, 2014

Detective: Father Brown.

Problem: Murder and disappearance of a man under guard.

420. "The Man in the Passage" *short story* in "The Wisdom of Father Brown"; EQMM February 1959

Detective: Father Brown.
Problem: Death by stabbing in a passage where three separate figures, other than the victim, were glimpsed but none could be identified.

421. "The Miracle of Moon Crescent" *short story* in "The Incredulity of Father Brown"
Detective: Father Brown.
Problem: Disappearance of a man from a guarded area.

422. "The Oracle of the Dog" *short story* in "The Incredulity of Father Brown"; EQMM July 1950; "The Locked Room Reader" U.S.: Random, 1968; "8 Keys to Murder" U.S.: Dell, 1970
Detective: Father Brown.
Problem: Death by stabbing in a guarded summer house.

423. "The Pursuit of Mr. Blue" *short story* in "The Scandal of Father Brown"
Detective: Father Brown.
Problem: Disappearance of an identifiable killer from a guarded sea pier.

424. "The Red Moon of Meru" *short story* in "The Secret of Father Brown"
Detective: Father Brown.
Problem: Disappearance of a diamond from a thief caught red-handed.

425. "The Salad of Colonel Gray" *short story* in "The Wisdom of Father Brown"
Detective: Father Brown.
Problem: Man attacked on three separate disembodied occasions by the curse of the monkey's tail.

426. "The Secret Garden" *short story* in "The Innocence of Father Brown"
Detective: Father Brown.
Problem: Appearance in a locked, guarded garden of a beheaded man (and head) and the disappearance from it of another man.

427. ✓ "The Shadow of the Shark" *short story* in "The Poet and the Lunatics" U.K.: Cassell, 1929; U.S.: Dodd, 1929
Detective: Gabriel Gale.
Problem: Death by stabbing on an unmarked stretch of sand.

428. "The Song of the Flying Fish" *short story* in "The Secret of

Father Brown"
Detective: Father Brown.
Problem: Theft of some valuable golden fish from a guarded room.

429. "The Soul of the Schoolboy" *short story* in "The Man Who Knew Too Much"
Detective: Horne Fisher.
Problem: Disappearance of a valuable silver coin from behind a screen during a light failure.

430. "The Three Tools of Death" *short story* in "The Innocence of Father Brown"
Detective: Father Brown.
Problem: Death of a man killed as if by a blow of superhuman strength.

431. "The Tower of Treason" *short story* in "The Man Who Knew Too Much"; EQMM December 1950
Detective: Horne Fisher.
Problem: Disappearance of diamonds from a casket house in a carefully guarded roof garden.

432. "The Vanishing of Vaudrey" *short story* in "The Secret of Father Brown"
Detective: Father Brown.
Problem: Disappearance of a man from a village street under observation.

433. "The Vanishing Prince" *short story* in "The Man Who Knew Too Much"
Detective: Horne Fisher.
Problems: (1) Disappearance of a man from a locked garden. (2) Shooting of two detectives looking into a tower room and subsequent disappearance of their murderer.

434. "The Wrong Shape" *short story* in "The Innocence of Father Brown"
Detective: Father Brown.
Problem: Death by stabbing in a locked room.

Child, Charles B.

435. "The Man Who Wasn't There" *short story* in EQMM, April 1969; "The Sleuth of Baghdad, Crippen & Landru, 2002
Detective: Inspector Chafik.
Problem: Footprints made each night on stairs by man who

wasn't there.

436. "The Thumbless Man" *short story* in Collier's, January 21, 1955 as "The Invisible Killer"; EQMM, December 1961; "The Sleuth of Baghdad, Crippen & Landru, 2002

Detective: Inspector Chafik.

Problem: Death by strangulation of a man crawling along a narrow tunnel at the end of which was no living person.

Child, Nellise

437. MURDER COMES HOME *novel* U.K.: Collins, 1933; U.S.: Knopf, 1933

Detective: Jerry Irish.

Problem: Death by asphyxiation in a locked room.

Chipperfield, Robert Orr (Isabelle Ostrander, q.v.)

438. ABOVE SUSPICION *novel* U.K.: Hurst, (1923); U.S.: McBride, 1923

Detective: Geoff Peters.

Problem: Death by blunt instrument of a man in unmarked sand.

Christie, Agatha

439. CURTAIN *novel* U.K.: Collins, 1975; U.S.: Dodd, 1975

Detective: Hercule Poirot.

Problem: Death by shooting in a locked room.

440. MURDER FOR CHRISTMAS *novel* U.S.: Dodd, 1938; U.K. (as "Hercule Poirot's Christmas"): Collins, 1939

Detective: Poirot.

Problem: Death by throat cutting in a locked room.

441. MURDER IN MESOPOTAMIA *novel* U.K.: Collins, 1936; U.S.: Dodd, 1936

Detective: Poirot.

Problem: Death by blunt instrument in a bedroom under observation.

442. TEN LITTLE NIGGERS *novel* U.K.: Collins, 1939; U.S. (as "And Then There Were None"): Dodd, 1940; (as "Ten Little Indians") U.S.: Pocket, 1965

Detective: Sir Thomas Legge.

Problem: Death by various means of ten people—out of ten—on an isolated island.

443. ✓ WHY DIDN'T THEY ASK EVANS? *novel* U.K.: Collins, 1934; U.S. (as "The Boomerang Clue"): Dodd, 1935 *Detectives:* Bobby Jones and Lady Frances Derwent.

Problem: Death by shooting in a locked room.
Comment: Possibly the author's best book in which a pair of silly young asses do the detecting. All the Christie magic in this relatively early book.

444. "At the 'Bells and Motley'" *short story* in "The Mysterious Mr. Quinn" U.K.: Collins, 1930, and U.S.: Dodd, 1930; "Surprise! Surprise!" U.S.: Dodd, 1965
Detectives: Harley Quinn and Mr. Satterthwaite.
Problem: Disappearance of a man from gardens under observation.

445. "The Blue Geranium" *short story* in "The Thirteen Problems" U.K.: Collins, 1932; "The Tuesday Club Murders" U.S.: Dodd, 1933; "13 for Luck!" U.S.: Dodd, 1961, and U.K.: Collins, 1936; EQMM March 1959; "13 Clues for Miss Marple" U.S.: Dodd, 1966
Detective: Miss Marple.
Problem: Death by poisoning in a locked room.

446. "Dead Man's Mirror" *short story* in "Murder in the Mews" U.K.: Collins, 1937; "Dead Man's Mirror" U.S.: Dodd, 1966; EQMM February 1966 as "Hercule Poirot and the Broken Mirror"
Detective: Poirot.
Problem: Death by shooting in a locked room.

447. "The Dream" *short story* in "The Regatta Mystery" U.S.: Dodd, 1939; EQMM December 1964; "The Adventure of the Christmas Pudding" U.K.: Collins, 1960; "Big Book of Locked-Room Mysteries", Black Lizard, 2014
Detective: Poirot.
Problem: Death by shooting in a room under observation.

448. "Greenshaw's Folly" *short story* in "The Adventure of the Christmas Pudding"; "Double Sin and Other Stories" U.S.: Dodd, 1961
Detective: Miss Marple.
Problem: A woman was shot with an arrow while all the suspects were either absent or locked in their rooms.

449. "The Idol House of Astarte" *short story* in "The Thirteen Problems"; "The Tuesday Club Murders"
Detective: Marple.
Problem: Death by stabbing by invisible agency when no one

was standing near victim.

450. "The Market Basing Mystery" *short story* in "Poirot's Early Cases" U.K.: Collins, 1974; U.S. (as "Hercule Poirot's Early Cases"): Dodd, 1974
Detective: Poirot.
Problem: Death by shooting in a locked room.

451. "Miss Marple Tells a Story" *short story* in "The Regatta Mystery"
Detective: Marple.
Problem: Death by stabbing in a room under observation.

452. "Problem at Sea" *short story* in "The Regatta Mystery"; "Poirot's Early Cases"; "Hercule Poirot's Early Cases"
Detective: Poirot.
Problem: Death by stabbing in a locked cabin.

453. "The Regatta Mystery" *short story* in "The Regatta Mystery"; "13 for Luck!"; EQMM July 1977
Detective: Parker Pyne.
Problem: Disappearance of a diamond under observation.

Clark, Benjamin S.

454. "Sunshine, Sunshine" *short story* in The Baker Street Journal Christmas Annual 1960
Detective: Sherlock Holmes.
Problem: Disappearance of a man from his own home.

Clark, Douglas

455. DEATH AFTER EVENSONG *novel* U.K.: Cassell, 1969; U.S.: Stein, 1970
Detective: Detective Chief Inspector Masters.
Problem: Man shot dead but no sign of the bullet.

Clarke, Laurence

456. ✓ "Flashlight" *short story* in The Strand Magazine, May 1918
Detective: Terence Milner, Admiralty secret service.
Problem: Signal flares are being sent up to the sky apparently from a hill that is surrounded by troops and proves to be absolutely spy-free.

Clason, Clyde B.

457. BLIND DRIFTS *novel* U.S.: Doubleday, 1937
Detective: Prof. Theocritus Lucius Westborough.
Problem: Disappearance of a gun, which had just caused serious injury, in the confines of an underground mining chamber under

constant observation.

458. DRAGON'S CAVE *novel* U.S.: Doubleday, 1939; U.K.: Heinemann, 1940
Detective: Professor Westborough.
Problem: Disappearance of a man from a locked, guarded room surrounded by unmarked snow.

459. THE FIFTH TUMBLER *novel* U.S.: Doubleday, 1936; U.K.: Heinemann, 1937
Detective: Westborough.
Problem: Ability to leave a door locked with a booby trap on the inside of the door.

460. GREEN SHIVERS *novel* U.S.: Doubleday, 1941; U.K.: Heinemann, 1948
Detective: Westborough.
Problem: Death by shooting in a guarded room.

461. THE MAN FROM TIBET *novel* U.K.: Heinemann, 1938; U.S.: Doubleday, 1938
Detective: Westborough.
Problem: Death by induced heart attack in a locked room.

462. THE PURPLE PARROT *novel* U.K.: Heinemann, 1937; U.S.: Doubleday, 1937
Detective: Westborough.
Problem: Death by stabbing in a locked and guarded room.

463. ✓ THE WHISPERING EAR *novel* U.S.: Doubleday, 1938; U.K.: Heinemann, 1939
Detective: Westborough.
Problem: Death by shooting in a locked bathroom.

Cobban, James MacLaren

464. ✓ THE TERROR BY NIGHT *novel* U.K.: Long, 1905
Detectives: Mr. Townshend, private detective, Mr. Maundslay, ghost hunter, and Dr. Montague Smith.
Problem: Appearance and disappearance of a ghostly figure in a wire mask outside and from within locked rooms, plus defenestration of victims from within locked rooms.

Coe, Tucker (Donald E. Westlake, q.v.)

465. MURDER AMONG CHILDREN *novel* U.S.: Random, 1968; U.K.: Souvenir, 1968
Detective: Mitchell Tobin.
Problem: Death by stabbing in a locked room.

Coffin, Peter (Jonathan Latimer, q.v.)

466. ✓ THE SEARCH FOR MY GREAT-UNCLE'S HEAD *novel* U.S.: Doubleday, 1937
Detectives: Prof. Peter Coffin and Colonel Black.
Problem: Movement of a murderer across a mud-strewn yard without leaving tracks.

Cogswell, Theodore R.

467. "Impact with the Devil" *short story* in Fantasy & Science Fiction, November 1956; "Deals with the Devil" U.S.: Dodd, 1958; U.K.: Faber, 1959
Problem: To extricate a demon trapped inside a pentacle inside a locked bank vault.

Cole, G.D.H. & M.

468. DISGRACE TO THE COLLEGE *novel* U.K.: Hodder, 1937
Detective: The Hon. Everard Blatchington.
Problem: Death by shooting in a locked room.

469. "In a Telephone Cabinet" *short story* in "Superintendent Wilson's Holiday" U.K.: Collins, 1928, and U.S.: Payson, 1929; "The Big Book of Detective Stories" U.K.: Clowes, c. 1935; AHMM, March 1983; "Big Book of Locked-Room Mysteries", Black Lizard, 2014
Detective: Superintendent Wilson.
Problem: Death by shooting in a locked house.

470. "Too Clever by Half" *short story* in "Detection Medley" U.K.: Hutchinson, (1939); "Line-Up" U.S.: Dodd, 1940
Detective: Dr. Benjamin Tancred.
Problem: Death by shooting in a locked room.

Coles, Manning

471. ✓ "The Case of the Six Indignant Footmen" *short story* in "Nothing to Declare" U.S.: Doubleday, 1960
Detective: Tommy Hambledon.
Problem: Disappearance of a headless "ghost" who had just stolen a quantity of jewellery in a moonlit room.

Colin, Aubrey

472. ✓ HANDS OF DEATH *novel* U.K.: Hammond, 1963 *Detective:* Inspector Bill Murray.
Problem: Death by gassing in a locked room.

Collins, Hunt (see also McBain, Ed)

473. ✓ "A Hanging We Will Go!" *short story* in Smashing Detective,

September 1952; "Smashing Detective Stories (UK) #5", 1952
Detectives: Inspector Westover and Sergeant Dawes of Scotland Yard.
Problem: Death by hanging inside a locked room.

Collins, Michael (Dennis Lynds, q.v.)

474. "No One Likes To Be Played for a Sucker" *short story* in EQMM, July 1969; "Ellery Queen's Anthology #29", Davis, 1975; "All But Impossible!" U.S.: Ticknor, 1981
Detective: Dan Fortune.
Problem: Death by shooting in a room leading on to a storeroom in which the main suspect is found locked.

Collins, Michelle

475. ✓ MURDER AT WILLOW RUN *novel* U.S.: Zebra, 1979
Detective: Megan Marshall, art-gallery director, all-American girl, and candidate for silliest sleuth of the season.
Problem: Death by stabbing in a locked bedroom.
Adey Comment: Amateurishly written puzzle novel in which pictures also supposedly give clues to the solution. If they do, they are certainly not explained and were not clear to me.
Skupin Comment: It is amateurishly written, but the pictures do give clues to the solution. This is a Zebra Mystery Puzzler with the solution sealed at the back, and a place for the reader to write their own solution before breaking the seal.

Collins, Wilkie

476. "A Terribly Strange Bed" *short story* in Household Words, February 1852; "After Dark" U.K.: Smith, 1856; Germany: Tauchnitz, 1856; "Death Locked In" U.S.: IPL, 1987; AHMM, November, 1991; "Big Book of Locked-Room Mysteries", Black Lizard, 2014
Detective: Mr. Faulkner.
Problem: Attempted murder in a locked room at an inn.

Commings, Joseph (see also Craven, Monte)

477. ✓ "Assassination—Middle East" *short story* in MSMM, May 1981
Detective: Sen. Brooks U. Banner.
Problem: Disappearance of a robed figure from a house into which it had been seen to withdraw.
478. "Betrayal in the Night" *short story* in Mystery Digest,

January/February 1963
Detective: Senator Banner.
Problem: Death of a man who comes out of a locked room and, just before dying, says that the murderer is inside the room. There is no one there, however.

479. ✓ "The Black Friar Murders" *short story* in Ten Detective Aces, January 1948
Detective: Mayor Thomas Landin.
Problem: Disappearance of a shadowy, black-cowled monk from within a locked cell.
Comment: Another virtually lost tale in which the detective is really, and quite obviously, Senator Banner, although the magazine editor insisted on the strange metamorphosis into Mayor Landin. Excellent and atmospheric.

480. "Bones for Davy Jones" *short story* in "Crooks' Tour" U.S.: Dodd, 1953, and U.K.: Macdonald, 1954; "The Locked Room Reader" U.S.: Random, 1968; "8 Doors to Death" U.S.: Dell, 1970; originally in Mystery Digest as "The Diver and the Witch" by Monte Craven
Detective: Captain Tom Pepper.
Problem: Death by stabbing of a diver who had dived to inspect a recently sunken vessel.

481. "Castanets, Canaries and Murder" *short story* in Mystery Digest, January/February 1962; "Banner Deadlines", Crippen & Landru, 2004
Detective: Senator Banner.
Problem: Death of a film actor who went behind a black screen with white walls on either side of it. Playback of the film showed no one going to the screen, and the evidence was that there was no one already there before the victim.

482. "Death by Black Magic" *short story* in Ten Detective Aces, November 1948; "Four-&-Twenty Bloodhounds" U.S.: Simon, 1950; U.K.: Hammond, (1951); "Sleight of Crime" U.S.: Regnery, 1977; "Banner Deadlines"
Detective: Banner.
Problems: (1) Disappearance of a man from a guarded roof.
(2) Death by strangulation of a magician in a magic cabinet.

483. ✓ "Death Shapes the Frame" *short story* in Private Detective Stories, February 1949

Detective: Matt Tudor.
Problem: Disappearance of the murder weapon from within the locked apartment in which a fatal stabbing had recently taken place.

484. "The Devil's Cousin" *short story* in Mystery Digest, July/August 1959; originally published as "Ghost in the Gallery"
Detective: Senator Banner.
Problems: (1) Disappearance of a man from a guarded room.
(2) Disappearance of a man from a guarded building.

485. ✓ "Dressed to Kill" *short story* in MSMM, March 1982
Detective: Banner.
Problem: Deaths of three women by apparently invisible agency.

486. "The Female Animal" *short story* in Mystery Digest, January 1958
Detective: Banner.
Problem: Death by poison in a locked room.

487. ✓ "Fingerprint Ghost" *short story* in 10-Story Detective Magazine, May 1947; "Banner Deadlines"
Detective: Banner.
Problem: Death by stabbing in a darkened séance chamber, outside which also in complete darkness witnesses in strait-jackets kept an unbroken circle of touching feet. When the victim was found, the prints on the knife belonged to no one in the room.

488. ✓ "The Fire Dragon Caper" *short story* in MSMM, May 1984
Detective: Banner.
Problems: (1) Disappearance of 30,000 gold sovereigns from a guarded workshop.
(2) Death by shooting in a vault under constant observation after the shot was heard.

489. "The Giant's Sword" *short story* in Mystery Digest, May/June 1963; "Banner Deadlines"
Detective: Banner.
Problem: Victim thrust through with a giant sword too large for one man to use as a thrusting weapon.

490. ✓ "Ghost in the Gallery" *short story* in Ten Detective Aces, July 1949; "The Art of the Impossible" U.K.: Xanadu, 1990; U.S.: "Murder Impossible" U.S.: Carroll, 1990

Comment: Reprinted as "The Devil's Cousin." See Item 484.

491. "The Glass Gravestone" *short story* in The Saint Mystery Magazine, October 1966; "Big Book of Locked-Room Mysteries", Black Lizard, 2014
Detective: Banner.
Problem: Death by throat cutting with no one near the victim at the time of the murder.

492. ✓ "The Grand Guignol Caper" *short story* in MSMM, November 1984
Detective: Banner.
Problem: The emergence of a vampire killer from a mausoleum locked for 150 years.
Comment: Another excellent atmospheric Banner tale written more than thirty years before its eventual publication.

493. "Hangman's House" *short story* in Mystery Digest, November/December 1962
Detective: Banner.
Problem: Dead body hanging from a chandelier with only the victim's footprints in the dust below.

494. ✓ "Hate Laughs at Locksmiths" *short story* in Ten Detective Aces, December 1947
Detective: Doc Vincent.
Problems: (1) Death by stabbing in a locked room in which the victim and the three suspects were together after being examined by a fluoroscope before they entered to prove that no weapon had been taken in.
(2) Exit, later, from the same locked room after similar fluoroscope examination to obviate the possibility of a key being taken in.

495. "Hot Bullets" *short story* in Mystery Digest, May/June 1960
Detective: The Great Jannings—Master of Magic.
Problem: See Item 505; a rewrite changing the name of the magician.

496. "Intermission" *short story* in Mystery Digest, November/December 1961
Detective: Faust the Great—Master of Magic
Problem: See Item 505; a rewrite changing the name of the magician.

497. ✓ "The Invisible Clue" *short story* in Hollywood Detective,

April 1950
Detective: Senator Banner.
Problem: Death by shooting in a locked and guarded twelve-feet-square brick well house.

498. "The Last Samurai" *short story* in The Saint Mystery Magazine (U.K.), July 1963
Detective: Banner.
Problem: Disappearance of a prisoner from a guarded room.

499. ✓ "The Moving Finger" *short story* in MSMM, April 1968
Detective: Banner.
Problem: Concealment of messages between two lovers in rooms which were carefully searched.

500. ✓ "Murder of a Mermaid" *short story* in MSMM, August 1982
Detective: Banner.
Problem: Death by drowning in a swimming pool of an extremely fit champion swimmer.

501. ✓ "Murder Under Glass" *short story* in 10-Story Detective Magazine, March 1947; "Banner Deadlines"
Detective: Banner.
Problem: Death by stabbing in a sealed glass room.

502. "Murderer's Progress" *short story* in Mystery Digest, November/December 1960
Detective: Banner.
Problem: A gun is fired in a guarded room in which two men are sitting. One walks out and there is no sign of the other man or the bullet.

503. ✓ "Nobody Loves a Fat Man" *short story* in MSMM, June 1980
Detective: Banner.
Problem: Concealment of a capsule containing microfilm in a house searched from top to bottom.

504. "Open to Danger" *short story* in Mystery Digest, July/August 1962
Detective: Banner.
Problem: Stabbing and shooting by invisible means.

505. "Paging Mr. Blitzen!" *short story* in Mystery Digest, September 1957
Detective: Blitzen the Great.
Problems: (1) Death by shooting in a locked room.
(2) Disappearance of a valuable deck of tarot cards from the

locked room.

Note: Items 495 and 496 are the same story with the detective's name changed.

506. ✓ "The Scarecrow Murders" *short story* in 10-Story Detective Magazine, April 1948

Detective: Senator Banner.

Problem: Death by shotgun and a trail of shoe prints that led directly to the shoes belonging to a scarecrow in the middle of an otherwise unmarked field.

507. "Serenade to a Killer" *short story* in Mystery Digest, July 1957; "Crime at Christmas" U.K.: Thorsons, 1988

Detective: Banner.

Problem: Death by shooting in an outhouse surrounded by snow unmarked save by the victim's footprints.

508. ✓ "The Spectre on the Lake" *short story* in 10-Story Detective Magazine, July 1947

Detective: Banner.

Problem: Death by shooting of two men alone in a boat in the middle of a lake, when no gun was taken on board and none found after the event.

509. "Through the Looking Glass" *short story* in "Big Time Mysteries" U.S.: Dodd, 1958

Detective: Banner.

Problems: (1) Disappearance of a boy in a fairground mirror room.

(2) Destruction of the mirrors within a locked mirror room.

510. "The X Street Murders" *short story* in Mystery Digest, March/April 1962; "Death Locked In" U.S.: IPL, 1987; "Banner Deadlines"; The Mammoth Book of Perfect Crimes and Impossible Mysteries", UK: Constable and Robinson, 2006, US: Carroll and Graf, 2007

Detective: Banner.

Problem: A murder by pistol shot is carried out and seconds later a sealed envelope in the intercommunicating room is opened to reveal the smoking murder weapon.

Commings, Joseph, and Edward D. Hoch

511. ✓ "Stairway to Nowhere" *short story* in MSMM, November 1979; "Banner Deadlines"

Detective: Senator Banner.

Problems: (1) Disappearance of a girl heard to proceed only part way up a set of stairs.
(2) Theft of a huge diamond from a display case shattered only seconds before by a bomb blast.

Conaway, Jim

512. THEY DO IT WITH MIRRORS *novel* U.S.: Belmont, 1977
Detective: Jana Blake.
Problem: Disappearance of a child from a magician's cabinet in full view of an audience.

Conde, Philip

513. MYSTERY OF THE VANISHING AERODROME *novel* U.K.: Wright, 1939
Detectives: Dick Pemberty and Peter Webb.
Problem: Disappearance of an aerodrome.

Connington, J. J.

514. In WHOSE DIM SHADOW *novel* U.K.: Hodder, 1935; U.S. (as "The Tau Cross Mystery"): Little, 1935
Detective: Sir Clinton Driffield.
Problem: Death by shooting in a locked room.

Conrad, Joseph

515. "The Inn of the Two Witches" *short story* in The Pall Mall Magazine, March, 193; "Within the Tides" U.K.: Dent, 1915; "The Complete Short Stories of Joseph Conrad" U.K.: Hutchinson, (1935); The Saint Mystery Magazine, January, 1959
Detective: Edgar Byrne.
Problem: Murder and attempted murder in a locked room at an inn.

Conyers, Dorothea

516. ✓ "The Poisoning of Hector Alhuson" *short story* in "Hunting and Hunted" U.K.: Hutchinson, 1930
Detective: Mervyn Henderson.
Problem: Death by poisoning of a man who had, during the course of a meal, eaten and drunk only the same as everyone else.

Copper, Basil

517. ✓ "The Adventure of the Defeated Doctor" *short story* in "The Further Adventures of Solar Pons" U.S.: Pinnacle, 1979; U.K.: L.S.P. Books, 1979

Detective: Solar Pons.
Problem: Death by blunt instrument in a locked studio.

Cornier, Vincent

518. ✓ "The Brother of Heaven" *short story* in Pearson's Magazine, October 1933; EQMM, December 1948; "Duel of Shadows", Crippen & Landru, 2011
Detective: Barnabas Hildreth.
Problem: Death by stabbing on a patch of muddy floor on which only the victim's footprints were evident.

519. ✓ "The Courtyard of the Fly" *short story* in Pearson's Magazine, July 1937; "The Art of the Impossible" U.K.: Xanadu, 1990; "Murder Impossible" U.S.: Carroll, 1990
Detective: Superintendent Hamilton.
Problem: Theft of a rope of pearls by a large, brightly coloured fly that flew in through an open window.

520. ✓ "Dust of Lions" *short story* in Pearson's Magazine, April 1933
Detective: Professor Wanless.
Problem: Involuntary conflagration of a number of people and animals at various points across the globe.

521. ✓ "The Flying Hat" *short story* in The Storyteller, May 1929; "The Best Detective Stories of the Year 1929" U.K.: Faber, 1930; U.S.: "Big Book of Locked-Room Mysteries", Black Lizard, 2014
Detectives: Sir Richard Brantingham and Lord Passingford.
Problem: Injury by a stabbing blow from above. The killer left no footprints in the snow.

522. ✓ "The Million Water" *short story* in Britannia & Eve, August 1932
Detective: None.
Problem: Survival of three men in an open boat in the middle of the Gulf of Mexico by drinking water taken only from the sea.

523. ✓ "The Monster" *short story* in EQMM, February 1951; "Duel of Shadows"
Detective: Barnabas Hildreth.
Problem: (non-impossible) How, under a capital-punishment system, could a sane, self-confessed murderer have his sentence of death justifiably quashed and rendered null and void.

524. "The Shot That Waited" *short story* in EQMM, September 1947;

(as "The Mystery of the Westmacott Bullet") "Anthology 1969" U.S.: Davis, 1968; originally as "The Duel of Shadows" Pearson's Magazine, April 1934; "Duel of Shadows"; The Mammoth Book of Perfect Crimes and Impossible Mysteries", UK: Constable and Robinson, 2006, US: Carroll and Graf, 2007
Detective: Hildreth.
Problem: Wounding by a 200-year-old bullet in a room in which the victim was alone.

525. ✓ "The Space-Time Masterpiece" *short story* in The Storyteller, April 1936
Detective: Hildreth.
Problems: (1) Death from a broken neck by reason of a fall with a horse brought down by an apparently invisible agency.
(2) Various ghostly manifestations of priories, cavaliers, etc.

Courtier, Sidney Hobson

526. ✓ THE GLASS SPEAR *novel* U.S.: Wyn, 1950; U.K.: Dakers, 1952
Detective: Ambrose Mahon.
Problem: Death by stabbing in a locked museum.

Cousins, E. G.

527. ✓ DEATH BY MARRIAGE *novel* U.K.: Gifford, 1959
Detective: Col. Richard Bame.
Problem: Death by drowning in a locked bathroom.

Craven, Monte (Joseph Commings, q.v.)

528. "The Bewitched Terrace" *short story* in Mystery Digest Magazine, July 1958
Detective: Senator Banner.
Problem: Appearance and disappearance of a wraithlike figure in a locked séance room with a twenty-storey balcony window, together with levitation to the balcony of a nearby block.

529. "The Fraudulent Spirit" *short story* in Mystery Digest, September/October 1960
Detective: Banner.
Comment: Same story as Item 528.

530. "I'm No Hero" *short story* in Mystery Digest, November/December 1961
Detective: Guy Sayre, the taxi driver.
Problem: Death by two bullets in the heart of a woman alone in the back of a taxi.

Crawfurd, Oswald

531. "The Flying Man" *short story* in "The Revelations of Inspector Morgan" U.K.: Chapman, 1906; U.S.: Dodd, 1907
Detective: Detective-Inspector Morgan.
Problem: Murder in a snow-bound lane with no footprints to account for the murderer.

Crispin, Edmund

532. THE CASE OF THE GILDED FLY *novel* U.K.: Gollancz, 1944; U.S. (as "Obsequies at Oxford"): Lippincott, 1945
Detective: Prof. Gervase Fen.
Problem: Death by shooting in a room constantly under observation.

533. THE MOVING TOYSHOP *novel* U.K.: Gollancz, 1946; U.S.: Lippincott, 1946
Detective: Fen.
Problems: (1) Disappearance of a toyshop.
(2) Death by asphyxiation in a room under observation.

534. SWAN SONG *novel* U.K.: Gollancz, 1947; U.S.: Walker, 1980; (as "Dead and Dumb") Lippincott, 1947
Detective: Fen.
Problem: Death by hanging in a guarded area.

535. "Beware of the Trains" *short story* in "Beware of the Trains" U.K.: Gollancz, 1953, and U.S.: Walker, 1962; (as "Nine Minus Nine Equals One") in EQMM, March 1951; "Big Book of Locked-Room Mysteries", Black Lizard, 2014
Detective: Fen.
Problem: Disappearance of an engine driver from a guarded railway station.

536. "The Name on the Window" *short story* in "Beware of the Trains"; EQMM, February 1953; "Ellery Queen's Blighted Dwellings" U.S.: Davis, 1986
Detective: Fen.
Problem: Death in a pavilion surrounded by snow with no footprints apart from the dead man's.

537. "Too Clever for Scotland Yard" *short story* in EQMM, September 1960; (as "Death Behind Bars") in "Fen Country" U.K.: Gollancz, 1979; U.S.: Walker, 1980
Detective: Assistant Commissioner John Kirkbride, CID.
Problem: Death by poisoning in a locked prison cell.

Crofts, Freeman Wills

538. THE END OF ANDREW HARRISON *novel* U.K.: Hodder, 1938; U.S. (as "The Futile Alibi"): Dodd, 1938
Detective: Chief Inspector French.
Problem: Death by gassing in a locked boat cabin.

539. SUDDEN DEATH *novel* U.K.: Collins, 1932; U.S.: Harper, 1932
Detective: Inspector French.
Problem: Deaths by gassing in a locked room (2).

Crombie, Michael

540. THE SEALED ROOM MURDER *novel* U.K.: Arthur Gray, (1934)
Detectives: Larry Milner and Sergeant Evans.
Problem: Death by stabbing in a locked room.

Cross, Mark

541. THE FOUR AT BAY *novel* U.K.: Ward, 1939
Detectives: Daphne Wrayne and the Adjustors.
Problem: Death by suffocation in a locked room.

542. THE JAWS OF DARKNESS *novel* U.K.: Ward, 1952
Detectives: Wrayne and the Adjustors.
Problem: Death by projectile into the brain but no traces of the projectile.

543. MURDER IN THE AIR *novel* Ward, 1943
Detectives: Wrayne and the Adjustors.
Problem: Death by poisoning while in the open air with no indication of how the poison was administered.

544. MURDER IN THE POOL *novel* U.K.: Ward, 1941
Detectives: Wrayne and the Adjustors.
Problems: (1) Death by drowning in a pool in which the victims swam alone.
(2) Disappearance of a ten-foot-high figure of a black monk.

545. THE WAY OF THE FOUR *novel* U.K.: Ward, 1936
Detectives: Wrayne and the Adjustors.
Problem: Disappearance of jewels from an unbreakable safe.

Crossen, Ken (see also Foster, Richard)

546. ✓ THE CASE OF THE CURIOUS HEEL *novel* in Baffling Detective Mysteries, 1942; U.S.: Eerie Series, 1944
Detectives: Jason Jones and Necessary Smith.
Problem: Death by shooting in a locked lavatory.

547. ✓ THE CASE OF THE PHANTOM FINGERPRINTS *novel* U.S.: Eerie Series, 1945

Detectives: Jones and Smith.
Problem: Disappearance, after a fingerprinting session, of one of those fingerprinted, and no marks in the surrounding snow to show how he had got away.

Cruickshank, Charles

548. THE TANG MURDERS *novel* U.K.: Hale, 1976
Detective: Jack Griffin.
Problem: Disappearance from a carefully guarded estate of a number of large and valuable pieces of porcelain.

Cumberland, Marten

549. ✓ SOMEONE MUST DIE *novel* U.K.: Hurst, 1940
Detective: Commissaire Satumin Dax of the Paris police.
Problem: Death by stabbing in a locked room.

550. "The Diary of Death" *short story* in "The Best Detective Stories of the Year 1928" U.K.: Faber, 1929; "The Best English Detective Stories of 1928" U.S.: Liveright, 1929; EQMM, January 1943
Detectives: Loreto Santos and Inspector Comfort.
Problem: Death by stabbing in a locked room.

Cummings, Ray

551. "The Confession of Rosa Vitelli" *short story* in The Sketch, Aug. 19,1925; "Tales from the Scientific Crime Club" U.K.: Ferret, 1979; "Big Book of Locked-Room Mysteries", Black Lizard, 2014
Detectives: Members of the Scientific Crime Club.
Problem: Death by gassing in a locked room.

Cunningham, A. B.

552. THE DEATH OF A WORLDLY WOMAN *novel* U.S.: Dutton, 1948
Detective: Sheriff Jess Roden.
Problem: Death by poisoning in a locked room.

553. ✓ WHO KILLED PRETTY BECKY LOW? *novel* U.S.: Dutton, 1951
Detective: Roden.
Problem: Death by stabbing in a locked room.

Curtis, Richard

554. "Odds Bodkins and the Locked Room Caper" *short story* in EQMM, January 1969
Detective: Godfrey "Odds" Bodkins.
Problem: Conveyance of messages into a betting-office room when no personal transmitter would work and no telephone or

other calls are allowed to clients.

D

Dallas, Walter

555. "The Mysterious Mirror" *short story* in MSMM, April 1964; MSMM (U.K.), October 1964 *Detective:* George Lombard Squire, banker.
Problem: Theft of valuable jewels from a locked hotel suite.

Dalman, Max

556. THE HIDDEN LIGHT *novel* U.K.: Ward, 1937
Detective: David Marchant.
Problem: Death by shooting in a locked room.

557. VAMPIRE ABROAD *novel* U.K.: Ward, 1938
Detectives: Colonel Cheddington and Superintendent Wilkins.
Problems: (1) Murder in a locked room.
(2) Victim had been drained of blood.

Daly, Elizabeth

558. MURDERS IN VOLUME 2 *novel* U.S.: Farrar, 1941; U.K.: Eyre, 1943
Detective: Henry Gamadge.
Problem: Disappearance of a girl from a closed-in garden.

D'Amato, Barbara

559. ✓ THE HANDS OF HEALING MURDER *novel* U.S.: Charter, 1980
Detective: Dr. Gerritt DeGraaf.
Problem: Death by stabbing through the temple with a scalpel in a room occupied only by eight bridge players. No one else could have entered the room, but the fingerprints on the scalpel did not match any of the room's occupants.

560. ✓ HARD TACK *novel* U.S.: Scribners, 1991
Detective: Cat Marsala.
Problem: Death by throat cutting in a locked cabin.

Danesford, Earle

561. ✓ "Beyond the Second Door" *short story* in The Violet Magazine, Dec. 25, 1926
Detective: Marise Overton.
Problem: Death by stabbing inside a locked room.

Daniel, Roland

562. THE BROWN MURDER CASE *novel* U.K.: Shaylor, 1930; reprint U.K.: Wright, (1930)
Detectives: Chief Inspector Neville Langham and Sergeant Hopkins.
Problem: Death by hanging in a locked room.

563. THE ROSARIO MURDER CASE *novel* U.K.: Brentanos, 1930; reprint U.K.: Wright, 1930
Detective: Chief Inspector Langham.
Problem: Murder of two people by gunshot but only one shot was heard.

Daniels, Norman A.

564. ✓ "Enigma of the Talkative Wraith" *short story* in 10-Story Detective Magazine, May 1942
Detective: Jimmy Ross.
Problem: Disappearance of a house in which our hero finds a dying man.

Dark, Rex

565. ✓ DEAD MEN TELL... *novel* U.K.: Wright, 1937
Detectives: Inspector Sam Thackeray and Bartholomew Dane.
Problem: Disappearance of a dead body from a room under constant surveillance.

566. ✓ THE INVISIBLE HAND *novel* U.K.: Wright, 1937
Detectives: Thackeray and Dane.
Problem: Death by stabbing in open space with nobody near the victim.

567. ✓ THE TREMLOW MURDER CASE *novel* U.K.: Wright, 1938
Detectives: Thackeray and Dane.
Problem: Death by stabbing in a locked theatre dining room.

568. ✓ THE WARDUR STREET MYSTERY *novel* U.K.: Wright, 1936
Detectives: Thackeray and Dane.
Problem: Various deaths by unknown means, including one in which the victim was in bed in a bedroom under close guard.

Davies, L. P.

569. ✓ ADVENTURE HOLIDAYS, LTD. *novel* U.S.: Doubleday, 1970
Detectives: Peter Cullimore and Donald Lomax.
Problem: Appearance and disappearance of a car along a stretch of open country road.

Davis, Frederick C.

570. NIGHT DROP *novel* U.S.: Doubleday, 1955; U.K. (as by Stephen Ransome): Gollancz, 1956
Detectives: Schyler Cole and Luke Speare.
Problem: Disappearance of money from envelopes posted into a guarded, locked room.

Davis, Robert Hart

571. "The Ghost Rider Affair" *short story* in The Man From U.N.C.L.E. Magazine, July 1966
Detectives: Napoleon Solo and Iliya Kuryakin.
Problem: Disappearance of two trains—among other thing: from a stretch of track.

572. ✓ "The Pawns of Death" *short story* in Charlie Chan Mystery Magazine, August 1974
Detective: Charlie Chan.
Problem: Death by shooting in a locked hotel bedroom.
Skupin Comment: "Robert Hart Davis" is a house name; this story was written by Bill Pronzini and Jeffrey M. Wallman (q.v.)

Davis, Tech

573. ✓ TERROR AT COMPASS LAKE *novel* U.S.: Doubleday, 1935
Detective: Aubrey Nash.
Problem: Death by stabbing in a locked bedroom.

Dawe, Carlton

574. THE BLACK SPIDER *novel* U.K.: Nash, 1911
Detective: Reginald Cosway.
Problem: Thefts of various jewels from locked hotel rooms.

deFord, Miriam Allen

575. "Time Trammel" *short story* in Fantasy & Science Fiction, November 1956; "Deals with the Devil" U.S.: Dodd, 1958, and U.K.: Faber, 1959; "The Locked Room Reader" U.S.: Random, 1968; "8 Doors to Death" U.S.: Dell, 1970
Problem: Disappearance from a locked cell.

de la Torre, Lillian

576. "The Disappearing Servant Wench" *short story* in "Villainy Detected" U.S.: Appleton, 1947; "Four and Twenty Bloodhounds" U.S.: Simon, 1950, and U.K.: Hammond, 1951; "Cream of the Crime" U.S.: Holt, 1962, and U.K.: Harrap, 1964; "The Return of Dr. Sam: Johnson" U.S.: IPL, 1985
Detective: Dr. Sam: Johnson.

Problem: Disappearance of a serving wench.

577. ✓ "Murder Lock'd In" *short story* in EQMM, Dec. 1, 1980; "The Return of Dr. Sam: Johnson"
Detective: Dr. Johnson.
Problem: Death by blunt instrument and strangling in a locked room.

578. "The Triple Lock'd Room" *short story* in EQMM, January 1952; "The Detections of Dr. Sam: Johnson" U.S.: Doubleday, 1960; "All But Impossible!" U.S.: Ticknor, 1981
Detective: Dr. Johnson.
Problem: Death by stabbing in a locked room.

Dean, Gregory

579. ✓ MURDER ON STILTS *novel* U.S.: Hillman, 1939
Detective: Commissioner Benjamin Stone.
Problem: Death by shooting in a locked room.

DeAndrea, William L.

580. ✓ KILLED ON THE ROCKS *novel* U.S.: Mysterious, 1990
Detective: Matt Cobb, media man.
Problem: A body found in an area of otherwise unmarked snow.

Delannoy, Burford

581. ✓ M.R.C.S. *novel* U.K.: Ward, 1903
Detective: John Garden.
Problem: Disappearance of a dead body from within a locked suite of rooms into which one of the killers had placed the only key after exiting and locking the door.

Dellbridge, John

582. "The Fire That Was Quenched" *short story* in "Searchlight on Hambledon" U.K.: Hurst, (1947)
Detective: Inspector Hambledon.
Problem: Death by asphyxiation and burning in a locked room.

Dennis, Robert C.

583. ✓ "Murder in the Mails" *short story* in Black Mask, November 1946
Detective: Willie Carmody and Margaret O'Leary
Problems: Disappearance (twice) of a thief between the first and third floors of an apartment building.

Derleth, August

584. "The Adventure of the Devil's Footprints" *short story* in "The Return of Solar Pons" U.S.: Mycroft, 1958; (as "The Devil's

Footprints") in Double-Action Detective Stories, No. 4, 1956
Detective: Solar Pons.
Problem: Disappearance of a man in unmarked snow apart from "devil's tracks."

585. "The Adventure of the Grice-Patterson Curse" *short story* in Pursuit Detective Story Magazine, November 1956; "The Return of Solar Pons"
Detective: Pons.
Problem: Several deaths by strangulation in a locked room. The one window open was not used to gain entrance.

586. "The Adventure of the Late Mr. Faversham" *short story* in Dragnet Magazine, December 1929; "In Re Sherlock Holmes" U.S.: Mycroft, 1945; "Regarding Sherlock Holmes" U.S.: Pinnacle, 1974; "The Adventures of Solar Pons" U.K.: Robson, 1975
Detective: Pons.
Problem: Disappearance of a man from a house under observation.

587. "The Adventure of the Lost Locomotive" *short story* in "The Memoirs of Solar Pons" U.S.: Mycroft, 1951
Detective: Pons.
Problem: Disappearance of a railway locomotive on a confined stretch of track.

588. "The Adventure of the Missing Tenants" *short story* in Dragnet Magazine, 1929; "The Chronicles of Solar Pons" U.S.: Mycroft, 1973, and U.K.: Robson, 1975
Detective: Pons.
Problem: Disappearance of a tenant from a house surrounded by unmarked snow.

Desmond, Hugh

589. FANFARE FOR MURDER *novel* U.K.: Wright, 1961
Detective: Alan Fraser.
Problem: Death by poison in a locked room.

590. THE JACARANDA MURDERS *novel* U.K.: Wright, 1951
Detectives: Ex-Detective Inspector Dunning and reporter Andrew Robertson.
Problems: (1) Death by strangulation in a locked room.
(2) Death by shooting in a room containing only the victim.

591. ✓ A PACT WITH THE DEVIL *novel* U.K.: Wright, 1952

Detective: Alan Fraser.

Problem: Death by unknown means in a railway compartment in which the victim and an innocent witness were the only people present.

Des Ormeaux, J. J. (Forest Rosaire)

592. ✓ "The Astral Assassin" *short story* in Street & Smith's Detective Story Magazine, September 1939; "Detective Story Annual 1942", Street & Smith, 1942

Detective: Hugh Calvert.

Problem: Death by poisoning by invisible agent.

593. ✓ "The Poisoned Bowl" *short story* in Street & Smith's Clues-Detective Stories, April 1939

Detective: Captain Corrigan.

Problem: Death by poison by invisible agency.

Detection Club

594. ✓ "Behind the Screen" *novelette* in The Listener, 1930; "The Scoop and Behind the Screen" U.K.: Gollancz, 1983; U.S.: Harper, 1983

Detectives: Inspector Rice (official), Wilfred Hope and Mr. Parsons (amateur).

Problem: Death by stabbing behind a screen in a room in which the movements of all concerned were apparently accounted for.

Detzer, Karl W.

595. ✓ "Through Bolted Doors" *short story* in "True Tales of the D.C.I." U.S.: Bobbs, 1925; "The World's Best One Hundred Detective Stories" U.S.: Funk, 1929

Detectives: The narrator and Papa Chenon, gendarme.

Problem: Death by shooting in a room with the door and window shutter locked on the inside.

Dibdin, Michael

596. ✓ VENDETTA *novel* U.K.: Faber, 1990

Detective: Inspector Aurelio Zen.

Problem: Death by shooting in a remote farm house cum top-security fortress totally guarded from the outside and quite impenetrable, the whole event being immortalised on videotape.

Dickinson, Peter

597. THE POISON ORACLE *novel* U.K.: Hodder, 1974; U.S.: Pantheon, 1974

Detective: Wesley Morris.

Problem: Death by poisoning in a locked zoo.

Dickson, Carter (see also Carr, John Dickson)

598. AND SO TO MURDER *novel* U.S.: Morrow, 1940; U.K.: Heinemann, 1941
Detective: Sir Henry Merrivale ("H.M.").
Problem: No impossible crime in this story, but a rather nasty affair involving sulfuric acid poured down a speaking tube and a poisoned cigarette.

599. BEHIND THE CRIMSON BLIND *novel* U.K.: Heinemann, 1952; U.S.: Morrow, 1952
Detective: Merrivale.
Problems: (1) Ability of a thief to escape while holding a large iron chest.
(2) Disappearance of diamonds and the iron chest from a room under guard.

600. THE BOWSTRING MURDERS *novel* U.S. (as by Carr Dickson): Morrow, 1933; U.K.: Heinemann, 1934
Detective: John Gaunt.
Problem: Death by strangulation in a hall, the only entrance to which is under observation.

601. THE CAVALIER'S CUP *novel* U.S.: Morrow, 1953; U.K.: Heinemann, 1954
Detective: Sir Henry Merrivale.
Problem: Movement of a valuable cup inside a locked room.

602. THE CURSE OF THE BRONZE LAMP *novel* U.S.: Morrow, 1945; U.K. (as "Lord of the Sorcerers"): Heinemann, 1946
Detective: Merrivale.
Problem: Disappearance of a person while footsteps were within hearing distance.

603. DEATH IN FIVE BOXES *novel* U.K.: Heinemann, 1938; U.S.: Morrow, 1938
Detective: Merrivale.
Problem: Death by poisoning in a locked room.

604. FEAR IS THE SAME *novel* U.K.: Heinemann, 1956; U.S.: Morrow,1956
Detective: Philip Clavering, Earl of Glenarvon.
Problem: No impossible crime; a historical mystery set in Regency London.

605. THE GILDED MAN *novel* U.K.: Heinemann, 1942; U.S.: Morrow,

1942; (as "Death and the Gilded Man") U.S.: Pocket, 1947
Detective: Sir Henry Merrivale.
Problem: Not an impossible-crime story. The problem is: Why would a man burgle his own house and get stabbed in the attempt?

606. A GRAVEYARD TO LET *novel* U.S.: Morrow, 1949; U.K.: Heinemann, 1950
Detective: Merrivale.
Problem: Disappearance of a man who jumped fully clothed into a swimming pool.

607. He WOULDN'T KILL PATIENCE *novel* U.K.: Heinemann, 1944; U.S.: Morrow, 1944
Detective: Merrivale.
Problem: Death by gassing in a locked room, with all edges to doors and windows sealed on the inside with gummed paper.

608. The JUDAS WINDOW *novel* U.K.: Heinemann, 1938; U.S.: Morrow, 1938; (as "The Crossbow Murder") U.S.: Berkley, 1964
Detective: Merrivale.
Problem: Death by bow and arrow in a locked room.

609. THE MAGIC LANTERN MURDERS *novel* U.K.: Heinemann, 1936; U.S. (as "The Punch and Judy Murders"): Morrow, 1937
Detective: Merrivale.
Problem: Not quite an impossible-crime problem, but we do have the case of the two identical corpses, counterfeiting, disguised clergymen, and guillotine windows.

610. MURDER IN THE SUBMARINE ZONE *novel* U.K.: Heinemann, 1940; (as "Murder in the Atlantic") World, 1959; U.S. (as "Nine—and Death Makes Ten"): Morrow, 1940
Detective: Merrivale.
Problem: Murder on an ocean liner where the killer left fingerprints that did not relate to any of the crew members or passengers.

611. MY LATE WIVES *novel* U.S.: Morrow, 1946; U.K.: Heinemann, 1947
Detective: Merrivale.
Problem: Disappearance of several women whose bodies cannot be found.

612. NIGHT AT THE MOCKING WIDOW *novel* U.S.: Morrow, 1950; U.K.: Heinemann, 1951

Detective: Merrivale.
Problem: Disappearance of the menacing "widow" figure from a locked bedroom.

613. THE PLAGUE COURT MURDERS *novel* U.S.: Morrow, 1934; U.K.: Heinemann, 1935
Detective: Merrivale.
Problem: Death by shooting in a locked room.

614. THE READER IS WARNED *novel* U.K.: Heinemann, 1939; U.S.: Morrow, 1939
Detective: Merrivale.
Problem: Deaths by invisible means.

615. THE RED WIDOW MURDERS neve/U.K.: Heinemann, 1935; U.S.: Morrow, 1935
Detective: Merrivale.
Problem: Death by poison in a guarded room.

616. SEEING IS BELIEVING *novel* U.S.: Morrow, 1941; U.K.: Heinemann, 1942; (as "Cross of Murder") U.K.: World, 1959
Detective: Merrivale.
Problem: During a hypnotic display a man is murdered with a knife that was earlier demonstrated to be made of rubber.

617. SHE DIED A LADY *novel* U.K.: Heinemann, 1943; U.S.: Morrow, 1943
Detective: Merrivale.
Problem: Death by shooting at close range at a lovers' leap with footprints of the victims only.

618. THE SKELETON IN THE CLOCK *novel* U.S.: Morrow, 1948; U.K.: Heinemann, 1949
Detective: Merrivale.
Problem: Death of a man who suddenly pitches off a high flat roof on which he stood alone.

619. THE TEN TEACUPS *novel* U.K.: Heinemann, 1937; U.S. (as "The Peacock Feather Murders"): Morrow, 1937
Detective: Merrivale.
Problems: (1) Death by shooting (twice) in a locked, guarded room.
(2) Death by stabbing by an invisible murderer.

620. THE UNICORN MURDERS *novel* U.S.: Morrow, 1935; U.K.: Heinemann, 1936
Detective: Merrivale.

Problem: Murder of a man by a close-range humane killer, with metal bolt that is afterwards extracted. No killer is seen despite clear visibility of the victim as he is killed.

621. THE WHITE PRIORY MURDERS *novel* U.S.: Morrow, 1934; U.K.: Heinemann, 1935
Detective: Merrivale.
Problem: Death by blunt instrument in a pavilion surrounded by unmarked snow.

622. "Blind Man's Hood" *short story* in "The Department of Queer Complaints" U.K.: Heinemann, 1940, and U.S.: Morrow, 1940; (as "To Wake the Dead") EQMM, December 1966; "Murder for Christmas" U.S.: Mysterious, 1982; "Big Book of Locked-Room Mysteries", Black Lizard, 2014
Detective: None.
Problem: Death by throat cutting and burning in a house surrounded by unmarked snow.

623. "The Crime in Nobody's Room" *short story* in "Detection Medley" U.K.: Hutchinson, (1939); "Line-Up" U.S.: Dodd, 1940; "The Department of Queer Complaints"; "101 Years' Entertainment" U.S.: Little, 1941; "Merrivale, March and Murder", Crippen & Landru, 1991
Detective: Colonel March.
Problem: Murder in a room that didn't exist.

624. "Death in the Dressing Room" *short story* in "The Department of Queer Complaints"; "Merrivale, March and Murder"
Detective: March.
Problem: Death by stabbing, in a room, with no apparent opportunity for the murder to be done, after the victim had performed in a cabaret.

625. ✓ "The Diamond Pentacle" *short story* in The Times, Nov. 15, 1939; "Merrivale, March and Murder"
Detective: None.
Problem: Entrance effected into a room bolted at the door and barred at the windows.

626. "Error at Daybreak" *short story* in "The Second Century of Detective Stories" U.K.: Hutchinson, (1938); "The Department of Queer Complaints"; (as "The Lion's Paw") EQMM July 1967; "Merrivale, March and Murder"
Detective: March.

Problem: Death by stabbing in an inaccessible stretch of beach.

627. "The Footprint in the Sky" *short story* in "The Department of Queer Complaints"; EQMM, November 1958; "Rogues' Gallery" U.S.: Doubleday, 1969; "Merrivale, March and Murder"
Detective: March.
Problem: Attempted murder in a snow-surrounded house. The only prints to it belonged to a nonguilty party, apart from one print on top of a hedge.

628. "Hot Money" *short story* in "The Department of Queer Complaints"; EQMM, April 1966; "Merrivale, March and Murder"
Detective: March.
Problem: Disappearance of a mound of paper money within a locked room.

629. "The New Invisible Man" *short story* in "The Department of Queer Complaints"; (as "The Man Who Saw the Invisible") EQMM, December 1967; "Whodunit? Houdini?" U.S.: Harper, 1976; "Merrivale, March and Murder"
Detective: March.
Problem: Shooting of a man by a gun held by the gloves of an invisible man.

630. "New Murders for Old" *short story* in "The Department of Queer Complaints"; (as "The One Real Horror") EQMM, August 1966; "Merrivale, March and Murder"
Detective: Hargreaves.
Problem: Man on world cruise reads of his own death.

631. "The Other Hangman" *short story* in "A Century of Detective Stories" U.K.: Hutchinson, (1935); "The Department of Queer Complaints"; EQMM, January 1965; "Fell and Foul Play", Crippen & Landru, 1991
Problem: (Nonimpossible)
Skupin Comment: Ingenious story about how a man is killed legally without possibility of prosecution

632. "Persons or Things Unknown" *short story* in "Detection Medley"; "Line-Up"; "The Department of Queer Complaints"; "Murder by Experts" U.S.: Ziff, 1947, and U.K.: Low, 1950; "Fell and Foul Play"
Detective: The host.
Problem: Death by stabbing in a room where no weapon could be found.

633. "The Silver Curtain" *short story* in "The Department of Queer Complaints"; EQMM, April 1960; "Merrivale, March and Murder"; "The Mammoth Book of Locked-Room Mysteries and Impossible Crimes", UK: Constable and Robinson, 2000, US: Carroll and Graf
Detective: March.
Problem: Death by stabbing in the neck in an empty street.

Dickson, Carter, and John Rhode

634. DROP TO HIS DEATH *novel* U.K.: Heinemann, 1939; U.S. (as "Fatal Descent"): Dodd, 1939
Detective: Dr. Horatio Glass.
Problem: Death by shooting in a closed elevator.

Didelot, Francis

635. THE TENTH LEPER *novel* U.K.: Macdonald, 1962
Detective: Commissaire Bignon.
Problem: Death by stabbing in a locked room.

Didelot, Roger Francis

636. MURDER IN THE BATH *novel* U.S.: Lippincott, 1933
Detectives: Commissioner Santelli and Inspector Lecain.
Problem: Death by strangulation in a locked bathroom.

Diehl, V. Vidal

637. ✓ "The Room 31 Riddle" *short story* in The 20 Story Magazine, between 1922 and 1940
Detective: Inspector Gibson, C.I.D.
Problem: Death by stabbing in a locked hotel room.

Dillard, R.H.W.

638. THE BOOK OF CHANGES *novel* U.S.: Doubleday, 1974
Detective: Sir Hugh Fitz-Hyffen.
Problem: Death of a man inside a locked room that could only be locked from the outside, yet the sole key was in the victim's stomach.

"Diplomat" (John Franklin Carter)

639. MURDER IN THE EMBASSY *novel* U.S.: Cape, 1930; U.K.: Harrap, 1931
Detective: Dennis Tyler.
Problem: Death by blunt instrument in a locked room.

Dix, Maurice

640. MURDER AT GRASSMERE ABBEY *novel* U.K.: Ward, 1933
Detectives: Inspector Gordon Frewin and Chief Inspector James

Miller.

Problem: Death by gunshot in a locked room.

Dolphin, Rex

641. "The Phantom Guest" *short story* in Edgar Wallace Mystery Magazine, Vol. 1, No. 1, October 1964

Detective: An unnamed police inspector.

Problem: Disappearance of heavy suitcases from a guarded room.

Donavan, John (Nigel Morland, q.v.)

642. THE CASE OF THE TALKING DUST *novel* U.K.: Hale, 1938; U.S.: Mystery House, 1941

Detectives: Inspector Cross and Sergeant Lamb.

Problem: The discovery of a recently dead body in a derelict shop covered with apparently undisturbed dust.

643. THE DEAD HAVE NO FRIENDS *novel* U.K.: Home, 1952

Detective: Sir Benjamin Scarle.

Problem: Death by poisoning in a locked study.

Donovan, Dick (J. E. Preston Muddock)

644. "Find the Missing Man" *competition short story* in All Sorts Magazine, 1898

Detective: The reader.

Problem: Disappearance of a murdered man from the locked room in which his murderer was also locked.

645. ✓ "The Saltmarket Murder Case" *short story* in "The Man-Hunter" U.K.: Chatto, 1888; U.S.: Lovell, 1891

Detective: Dick Donovan.

Problem: Two murders in a suite of rooms approached through a locked shop door.

Dorrington, Albert

646. ✓ THE RADIUM TERRORS *novel* U.K.: Nash, 1912; U.S.: Doubleday, 1912

Detective: Gifford Renwick.

Problem: Disappearance, virtually under the nose of one innocent witness, of a vial of radium.

Doty, William L.

647. ✓ BUTTON, BUTTON... *novel* U.S.: Our Sunday Visitor, 1979

Detective: Monsignor Thomas O. McGillicuddy.

Problem: Death by throat cutting in a locked cabin.

Dowie, W. Kesterton

648. ✓ "The Casallis Mystery" *short story* in Pearson's Weekly Extra Christmas Number, 1892, and Pearson's Weekly, Jan. 21,1893

Detective: Not known.

Problem: Disappearance from a locked room.

Downey, Edmund

649. ✓ THE UGLY MAN *novel* U.K.: Downey, 1896

Detective: Walter Tandy.

Problem: Disappearance of a great emerald from the secret pocket in a young man's coat and its subsequent reappearance in the guttering of a large house.

Doyle, Adrian Conan and John Dickson Carr (q.v)

650. "The Adventure of the Deptford Horror" *short story* in "The Exploits of Sherlock Holmes" U.K.: Murray, 1954; U.S.: Random, 1954

Detective: Sherlock Holmes.

Problem: Death by fright caused by an invisible agent.

651. "The Adventure of the Sealed Room" *short story* in "The Exploits of Sherlock Holmes"

Detective: Holmes.

Problem: Death by shooting in a locked room.

Doyle, Sir Arthur Conan

652. "The Adventure of the Speckled Band" *short story* in The Strand Magazine, February 1892; "The Adventures of Sherlock Holmes" U.K.: Newnes, 1892; U.S.: Harper, 1892; "Tantalizing Locked Room Mysteries" U.S.: Walker, 1982; "Big Book of Locked-Room Mysteries", Black Lizard, 2014

Detective: Sherlock Holmes.

Problem: Death by fright in a locked bedroom.

653. "J. Habakuk Jephson's Statement" *short story* in "Dreamland and Ghostland" U.K.: Redway, (1887), three volumes; "Strange Stories of Coincidence" U.K.: Redway, 1888 (reissue of volume two of "Dreamland and Ghostland"); "The Captain of the Polestar" U.K.: Longmans, 1890

Problem: The mystery of the "Marie Celeste."

654. "The Problem of Thor Bridge" *short story* in The Strand Magazine, February 1922; "The Case-Book of Sherlock Holmes" U.K.: Murray, 1927, and U.S.: Doran, 1927

Detective: Sherlock Holmes.
Problem: Death by shooting on a bridge; the weapon was absent.

655. "The Story of the Lost Special" *short story* in The Strand Magazine, August 1898; "Round the Fire Stories" U.K.: Smith, 1908, and U.S.: MacClure, 1908; U.S.: "The Black Doctor and Other Tales of Terror and Mystery", Doran, 1925; (as "The Mystery of the Lost Special") "Death Locked In" U.S.: IPL, 1987
Detective: (Sherlock Holmes).
Problem: Disappearance of a train from a stretch of line guarded at both ends.

Dresser, Davis (see also Halliday, Michael)

656. "Murder Takes a Ride" *short story* in Mystery Book Magazine, January 1946
Detective: Steve Random.
Problem: Disappearance of an old man with a broken hip from a hotel bedroom locked on the inside.

Drew, Ronald

657. THE PHANTOM CAR *juvenile novel* U.K.: Cooke, 1925
Detectives: Harry Wardon and Tommy Potts.
Problem: Disappearance of a car from a guarded stretch of road.

Drummond, Hamilton

658. ✓ ROOM FIVE *novel* U.K.: Ward, 1904
Detective: George Vore.
Problem: Death of two men by poison in a locked room.

Drummond, John (John Newton Chance, q.v.)

659. At 60 MPH *novel* SBL No. 94 (3rd series) U.K.: Amalgamated, 1945
Detective: Sexton Blake.
Problem: Death by stabbing in a locked railway carriage on a moving train.

660. ✓ THE CASE OF THE MAN WITH NO NAME *novel* SBL No. 246 (3rd series) U.K.: Amalgamated, 1951
Detective: Blake.
Problem: Fall of a dead body from the otherwise unoccupied roof of a building.

661. ✓ THE PAINTED DAGGER *novel* SBL No. 86 (3rd series) U.K.: Amalgamated, 1944
Detective: Blake.
Problem: Death by stabbing in a theatre box under constant

observation.

662. THE RIDDLE OF THE MUMMY CASE *novel* SBL No. 100 (3rd series) U.K.: Amalgamated, 1945
Detective: Blake.
Problem: Robbery from a tightly sealed museum.

663. ✓ The Secret of the Sixty Steps *novel* SBL No. 213 (3rd series) U.K.: Amalgamated, 1950
Detective: Blake.
Problem: A small model plane containing only a thimbleful of fuel crashes into a tall, sturdy brick tower that is blown to smithereens.

664. ✓ THE TOWN OF SHADOWS *novel* SBL No. 182 (3rd series) U.K.: Amalgamated, 1948
Detective: Blake.
Problems: (1) Death by shooting by a killer who then left no footprints.
(2) Ability of a driver to drive at good speed through thick fog that should have reduced his speed to a snail's pace.

Dudley, Ernest

665. ✓ "The Case of the Man Who Was Too Clever" *short story* in "Meet Dr. Morelle" U.K.: Long, 1943
Detective: Dr. Morelle.
Problem: Death by poison in a locked bathroom.

Duncan, David

666. THE SHADE OF TIME *novel* U.S.: Random, 1946; U.K.: Grey Walls Press, 1948
Detective: Jim Quigley.
Problem: Man shot by an arrow while inside a locked laboratory.

Dunn, J. Allan

667. ✓ "Jimmy Dugan Figures Out the Impossible Crime" *short story* in Detective Weekly, No. 214, March 27, 1937
Detective: Jimmy Dugan, plainclothes policeman.
Problem: Robbery from a safe in plain view at all times.

Dunsany, Lord

668. "Near the Back of Beyond" *short story* in EQMM, November 1955; EQMM UK, November 1955; EQMM Australia, January 1956
Narrator: Joseph Jorkens.
Problem: Escape of a condemned man from a locked, guarded

prison cell.

669. "The Two Bottles of Relish" *short story* in "Powers of Darkness" U.K.: Allan, 1934; "101 Years' Entertainment" U.S.: Little, 1941; EQMM, March 1951; "The Little Tales of Smethers" U.K.: Jarrolds, 1952; Suspense (UK), December 1959; "Perfect Crimes" U.S.: St. Martin's, 1989; "Big Book of Locked-Room Mysteries", Black Lizard, 2014
Detective: Linley.
Problem: Disappearance of a girl from a bungalow under observation.

Dupree, Morrison

670. A TAP ON THE SHOULDER *novel* U.S.: Doubleday, 1929
Detective: Dr. Andrew Stoughton.
Problem: Death by blunt instrument in a locked room.

Durham, David (Roy Vickers, q.v.)

671. ✓ "The Great Kabul" *short story* in "The Exploits of Fidelity Dove" U.K.: Hodder, 1924; U.K. (as by Roy Vickers): Newnes, 1935
Criminal: Fidelity Dove.
Problem: The concealment in a house of a great diamond and the inability of those searching for it there to find it.

672. ✓ "The Gulverbury Diamonds" *short story* in "The Exploits of Fidelity Dove"; "Big Book of Locked-Room Mysteries", Black Lizard, 2014
Criminal: Dove.
Problem: Disappearance of diamonds from a room under guard.

673. ✓ "Proverbs and Profits" *short story* in "The Exploits of Fidelity Dove"
Criminal: Dove.
Problem: Return of tapestries to a room under constant guard.

Durham, Mary

674. MURDER HATH CHARMS *novel* U.K.: Skeffington, (1948)
Detective: Inspector Rodney Hilton.
Problem: Death by strangulation in a room to which both entrances were guarded.

Dutton, Charles J.

675. ✓ THE CIRCLE OF DEATH *novel* U.K.: Hurst, 1933; U.S.: Dodd, 1933
Detective: Prof. Harley Manners.

Problem: Deaths by poisoning introduced by unknown means.

676. THE CROOKED CROSS *novel* U.S.: Dodd, 1926
Detective: John Bartley.
Problem: Death by stabbing in a locked library.

677. THE SHADOW ON THE GLASS *novel* U.S.: Dodd, 1923; U.K.: Jenkins, 1925
Detective: Bartley.
Problem: Death by blunt instrument in a locked library.

678. THE UNDERWOOD MYSTERY *novel* U.S.: Dodd, 1921; U.K.: Robinson, 1922
Detective: Bartley.
Problem: Death by shooting in a locked library.

Dyer, George

679. THE CATALYST CLUB *novel* U.S.: Scribners, 1936; U.K.: Heinemann, (1937)
Detectives: The members of the Catalyst Club.
Problem: Death by mutilation; no marks of an attacker.

680. THE THREE-CORNERED WOUND *novel* U.S.: Houghton, 1931; U.K.: Skeffington, (1932)
Detective: Dr. Ben Starrett.
Problem: Death by stabbing. No assailant near the victim and no weapon to be found afterwards.

E

Eadie, Arlton

681. "The Clue from Mars" *short story* in The Detective Magazine, Feb. 1, 1924
Detective: Wayman Instone.
Problem: Death by blunt instrument in a locked observatory.

East, Roger

682. ✓ TWENTY-FIVE SANITARY INSPECTORS *novel* U.K.: Collins, 1935
Detective: Ex-Superintendent Simmonds of Scotland Yard.
Problem: Death by stabbing in a room under constant guard.

Eastman, Roy

683. THE MYSTERIES OF BLAIR HOUSE *novel* U.S.: Conjure, 1948
Detectives: Harrison Holt and Bobby Weatherby.
Problem: Death by shooting in a locked, sealed basement.

Eaton, Herbert

684. "The Adventure of the Addleton Tragedy" *short story* in "The Non-Canonical Sherlock Holmes" U.S.: Pontine, 1975
Detective: Sherlock Holmes.
Problem: Death by shooting in a drawing room with all entrances watched.

Eberhardt, Walter

685. THE JIG-SAW PUZZLE MURDER *novel* U.S.: Grosset, 1933; U.K.: Puzzle Books, (1933)
Detective: Inspector Watterson.
Problem: Death by shooting while under observation. Nothing was seen or heard by the witnesses present.

Eberhart, Mignon G.

686. THE MYSTERY OF HUNTING'S END *novel* U.S.: Doubleday, 1930; U.K.: Heinemann, 1931
Detective: Lance O'Leary.
Problem: Death by shooting in a room under continuous observation.

687. ✓ "The Calico Dog" *short story* in The Delineator, September 1934; "The Cases of Susan Dare" U.K.: Lane, 1935, and U.S.: Doubleday, 1934; Rex Stout Mystery Magazine, February 1946; Rex Stout Mystery Magazine (Canada); "Crime on Her Mind" U.S.: Pantheon, 1975; U.K.: Joseph, 1976
Detective: Susan Dare.
Problem: Death by shooting in a hotel room in which no one else appeared to be.

Eden, Dorothy

688. THE DEADLY TRAVELLERS *novel* U.K.: Macdonald, 1959; U.S.: Ace, 1966
Detective: Kate Tempest, artist.
Problem: Disappearance of a child from a moving train.

Ekström, Jan

689. ✓ DEADLY REUNION *novel* U.S.: Scribners, 1983; U.K. (as "The Ancestral Precipice"): Macmillan, 1983
Detective: Inspector Bertil Durell.
Problem: Death by carbon-monoxide poisoning in a locked room.

Eldredge, Gilbert

690. MURDER IN THE STRATOSPHERE *novel* U.S.: Phoenix, 1940

Detectives: Chip Carpenter and Thibault Parew.
Problems: (1) Disappearance of a man from an aeroplane flying at high altitude.
(2) Death by poison in a room under observation.

Ellin, Stanley

691. ✓ "The Twelfth Statue" *short story* in EQMM, February 1967; "Kindly Dig Your Grave" U.S.: Davis, 1975; "The Specialty of the House" U.S.: Mysterious, 1979; "Deadly Arts" U.S.: Arbor, 1985; "Big Book of Locked-Room Mysteries", Black Lizard, 2014
Detective: Mel Gordon, screenwriter.
Problem: Disappearance of a film producer from within a guarded film set.

Ellington, Richard

692. ✓ EXIT FOR A DAME *novel* U.S.: Morrow, 1951; U.K.: Board man, 1954
Detective: Steve Drake, private eye.
Problems: (1) Movement seen through a window of a woman dead more than a week.
(2) Disappearance of a woman into thin air.
(3) Disappearance of a maid from a study under constant observation.

Elliot, Bruce

693. ✓ YOU'LL DIE LAUGHING *novel* U.S.: Five Star, 1945; Ramble House, 2006
Detective: Lieutenant Brissk.
Problem: Disappearance of a man from a bedroom into which he had been seen to enter seconds before and the discovery of his dead body minutes later in an adjacent room.

694. ✓ "Death Paces the Widow's Walk" *short story* in The Shadow, October 1944; Street & Smith's Detective Monthly (U.K.), January 1958
Detective: Nick Carter.
Problems: (1) Death by shooting in a locked room.
(2) Disappearance of a man from a house under constant surveillance.

Elston, Allan Vaughan

695. "The Shanghaied Ship" *short story* in Adventure, December 1933

Detective: The Great Garlow, magician.
Problems: (1) Theft of a ton of gold from an ocean-going yacht. (2) Survival of a drugged man thrown overboard from that yacht.

Elvy, C.

696. THE MAGIC OF CHEZ FINNIE *novel* U.K.: Stockwell, 1967
Detective: Inspector Slade.
Problem: Disappearance of an actress from a stage between curtain calls.

Ephesian (Bechhofer Roberts)

697. ✓ Chapter XIII in "A.B.C. Investigates" *(short story)* U.K.: Jarrolds, 1937
Detective: A.B.C. Hawkes.
Problem: Death by poisoning in a locked laboratory.

Essex, Richard

698. SLADE OF THE YARD *novel* U.K.: Jenkins, 1932; U.S.: McBride, 1933
Detective: John Darrell, alias "Slade of the Yard."
Problem: Death by shooting in a locked study.

Ethan, John B.

699. ✓ THE BLACK GOLD MURDERS *novel* U.S.: Detective Book Club, 1959; Pocket, 1960
Detective: Victor Grant.
Problem: Theft of valuable strip maps from a locked map room with a hidden camera that failed to film anything incriminating.

700. MURDER ON WALL STREET *novel* U.S.: Mill, 1960
Detective: Victor Grant.
Problem: Death by shooting in a locked room.

Evans, Gwyn

701. THE CASE OF THE CLIMBING CORPSE *novel* U.K.: Wright, (1939)
Detectives: Chester Brett and Splash Page, reporter.
Problem: Death by stabbing in and disappearance from a locked upper-storey hotel room.

702. THE CASE OF THE CRIMSON CONJUROR *novel* SBL No. 171 (2nd series) U.K.: Amalgamated, 1928; reprinted as SBL No. 723 (2nd series) U.K.: Amalgamated, 1940
Detective: Sexton Blake.
Problem: Death by stabbing in a locked room.

703. THE CRYSTAL CELL *novel* SBL No. 313 (2nd series) U.K.: Amalgamated, 1931

Detective: Blake.

Problems: (1) Death by shooting in a room in which the only other occupant is innocent.

(2) Death by stabbing in a sealed glass cell.

704. ✓ THE HANGING JUDGE *novel* U.K.: Wright, 1936

Detective: Chester Brett.

Problem: Exactly the same as in Evans's "The Silent Jury," Item 707.

705. THE HOMICIDE CLUB *novel* U.K.: Shaylor, 1931; U.S.: Dial, 1932

Detectives: Bill Kellaway and Bannerhead Bruce.

Problem: Theft of valuable jewels from a guarded stage plunged suddenly in darkness.

706. THE IRON MASK *novel* U.K.: Wright, 1938

Detective: Double-O Day.

Problem: Death by stabbing in a sealed glass cell.

707. ✓ THE SILENT JURY *novel* SBL (2nd series) No. 221 U.K.: Amalgamated, 1930

Detective: Sexton Blake.

Problem: Multiple murder of an entire jury in a jury room guarded by police.

708. ✓ "Black Magic" *novelette* in The Union Jack, No. 1101, Nov. 15, 1924

Detective: Blake.

Problem: A witch is observed flying through the air at night on a broomstick.

709. ✓ "Eclipse!" *novelette* in The Union Jack No. 1237, July *2,* 1937

Detective: Blake.

Problem: A victim shot dead by a powerful rifle in the middle of a total eclipse, in a crowd, in dead silence, when it seemed impossible that he could have been singled out in the dark.

710. ✓ "The Man with the Scarlet Skull" *short story* in Detective Weekly, No. 103, Feb. 9, 1935; "The Man with the Scarlet Skull" U.K.: Wright, 1935

Detective: Quentin Ellery Drex ("QED").

Problem: A witch is observed flying on a broomstick and emitting unearthly laughter.

711. ✓ "The Pool of Secrets" *short story* in Detective Weekly, No.

105, Feb. 23, 1935; "The Man with the Scarlet Skull"
Detective: Drex.
Problems: (1) Victim falling into a haunted pool resurfaces moments later as skeleton, but when the pool is cleared nothing sinister is found.
(2) The figure of a woman in a bridal veil is seen in the water.

Evans, Howel

712. ✓ "The Murder in the Flat" *short story* (Chapter 4 to 6) in "The Murder Club" U.K.: Jarrolds, 1924; U.S.: Putnam, 1925
Detectives: The Murder Club.
Problem: The strangling of a woman by a pair of hands of unusually large size and certainly much bigger than those of the main suspect.

713. ✓ "Number One Brings a Gift" *short story* (Chapter 6 to 7) in "The Murder Club"
Detectives: The Murder Club.
Problem: Death by stabbing with a sharpened knitting needle of a man on his own in the back of a moving taxi.

Everton, Francis

714. INSOLUBLE *novel* U.K.: Collins, 1934
Detective: Peter Lindsay.
Problem: Death by poisoning in a locked bedroom.

F

Fairleigh, Runa (L. A. Morse)

715. ✓ AN OLD-FASHIONED MYSTERY *novel* U.S.: Avon, 1983; Canada: Dennys, 1983
Detectives: Sebastian and Violet Cornichon.
Problem: Death by blunt instrument in a locked room.

Fearn, John Russell

716. ✓ MERRIDREW MARCHES On *novel* U.K.: World's Work, 1951
Detective: Mayor Jenkinson Talbot Merridrew, a 300-pound English butler in the midwest.
Problem: Death by poison gas in undisturbed desert sand.

717. ✓ "Chamber of Centuries" *short story* in Thrilling Mystery, September 1940
Detective: Jane Melrose.
Problem: Appearance, once a year at a particular time, of the

ghost of a man in a locked room.

718. "Robbery Without Violence" *novelette* in Toronto Star Weekly, Dec. 14, 1957
Detective: Sawley Gerson, scientist.
Problem: Disappearance of gold bullion from a locked bank vault.

719. "Within That Room" *novelette* in Toronto Star Weekly, Jan. 19, 1946
Detective: Dick Wilmott.
Problem: (1) Mental assault in a room containing no one but the victim.
(2) Appearance, once a year at a particular time, of the ghost of a man in a locked room.

Feeny, Alfred

720. ✓ "The Mystery of the Round House" *short story* in "By a Vanished Hand" U.K.: Ward, 1906
Detective: None.
Problem: Disappearance of several travellers from a locked room.

Ferguson, John

721. THE GROUSE MOOR MYSTERY *novel* U.K.: Collins, 1934; U.S. (as "The Grouse Moor Murder"): Dodd, 1934
Detective: Francis MacNab.
Problem: Death by shooting in a locked library.

Fieldhouse, W. L.

722. ✓ "Murder Under the Christmas Tree" *short story* in MSMM, December 1980
Detective: Maj. Clifford Lansing.
Problem: Death by blunt instrument in an upper-storey room from which no one was seen to emerge.

Fielding, A.

723. THE CLUNY PROBLEM *novel* U.K.: Collins, 1928; U.S.: Knopf, 1929
Detective: Chief Inspector Pointer.
Problem: Murder of two men in a locked room.

724. ✓ THE FOOTSTEPS THAT STOPPED *novel* U.K.: Collins, 1926; U.S.: Knopf, 1926
Detective: Chief Inspector Pointer.
Problem: Death by shooting at point-blank range of a woman

who had apparently, and inexplicably, put up no struggle at all.

Findler, Gerald

725. "The House of Screams" *short story* in Doidge's Western Counties Annual, 1932; "The Art of the Impossible" U.K.: Xanadu, 1990; "Murder Impossible" U.S.: Carroll, 1990; "Resorting to Murder", U.K.: British Library, 2015; U.S.: Poisoned Pen Press, 2015
Detective: The narrator.
Problem: Screams heard in a house where the former owner killed his wife and later himself.

Fitzgerald, Nigel

726. ✓ THE STUDENT BODY *novel* U.K.: Collins, 1958
Detective: Superintendent Duffy.
Problem: Death by stabbing inside a locked room, outside which as an extra precaution talcum powder had been sprinkled and still lay undisturbed.

727. ✓ SUFFER A WITCH *novel* U.K.: Collins, 1958
Detective: Superintendent Duffy.
Problem: Disappearance of a girl from a post office and adjoining yard under constant observation.

Fitzsimmons, Cortland

728. 70,000 WITNESSES *novel* U.S.: McBride, 1931
Detective: Ketheridge.
Problem: Deaths of two football players during a game, without bodily contact or injury marks to account for the deaths.

Flanagan, Thomas

729. "The Fine Italian Hand" *short story* in EQMM, May 1949; "The Queens' Awards 4th Series" U.S.: Little, 1949, and U.K.: Gollancz, 1951; "The Locked Room Reader" U.S.: Random, 1968; "8 Doors to Death" U.S.: Dell, 1970
Detective: Niccolo Machiavelli.
Problem: Theft of jewels from a guarded room.

Fleming, Joan

730. ✓ POLLY PUT THE KETTLE ON *novel* U.K.: Hutchinson, 1952
Detective: Inspector Hope.
Problem: Death by gassing in a locked room.

Fletcher, Henry

731. THE NORTH SHORE MYSTERY *novel* U.K.: Swan Sonnenschein, 1899

Detective: Constable Hobbs.
Problem: Death by stabbing in a locked room.

Flinn, Denny Martin

732. ✓ SAN FRANCISCO KILLS *novel* U.S.: Bantam, 1991
Detective: Spencer Holmes, a certain famous consultant's grandson.
Problem: Death by shooting at an outdoor wedding where it would have been impossible for anyone attending or viewing from the house or grounds not to have been seen doing the shooting.

Flora, Fletcher

733. ✓ "A Word for Murder" *short story* in MSMM, October 1964; "Homicide Department" U.K.: N.E.L., 1968
Detective: Lt. Joseph Marcus.
Problem: Death by a hard, smooth object of a man in the act of cutting his lawn, and no sign of the object in question.

Flynn, Brian

734. THE CASE OF THE BLACK TWENTY-TWO *novel* U.K.: J. Hamilton, (1928); U.S.: Macrae, 1929
Detective: Anthony Bathurst.
Problem: Death by blunt instrument in a locked library.
735. INVISIBLE DEATH *novel* U.K.: J. Hamilton, 1929
Detective: Bathurst.
Problem: Death by poisoning by an invisible agency.
736. MURDER EN ROUTE *novel* U.K.: Long, 1930; U.S.: Macrae, 1932
Detective: Bathurst.
Problem: Death by strangulation on the top deck of an open-topped double-decker bus, unoccupied apart from the victim.
737. THE SPIKED LION *novel* U.K.: Long, 1933; U.S.: Macrae, 1934; in Mystery League, December 1933
Detective: Bathurst.
Problem: Death by poison in a locked bedroom.

Footner, Hulbert

738. UNNEUTRAL MURDER *novel* U.K.: Collins, 1944; Harper, 1944
Detective: Lee Mappin.
Problem: Disappearance of a man from within a locked hotel room.
739. "The Ashcomb Poor Case" *short story* in "Madame Storey"

U.K.: Collins, 1926; U.S.: Doran, 1926; "Big Book of Locked-Room Mysteries", Black Lizard, 2014
Detective: Madame Rosika Storey.
Problem: Death by shooting in a house containing the victim and three other innocent people and forbidden to outsiders by a burglar alarm guarding all exits.

740. "The Scrap of Lace" *short story* in "Madame Storey"
Detective: Storey.
Problem: Death by poisoning in a locked room.

Forbes, Colin

741. ✓ THE GREEK KEY *novel* U.K.: Collins, 1989
Detective: Tweed, Deputy Director of British Secret Intelligence Service.
Problem: Death by decapitation in a guarded building from which no one was observed to leave.

Ford, Leslie (see also Frome, David)

742. ✓ "Death Stops at a Tourist Camp" *novelette* in The American Magazine, April 1936; The Saint Mystery Magazine (U.S.), October 1955; The Saint Detective Magazine (Australia), February 1956; The Saint Detective Magazine (UK), April 1956; The Saint Mystery Library No. 7, 1959; "Baker's Dozen" U.S.: Bonanza, 1987; (as "The Bridge Camp Mystery") Story-Teller Magazine, September 1936
Detective: Dr. Porteus Alexander Harp, Professor of Geology.
Problem: Appearance of a corpse in a cabin vacated only seconds before by our heroine.

Forrest, Norman (Nigel Morland, q.v.)

743. ✓ DEATH TOOK A PUBLISHER *novel* U.K.: Harrap, 1936; U.S.: Hillman, 1938
Detective: Inspector Grief and John Finnegan, head of the Department of Forensic Medicine, Chemistry and Toxicology.
Problem: Two deaths by poisoning inside locked and guarded rooms.

Forrest, Richard

744. A CHILD'S GARDEN OF DEATH *novel* U.S.: Bobbs, 1975; U.K.: Hale, 1979
Detectives: Lyon Wentworth and Rocco Herbert.
Problem: Death by shooting in a locked office.

745. ✓ THE DEATH AT YEW CORNER *novel* U.S.: Holt, 1980; U.K.:

Hale, 1981
Detectives: Lyon and Bea Wentworth.
Problem: Death by suffocation in a locked room.

746. ✓ DEATH ON THE MISSISSIPPI *novel* U.S.: St. Martin's, 1989
Detectives: Lyon and Bea Wentworth.
Problem: Disappearance of a large houseboat from a stretch of river guarded at each end by a manned bridge.

747. DEATH THROUGH THE LOOKING GLASS *novel* U.S.: Bobbs, 1978; U.K.: Hale, 1979
Detective: Lyon Wentworth.
Problem: Disappearance of a plane seen to go into the sea.

Forsyte, Charles

748. ✓ DIPLOMATIC DEATH *novel* U.K.: Cassell, 1961; U.S.: Morrow, 1961
Detective: Inspector Richard Left.
Problem: The closing of a safe door in a sealed room that had been seen to be open when the room was sealed.

749. DIVING DEATH *novel* U.K.: Cassell, 1962; U.S. (as "Dive into Danger"): Morrow, 1962
Detective: Inspector Richard Left.
Problem: Shooting of a diver with a spear gun when all suspects were under observation.

750. MURDER WITH MINARETS *novel* U.K.: Cassell, 1968
Detective: Christopher Milner-Brown, archaeologist.
Problem: Death by induced heart attack in a locked bathroom.

Foster, John

751. ✓ WATCH All NIGHT *novel* U.K.: Puffin, 1980
Detective: Tess Eveling, aged about 16.
Problem: Disappearance of a hotel room and the man in it. *Comment:* Written for the teenage market.

Foster, R. Francis

752. SOMETHING WRONG AT CHILLERY *novel* U.K.: Nash, 1931; U.S. (as "The Mystery at Chillery"): Fiction League, 1931; U.K. (as "The Chillery Court Mystery"): Mellifont, 1936
Detective: Anthony Ravenhill.
Problem: Death by strangulation in a locked room.

Foster, Richard (Ken Crossen, q.v.)

753. ✓ THE INVISIBLE MAN MURDERS *novel* U.S.: Five Star, 1945; Canada: Crown, 1946

Detective: Chin Kwang Kham, Tibetan private eye.

Problems: (1) Appearance as witnesses watched of the invisible man's blood-red footprints on a white carpet just after a fatal shooting on a film set.

(2) Appearance, again as witnesses watched, of the invisible man's footprints on a beach just after a further fatal shooting.

754. ✓ THE LAUGHING BUDDHA MURDERS *novel* U.S.: Vulcan, 1944

Detective: Chin Kwang Kham.

Problem: Disappearance of a gold Buddha from a locked room that had also contained three bronze Buddhas.

Frances, Stephen

755. THE ILLUSIONIST *novel* U.K.: Mayflower, 1970

Detective: The Magnificent Saki, magician.

Problem: Disappearance of the magician from a sealed stone coffin submerged in water.

Franklin, Eugene (Franklin Bandy)

756. MURDER TRAPP *novel* U.S.: Stein, 1971

Detectives: Berkeley Barnes and Larry Howe.

Problem: Non-impossible. Included here because the synopsis in the paperback edition indicated, erroneously, that a locked-room murder was involved.

Fraser, T. A.

757. "The Pink Carnation" *short story* in "The Eye of Jinas" U.K.: Fraser, 1923

Detective: Hudson of Harley Street.

Problem: Death by poisoning in a locked room.

Freeman, R. Austin

758. THE JACOB STREET MYSTERY *novel* U.K.: Hodder, 1942; U.S. (as "The Unconscious Witness"): Dodd, 1942

Detective: Dr. Thorndyke.

Problem: Death by poison in a locked room.

759. "The Aluminium Dagger" *short story* in "John Thorndyke's Cases" U.K.: Chatto, 1909; "Dr. Thorndyke's Cases" U.S.: Dodd, 1931; "Crimes and Clues" U.S.: Prentice, 1978; "Big Book of Locked-Room Mysteries", Black Lizard, 2014

Detective: Thorndyke.

Problem: Death by a dagger wound in a room with the door

locked on the inside and the windows, although open, inaccessible and forty feet above the ground.

Freesland, Wilson S.

760. "Treachery Tarmac" *short story* in Battle Aces, April 1932
Detective: Clem Eads.
Problem: Disappearance of three bombers about to land on a World War One landing strip when our hero was knocked out.

Friend, Ed

761. THE CORPSE IN THE CASTLE *novel* U.S.: Lancer, 1970
Detectives: Jonathon and Vanessa Arcane.
Problem: Entrance and murder there of an intruder in the apparently impregnable fortress of an eccentric millionaire.

Frome, David (see also Ford, Leslie)

762. ✓ "Policeman's Cape" *short story* in "Fifty Famous Detectives of Fiction" U.K.: Odhams, c. 1937; "World's Great Detective Stories" U.S.: World, 1943
Detective: Evan Pinkerton.
Problem: Death by stabbing in a street in which no one else had passed at the time of death.

Frost, Kelman

763. DEATH REGISTERS AT THE EAGLE ARMS *novel* U.K.: Oberon, c. 1948
Detective: Inspector Hynd.
Problem: Death by blunt instrument in a locked bathroom.

764. "The Late Edition" *short story* in Clues #2, March 1928; "The Best Detective Stories of the Year 1928" U.K.: Faber, 1929
Detective: Dr. Francis Farrar.
Problem: Death by gassing in a locked room.

Fuller, John

765. ✓ "A Mushroom Mystery" *short story* in "The Adventures of Speedfall" U.K.: Salamander, 1985
Detective: Speedfall.
Problem: Death by blunt instrument in a locked room. *Comment:* From one of my favourite modern short-story volumes and containing two of my favourite weird and science-fiction stories, "Wriggly Porridge" and "The Smallest Ghost in the World."

Fuller, Timothy

766. THIS IS MURDER, MR. JONES *novel* U.S.: Little, 1943; U.K.: Heinemann, 1944

Detective: Jupiter Jones.
Problem: Death by throat cutting in a locked bathroom.

Furnivall, Gordon

767. THE TRACKER TRACKED *novel* U.K.: Jenkins, 1928
Detective: Dr. Sebastian Long.
Problem: Death by wrist slashing in a locked bathroom.

Futrelle, Jacques

768. "The Case of the Mysterious Weapon" *short story* in EQMM, October 1950; (as "An Absence of Air") in "The Art of the Impossible" U.K.: Xanadu, 1990, and "Murder Impossible" U.S.: Carroll, 1990; originally as "Vacuum" in The Storyteller, December 1922
Detective: Prof. S.F.X. van Dusen, "The Thinking Machine"
Problem: Deaths of three people by unknown means, the symptoms being complete absence of air from the body and a puncture mark in one cheek.

769. "The Crystal Gazer" *short story* in "The Thinking Machine on the Case" U.S.: Appleton, 1908; U.K. (as "The Professor on the Case") Nelson, 1909; "Best Thinking Machine Detective Stories" U.S.: Dover, 1973
Detective: The Thinking Machine.
Problem: Vision of death by stabbing seen in a crystal ball.

770. "The Flaming Phantom" *short story* in "The Thinking Machine" U.K.: Chapman, 1907, and U.S.: Dodd, 1907; "Best Thinking Machine Detective Stories"
Detective: The Thinking Machine.
Problem: Appearance, apparent indestructibility, and disappearance of a flaming figure in a derelict house.

771. "The House That Was" *short story* in EQMM (U.S.), June 1952; "Death Locked In" U.S.: IPL, 1987
Detective: The Thinking Machine.
Problem: Appearance of a road not shown on the map, subsequent disappearance of that road and a house and its inmates nearby.

772. "Kidnapped Baby Blake, Millionaire" *short story* in "Best Thinking Machine Detective Stories"
Detective: The Thinking Machine.
Problem: Disappearance of a young child whose footprints lead out into otherwise unmarked snow, then suddenly stop.

773. "The Lost Radium" *short story* in "The Thinking Machine on the Case" ("The Professor on the Case"); "Best Thinking Machine Detective Stories"
Detective: The Thinking Machine.
Problem: Theft of a small container of radium from a guarded laboratory.

774. "The Missing Necklace" *short story* in "The Thinking Machine on the Case" ("The Professor on the Case"); "Best Thinking Machine Detective Stories"
Detective: The Thinking Machine.
Problem: Disappearance of a valuable necklace from a boat that was carefully searched when it docked.

775. "The Phantom Motor Car" *short story* in Associated Sunday Magazine, November 11 1906 (as "Problem of the Phantom Auto"); "The Thinking Machine on the Case" ("The Professor on the Case"); "Best Thinking Machine Detective Stories"; "Big Book of Locked-Room Mysteries", Black Lizard, 2014
Detective: The Thinking Machine.
Problem: Disappearance of a motor car at night from a guarded stretch of road with only one exit and that too small to accommodate a car.

776. "The Problem of Cell 13" *short story* in "The Thinking Machine"; "Best Thinking Machine Detective Stories"; "Tantalizing Locked Room Mysteries" U.S.: Walker, 1982; "Big Book of Locked-Room Mysteries", Black Lizard, 2014
Detective: The Thinking Machine.
Problem: Escape from a locked, guarded cell.

777. "The Problem of the Stolen Reubens" *short story* in Associated Sunday Magazine, February 17 1907; EQMM, Spring 1942; "Best Thinking Machine Detective Stories"
Detective: The Thinking Machine.
Problem: Theft of a valuable canvas from a guarded gallery.

778. ✓ "The Roswell Tiara" *short story* in The Storyteller, c. 1906-7; "Great Cases of the Thinking Machine" U.S.: Dover, 1976
Detective: The Thinking Machine.
Problem: Theft of a diamond from a tiara in a locked safe in a locked suite of which two women were the only occupants.

779. "The Scarlet Thread" *short story* in "The Thinking Machine"; "Best Thinking Machine Detective Stories"

Detective: The Thinking Machine.
Problem: Death by gassing in a locked bedroom.

780. "The Vanishing Man" *short story* in EQMM, November 1949; "Ellery Queen's Lost Men" U.S.: Davis, 1983
Detective: The Thinking Machine.
Problem: Disappearance of a man from a locked or guarded upper-storey room.

Futrelle, May

781. "The Grinning God" *short story* in EQMM, June 1952; "Death Locked In" U.S.: IPL, 1987
Comment: The story by Jacques Futrelle's wife that posed the problem in Item 771, "The House That Was."

G

Gainsley, Sidney

782. LOVE AND DR. HAWKINS *novel* U.K.: Brown, 1945
Detective: Dr. Hawkins.
Problem: Death by stabbing in a locked room.

Gallon, Tom

783. ✓ "The Mystery of the Locked Room" *short story* in The Pictorial Magazine, June 3, 1905
Detective: Enoch Voyce.
Problem: The theft of a diamond necklace from within a locked hotel bedroom.

Gardiner, Dorothy

784. THE TRANSATLANTIC GHOST *novel* U.K.: Harrap, 1933; U.S.: Doubleday, 1933
Detective: Mr. Watson.
Problem: Death by gunshot in a locked, "haunted" room.

Gardner, Curtiss W.

785. ✓ "Death's Bright Angel" *short story* in Street & Smith's Detective Story, January 1948; "Detective Story Annual 1949", Street & Smith, 1949; Street & Smith's Detective Story (UK), February 1949
Detective: Leonard Mace.
Problem: Death by shooting in a prison tower by an angel of death seen to soar through the air "like a swallow in flight."

786. ✓ "In Bed We Die" *short story* in Dime Mystery, July 1944

Detective: Valentine Vickers, specialist in the impossible.
Problem: Death by electrocution in a bed on a night when a storm had taken out the house's main electrical power supply provided by a hydroelectric plant.

787. ✓ "Satan's Insidious Chessmen" *short story* in Dime Mystery, January 1944; Strange Detective Mysteries (Canada), February 1944
Detective: Vickers.
Problem: Death by poisoned dart in a room in which the victim was alone and playing chess with an automaton.

788. ✓ "Sorcery in the Death House" *short story* in Dime Mystery, September 1943; Strange Detective Mysteries (Canada), October 1943
Detective: Vickers.
Problem: Disappearance, during a temporary blackout, of a condemned man from a locked, guarded death house.

Gardner, Erle Stanley

789. THE CASE OF THE QUEENLY CONTESTANT *novel* U.S.: Morrow, 1967; U.K.: Heinemann, 1973
Detective: Perry Mason.
Comment: Listed here simply because an advertisement for the book stated that it was a locked-room murder. It was not.

790. "Bird in the Hand" *short story* in EQMM, December 1953; "The Hardboiled Dicks" U.S.: Sherbourne, 1965; U.K.: Boardman, 1967; Detective Fiction Weekly, April 9 1932; "Big Book of Locked-Room Mysteries", Black Lizard, 2014
Detective (and villain): Lester Leith.
Problems: Disappearance from a hotel under observation of (1) a large chest, (2) some valuable diamonds.

791. "The Case of the Runaway Blonde" *short story* in "Two Clues" U.S.: Morrow, 1937; U.K.: Cassell, 1951
Detective: Sheriff Bill Eldon.
Problem: Death by stabbing in a ploughed field where there are no footprints made by the murderer.

792. "The Exact Opposite" *short story* in EQMM, October 1951; originally in a Popular Publications magazine in 1939; "Tantalizing Locked Room Mysteries" U.S.: Walker, 1982
Detective: Lester Leith.
Problem: Death by throat cutting in a locked, guarded room.

Garrett, Randall

793. TOO MANY MAGICIANS *novel* U.S.: Doubleday, 1967; Macdonald, 1968
Detective: Lord Darcy.
Problem: Death by stabbing in a locked room.

794. "The Ipswich Phial" *short story* in Analog, December 1976; "Lord Darcy Investigates" U.S.: Ace, 1981
Detective: Darcy.
Problem: Death by shooting on unmarked sand.

795. "A Matter of Gravity" *short story* in Analog, October 1974; "Lord Darcy Investigates"; "Alfred Hitchcock's Anthology #14", Davis, 1983
Detective: Darcy.
Problem: Death by defenestration from a high room in a locked tower.

796. "The Muddle of the Woad" *short story* in Analog, June 1965; "Murder and Magic" U.S.: Ace, 1979
Detective: Darcy.
Problem: Appearance of a dead, woad-covered body within a locked workshop.

797. "The Sixteen Keys" *short story* in Fantastic, May 1976; "Lord Darcy Investigates"
Detective: Darcy.
Problem: (non-impossible) Death and disappearance of valuable documents in a locked house.

798. "A Stretch of the Imagination" *short story* in "Men and Malice" U.K.: Doubleday, 1973; "Murder and Magic" U.S.: Ace, 1979
Detective: Darcy.
Problem: Death by hanging in a room under constant observation.

Gayle, Newton

799. MURDER IN THE HAUNTED SENTRY-BOX *novel* U.K.: Gollancz, 1935; U.S. (as "The Sentry-Box Murder"): Scribners, 1935
Detective: James Greer.
Problem: Death by shooting in a sentry-box under constant observation.

Gellibrand, Edward

800. ✓ THE END OF A CIGARETTE *novel* U.K.: Long, 1924
Detective: Horace Draper and Kenneth O'Brien.

Problem: Death by shooting in a locked library.

801. The Windblow Mystery *novel* U.K.: J. Hamilton, (1926)
Detective: Kenneth O'Brien.
Problem: Death by hanging in a haunted room. The other house occupants were locked in their rooms.

Gerard, Francis

802. The Mind of John Meredith *novel* U.K.: Macdonald, 1946
Detective: Sir John Meredith.
Problem: Nonimpossible. Included here because of its werewolf theme and the eventual rational explanation to it.

803. Sorcerer's Shaft *novel* U.K.: Macdonald, 1947
Detective: Meredith.
Problem: Death by defenestration from a tower balcony approached through a door that was locked on the inside.

Gibbons, H.H.C.

804. "The Third Key, or, The Clue of the Horoscope" *novel* in SBL No. 329, April 1924
Detective: Sexton Blake.
Problem: Murder inside a locked house.

805. "The House of the Horoscope" *novelette* in The Union Jack, Jan. 24, 1925
Detective: Blake.
Problem: Disappearance of a man from a room in a locked house.

Gibson, Walter B.

806. ✓ "The Green Ghoul" *short story* in Games, October 1983
Detective: Bud Harroway.
Problem: Death by shooting in and theft of valuables from a locked, guarded vault.

807. "One Night in Paris" *short story* in The Saint Mystery Magazine, November 1955; The Saint Detective Magazine (Australia), January 1956; The Saint Detective Magazine (UK), March 1956; "Whodunit? Houdini?" U.S.: Harper, 1976
Detective: The Great Gerard.
Problem: Death by stabbing in a locked curio room.

Gielgud, Val, and Eric Maschwitz

808. ✓ The First Television Murder *novel* U.K.: Hutchinson, 1940
Detective: Simon Spears.

Problem: Death by shooting with a gun bearing fingerprints of an actress who was doing a live television broadcast several miles away at the time of the shooting.

Gilbert, Anthony

809. DEATH KNOCKS THREE TIMES *novel* U.K.: Collins, 1949; U.S.: Random, 1950
Detective: Arthur Crook, lawyer.
Problem: Death by blunt instrument in a locked bathroom.

Gilbert, Kenneth

810. ✓ "Murder Is Aboard!" *short story* in Pocket Detective, February 1937
Detective: Jimmy Brennon.
Problem: Death by shooting in a locked cabin.

Gilbert, Michael

811. CLOSE QUARTERS *novel* U.K.: Hodder, 1947; U.S.: Walker, 1963
Detectives: Inspector Hazelrigg and Sergeant Pollock.
Problem: Murder in a guarded area where those present are generally alibied.

812. DEATH IN CAPTIVITY *novel* U.K.: Hodder, 1952; U.S. (as "The Danger Within"): Harper, 1952
Detective: Cuckoo Goyles.
Problem: Death by suffocation of the only man in an escape tunnel that could only be entered with the help of at least three men.

813. "The Coulman Handicap" *short story* in Argosy (UK), April 1958; EQMM, May 1975; "Ellery Queen's Anthology Fall-Winter 1980" U.S.: Davis, 1980; "Young Petrella" U.K.: Hodder 1988
Detective: Sergeant Petrella.
Problem: Disappearance of a woman from a public house under constant observation.

Gillespie, Robert

814. ✓ THE CROSSWORD MYSTERY *novel* U.K.: Constable, 1979; U.S.: Raven, 1980
Detective: Rocky Caputo, crossword-puzzle compiler.
Problem: Death by starvation in a locked apartment.

Gillmore, Rufus

815. THE EBONY BED MURDER *novel* U.S.: Mystery League, 1932

Detective: Griffin Scott, psychologist.
Problem: Death by shooting in a locked room.

Glasby, John S. (see also Merak, A. J.)

816. ✓ "Cyanide for Christmas" *short story* in "Mystery for Christmas" U.K.: O'Mara, 1990
Detective: Inspector Challon.
Problem: Death by poisoning in a locked vault.

Godfrey, Ellen

817. ✓ MURDER BEHIND LOCKED DOORS *novel* U.S.: St. Martin's, 1988
Detective: Jane Tregar.
Problem: Death by poisoning in a locked computer room.

Godfrey, Peter

818. "A Dagger of the Mind" *short story* in "Rolf Le Roux", Publicitas, 1950; EQMM (U.S.), March 1951; EQMM (Australia) July 1953; "The Newtonian Egg and Other Stories", Crippen & Landru, 2002
Detective: Rolf Le Roux.
Problem: Disappearance of the murder weapon from a locked room in which a man's throat has just been cut and in which the murderer has been apprehended almost at once.

819. ✓ "The Flung-Back Lid" *short story* in "John Creasey's Crime Collection 1979" U.K.: Gollancz, 1979; "Best Detective Stories of the Year-1980" U.S.: Dutton, 1980; The Mammoth Book of Perfect Crimes and Impossible Mysteries" U.K.: Constable and Robinson, 2006, U.S.: Carroll and Graf, 2007; "The Newtonian Egg and Other Stories", Crippen & Landru, 2002; "Big Book of Locked-Room Mysteries", Black Lizard, 2014
Detective: Rolf le Roux.
Problem: Death by stabbing in a cable car in which the victim was the only occupant.

820. "Kill and Tell" *short story* in "Rolf Le Roux"; EQMM (U.S.), January 1950; EQMM (Australia), May, 1954; "The Newtonian Egg and Other Stories"
Detective: Rolf le Roux.
Problem: Death by poisoning in a locked room.

821. "The Newtonian Egg" *short story* in EQMM (U.S.), December 1951; "All But Impossible!" U.S.: Ticknor, 1981; "The Newtonian Egg and Other Stories"

Detective: Rolf le Roux.

Problem: Death by poisoning after eating a hard-boiled egg (the "locked room" in the case).

822. ✓ "Out of This World" *short story* in "Death Under the Table" U.K.: S. A. Scientific Pub., 1954; "Death Locked In" U.S.: IPL, 1987

Comment: An earlier version of Item 819, "The Flung-Back Lid."

Gollomb, Joseph

823. ✓ THE GIRL IN THE FOG *novel* U.S.: Boni, 1923; U.K.: Long, 1924

Detective: Inspector Barton Hawley.

Problem: Death by throat cutting with, on the throat, fingerprints of a man found to have been executed days before.

Goodchild, George (see also Templeton, Jesse)

824. ✓ CAULDRON, BUBBLE *novel* U.K.: Macdonald, 1946

Detective: Inspector Laurence Ogilvie.

Problem: Death by unknown means, supposedly by black magic.

825. ✓ COMPANION TO SIRIUS *novel* U.K.: Rich, 1949

Detective: Chief Inspector McLean.

Problem: How can a painter paint an intricately detailed picture of a room in a house that he has never visited.

826. ✓ Chapter V of "McLean Keeps Going" *short story* U.K.: Hodder, 1941

Detective: McLean.

Problem: Man with heart condition is sadly affected by a picture of Saint Sebastian that appears to him to bleed real blood but appears normal to everyone else.

827. ✓ Chapter X of "McLean Investigates" *short story* U.K.: Hodder, 1930

Detective: McLean.

Problem: Death by gassing in a locked kitchen.

828. Chapter XII of "Well Caught, McLean!" *short story* U.K.: Rich, 1953

Detective: McLean.

Problem: Death by shooting in a locked upper-storey bedroom.

829. Chapter XVII of "McLean Remembers!" *short story* U.K.: Hodder, 1936

Detective: McLean.

Problem: Death by gassing in a study with door bolted on the inside.

830. Chapter XII of "McLean of Scotland Yard" *short story* U.K.: Hodder, (1929)

Detective: McLean.

Problem: Death by shooting in a closed lift.

Goodhue, Stoddard

831. ✓ "The Locked Room" *short story* in Everybody's Magazine (U.S.), June 1922

Detective: Dr. Goodrich, physician.

Problem: Death by shooting in a locked suite.

Gore-Brown, Robert

832. ✓ DEATH ON DELIVERY *novel* U.K.: Collins, 1929; U.S. (as "By Way of Confession"): Doubleday, 1930

Detective: Lucien Clay.

Problem: Death by poison in a garden room under constant observation.

Goyne, Richard

833. THE CRIME PHILOSOPHER *novel* U.K.: Paul, (1945)

Detectives: The Padre and Pamela.

Problem: Death by stabbing in a locked room.

Graeme, Roderic

834. ✓ SALUTE TO BLACKSHIRT *novel* U.K.: Hutchinson, 1954

Detective: Richard Verrell, "Blackshirt."

Problem: Theft of a collection of art treasures from an apparently burglarproof exhibition room—which Blackshirt himself had failed to penetrate.

Grange, A. Demain

835. ✓ "The Round Room Horror" *short story* in Everybody's Story Magazine, No. 17, March 1911

Detective: Montague Steel.

Problem: Death by stabbing in a locked and bolted room.

Grant, Maxwell

836. HIDDEN DEATH *novel* in The Shadow Mystery Magazine, September 1932; U.S.: Bantam, 1970

Detective: The Shadow (Lamont Cranston).

Problem: Death by shooting in a locked room.

837. ✓ THE HOUSE THAT VANISHED *novel* in The Shadow Mystery

Magazine, October 15, 1935
Detective: The Shadow.
Problem: Disappearance of a house visited on the previous day by two men.

838. "Room 1313" *novelette* in The Shadow Mystery Magazine (U.K.), October 1954
Detective: The Shadow.
Problem: Disappearance of a floor (the 13th) and a room (number 1313) from a multistorey-apartment block.

Gray, Berkeley (see also Brooks, E. S., and Gunn, Victor)

839. CALAMITY CONQUEST *novel* U.K.: Collins, 1965
Detective: Norman Conquest.
Problem: A burglary in which every door and window of the house was fitted with alarms and yet no alarm rang.

Gray, Curme

840. MURDER IN MILLENNIUM VI *novel* U.S.: Shasta, 1951
Detective: Victor Mitchel.
Problem: Death by invisible agency.

Gray, Harold

841. "Murder in the Library" *short story* in Mirage, November 1933
Detective: Hawkshaw and Watson.
Problem: Murder within a locked room.

Gray, Rod

842. ✓ LAY ME ODDS *novel* U.S.: Tower, 1967; U.K.: K&G, 1968
Detective: Eve Drum, agent of LUST (League of Underground Spies and Terrorists).
Problem: Death by shooting with an antique duelling pistol inside a locked library.

Grayle, Hubert

843. "Three White Hairs" *short story* in The Ludgate Magazine, April 1893
Detective: Mr. Fordham.
Problem: Thefts of valuable jewellery from a locked room.

Greeley, Andrew M.

844. ✓ HAPPY ARE THE MEEK *novel* U.S.: Warner, 1985
Detective: Father Blackie Ryan.
Problem: Death by stabbing in a locked museum.

845. ✓ HAPPY ARE THOSE WHO SEARCH FOR JUSTICE *novel* U.S.: Mysterious, 1987

Detective: Ryan.

Problem: Death by shooting in a locked cabin aboard a harbour-moored yacht from which no one was seen to exit.

Green, Alan

846. THEY DIED LAUGHING *novel* U.S.: Simon, 1952; U.K.: Panther, 1957

Detectives: Arthur Hutch and John Hugo.

Problem: Death by shooting in a locked room.

847. WHAT A BODY! *novel* U.S.: Simon, 1949; U.K.: Redman, 1950

Detectives: Hutch and Hugo.

Problem: Death by gunshot in a room, locked and sealed but for a small opening, at the top of a window. The wound was in a position impossible to hit through the gap in the window, and there was an unmarked pyjama top over the wound.

Green, Anna Katherine

848. BEHIND CLOSED DOORS *novel* U.S.: Putnam, 1888; U.K.: Routledge, 1888

Detective: Ebenezer Gryce.

Problem: Nonimpossible story of suicide, murder, and impersonation; included here because of the misleading nature of the title.

849. ✓ THE FILIGREE BALL *novel* U.S.: Bobbs, 1903; U.K.: Unwin, 1904

Detective: Unnamed police officer.

Problem: Death by blunt instrument in a library in which, each time, only the victim was present.

850. INITIALS ONLY *novel* U.S.: Dodd, 1911; U.K.: Nash, 1912

Detectives: Ebenezer Gryce and Sweetwater.

Problem: Death by stabbing in a locked room—with one window open—and in a guarded area.

851. ✓ MISS HURD: AN ENIGMA *novel* U.S.: Putnam, 1894

Detective: None as such.

Problem: Disappearance of a woman from a house surrounded by unbroken flat countryside that gave her no time to reach the horizon in the time available.

Greene, Graham

852. ✓ "Murder for the Wrong Reason" *short story* in The Graphic 1929; "The Last Word" U.K.: Reinhardt, 1990

Detective: Inspector Mason.

Problem: Death by stabbing in a locked room.

Greenwald, Ken

853. ✓ "The Case of the Uneasy Chair" *short story* in "The Lost Adventures of Sherlock Holmes" U.S.: Mallard, 1989
Detective: Sherlock Holmes.
Problem: Death by stabbing in a room under constant surveillance.

Gregory, Hylton

854. ✓ THE SIGN OF THE BLACK FEATHER *novel* SBL No. 667 (2nd series) U.K.: Amalgamated, 1939
Detective: Sexton Blake.
Problem: Death by shooting in a locked room.

Grey, Robin

855. ✓ PUZZLE IN PORCELAIN *novel* U.S: Duell, 1945; (as by Elizabeth Gresham) Curtis, 1973
Detective: Hunter Lewis, handyman.
Problem: Death from an apparent rattlesnake bite but with the puncture marks higher on the body than any snake could reach.

Grey, Vivian

856. "The Bhudda Case" *short story* in "Stories of Scotland Yard" U.K.: Everett, 1906
Detective: Inspector Wall.
Problem: Death by shooting in a locked room.

Gridban, Volsted (John Russell Fearn, q.v.)

857. THE LONELY ASTRONOMER *novel* U.K.: Scion, 1954
Detective: Adam Quirke, scientist.
Problem: Death by brain damage and strangulation in an upper floor of a guarded observatory.

858. THE MASTER MUST DIE *novel* U.K.: Scion, 1953
Detective: Adam Quirke.
Problem: Death by poisoning in a locked strong-room.

Griffin, Vincent

859. ✓ "Martin Speed Unveils the Invisible Death" *short story* in "Schoolboy's Album, 1957" U.K.: Swan, 1957
Detective: Martin Speed.
Problem: Death by poison in a locked room.

Groc, Leon

860. THE BUS THAT VANISHED *novel* U.S.: Macaulay, 1928
Detective: Henri Henry.

Problem: Disappearance of a bus in a restricted area.

Groner, Augusta

861. THE MAN WITH THE BLACK CORD *novel* U.K.: Chatto, 1911; U.S.: Duffield, 1911
Detective: Joe Muller.
Problem: Disappearance of a man from a locked, bolted room.

Guise, Stanley

862. THE FALCON MYSTERY *novel* U.K.: Long, 1930
Detective: Frank Despard.
Problem: Death by stabbing in a locked pavilion. Key attached to the body of the victim.

Gumley, F. W.

863. THE MYSTERY OF THE LOCKED ROOM *juvenile novel* U.K.: Dawson, 1946
Detectives: Hamilton, Hutchinson, and Rice of the Fourth Form.
Problem: Lights seen in a locked room.

Gunn, Victor (see also Brooks, E. S.; Gray, Berkeley, and Ross, Carlton)

864. DEATH ON SHIVERING SANDS *novel* U.K.: Collins, 1946
Detective: Bill "Ironsides" Cromwell, chief inspector.
Problem: Disappearance of a man whose footprints lead to a hole in the middle of a frozen but very shallow pond.

865. DEVIL IN THE MAZE *novel* U.K.: Collins, 1961
Detective: Cromwell.
Problem: Disappearance of a man from within a maze, the only entrance of which was under observation.

866. THE PAINTED DOG *novel* U.K.: Collins, 1955
Detective: Cromwell.
Problem: Death by shooting in a locked room.

867. "Death in December" *short story* in "Ironsides Sees Red" U.K.: Collins, 1943
Detective: Cromwell.
Problem: Disappearance of a man from a snow-covered area without leaving tracks.

868. "On the Road to Gallow's Cross" *novelette* in "Three Dates with Death" U.K.: Collins, 1947
Detective: Cromwell.
Problem: Death by poisoning by invisible agency aboard a bus.

Gurdon, J. E.

869. "The Monkey Trick" *short story* in "The Monkey Trick" U.K.: Newnes, (1936); "Big Book of Locked-Room Mysteries", Black Lizard, 2014
Detective: Police Sergeant Dunsterman.
Problem: The landing and taking off of an apparently unmanned aircraft.

H

Hale, Christopher

870. WITCH WOOD *novel* U.S.: Doubleday, 1940; U.K.: Boardman, 1946
Detective: Lt. Bill French.
Problem: Death by shooting in a locked cabin.

Halliday, Brett (Davis Dresser, q.v.)

871. ✓ "The Scent of Death" *short story* in MSMM, April 1979
Detective: Mike Shayne.
Problem: Death by shooting in a warehouse locked at all exits except one, which the dead body was blocking.

Hamilton, Henrietta

872. THE TWO HUNDRED GHOST *novel* U.K.: Hodder, 1956
Detectives: Sally Merton and Johnny Heldar.
Problem: Appearance and disappearance of the "two hundred" ghost in an area of an old building from which disappearance seemed impossible.

Hammett, Dashiell

873. ✓ "Tom, Dick or Harry" *short story* in "The Creeping Siamese" U.S.: Jonathan, 1950; originally as "Mike or Alice or Rufus" from Black Mask, January 1925; "Big Book of Locked-Room Mysteries", Black Lizard, 2014
Detective: The Continental Op.
Problem: Disappearance of a young male thief from a section of an apartment block that was under constant surveillance and that had no fire escape.

Hanshew, Mary E. and Thomas W.

874. THE AMBER JUNK *novel* U.K.: Hutchinson, (1924); U.S. (as "The Riddle of the Amber Ship"): Doubleday, 1924
Detective: Hamilton Cleek.

Problem: Various disappearances, and a death preceded by a scream, in a locked house.

875. THE FROZEN FLAME *novel* U.K.: Simpkin, 1920; U.S. (as "The Riddle of the Frozen Flame"): Doubleday, 1920
Detective: Cleek.
Problem: Disappearance of a man whose footprints stop abruptly in marshy ground.

876. THE HOUSE OF DISCORD *novel* U.K.: Hutchinson, (1922); U.S. (as "The Riddle of the Spinning Wheel"): Doubleday, 1922
Detective: Cleek.
Problem: Death by gunshot in a suddenly darkened room, with no sign of the weapon.

877. ✓ "An Interrupted Holiday" *short story* in "The Riddle of the Mysterious Light" U.S.: Doubleday, 1921; originally as "The Riddle of the Fire Opal" in Short Stories Magazine, August 1915
Detective: Cleek.
Problem: Death by unknown hand in a locked, steel-lined room.

878. ✓ "The Mystery of the 'Rope of Fear' " *short story* in Short Stories Magazine, December 1919; "The Riddle of the Mysterious Light"
Detective: Cleek.
Problem: Death of a watchman and disappearance of money from a guarded vault.

879. ✓ "The Mystery of the Rose of Fire" *short story* in "The Riddle of the Mysterious Light"
Detective: Cleek.
Problem: Death by poisoning in a locked room.

880. ✓ "The Priceless Statue That Vanished" *short story* in "The Riddle of the Mysterious Light"
Detective: Cleek.
Problem: Disappearance of a large, life-size statue from a locked museum.

881. ✓ "The Riddle of the Marble Hand" *short story* in Short Stories Magazine, February 1920
Detective: Cleek.
Problem: Strangulation in a locked room, apparently by the hand of a marble statue that left no fingerprints.

882. ✓ "The Riddle of the Painted Shrine" *short story* in Short

Stories Magazine, November 1919
Detective: Cleek.
Problem: Disappearance of a formula from a room surrounded by six feet of cement, and the only door guarded.

883. ✓ "The Riddle of the Silver Death" *short story* in Short Stories Magazine, March 1920; EQMM August 1951
Detective: Cleek.
Problem: Death by poison in a locked and guarded room.

Hanshew, Thomas W.

884. Chapters XXVI to XXX *short story* in "Cleek of Scotland Yard" U.K.: Cassell, 1914; U.S.: Doubleday, 1914
Detective: Hamilton Cleek.
Problem: Death by poisoning in a locked fortification—the Stone Drum—with no openings except arrow slits.

885. ✓ "The Mystery of the Amsterdam Diamonds" *short story* in Short Stories Magazine, June 1914
Detective: Cleek.
Problem: The smuggling of diamonds from a ship when the smuggler is rigorously searched on disembarkation.

886. ✓ "The Mystery of the Fadeless Tints" *short story* in Short Stories Magazine, July 1914
Detective: Cleek.
Problem: Disappearance on a moonlit night and apparently in midair of a man seen by witnesses to perform a somersault.

887. ✓ "The Mystery of the Glass Tubes" *short story* in Short Stories Magazine, October 1914
Detective: Cleek.
Problem: (1) The secreting of smuggled saccharin despite rigorous search of ships and people.
(2) A match struck by an invisible agency.

888. ✓ "The Mystery of the Sealed Art Gallery" *short story* in Short Stories Magazine, November 1914
Detective: Cleek.
Problem: Disappearance of a man and jewels from a locked gallery.
Comment: Noted critic and Cleek fancier Douglas G. Greene regards this as "an extraordinary story."

889. "The Mystery of the Steel Room" *short story* in "The Man of the Forty Faces" U.K.: Cassell, 1910; U.S. (as "Cleek, The

Master Detective"): Doubleday, 1918; "The World's Best One Hundred Detective Stories" U.S.: Funk, 1929
Detective: Cleek.
Problem: Death by poisoning in a locked room.

890. "The Riddle of the 5.28" *short story* in "The Man of the Forty Faces" and "Cleek, The Master Detective"; "Challenge to the Reader" U.S.: Stokes, 1938
Detective: Cleek.
Problem: Death by shooting in a locked railway carriage surrounded by unmarked snow.

891. ✓ "The Riddle of the Globes of Darkness" *short story* in Short Stories Magazine, February 1916
Detective: Cleek.
Problem: Substitution, while apparently in full view, of fake pearls for real ones.

892. ✓ "The Riddle of the Golden Rain" *short story* in Short Stories Magazine, April 1915
Detective: Cleek.
Problem: Death by unknown means within a locked and guarded room.

893. ✓ "The Riddle of the Laughing Girl" *short story* in Short Stories Magazine, June 1915
Detective: Cleek.
Problem: Laughter from an undiscernible source preceding death by unknown means.

894. ✓ "The Riddle of the Lost Stradivarius" *short story* in Short Stories Magazine, August 1914
Detective: Cleek.
Problem: Theft of a violin and case from a locked and sealed safe in a locked and sealed room.

895. ✓ "The Riddle of the Octagonal Room" *short story* in Short Stories Magazine, September 1914
Detective: Cleek.
Problem: Disappearance from a locked and guarded room.

896. ✓ "The Riddle of the Scarlet Monk" *short story* in Short Stories Magazine, March 1916
Detective: Cleek.
Problem: Death by asphyxiation in a locked room.

897. ✓ "The Riddle of the Seacliffe Farm" *short story* in Short

Stories Magazine, May 1916
Detective: Cleek.
Problems: (1) Poisoning in a locked room.
(2) Disappearance from a locked room.

898. ✓ "The Riddle of the Siva Stones" *short story* in "The Man of the Forty Faces" and "Cleek, The Master Detective"
Detective: Cleek.
Problem: Death by stabbing in a locked room.

899. ✓ "The Riddle of the Stones of Flame" *short story* in Short Stories Magazine, April 1916
Detective: Cleek.
Problem: Various stabbings and poisonings in a locked room.

900. ✓ "The Valehampton Riddle" *short story* in Cassell's Magazine of Fiction, c. 1912; "The Riddle of the Mysterious Light" (as Chapters 1-16)
Detective: Cleek.
Problem: Disembodied ringing of bells in a church tower after the ropes had been removed.

Harding, Eric

901. ✓ PRAY FOR THE DAWN *novel* U.K.: Low, 1946
Detective: Toby Judd.
Problem: A black dwarf dead for ten years is seen to breathe and perspire prior to disappearing from his coffin and apparently going on a murderous rampage.

Harding, Ronald S. L.

902. THE LIBRARY OF DEATH *novel* U.K.: Modern, (1938), U.S. Ramble House, 2011
Detective: Inspector Richardson.
Problem: Death by shooting in a locked room.

Hardinge, Rex (see also "Capstan")

903. ✓ THE GARGOYLE OF PENGELLY *novel* SBL No. 160 (3rd series) U.K.: Amalgamated, 1952
Detective: Sexton Blake.
Problem: Disappearance of an entire corridor inside a lonely house in Cornwall.

904. ✓ MURDER TO MUSIC *novel* in Detective Weekly, Oct. 2, 1937
Detectives: Tim McGee and ex-Chief Inspector Flynn.
Problem: Death by shooting in a cabin locked and under surveillance when those outside heard the shot and the victim crashing

onto the keys as he is killed.

905. ✓ THE PRISONER OF THE MANOR *novel* SBL No. 273 (3rd series) U.K.: Amalgamated, 1952
Detective: Sexton Blake.
Problem: Disappearance of a room from within a lovely old house.

906. THE PROBLEM IN CIPHERS *novel* U.K.: Wright, 1952; also published as a "Streamline" paperback
Detective: Murphy and McTavish.
Problem: Death by shooting in a locked cipher room.

907. ✓ THE RIDDLE OF THE INVISIBLE MENACE *novel* SBL No. 315 (3rd series) U.K.: Amalgamated, 1954
Detective: Sexton Blake.
Problems: Deaths by poison by invisible agency.

908. THE RIDDLE OF THE SEALED ROOM *novel* SBL No. 176 (3rd series) U.K.: Amalgamated, 1948
Detective: Blake.
Problem: Death by shooting in a locked room.

909. ✓ "The Affair of the Colonel's Vengeance" *short story* in Detective Weekly, Nov. 6, 1937; also as "Back to Front" in "The Polite Pirate" (as by "Capstan") U.K.: Wright, 1938
Detective: Don Alverado y Miraflores Smith.
Problem: Shooting of two men by another witnessed to have fired with his right hand, even though his right hand was too badly injured to fire a pistol and he claims not to have shot the two men.

910. ✓ "The Cinema Murder Mystery" *short story* in Detective Weekly, Dec. 4, 1937; also as "In the Dark" in "The Polite Pirate"
Detective: Smith.
Problem: Death by steel dart shot by air rifle in a darkened cinema but with no air rifle found on the premises.

911. ✓ "The Strange Affair of the Dagger of Fate" *short story* in Detective Weekly, Nov. 20, 1937; also as "How Fate Intervened" in "The Polite Pirate"
Detective: Smith.
Problem: Death by knife wound in the back of the neck in a Swiss alley under constant observation.

Harrington, Neil

912. "Too Much Evidence" *short story* in MSMM, February 1969
Detective: Alexander Fallon.
Problem: Disappearance of a murder weapon from an adjoining room to which the killer had gone immediately after shooting his victim and which was under constant observation. A gun was found on him, but the fatal bullet did not match it.

Harris-Burland, J. B.

913. THE CURSE OF CLOUD *novel* U.K.: Chapman, 1914
Detective: Inspector Strode.
Problem: Disappearance of a man from within a locked room.

914. THE SHADOW OF MALREWARD *novel* U.K.: Chapman, 1911; U.S.: Knopf, 1919
Detective: Richard Loryat.
Problem: Death by shooting in a locked room.

Harrison, Barbara

915. ✓ A COLD NIGHT'S DEATH *novel* U.S.: Award, 1973
Detectives: Dr. Robert Jones and Dr. Frank Enari, research scientists.
Problem: Death in a remote experimental station 15,000 feet above the world where only the dead scientist and his experimental monkeys had been living.

Harrison, Michael

916. "The Facts in the Case of the Missing Diplomat" *short story* in EQMM, April 1968; "The Exploits of the Chevalier Dupin" U.S.: Mycroft, 1968; "The Murder in the Rue Royale" U.K.: Tom Stacey, 1972
Detective: C. Auguste Dupin.
Problem: Disappearance of a man from a courtyard under observation.

Harrison, Van

917. "Alibi" *short story* in "Best Crime Stories" U.K.: Faber, 1934
Detective: Detective Inspector Bryson.
Problem: Death by shooting in a locked room.

Hart, Carolyn G.

918. ✓ DEATH ON DEMAND *novel* U.S.: Bantam, 1987
Detectives: Annie Laurence, bookseller, & Max Darling, swain.
Problem: Death from a dart thrown with deadly accuracy in a

pitch-black room.

Harvey, Marion

919. ✓ THE ARDEN MYSTERY *novel* U.K.: Brentanos, 1925
Detective: Graydon McKelvie.
Problem: Death by stabbing in a locked room.

920. ✓ THE HOUSE OF SECLUSION *novel* U.S.: Small, 1925; U.K.: Wright, 1935
Detective: McKelvie.
Problem: Death by stabbing in the vault of a locked and guarded house.

921. ✓ THE MYSTERY OF THE HIDDEN ROOM *novel* U.S.: Clode, 1922; U.K.: Brentanos, 1923
Detective: McKelvie.
Problem: Death by shooting in an apparently inaccessible room.

Haughey, Thomas Brace

922. ✓ THE CASE OF THE INVISIBLE THIEF *novel* U.S.: Bethany, 1978
Detective: Geoffrey Weston.
Problem: Theft of secret papers from a locked laboratory.

Hawk, John

923. THE LOCKED DOOR *novel* U.K.: Skeffington, (1929); U.S. (as "It Was Locked"): Farrar, 1930
Detective: Inspector Linscott.
Problem: Death by stabbing in a locked room.

Hawthorne, Julian (q.v. Anonymous, entry 58)

924. ✓ "Greaves' Disappearance" *short story* in "Six Cent Sam's" U.S.: Price, 1893; "Mr. Dunton's Invention" U.S.: Merriman, 1896; "Big Book of Locked-Room Mysteries, Black Lizard, 2014
Detective: Sam.
Problem: Disappearance of a man from a busy street.

Hawton, Hector

925. ✓ DEATH OF A WITCH *novel* U.K.: Ward, 1952
Detectives: Peter and Susan Maxwell.
Problem: Death by poisoned dart in a locked bathroom.

Hayter, Cecil

926. "The Clue of the Burnt Candle" *short story* in The Penny Pictorial Magazine, Feb. 23, 1918
Detective: Derwent Duff.

Problem: Death by shooting in a locked room.

927. ✓ "The Maddox House Murder" *short story* in The Red Magazine

Detective: Mortimer Kane.

Problem: Death by blunt instrument in a bolted office suite.

928. "The Mystery of the Locked Door" *short story* in The Penny Pictorial Magazine, May 4, 1918

Detective: Derwent Duff.

Problem: Death by stabbing in a locked bedroom.

Heard, Gerald

929. THE NOTCHED HAIRPIN *novel* U.S.: Vanguard, 1949; U.K.: Cassell, 1951

Detective: Mr. Mycroft.

Problem: Death by stabbing in a walled garden under guard.

Heath, Eric

930. MURDER IN THE MUSEUM *novel* U.S.: Hillman, 1939

Detective: Cornelius ("Copey") Clift, Jr.

Problem: Death by poisoning in a locked museum.

931. MURDER OF A MYSTERY WRITER *novel* U.S.: Arcadia, 1955

Detective: Dr. Wade Anthony.

Problem: Murder by shooting in a darkened room where none of the suspects had access to a gun.

Hecht, Ben

932. "Mystery of the Fabulous Laundryman" *short story* in "Best Mysteries of the Year" U.K.: Faber, 1933; "Actor's Blood" U.S.: Covici, 1936; EQMM, June 1954; EQMM (U.K.), June 1954; EQMM (Australia), June 1954; "Ellery Queen's Best Bets" U.S.: Pyramid, 1972

Detective: Dick McCarey.

Problem: Death by shooting in a locked room.

Heidenfeld, W.

933. "The Unpleasantness at the Stooges Club" *short story* in EQMM, February 1953; EQMM (Australia) April 1953

Detectives: Dr. Watson, Captain Hastings, Mr. Riccardo, Nikki Porter, Squire Randolph, and other stooges.

Problem: Death by shooting in a locked house.

Henderson, Donald

934. "The Sealed Room" *playlet* in "The Trial of Lizzie Borden" U.K.: Hurst, (1946)

Detective: Inspector Thorne.
Problem: A series of murders of young blondes—all in locked rooms.

Herne, Huxley

935. THE TANGLED MIRACLE *novel* U.K.: Nelson, 1936
Detective: Mortimer Hood, scientist.
Problem: Disappearance of an unclothed priestess from a temple, shortly after she had announced that, like Enoch and Elijah, she would soon be received up into heaven.

Hershman, Morris

936. "When a Felon Needs a Friend" *short story* (as by Arnold English) in MSMM, February 1958; "The Locked Room Reader" U.S.: Random, 1968; "8 Keys to Murder" U.S.: Dell, 1970
Detective: None.
Problem: Disappearance from—and reappearance into—a locked prison cell.

Herring, Paul

937. ✓ THE MURDER OF MARGOT MIDNIGHT *novel* U.K.: Low, 1932; U.S. (as "The Midnight Murder"): Lippincott, 1932
Detectives: Inspector Bow and Captain Keetch of the Jewel Insurance Bureau.
Problem: Death by shooting in a locked morning room.

Hewitt, Lewen

938. ✓ "The Twisted Bullet" *short story* in Detective Story Magazine February 12 1921; The Novel Magazine, June 1921; Best Detective Magazine June 1932
Detective: Balbane, the magician.
Problem: Death by shooting in a darkened room during a séance in which all the participants held hands.

Heyer, Georgette

939. ENVIOUS CASCA *novel* U.K.: Hodder, 1941; U.S.: Doubleday, 1941
Detective: Inspector Hemingway.
Problem: Death by stabbing in a locked room.

Hibberd, Lionel

940. ✓ "The Mysterious Presence" *short story* in "The Mysterious Presence and Other Stories" U.K.: Stockwell, 1926
Detective: Hetherington.
Problem: Death by poisoning in a locked room.

Hill, Frederick T.

941. THE ACCOMPLICE *novel* U.S.: Harper, 1905
Detective: Deake Gilbert.
Problem: Death by stabbing in a locked study.

Hill, Headon (Francis Edward Grainger)

942. A ROGUE IN AMBUSH *novel* U.K.: Ward, 1911
Detective: Elisha Crowe.
Problem: Death by shooting in a study under observation at all exits.

943. "The Bayswater Boarding House" *short story* in "Radford Shone" U.K.: Ward, 1908
Detective: Radford Shone.
Problem: Death by stabbing in a locked bedroom.

944. "The Guest House at Lugard Grange" *short story* in The Million, Dec. 24, 1892
Detective: None.
Problem: Attempted murder by asphyxiation in a locked room.

Hill, Reginald

945. ✓ "There Are No Ghosts in the Soviet Union" *short story* in "There Are No Ghosts in the Soviet Union" U.K.: Collins, 1987; U.S.: Foul Play, 1988
Detective: Inspector Lev Chislenko.
Problem: A man is pushed into a lift and promptly disappears through the floor.

Hills, Hazel

946. "The Unlocked Room" *short story* in EQMM, September 1946; EQMM (Australia), December 1947; EQMM (UK) May 1958
Detective: Mr. Riddle, man of all work.
Problem: Death by throat cutting in a locked room.

Hobart, Donald Bayne

947. THE CELL MURDER MYSTERY *novel* U.S.: Fiction League, 1931
Detective: Chief Kenny.
Problem: Death by stabbing in a locked prison.

Hoch, Edward D.

948. ✓ "The Avenger from Outer Space" *short story* in EQMM, October 1979
Detective: Simon Ark.
Problem: Death by lightning bolt of various Russian and American astronauts.

949. ✓ "The Bad Samaritan" *short story* in AHMM, Dec. 9, 1981; "John Creasey's Crime Collection 1989" U.K.: Gollancz, 1989
Detective: G. K. Chesterton.
Problem: Disappearance of a circus that a witness heard passing as he and the victim were attacked by a clown.
Comment: The background to this is quite fascinating. In a spoof article in an American fanzine, author Bill Pronzini announced that he had found a lost John Dickson Carr novel in which, inter alia, a whole circus had been made to disappear. The book, of course, never existed, but Ed Hoch took up the challenge, wrote this story, and made the narrator one Jack Foxx, Pronzini's most famous pseudonym.

950. ✓ "Behind Closed Doors" *short story* in Woman's World (U.S.), May 1982
Detective: Sergeant Romano.
Problem: Disappearance of a girl's apartment and flatmate while she was away on a short trip.

951. "Captain Leopold and the Ghost-Killer" *short story* in EQMM, August 1974; "Leopold's Way" U.S.: Southern Illinois University, 1985
Detective: Captain Leopold.
Problem: Death by shooting by an identified man who was later reported by another witness (a policeman) to have been killed in a road accident that had occurred before the shooting.

952. "Captain Leopold and the Impossible Murder" *short story* in EQMM, December 1976; (as "The Impossible Murder") in "The Art of the Impossible" U.K.: Xanadu, 1990; "Murder Impossible" U.S.: Carroll, 1990
Detective: Leopold.
Problem: Death by strangulation in a closed car in a traffic jam. When the door of the car was opened, only the victim was inside it.

953. ✓ "Captain Leopold and the Vanishing Men" *short story* in EQMM, July 1979; "Prime Suspects" U.S.: Ivy, 1987
Detective: Leopold.
Problem: Disappearance of two men in eye-catching suits from respectively a café and a police station when their clothing would have clearly identified them.

954. "Day of the Wizard" *short story* in The Saint Mystery Magazine

(U.K.), August 1963; "Locked Room Puzzles" U.S.: Academy, 1986
Detective: Simon Ark.
Problem: Appearance of a drugged girl inside a locked closet.

955. ✓ "The Flying Fiend" *short story* in EQMM, Mid-July, 1982
Detective: Sir Gideon Parrot.
Problem: Several deaths by throat cutting where the bodies are found on unmarked sand.

956. "The Hoofs of Satan" *short story* in Famous Detective Stories, February 1956; "Crimes Across the Sea" U.S.: Harper, 1964, and U.K.: Harrap, 1965; "City of Brass" U.S.: Leisure, 1971
Detective: Simon Ark.
Problem: The presence of tracks, apparently neither human nor animal.

957. "The Impossible 'Impossible Crime'" *short story* in EQMM, April 1968; "Ellery Queen's Murder Menu" U.K.: Gollancz, 1969, and U.S.: World, 1969; "Realm of the Impossible", Locked Room International, 2017
Detective: Henry Bowfort.
Problem: Death by shooting in a snowbound hut with only the victim and one innocent witness present.

958. "Interpol: The Case of the Modern Medusa" *short story* in EQMM, November 1973; "Tales of Espionage" U.S.: Castle, 1989
Detectives: Sebastian Blue and Laura Charme.
Problem: Death by stabbing with a trident in a room under constant observation.

959. "Interpol: The Case of the Musical Bullet" *short story* in EQMM, March 1974; "Tales of Espionage"
Detectives: Blue and Charme.
Problem: Death by shooting in a stationary aircraft about to take off and after stringent screening and security measures.

960. ✓ "The Invisible Intruder" *short story* in EQMM, Mid-December 1984; "Lady on the Case" U.S.: Bonanza, 1988
Detective: Libby Knowles.
Problem: Death by throat cutting in a locked room.

961. ✓ "Lady of the Impossible" *short story* in EQMM, May 20, 1981
Detective: Sir Gideon Parrot.

Problem: Disappearance of a woman from a locked bedroom in which she was heard to shout for help and glass was heard to break.

962. "The Leopold Locked Room" *short story* in EQMM, October 1971; "Ellery Queen's Mystery Bag" U.S.: World, 1972, and U.K.: Gollancz, 1973; "Tantalizing Locked Room Mysteries" U.S.: Walker, 1982; "Leopold's Way"
Detective: Captain Leopold.
Problem: Death by shooting in a locked room, with only Captain Leopold present as an innocent witness.

963. ✓ "The Locked Room Cipher" *short story* in "Who Done It? Houdini!" U.S.: Houghton, 1980
Detective: Ross Calendar, newspaper columnist.
Problem: Death by shooting in a locked room, the whole observed live on closed-circuit television.

964. "The Long Way Down" *short story* in AHMM, February 1965; "Best American Detective Stories of the Year 16th Series" U.S.: Dutton, 1966; "Best Detective Stories of the Year 21st Series" U.K.: Boardman, 1967; "The Locked Room Reader" U.S.: Random, 1968; "8 Doors to Death" U.S.: Dell, 1970; "Fifty Years of Crime and Suspense", Pegasus, 2006
Detective: McLove.
Problem: Disappearance—and later reappearance—of a man who had thrown himself from an upper-storey window.

965. "The Magic Bullet" *short story* in Argosy, January 1969; "Best Detective Stories of the Year 24th Annual Collection" U.S.: Dutton, 1970; "Death Locked In" U.S.: IPL, 1987
Detective: Harry Ponder.
Problem: Death by shooting in a locked, bulletproof car.

966. "The Man from Nowhere" *short story* in Famous Detective Stories, June 1956; Startling Mystery Stories, Summer 1967; "The Quests of Simon Ark" U.S.: Mysterious, 1984; "Big Book of Locked-Room Mysteries", Black Lizard, 2014
Detective: Simon Ark.
Problem: Death by stabbing in snow with only the victim's footprints.

967. ✓ "A Melee of Diamonds" *short story* in AHMM, April 1972; "Leopold's Way"
Detective: Captain Leopold.

Problems: (1) Disappearance of diamonds under constant observation from the moment they were stolen in a smash-and-grab raid.

(2) Disappearance of diamonds from a kitchen that no one left.

968. "Murder Offstage" *short story* in EQMM, January 1969; "Ellery Queen's Grand Slam" U.S.: World, 1970, and U.K.: Gollancz, 1971

Detective: Paul Drayer.

Problem: Disappearance of some photograph negatives from a room under constant observation.

969. "Picnic at Midnight" *short story* in MSMM, October 1969

Detective: Gaines.

Problem: Disappearance of diamonds from a guarded room.

970. ✓ "Prisoner of Zerfall" *short story* in Espionage, November 1985

Detective: Simon Ark.

Problem: Disappearance of an elderly prisoner from a high-walled prison yard in which he walked alone.

971. "The Problem of Cell 16" *short story* in EQMM, March 1977; "Diagnosis Impossible", Crippen & Landru, 1996

Detective: Dr. Sam Hawthorne.

Problem: Disappearance of a master criminal, the Eel, from a locked cell.

972. ✓ "The Problem of the Blue Bicycle" *short story* in EQMM, April 1991; "Nothing is Impossible", Crippen & Landru, 2014

Detective: Hawthorne.

Problem: Disappearance of a girl from a bike that she rode around a corner just ahead of a group of fellow cyclists and with no cover near where the bike had been abandoned.

973. ✓ "The Problem of the Body in the Haystack" *short story* in EQMM, August 1983; "More Things Impossible", Crippen & Landru, 2006

Detective: Hawthorne.

Problem: The concealment towards the top of a tarpaulin-covered haystack of a body when no one had been seen to remove the tarpaulin to put the body there after the victim had been seen working to tie down the last of the tarpaulin.

974. ✓ "The Problem of the Bootlegger's Car" *short story* in EQMM, July 1982; "More Things Impossible"

Detective: Hawthorne.
Problem: Disappearance of a man from a car into which he was seen to get.

975. ✓ "The Problem of the Boston Common" *short story* in EQMM, August 1979; "Murder in New England" U.S.: Castle, 1989; "More Things Impossible"
Detective: Hawthorne.
Problem: Death by poisoned dart on a common on which all people were subject to close police scrutiny.

976. "The Problem of the Christmas Steeple" *short story* in EQMM, January 1977; "The Twelve Crimes of Christmas" U.S.: Avon, 1981; "Diagnosis Impossible"
Detective: Hawthorne.
Problem: Death by stabbing in a locked steeple with one witness present but physically incapable of performing the deed.

977. "The Problem of the Country Inn" *short story* in EQMM, September 1977; "Diagnosis Impossible"
Detective: Hawthorne.
Problem: Disappearance of a man from a passage at the end of which was a door locked on the inside.

978. "The Problem of the County Fair" *short story* in EQMM, February 1978; "Uncollected Crimes" U.S.: Walker, 1987; "Diagnosis Impossible"
Detective: Hawthorne.
Problem: A dead body found inside a sealed time capsule that had shortly before been seen not to contain a dead body.

979. ✓ "The Problem of the Courthouse Gargoyle" *short story* in EQMM, June 3, 1980; "More Things Impossible"
Detective: Hawthorne.
Problem: Poisoning from a glass of water that it seemed impossible for anyone but the victim to have touched.

980. "The Problem of the Covered Bridge" *short story* in EQMM, December 1974; "All But Impossible!" U.S.: Ticknor, 1981; "Diagnosis Impossible"
Detective: Hawthorne.
Problem: Disappearance of a horse and buggy from a covered bridge to which their snow tracks lead but do not emerge.

981. ✓ "The Problem of the Crying Room" *short story* in EQMM, November 1984; "Nothing is Impossible"

Detective: Hawthorne.

Problem: Gunshot wound in a room in which only the victim and the detectives were present and by means of a gun that was apparently held by the sheriff for the whole of the relevant period.

982. ✓ "The Problem of the Curing Bam" *short story* in EQMM, August 1987; "Nothing is Impossible"

Detective: Hawthorne.

Problem: Disappearance of a weapon used in a fatal throat cutting when there had apparently been no opportunity for anyone in the bam to secrete or get rid of anything.

983. ✓ "The Problem of the Dying Patient" *short story* in EQMM, December 1989; "Nothing is Impossible"

Detective: Hawthorne.

Problem: Death by cyanide poisoning when the victim had just taken a harmless pill with a simple glass of water.

984. ✓ "The Problem of the Fatal Fireworks" *short story* in EQMM, May 1985; "Tales from Ellery Queen's Mystery Magazine" U.S.: Harcourt, 1986; "Nothing is Impossible"

Detective: Hawthorne.

Problem: The appearance of a stick of dynamite in a sealed package supposedly containing harmless firecrackers.

985. ✓ "The Problem of the General Store" *short story* in EQMM, November 1979; "More Things Impossible"

Detective: Hawthorne.

Problem: Death by shooting in a locked store.

986. ✓ "The Problem of the Gingerbread Houseboat" *short story* in EQMM, Jan. 28, 1981; "More Things Impossible"

Detective: Hawthorne.

Problem: Disappearance of four people from a floating houseboat under observation from the shore.

987. ✓ "The Problem of the Graveyard Picnic" *short story* in EQMM, June 1984; "Nothing is Impossible"

Detective: Hawthorne.

Problem: Fall of a woman from a bridge into a creek with nothing to account for the fall.

988. ✓ "The Problem of the Gypsy Camp" *short story* in EQMM, Jan.1, 1982; "More Things Impossible"

Detective: Hawthorne.

Problems: (1) Finding of a freshly buried bullet in the heart of a corpse with no entry in front or rear to account for its presence. (2) Disappearance of a gypsy encampment under surveillance.

989. "The Problem of the Haunted Bandstand" *short story* in EQMM, January 1976; "Diagnosis Impossible"
Detective: Hawthorne.
Problem: Disappearance, in a puff of smoke, of a hooded figure who had just stabbed the mayor on a crowded bandstand.

990. ✓ "The Problem of the Haunted Tepee" *short story* in EQMM, December 1990; "Nothing is Impossible"
Detective: Hawthorne.
Problem: Mysterious deaths in a tepee into which no outsider went after it was closed.

991. "The Problem of the Hunting Lodge" *short story* in EQMM, May 1983; "Beastly Tales" U.S.: Wynwood, 1989; "More Things Impossible"
Detective: Hawthorne.
Problem: Death by blunt instrument in a lodge surrounded by snow, with no footprints to account for the killer.

992. ✓ "The Problem of the Invisible Acrobat" *short story* in EQMM, Mid-December 1986; "Nothing is Impossible"
Detective: Hawthorne.
Problem: Disappearance of an acrobat while performing in a troupe on the high wire.

993. "The Problem of the Little Red Schoolhouse" *short story* in EQMM, September 1976; "Dark Lessons" U.S.: Macmillan, 1985; "Diagnosis Impossible"
Detective: Hawthorne.
Problem: Disappearance of a red-haired boy from a swing in a schoolyard under constant surveillance.

994. "The Problem of the Lobster Shack" *short story* in EQMM, September 1975; "Diagnosis Impossible"
Detective: Hawthorne.
Problem: Death of an escapologist by throat cutting in a locked lobster shack.

995. "The Problem of the Locked Caboose" *short story* in EQMM, May 1976; "Midnight Specials" U.S.: Bobbs, 1977; "Diagnosis Impossible"
Detective: Hawthorne.

Problem: Death by stabbing in, and theft from, a locked caboose.

996. ✓ "The Problem of the Octagon Room" *short story* in EQMM, Oct. 7,1981; "The Year's Best Mystery and Suspense Stories-1982" U.S.: Walker, 1982; "More Things Impossible"
Detective: Hawthorne.
Problem: Death by stabbing in a locked octagon room.

997. "The Problem of the Old Gristmill" *short story* in EQMM, March 1975; "Diagnosis Impossible"
Detective: Hawthorne.
Problem: Disappearance of books and records from a locked trunk.

998. "The Problem of the Old Oak Tree" *short story* in EQMM, July 1978; "Diagnosis Impossible"; "Big Book of Locked-Room Mysteries", Black Lizard, 2014
Detective: Hawthorne.
Problem: Death by strangulation of a stuntman who was alive when he parachuted out of his plane but upon landing was found to have been strangled.

999. ✓ "The Problem of the Pilgrims Windmill" *short story* in EQMM, Sept. 10, 1980; "More Things Impossible"
Detective: Hawthorne.
Problem: Death or injury by conflagration in a windmill occupied only by the injured or dead victims.

1000. ✓ "The Problem of the Pink Post Office" *short story* in EQMM, June 17, 1987; "More Things Impossible"
Detective: Hawthorne.
Problem: Disappearance of an envelope from a post office in which all the occupants were carefully searched.

1001. ✓ "The Problem of the Protected Farmhouse" *short story* in EQMM, May 1990; "Nothing is Impossible"
Detective: Hawthorne.
Problem: Death by blunt instrument inside a locked farmhouse guarded by an electrified fence and a dog.

1002. "The Problem of the Revival Tent" *short story* in EQMM, November 1978; "More Things Impossible"
Detective: Hawthorne.
Problem: Death by sword-thrust in a tent unoccupied but for the victim (and Dr. Sam Hawthorne!).

1003. ✓ "The Problem of Santa's Lighthouse" *short story* in EQMM,

December 1983; "More Things Impossible"
Detective: Hawthorne.
Problem: Death by stabbing on top of a lighthouse in which the victim appeared to be alone.

1004. ✓ "The Problem of the Sealed Bottle" *short story* in EQMM, September 1986; "Nothing is Impossible"
Detective: Hawthorne.
Problem: Death by poisoning from the contents of a sealed bottle, freshly opened.

1005. ✓ "The Problem of the Snowbound Cabin" *short story* in EQMM, December 1987; "Murder and Mystery in Maine" U.S.: December, 1989; "Nothing is Impossible"
Detective: Hawthorne.
Problem: Death by stabbing in a snowbound cabin with no tracks leading in or out.

1006. ✓ "The Problem of the Thunder Room" *short story* in EQMM, April 1988; "Nothing is Impossible"
Detective: Hawthorne.
Problem: A witness identifies as the perpetrator of a fatal blunt-instrument attack a young, blond-haired woman with whom Dr. Hawthorne himself had been just before the crime was committed and at a distance that would have taken at least fifteen minutes to cover.

1007. ✓ "The Problem of the Tin Goose" *short story* in EQMM, December 1982; "More Things Impossible"
Detective: Hawthorne.
Problem: Death by stabbing of an aircraft pilot in the locked cabin of an aircraft that had just landed.

1008. ✓ "The Problem of the Unfinished Painting" *short story* in EQMM, February 1986; "Nothing is Impossible"
Detective: Hawthorne.
Problem: Death by strangulation in a studio under constant observation.

1009. "The Problem of the Voting Booth" *short story* in EQMM, December 1977; "Diagnosis Impossible"
Detective: Hawthorne.
Problem: Death by stabbing in a voting booth under constant observation.

1010. ✓ "The Problem of the Whispering House" *short story* in

EQMM, April 1979; "Ellery Queen's Blighted Dwellings" U.S.: Davis, 1986; "More Things Impossible"
Detective: Hawthorne.
Problem: Death by stabbing in a room under constant observation and into which the victim had been seen to recently enter, though when discovered minutes later was found to have been dead for fifteen to twenty hours.

1011. ✓ "The Return of the Speckled Band" *short story* in "The New Adventures of Sherlock Holmes" U.S.: Carroll, 1987; U.K.: Arlington, 1988
Detective: Sherlock Holmes.
Problem: Disappearance of a deadly snake that was believed to have just inflicted on the victim a fatal bite.

1012. "The Sorceress of the Sea" *short story* in EQMM, Aug. 18, 1980
Detective: Simon Ark.
Problem: Appearance of a sorceress from the depths of the ocean.

1013. "The Spy and the Snowman" *short story* in EQMM, Nov. 3, 1980; "Tales of Espionage" U.S.: Castle, 1989
Detective: Rand.
Problem: Death of a man seen just previously to disappear into a fake snowman in a patch of snow unmarked but for his own footprints.

1014. "The Spy Who Walked Through Walls" *short story* in EQMM, November 1966
Detective: Rand.
Problem: Theft of top-secret blueprint carbons from an office under constant surveillance.

1015. "The Stalker of Souls" *short story* in "Stalkers" U.S.: Dark Harvest, 1989; Roc/Penguin, 1990
Detective: Simon Ark.
Problem: Footsteps are clearly heard by an eventual murder victim when there is no human agency to account for them.

1016. "The Stolen Sapphire" *short story* in "The Monkey's Clue/The Stolen Sapphire" U.S.: Grosset, 1978
Detective: Tommy Preston.
Problem: Disappearance of a sapphire from a science fair.

1017. "The Sweating Statue" *short story* in "Detectives A to Z" U.S.:

Bonanza, 1985; "Murder Most Sacred" U.S.: December, 1989
Detective: Monsignor Thomas Xavier.
Problem: A wooden church statue that sweated.

1018. "The Terrier Recognition" *jigsaw puzzle* U.S.: IPL, 1986
Detective: Reynolds.
Problem: Disappearance of a roll of blueprints, three feet long, from an embassy suite undergoing refurbishment and where all workers and likely hiding places had been checked.

1019. "The Theft from the Empty Room" *short story* in EQMM, September 1972; "Ellery Queen's Crookbook" U.S.: Random, 1974; "The Thefts of Nick Velvet" U.S.: Mysterious, 1978
Detective: Nick Velvet.
Problem: The thief under contract to steal something of value from a room that is apparently empty.

1020. "The Theft of the Bermuda Penny" *short story* in EQMM, June 1975; "The Thefts of Nick Velvet"; "Big Book of Locked-Room Mysteries", Black Lizard, 2014
Detective: Velvet.
Problem: Disappearance of a man from a closed car travelling at speed and leaving his rear seat belt still fastened.

1021. ✓ "The Theft of the White Queen's Menu" *short story* in EQMM, March 1983; "The Velvet Touch", Crippen & Landru, 2000
Detective: Velvet.
Problems: (1) Disappearance of a roomful of furniture in a matter of minutes.
(2) Disappearance of a roulette wheel from a busy casino.
(3) Disappearance of a printed menu card practically out of someone's hands.

1022. "The Theft of the Venetian Window" *short story* in EQMM, November 1975; "Ellery Queen's Searches and Seizures" U.S.: Dial, 1977; "The Velvet Touch"
Detective: Velvet.
Problem: Death by throat slitting in a locked room.

1023. "The Tomb at the Top of the Tree" *short story* in MSMM, June 1969
Detective: George Gordon.
Problem: A man climbed to the top of a tree and disappeared.

1024. ✓ "The Vanished Steamboat" *short story* in EQMM, May 1984;

"The Year's Best Mystery and Suspense Stories-1985" U.S.: Walker, 1985; "The Ripper of Storyville", Crippen & Landru, 1997

Detective: Ben Snow, gunfighter.

Problem: Disappearance of a large steamboat from a particular stretch of river.

1025. "The Vanishing of Velma" *short story* in AHMM, August 1969; "Leopold's Way"

Detective: Captain Leopold.

Problem: Disappearance of a girl from a Ferris wheel under observation.

1026. ✓ "The Weapon out of the Past" *short story* in EQMM, April 7, 1980

Detective: Simon Ark.

Problem: Death by knife wound in a room unoccupied but for the victim by a knife that had disappeared in flight 200 years before.

1027. "The Witch Is Dead" *short story* in Famous Detective Stories, April 1956; "The Judges of Hades" U.S.: Leisure, 1971

Detective: Ark.

Problem: Death by self-conflagration in a locked trailer.

1028. ✓ "The Witch of Park Avenue" *short story* in EQMM, August 1982; "The Quests of Simon Ark"

Detective: Ark.

Problem: Death by poison of a man stuck by himself in a revolving door.

Hocking, Joseph

1029. THE CASE OF MISS DUNSTABLE *novel* U.K.: Hodder, (1923); Wright, (1936)

Detective: Jaspar Poole.

Problem: Disappearance of a girl from within a locked house.

Hodges, Carl G.

1030. "Sixteen Pounds of Murder" *short story* in Thrilling Detective Magazine (U.K.), March 1947

Detective: Dwight Berke.

Problem: All suspects to a murder were locked in their rooms, yet one escaped and killed.

Hodgson, William Hope

1031. ✓ "Bullion!" *short story* in Everybody's Weekly, March

11,1911; "The Art of the Impossible" U.K.: Xanadu, 1990; "Murder Impossible" U.S.: Carroll, 1990
Detective: Mr. James, second mate aboard a Melbourne-London clipper.
Problem: Disappearance and reappearance of a bullion box and subsequent substitution of lead for gold in a number of such boxes while in a sealed and guarded bullion room.

1032. ✓ "The Haunting of the Lady Shannon" *short story* in "Out of the Storm" U.S.: Grant, 1975
Detective: None.
Problem: Death by stabbing on the bridge of a ship on which the victim stood apparently alone.

1033. "The Horse of the Invisible" *short story* in The Idler, April 1910; "Carnacki the Ghost-finder" U.K.: Nash, 1913, and U.S.: Mycroft, 1947; "The Rivals of Sherlock Holmes" U.S.: Pantheon, 1971, and U.K.: Bodley, 1971; Sherlock Holmes: The Detective Magazine #24, 1998
Detective: Carnacki.
Problem: The sounds of a horse within a guarded house.

1034. ✓ "The Inn of the Black Crow" *short story* in The Red Magazine, Oct. 1, 1915; "Tales of Land and Sea" U.K.: Murqi,1984
Detective: John Dory, secret exciseman.
Problem: Death by unknown means in a locked bedroom of the inn.

1035. "The Thing Invisible" *short story* in The New Magazine (UK), January 1912; "Carnacki the Ghostfinder," both editions; MSMM, January 1973; "Big Book of Locked-Room Mysteries", Black Lizard, 2014
Detective: Carnacki.
Problem: Injury by stabbing in a chapel under constant observation.

Hoffman, E.TA.

1036. ✓ "Mademoiselle De Scuderi" *novelette* in "Weird Tales" U.S.: Scribners, 1928 *Protagonist:* Mademoiselle De Scuderi.
Problem: Death by stabbing in locked apartments when the accused, also present in the apartments, claimed that the victim had been wounded elsewhere and carried home by himself although the unmistakable noise of the lock had not been heard by the people occupying the ground-floor apartments.

Holding, James

1037. "The Philippine Key Mystery" *short story* in EQMM, February 1968; "When Last Seen" U.S.: Harper, 1977; "The Zanzibar Shirt Mystery and Other Stories", Crippen & Landru, 2018
Detectives: Marvin Leroy and King Danforth.
Problem: Escape of a prisoner from a locked cell to which the guard had the only key.

Holman, Hugh

1038. SLAY THE MURDERER *novel* U.S.: Mill, 1946; U.K.: Foulsham, 1950
Detective: Sheriff Macready.
Problem: Death by poison/stabbing in a locked room.

1039. UP THIS CROOKED WAY *novel* U.S.: Mill, 1946; U.K.: Foulsham, 1951
Detective: Macready.
Problem: Death by stabbing in a room under constant observation.

Holmes, H. H. (see also Boucher, Anthony)

1040. NINE TIMES NINE *novel* U.S.: Duell, 1940
Detectives: Sister Ursula and Lt. Terence Marshall.
Problem: Death by shooting in a locked room.

1041. ROCKET TO THE MORGUE *novel* U.S.: Duell, 1942
Detectives: Sister Ursula and Marshall.
Problem: Death by stabbing in the back in a locked room.

Holt, Samuel

1042. ✓ WHAT I TELL YOU THREE TIMES IS FALSE *novel* U.S.: Tor, 1987
Detective: Samuel Holt.
Problem: Death by smothering in a locked suite of rooms.

Hopkins, Nevil Monroe

1043. "The Investigation at Holman Square" *short story* in "The Strange Cases of Mason Brant" U.S.: Lippincott, 1916; U.K. (on its own as a separate book): Modern Publishing Co., c. 1936
Detective: Mason Brant.
Problem: Death by shooting of victim alone in a room under observation.

1044. "The Moyett Case" *short story* in "The Strange Cases of Mason Brant"
Detective: Mason Brant.

Problem: The driving of a car by a man found to be dead.

1045. "The Mystery in the North Case" *short story* in "The Strange Cases of Mason Brant"
Detective: Mason Brant.
Problem: Death by head wound in a locked room.

Horler, Sydney

1046. DEATH AT COURT LADY *novel* U.K.: Collins, 1936
Detective: Sir Charles Knightley, pathologist.
Problem: Death by strangulation in a locked room.

1047. "The Death of Allan Mandeville" *short story* in "The Man Who Shook the Earth" U.K.: Hutchinson, (1933)
Detective: Knightley.
Problem: Death by strangulation in a locked room.

1048. ✓ "The Red-Haired Death" *novelette* in "The Destroyer" U.K.: Hodder, 1938; MacKill's Mystery Magazine v4 #4 1954; MacKill's Mystery Magazine (US) Aug 1954
Detective: Inspector Neilson.
Problem: Death in snow with no footmarks leading from the body.

Hornig, Doug

1049. ✓ THE DARK SIDE *novel* U.S.: Mysterious, 1986
Detective: Loren Swift.
Comment: The blurb on the paperback edition repeats a Booklist comment: "A deft combination of locked room mystery —..." I was unable to detect the locked-room situation thus reported.

Horton, Mileson, and Thomas Pembroke

1050. "Behind Locked Doors" *short story* in "Photocrimes" U.K.: Barker, (1936)
Detective: Sergeant Ellis.
Problem: Death by poisoning in a locked room.

Hougham, Arthur

1051. "The Night of the Garter" *short story* in "Best Detective Stories" U.K.: Faber, 1929
Detective: Amadour Bevan, antique dealer.
Problem: Attempted murder in a locked, "haunted" room.

Hubbell, Ned

1052. ✓ "The Case of the Scientific Recluse" *short story* in "The Adventures of Creighton Holmes" U.S.: Popular, 1979
Detective: Creighton Holmes, grandson of the maestro.

Problem: Death by gassing in a locked room.

Huggins, Roy

1053. "Appointment with Fear" *short story* in "77 Sunset Strip" U.S.: Dell, 1959, and U.K.: World, 1960; originally in The Saturday Evening Post
Detective: Stuart Bailey.
Problem: Apparent death by strangulation in a locked bedroom.

1054. ✓ "Aunt Willie's Ghost" *short story* in Conflict, Fall 1953
Detective: Jim Hane.
Problem: Death by gassing in a locked bedroom.

1055. "Death and the Skylark" *short story* in "77 Sunset Strip"; originally in Esquire, 1952; EQMM, April 1964; EQMM (UK) Aug 1964; EQMM (Australia) October 1964
Detective: Stuart Bailey.
Problem: Death by shooting on a boat where all suspects are alibied.

1056. "Now You See It" *short story* in "77 Sunset Strip"; originally in The Saturday Evening Post
Detective: Bailey.
Problem: Disappearance of murder weapon, a dagger, from a guarded room in which all suspects were carefully searched.

Hughes, Russell

1057. ✓ "Seeing Is Believing" *short story* in EQMM, July 1944
Detective: Wilmurt Robin.
Problem: Theft of a valuable chalice from a room under constant observation.

Hume, Fergus

1058. ✓ THE LAST STRAW *novel* U.K.: Hutchinson, 1932
Detective: Detective Sergeant O'Byrne.
Problem: Death by stabbing in a locked room.

Hurst, S.B.H.

1059. "The Pagoda of Gold" *short story* in Adventure, May 15, 1931
Detective: "Bugs" Horace Sinnat.
Problem: Disappearance of gold and jewels from off the top of a tall, smooth-sided, unclimbable pagoda.

Hutchinson, Horace

1060. THE FOREIGN SECRETARY WHO VANISHED *novel* U.K.: Hutchinson, (1927)
Detective: Emil Tabor.

Problem: Disappearance of the foreign secretary from a moving car that stopped outside his own house.

1061. THE GREENWELLS GLORY CASE *novel* U.K.: Hutchinson, (1924)
Detective: Inspector Spens.
Problem: Death by shooting in a locked room.

Huxley, Elspeth

1062. ✓ MURDER AT GOVERNMENT HOUSE *novel* U.K.: Methuen, 1937; U.S.: Harper, 1937
Detective: Superintendent Vachell.
Problem: Death by strangulation in a room under constant guard.

Hyne, C. J. Cutcliffe

1063. "The Looting of the Specie-Room" *short story* in "Mr. Horrocks, Purser" U.K.: Methuen, 1902
Detective: Mr. Horrocks.
Problem: Thefts from a locked specie room.

I

Ingemann, Bernhard S.

1064. "The Sealed Room" *short story* in "Library of the World's Best Mystery and Detective Stories" U.S.: Review, 1907; "The Lock and Key Library" U.S.: Review, 1909
Detective: None.
Problem: The enigma of a room locked for many years and reputed to contain all manner of treasures or horrors.

Innes, Michael

1065. ✓ APPLEBY AND HONEYBATH *novel* U.K.: Gollancz, 1983; U.S.: Dodd, 1983
Detectives: Sir John Appleby and Charles Honeybath.
Problem: Disappearance of a dead body from a locked library.

1066. THERE CAME BOTH MIST AND SNOW *novel* U.K.: Gollancz, 1940; U.S. (as "A Comedy of Terrors"): Dodd, 1940
Detective: Appleby.
Problem: Gunshot wound administered while the gun was not in anyone's possession.

1067. "A Derby Horse" *short story* in "Appleby Talking" U.K.: Gollancz, 1954; "Dead Man's Shoes" U.S.: Dodd, 1954; "Deadly Odds" U.K.: Souvenir, 1986

Detective: Appleby.

Problem: Disappearance of a horse from a locked and moving horse box.

1068. "The Sands of Thyme" *short story* in MacKill's Mystery Magazine, February 1953; MacKill's Mystery Magazine (US), February 1953; The Creasey Mystery Magazine, March 1957 "Appleby Talking" and "Dead Man's Shoes"; "Big Book of Locked-Room Mysteries", Black Lizard, 2014

Detective: Appleby.

Problem: Death by shooting on a beach when the sand was unmarked by prints other than the victim's.

Irish, William (Cornell Woolrich, q.v.)

1069. ✓ "All at Once, No Alice" *short story* in Argosy, March 2, 1940; EQMM, November 51; Verdict, July 1953; "Eyes That Watch You" U.S.: Rinehart, 1952; "Big Book of Locked-Room Mysteries", Black Lizard, 2014

Detective: Ainslie.

Problem: Disappearance of a bride on her wedding night from a hotel room where afterwards all the staff and the hotel register, etc., deny her presence.

1070. "The Room with Something Wrong" *short story* in "Somebody on the Phone" U.S.: Lippincott, 1950; (as "Mystery in Room 913") in Detective Fiction Weekly, June 4, 1938; as "The Suicide Room" (by Woolrich) and "The Murder Room" (by Irish) in EQMM, December 1949 (there split into two parts)

Detective: Striker.

Problem: Deaths (four) by defenestration from a locked ninth-storey hotel room.

Irving, Charles

1071. "Locked Room" *short story* in The Evening Standard, July 5, 1951

Detective: Inspector Sims.

Problem: Death by shooting in a locked study.

Irwin, Wallace

1072. THE JULIUS CAESAR MURDER CASE *novel* U.S.: Appleton, 1935

Detective: Publius Manlius Scribo.

Problem: Death by stabbing by invisible agency.

J

Jackson, Lewis

1073. ✓ THE GIRL OF DESTINY *novel* in The Union Jack 1270, Feb. 18, 1928
Detective: Sexton Blake.
Problem: Robbing of a safe requiring two separate keys, located on a guarded upper floor of a building, guarded at all ground-floor entrances, and the shooting of one of the key holders on a floor below when the safe guard heard nothing.

1074. ✓ THE TENANT OF NO. 13 *novel* SBL No. 114 (3rd series) U.K.: Amalgamated, 1946
Detective: Blake.
Problem: Death by gassing in a locked hotel room in which all exits had been sealed from the inside.

Jackson, Wallace

1075. THE ZADDA STREET AFFAIR *novel* U.K.: Low, (1934)
Detective: Archibald Penny.
Problem: Death by stabbing in a derelict boarded-up house in which all floors are covered with a thick, unmarked layer of dust.

Jacobs, T.C.H.

1076. ✓ APPOINTMENT WITH THE HANGMAN *novel* U.K.: Paul, 1936; U.S.: Macaulay, 1936
Detectives: Reggie Ruggles and Sergeant Trotter.
Problem: Various disappearances from a locked séance room, elemental materialisation, levitation, etc., and a series of inexplicable deaths. Not to mention a talking cat!

1077. BLACK TRINITY *novel* U.K.: Long, 1959
Detective: Dr. Ian McAndrew.
Problem: Death by decapitation in a locked room.

1078. ✓ THE TERROR OF TORLANDS *novel* U.K.: Paul, 1930
Detectives: Capt. Jacques Radford and Tony Anderson.
Problem: Disappearance of a wad of money from a room in which several people kept guard.

James, Francis

1079. "The Death Bead" *short story* in Detective Book, May 1930
Detective: Prentice.
Problem: Death by poison in a locked room.

Janifer, Laurence M., and Michael Kurland

1080. ✓ "Elementary" *short story* in "Shared Tomorrows" U.S.: St.

Martin's, 1979; originally in The Magazine of Fantasy & Science Fiction

Detective: None.

Problem: Death by shooting in the locked office of a literary agent.

Jenkins, Herbert

1081. "The Strange Case of Mr. Challoner" *short story* in "Malcolm Sage, Detective" U.K.: Jenkins, 1921; U.S.: Doran, 1921

Detective: Malcolm Sage.

Problem: Death by stabbing in a locked library.

Jepson, Edgar

1082. "The House That Paid No Rent" *short story* in "Garthoyle Gardens" U.K.: Hutchinson, 1913; U.S. (as "Alice Devine"): Bobbs, 1916

Detective: Lord Rupert Garthoyle.

Problem: Disappearance of a woman from within a locked room.

Comment: The Ellery Queen bibliography of the detective short story gives the American title of "Garthoyle Gardens" as "The Garden at 19." That is incorrect; "The Garden at 19" is the American edition of "No. 19," a completely different book.

Jepson, Edgar, and Robert Eustace

1083. "The Tea Leaf" *short story* in The Strand Magazine, October 1925; "Great Short Stories of Detection, Mystery and Horror" U.K.: Gollancz, 1928; "101 Years' Entertainment" U.S.: Little, 1941; "Detective Stories" U.S.: Octopus, 1980; AHMM February 2000; "The Big Book of Locked-Room Mysteries", Black Lizard 2014; "Capital Crimes", UK: British Library, 2015, US: Poisoned Pen Press, 2015

Detective: Ruth Kelstern.

Problem: Death by stabbing in a room (in a Turkish bath) under observation.

Johns, Ayresome

1084. ✓ PATTERN OF TERROR *novel* U.K.: Privately published, 1987

Detectives: John Anderson, ace investigator of the Antiquarian Booksellers Society of Great Britain, and Ninian Loftus and Stanford Maine, sleuth hounds.

Problems: (1) Death by shooting through the heart but with no external wound to correspond with the heart wound.

(2) Death by poisoning introduced by unknown means.
(3) Various locked-room murders, actual and proposed.

Johnson, Evelyn, and Gretta Palmer

1085. "Alley-Oop" *short story* in "Murder" U.S.: Covici, 1928; "Murder and Mystery" U.K.: Richards, 1929
Detective: John Waterbury.
Problem: Death by knife wound in a locked dressing room with nine-foot walls but no ceiling.

1086. "The Double Dealer" *short story* in "Murder" and "Murder and Mystery"
Detective: None.
Problem: Death by shooting in a locked room.

1087. "Mr. Southeby's Great Day" *short story* in "Murder" and "Murder and Mystery"
Detective: Mr. Southeby.
Problem: Death by stabbing in a locked cabin.

Johnson, Maurice C.

1088. DAMNING TRIFLES *novel* U.S.: Knopf, 1932; Ramble House, 2014
Detective: Bob Rollins.
Problem: Death by poisoning in a locked laboratory.

Johnston, Frank

1089. LI KWANG'S DAGGER *novel* U.K.: Wright, (1936)
Detective: Inspector Dursley.
Problems: (1) Death by stabbing in a locked study.
(2) Death by shooting in a locked inner room to the locked study.

Johnston, Jane

1090. ✓ PAINT HER FACE DEAD *novel* U.S.: St. Martin's, 1987
Detective: Louisa Evans, investigative reporter.
Problem: Death from a poisoned capsule that apparently could not have been passed to the victim.

Jones, Eugene

1091. WHO KILLED GREGORY? *novel* U.S.: Stokes, 1928; U.K. (as "The Last Clue"): Selwyn, 1931
Detective: Byron Hughes.
Problem: Death by unknown means in a locked room.

Jones, G. Wayman (house name)

1092. "The Black Bat's Invisible Enemy" by Norman A. Daniels (q.v.), *novelette* in Black Book Detective Magazine, September

1941; Greece: Hanos Publications
Detective: The Black Bat (Anthony Quinn).
Problems: (1) Disappearance of money from a locked vault.
(2) Death by poisoning in a locked laboratory.
(3) Disappearance of jewellery from a store under guard.
(4) Death by shooting in a locked room.
(5) Disappearance of a valuable tiara from an auction room under guard.

Jorricks, Handon C.

1093. "Hocus Pocus at Drumis Tree" *short story* in EQMM, April 1966; "The Anagram Detectives" (as by Norma Schier) U.S.: Mysterious, 1979
Detective: Sir Marvin Rhyerlee.
Problem: Death by poisoning by invisible agency.

Joseph-Renaud, Jean

1094. DR. MEPHISTO *novel* U.K.: Hutchinson, (1929)
Detectives: Monsieur Hignette and Dr. Mephisto.
Problems: (1) Death by stabbing in a locked strong room that could only be locked from the outside but the only keys to which were found inside, near the corpse.
(2) Death by shooting in a room in which the victim was surrounded by police officials when he died.

1095. THE PHANTOM VIOLIN *novel* Eire: Metropolitan, 1948
Detective: Monsieur Chenavard (Pere Bilboquet).
Problem: Death by strangulation in a locked room.

1096. ✓ "The Vengeance of Sewek" *short story* in Hutchinson's Mystery-Story Magazine, July 1923
Detective: Christophe Rozès.
Problem: Death by stabbing in a locked room belonging to an Egyptologist.

Joyce, Cyril

1097. ✓ ERRANT SLEUTH *novel* U.K.: Hale, 1983
Detective: Greg Allard, American actor and former CIA man.
Problem: Death by axe in a locked room.

Juta, Sir Henry

1098. OFF THE TRACK *novel* U.K.: Hutchinson, (1925)
Detective: Ronald Fraser.
Problem: Death by stabbing in a locked consulting room.

K

Kallen, Lucille

1099. ✓ C. B. GREENFIELD: THE TANGLEWOOD MURDERS *novel* U.K.: Collins, 1980; U.S.: Wyndham, 1980
Detectives: C. B. Greenfield and Maggie Rome.
Problem: Death of an orchestra leader by unknown means.

Kaminsky, Stuart

1100. ✓ NEVER CROSS A VAMPIRE *novel* U.S.: St. Martin's, 1980
Detective: Toby Peters.
Problem: Death by shooting in a locked room.

Kane, Henry

1101. TOO FRENCH AND TOO DEADLY *novel* U.S.: Avon, 1955; (as The Narrowing Lust") U.K.: Boardman, 1956, and U.S. (in The Locked Room Reader"): Random, 1968; "8 Doors to Death" U.S.: Dell, 1970
Detective: Peter Chambers.
Problem: Death by shooting in a locked office inside a locked garage.

1102. "Suicide Is Scandalous" *short story* in "Report for a Corpse" U.S.: Simon, 1948, and U.K.: Boardman, 1951; "Murder of a Park Avenue Playgirl" U.S.: Avon, 1957; "The Mammoth Book of Private Eye Stories" U.S.: Robinson, 1988; originally in Esquire
Detective: Chambers.
Problem: Death by shooting in a locked room.

1103. "Slaughter on a Sunday" *short story* in "Trilogy in Jeopardy" U.K.: Boardman, 1955; "Trinity in Violence" U.S.: Avon, 1955; (as "The Wrong Touch") in "The Name Is Chambers" U.S.: Pyramid, 1957
Detective: Chambers.
Problem: Death by shooting in a locked apartment to which only the owner had a key.

1104. "Watch the Jools" *short story* in "Death on the Double" U.S.: Avon, 1957; U.K.: Boardman, 1958
Detective: Chambers.
Problem: Death by drowning in a room with both exits under observation.

Kantor, MacKinlay

1105. "The Light at Three O'Clock" *short story* in Real Detective

Tales, 1930; The Saint Detective Magazine, April 1956; The Saint Detective Magazine (UK), August 1956; "It's About Crime" U.S.: Signet, 1960; "Tantalizing Locked Room Mysteries" U.S.: Walker, 1982

Detective: Matt Edwards, hotel manager.

Problem: Disappearance of a man from a locked apartment room.

1106. "Nobody Saw Him Fall" *short story* in Detective Fiction Weekly, 1933; "It's About Crime"

Detective: Daniel Ross.

Problem: Death by blunt instrument in a room in which no suitable instrument could be found or from which one appeared to have been removed.

1107. "The Strange Case of Steinkelwintz" *short story* in Chicago Daily News Midweek, 1929; "It's About Crime"; "Big Book of Locked-Room Mysteries", Black Lizard, 2014

Detective: Max Grame.

Problem: Disappearance of a baby grand piano from a second-storey room.

1108. "Wolf! Wolf!" *short story* in Real Detective Tales, 1932; "It's About Crime"

Detective: Lt. Cliff Kennedy.

Problem: Death by shooting from an inaccessible balcony into a room in which only the victim sat.

Karta, Nat

1109. VISION SINISTER *novel* U.K.: Dragon, 1954

Detectives: Inspector Garth and Dr. Carruthers.

Problem: Death by stabbing in a locked laboratory and subsequent and immediate disappearance from the room of the victim, assailant, and all the laboratory equipment.

Note: The earlier Garth/Carruthers novels are listed under John Russell Fearn's Hugo Blayn pen name; Nat Karta is a house name employed by Fearn on this occasion.

Keating, H.R.F.

1110. ✓ GO WEST, INSPECTOR GHOTE *novel* U.K.: Collins, 1981; U.S.: Doubleday, 1981

Detective: Inspector Ghote.

Problem: Death by throat cutting in a room under constant observation.

1111. ✓ THE PERFECT MURDER *novel* U.K.: Collins, 1964; U.S.: Dutton, 1965
Detective: Inspector Ghote.
Problem: Disappearance of a one-rupee note—out of ten such notes—from a desk drawer in an office under constant surveillance.

1112. ✓ "The Locked Bathroom" *short story* in EQMM, June 2, 1980; "Big Book of Locked-Room Mysteries", Black Lizard, 2014
Detective: Mrs. Craggs, charwoman.
Problem: Disappearance of a man from a bathroom under constant observation.

Keeler, Harry Stephen

1113. ✓ THE CASE OF THE TWO STRANGE LADIES *novel* U.S.: Phoenix, 1943; Ramble House, 2009; U.K. (as "Two Strange Ladies"): Ward, 1945
Detective: Bob Landell.
Problem: Disappearance of a diamond necklace from a room under constant observation.

1114. ✓ CHEUNG, DETECTIVE *novel* U.K.: Ward, 1938; U.S. (as "Y. Cheung, Business Detective"): Dutton, 1939
Detective: Y. Cheung.
Problem: Passing of confidential information from a room under constant guard.

1115. THE MARCEAU CASE *novel* U.S.: Dutton, 1936; Ramble House, 2009; U.K.: Ward, 1936
Detectives: Alec Snide (Alex Nide) and Xenius Jones.
Problem: Death by garotting in an unmarked area of rolled loam.

1116. THE VANISHING GOLD TRUCK *novel* U.S.: Dutton, 1941; Ramble House, 2009; U.K.: Ward, 1942
Detective: Sheriff Bugrus Duckhouse.
Problem: Disappearance of a large truck from a stretch of road under observation at both ends.

1117. X JONES OF SCOTLAND YARD *novel* U.S.: Dutton, 1936; Ramble House, 2009; U.K. (as "X Jones"): Ward, 1936
Detective: Xenius Jones.
Problem: As for Item 1115, "The Marceau Case," to which this is a companion book.

1118. "The Hand of God" *short story* in "20 Great Tales of Murder" U.S.: Random, 1951; U.K.: Hammond, 1952

Detective: Dr. Burkhalter.

Problem: Death by stabbing in a locked room.

Keeler, Harry Stephen, and Hazel Goodwin

1119. THE STRANGE WILL *novel* U.K.: Ward, 1949; U.S. Ramble House, 2009

Detective: Dr. Everett Edwards

Problem: Death by shooting in a locked room.

Keene, Carolyn

1120. THE MYSTERY OF THE LOCKED ROOM *juvenile novel* U.S.: Grosset, 1938

Detectives: The Dana Girls.

Problem: There are no impossible crimes in this book and nothing to commend it to adult readers.

Kelsey, Vera

1121. WHISPER MURDER! *novel* U.S.: Doubleday, 1946

Detective: Dan Cumberland, newsman.

Problem: Death by poisoning in a locked house.

Kelso, Jack

1122. ✓ THE MURDER OF COLONEL NEVILLE *novel* U.K.: Popular, c. 1935

Detective: Reginald Delamere.

Problem: Death by shooting in a locked room.

Kendrick, Baynard

1123. ✓ BLIND MAN'S BLUFF *novel* U.S.: Little, 1943; U.K.: Methuen, 1944

Detective: Capt. Duncan Maclain.

Problem: Death by defenestration from buildings in which the victims were alone.

1124. DEATH KNELL *novel* U.S.: Morrow, 1945; U.K.: Methuen, 1946

Detective: Maclain.

Problem: Death by shooting on a fourteenth-floor-apartment balcony on which the only person was the victim.

1125. ✓ THE IRON SPIDERS *novel* U.S.: Greenberg, 1936; U.K.: Methuen, 1938; (as "The Iron Spiders Murder") U.S.: Dell, 1944

Detective: Deputy Sheriff Stan Rice.

Problem: Entry into and exit from a locked suite of rooms of a murderer.

Kenealy, Arabella

1126. "The Villa of Simpkins" *short story* in The Ludgate Magazine,

1896; "Belinda's Beaux" U.K.: Bliss, 1897

Detective: Lord Syfret.

Problem: Death by poisoning in a locked room.

Kennedy, Douglas

1127. "Footprints in the Snow" *short story* in "13 Strange Tales" U.K.: Lawson, 1946

Detective: Unnamed narrator.

Problem: Death by stabbing in a room locked but for an open window. Tracks in the snow outside led to a blank wall and then stopped.

Kennedy, Milward

1128. THE CORPSE ON THE MAT *novel* U.K.: Gollancz, 1929; U.S. (as "The Man Who Rang the Bell"): Doubleday, 1929

Detective: Merriman.

Problem: Death by stabbing in an empty hall. The corpse was discovered by a flat owner who answered a ring at his doorbell and found a corpse on the mat.

1129. ✓ DEATH TO THE RESCUE *novel* U.K.: Gollancz, 1931

Detective: Gregory Amor.

Problem: Death by hanging from a balcony of a high, locked tower.

1130. HALF-MAST MURDER *novel* U.K.: Gollancz, 1930; U.S.: Doubleday, 1930

Detective: Superintendent Guest.

Problem: Death by stabbing in a locked, inaccessible summer house.

Kenrick, Tony

1131. A TOUGH ONE TO LOSE *novel* U.K.: Joseph, 1972; U.S.: Bobbs, 1972

Detective: Bill Verecker, lawyer.

Problem: Disappearance on an inland flight of a jumbo jet.

Kersh, Gerald

1132. "The Crewel Needle" *short story* in Esquire, 1953; "Guttersnipe" U.K.: Heinemann, 1954; (as "Open Verdict") EQMM, October 1959; "Big Book of Locked-Room Mysteries", Black Lizard, 2014

Detective: The narrator, a former policeman.

Problem: Death by stabbing through the skull with a needle in a locked room in which the victim's only companion was a little girl, aged eight years.

Kilvington, Edwin

1133. A MYSTERY IN GLASS *novel* U.K.: Houghton, 1931
Detective: Crispin Quane, professor of psychology.
Problem: Death by shooting in a room under constant guard.

Kincaid, H. C.

1134. "Murder on a Bet" *short story* in EQMM, November 1950
Detective: "Doc" Kay.
Problem: Death by poisoning in a locked room.

King, C. Daly (see also Phelan, Jeremy)

1135. ARROGANT ALIBI *novel* U.K.: Collins, 1938; U.S.: Appleton, 1939
Detective: Lt. Michael Lord.
Problem: Death by stabbing in a locked room.

1136. CARELESS CORPSE *novel* U.K.: Collins, 1937
Detective: Deputy-Inspector Michael Lord.
Problem: Death by poisoning in guarded areas.

1137. ✓ "The Episode of the Absent Fish" *short story* in EQMM, April 1979; "The Complete Curious Mr. Tarrant", Crippen & Landru, 2003
Detective: Trevis Tarrant.
Problem: Death by blunt instrument on a penthouse terrace accessible only by an automatic lift that was used by the first person to discover the body who could then find no trace of a third party on the terrace.

1138. "The Episode of the Codex Curse" *short story* in "The Curious Mr. Tarrant" U.K.: Collins, 1935, and U.S.: Dover, 1977; "Murder: Plain and Fanciful" U.S.: Sheridan, 1948; "The Complete Curious Mr. Tarrant"; "Big Book of Locked-Room Mysteries", Black Lizard, 2014
Detective: Tarrant
Problem: Disappearance of a codex from within a locked room with a witness in attendance.

1139. "The Episode of the Headless Horror" *short story* in "The Curious Mr. Tarrant"; "The Complete Curious Mr. Tarrant"
Detective: Tarrant.
Problem: Appearance at intervals of headless torsos on one particular road. No indication of how or by whom and no trace of the heads.

1140. "The Episode of the Man with Three Eyes" *short story* in "The Curious Mr. Tarrant"; "The Complete Curious Mr. Tarrant"
Detective: Tarrant.
Problem: Murder of a woman in a confined area. Neither of her companions was the murderer.

1141. "The Episode of the Nail and the Requiem" *short story* in "The Curious Mr. Tarrant"; "Tales of Detection" U.K.: Dent, 1936; (as "The Nail and the Requiem") EQMM, May, 1944; "The Complete Curious Mr. Tarrant"
Detective: Tarrant.
Problem: Murder in a locked room.

1142. "The Episode of the Tangible Illusion" *short story* in "The Curious Mr. Tarrant"; "The Complete Curious Mr. Tarrant"
Detective: Tarrant.
Problem: Haunting of a house by footsteps that follow on the stairs and a ghostly vision in an upper room.

1143. "The Episode of 'Torment IV'" *short story* in "The Curious Mr. Tarrant"; "Fifty Famous Detectives of Fiction" U.K.: Od- hams, 1938; AHMM, April 1990; "The Complete Curious Mr. Tarrant"; "Big Book of Locked-Room Mysteries", Black Lizard, 2014
Detective: Tarrant.
Problem: Each time *Torment IV* sails, she is abandoned by her crew, none of whom survive.

1144. "The Episode of the Vanishing Harp" *short story* in "The Curious Mr. Tarrant"; AHMM August 1987; "The Complete Curious Mr. Tarrant"
Detective: Tarrant.
Problem: Disappearance of an ancient harp from within a locked room.

1145. "Lost Star (The Episode of the Little Girl Who Wasn't There)" *short story* in EQMM, September 1944; "The Complete Curious Mr. Tarrant"; "Fifty Years of the Best From Ellery Queen's", Carroll & Graf, 1991
Detective: Tarrant.
Problem: Disappearance of an actress from within a guarded area.

King, Frank

1146. DEATH CHANGES HIS MIND *novel* U.K.: Hale, 1953

Detective: Dr. Frank King.
Problem: Murder in a locked room.

1147. DEATH OF A CLOVEN HOOF *novel* U.K.: Hale, 1951
Detective: King.
Problem: Death by stabbing in a room where an alarm sounds at any footfall; the room is empty, but for the corpse, moments after the alarm has sounded.

1148. THE GHOUL *novel* U.K.: Bles, 1928; U.S.: Watt, 1929
Detective: Paul Grendon.
Problem: Various disappearances in various disguises—and one murder by stabbing in a pitch black room—by a master villain, the Ghoul.

1149. TERROR AT STAUPS HOUSE *novel* U.K.: Bles, 1927; U.S.: Watt, 1929
Detective: Inspector Chambers.
Problem: Death by poisoning in a locked bedroom.

King, Rufus

1150. ✓ THE CASE OF THE CONSTANT GOD *novel* U.S.: Doubleday, 1936; U.K.: Methuen, 1938
Detective: Lieutenant Valcour.
Problem: Disappearance of a killer from a yacht that was searched from stem to stern.
Comment: On this performance King appears to be a writer of the first rank. Dryly humorous narrative and dialogue, an unusual plot line, a neat twist at the end, and a quietly competent detective. Surprising that he is so comparatively little known.

King, Sherry (R. Sherwood King)

1151. ✓ BETWEEN MURDERS *novel* U.S.: Appleton, 1935; U.K. (as "Death Carries a Cane"): Cherry Tree, 1941
Detectives: James Gaylord Durstine, retired lawyer, Robert Lord, and Tattersal, state attorney.
Problem: Death by poisoning, with the poison introduced by unknown means.

King, Stephen

1152. ✓ "The Doctor's Case" *short story* in "The New Adventures of Sherlock Holmes" U.S.: Carroll, 1987; U.K.: Arlington, 1988; "Big Book of Locked-Room Mysteries", Black Lizard, 2014
Detectives: Sherlock Holmes and Dr. Watson.
Problem: Death by stabbing in a locked room.

Knight, L. A.

1153. NIGHT EXPRESS MURDER *novel* U.K.: Low, (1936)
Detective: Colby Stack.
Problem: Death by carbon-monoxide poisoning in a locked train compartment.

Knox, E. V. ("Evoe")

1154. ✓ "Tomkinson's Bird Story" *short story* in "Fancy Now!" U.K.: Methuen, 1924; "It Occurs to Me" U.K.: Methuen, 1926
Detective: None.
Problem: Death by stabbing in a locked upper-story flat with only one apparently inaccessible window open.
Comment: Humorous story by a well-known parodist who was the brother of Ronald Knox.

Knox, Ronald A.

1155. THE THREE TAPS *novel* U.K.: Methuen, 1927; U.S.: Simon, 1927
Detective: Miles Bredon, insurance investigator.
Problem: Death by gassing in a locked bedroom.

1156. "The Adventure of the First Class Carriage" *short story* in The Strand Magazine, February 1947; "The Sherlock Holmes Scrapbook" U.K.: N.E.L., 1975; "The Further Adventures of Sherlock Holmes" U.K.: Penguin, 1985
Detective: Sherlock Holmes.
Problem: Disappearance of a man from a railway carriage under observation.

1157. "Solved by Inspection" *short story* in "Great Short Stories of Detection, Mystery and Horror, Second Series" U.K.: Gollancz, 1931; "My Best Detective Story" U.K.: Faber, 1931; "101 Years' Entertainment" U.S.: Little, 1941; "The Fifth Bedside Book of Great Detective Stories" U.K.: Baker, 1981
Detective: Miles Bredon.
Problem: Death by starvation in a locked gymnasium.

Kroder, Conroy

1158. ✓ "The Ghost Intrigue" *short story* in Adventure, Dec. 20, 1923
Detective: Stitt.
Problem: Death by shooting from within a room found seconds later to be empty and with all possible exits locked or under constant view.

Krohn, William

1159. "The Impossible Murder of Dr. Satanus" *short story* in EQMM, April 1965; "The Mammoth Book of Perfect Crimes and Impossible Mysteries", U.K.: Constable and Robinson, 2006; U.S.: Carroll and Graf, 2007
Detective: Richard Sheilan.
Problem: Death by stabbing in a locked lift.

Kronmueller, Colleen

1160. ✓ "Partners in Crime" *short story* in Woman's World (U.S.), May 25, 1982
Detective: Sergeant Jay.
Problem: Theft of a giant ruby from a tightly guarded museum.

Kummer, Frederic Arnold

1161. THE GREEN GOD *novel* U.S.: Watt, 1911
Detective: Owen Morgan.
Problem: Death by blunt instrument in a locked bedroom.

Kurland, Michael

1162. ✓ TEN LITTLE WIZARDS *novel* U.S.: Ace, 1988
Detective: Lord Darcy.
Problem: (1) Death by stabbing in a locked room.
(2) Death by throat cutting on a freshly shellacked floor on which were only the victim's footprints.
(3) Death by running through with a pike in a room to which all entrances were guarded either by men or a locked door.
Comment: A worthy successor to the Randall Garrett Lord Darcy tales, even if the impossible crimes are a letdown.

L

Lambert, Rosa and Dudley

1163. MONSIEUR FAUX-PAS *novel* U.K.: Wishart, 1928; (as "Death Goes to Brussels"): Nelson, 1937
Detective: Glyn Morgan.
Problem: Murder by defenestration from a locked room.

L'Amour, Louis

1164. ✓ "The Hills of Homicide" *short story* in Detective Tales, May 1949; "The Hills of Homicide" U.S.: Bantam, 1983; U.S.: Carroll, 1983; U.K.: Corgi, 1985

Detective: Unnamed private eye.
Problem: Death by stabbing in a house approached from one side by a narrow track under constant observation and from the other by a sheer cliff.
Comment: Interesting and worthwhile story, but the publishing history of the books is even more interesting. The Bantam edition is the authorised one, with author's notes, foreword, and publishing history, but may have actually been preceded by the Carroll & Graf edition that contains fewer stories and, as the author angrily points out, was unauthorised and had no backing of his.

Landon, Herman

1165. ✓ MYSTERY MANSION *novel* U.K.: Cassell, 1928
Detectives: Peterkin the valet, Donald Chadmore, ex-con, and Milliken, the policeman.
Problem: Death by stabbing in a locked and bolted library in which the innocent Chadmore was alone with the victim.

1166. ✓ WHISPERING SHADOWS *novel* U.K.: Jarrolds, 1930; U.S. (as "Three Brass Elephants"): Liveright, 1930
Detective: Napoleon Brown.
Problem: Disappearance of a red-and-black room that had contained a body later found elsewhere in the same house.

Larbalestier, P. G.

1167. "Psychic Death?" *short story* in "Officer, That's Your Man" U.K.: Gifford, 1947
Detective: Inspector Meredith.
Problem: Death by poisoning during a séance with no apparent means of introducing the poison.

Lariar, Lawrence

1168. ✓ DEATH PAINTS THE PICTURE *novel* U.S.: Phoenix, 1943; (as "Death Is the Host") Crime Novel Selection, 1943
Detective: Homer Bull.
Problem: Death by shooting in a locked room.

LaSpina, Greye

1169. ✓ "Vampire Bite" *short story* in Bull's-Eye Detective, Vol. 1, No. 2, Spring 1939
Detective: Dr. Arnold Hampton.
Problem: Deaths by unknown means in a locked bedroom,

where the victims' bodies were left virtually bloodless.

Latimer, Jonathan (see also Coffin, Peter)

1170. BLACK IS THE FASHION FOR DYING *novel* U.S.: Random, 1959; U.K. (as "The Mink-Lined Coffin"): Methuen, 1960
Detective: Richard Blake, scriptwriter.
Problem: Death by shooting during a filming sequence under observation.

1171. THE DEAD DON'T CARE *novel* U.K.: Methuen, 1938; U.S.: Doubleday, 1938
Detectives: William Crane and Thomas O'Rourke.
Problem: (1) Death by poisoning in a locked bedroom.
(2) Disappearance of a cardboard box full of money from beneath a bridge under constant observation.

1172. HEADED FOR A HEARSE *novel* U.S.: Doubleday, 1935; U.K.: Methuen, 1936; U.S. (as "The Westland Case"): Sun Dial, 1938
Detectives: Crane and Doc Williams.
Problem: Death by shooting in a locked room.

1173. MURDER IN THE MADHOUSE *novel* U.S.: Doubleday, 1934; U.K.: Hurst, (1935)
Detective: Crane.
Problem: Manner in which a body was cast down from a room with only one, apparently inaccessible, window.

Lauriston, Victor

1174. THE TWENTY-FIRST BURR *novel* U.S.: Doran, 1922
Detective: Harry Burnville.
Problem: Death by poisoning in a room containing no one but the victim.

Leblanc, Maurice

1175. THE DOUBLE SMILE *novel* U.K.: Skeffington, (1933); U.S. (as "The Woman with Two Smiles"): Macaulay, 1933
Detective: Monsieur Raoul (i.e., Arsène Lupin).
Problem: Death by invisible blunt instrument with all persons present under observation.

1176. ✓ "Arsène Lupin in Prison" *short story* in "The Exploits of Arsène Lupin" U.S.: Harper, 1907, and U.K.: Cassell, 1910; "The Seven of Hearts" U.K.: Cassell, 1908; "Big Book of Locked-Room Mysteries", Black Lizard, 2014
Detective: Prince Sergi Renine (Arsène Lupin).
Problem: Theft of valuable paintings and other objets d'art from

a locked and guarded castle.

1177. ✓ "Edith of the Swan-neck" *short story* in "The Confessions of Arsène Lupin" U.K.: Miller, 1912; U.S.: Doubleday, 1913; Walker, 1967
Detective: Chief Inspector Ganimard.
Problem: Theft of tapestries from a guarded gallery.

1178. "Footprints in the Snow" *short story* in "The Eight Strokes of the Clock" U.K.: Cassell, 1922, and U.S.: Macaulay, 1922; "The Great Detective Stories" U.S.: Scribners, 1927; "Foreign Bodies", British Library, 2017
Detective: Prince Sergi Renine (Arsène Lupin)
Problem: Apparent murder and disappearance of a man from a house surrounded by snow

1179. ✓ "The Invisible Prisoner" *short story* in "The Confessions of Arsène Lupin"
Detective: Arsène Lupin.
Problem: Disappearance of a man on farmland under constant surveillance.

1180. ✓ "The Queen's Necklace" *short story* in "The Exploits of Arsène Lupin"
Detective: The Cavaliere Floriani.
Problem: Disappearance of a diamond necklace from a locked bedroom.

1181. ✓ "Thérèse and Germaine" *short story* in "The Eight Strokes of the Clock" U.K.: Cassell, 1922; U.S.: Macaulay, 1922
Detective: Prince Sergi Renine (Arsène Lupin).
Problem: Death by stabbing of a man in a cabin under constant surveillance.

Le Carré, John

1182. A MURDER OF QUALITY *novel* U.K.: Gollancz, 1962; U.S.: Walker, 1962
Detective: George Smiley.
Problem: Death by blunt instrument in a house surrounded by snow, with no footprints to account for the killer's arrival or departure.

Lee, Gerald

1183. MURDER AND MUSIC *novel* Eire: Talbot, 1943
Detective: Inspector Crowley, "The Crow."
Problem: Death by poison gas in a locked study.

Lee, Gypsy Rose

1184. THE G-STRING MURDERS *novel* U.S.: Simon, 1941; U.K. (as "The Strip-Tease Murders"): Lane, 1943; U.S. (as "Lady of Burlesque): Tower, 1942
Detective: Biff Brannigan.
Problem: Death by poison in a room, the door of which is wax-sealed.

Le Fanu, J. Sheridan

1185. A LOST NAME *novel* U.K.: Bentley, 1868 (three volumes)
Problem: Death by throat cutting in a locked bedroom.

1186. UNCLE SILAS *novel* U.K.: Bentley, 1864 (three volumes); U.S.: Dover, 1966
Detective: (Maud Ruthyn).
Problem: Death by blunt instrument in a locked bedroom.

1187. "The Evil Guest" *novelette* in "Ghost Stories and Tales of Mystery" Eire: M'Glashan, 1851; (as a separate volume) U.K.: Downey, (1895)
Comment: A shorter version of "A Lost Name" (Item 1185).

1188. "The Murdered Cousin" *short story* in "Ghost Stories and Tales of Mystery"
Detective: None.
Problem: Death in a locked room.

1189. "A Passage in the Secret History of an Irish Countess" *short story* in The Dublin University Magazine, November 1838; "The Purcell Papers" U.K.: Bentley, 1880 (three volumes); "The Watcher" U.K.: N.E.L., 1974; "Death Locked In" U.S.: IPL, 1987
Detective: None.
Problem: Death by blunt instrument in a locked bedroom.

1190. "Some Account of the Latter Days of the Honourable Richard Marston of Dunoran" *short story* in The Dublin University Magazine, 1848
Comment: Shorter version of "A Lost Name" (Item 1185).

Lejeune, Anthony

1191. ✓ KEY WITHOUT A DOOR *novel* U.K.: Macmillan, 1988; U.S.: Doubleday, 1989
Detective: Prof. James Glowery.
Problem: Disappearance of a man in pajamas from outside his front door.

1192. Mr. DIABOLO *novel* U.K.: Macdonald, 1960

Detectives: Alastaire Burke and Arthur Blaise.

Problems: (1) Disappearance of Mr. Diabolo from a guarded area.

(2) Death by strangulation in a locked room.

Lenehan, J. C.

1193. THE MANSFIELD MYSTERY *novel* U.K.: Jenkins, 1932

Detective: Norma Glen, reporter.

Problem: Death by shooting in a locked study.

Lequeux, William

1194. ✓ THE CLOSED BOOK *novel* U.K.: Methuen, 1904; U.S.: Smart Set, 1904

Detective: Allan Kennedy, writer.

Problems: Various collapses and deaths from an unknown source.

1195. THE CRYSTAL CLAW *novel* U.K.: Hodder, 1924; U.S.: Macaulay, 1924

Detective: Rex Yelverton.

Problem: Disappearance of a man from a room locked on the inside.

1196. ✓ THE RED ROOM *novel* U.K.: Cassell, 1909; U.S.: Little, 1911

Detective: Kershaw Kirk.

Problem: Death by stabbing in a locked laboratory.

1197. "The Elusive Clue" *short story* in "The Crimes Club" U.K.: Nash, 1927

Detectives: Members of The Crimes Club.

Problem: Death by blunt instrument in a locked room.

1198. "A Secret of the Underworld" *short story* in Hutchinson's Mystery Story Magazine December 1926; "The Crimes Club"

Detectives: Members of The Crimes Club.

Problem: Death by garrotting in a locked library.

Leroux, Gaston

1199. BALAOO *novel* U.K.: Hurst, 1913

Detective: Balaoo, an educated pithecanthrope (half man, half ape).

Problem: Death by strangulation in a guarded premises by a killer who left footprints on the ceiling.

1200. THE MAN WHO CAME BACK FROM THE DEAD *novel* U.K.: Nash, 1916

Comment: A story of ghosts, séances, disappearances, impersonations, and murders. The crimes are bizarre but not strictly speaking impossible.

1201. THE MYSTERY OF THE YELLOW ROOM *novel* U.K.: Daily Mail, 1908; U.S.: Brentanos, 1908
Detective: Joseph Rouletabille, reporter.
Problems: (1) Attack by blunt instrument in a locked bedroom. (2) Disappearance of a man pursued to the intersection of 4 corridors—with one pursuer coming from each direction!

1202. THE PERFUME OF THE LADY IN BLACK *novel* U.K.: Daily Mail, 1909; U.S.: Brentanos, 1909
Detective: Rouletabille.
Problem: The appearance of a body within locked quarters with all persons within the area accounted for.

1203. ✓ THE PHANTOM OF THE OPERA *novel* U.K.: Mills, 1911; U.S.: Bobbs, 1911
Detective: None as such.
Problem: Disappearance of an envelope full of money while under constant observation in a theatre box.

Leslie, Charles

1204. "The Case of Miss Barracombe" *short story* in Tit-Bits Novels, 1915
Detective: Dr. Petrie.
Problem: Death by stabbing in a locked bedroom.

Leslie, Francis

1205. ✓ STUDY OF DEATH *novel* U.K.: Hurst, 1943
Detective: Jimmy Langtry.
Problem: Death by shooting in a locked study.

Leverage, Henry

1206. WHISPERING WIRES *novel* U.S.: Moffat, 1918
Detective: Triggy Drew.
Problem: Death by shooting in a locked library.

Levinrew, Will

1207. DEATH POINTS A FINGER *novel* U.S. & U.K.: Mystery League, 1933
Detective: Prof. Herman Brierly.
Problem: Death by shooting in a locked room.

1208. MURDER ON THE PALISADES *novel* U.S.: McBride, 1930; U.K.: Gollancz, 1930; U.S. (as "The Wheelchair Corpse"): Bart, 1946

Detective: Brierly.
Problem: Death by an unseen blunt instrument in a room under observation.

Lewis, Alfred Henry

1209. "The Man Who Flew" *short story* in "Confessions of a Detective" U.S.: Barnes, 1906
Detective: Inspector Val.
Problem: Disappearance of a man from a snow-covered area with only the victim's tracks leading to the body.

Lewis, Jack

1210. ✓ THE RED HEART OF THE INCAS *novel* SBL No. 86 (1st series) U.K.: Amalgamated, 1919
Detective: Sexton Blake.
Problem: Disappearance of a fabulous jewel from a locked suitcase.

Lewis, Ken

1211. ✓ "Sharon's Shawl" *short story* in Doc Savage Magazine, September/October, 1947; Street & Smith's Detective Monthly (UK), November 1956
Detective: Uncle Joss.
Problem: Death, presumed suicide, by shooting of a girl alone in a canoe.

Limnelius, George

1212. THE MEDBURY FORT MURDER *novel* U.K.: Benn, 1929; U.S.: Doubleday, 1929
Detective: Chief Inspector McMaster.
Problem: Death by stabbing in a locked bedroom.

Lipman, Clayre and Michael

1213. "Man Out of Time" *short story* in Malcolm's, March 1954
Detective: George Washington Neff, U.N. Division of Interplanetary Defence.
Problem: Murder by blunt instrument, leaving the victim with fifteen feet of untouched ground all around.

1214. "The Walking Corpse" *short story* in EQMM, September 1950; "Best Detective Stories of the Year 1951" U.S.: Dutton, 1951; "Best American Detective Stories of the Year 1951" U.K.: Boardman, 1952
Detective: Neff.
Problem: Death, disappearance, and reappearance of a man

whose vital organs, on analysis, prove not to be human.

Livingston, Armstrong

1215. TRACKLESS DEATH *novel* U.K.: Skeffington, (1930); U.S.: Bobbs, 1930
Detectives: Kitty Doyle and Peter Creighton.
Problem: Death, from a broken spine, and multiple injuries in a muddy field that bore no tracks.

Livingston, Jack

1216. ✓ DIE AGAIN, MACREADY *novel* U.K.: Macmillan, 1984; U.S.: St. Martin's, 1984
Detective: Joe Binney.
Problem: Death by hanging in a locked room.

Locke, G. E.

1217. THE SCARLET MACAW *novel* U.S.: Page, 1923
Detective: Miss Mercedes Quero.
Problem: Death by poisoning in a locked room.

Locke, George

1218. ✓ "The Channel Tunnel Mystery" *short story* in Ferret Fantasy's December 1990 catalogue
Detective: Morlock Tomes.
Problem: Disappearance of a train, fully laiden, from a Victorian channel tunnel.

1219. ✓ "A Nineteenth Century Debacle" *short story* U.K.: Ferret, 1979; "The Art of the Impossible" U.K.: Xanadu, 1990; "Murder Impossible" U.S.: Carroll, 1990 *Detective:* Tomes.
Problem: The naked body of a man falls from the air at almost the exact moment when 300 miles away at sea he is reported to have been washed overboard from his boat.

Long, Amelia Reynolds

1220. DEATH LOOKS DOWN *novel* U.S.: Ziff, 1944
Detectives: Edward Trelawney and "Peter" Piper.
Problem: A non-impossible murder. Often mistaken for a locked- room mystery because of its Edgar Allan Poe theme and a section headed "The Murders in the Rue Morgue." The reference, however, is to the means of stowing the body (i.e., up a chimney), and the book is otherwise unremarkable.

1221. THE HOUSE WITH GREEN SHUDDERS *novel* U.S.: Phoenix, 1950
Detective: Stephen Carter.
Problem: Appearance and disappearance of a mysterious room

from an old house.

1222. MURDER BY MAGIC *novel* U.K.: Grafton, 1947; U.S.: Phoenix, 1947

Detective: Carter.

Problem: Death by stabbing in a locked room.

Long, Max

1223. ✓ THE LAVA FLOW MURDERS *novel* U.S.: Lippincott, 1940

Detective: Komako Koa, Hawaiian peace officer.

Problem: Presence in a house of a ball of intensely hot lava clinker that was seen to roll down the stairs from the top to the ground floor.

Longyear, Barry

1224. ✓ "Slaughterhouse" *short story* in AHMM, July 1979; The Mammoth Book of Perfect Crimes and Impossible Mysteries", UK: Constable and Robinson, 2006, US: Carroll and Graf, 2007

Detective: Inspector Cockeral.

Problem: Death by shooting in a locked, impregnable bedroom defended by electrically operated bolts and such like.

Lonstar, Conway

1225. "The Weapon from Nowhere" *short story* in EQMM, November, 1970; "Sleight of Crime" U.S.: Regnery, 1977; "The Anagram Detectives" Mysterious, 1979

Detective: Maitre Glenthier.

Problem: Death by stabbing by invisible agency.

Lorac, E.C.R. (see also Carnac, Carol)

1226. ROPE'S END, ROGUE'S END *novel* U.K.: Collins, 1942

Detective: Chief Inspector Macdonald.

Problem: Death by shooting in a locked upper-storey room.

Lore, Phillips

1227. ✓ MURDER BEHIND CLOSED DOORS *novel* U.S.: Playboy, 1980

Detective: Leo Roi, millionaire attorney.

Problems: (1) Death by strangulation in a locked coach-house studio.

(2) Death by shooting in the same locked coach house.

(3) Death by stabbing in a locked theatre.

(4) Attempted murder by poison inside a locked elevator.

Lovesey, Peter

1228. ✓ A CASE OF SPIRITS *novel* U.K.: Macmillan, 1975; U.S.: Dodd, 1975

Detective: Sergeant Cribb.

Problem: Death by electrocution during a séance in which the victim was wired up to a system via a transformer capable of giving a small shock only and no more.

Lutz, John

1229. ✓ "The Case of the Canine Accomplice" *short story* in AHMM, March 3, 1982; (as "It's a Dog's Life") in "The Art of the Impossible" U.K.: Xanadu, 1990, and "Murder Impossible" U.S.: Carroll, 1990

Detectives: Milo Morgan and Sam, his dog.

Problem: Disappearance of a gun from the scene of the crime when the criminal seemed to have no time to get rid of it.

1230. "The Crooked Picture" *short story* in Man from U.N.C.L.E. magazine, November 1967; "MSMM Annual #3 1973", Renown 1973; "Tricks and Treats" U.S.: Doubleday, 1976; "101 Mystery Stories" U.S.: Avenel, 1986; "Big Book of Locked-Room Mysteries", Black Lizard, 2014

Detective: Louis Bratten.

Problem: Death by stabbing in a locked room.

Lynds, Dennis (see also Arden, William, and Collins, Michael)

1231. "No Way Out" *short story* in MSMM, February 1964; MSMM (UK), February 1964; "Best Detective Stories of the Year: 20th Annual Collection" U.S.: Dutton, 1965; "The Mammoth Book of Locked-Room Mysteries and Impossible Crimes", UK: Constable and Robinson, 2000, US: Carroll and Graf; "Slot Machine Kelly", Crippen & Landru 2005; "Big Book of Locked-Room Mysteries", Black Lizard, 2014

Detective: Slot-Machine Kelly.

Problem: Disappearance of rubies under constant guard.

Lynwood, Leslie

1232. "The Mystery of the Cape Mail" *short story* in "Lester Grayling, K.C." U.K.: Bale, 1921

Detective: Lester Grayling, lawyer.

Problem: Disappearance of a vanload of gold bullion from a heavily guarded express.

Lyon, Dana

1233. "The Impossible Murder" *short story* in "Eat, Drink and Be Buried" U.S.: Viking, 1956; "For Tomorrow We Die" U.K.: Macdonald, 1958; (as "Six Stories in Search of a Solution")

EQMM, July 1960
Detective: Officer Hogan.
Problem: Death by shooting in a locked house.

M

M.M.B.

1234. "The Mystery of the Hotel de L'Orme" *short story* in London Society magazine, August 1862; "Death Locked In" U.S.: IPL, 1987
Detective: Louis.
Problem: Death by suffocation in a locked upper-storey bedroom.

McBain, Ed (see also Hunter, Evan)

1235. KILLER'S WEDGE *novel* U.S.: Simon, 1959; U.K.: Boardman, 1961
Detective: Steve Carella.
Problem: Death from a broken neck in a locked room.

McCloy, Helen

1236. DESIGN FOR DYING *novel* U.K.: Heinemann, 1938; U.S. (as "The Dance of Death"): Morrow, 1938
Detective: Dr. Basil Willing.
Problem: Death by heat stroke in the middle of a snow-bound winter.

1237. THE FURTHER SIDE OF FEAR *novel* U.K.: Gollancz, 1967; U.S.: Dodd, 1967
Detective: Inspector Devlin.
Problem: Entry of an intruder into a barred and bolted flat.

1238. Mr. SPLITFOOT *novel* U.S.: Dodd, 1968; U.K.: Gollancz, 1969
Detective: Dr. Basil Willing.
Problem: Death by stabbing in a room under constant observation.

1239. A QUESTION OF TIME *novel* U.K.: Gollancz, 1971; U.S.: Dodd, 1971
Detective: Alfred Neroni.
Problem: Death from fright in a locked ballroom.

1240. THROUGH A GLASS, DARKLY *novel* U.S.: Random, 1950; U.K.: Gollancz, 1951
Detective: Dr. Basil Willing.

Problem: Appearance of a woman's doppelganger.

1241. "Through a Glass, Darkly" *short story* in EQMM, September 1948; "The Queens' Awards Third Series" U.S.: Little, 1948, and U.K.: Gollancz, 1950; "All But Impossible!" U.S.: Ticknor, 1981; "The Pleasant Assassin", Crippen & Landru, 2003
Comment: Short-story version of Item 1240.

MacClure, Victor

1242. DEATH BEHIND THE DOOR *novel* U.K.: Harrap, 1933; U.S.: Houghton, 1933
Detective: Archie Burford.
Problem: Death by shooting in a cloakroom in which the victim was alone.

McCombs, R.L.F.

1243. CLUE IN TWO FLATS *novel* U.S.: Mystery House, 1940; U.K.: Eldon, 1942
Detective: Richard Deming, violinist.
Problem: Death by strangulation in a locked room.

McCulley, Johnston

1244. THE BLACK STAR *novel* U.S.: Chelsea, 1921; U.K.: Hutchinson, (1924)
Detectives: Roger and Robert Verbeck.
Problems: (1) Disappearance of a master criminal from within a locked vault.
(2) Materialisation of the master criminal inside a locked house surrounded by show.

Mcdonald, Gregory

1245. ✓ FLETCH'S MOXIE *novel* U.S.: Warner, 1982; U.K.: Gollancz, 1983
Detective: Fletch.
Problem: Death by stabbing in front of TV cameras when only one other person appears to have been near enough to do it—but she didn't.

MacDonald, Philip (see also Porlock, Martin)

1246. THE CHOICE *novel* U.K.: Collins, 1931; U.S. (as "The Polferry Riddle"): Doubleday, 1931; U.K.: (as "The Polferry Mystery"): Collins, 1932
Detective: Anthony Gethryn.
Problem: Death by drowning in a locked bathroom.

1247. THE CRIME CONDUCTOR *novel* U.S.: Doubleday, 1931; Collins,

1932

Detective: Gethryn.

Problem: Death by drowning in a locked bathroom.

1248. RYNOX *novel* U.K.: Collins, 1930; U.S. (as "The Rynox Murder Mystery"): Doubleday, 1931; U.K. (as "The Rynox Mystery"): Collins, 1932

Detective: Superintendent Shanter.

Problem: Death by shooting by an untraceable killer in what could have been a guarded area.

1249. THE WHITE CROW *novel* U.K.: Collins, 1928; U.S.: Dial, 1928

Detective: Gethryn.

Problem: Death by shooting in a locked office.

MacDonald, William Colt

1250. ✓ SIX-SHOOTER SHOWDOWN *novel* U.S.: Sun Dial, 1940

Detectives: Rainbow Rhodes and Frosty Ferguson.

Problem: Theft of gold from a sealed sack.

McDougald, Roman

1251. THE BLUSHING MONKEY *novel* U.S.: Simon, 1953; U.K.: Boardman, 1953

Detective: Philip Cabot.

Problems: (1) Death by stabbing in a room with all exits unlocked but from which, after an initial flesh wound, the victim apparently made no attempt to escape.

(2) Death by throat cutting in a locked bathroom.

MacEwan, Walter

1252. ✓ "The Mystery of Wo Tak" *short story* in "The Adventures of Clay Fisk" U.K.: Leng, 1906

Detective: None.

Problem: Death by blunt instrument in a cabin in which the victim had been alone.

McFarlane, Arthur E.

1253. BEHIND THE BOLTED DOOR? *novel* U.K.: Nash, 1916; U.S.: Dodd, 1916

Detective: Dr. Henry Laneham, nerve specialist.

Problem: Death by electrocution in a locked room with a swimming pool.

McGinity, James Patrick

1254. ✓ "The Tortoise" *short story* in "Whirlpools" U.K.: Stockwell, 1925

Detective: Gerald Claxton.
Problem: Death from asphyxiation in a room in which no gas or source of gas could be found.

MacIsaac, Fred

1255. ✓ THE WINGED MURDERER *novel* U.K.: Sovereign, 1939
Detective: Dick Hadden.
Problem: Death by stabbing in a constantly guarded upper-storey office.

Mackenzie, Scobie

1256. ✓ THREE DEAD, ONE HURT... *novel* U.S.: Eyre, 1934
Detective: Inspector Mullins.
Problem: Death by shooting in a locked library.

Mackenzie, W. A.

1257. THE FLOWER O' THE PEACH *novel* U.K.: Ward, 1916
Detective: "Slow and Sure" Jackson.
Problem: Death by stabbing in a locked room.

MacLeod, Adam Gordon

1258. ✓ THE MARLOE MANSIONS MURDER *novel* U.K.: Harrap, 1928; U.S.: Dial, 1928
Detectives: Bobby Burrill and Sir William Burrill.
Problem: Disappearance of various people from within a locked apartment.

McMorrow, Will

1259. "The House with the Red Door" *short story* in Dime Detective, July 1938
Detective: Bradley Austin.
Problem: Infiltration of a locked house and subsequent disappearance of the house.

Magnay, Sir William

1260. ✓ THE CLOAK OF DARKNESS *novel* U.K.: Ward, 1918
Detective: Mr. Rolf, Commissioner of Criminal Investigation.
Problem: Disappearance of a lady from a moving brougham in which she sat alone.
1261. THE HUNT BALL MYSTERY *novel* U.K.: Ward, 1918; U.S.: Brentanos, 1918
Detective: Major Freeman.
Problem: Death by stabbing in locked room.

Mallory, Arthur

1262. APPERSON'S FOLLY *novel* U.S.: Chelsea, 1930

Detective: Dr. Montgomery.
Problems: (1) Death by defenestration from the window of an unoccupied cupola.
(2) Death by blunt instrument in a locked room.

March, William

1263. "The Bird House" *short story* in EQMM, February 1954; EQMM (UK) February 1954; EQMM (Australia) April 1954; "Ellery Queen's Best Bets" U.S.: Pyramid, 1972; "Tantalizing Locked Room Mysteries" U.S.: Walker, 1982; "Ellery Queen's Anthology #19: Davis, 1970, "Ellery Queen's Anthology #57", Davis, 1987
Detective: John Littleton, lawyer.
Problem: Death by shooting in a locked room.

Mark, Ted

1264. REGINA BLUE *novel* U.S.: Dell, 1972
Detective: Regina Blue.
Problem: Death by stabbing in a locked room.

Markham, Virgil

1265. THE DEAD ARE PROWLING *novel* U.K.: Collins, 1934
Detective: Ed Bond, newspaperman.
Problem: Appearance and disappearance of ghostly figures in guarded areas.

1266. ✓ THE DEADLY JEST *novel* U.K.: Collins, 1935
Detective: Ex-Inspector Myles Rusby.
Problems: (1) Disappearance of a man from outside a shaded window with no apparent avenue of escape.
(2) Death by shooting by invisible agency.

1267. DEATH IN THE DUSK *novel* U.K. and U.S.: Knopf, 1928
Detectives: Superintendent Salt and Paula Lebetwood.
Problem: Deaths (two) by blunt instrument in an area where there were no other people.

1268. THE DEVIL DRIVES *novel* U.K.: Collins, 1932; U.S.: Knopf, 1932; Ramble House, 2007
Detective: George Peters, ex-prison warden.
Problem: Death by drowning in a locked cabin.

1269. INSPECTOR RUSBY'S FINALE *novel* U.K.: Collins, 1933; U.S.: Farrar, 1933
Detective: Inspector Myles Rusby.
Problem: Disappearance of a party of guests from an isolated

country house.

1270. ✓ SHOCK! *novel* U.K.: Collins, 1930; U.S. (as "The Black Door"): Knopf, 1930
Detectives: Inspector Frost and American ingénue Toni Stapleton.
Problem: Disappearance of suspect from room under constant observation.

Marsh, Ngaio

1271. ✓ DEATH AND THE DANCING FOOTMAN *novel* U.S.: Little, 1941; U.K.: Collins, 1942
Detective: Chief Inspector Roderick Alleyn.
Problem: Death by blunt instrument in a room that no one left during a period when both exits were under surveillance.

1272. DEATH OF A FOOL *novel* U.S.: Little, 1956; U.K. (as "Off with His Head"): Collins, 1957
Detective: Alleyn.
Problem: Death by decapitation in the middle of a morris-dancing exhibition.

1273. "I Can Find My Way Out" *short story* in EQMM, August 1946; "The Queen's Awards" U.S.: Little, 1946, and U.K.: Gollancz, 1948; EQMM (Australia), November 1947; "Death Locked In" U.S.: IPL, 1987; "The Collected Short Fiction of Ngaio Marsh" U.S.: IPL, 1989; "Fifty Years of the Best From Ellery Queen's", Carroll & Graf, 1991
Detective: Alleyn.
Problem: Death by gassing in a locked dressing room.

Martel, Charles

1274. ✓ "Hanged by the Neck: A Confession" *short story* in "The Detective's Notebook" U.K.: Ward, 1860; "A Treasury of Victorian Detective Stories" U.S.: Scribners, 1979
Detective: Narrator.
Problem: Death by throat cutting in a locked bedroom.

Martell, Francis

1275. ✓ "Blank Walls" *short story* in 20-Story Magazine, June 1936
Detective: Superintendent Southgate.
Problem: Disappearance of a man from a narrow, dark alley guarded at both ends.

Martin, A. E.

1276. DEATH IN THE LIMELIGHT *novel* U.S.: Simon, 1946; U.K.:

Reinhardt, 1956

Detective: Inspector Gormley.

Problem: (1) Death by gassing in a locked room. (2) Stabbing on stage in full view of audience

1277. "The Flying Corpse" *short story* in EQMM, September 1947; "The Queens' Awards Second Series" U.S.: Little, 1947; EQMM (Australia), May 1950; U.K.: Gollancz, 1949; "Big Book of Locked-Room Mysteries", Black Lizard, 2014

Detectives: Mona and Rodney.

Problem: Discovery of a dead, naked man in a patch of unmarked soft earth.

Martin, Aylwin Lee

1278. ✓ DEATH FOR A HUSSY *novel* U.S.: Graphic, 1952

Detective: Matt Hughes, attorney.

Problem: Death by shooting in a locked room with a window overlooking a deep, inaccessible canyon.

Martyn, Wyndham

1279. THE DEATH FEAR *novel* U.K.: Jenkins, 1929; U.S.: McBride, 1929

Detective: Anthony Trent.

Problem: Death by blunt instrument in a locked library.

Maschwitz, Eric, and Bevis Winter

1280. LITTLE RED MONKEY *novel* U.K.: Jenkins, 1953

Detective: Major Colin Currie.

Comment: The blurb on the dust wrapper suggests a murder in a locked room. However, the problem is really how did someone trick his way into the murder room. The novelisation of a highly successful television espionage serial, but very run of the mill.

Mason, Van Wyck

1281. SPIDER HOUSE *novel* U.S.: Mystery League, 1932; U.K.: Hale, 1959

Detective: Captain Catlin.

Problem: Disappearance of a murder gun from a guarded suite of rooms.

Massey, Morrell

1282. ✓ LEFT HAND LEFT *novel* U.K.: Hutchinson, 1932; U.S.: Penn 1932

Detective: Thornton Zane, analyst of mystery.

Problem: Disappearance from a fast-moving train of a villain later found to have somehow survived with nothing worse than a broken arm.

Masterman, Walter S.

1283. THE BORDER LINE *novel* U.K.: Jarrolds, 1936; U.S.: Dutton, 1937; Ramble House, 2009
Detective: Dick Selden.
Problem: Strangulation of two strong men when all present, bar one woman and two children, were accounted for.

1284. THE CURSE OF THE RECKAVILES *novel* U.K.: Methuen, 1927; U.S.: Dutton, 1927; U.K. (as "The Crime of the Reckaviles"): Methuen, 1934
Detective: Chief Inspector Sinclair.
Problem: Death by stabbing in a locked room.

1285. ✓ THE FLYING BEAST *novel* U.K.: Jarrolds, 1932; U.S.: Dutton, 1932; Ramble House, 2009
Detective: Sir Arthur Sinclair.
Problem: Death by poisoning when it seemed that no one could have got at the victim's drinking glass.

1286. THE GREEN TOAD *novel* U.K.: Gollancz, 1928; U.S.: Dutton, 1929; Ramble House, 2009
Detective: Chief Constable Hendon.
Problem: Death by blunt instrument and prints left as though by a monstrous toad.

1287. THE NAMELESS CRIME *novel* U.K.: Jarrolds, 1932; U.S.: Dutton, 1932
Detective: Superintendent (later Sir Arthur) Sinclair.
Problem: Death by stabbing in a locked room.

1288. THE SECRET OF THE DOWNS *novel* U.K.: Jarrolds, (1938); U.S.: Dutton, (1939)
Detective: Sinclair.
Problem: In full view of a shoreline audience, a man is apparently pulled off his boat by an unseen agency.

1289. ✓ 2 L.O. *novel* U.K.: Gollancz, 1928; U.S.: Dutton, 1928; U.K. (as "Blood on the Floor"): Newnes, 1935
Detective: Sinclair.
Problem: Death by shooting behind a locked study door.

1290. THE WRONG LETTER *novel* U.K.: Methuen, 1926; U.S.: Dutton, 1926

Detective: Sylvester Collins.
Problem: Death by shooting in a locked library.

Mathews, J. J.

1291. "Death Opens Tonight" *short story* in Double-Action Detective and Mystery Stories, Winter 1957-8
Detective: Ford J. Ash.
Problem: Death by poisoning of a man under guard, before a carefully watched audience.

Mathews, Nieves

1292. SHE DIED WITHOUT LIGHT *novel* U.K.: Hodder, 1956
Detective: Dr. Hal Phillips.
Problem: Death by poisoning in a locked room.

Mathieson, Theodore

1293. THE DEVIL AND BEN FRANKLIN *novel* U.S.: Simon, 1961
Detective: Ben Franklin.
Problem: Death by sword-thrust in a locked room.

1294. "Leonardo da Vinci, Detective" *short story* in EQMM, January, 1959; EQMM (Australia), March 1959; "The Great 'Detectives'" U.S.: Simon, 1960
Detective: Leonardo da Vinci.
Problem: Death by stabbing in an open field by an invisible agency.

1295. "Omar Khayyam, Detective" *short story* in EQMM, February 1960; EQMM (Australia), April 1960; EQMM (UK) April 1960; "The Great 'Detectives'"
Detective: Omar Khayyam.
Problem: Death by stabbing in a locked turret room.

Matthews, Clayton

1296. ✓ "Into Thin Air" *short story* in AHMM, October 1978
Detective: Lincoln Plummer, private detective.
Problem: Disappearance of a woman from a swimming pool under constant observation.

Mavity, Nancy Barr

1297. ✓ THE OTHER BULLET *novel* U.S.: Doubleday, 1930; U.K.: Collins, 1931
Detective: Peter Piper, newsman.
Problem: The victim was hit by two shots but shortly afterwards was found to be in a state of rigor mortis.

Maxon, P. B.

1298. ✓ THE WALTZ OF DEATH *novel* U.S.: Mystery House, 1941
Detective: Lander.
Problem: Death by unknown means of a man listening to a piece of piano music being played.

Meade, L. T.

1299. THE RED RUTH *novel* U.K.: Laurie, (1907)
Detective: Rudolph Grey.
Problem: Poisoning when the victim was on his/her own.

1300. ✓ "The Face of the Abbot" *short story* in "The Sorceress of the Strand" U.K.: Ward, 1903; "Rivals of Sherlock Holmes" U.S.: Castle, 1978
Detective: Dixon Druce.
Problem: Appearance of a ghostly abbot's face at the window of a castle room in which the only occupant was searched immediately afterwards.

1301. ✓ "The Talk of the Town" *short story* in "The Sorceress of the Strand"
Detectives: Eric Vandeleur and Dixon Druce.
Problem: Poisoning by unknown means of a lecturer standing alone on a platform.

Meade, L. T., and Robert Eustace

1302. ✓ "The Eight-Mile Lock" *short story* in "A Master of Mysteries" U.K.: Ward, 1898
Detective: John Bell, ghost exposer.
Problem: A mysterious disembodied voice heard in a lock with no boats in it.

1303. ✓ "How Siva Spoke" *short story* in "A Master of Mysteries"
Detective: Bell.
Problem: A voice emanating from an Indian statue.

1304. ✓ "The Invisible Enemy" *short story* in The Storyteller, c. 1906/07
Detective: Prof. Christopher Ekshaw.
Problem: Deaths by unknown poison introduced by unknown means.

1305. ✓ "The Man Who Disappeared" *short story* in "Silenced" U.K.: Ward, 1904; EQMM, May 1948; "Death Locked In" U.S.: IPL, 1987
Detectives: Dr. Garland and Inspector Frost.

Problem: Disappearance of a man seen to enter a closely guarded house.

1306. ✓ "Mr. Bovey's Unexpected Will" *short story* in The Harmsworth Magazine, 1899/1900; "Crime on Her Mind" U.S.: Pantheon, 1975; U.K.: Joseph, 1976
Detective: Florence Cusack.
Problem: Disappearance of a large quantity of gold from a pawnbroker's shop that was rigorously searched.

1307. ✓ "The Mystery of the Circular Chamber" *short story* in "A Master of Mysteries"; "Master Detective Stories" U.S.: Clode, 1929
Detective: John Bell.
Problem: Death by unknown means in a reputedly haunted room.

1308. ✓ "The Mystery of the Felwyn Tunnel" *short story* in "A Master of Mysteries"
Detective: Bell.
Problem: Death by unknown means of workers near the Felwyn tunnel.

1309. "The Mystery of the Strong Room" *short story* in "The Brother hood of the Seven Kings" U.K.: Ward, 1899; "Big Book of Locked-Room Mysteries", Black Lizard, 2014
Detective: Norman Head.
Problem: Theft of jewellery from a burglar-proof safe.

1310. ✓ "To Prove an Alibi" *short story* in "A Master of Mysteries"
Detective: John Bell.
Problem: Attempted murder by suffocation in a locked turret room.

1311. "The Secret of Emu Plain" *short story* in Cassell's Magazine, December 1898 (as a competition story); "The Oracle of Maddox Street" U.K.: Ward, 1904; "Dead Witness" U.S.: Penguin, 1990
Detective: BelMournfulearance of various men near a great rock on an open plain.

1312. ✓ "The Warder of the Door" *short story* in "A Master of Mysteries"; "The Supernatural Solution" U.S.: Taplinger, 1976; "Realm of the Impossible", Locked Room International, 2017
Detective: Bell.
Problem: The opening and closing of a door according to

whether or not an ancient coffin was within or without an equally ancient cell.

Meadows, Patrick

1313. "Murder in a Locked Box" *short story* in EQMM, August 1969
Detective: Chief Delancey.
Problem: Death by poisoning in a locked cell.

Mearson, Lyon

1314. PHANTOM FINGERS *novel* U.S.: Macaulay, 1927; U.K.: Hutchinson, (1929)
Detective: Steve Muirhead.
Problem: Death by strangulation by invisible agency in front of a full theatre audience.

1315. ✓ "The Secret of the Dismembered Hand" *short story* in True Detective Mysteries, January 1928
Detective: The Old Inspector.
Problem: Disappearance of a writer from within a study under constant observation.

Mee, Huan (Walter E. and Charles H. Mansfield)

1316. ✓ "The Act of an Anarchist" *short story* in The Penny Pictorial Magazine, 1905; "Solving the Unsolvable" U.K.: Ferret, 1980
Detective: None.
Problem: Death and devastation in a study caused by an apparently noiseless bomb.

1317. ✓ "The Bloomsbury Tragedy" *short story* in The Penny Pictorial Magazine, 1905; "Solving the Unsolvable"
Detective: *None.*
Problem: Death by stabbing in a locked room.

1318. ✓ "The Body That Vanished" *short story* in The Penny Pictorial Magazine, 1905; "Solving the Unsolvable"
Detective: None.
Problem: Disappearance of a corpse from a room under constant watch from inside and inaccessible from outside by anyone trying to carry out a body.

1319. ✓ "The Great Gold Robbery" *short story* in The Penny Pictorial Magazine, 1905; "Solving the Unsolvable"
Detective: John Dawes, private detective.
Problem: Disappearance of gold bars from a liner's bullion room.

1320. ✓ "How the Restowe Diamonds Disappeared" *short story* in

The Penny Pictorial Magazine, 1905; "Solving the Unsolvable"
Detective: Sergeant Foskett.
Problem: Theft of diamonds from a room under constant observation.

1321. ✓ "Monsieur Roche's Defeat" *short story* in "A Diplomatic Woman" U.K.: Sands, 1900; U.S.: Harper, 1900
Detective: Aide Lerestrelle.
Problem: Disappearance of a sealed, written document from a locked safe and its replacement by blank paper.

1322. ✓ "The Tragedy in the Train" *short story* in The Penny Pictorial Magazine, 1905; "Solving the Unsolvable"
Detective: None.
Problem: Death by shooting of a man alone in a railway compartment.

Mengchu, Master Ling

1323. "Lazy Dragon the Master Thief" *short story* in "The Lecherous Academician" U.K.: Rapp, 1973
Thief: Lazy Dragon.
Problem: Theft of a decanter from a sealed house.

Merak, A. J. (see also Glasby, John S.)

1324. THIS TIME FOREVER *novel* U.K.: Spencer, 1957
Detectives: Johnny Merak and Dawn Grahame.
Problem: Death by hydrocyanic-acid poisoning in a locked room.

Meriton, Peter

1325. ✓ CAPTAIN DACK *novel* U.K.: Hurst, 1939
Detective: Captain Dack.
Problem: Disappearance of a fully manned ship while at sea.

Metcalfe, Herbert

1326. THE PACKET OF DEATH *novel* U.K.: Church, 1967
Detective: Inspector John Heenan.
Problem: Death by poisoning in a guarded office.

Miller, Elizabeth York

1327. THE MARK OF YEKEL *novel* U.K.: Bles, 1927
Detective: Frank Yardley.
Problem: Death by stabbing in a locked bedroom.

Mitchelson, Austin, and Nicholas Utechin

1328. HELLBIRDS *novel* U.K.: Paramount, 1976; U.S.: Belmont, 1976
Detective: Sherlock Holmes.

Problem: Disappearance of a spy from a locked and guarded cell.

Mitford, C. Guise

1329. THE HIDDEN MASK *novel* U.K.: Greening, 1914
Detective: Greatorex.
Problem: Disappearance from a bedroom of a sinister dwarf who moments before had been seen to enter it and heard to shoot its occupant. All exits except the door were locked on the inside.

Monro, Gavin

1330. ✓ MARKED WITH A CROSS *novel* U.K.: Hale, 1968
Detective: Inspector Hinkley.
Problem: Death by poisoning in a waiting room in which the victim had been well away from all the other occupants.

Moody, Helen Wills, and Robert Murphy

1331. ✓ DEATH SERVES AN ACE *novel* U.K.: Hutchinson, 1939; U.S.: Scribners, 1939
Detective: Chief Inspector MacMasters.
Problem: Death from poison in the middle of a Wimbledon tennis match.

Morland, Nigel (see also Donavan, John, and Forrest, Norman)

1332. THE CLUE OF THE BRICKLAYER'S AUNT *novel* U.K.: Cassell, 1936; U.S.: Farrar, 1937
Detective: Mrs. Pym.
Comment: The book contains a sequence in which a house is entered by the use outside of a pair of pliers to turn a key in a lock inside.

1333. THE CORPSE ON THE FLYING TRAPEZE *novel* U.K.: Cassell, 1941; U.S.: Farrar, 1941
Detective: Pym.
Problem: Decapitation of a trapeze artist by an invisible assailant.

1334. DEATH WHEN SHE WAKES *novel* U.K.: Evans, 1951
Detective: Inspector Rory Luccan.
Problem: Death by poisoning in a locked room.

1335. A GIRL DIED SINGING *novel* U.K.: Evans, 1952
Detective: Luccan.
Problem: Death by throat cutting in a great glass tank where other people swam but no knife could be found.

1336. THE LADY HAD A GUN *novel* U.K.: Cassell, 1951

Detective: Mrs. Pym.

Problem: A car, at the scene of a killing, apparently driven by an Egyptian mummy more than 2,000 years old.

1337. THE MOON MURDERS *novel* U.K.: Cassell, 1935

Detective: Pym.

Problem: Death by poisoning in a locked room.

1338. ✓ "The Case of the Impossible Theft" *short story* in "The Case of the Innocent Wife and Other Mrs Pym Stories" U.K.: Martin, (1947)

Detective: Pym.

Problem: Theft of an invaluable vase from a locked flat.

1339. "The Curious Death" *short story* in "Mrs Pym of Scotland Yard" U.K.: Vallancey, 1946

Detective: Pym.

Problem: Death by poisoning in a room under constant observation.

1340. "The Faded Moquette" *short story* in The Saint Mystery Magazine (U.K.), September 1966; The Saint Mystery Magazine (U.S.), September 1966

Detective: Pym.

Problem: Death by poisoning in a sealed railway compartment.

1341. "The Haunting of Craig Tara" *short story* in Edgar Wallace Mystery Magazine, February 1965; "John Creasey's Mystery Bedside Book" U.K.: Hodder, 1973; "Mrs Pym and Other Stories" U.K.: Ellis, 1976

Detective: Inspector Garrick.

Problem: Death by throat cutting of one of three men locked in a haunted room. Each man had been rigorously searched and the room was guarded at all exits.

1342. "The Impossible Crime" *short story* in "26 Three Minute Thrillers" U.K.: Martin, c. 1946

Detective: Mrs. Pym.

Problem: Death by poison in a locked office.

1343. "Murder by the Mile" *short story* in The Evening News, Dec. 14, 1977

Detective: Sergeant Johnny Lamb.

Problem: Death by being pushed over the edge of a quarry of a man whose brother, the main suspect, was immobile due to a spinal injury and could not have walked the half mile to the quarry.

1344. "The Phantom Killer" *short story* in "26 Three Minute Thrillers"
Detective: Mrs. Pym.
Problem: Death by poison of a surfer while out surfing.

1345. "The Rotherhithe Miracle" *short story* in "Mrs Pym of Scotland Yard"
Detective: Pym.
Problem: Noise and commotion made by a totally paralysed woman.

1346. "Sealed-Up Clue" *short story* in The Evening Standard, 1961; (as "The de Rougement Case") EQMM, September 1978, and "Ellery Queen's Eyewitnesses" U.S.: Davis, 1982
Detective: Jean Soustrelle.
Problem: Death by gassing in a locked room sealed on the inside with tape.

Morris, T. B.

1347. THE PAPYRUS MURDERS *novel* U.K.: Hale, 1958
Detective: Dr. John Tarleton.
Comment: There's some action centreing around a locked museum mysteriously entered, but it eventually turns out that the killer waited until someone opened one of the doors and went in.

Morrison, Arthur

1348. ✓ "The Case of the Admiralty Code" *short story* in "The Red Triangle" U.K.: Nash, 1903; U.S.: Page, 1903
Detective: Martin Hewitt.
Problem: Disappearance of secret Admiralty papers that were either in a locked safe or in a locked room and under constant guard.

Morrison, Hugo

1349. The LOW ROAD *novel* U.K.: Methuen, 1930
Detective: The Hon. James "Kipper" Herring.
Problem: Death by strangulation in a locked room where the only witness was apparently physically incapable of doing the deed.

Morton, Guy

1350. THE PERRIN MURDER CASE *novel* U.K.: Skeffington, (1930); U.S.: Greenberg, 1934
Detective: Konrad Roque.

Problem: Death by stabbing in a locked room.

Morton, William

1351. THE MYSTERY OF THE HUMAN BOOKCASE *novel* U.K.: Hurst, (1931); U.S.: Mason, 1931

Detectives: Kirker Cameron, Commissioner of Police, and Jerome Bland, District Attorney.

Problem: Death by poisoning in a locked room.

Moye, Wayne, and John Polley

1352. ✓ "A Bookman's Christmas Carol" *short story* in U.S.: Moye Polley, 1981

Detectives: Kedge, a bookseller, and Detective Lestrade.

Problem: Murder in a locked bookshop.

Muir, Augustus

1353. "The Condemning Eye" *short story* in "Raphael, M.D." U.K.: Methuen, 1935

Detective: Dr. Louis Raphael.

Problem: Death by shooting in a locked cellar.

1354. "The Kestar Diamond Case" *short story* in "Raphael, M.D."; "The Big Book of Locked-Room Mysteries", U.S.: Black Lizard, 2014

Detective: Raphael.

Problem: Death by blunt instrument in a locked room.

1355. "The Terror of the Purple Room" *short story* in "Raphael, M.D."

Detective: Raphael.

Problem: Death by throat cutting in a locked bedroom.

Muller, Marcia

1356. ✓ THE TREE OF DEATH *novel* U.S.: Walker, 1983

Detective: Elena Oliverez, museum curator.

Problem: Death by blunt instrument in the locked museum.

Munro, John

1357. ✓ THE CATWALK KILL *novel* U.K.: Hale, 1985

Detectives: Sgt. Leo Farrell and Detective Vic Henderson.

Problem: Death of a fashion model, by shooting, on a floodlit catwalk, but no one heard the shot or saw the gunman, and no weapon could be found.

Murphy, Warren B.

1358. LEONARDO'S LAW *novel* U.S.: Carlyle, 1978

Detective: Dr. David Vincent Leonardo.

Problem: Death by blunt instrument in a locked room.

Murray, Robert

1359. ✓ THE FOUR GUESTS MYSTERY *novel* in The Union Jack, Oct. 8, 1932
Detective: Sexton Blake.
Problem: Various deaths by stabbing in a locked study.

Myers, Isabel Briggs

1360. MURDER YET TO COME *novel* U.K.: Gollancz, 1930; U.S.: Stokes, 1930
Detective: Peter Jerningham, playwright.
Problem: Death by blunt instrument in a locked room.

N

Narcejac, Thomas

1361. "The Red Orchid" *short story* in EQMM, January, 1961; "The Misadventures of Ellery Queen", Wildside, 2018
Detective: Nero Wolfe.
Problem: Death by poison in a locked room.

Nathenson, Joseph

1362. ✓ A PUZZLE FOR EXPERTS *novel* U.S.: S.O.S. (Los Angeles), 1985
Detective: Lieutenant Kupferman.
Problem: Death by shooting in a locked room.

Neuman, Fredric

1363. ✓ THE SECLUSION ROOM *novel* U.S.: Viking, 1978; U.K.: Gollancz, 1979
Detective: William Moore, policeman.
Problem: Death by strangulation inside a locked seclusion room in a psychiatric hospital.

Newell, Audrey

1364. ✓ WHO KILLED CAVELOTTI? *novel* U.S.: Century, 1930
Detective: Patrick Michael Doyle, of the homicide squad.
Problem: Death by stabbing in a room where the only witness was innocent.

Newton, Douglas

1365. "Watch Your Step" *short story* in Tit-Bits, Feb. 13, 1932
Detective: An unnamed police inspector.
Problem: Death by shooting in a locked office.

Nichols, Beverley

1366. THE MOONFLOWER *novel* U.K.: Hutchinson, 1955; U.S. (as "The Moonflower Murder"): Dutton, 1955
Detective: Mr. Green.
Problem: Death by induced heart attack in a locked hot-house.

1367. THE RICH DIE HARD *novel* U.K.: Hutchinson, 1957; U.S.: Dutton, 1958
Detective: Green.
Problem: Death by shooting in a locked bedroom.

Niven, Larry

1368. ✓ THE PATCHWORK GIRL *novel* U.S.: Ace, 1980
Detective: Gil Hamilton, special ARM investigator.
Problem: Wounding of a man inside a moonbase complex by laser beam fired from outside the complex when the only person outside was innocent of the attack.

1369. ✓ "ARM" *short story* in Epoch (anthology), published in 1975; "The Long Arm of Gil Hamilton" U.S.: Ballantine, 1976; "The 13 Crimes of Science Fiction" U.S.: Doubleday, 1979
Detective: Hamilton.
Problem: Death by blunt instrument in an apartment from which the only reasonable exit was via an elevator, which had not been so used.

Noble, James A.

1370. ✓ "Involuntary Suicide" *short story* in AHMM, April 1985
Detectives: Winnie and Thatcher.
Problem: Death by gassing in a locked room.

Noel, Atanielle Annyn

1371. ✓ SPEAKER TO HEAVEN *novel* U.S.: Baen, 1988
Detective: Wolf.
Problem: Death within a locked tower, plus at least one later death in a room under constant observation.

Nolan, J. Vincent

1372. ✓ MURDER WALKS ALONE *novel* Eire: Grafton, 1945
Detective: Edmond MacKell, private eye.
Problem: Various disappearances from a locked room previously minutely examined by the indefatigable MacKell.

O

Oates, Joyce Carol

1373. ✓ MYSTERIES OF WINTERTHURN *novel* U.K.: Cape, 1984; U.S.: Dutton, 1984
Detective: Xavier Kilgarvan.
Problem: Death by mutilation of a babe in arms in a locked room.

O'Brien, Fitz-James

1374. "The Diamond Lens" *short story* in The Atlantic Monthly, 1858; "The Poems and Stories of Fitz-James O'Brien" U.S.: Osgood, 1881; "The Diamond Lens and Other Stories" U.K.: Ward & Downey, 1887; "Famous Mystery and Detective Stories" U.S.: Blue Ribbon, 1938
Detective: None.
Problem: Death by stabbing in a locked room.

Odlum, Jerome

1375. NINE LIVES ARE NOT ENOUGH *novel* U.S.: Sheridan, 1940; U.K.: Boardman, 1944
Detective: O'Sullivan, newspaperman.
Problem: Death by shooting in a locked room.

O'Duffy, Eimar

1376. ✓ THE SECRET ENEMY *novel* U.K.: Bles, 1932
Detective: Roy Thacker, poet.
Problem: Disappearance of the Phantom Burglar through an open window and across a wide flower bed without leaving prints.

1377. "The Glass Panel" *short story* in "Thrills, Crimes and Mysteries" U.K.: Associated Newspapers, 1936
Detective: Bradley.
Problem: Death by stabbing in a locked room.

Olde, Nicholas (Amian Lister Champneys)

1378. "The Invisible Weapon" *short story* in "The Incredible Adventures of Rowland Hern" U.K: Heinemann, 1928; U.S. Ramble House, 2009; "Big Book of Locked-Room Mysteries", Black Lizard, 2014
Detective: Rowland Hern.
Problem: Death by blunt instrument in a completely empty room under constant observation.

Oliver, Anthony

1379. ✓ THE ELBERG COLLECTION *novel* U.K.: Heinemann, 1985; U.S.: Doubleday, 1985
Detectives: Ex-Detective Inspector John Webber and Welsh widow Lizzie Thomas.
Problem: Death by conflagration on a stretch of beach on which the victims were alone.

Olsen, Jack

1380. ✓ MISSING PERSONS *novel* U.S.: Atheneum, 1981; U.K.: Hale, 1982
Detectives: Sgt. John Boon and Officer Tally Wickham.
Problem: Disappearance of various visitors to a police building.

Oppenheim, E. Phillips

1381. SIR ADAM DISAPPEARED *novel* U.K.: Hodder, 1939; U.S.: Little, 1939
Detective: Inspector Snell.
Problem: Disappearance of an old man from a club in which he was never left alone long enough to effect an exit.

1382. ✓ "The Thirteenth Card" *short story* in "Slane's Long Shots" U.K.: Hodder, 1930, and U.S.: Little, 1930; "Fifty Famous Detectives of Fiction" U.K.: Odhams, c. 1937
Detective: Sir Jasper Slane.
Problem: Disappearance of a man from a guarded block of apartments.

Orde-Powlett, Nigel

1383. ✓ THE CAST TO DEATH *novel* U.K.: Benn, 1932; U.S.: Houghton, 1932
Detectives: Superintendent Farnis and Anthony Rillington.
Problem: Death by stabbing by a stretch of river to which all approaches were under watch.

1384. ✓ DRIVEN DEATH *novel* U.K.: Benn, 1933
Detective: Anthony Rillington.
Problem: Death of a man during a shoot when it appeared that all other parties were accounted for and could not have committed the murder.

Ormerod, Roger

1385. ✓ AN OPEN WINDOW *novel* U.K.: Constable, 1988
Detective: Ex-Detective Inspector Richard Patton.
Problem: Death by defenestration from a locked bedroom

through a conservatory roof.

1386. ✓ A SPOONFUL OF LUGER *novel* U.K.: Hale, 1975
Detective: George Coe, ex-policeman private eye.
Problem: The finding of a murder weapon in a locked box to which the only available key had been swallowed by the victim just before his death.

1387. ✓ THE WEIGHT OF EVIDENCE *novel* U.K.: Hale, 1978
Detectives: David Mallin and George Coe.
Problems: (1) Disappearance of a man from a shed, the door of which was right next to a fence.
(2) Death by shooting in a cellar bolted on the inside.

O'Rourke, Frank

1388. THE ABDUCTION OF VIRGINIA Lee *novel* U.S.: Lippincott, 1970
Detective: None.
Problem: Disappearance of a railroad car from a section of line.

Orr, Clifford

1389. THE WAILING ROCK MURDERS *novel* U.S.: Farrar, 1932; U.K.: Cassell, 1933
Detective: Spider Meech.
Problem: Death by stabbing in a locked cupola.

Ostrander, Isabel (see also Chipperfield, Robert Orr)

1390. THE CLUE IN THE AIR *novel* U.S.: Watt, 1917; U.K.: Skeffington, (1920)
Detectives: Timothy McCarty and Wade Terhune.
Problem: Death by defenestration from within a locked flat.

Oursler, Will

1391. ✓ MURDER MEMO: THE CARL HOUSTON CASE *novel* U.S.: Simon, 1950
Detective: Michael La Rue, first grade NYPD.
Problem: Death by shooting in a locked ninth-storey apartment room.

Ozaki, Milton (see also Saber, Robert O.)

1392. THE CUCKOO CLOCK *novel* U.S.: Ziff, 1946; (as "Too Many Women") Handi-Books, 1950
Detective: Professor Caldwell, head of psychology department.
Problem: Death by stabbing in a locked room.

P

Padgett, Lewis

1393. ✓ THE DAY HE DIED *novel* U.S: Duell, 1947
Detective: None.
Problem: The insertion of plagiarised paragraphs into the typescripts of an author who lived in a locked apartment to which she had the only key for the door, which was also chained.

Page, Stanley Hart

1394. FOOL'S GOLD *novel* U.S.: Knopf, 1933; U.K.: Paul, (1934)
Detective: Christopher Hand.
Problem: Death by blunt instrument in a locked laboratory.

1395. ✓ SINISTER CARGO *novel* U.S.: Knopf, 1932; U.K.: Paul, 1933
Detective: Hand.
Problem: Death by shooting in a room in which one innocent person is the only other occupant, no shots came through the open door, and therefore the fatal shot could not be accounted for.

Paige, Peter

1396. ✓ "Death Is from Hunger" *short story* in Dime Detective Magazine, April 1942; Dime Detective Magazine Canada, October 1942
Detective: Cash Wale.
Problem: Death by starvation of a woman seen to eat a large meal only hours previously.

Palmer, Stuart

1397. DEATH IN GREASE PAINT *novel* U.K.: Collins, 1956; U.S. (as "Unhappy Hooligan"): Harper, 1956
Detective: Howard Rook.
Problem: Death by shooting in a locked room.

1398. ✓ "The Monkey Murder" *short story* in EQMM, January 1947; EQMM (Australia), February 1949; "The Monkey Murder and Other Hildegarde Withers Stories" U.S.: Bestseller, 1950
Detective: Hildegarde Withers.
Problem: Death by strangling in a locked room.

1399. "The Riddle of the Yellow Canary" *short story* in Mystery, April, 1934; "Great American Detective Stories" U.S.: World, 1945; "The Riddles of Hildegarde Withers" U.S.: Jonathan, 1947
Detective: Withers.

Problem: Death by poisoning in a locked office.

Papazoglou, Orania

1400. ✓ SWEET, SAVAGE DEATH *novel* U.S.: Doubleday, 1984
Detective: Patience Campbell McKenna, romantic novelist.
Problem: Death by stabbing in a locked apartment.

Parkhill, Forbes

1401. "Partners in Disaster" *short story* in Detective Book, May 1930
Detective: Bruce Gordon.
Problem: Murder in a locked room.

Parsons, Anthony

1402. ✓ The Bad Man of Cairo *novel* SBL No. 251 (3rd Series) U.K.: Amalgamated, 1951
Detective: Sexton Blake.
Problem: Appearance of a dead body within the heavily guarded courtyard of an Egyptian university.

1403. ✓ The Harem Mystery *novel* SBL No. 671 (2nd series) U.K.: Amalgamated, 1939
Detective: Blake.
Problem: Death by stabbing of a white woman inside a harem to which all three entrances were barred.

1404. ✓ The Mystery of the Crooked Gift *novel* SBL No. 221 (3rd series) U.K.: Amalgamated, 1950
Detective: Blake.
Problem: Death by unseen hand and, at the same time and place, the rendering unconscious of a would-be assassin who was under the impression that he alone had planned the victim's death.

1405. ✓ THE RIDDLE OF THE INDIAN ALIBI *novel* SBL No. Ill (3rd series) U.K.: Amalgamated, 1946
Detective: Blake.
Problem: Death by blunt instrument, a ruler with the only fingerprints on it those of a man with the cast-iron alibi of being in a police cell.

1406. ✓ THE RIDDLE OF THE RAJAH'S CURIOS *novel* SBL No. 198 (3rd series) U.K.: Amalgamated, 1949
Detective: Blake.
Problem: The landing of a plane and subsequent almost immediate discovery that the pilot had been dead for several hours.

1407. ✓ "A Sleeping Draught" *short story* in The Strand, July 1929; "Great Short Stories of Detection, Mystery and Horror: Part V" U.K.: Gollancz, 1939
Detective: Major Coleman.
Problem: Death by strangulation in a locked room.

Paul, Barbara

1408. ✓ HE HUFFED AND HE PUFFED *novel* U.K.: Macmillan, 1989; U.S.: Scribners, 1989
Detectives: Sergeants Marian Larch and Ivan Malecki.
Problem: Death by stabbing in a locked library.

Peach, L. du Garde

1409. "The 'Mary Celeste'" *play* in "Radio Plays" U.K.: Newnes, (1931)
Problem: The "Marie Celeste" mystery.

1410. "The Perfect Alibi" *play* in "The Collected Plays of L. du Garde Peach, Volume IV" U.K.: Countrygoer, 1955
Detective: Inspector Clark.
Problem: Escape from a cell of "Ubique," an escape artist who is handcuffed, roped, etc.

Peirce, J. F.

1411. "Cassandra's Castle; or, The Devious Disappearances" *short story* in EQMM, May 1975
Detective: William Shakespeare, playwright.
Problems: Disappearance of a midget and five boy actors from a castle on a moated island under constant guard.

1412. ✓ "The Magician's Wife" *short story* in "All But Impossible!" U.S.: Ticknor, 1981
Detective: Captain Zachary.
Problem: Disappearance of a magician's female assistant from a coffin in which she had just been sawn in half.

Pelletier, Bruce D.

1413. "The Hedgehog and the Fox" *short story* in EQMM, April 1961; EQMM (UK), October 1961
Detectives: John Balfour, professor of Moral Philosophy, and Inspector Ishikawa, of the Tokyo Metropolitan Police.
Problem: Death by stabbing by invisible agent.

Pendower, Jacques

1414. ✓ OUT OF THIS WORLD *novel* U.K.: Hale, 1966
Detective: Robert Maine.

Problem: Levitation, walking on air, and disappearance in part through locked windows.

Penny, Rupert

1415. POLICEMAN'S EVIDENCE *novel* U.K.: Collins, 1938; U.S. Ramble House, 2007
Detective: Chief Inspector Beale.
Problem: Death by stabbing in a locked room.

1416. SEALED ROOM MURDER *novel* U.K.: Collins, 1941; U.S. Ramble House, 2007
Detective: Beale.
Problem: Death by stabbing in a locked room.

Pentecost, Hugh (see also Philips, Judson)

1417. THE DAY THE CHILDREN VANISHED *novel* U.S.: Pocket, 1976; U.K.: Hale, 1977
Detective: Clyde Haviland.
Problem: Disappearance of a bus from a stretch of road without exit points.

1418. "The Day the Children Vanished" *short story* in This Week Magazine, 1958; "Best American Detective Stories of the Year—Tenth Series" U.K.: Boardman, 1960; EQMM, June 1963; EQMM (UK), October 1963, EQMM (Australia), December 1963; "Ellery Queen's Anthology #25", Davis, 1973; "All But Impossible!" U.S.: Ticknor, 1981; "Murder in New England" U.S.: Castle, 1989; "Big Book of Locked-Room Mysteries", Black Lizard, 2014
Detective: Haviland.
Problem: Disappearance of a bus from a stretch of road without exit points.

Peppé, Frank

1419. ✓ THE RIDDLE IN WAX *novel* U.K.: Paget, c. 1950
Detective: Steve Bradshaw.
Problem: Disappearance of two people on whom an invisibility ray gun was trained.

Perowne, Barry

1420. "The Blind Spot" *short story* in EQMM, November 1945; EQMM "Overseas Edition for the Armed Forces", November, 1945; EQMM (Australia) October, 1947; Ellery Queen's Anthology #47", Davis, 1983; "Tantalizing Locked Room Mysteries" U.S.: Walker, 1982; "The Art of the Impossible"

U.K.: Xanadu, 1990; "Murder Impossible" U.S.: Carroll, 1990
Detective: None.
Problem: Death by stabbing in a locked room.

Perry, James D.

1421. ✓ MURDER WALKS THE CORRIDOR *novel* U.S.: Macmillan, 1937; U.K. (as "Corridor of Fear"): Constable, 1937
Detective: Dr. North.
Problem: Death of two embracing victims by electrocution in the middle of the garden of a mental hospital.

Perry, Tyline

1422. THE NEVER SUMMER MYSTERY *novel* U.S.: King, 1932
Detective: Sheriff Gus Flowers.
Problem: Death by shooting in a room under observation.

1423. THE OWNER LIES DEAD *novel* U.K.: Gollancz, 1930; U.S.: Covici, 1930
Detective: Sheriff MacFarland.
Problem: Death by shooting in a mine under constant observation.

Peters, Elizabeth

1424. ✓ "The Locked Tomb Mystery" *short story* in "Sisters in Crime" U.S.: Berkley, 1989; "Mammoth Book of Egyptian Whodunits", Carroll & Graf, 2002; "Realm of the Impossible", Locked Room International, 2017
Detective: Amenhotep Sa Hapu, Egyptian priest.
Problem: Theft of gold and other valuables from and desecration of a locked Egyptian tomb.

Peters, Steven

1425. "George Washington, Detective" *short story* in EQMM, August 1967
Detective: George Washington.
Problem: Disappearance of a spy from within a locked room.

Peterson, Charles

1426. ✓ "The Adventure of the Mocking Devil" *short story* in MSMM, January 1982
Detectives: Mr. Holbrook and Mr. Wilson, behind whose assumed names lurk two very much more illustrious.
Problem: Death by shooting on a stretch of unmarked beach.

Pettee, Florence M.

1427. ✓ THE PALGRAVE MUMMY *novel* U.K.: Skeffington, 1929;

U.S.: Payson, 1929
Detective: Digby Gresham.
Problems: (1) Change of a young woman into a likeness of a shrivelled mummy.
(2) Appearance of spots of blood on various people, including the mummy itself.

1428. ✓ "Death Laughs at Walls" *short story* in Detective Classics Magazine, January 1930; "Son of Gun in Cheek" U.S.: Mysterious, 1987
Detective: Gresham.
Problem: Death by unknown means in a locked study.

Phelan, Jeremy (C. Daly King, q.v.)

1429. ✓ "The Episode of the Perilous Talisman" *short story* in The Magazine of Fantasy & Science Fiction, February 1951; "The Complete Curious Mr. Tarrant", Crippen & Landru, 2003
Detective: Trevis Tarrant.
Problem: Deaths by unknown means when victims on their own opened a strange box found in the Great Pyramid.

Philips, Judson (see also Pentecost, Hugh)

1430. "Room Number Twenty-Three" *short story* in Flynn's, June 20, 1925; EQMM, June 1949; "Maiden Murders" U.S.: Harper, 1952, and U.K.: Hammond, 1953; "Big Book of Locked-Room Mysteries", Black Lizard, 2014
Detective: James Bellamy.
Problem: Disappearance of a woman from a hotel room under observation.

Phillips, Mark (Randall Garrett, q.v., and Laurence M. Janifer)

1431. THE IMPOSSIBLES *novel* U.S.: Pyramid, 1963
Detective: Kenneth Malone, FBI agent.
Problem: Various disappearances and thefts from locked rooms, together with Cadillacs with the apparent ability to drive themselves.

Phillpotts, Eden

1432. A CLUE FROM THE STARS *novel* U.K.: Hutchinson, (1932); U.S.: Macmillan, 1932
Detective: Inspector Thomas Warner.
Problem: Disappearance of a man—and his scent—from the middle of an open field.

1433. THE GREY ROOM *novel* U.K.: Hurst, (1921); U.S.: Macmillan,

1921

Detective: Signor Mannetti.

Problem: Death by poisoning in a locked room.

1434. THE MARYLEBONE MISER *novel* U.K.: Hutchinson, (1926); U.S. (as "Jig-Saw"): Macmillan, 1926

Detective: John Ringrose.

Problem: Death by stabbing in a locked room.

1435. ✓ A TIGER'S CUB *novel* U.K.: Arrowsmith, 1892

Detective: Richard Silver.

Problem: Disappearance of a man from inside a locked Treasure House.

1436. "The Witching Hour" *short story* in "Once Upon a Time" U.K.: Hutchinson, 1936

Detective: Inspector Edward Maine.

Problem: The movement of a corpse inside a glass-topped coffin that could only be opened from the inside, the coffin itself being inside a locked chapel.

Pierce, Frank Richardson

1437. "A Ton of Gold" *short story* in Argosy Weekly, May 20, 1939

Detective: No-Shirt McGee.

Problem: Disappearance of a ton of gold from within a moving steamship.

Pink, Hal

1438. THE RODEO MURDER MYSTERY *novel* U.K.: Hutchinson, (1941)

Detective: Inspector Docker.

Problem: Death by shooting while astride a wildly bucking bronco.

Piper, H. Beam

1439. MURDER IN THE GUNROOM *novel* U.S.: Knopf, 1953

Detective: Col. Jefferson Davis Rand.

Comment: The dust-wrapper blurb suggests that a locked-room murder by shooting is involved. However, the simple explanation is that the killer exited through another door that wasn't locked.

Platts, A. Monmouth (see also Berkeley, Anthony)

1440. ✓ CICELY DISAPPEARS *novel* U.K.: Long, 1927

Detective: Stephen Munro, temporary footman.

Problem: Disappearance of a young woman from within a blacked-out room during a séance experiment.

Pleasants, W. Shepard

1441. THE STINGAREE MURDERS *novel* U.S.: Mystery League, 1932
Detective: Paul Green.
Problems: (1) Death by stabbing of a man alone in a boat and in plain view.
(2) Disappearance of a knife plunged deep into a boat's woodwork and demonstrably not extractable by human hands.
(3) Death by drowning of a man pulled from his boat by an invisible agent.

Plum, Mary

1442. MURDER AT THE HUNTING CLUB *novel* U.K.: Eyre, 1932; U.S.: Harper, 1932
Detective: John Smith.
Problem: Death by stabbing in the centre of a lake under constant observation.

Plumptre, Anne and Annabella

1443. ✓ "The Spectre of Presburg" *novelette* in "Tales of Wonder, of Humour, and of Sentiment; Original and Translated" U.K.: Colburn, 1818
Detective: Captain Storkenheim.
Problems: (1) Disappearance from a room under constant observation of an army officer later discovered to have been killed in battle earlier.
(2) Appearance of giants in a misty mountain pass.

Plunkett, Cyril

1444. ✓ "The Guest" *short story* in EQMM, September 1944
Detectives: Joe and Jeri Jones.
Problem: Death by throttling in a locked sewing room.

Poate, Ernest M.

1445. BEHIND LOCKED DOORS *novel* U.S.: Chelsea, 1923
Detective: Dr. Bentiron.
Problem: Death by stabbing in a locked suite of rooms inhabited by the victim and a number of other people innocent of his murder.

Poe, Edgar Allan

1446. "The Murders in the Rue Morgue" *short story* in Graham's Magazine, April 1841; "Tales" U.K. and U.S.: Wiley, 1845; Scientific Detective, May, 1946; "Tantalizing Locked Room Mysteries" U.S.: Walker, 1982; "Detectives A to Z" U.S.:

Bonanza, 1985; "Big Book of Locked-Room Mysteries", Black Lizard, 2014
Detective: Chevalier C. Auguste Dupin.
Problem: Death by throttling in a locked room.

Pond, E. J.

1447. THE INCE MURDER CASE *novel* U.K.: Heritage, 1934
Detective: Inspector Wayne.
Problem: Death by shooting in a locked room.

Popplewell, Jack

1448. DEAD EASY *play* U.K.: French, 1975
Detective: Lily Piper, office cleaner.
Problem: Death by shooting in a locked room.

Porges, Arthur

1449. "Another Adventure of Stately Homes" *short story* in The Saint Mystery Magazine (UK), November 1961; The Saint Mystery Magazine, September 1964; "Three Porges Parodies and a Pastiche" U.S.: Magico, 1988; "The Adventures of Stately Homes and Sherman Horn", The Battered Silicon Despatch Box, 2008
Detective: Stately Homes.
Problem: Murder in a locked room.

1450. ✓ "The Bet" *short story* in "Alfred Hitchcock's Mystery Sampler", Davis, Fall 1966; AHMM, March 1967
Detective: Ben Joyce, insurance-claims investigator.
Problem: Death by being hit on the head by a ten-pound metal ball suspended by a wire from the ceiling but with the victim at a point where it was physically impossible, if only by a fraction of an inch, for him to be hit by the ball. No one was in the room with the victim at the time of his death.

1451. "Birds of One Feather" *short story* in AHMM, January 1963; "No Killer Has Wings"; Richard Simms, 2017
Detective: Dr. Joel Hoffman.
Problem: Death by cyanide poisoning. No apparent means of introducing the poison.

1452. ✓ "Blood Will Tell" *short story* in AHMM, February 1964; "Alfred Hitchcock's Anthology #23", Davis 1987; "Alfred Hitchcock's A Brief Darkness" U.S.: Castle, 1988; "These Daisies Told", Richard Simms, 2018
Detective: Prof. Ulysses Price Middlebie.

Problem: How to obtain a sample of blood from a murder suspect unwilling and within his rights not to give it.

1453. "Breath of Suspicion" *short story* in The Man from U.N.C.L.E. Magazine, January 1967
Detective: George Fort Elgin.
Problem: Disappearance of a ruby from an apartment under constant observation.

1454. "Coffee Break" *short story* in AHMM, July 1964; "Alfred Hitchcock's Anthology #11", Davis 1982; "The Art of the Impossible" U.K.: Xanadu, 1990; "Murder Impossible" U.S.: Carroll, 1990; "These Daisies Told"
Detective: Professor Middlebie.
Problem: Death by poisoning in a locked room.

1455. ✓ "The Cunning Cashier" *short story* in The Girl From U.N.C.L.E. Magazine, April 1967
Detective: Julian Morse Trowbridge.
Problem: Disappearance of $100,000 from a house and grounds that the money cannot have left.

1456. "Dead Drunk" *short story* in AHMM, December 1959; "Alfred Hitchcock's Grave Suspicions" U.S.: Davis, 1984; "No Killer Has Wings"
Detective: Dr. Joel Hoffman.
Problem: Death by poisoning with phosgene gas in a locked room.

1457. ✓ "The Deadly Cherub" *short story* in Shell Scott Mystery Magazine, March 1966
Detectives: Sheriff Danny Bowen and Lloyd Pearson, artist.
Problem: Death by strangulation of a big, fit man when the marks on the neck indicated that the killer was a child.

1458. "The Devil Will Surely Come" *short story* in EQMM, October 1964; EQMM (UK), February 1964, EQMM (Australia), April 1964
Detective: None.
Problem: The existence of devil's hoof prints up a sheer castle wall.

1459. ✓ "Fire for Peace" *short story* in Ed McBain's 87th Precinct Mystery Magazine, May 1975; "These Daisies Told"
Detective: Professor Middlebie.
Problem: The starting of fires in a heavily guarded plant where

chemical-warfare materials were manufactured.

1460. ✓ "First Degree Murder" *short story* in MSMM, March 1962
Detective: Dr. Alfred Lewis, pathologist.
Problem: Death by shooting when the only other person in the vicinity claimed to have been at the top of a nearby peak after a three-hour climb and produced photographs taken from the peak just after the murder.

1461. "Her Last Bow—An Adventure of Stately Homes" *short story* in EQMM, February 1957; EQMM (UK), February 1957, EQMM (Australia), April 1957; "Three Porges Parodies and a Pastiche"; "The Adventures of Stately Homes and Sherman Horn"
Detective: Stately Homes.
Problem: Death by dismemberment in a cellar concreted up apart from a hole five inches in diameter.

1462. "Horse-Collar Homicide" *short story* in AHMM, January 1960; "Alfred Hitchcock's Death Bag" U.S.: Davis, 1969; "No Killer Has Wings"
Detective: Dr. Joel Hoffman.
Problem: Death of a man by unseen agency while sticking his head through a horse collar.

1463. ✓ "The Impossible Gulf" *short story* in MSMM, October 1975
Detective: Cyriack Skinner Grey.
Problem: A dead body found in an area of ground with no marks to show how it got there.

1464. "In Compartment 813" *short story* in EQMM, June 1966; "All-Star Lineup—22nd Mystery Annual" U.S.: N.A.L, 1967; U.K.: Gollancz, 1968
Detective: Arsène Lupin.
Problem: Disappearance of a ruby from a room under constant guard.

1465. ✓ "The Indian Diamond Mystery" *short story* in EQMM (U.S.), June 1965
Detective: Celery Green.
Problem: Disappearance of a fabulous diamond from a house under surveillance.

1466. "The Invisible Tomb" *short story* in AHMM, February 1967; "Alfred Hitchcock's Anthology #14", Davis, 1983; "Alfred Hitchcock: Portals of Murder" U.S.: Galahad, 1988

Detective: Trowbridge.
Problem: Disappearance of a woman from a thoroughly searched, well-observed private house.

1467. "Lost Gun" *short story* in AHMM, May 1971; "Alfred Hitchcock's Shrouds and Pockets" U.S.: Davis, 1988
Detective: Chester Payne Middleton.
Problem: Death by shooting—but the pistol that fired the shot has disappeared.

1468. "The Missing Body" *short story* in MSMM, January 1967
Detective: Trowbridge.
Problem: Disappearance of a body from a house and plot of land from which the body could not have been removed.

1469. "The Missing Bow" *short story* in AHMM, November 1963; "Alfred Hitchcock's Mystery Sampler Fall 1964", Davis, 1964; "This Days's Evil and Other Tales of Suspense" U.S.: Four Square, 1967; "These Daisies Told"
Detective: Professor Middlebie.
Problem: Murder by arrow projected by a one-armed archer. No bow can be found in the confined area from which the arrow was projected.

1470. "A Model Crime" *short story* in AHMM, August 1964; "These Daisies Told"
Detective: Professor Middlebie.
Problem: Disappearance of transistors from a top-security establishment.

1471. "Murder of a Priest" *short story* in EQMM, September 1967
Problem solver: Lieutenant Selby.
Problem: Murder of a prisoner inside a locked, guarded prison cell.

1472. "Murder on Video Tape" *short story* in The Saint Mystery Magazine (U.K.), March 1966
Detective: Capt. Glenn Fraser.
Problem: Poisoning of an artiste on stage in view of full audience.

1473. "No Killer Has Wings" *short story* in AHMM, January 1961; "Best Detective Stories of the Year—16th Annual Collection" U.S.: Dutton, 1961; "Best American Detective Stories of the Year 1961" U.K.: Boardman, 1962; The Mammoth Book of Perfect Crimes and Impossible Mysteries", UK: Constable and

Robinson, 2006, US: Carroll and Graf, 2007; "No Killer Has Wings"
Detective: Dr. Joel Hoffman.
Problem: Murder by blunt instrument (ebony cane) on an unmarked stretch of sand.

1474. "The Puny Giant" *short story* in AHMM, November 1964; "These Daisies Told"
Detective: Professor Middlebie.
Problem: Woman killed by repeated blows with a block of concrete too heavy to lift.

1475. "A Puzzle in Sand" *short story* in AHMM, February; "No Killer Has Wings"
Detective: Dr. Joel Hoffman.
Problem: Death by shooting at close range. The only footprints belong to someone who did not kill the dead man.

1476. ✓ "The Scientist and the Exterminator" *short story* in AHMM, November 1974; "Killers at Large" U.S.: Dell, 1978; "The Curious Cases of Cyriack Skinner Grey", Richard Simms, 2009
Detective: C. S. Grey.
Problem: Death by cyanide poisoning in a strongly guarded hotel room.

1477. "The Scientist and the Invisible Safe" *short story* in MSMM, May 1967; "The Curious Cases of Cyriack Skinner Grey"
Detective: Grey.
Problem: Disappearance of a diamond from a guarded room, later minutely searched, as also is the room's only occupant.

1478. "The Scientist and the Missing Pistol" *short story* in MSMM, January 1975; "The Curious Cases of Cyriack Skinner Grey"
Detective: Grey.
Problem: Disappearance of a murder gun from a locked room containing only the victim and his killer.

1479. "The Scientist and the Multiple Murderer" *short story* in MSMM, February 1967; "The Curious Cases of Cyriack Skinner Grey"
Detective: Grey.
Problem: Death by electrocution in a rooftop swimming pool inaccessible from below.

1480. ✓ "The Scientist and the Platinum Chain" *short story* in AHMM, September 1974; "The Curious Cases of Cyriack Skinner Grey"

Detective: Grey.
Problem: Disappearance of a platinum chain from a building from which it could not have been removed.

1481. ✓ "The Scientist and the Stolen Rembrandt" *short story* in AHMM, February 1975; "Alfred Hitchcock's No Harm Undone" U.S.: Davis, 1985; "The Curious Cases of Cyriack Skinner Grey"
Detective: Grey.
Problem: Disappearance of a stolen masterpiece on board a small oceangoing vessel.

1482. ✓ "The Scientist and the Time Bomb" *short story* in AHMM, August 1974; "Alfred Hitchcock's Words of Prey" U.S.: Davis, 1986; "The Curious Cases of Cyriack Skinner Grey"
Detective: Grey.
Problem: Ability of a man, dead some fifteen years, to destroy a large building by a bomb, despite the keenest of searches to locate it.

1483. ✓ "The Scientist and the Two Thieves" *short story* in AHMM, June 1974; "The Curious Cases of Cyriack Skinner Grey"
Detective: Grey.
Problem: Disappearance of a bag of diamonds in the clutches of a thief trapped in a blind alley.

1484. "The Scientist and the Vanished Weapon" *short story* in MSMM, March 1966; "101 Mystery Stories" U.S.: Avenel, 1986; "The Curious Cases of Cyriack Skinner Grey"
Detective: Grey.
Problem: Disappearance of a gun from a room and garden under close observation.

1485. "The Scientist and the Wife Killer" *short story* in MSMM, January 1966; "The Curious Cases of Cyriack Skinner Grey"
Detective: Grey.
Problem: Death by electrocution in a locked bathroom.

1486. ✓ "The Silent Death" *short story* in MSMM, July 1968
Detective: Sheriff Gunter.
Problem: Deaths of a family of twelve in their beds by unknown means.

1487. "A Sticky Case" *short story* in MSMM, April 1967
Detective: Trowbridge.
Problem: Disappearance of a murder gun from guarded murder room.

1488. "The Symmetrical Murder" *short story* in AHMM, December 1964; "These Daisies Told"
Detective: Professor Middlebie.
Problem: Murder by blunt instrument on a roofed balcony. The doors leading to the balcony were locked. The balcony was twenty feet above the ground and inaccessible.

1489. "These Daisies Told" *short story* in AHMM, December 1962; "Alfred Hitchcock Presents: I Am Curious (Bloody)" U.S.: Dell, 1971; "These Daisies Told"
Detective: Middlebie.
Problem: Disappearance of a woman's body from within the confines of a guarded room.

1490. "To Barbecue a White Elephant" *short story* in AHMM, October 1964; "These Daisies Told"
Detective: Middlebie.
Problem: Fire started by an arsonist six weeks after a house was securely locked and barred.

1491. ✓ "The Unguarded Path" *short story* in MSMM, January 1963; "These Daisies Told"
Detective: Middlebie.
Problem: Attempted murder by a syndicate hit man of a witness under constant guard in a house-fortress.

1492. "The Unnatural Cause" *short story* in Tightrope Magazine, June 1960
Detectives: Lieutenant Benn and Peter Loret, pathologist.
Problem: Severe disability induced in an office under surveillance.

1493. "The Unsolvable Crime" *short story* in EQMM, March 1964; EQMM (UK), July 1964; EQMM (Australia), September, 1964
Detective: Captain Corbett (retired).
Problem: Disappearance of a special powdered form of platinum from a guarded area where all entrances and exits are monitored.

Porlock, Martin (Philip MacDonald, q.v.)

1494. MYSTERY AT FRIAR'S PARDON *novel* U.K.: Collins, 1931; U.S.: Doubleday, 1932
Detective: Charles Fox-Browne.
Problem: Death by drowning in a locked room.

Post, Melville Davisson

1495. "The Bradmoor Murder" *short story* in "The Garden in Asia" U.K.: Brentanos, 1929; "The Bradmoor Murder" U.S.: Sears, 1929; Great Detective, June 1933; "Big Book of Locked-Room Mysteries", Black Lizard, 2014
Detective: Henry Marquis.
Problem: Death by shooting in a locked room.

1496. "The Doomdorf Mystery" *short story* in "Uncle Abner" U.S.: Appleton, 1918, and U.K.: Tom Stacey, 1972; "The Detective in Fiction" U.K.: Bell, 1931; "The Locked Room Reader" U.S.: Random House, 1968; "8 Keys to Murder" U.S.: Dell, 1970; "The Complete Uncle Abner" U.S.: The Mystery Library, (1977); "Great American Mystery Stories of the Twentieth Century" U.S.: Franklin, 1989; "The Mammoth Book of Locked-Room Mysteries and Impossible Crimes", UK: Constable and Robinson, 2000, US: Carroll and Graf; "Big Book of Locked-Room Mysteries", Black Lizard, 2014
Detective: Uncle Abner.
Problem: Death by shooting in a locked room.

1497. "The Garden in Asia" *short story* in "The Garden in Asia" and "The Bradmoor Murder"
Detective: Henry Marquis (?).
Problem: Disappearance of a locomotive from within a collapsed tunnel.

1498. "The Hidden Law" *short story* in Metropolitan Magazine, August 1914; "Uncle Abner, Master of Mysteries" U.S.: Appleton, 1918, and U.K.: Tom Stacey, 1972; The Saint Mystery Magazine, September, 1959; "The Complete Uncle Abner"; "Realm of the Impossible", Locked Room International, 2017
Detective: Uncle Abner.
Problem: Disappearance of a miser's gold pieces from within a locked house.

1499. "The Nameless Thing" *short story* in "The Nameless Thing" U.S.: Appleton, 1912
Detectives: Judge Flint, Father Jerome, and Dr. Lennard.
Problem: Death by blunt instrument in a locked room.

Post, Roy, and Austin Ripley

1500. "The Case of the Missing Knife" *short story* in EQMM, January

1943
Detective: Professor Fordney.
Problem: Disappearance of a murder knife from a train car under guard.

Powell, Talmage

1501. ✓ "The Disappearance of Maggie" *short story* in "Dark Lessons" U.S.: Macmillan, 1984
Detective: Sheriff David Landsburg.
Problem: Disappearance of a child from a school bus.

Pratt, Fletcher

1502. DOUBLE JEOPARDY *novel* U.S.: Doubleday, 1952
Detective: Agent George Helmfleet Jones.
Problem: Theft of a large sum of money during the flight of a sealed rocket in which no man could survive.

Priestley, J. B.

1503. MYSTERY AT GREENFINGERS *play* U.K. and U.S.: French, 1937
Detective: Robert Crowther.
Problem: Disappearance of a woman from a locked room.

Pronzini, Bill (See also Davis, Robert Hart)

1504. ✓ BONES *novel* U.S.: St. Martin's, 1985
Detective: Nameless.
Problem: Death by shooting in a locked study.

1505. ✓ HOODWINK *novel* U.S.: St. Martin's, 1981; U.K.: Hale, 1987
Detective: Nameless.
Problems: (1) Death by shooting in a locked hotel room.
(2) Death by axe wound in a locked shed.

1506. ✓ SCATTERSHOT *novel* U.S.: St. Martin's, 1982
Detective: Nameless.
Problems: (1) Death by stabbing in a locked car under constant observation.
(2) Death by shooting in a cottage where all exits were either locked or under constant observation.
(3) Theft of a ring from a locked room under constant guard and where, after the theft, a broken window indicated that it had been broken from the inside.

1507. ✓ "Ace in the Hole" *short story* in "Mean Streets" U.S.: Mysterious, 1986
Detective: Nameless.

Problem: Disappearance of a gun and some incriminating documents from a locked room in which the killer and victim were still inside.

1508. "An Almost Perfect Hiding Place" *short story* in MSMM, October 1969
Detective: Boone.
Problem: Disappearance of murder gun from a guarded murder room.

1509. "The Arrowmont Prison Riddle" *short story* in AHMM, October 1976; "All But Impossible!" U.S.: Ticknor, 1981; "Alfred Hitchcock Tales of Terror" U.S.: Galahad, 1986
Detective: Buckmaster Gilloon.
Problem: Disappearance of a man/corpse from the end of a gallows drop under constant observation.

1510. ✓ "Booktaker" *short story* in "Case File" U.S.: St. Martin's, 1983; "Locked Room Puzzles" U.S.: Academy, 1986
Detective: Nameless.
Problem: Theft of valuable maps and documents from a bookstore protected by an electronic surveillance system.

1511. ✓ "Cat's-Paw" *short story* U.S.: Waves Press, 1983; "Graveyard Plots" U.S.: St. Martin's, 1985; "Spadework", Crippen & Landru, 1996
Detective: Nameless.
Problem: Death by shooting in a locked animal cage inside a zoo's lion house under constant observation.

1512. ✓ "Dead Man's Slough" *short story* in AHMM, May 21, 1980; "Case File"
Detective: Nameless.
Problem: Disappearance of a man seen to wade out to a small, uninhabited island.

1513. ✓ "A Killing in Xanadu" *short story* U.S.: Waves Press, 1980; "Detectives A to Z" U.S.: Bonanza, 1985
Detective: Nameless.
Problem: Death by shooting in a cottage where all exits were either locked or under constant observation.

1514. ✓ "A Nice Easy Job" *short story* in EQMM, November 1979
Detective: Nameless.
Problem: Theft of a ring from a locked room under constant guard and where, after the theft, a broken window indicated that

it had been broken from the inside.

1515. ✓ "The Perfect Crime" *short story* in MSMM, July 1968
Detective: Sheriff Aubrey Canfield.
Problem: Death by defenestration from an upper window of a locked house.

1516. ✓ "The Private Eye Who Collected Pulps" *short story* in EQMM, February 1979; (as "The Pulp Connection") in "Case File"; "The Mammoth Book of Locked-Room Mysteries and Impossible Crimes", UK: Constable and Robinson, 2000, US: Carroll and Graf
Detective: Nameless.
Problem: Death by stabbing in a locked room.

1517. "Proof of Guilt" *short story* in EQMM, December 1973; "Graveyard Plots" U.S.: St. Martin's, 1990; "The Art of the Impossible" U.K.: Xanadu, 1990; "Murder Impossible" U.S.: Carroll, 1990; The Mammoth Book of Perfect Crimes and Impossible Mysteries", U.K.: Constable and Robinson, 2006, U.S.: Carroll and Graf, 2007
Detectives: Jack Sherrard and his partner, the narrator.
Problem: Death by shooting in a guarded room in which the victim and one other person, but no weapon, were found.

1518. ✓ "Something Wrong" *short story* in "Small Felonies" U.S.: St. Martin's, 1988
Detective: Nameless.
Problem: Planting of explosives in a locked and barred apartment.

1519. ✓ "The Terrarium Principle" *short story* in EQMM, April 22, 1987; "Small Felonies"
Detectives: Jerry and Andrea Parker.
Problem: Disappearance of a gun from a room in which it had just been used to kill a man.

1520. ✓ "Thin Air" *short story* in AHMM, May 1979; "Death Locked In" U.S.: IPL, 1987
Detective: Nameless.
Problem: Death by stabbing in a closed car under constant observation.

1521. ✓ "Where Have You Gone, Sam Spade?" *short story* in AHMM, Jan. 30, 1980; "Case File"; "Big Book of Locked-Room Mysteries", Black Lizard, 2014

Detective: Nameless.
Problem: Death by shooting in a locked warehouse.

Pronzini, Bill, and Jeffrey Wallmann

1522. "The Half-Invisible Man" *short story* in EQMM, May 1974; "Great Modern Police Stories" U.S.: Walker, 1986
Detective: Patrolman Fred Gallagher.
Problem: Death by shooting in a locked motel room.

Pronzini, Bill, and Marcia Muller

1523. ✓ "Cache and Carry" *short story* in "Small Felonies" U.S.: St. Martin's, 1988
Detectives: Sharon McCone and Nameless.
Problem: Theft and disappearance of cash from an office under continuous surveillance.

Pronzini, Bill, and Michael Kurland

1524. ✓ "Vanishing Act" *short story* in AHMM, January 1976; "Tantalizing Locked Room Mysteries" U.S.: Walker, 1982; "Deadly Arts" U.S.: Arbor, 1985
Detective: Christopher Steele, magician.
Problem: Disappearance of a man from a dressing-room under observation.

Pruyn, Leonard

1525. "Dinner at Garibaldi's" *short story* in Malcolm's, March 1954; "The Art of the Impossible" U.K.: Xanadu, 1990; "Murder Impossible" U.S.: Carroll, 1990
Detective: Joachim Andreas.
Problem: Death of a prominent gourmet by starvation.

Puccetti, Roland

1526. THE TRIAL OF JOHN AND HENRY NORTON *novel* U.K.: Hutchinson, 1973
Detective: Harvey Shapman, lawyer.
Problem: (non-impossible) Death by blunt instrument in a locked house protected by a burglar-alarm system when only the victim and one other innocent person were present.

Punshon, E. R.

1527. SIX WERE PRESENT *novel* U.K.: Gollancz, 1956
Detective: Bobby Owen.
Problem: Death by stabbing around a darkened séance table where no one appeared to have possessed a weapon or to be near enough to have used it.

Q

Queen, Ellery

1528. THE AMERICAN GUN MYSTERY *novel* U.K.: Gollancz, 1933; U.S.: Stokes, 1933
Detective: Ellery Queen.
Problem: Disappearance of a murder gun from a sportsdome at which every person is carefully searched.

1529. THE CHINESE ORANGE MYSTERY *novel* U.K.: Gollancz, 1934; U.S.: Stokes, 1934
Detective: Queen.
Problem: Death by blunt instrument in a room with a locked door.

1530. THE DOOR BETWEEN *novel* U.K.: Gollancz, 1937; U.S.: Stokes, 1937
Detective: Queen.
Problem: Death by stabbing in a room under constant observation.

1531. ELLERY QUEEN, MASTER DETECTIVE *novel* U.S.: Grosset, 1941; U.S. (as "The Vanishing Corpse"): Pyramid, 1968
Detective: Queen.
Problem: Death by stabbing in a guarded room.

1532. THE KING IS DEAD *novel* U.K.: Gollancz, 1952; U.S.: Little, 1952
Detective: Queen.
Problem: Wounding by shooting in a locked strong room. Both occupants and the room were thoroughly searched without success.

1533. "The Adventure of the Dead Man's Cavern" *radio play* 1944
Detective: Queen.
Problem: Death by strangulation in a cave at the entrance to which were a door to which only the victim had a key and à patch of soft mud that bore only the victim's footprints. The only other exit was a window at the rear that was inaccessible from every outside direction.

1534. "The Adventure of the Frightened Star" *play* in EQMM, Spring 1942
Detective: Queen.

Problem: Death by shooting in a locked bungalow.

1535. "The Adventure of the House of Darkness" *short story* in American Magazine, February 1935; "The New Adventures of Ellery Queen" U.K.: Gollancz, 1940; U.S.: Stokes, 1940
Detective: Queen.
Problem: Death by accurate shooting in a pitch-black room.

1536. "The Adventure of the Man Who Could Double the Size of Diamonds" *short play* in EQMM, May 1943; "Death Locked In" U.S.: IPL, 1987; "The Adventure of the Murdered Moths and Other Mysteries"; Crippen & Landru, 2005
Detective: Queen.
Problem: Theft of diamonds from a strong room, the only occupant of which has been rigorously searched.

1537. "The Adventure of the Meanest Man in the World" *play* in EQMM, July 1942
Detective: Queen.
Problem: Death by stabbing in a room under constant observation.

1538. "The Adventure of the One-Legged Man" *play* in EQMM, November 1943
Detective: Queen.
Problem: Tracks made in the snow by a one-legged man apparently without a stick or crutch and inside an electrically fenced area.

1539. "The Dauphin's Doll" *short story* in (as "With the Compliments of Comus") EQMM, December 1948; "Calendar of Crime" U.K.: Gollancz, 1952, and U.S.: Little, 1952; "The Twelve Crimes of Christmas" U.S.: Avon, 1981
Detective: Queen.
Problem: Theft of a doll and diamond from a tightly guarded display stand in a department store.

1540. "The Disappearance of Mr. James Phillimore" *short story* in "The Misadventures of Sherlock Holmes" U.S.: Little, 1944
Detective: Ellery Queen.
Problem: Disappearance of a man from a house under close and constant observation.

1541. "Double Your Money" *short story* in (as "The Vanishing Wizard") This Week, Sept. 30, 1951; EQMM, September 1955; "Q.B.I.: Queen's Bureau of Investigation" U.K.: Gollancz,

1955, and U.S.: Little, 1955
Detective: Queen.
Problem: Disappearance of a man from a locked and guarded office.

1542. "E = Murder" *short story* in EQMM, May 1961; "Queens Full" U.S.: Random, 1965, and U.K.: Gollancz, 1966; "With Malice Toward All" U.S.: Putnam, 1968, and U.K.: Macmillan, 1969; "101 Mystery Stories" U.S.: Avenel, 1986
Detective: Queen.
Problem: Death by stabbing in a guarded suite.

1543. "The Lamp of God" *short story* in (as "The House of Haunts") Detective Story, November 1935; "The New Adventures of Ellery Queen"; "Detectives A to Z" U.S.: Bonanza, 1985; "Big Book of Locked-Room Mysteries", Black Lizard, 2014
Detective: Queen.
Problem: Disappearance of a house from open countryside.

1544. "Object Lesson" *short story* in (as "The Blackboard Gangsters") in The Saturday Evening Post, Sept. 11, 1955; (as "Kid Stuff') in "For Love or Money" U.S.: Doubleday, 1957, and U.K.: MacDonald, 1959; "Q.E.D.: Queen's Experiments in Detection" U.S.: N.A.L., 1968, and U.K.: Gollancz, 1969; "Masterpieces of Mystery: Choice Cuts" U.S.: Davis, 1979
Detective: Queen.
Problem: Theft of seven dollar bills from a classroom in which all places and persons are searched.

1545. "Snowball in July" *short story* in "Q.B.I.: Queen's Bureau of Investigation"; previously in EQMM, July 1956; originally (as "The Phantom Train") in This Week, Aug. 31, 1952; "All But Impossible!" U.S.: Ticknor, 1981
Detective: Queen.
Problem: Disappearance of a train from an area of track under surveillance.

1546. "The Three Widows" *short story* in (as "Murder Without Clues") in This Week, Jan. 29,1950; EQMM, January 1952; "Q.B.I.: Queen's Bureau of Investigation"; "Masterpieces of Mystery: The Grand Masters Up to Date" U.S.: Davis, 1979
Detective: Queen.
Problem: Death by poisoning in a guarded bedroom where all foodstuffs, toothpaste, etc., are carefully examined before

consumption/use.

1547. "The Case of His Headless Highness" *jigsaw puzzle* U.S.: Janus Games, 1973
Detective: Ellery Queen.
Problem: Death by beheading in a locked room belonging to a recluse.

"Queen, Ellery" (house name; now known to be by John Holbrook Vance)

1548. A ROOM TO DIE IN *novel* U.S.: Pocket, 1965; U.K.: Kinnell, 1987
Detectives: Inspector Tarr and Ann Nelson.
Problem: Death by shooting in a locked study.

Quin, B. G.

1549. THE PHANTOM MURDERER *novel* U.K.: Hutchinson, (1932)
Detective: Clarkson-Perry.
Problem: Death by shooting in a locked room.

Quinn, Jake

1550. THE UNDERTAKER *novel* U.S.: Leisure, 1974
Detective: Shannon.
Problem: A vanisher novel in which seven famous blonde beauties mysteriously disappear. In fact, they have been kidnapped and transported to a Caribbean island from which they are eventually rescued by our hero—after the inevitable preliminaries.

Quiroule, Pierre (W.W. Sayer)

1551. THE CASE OF THE BISMARCK MEMOIRS *novel* U.K.: Fleetway, 1966
Detective: Sexton Blake.
Problem: Death by shooting in a room under observation.

1552. "The Clayton Moat Mystery" *novelette* in The Union Jack No. 1103 (Nov. 29, 1924)
Detective: Granite Grant of the Secret Service.
Problem: Death by shooting in a locked room.

1553. "The Mystery of the Random Bullet" *novelette* in The Union Jack No. 1087 (Aug. 9, 1924)
Detectives: Granite Grant and Sexton Blake.
Problem: Death by shooting in a room under observation.

R

Radcliffe, Ann

1554. ✓ THE MYSTERIES OF UDOLPHO *novel* U.K.: Wogan, 1794
Detective: None.
Problem: Disappearance of a man from within a locked room.

Radford, E. and M. A.

1555. ✓ DEATH OF A FRIGHTENED EDITOR *novel* U.K.: Hale, 1959
Detective: Dr. Manson.
Problem: Death by strychnine poisoning, which acts within fifteen minutes of swallowing, when the victim had eaten or drunk nothing for an hour.

1556. ✓ WHO KILLED DICK WHITTINGTON? *novel* U.S.: Melrose, 1947
Detective: Chief Detective Inspector Dr. Manson.
Problem: Death of an actress on stage alone apart from her stage cat.

1557. ✓ Chapters 2-5 *short story* in "Death and the Professor" U.K.: Hale, 1961
Detectives: Prof. Marcus Stubbs and the other members of the Dilettantes' Club.
Problem: Death by shooting in a locked room.

1558. ✓ Chapters 6-9 *short story* in "Death and the Professor"
Detectives: Stubbs and the Dilettantes' Club.
Problem: Death from poisoning of a man who drank coffee from the same source and ate one half of a bisected sandwich while his companion did exactly the same and was unaffected.

1559. ✓ Chapters 10-15 *short story* in "Death and the Professor"
Detectives: Stubbs and the Dilettantes' Club.
Problem: Death of four men by morphine poisoning in a room guarded on the outside and where the only consumables present—liquor, water, and oranges—contained no poison.

1560. ✓ Chapters 16-19 *short story* in "Death and the Professor"
Detectives: Stubbs and the Dilettantes' Club.
Problem: Death by induced heart attack in a locked railway-carriage compartment.

1561. ✓ Chapters 25-29 *short story* in "Death and the Professor"
Detectives: Stubbs and the Dilettantes' Club.
Problem: The inexplicable falling asleep of various persons, thus allowing various crimes, usually theft, to take place.

1562. ✓ Chapters 30-33 *short story* in "Death and the Professor"
Detectives: Stubbs and the Dilettantes' Club.
Problem: Death by strangulation in a guarded apartment.

1563. ✓ Chapters 34-38 *short story* in "Death and the Professor"
Detectives: Stubbs and the Dilettantes' Club.
Problem: A victim proved at post mortem to have died at 7:30 p.m. was seen alive three hours later.

Radnor, Alan

1564. THE CASE OF THE VANISHING HOUSE *novel* U.K.: Star, 1978
Detectives: Dick Barton, special agent, Snowey White, and Jock Anderson.
Problem: Disappearance of a house.

Rafferty, S. S.

1565. "Murder by Scalping or The Invisible Indian" *short story* in EQMM, July 1973; "Tricks and Treats" U.S.: Doubleday, 1976; "Ellery Queen's Anthology, Fall-Winter 1982" U.S.: Davis, 1982
Detective: Captain Cork.
Problem: Death by scalping in a cabin under constant observation.

Raison, Milton M.

1566. MURDER IN A LIGHTER VEIN *novel* U.S.: Murray, 1947
Detective: Tony Woolrich, drama critic.
Problem: Death of a man alone at a microphone.

Randall, William R.

1567. ✓ THE SYNDICATE MURDERS *novel* U.S.: Greenberg, 1935
Detective: Mortimer Drexel, newspaper reporter.
Problem: Death from unknown means, in front of witnesses, and according to a prediction.

Rawson, Clayton (see also Towne, Stuart)

1568. DEATH FROM A TOP HAT *novel* U.K.: Collins, 1938; U.S.: Putnam, 1938
Detective: The Great Merlini.
Problems: (1) Death by strangulation in a locked room (twice). (2) Disappearance from a taxi under surveillance.

1569. THE FOOTPRINTS ON THE CEILING *novel* U.K.: Collins, 1939; U.S.: Putnam, 1939
Detective: Merlini.
Problems: (1) Footprints on the ceiling of the room where the

corpse is discovered.

(2) Bullet apparently fired around a corner.

1570. THE HEADLESS LADY *novel* U.S.: Putnam, 1940; U.K.: Collins, 1942

Detective: Merlini.

Problem: Escape from an electrically controlled double-locked prison cell.

1571. NO COFFIN FOR THE CORPSE *novel* U.S.: Little, 1942; U.K.: Stacey, 1972

Detective: Merlini.

Problem: Death by shooting in a guarded room. One witness was present—but no weapon.

1572. "The Clue of the Broken Legs" *short story* in EQMM, January and April, 1947; "The Great Merlini" U.S.: Gregg, 1979; "The Compleat Great Merlini Saga"; Battered Silicon Despatch Box;

Detective: Merlini.

Problem: Death by shooting in a room with locked windows and a guarded door.

1573. "From Another World" *short story* in EQMM, June 1948; "The Quintessence of Queen: A Magnum of Mysteries" U.S.: Random, 1962, and U.K.: Gollancz, 1963; "Whodunit? Houdini?" U.S.: Harper, 1977; "The Great Merlini"; "All But Impossible!" U.S.: Ticknor, 1981; "Locked Room Puzzles" U.S.: Academy, 1986; "The Compleat Great Merlini Saga"

Detective: Merlini.

Problem: Death by stabbing in a locked room to which all doors and windows were sealed with tape.

1574. "Merlini and the Vanished Diamonds" *short story* in EQMM, October 1955; EQMM, November 1970; "The Great Merlini"; "The Compleat Great Merlini Saga"

Detective: Merlini.

Problem: Disappearance of diamonds from a ship's cabin under constant observation.

1575. "Miracles—All in the Day's Work" *short story* in EQMM, October 1958; "14th Mystery Annual" U.S.: Random, 1959; "Ellery Queen's Choice 14th Series" U.K.: Collins, 1961; "The Great Merlini"; "The Compleat Great Merlini Saga"

Detective: Merlini.

Problem: Death by stabbing in an office under constant

observation.

1576. "Nothing Is Impossible" *short story* in EQMM, July 1958; "The Locked Room Reader" U.S.: Random, 1968; "8 Keys to Murder" U.S.: Dell, 1970; "The Great Merlini"; "Big Book of Locked-Room Mysteries", Black Lizard, 2014; "The Compleat Great Merlini Saga"
Detective: Merlini.
Problem: Death by shooting in a locked room containing an unconscious nude man but no murder weapon.

1577. "Off the Face of the Earth" *short story* in EQMM, September 1949; "The Queen's Awards Fourth Series" U.S.: Little, 1949, and U.K.: Gollancz, 1951; "Butcher, Baker, Murder-Maker" U.S.: Knopf, 1954, and U.K.: Macdonald, 1956; "The Great Merlini"; "Death Locked In" U.S.: IPL, 1987; "The Mammoth Book of Locked-Room Mysteries and Impossible Crimes", UK: Constable and Robinson, 2000, US: Carroll and Graf; "The Compleat Great Merlini Saga"
Detective: Merlini.
Problem: Disappearance of a man from a phone booth under constant observation.

1578. "The World's Smallest Locked Room" *short story* in EQMM, August 1971; "The Great Merlini"; "The Compleat Great Merlini Saga"
Detective: Merlini.
Problem: Poisoning during a meal at which none of the suspects touched the victim's food and drink.

Reed, P. Lea

1579. ✓ WHAT KILLED CHRISTOPHER SCAMMELL? *novel* U.K.: Bear, 1945
Detective: Valence Lane.
Problem: Death by unknown means (not poison) in a board-room meeting.

Rees, Arthur J.

1580. THE MOON ROCK *novel* U.K.: Lane, 1922; U.S.: Dodd, 1922
Detective: Detective Barrant of Scotland Yard.
Problem: Death by shooting in a locked room.

Reeve, Arthur B.

1581. "The Mystic Poisoner" *short story* in "The Treasure-Train" U.S.: Harper, 1917; U.K.: Collins, 1920

Detective: Craig Kennedy.
Problem: Death by poisoning in a locked room.

Reeves, John

1582. ✓ MURDER WITH MUSKETS *novel* U.S.: Doubleday, 1985
Detectives: Inspector Andrew Coggin and Sgt. Fred Sump.
Problem: Death by shooting by invisible agent while on stage in the execution scene from Tosca.

Reid, Allen F.

1583. "The Model Murder" *short story* in EQMM, May 1950
Detective: Lieutenant Blanchard.
Problem: Death by strangulation in a locked room.

Reid, Desmond (house name, Michael Moorcock)

1584. CARIBBEAN CRISIS *novel* U.K.: SBL No. 501 (4th series) U.K.: Amalgamated, 1962
Detective: Sexton Blake.
Problem: Death by stabbing in a submerged diving bell from which the other occupant had disappeared.

Reid, John

1585. ✓ "The Magician Kills" *short story* in "The Magician Kills and The Coffin Mystery" U.K.: Stockwell, 1942
Detective: Inspector Roseworth.
Problem: Disappearance of a man from within a locked room.

Reilly, Helen

1586. DEAD MAN CONTROL *novel* U.S.: Doubleday, 1936; U.K: Heinemann, 1937
Detective: Inspector Christopher McKee.
Problem: Death by shooting in a locked room in which an innocent person is also found.

Remenham, John

1587. SEA GOLD *novel* U.K.: Skeffington, (1930)
Detective: Inspector Badger.
Comment: Of relevance here because a murder is committed (by pouring molten gold down the victim's throat) after the room has been penetrated by unlocking the door lock with a key and drawing the bolts by means of looped wire pushed through holes bored through the door. Thus the problem is the reverse of the normal one. The author writes mystery and adventure stories, as opposed to detective stories, and on the strength of this one writes them very well.

Renard, Maurice

1588. ✓ THE SNAKE OF LUVERCY *novel* U.S.: Dutton, 1930
Detective: Jean Mareuil.
Problem: Death by snake bite inside a locked bedroom.

Resnicow, Herbert

1589. ✓ THE DEAD ROOM *novel* U.S.: Dodd, 1987
Detectives: Ed and Warren Baer.
Problem: Death by stabbing in the upper level of an anechoic chamber, the entrance to which at upper level was under constant observation and where the victim could not be reached by anyone on the lower level. The lower and upper levels were divided by a rope mesh floor.

1590. ✓ THE GOLD CURSE *novel* U.S.: St. Martin's, 1986
Detectives: Alexander and Norma Gold.
Problem: Death by stabbing of an opera singer on a darkened stage set under constant audience view and with all others on stage accounted for.

1591. ✓THE GOLD DEADLINE *novel* U.S.: St. Martin's, 1984; U.K.: Hale, 1985
Detectives: Alexander and Norma Gold.
Problem: Death by stabbing in a theatre box under constant guard.

1592. ✓ THE GOLD FRAME *novel* U.S.: St. Martin's, 1984; U.K.: Hale, 1986
Detectives: Alexander and Norma Gold.
Comment: At a point in the story reference is made to the murder being "impossible." In fact, it isn't, though in many ways I found it the most enjoyable of the Gold stories (to date).

1593. ✓ THE GOLD GAMBLE *novel* U.S.: St. Martin's, 1988
Detectives: Alexander and Norma Gold.
Problem: Death by asphyxiation of a victim in a theatre dining room on a floor on which only she and one other innocent person were believed to be. The theatre doorman monitored all other comings and goings and saw no one.

1594. ✓ THE GOLD SOLUTION *novel* U.S.: St. Martin's, 1983; U.K.: Hale, 1984
Detectives: Alexander and Norma Gold.
Problem: Death by stabbing in a locked, impenetrable studio at the top of a townhouse.

Rhode, John (see also Burton, Miles)

1595. DEATH IN HARLEY STREET *novel* U.K.: Bles, 1946; U.S.: Dodd, 1946

Detective: Dr. Priestley.

Problem: Death by poisoning in a dispensary under constant observation.

1596. INVISIBLE WEAPONS *novel* U.K.: Collins, 1938; U.S.: Dodd, 1938

Detective: Priestley.

Problem: Death by blunt instrument in a guarded bathroom.

1597. POISON FOR ONE *novel* U.K.: Collins, 1934; U.S.: Dodd, 1934

Detective: Priestley.

Problem: Death by poison in a locked room.

1598. TRAGEDY AT THE UNICORN *novel* U.K.: Bles, 1928; U.S.: Dodd, 1928

Detective: Priestley.

Problem: Death by poison in a locked room.

1599. TWICE DEAD *novel* U.K.: Bles, 1960; U.S.: Dodd, 1960

Detective: Priestley.

Problem: Death by carbon-monoxide poisoning in a locked house containing innocent persons only.

Rice, Craig

1600. THE BIG MIDGET MURDERS *novel* U.S.: Simon, 1942

Detectives: John J. Malone, lawyer, and Jake and Helene Justus.

Problem: Disappearance of a midget's body from within a locked bull-fiddle case.

1601. "And Be Merry" *short story* in Manhunt, January 1954, Manhunt (UK), August 1954; Bloodhound Detective Story Magazine, May 1962

Detective: John J. Malone.

Problem: Death by poisoning in a locked room.

1602. "His Heart Could Break" *short story* in EQMM, March 1943; "To the Queen's Taste" U.S.: Little, 1946, and U.K.: Faber, 1949; EQMM (Australia), August, 1947; Verdict, June 1953, Verdict (UK), August, 1953; "The Name Is Malone" U.S.: Pyramid, 1958; The Saint Mystery Magazine, June, 1959; Edgar Wallace Mystery Magazine (US) March 1966; "The Locked Room Reader" U.S.: Random, 1968; "8 Keys to Murder" U.S.: Dell, 1970; "Murder and Mystery in Chicago" U.S.:

December, 1987
Detective: Malone.
Problem: Death by hanging in a locked cell.

1603. "One More Clue" *short story* in Manhunt, April 1958; "Best Detective Stories of the Year 14th Annual Collection" U.S.: Dutton, 1959; "Best American Detective Stories of the Year — Tenth Series" U.K.: Boardman, 1960; "Perfect Crime" U.S.: St. Martin's, 1989
Detective: Malone.
Problem: Death by gassing in a locked room.

Rich, Arthur T.

1604. THE CURATE FINDS THE CORPSE *novel* U.K.: Bear, 1945
Detective: Inspector Lightfoot.
Problem: Death by shooting in a locked room.

Rich, Willard

1605. BRAIN-WAVES AND DEATH *novel* U.S.: Scribners, 1940
Detective: Inspector Noonan.
Problem: Death by poisoning (two) in locked or guarded rooms.

Richardson, H. M.

1606. ✓ THE ROCK OF JUSTICE *novel* U.K.: Hutchinson, 1928
Detective: Robert Hutch.
Problem: Death by hanging in a locked room.

Richmond, Grace

1607. ✓ NURSE HANSON'S STRANGE CASE *novel* U.K.: Hale, 1987
Detective: Sally Hanson, nurse.
Problem: Opening of windows in a locked bedroom.

Rinehart, Mary Roberts

1608. HAUNTED LADY *novel* U.K.: Cassell, 1942; U.S.: Farrar, 1942
Detective: Policewoman Hilda Adams.
Problem: Death by stabbing in a room under guard.

Ritchie, Jack

1609. "Box in a Box" *short story* in AHMM, October 1977; "All But Impossible!" U.S.: Ticknor, 1981; "The Adventures of Henry Turnbuckle" U.S.: Southern Illinois University, 1987
Detectives: Ralph and the sergeant.
Problem: Death by shooting in a locked bedroom.

1610. "Pearls Before Wine" *short story* in MSMM, August 1968
Detective: Inspector Murdock.
Problem: Disappearance of pearls from a room suddenly

plunged momentarily into darkness.

1611. "Swing High" *short story* in AHMM, May 1965; "Little Boxes of Bewilderment" U.S.: St. Martin's, 1989
Detective: Unnamed police lieutenant, the narrator.
Problem: Death by defenestration where the body is found beneath a line of closed windows.

Robbins, Alan

1612. ✓ MURDER IN A LOCKED BOX *novel* U.S.: Ballantine, 1989
Detective: The reader.
Problem: Death of the Great Baldini, a magician, by drowning in a sack in a crate in a trunk while attempting to perform his triple-escape act. The impossibility was how did someone else manage to influence what went on inside those items during the attempt.

Robbins, Grenville

1613. ✓ "The Broadcast Body" *short story* in 20-Story Magazine, June 1936
Detective: Henry.
Problem: Disappearance of a professor from a guarded room in which he was carrying out a matter-transference experiment.

1614. "The Broadcast Murder" *short story* in "The Best Detective Stories of the Year 1929" U.K.: Faber, 1930
Detective: William Garland.
Problem: Death by strangulation and subsequent disappearance of a man from a locked broadcasting studio.

Roberts, Lee

1615. THE PALE DOOR *novel* U.S.: Dodd, 1955; U.K.: Foulsham, 1956
Detective: Chad Proctor, tough guy.
Problem: The synopsis to the British edition states "the murder had been committed in a house under constant guard." The synopsis writer, alas, had evidently not read the book, which is very routine.

Roberts, W. Adolphe

1616. ✓ THE HAUNTING HAND *novel* U.K.: Hutchinson, 1926; U.S.: Macaulay, 1926
Detectives: Margot Anstruther and Gene Valery.
Problem: Disappearance of a hand and arm that reached out from under a bed and could then not be found.

Robertson, Colin

1617. GHOST FINGERS *novel* U.K.: Ward, 1941
Detective: Mike Reed, newspaperman.
Problem: Death by gassing in a locked room.

1618. THE STALKING STRANGER *novel* U.K.: Ward, 1939
Detective: Chief Inspector John Martin.
Problem: Death by gassing in a locked bedroom.

Robertson, Muirhead

1619. A LOMBARD STREET MYSTERY *novel* U.K.: Bartholomew, 1888; U.K.: Blackett, c. 1890
Detective: Percival Montgomery.
Problem: Murder in a locked room.

Robeson, Kenneth (house name)

1620. BRAND OF THE WEREWOLF *novel* in Doc Savage Magazine, January 1934; U.K. and U.S.: Bantam, 1965
Detective: Doc Savage.
Problem: Rendering persons unconscious—and near to death—behind various locked doors, some of them aboard trains.

1621. THE DERRICK DEVIL *novel* in Doc Savage Magazine, February 1937; U.S.: Bantam, 1973
Detective: Doc Savage.
Comment: Not quite an impossible-crime story. However, it does involve mysterious jellylike creatures with the apparent power to absorb human bodies. They in fact prove to be a combination of balloons and sponge rubber manipulated by an evil human intelligence who absorbs his fellow beings in an acid bath.

1622. THE EVIL GNOME *novel* in Doc Savage Magazine, April 1940; U.S.: Bantam, 1976
Detective: Doc Savage.
Problem: Death by throat cutting, etc., by invisible agent in locked rooms, etc.

1623. FEAR CAY *novel* in Doc Savage Magazine, September 1934; U.K. and U.S.: Bantam, 1965
Detective: Doc Savage.
Problem: Disappearance of a man from a locked and guarded room in a high-storey building.

1624. THE FLAMING FALCONS *novel* in Doc Savage Magazine, 1939; U.S.: Bantam, 1968; U.K.: Bantam, 1969

Detective: Doc Savage.
Problem: Death by poisoning and conflagration behind a locked cabin door.

1625. THE MYSTIC MULLAH *novel* in Doc Savage Magazine, January 1935; U.S.: Bantam, 1965; U.K.: Bantam, 1966
Detective: Doc Savage.
Problem: Death by poisoning by great squirming nebulous floating shapes with the ability to disappear from all types of situations, including guarded corridors and rooms, etc.

1626. THE SEVEN AGATE DEVILS *novel* U.S.: Bantam, 1973
Detective: Doc Savage.
Problem: Death by stabbing in various locked rooms.

1627. THE SQUEAKING GOBLIN *novel* in Doc Savage Magazine, August 1934; U.K. and U.S.: Bantam, 1969
Detective: Doc Savage.
Problem: Death—or nonfatal penetration—by shooting with bullets that afterwards vanished.

Robinson, Gene D.

1628. ✓ "Hocus-Pocus Homicide" *short story* in 10-Story Detective, April 1945
Detective: Ned Cain.
Problem: Disappearance of a man from a locked trunk.

Rodd, Ralph

1629. SLEUTH O' THE WORLD *novel* U.K.: Collins, 1933
Detective: Anthea Jubb.
Problem: Death by shooting in a locked cottage.

Roe, C. F.

1630. ✓ DEATH BY FIRE *novel* U.K.: Headline, 1990
Detective: Dr. Jean Montrose.
Problem: Death by spontaneous combustion in a locked house.

Rogers, Joel Townsley

1631. THE RED RIGHT HAND *novel* U.S.: Simon, 1945; U.K.: Panther, c. 1956
Detectives: Prof. Adam MacCamerou and Dr. Henry Riddle.
Problem: Disappearance of a grey tourer and of a crazy murderer.

1632. ✓ "The Hanging Rope" *novelette* in New Detective Magazine, September 1946; "The Art of the Impossible" U.K.: Xanadu, 1990; "Murder Impossible" U.S.: Carroll, 1990

Detective: Kerry Ott, deaf playwright.

Problem: Death by blunt instrument and throat cutting of two people inside a locked apartment.

Rohmer, Sax (Arthur Sarsfield Ward, q.v.)

1633. ✓ DAUGHTER OF FU MANCHU *novel* U.K.: Cassell, 1931; U.S.: Doubleday, 1931

Detective: Nayland Smith.

Problem: Disappearance of a body from a locked hut.

1634. THE MOON IS RED *novel* U.K.: Jenkins, 1954; U.S.: Bookfinger, 1976

Detective: Inspector Ryder.

Problem: Death by strangulation of two women in locked rooms in upper storeys.

1635. THE MYSTERY OF DR. FU MANCHU *novel* U.K.: Methuen, 1913; U.S. (as "The Insidious Dr. Fu Manchu"): McBride, 1913

Detective: Nayland Smith.

Problem: Death by poison in a study under constant observation.

1636. THE QUEST OF THE SACRED SLIPPER *novel* U.K.: Pearson, 1919; U.S.: Doubleday, 1919

Detective: Inspector Bristol.

Problem: Death by decapitation in a locked room.

1637. ✓ "The Blue Monkey" *short story* in "The Haunting of Low Fennel" U.K.: Pearson, 1920

Detective: Mr. East.

Problem: Death by strangulation apparently—since there were no other footprints—carried out by a blue-porcelain monkey that had come to life.

1638. ✓ "Case of the Blue Rajah" *short story* in The New Magazine (UK) August 1913; "The Dream Detective" U.K.: Jarrolds, 1920; U.S.: Doubleday, 1925

Detective: Morris Klaw.

Problem: Disappearance of a fabulous diamond from a locked room in which all the inmates were almost immediately carefully searched.

1639. ✓ "Case of the Ivory Statue" *short story* in The New Magazine (UK) July 1913; "The Dream Detective"

Detective: Klaw.

Problem: Disappearance of a life-size ivory statue from a locked studio under almost constant observation.

1640. ✓ "Case of the Tragedies in the Greek Room" *short story* in The New Magazine (UK) April 1913; "The Dream Detective"; "Fifty Famous Detectives of Fiction" U.K.: Odhams, 1938
Detective: Klaw.
Problem: Death by poison in a locked museum.

1641. "The Squirrel Man" *short story* in "Tales of East and West" U.K.: Cassell, 1932 (not in the U.S. edition); "Many Mysteries" U.K.: Rich, 1933
Detective: Heatherley.
Problem: Death by shooting in a room under constant observation.

1642. "A White Orchid" *short story* in "The Sins of Severac Bablon" U.K.: Cassell, 1914; U.S.: Bookfinger, 1967
Detective: Inspector Sheffield.
Problem: Disappearance of a man from a locked room under constant observation.

Romano, Deane

1643. BANACEK *novel* U.S.: Bantam, 1973
Detective: Banacek.
Problem: Disappearance of a football player from beneath a massive fallen pile of opposing players.

Ronald, James

1644. CROSS MARKS THE SPOT *novel* U.K.: Hodder, 1933; reprint Rich, 1936
Detective: Julian Mendoza, reporter.
Problem: Death by shooting in a flat unoccupied by anyone but the victim.

1645. SIX WERE TO DIE *novel* U.K.: Hodder, 1932; U.S. (as by Kirk Wales): Mystery House, 1941
Detective: Dr. Daniel Britling.
Problems: (1) Death by poison and (2) wounding by shooting in guarded or locked rooms.

1646. THEY CAN'T HANG ME! *novel* U.K.: Rich, 1938; U.S.: Doubleday, 1938
Detectives: Alastair MacNab, newsman, and Superintendent Wrenn.
Problem: Death by shooting in a room under constant watch.

1647. ✓ "Too Many Motives" *short story* in 20 Story Magazine, April 1930; Hush, June 1931

Detective: Divisional-Surgeon Daniel Britling.
Problem: Death by shooting in a locked room.

Roos, Kelley

1648. THE BLONDE DIED DANCING *novel* U.S.: Dodd, 1956; U.K. (as "She Died Dancing"): Eyre, 1957
Detectives: Steve and Connie Barton.
Problem: Death by shooting in a guarded room.

1649. SAILOR, TAKE WARNING! *novel* U.S.: Dodd, 1944; U.K.: Hale, 1952
Detectives: Jeff and Haila Troy.
Problem: Appearance in and disappearance from a locked house of an intruder who attacked one of the occupants.

1650. "The Great Locked Room Mystery" *playlet* in "Mystery Writers' Annual, 1964"
Detectives: Wendell St. John and Inspector Trout.
Problem: Death in a locked room.

Roosevelt, Elliott

1651. ✓ MURDER IN THE OVAL OFFICE *novel* U.S.: St. Martin's, 1989
Detective: Mrs. Eleanor Roosevelt.
Problem: Death by shooting in the locked Oval Office at the White House.

Roscoe, Theodore

1652. I'LL GRIND THEIR BONES *novel* U.S.: Dodge, 1936; U.K.: Harrap, 1937
Detective: John H. W. Keats, news correspondent.
Problem: Death by shooting in a locked room.

1653. ✓ MURDER ON THE WAY! *novel* U.S.: Dodge, 1935; as "A Grave Must Be Deep" Canada/U.K., 1947; U.S.: as "A Grave Must Be Deep" Starmont House, 1989
Detectives: Edwin Edward Cartershall, painter; Patricia ("Pete") Dale, heiress; Lt. Nemo Narcisse of the Garde d'Haiti.
Problems: (1) Death by shooting in a locked room.
(2) Pursuit of a man through an underground tunnel into an enclosed room from which the man had disappeared.

1654. ✓ "I Was the Kid with the Drum" *short story* in Argosy, Oct. 30, 1937; "I Was the Kid with the Drum & Anywhere But Here" (by Eustace L. Adams) U.K.: Harry Green, c. 1938
Detective: Sheriff Whittier.
Problems: (1) A drum that beats on its own.

(2) Disappearance of a woman from within a house.

Rosenhayn, Paul

1655. "Through the Door" *short story* in "Joe Jenkins' Casebook" U.K.: Heinemann, 1930
Detective: Joe Jenkins.
Problem: Disappearance of a platinum bracelet from a locked workshop.

Ross, Carlton (Edwy Searles Brooks, q.v.)

1656. THE BLACK SKULL MURDERS *novel* U.K.: Swan, 1942
Detectives: Bill Morrow and Jacqueline ("Pinky") Pinker.
Problem: Attempted murder in a locked room.

Rossetti, H. F.

1657. ✓ "A Policeman's Soliloquies: Death of an Oxford Blue" *short story* in London Mystery Selection No. 37, June 1958
Detective: Unnamed narrator.
Problem: Death by gassing in a room bolted on the inside.

Rothwell, C. C. (as "A. Cone and Oil")

1658. ✓ "Adventures of Sherwood Hoakes. Adventure 1—An Interrupted Honeymoon" *short story* in Ludgate Weekly, April 9, 1892; "My Evening with Sherlock Holmes" U.K.: Ferret, 1981
Detective: Sherwood Hoakes.
Problem: Disappearance of a man before the very eyes of his wife.

Rowland, John

1659. CALAMITY IN KENT *novel* U.K.: Jenkins, 1950
Detective: Inspector Shelley.
Problem: Death by stabbing in a locked cliff-railway cabin.

1660. DEATH BENEATH THE RIVER *novel* U.K.: Jenkins, (1943)
Detective: Shelley.
Problem: Death by shooting of a man driving a car through a road tunnel.

1661. SUICIDE ALIBI *novel* U.K.: Jenkins, 1937
Detective: Shelley.
Problem: Death by shooting in a room under observation.

Rud, Anthony

1662. ✓ HOUSE OF THE DAMNED *novel* U.S.: Macaulay, 1934; originally published (as "The Death Messenger") in Two Book Detective Magazine, February-March 1934

Detective: Jiggers Masters.
Problem: Death by stabbing in unmarked snow.

1663. ✓ THE ROSE BATH RIDDLE *novel* U.S.: Macaulay, 1934
Detective: Masters
Problem: Death by freezing in a scalding-hot shower behind the locked door of a bathroom.

Russell, Ray

1664. ✓ INCUBUS *novel* U.S.: Morrow, 1976; U.K.: Sphere, 1977
Detective: Julian Trask.
Problem: Rape and murder of a woman housed in a locked dormitory inhabited only by females.

Rutherford, Douglas

1665. THE BLACK LEATHER MURDERS *novel* U.K.: Collins, 1966; U.S.: Walker, 1966
Detective: Jay Delany.
Comment: The blurb suggests that a taxi and its four occupants vanish as if by magic from a prehistoric site. In fact, it is a simple case of kidnapping and imprisoning in a subterranean cavern that takes place in this fast-paced thriller.

Ryerson, Florence, and Colin Clements

1666. ✓ FEAR OF FEAR *novel* U.K.: Skeffington, 1931; U.S.: Appleton, 1931
Detective: Jimmy Lane.
Problem: Death by unknown means in a locked séance room.

Ryland, John Knox

1667. ✓ THE EASTER GUESTS MYSTERY *novel* U.K.: Paul, 1935
Detective: Detective Inspector Rodway.
Comment: Advertising blurbs for this book indicate that a locked-room murder has been committed. It is true that a corpse is found behind the remains of a locked room in the shell of a burnt-out building, but the point seems to have been that the victim was locked in from the outside. So no impossible crime as such, though this is otherwise a surprisingly good, leisurely, golden-age police procedural, and from a virtually unknown writer.

S

Sabatini, Rafael

1668. ✓ "The Plague of Ghosts" *short story* in The Storyteller, September 1907
Detective: Capoulade, the thief.
Problem: The catching by a ghostly apparition of two bullets fired from a brace of horse-pistols.

Saber, Robert O. (Milton Ozaki, q.v.)

1669. THE BLACK DARK MURDERS *novel* U.K.: Jewel, 1949; U.S.: Handi-Books, 1949
Detective: Phil Keene.
Problem: Deaths by stabbing (3) in pitch-black conditions.

Sanders, Lawrence

1670. ✓ THE EIGHTH COMMANDMENT *novel* U.K.: N.E.L., 1986; U.S.: Putnam, 1986
Detective: Mary Lou "Dunk" Bateson.
Problem: Disappearance of a valuable coin from within a sealed cabinet under constant watch while it was being moved from its owner's home.

Sandys, James

1671. THE MAN WHO WASN'T THERE *novel* U.K.: Paul, 1953
Detective: Mr. Springfield, solicitor.
Problem: Death by shooting in a room where the killer went unseen by the one witness.

Sandys, Oliver

1672. ✓ "Scotland Yard" *short story* in "Chicane" U.K.: Long, 1912
Detectives: Lady Nannie Weybridge and Miss Maida Strangways.
Problem: Death by blunt instrument in a locked bathroom.

Sanger, Joan

1673. ✓ THE CASE OF THE MISSING CORPSE *novel* U.S.: Green Circle, 1936
Detectives: Peter Alcott and John Ellis.
Problems: (1) Disappearance of a man from a poker game during a brief blackout.
(2) Stabbing in a locked storeroom.

Sapper (H. C. McNeile)

1674. "The Horror at Staveley Grange" *short story* in Hutchinson's

Adventure Story Magazine September 1922; "The Saving Clause" U.S.: Doran, 1926, and U.K.: Hodder, 1927; "My Best Detective Story" U.K.: Faber, 1931; Mystery and Detection #1 1934

Detective: Ronald Standish.

Problem: Death by unknown means in a room entered only by the victim.

1675. "The Music Room" *short story* in "Ask for Ronald Standish" U.K.: Hodder, 1936

Detective: Standish.

Problem: Death by blunt instrument in a locked music room.

1676. "The Mystery of the Slip Coach" *short story* in "Ronald Standish" U.K.: Hodder, 1933

Detective: Standish.

Problem: Death by shooting in a closed (noncorridor) railway train compartment.

Sardou, Victorien

1677. "The Black Pearl" *short story* in "Three Romances" U.S. Brentanos, 1888; "The Lion's Skin" (as by Charles de Bernard) U.K.: Vizetelly, 1889

Detective: Cornelius Pump.

Problem: Theft of precious metal from a locked room.

Saunders, Hilary St. G.

1678. THE SLEEPING BACCHUS *novel* U.K.: Joseph, 1951

Detective: Raoul Weiler.

Problems: (1) Disappearance of a canvas from a guarded picture gallery.

(2) Disappearance of a man over an apparently unclimbable fence.

(3) Disappearance of a black maria from a section of road under surveillance.

Sawyer, Lynwood

1679. "The Shredded Rose" *short story* in EQMM, July 1978

Detective: Dr. Austin Lyle, professor emeritus of organic chemistry.

Problem: Death by poisoning in a locked bathroom.

Saxon, John A.

1680. ✓ "Death in a Crystal Casket" *short story* in Street & Smith's Detective Story Magazine, June 1945; Street & Smith's

Detective Story Magazine (U.K.), January 1953
Detective: Barney Allison.
Problem: Death of a magician by shooting, apparently through a crystal-glass coffin.

Sayers, Dorothy L.

1681. "The Haunted Policeman" *short story* in "Detection Medley" U.K.: Hutchinson, 1939; EQMM May 1952; "Striding Folly" U.K.: N.E.L., 1972; "Lord Peter" U.S.: Harper, 1972; "Masterpieces of Mystery: The Golden Age: Part One" U.S.: Davis, 1977
Detective: Lord Peter Wimsey.
Problem: Disappearance of a corpse and its environs as glimpsed through a keyhole.

1682. ✓ "The Poisoned Dow '08" *short story* in (as "The Poisoned Port") The Passing Show, Feb. 25, 1933; "Hangman's Holiday" U.K.: Gollancz, 1933, and U.S.: Harcourt, 1933; EQMM February 1948; "Masterpieces of Mystery: Amateurs & Professionals" U.S.: Davis, 1978; "Big Book of Locked-Room Mysteries", Black Lizard, 2014
Detective: Montague Egg, wine salesman.
Problem: Death by poison from a sealed bottle in a locked study.

1683. "Talboys" *short story* in "Striding Folly" and "Lord Peter"; "In the Teeth of the Evidence", Gollancz, 1972; EQMM December 1983
Detective: Lord Peter Wimsey.
Problem: Theft of peaches from a walled garden in which the thieves left no footprints.

Scarlett, Roger

1684. ✓ THE BEACON HILL MURDERS *novel* U.K.: Heinemann, 1930; U.S.: Doubleday, 1930
Detective: Inspector Kane.
Problem: Death by throat cutting in a room under police guard.

1685. MURDER AMONG THE ANGELLS *novel* U.S.: Doubleday, 1932
Detective: Kane.
Problem: Death by stabbing in a locked elevator.

Schweik, Robert C.

1686. "Imagine a Murder" *short story* in EQMM, June 1978
Detective: Prof. Paul Engel.
Problem: Death by shooting in a locked room.

Scott, Jeffry

1687. ✓ "Now You See It" *short story* in AHMM, Feb. 4, 1981
Detective: Lieutenant Farmer.
Problem: Disappearance of a leather bag full of jewellery from an alley in which the thief is apprehended.

Scott, Maxwell

1688. "The Hermit of the Rigi. An Adventure in the Air" *short story* in The Union Jack, c. 1894
Detective: Nelson Lee.
Problem: Death by strangulation in a chalet surrounded by unmarked snow.

1689. "The Professor's Gold. An Adventure Underground" *short story* in The Union Jack, Xmas 1894
Detective: Lee.
Problem: Disappearance of a man from a locked room.

Scott, R.T.M.

1690. THE BLACK MAGICIAN *novel* U.S.: Dutton, 1925; U.K: Heinemann, 1926
Detective: Aurelius (Secret Service) Smith.
Problem: Resurrection of a man seen and known to have been killed.

Scott, Sutherland

1691. DOCTOR DODDS' EXPERIMENT *novel* U.K.: Paul, 1956
Detective: Dr. Septimus Dodds.
Problem: Death by shooting in a locked room.

Scott, Will

1692. DISHER—DETECTIVE *novel* U.K.: Cassell, 1925; U.S. (as "The Black Stamp): Macrae, 1926
Detective: Disher.
Problem: Disappearance of a man from a room and house under surveillance.

1693. "The Locked Room" *short story* in The Passing Show, Sept. 3, 1932
Detective: Belinda "Britannica" Brown (Lindy).
Problem: Assault in a locked room.

1694. "The Vanishing House" *short story* in "Giglamps" U.K.: Cassell, 1924
Detective: Giglamps.
Problem: Disappearance of a house glimpsed by a witness to a

nearby murder.

Seaforth (George C. Foster)

1695. MISPRISION OF FELONY *novel* U.K.: Jenkins, 1941
Detective: Lady Jane Eastings.
Problem: Death by gassing in a locked room.

Seamark (Austin J. Small)

1696. THE MASTER MYSTERY *novel* U.S. (as by Austin J. Small): Doran, 1928; U.K.: Hodder, (1929)
Detective: Tommy Delayn.
Problem: Disappearance of rubies from a room under constant surveillance.

1697. ✓ THE WEB OF DESTINY *novel* U.K.: Hodder, 1929; U.S. (as "The Web of Murder" by Austin J. Small): Doubleday, 1929
Detective: Forrest Ord.
Problem: Disappearance of a woman from a locked and bolted inner room.

Selwyn, Francis

1698. CRACKSMAN ON VELVET *novel* U.K.: Deutsch, 1974; U.S.: Stein, 1974; (as "Sergeant Verity and the Cracksman") U.K.: Futura Books, 1975
Detective: Sgt. William Clarence Verity.
Problem: Theft of gold bullion from a locked, moving railway luggage van.

1699. ✓ SERGEANT VERITY AND THE BLOOD ROYAL *novel* U.K.: Deutsch, 1979; U.S.: Stein, 1979
Detective: Verity.
Problem: Theft of gold from the impregnable Philadelphia U.S. mint.

1700. SERGEANT VERITY AND THE IMPERIAL DIAMOND *novel* U.K.: Deutsch, 1975; U.S.: Stein, 1976
Detective: Verity.
Problem: Theft of a valuable diamond from a casket under constant surveillance.

1701. SERGEANT VERITY PRESENTS HIS COMPLIMENTS *novel* U.K.: Deutsch, 1977; U.S.: Stein, 1977
Detective: Verity.
Problem: Murder by shooting when it seemed that the bullet could only have come from a gun handled by the victim himself.

1702. "The Goblin Rapist of Dingley Dell" *short story* in Men Only,

December 1978
Detectives: Verity and Sergeant Samson.
Problem: Rape of various women, by a goblin, in unmarked snow.

Severy, Melvin L.

1703. THE DARROW ENIGMA *novel* U.K.: Richards, 1904; U.S.: Dodd, 1904
Detective: George Maitland.
Problem: Death by poisoning administered before witnesses by invisible agency.

1704. ✓ THE MYSTERY of JUNE 13TH *novel* U.K.: Stevens, 1905; U.S.: Dodd, 1905
Detective: Maitland.
Problem: (1) Disappearance of a clean-shaven man from a locked shack to which his footprints in the snow led and where the only occupant proved to be bearded.
(2) Disappearance of a freshly murdered corpse from a locked apartment.
(3) Escape of a man from the same locked apartment, now also sealed.

Shaffer, A. and P. (see also Antony, Peter)

1705. WITHERED MURDER *novel* U.K.: Gollancz, 1955; U.S.: Macmillan, 1956
Detective: Mr. Fathom.
Problem: Death by stabbing in a room under constant observation.

Shaffer, Anthony

1706. "Sleuth" *play* in "Best Mystery and Suspense Plays of the Modern Theatre" U.S.: Dodd, 1970; U.K.: Calder, 1971
Detective: St. John Lord Merridew.
Problem: Death in the centre of a red-dust tennis court, on which the murderer had left no footprints.

Shakley, Jay

1707. ✓ "The Villars-Manningham Papers" *short story* in "The Villars-Manningham Papers" Canada, 1978
Detective: Sherlock Holmes.
Problem: Death by shooting in a room under guard.

Shannon, Dell

1708. CRIME FILE *novel* U.S.: Morrow, 1974; U.K.: Gollancz, 1975

Detectives: Lt. Luis Mendoza and his associates.
Problem: Disappearance of a four-year-old girl from an apartment block under surveillance and subsequently searched.

1709. THE DEATH BRINGERS *novel* U.S.: Morrow, 1965; U.K.: Gollancz, 1966
Detective: Mendoza.
Problem: Death by shooting in a guarded area.

Shaw, Frank H.

1710. ✓ ATLANTIC MURDER *novel* U.K.: Mathews, 1932; U.S.: McBride, 1933
Detective: Captain Frazer of the "Ligerian."
Problem: Death by poison within locked cabins aboard ship.

Sheinin, Lev

1711. ✓ "The Hunting Knife" *short story* in "Diary of a Criminologist", Foreign Languages Publishing House 1956; EQMM, July, 1965
Detective: Unnamed investigator.
Problem: Death by stabbing of a man apparently standing on his own.

Simenon, Georges

1712. "The Little House at Croix-Rousse" *short story* in EQMM, November 1947; "Maiden Murders" U.S.: Harper, 1952, and U.K.: Hammond, 1953 (this translation by Anthony Boucher); as (an earlier translation) "The Case of Dr. Ceccioni" in Esquire, 1935, and October 1973; "Death Locked In" U.S.: IPL, 1987; "Big Book of Locked-Room Mysteries", Black Lizard, 2014
Detective: Joseph Leborgne.
Problem: Death by shooting in a locked and guarded house.

Simon, Robert A.

1713. THE WEEKEND MYSTERY *novel* U.S.: Watt, 1926; U.K.: Collins, 1927
Detective: Jimmy Wrome.
Problem: Death by shooting in a locked room.

Sims, George R.

1714. "An Infernal Machine" *short story* in "The Theatre of Life" U.K.: Fuller, 1881
Detective: None.
Problem: (non-impossible) Death by explosion in a locked room.

1715. ✓ "The Mystery of the Studio Suite" *short story* in "The Cabinet Minister's Wife" U.K.: Paul, 1910
Detective: Detective Inspector Hogarth.
Problem: Wounding by stabbing in a locked room.

Sjöwall, Maj, and Per Wahlöö

1716. THE LOCKED ROOM *novel* U.S.: Pantheon, 1973; U.K.: Gollancz, 1974
Detective: Martin Beck.
Problem: Death by shooting in a locked room.

Skene, Anthony

1717. ✓ THE £1,000,000 PLOT *novel* SBL No. 393 (2nd series) U.K.: Amalgamated, 1933
Detective: Sexton Blake.
Problem: Death by shooting in a locked room.

Skvorecky, Josef

1718. "The Case of the Horizontal Trajectory" *short story* in "The Mournful Demeanour of Lieutenant Boruvka" U.K.: Gollancz, 1973; U.S. "The Realm of the Impossible", Locked Room International, 2017
Detective: Lieutenant Boruvka.
Problem: Death by blunt instrument in a locked room.

1719. "Death on Needlespoint" *short story* in "The Mournful Demeanour of Lieutenant Boruvka"
Detective: Boruvka.
Problem: Death by stabbing of the lead climber on an apparently inaccessible peak.

1720. ✓ "Mistake in Hitzungsee" *short story* in "Sins for Father Knox" U.K.: Faber, 1989; U.S.: Norton, 1989
Detective: Eve Adam.
Problem: Death by blunt instrument in a locked room.

1721. "A Tried and Proven Method" *short story* in "The Mournful Demeanour of Lieutenant Boruvka"
Detective: Lieutenant Boruvka.
Problem: Death by falling from a cable car that arrives at its destination empty.

Sladek, John

1722. BLACK AURA *novel* U.K.: Cape, 1974; U.S.: Walker, 1979
Detective: Thackeray Phin.
Problems: (1) Disappearance from a locked lavatory.

(2) Levitation at night in the open at fourth-floor level.

1723. INVISIBLE GREEN *novel* U.K.: Gollancz, 1977; U.S.: Walker, 1979
Detective: Phin.
Problems: (1) Death by suffocation within a locked, guarded house.
(2) Death by blunt instrument with victim found in house while all suspects were known to be together in another house
(3) Death by stabbing in a guarded seaside house

1724. "By an Unknown Hand" *short story* in "The Times Anthology of Detective Stories" U.K.: Cape, 1972; "Maps: The Uncollected Stories of John Sladek"; Cosmos, 2003
Detective: Phin.
Problem: Death by strangulation in a locked, guarded room.

1725. ✓ "The Locked Room" *short story* in New Worlds Quarterly No. 4 (1972); "Keep the Giraffe Burning" U.K.: Panther, 1977
Detective: Fenton Worth.
Problem: Death within a locked room.

Slate, John (John Russell Fearn, q.v.)

1726. BLACK MARIA, M.A. *novel* U.K.: Rich, (1944)
Detective: Maria Black, school headmistress ("Black Maria").
Problem: Death by shooting in a locked library.

1727. DEATH IN SILHOUETTE *novel* U.K.: Rich, (1950)
Detective: Black.
Problem: Death by hanging in a locked cellar.

1728. FRAMED IN GUILT *novel* U.K.: Rich, (1948)
Detective: Superintendent Henshaw.
Problem: Death by stabbing in a locked office.

1729. ✓ THY ARM ALONE *novel* U.K.: Rich, 1947
Detective: Maria Black.
Problem: Death by blunt instrument of a man apparently not within reach of anyone else.

Slater, Will

1730. "The Affair of Peg-Top Leg" *short story* in "The Adventures of D'Arcy Dewpond, Detective" U.K.: Drane, (1927)
Detective: D'Arcy Dewpond.
Problem: Death by hanging in a locked room.

Slesar, Henry

1731. "The Case of the Shaky Snowman" *short story/jigsaw puzzle*

U.S.: Janus Games, 1973
Detective: Inspector Jiggs.
Problem: Death by stabbing in a guarded room where every visitor was searched before and after their visit, and no weapon was found.

1732. "The Case of the Snoring Skinflint" *jigsaw puzzle* U.S.: Janus, 1972
Detective: Jiggs.
Problem: Death by poisoning in a locked room.

1733. ✓ "Santa Claus and the Locked Room" *short story* in "Acrostic Mysteries" U.S.: Avon, 1985
Detective: Inspector Cross.
Problem: Appearance within a locked and guarded room of a collection of Christmas presents for a cynical little boy.

Smith, D. W.

1734. ✓ SERIOUS CRIMES *novel* U.K.: Macmillan, 1987; U.S. (as "The Silver Spoon Murders"): Stuart, 1988
Detective: Chief Inspector Harry Fathers.
Problem: Death by shooting in a locked parlour.

Smith, Derek

1735. WHISTLE UP THE DEVIL *novel* U.K.: Gifford, 1953, Thriller Book Club, 1953; U.S.: Locked Room International, 2014
Detective: Algy Lawrence.
Problems: (1) Death by stabbing in a locked, guarded room. (2) Death by strangulation in a locked, guarded cell.

Smith, Edgar D.

1736. "Killer in Khaki" *short story* in Detective Fiction Weekly February 1 1941; EQMM, August 1948; EQMM (Australia), December 1949
Detective: Ex-constable Private Enly.
Problem: Death by bayonetting, in an area guarded by sentries, by a murderer apparently invisible.

Smith, Edgar W.

1737. "The Disappearance of Mr. James Phillimore" *short story* in "A Baker Street Four-Wheeler" U.S.: Pamphlet House, 1944
Detective: Ronald Phillimore.
Problem: Disappearance of James Phillimore and his umbrella.

Smith, Evelyn E.

1738. "Really It Was Quite Simple" *short story* in EQMM, May 1953

Detectives: Sir Odo, Biestleigh, and Pottridge.
Problem: Disappearance of a man from a locked, guarded room.

Smith, H. Greenhough

1739. ✓ "The Case of Roger Carboyne" *short story* in The Strand Magazine, September 1892
Detective: Sergeant Wallis.
Problem: Disappearance of a man from a mountain track covered in otherwise unmarked snow and the subsequent discovery of his body on a higher plateau, again in otherwise unmarked snow.

Smith, J.C.S.

1740. ✓ NIGHTCAP *novel* U.S.: Atheneum, 1984; U.K.: Quartet, 1985
Detective: Quentin Jacoby.
Problem: Death by stabbing on a closed-off floor of a skyscraper in which the other three present were innocent.

Smith, L. Neil

1741. ✓ THEIR MAJESTIES' BUCKETEERS *novel* U.S.: Ballantine, 1981
Detective: Bucketeer-Inquirer Mav, a three-shouldered alien.
Problem: Death by explosion in a locked, windowless room.

Smith, Shelley

1742. ✓ HE DIED OF MURDER! *novel* U.K.: Collins, 1947; U.S.: Harper, 1948
Detective: Inspector Jacob Chaos.
Problem: Death by shooting in the middle of a ploughed field where the victim stood apparently alone.

Sobol, Donald J.

1743. ✓ "The Case of the Glass of Ginger Ale" *short story* in "Encyclopedia Brown and the Case of the Secret Pitch" U.S.: Nelson, 1965
Detective: Encyclopedia Brown, boy detective.
Problem: Appearance of ginger ale and disappearance of ice cubes from the same glass in a locked safe.
Comment: An earlier version of Item 1744.

1744. "The Case of the Locked Room" *short story* in "Two Minute Mysteries" U.S.: Scholastic, 1967
Detective: Dr. Haledjian.
Problem: Appearance of ginger ale and disappearance of ice cubes from the same glass in a locked safe.

Sorrel, Lucian

1745. ✓ "The Rajah of Lives" *short story* in Pearson's Weekly, Jan. 25, 1896
Detective: None.
Problem: Apparent ability of a rajah to kill his subjects by words and a light tap on the forehead.

Soutar, Andrew

1746. THE BLACK SPOT MYSTERY *novel* U.K.: Hutchinson, (1938)
Detective: Phineas Spinnet.
Problem: Death by stabbing in a locked room.

1747. THE HANGING SWORD! *novel* U.K.: Hutchinson, (1933)
Detective: Spinnet.
Problem: Death by shooting in a locked room.

1748. KHARDUNI *novel* U.K.: Hutchinson, (1933); U.S.: Macaulay, 1934
Detective: Kharduni.
Problem: Disappearance of a houseful of guests.

Spewack, Samuel

1749. ✓ THE SKYSCRAPER MURDER *novel* U.S.: Macaulay, 1928
Detectives: Inspector Marx and Dr. Rhinewald.
Problem: Death in a skyscraper apartment of a man not seen going up to it, and no more was the murderer seen either coming or leaving.

Sprigg, C. St. John

1750. CRIME IN KENSINGTON *novel* U.K.: Eldon, 1933; U.S. (as "Pass the Body"): Dial, 1933
Detective: Charles Venables, journalist.
Problem: Disappearance of two women from within a bedroom under surveillance. One woman was actually seen to be dragged back into the room by a gloved hand.

1751. DEATH OF A QUEEN *novel* U.K.: Nelson, 1935
Detective: Venables.
Problem: Death by strangulation in a room under constant guard.

1752. ✓ THE SIX QUEER THINGS *novel* U.K.: Jenkins, 1937; U.S.: Doubleday, 1937
Detective: Inspector Charles Morgan.
Problem: Death by poison taken in a glass of water poured from an apparently harmless tap.

1753. ✓ "Death at 8.30" *short story* in Detective Fiction Weekly May 25 1935; The Windsor Magazine, March 1936
Detective: Paule.
Problem: Death in a sealed bank vault under constant guard.

Stacpoole, W. H.

1754. "The Manufacturer" *short story* in "Three Boots" U.K.: Dean, (1897)
Detective: Sergeant Sharp.
Problem: Theft of gold bullion from a locked railway compartment.

Starrett, Vincent

1755. THE END OF MR. GARMENT *novel* U.S.: Doubleday, 1932
Detective: Walter Ghost.
Problem: Death by stabbing in a taxi under constant surveillance.

1756. "The Sealed Room" *short story* in "The Case Book of Jimmie Lavender" U.S.: Gold Label, 1944
Detective: Jimmie Lavender.
Problem: Death by shooting in a sealed room.

Steele, Chester K.

1757. ✓ THE HOUSE OF DISAPPEARANCES *novel* U.S.: Chelsea, 1927
Detective: Prof. Irving Spencer, blind detective.
Problem: Disappearance of several people from a house under observation.

Steele, Derwent

1758. THE PHANTOM SLAYER *novel* U.K.: Modern, (1935)
Detective: John Blackmore.
Problem: Death by poison gas in a locked flat.

Steele, Wilbur Daniel

1759. "The Yellow Cat" *short story* in "Land's End" U.S.: Harper, 1918; "Full Cargo" U.S.: Doubleday, 1951; "Purr-Fect Crime" U.S.: Lynx, 1989
Comment: One of the "Marie Celeste" breed of story. In this one, the salvage team eventually discover that there is a sole survivor hiding in the ship's rigging.

Steeman, Stanislas-André

1760. THE NIGHT OF THE 12TH-13TH *novel* U.S.: Lippincott, 1933
Detective: Wenceslas Vorobeitchik.
Problem: Death and wounding by shooting in a locked room in which only the two victims were found.

1761. SIX DEAD MEN *novel* U.S.: Farrar, 1932; U.K.: Hurst, (1933)
Detective: Vorobeitchik.
Problem: Death by stabbing in a closed elevator.

Stephens, Jessie Gunn

1762. ✓ "Dying Embers" *short story* in Woman's World (U.S.), Feb.12, 1985
Detective: Deputy Sheriff Conella.
Problem: Death from arsenic poisoning but no poison can be traced to food or drink.

Stephenson, Ralph

1763. BODY IN MY ARMS *novel* U.K.: Gifford, 1963
Detective: Peter Jackson, broadcaster.
Problem: Death by strangulation in a locked room.

1764. DARKEST DEATH *novel* U.K.: Gifford, 1964
Detectives: Stalky Heron and Charles Finch.
Problem: Death by shooting with an arrow in a locked room.

Stevenson, Burton E.

1765. ✓ THE RED CARNATION *novel* U.S.: Dodd, 1939, and U.K.: Cassell, 1940; U.S. (as "Death Wears a Carnation"): Mystery Novel of the Month, 1942
Detective: Antony Bigelow, columnist.
Problem: Death by shooting in a locked apartment.

Stevermer, C. J.

1766. ✓ THE DUKE AND THE VEIL *novel* U.S.: Ace Charter, 1987
Detective: Nicholas Coffin, alchemist.
Problem: Death by poison in a room under constant view.

Steward, Dwight

1767. ✓ "Genesis" *short story* in "Crime Wave" U.K.: Collins, 1981
Detective: Edgar Allan Poe.
Problem: Death by stabbing in a locked cellar.

Stone, Hampton

1768. ✓ THE GIRL WITH THE HOLE IN HER HEAD *novel* U.S.: Simon, 1949; U.K.: Boardman, 1958
Detectives: (Jeremiah) Gibson and Mac, assistant district attorneys.
Problem: Death by shooting in a locked room.

Stout, Rex

1769. "The Fourth of July Picnic" *short story* in "And Four to Go" U.S.: Viking, 1958; "Crime and Again" U.K.: Collins, 1959; (as

"The Fourth of July Murder") EQMM, August 1965; "Ellery Queen's Anthology, Spring-Summer 1979" U.S.: Davis, 1979

Detective: Nero Wolfe.

Comment: Advertised in its magazine appearance as a "locked tent" mystery, it is in fact a straightforward mystery in which the locking of the exit at the back of the tent only serves to limit the number of people who could have committed the crime.

Strahan, Kay Cleaver

1770. DEATH TRAPS *novel* U.K.: Gollancz, 1930; U.S.: Doubleday, 1930

Detective: Lynn MacDonald.

Problem: Death by carbon-monoxide poisoning in a locked room.

1771. FOOTPRINTS *novel* U.K.: Gollancz, 1929; U.S.: Doubleday, 1929

Detective: MacDonald.

Problem: Death by shooting in a house surrounded by unmarked snow and in which each suspect is locked into his room.

Straus, Ralph

1772. ✓ "The Room on the Fourth Floor" *short story* in "Fifty Master pieces of Mystery" U.K.: Odhams, 1937; "Alfred Hitchcock Presents: 14 Suspense Stories to Play Russian Roulette By" U.S.: Dell, 1964

Detective: The ex-Prime Minister.

Problem: Disappearance of a woman from a Parisian hotel at which she had arrived with her daughter. The following morning the daughter could find no trace of her mother and indeed all the hotel staff vehemently denied that she had been accompanied when she arrived.

Street, James

1773. CARBON MONOXIDE *novel* U.K.: Low, (1937)

Detectives: Superintendent Romer and aides.

Problem: Death by carbon-monoxide poisoning in a locked garage.

Strong, L.A.G.

1774. "The Case of the Red Cliff" *short story* in "Odd Man In" U.K.: Pitman, 1938

Detective: Peter Black.

Problem: Death by falling from a cliff, the top of which had sand marked only by the victim's prints.

Stuart, Donald (see also Verner, Gerald) (John Robert Stuart Pringle)

1775. THE SECRET OF THE SEALED ROOM *novel* SBL No. 470 (2nd series) U.K.: Amalgamated, 1935
Detective: Sexton Blake.
Problem: Death by shooting in a locked room.

1776. ✓ THE VILLAGE OF FEAR *novel* SBL No. 430 (2nd series) U.K.: Amalgamated, 1934
Detective: Blake.
Problem: Death by poisoning in a locked room.

1777. ✓ "The Clue of the Crimson Snow" *short story* in Detective Weekly, Dec. 23, 1933
Detective: Blake.
Problem: Death by shooting in an upper-storey bedroom under constant surveillance where, although the victim was slumped over the window sill and the window was open, the angle of the wound proved that the shot did not come from below.

Sturrock, Jeremy

1778. ✓ SUICIDE MOST FOUL *novel* U.K.: Hale, 1981; U.S. (as by J. G. Jeffreys): Walker, 1981
Detective: Jeremy Sturrock, Bow Street Runner.
Problem: Death by shooting in a room when all the exits were under constant watch.

1779. A WICKED WAY TO DIE *novel* U.K.: Macmillan, 1973; U.S. (as by J. G. Jeffreys): Walker, 1973
Detective: Sturrock.
Problem: Death by shooting in a locked room.

Stutley, S. J., and A. E. Copp

1780. THE MELBOURNE MYSTERY *novel* U.K.: Bodley, 1929
Detective: Trevelyan.
Problem: Death by shooting in a locked room.

Suter, John F.

1781. ✓ "The Fairy Ring" *short story* in EQMM, June 2, 1980
Detective: Uncle Abner.
Problem: Disappearance of a child from a fairy ring into the middle of which a bloodhound trailed him, but there the trail mysteriously ended.

1782. "The Impossible Theft" *short story* in EQMM, May 1964;

EQMM (UK) September 1964; EQMM (Australia) November 1964; Ellery Queen's Anthology #19 1970 "All But Impossible!" U.S.: Ticknor, 1981; "The Art of the Impossible" U.K.: Xanadu, 1990; "Murder Impossible" U.S.: Carroll, 1990

Detective: None.

Problem: Disappearance of an extremely valuable document from a locked room.

1783. "The Thousand Mile Shot" *short story* in EQMM November 1956; EQMM (UK) November 1956; EQMM (Australia) January 1957; "Big Time Mysteries" U.S.: Dodd, 1958

Detective: Walter Peterson.

Problem: Death in a one-man rocket in orbit 1,100 miles above the earth.

1784. "The Unlocked Room" *short story* in EQMM, July 1960; EQMM (UK) September 1960; "Crimes Across the Sea" U.S.: Harper, 1964; U.K.: Harrap, 1965

Detectives: Patrolman George Witmer and Col. Goliath Perrivale.

Problem: Death by strangulation in the only dry corner of a room that had just been varnished and on which no footprints have been made.

Sutherland, William

1785. BEHIND THE HEADLINES *novel* U.K.: Arrowsmith, 1933

Detective: Inspector Haskell.

Problem: Death by shooting in a locked room.

Swartwout, R. E.

1786. THE BOAT RACE MURDER *novel* U.K.: Grayson, 1933

Detective: Angus MacNair of Scotland Yard.

Problem: Death by drowning in a locked bathroom.

Swem, Charles Lee

1787. WEREWOLF *novel* U.K.: Hutchinson, (1928); U.S.: Doubleday, 1928

Detective: David Lee.

Comment: No impossible crime as such, but plenty of appearances, both in legend and present times, of mysterious, vengeful werewolf characters.

Sydney, George

1788. ✓ COUNTDOWN FOR MURDER *novel* SBL No. 493 (4th series) U.K.: Amalgamated, 1962

Detective: Sexton Blake.
Problem: Death by shooting in a sealed spacecraft in flight.

Sykes, W. Stanley

1789. "How Was the Knife Thrown?" *short puzzle story* in Hush Magazine No. 8, January 1931
Detective: A police sergeant.
Problem: Death by stabbing at a darkened seance when all the participants were holding hands.

1790. "The Locked Room" *short puzzle story* in Hush Magazine No. 10, March 1931 (solution is in No. 11, April 1931)
Detective: Sergeant Hall.
Problem: Death by stabbing in a locked room.

Symonds, F. Addington

1791. ✓ "The Riddle of the Locked Door" *short story* in The Penny Pictorial Magazine, Feb. 18, 1922
Detective: Marcus Bland.
Problem: Death by shooting in a locked room.

Symons, Julian

1792. "The Hiding Place" *short story* in "Murder! Murder!" U.K.: Fontana, 1961; (as "As If by Magic") EQMM, September 1963; "All But Impossible!" U.S.: Ticknor, 1981; "The Detections of Francis Quarles" Crippen & Landru, 2006
Detective: Francis Quarles.
Problem: Disappearance of a murderer from a guarded amusement pier.

1793. "The Impossible Theft" *short story* in EQMM, January 1966; "Drugged Cornet and Other Mystery Stories" U.S.: Dutton, 1973; "The Detections of Francis Quarles"
Detective: Quarles.
Problem: Disappearance of a string of pearls from a party at which everyone is subsequently and unsuccessfully searched.

1794. "Take That Body Out of the Library" *short article* in Suspense, July 1960
Detectives: Monty Languid and Inspector Numbskull.
Problem: Death by poisoning in a locked library.

T

Tack, Alfred

1795. ✓ FORECAST—MURDER *novel* U.K.: Long, 1967
Detective: David Crosbie, sales manager.
Problem: Death by poisoning in a locked hotel bedroom.

Talbot, Hake

1796. THE HANGMAN'S HANDYMAN *novel* U.S.: Simon, 1942; Ramble House, 2009
Detective: Rogan Kincaid.
Problems: (1) Man killed by a spoken curse and his body immediately becomes decomposed.
(2) Attempted murder in a locked room.

1797. RIM OF THE PIT *novel* U.S.: Simon, 1944; U.K.: Stacey, 1972; Ramble House, 2009
Detective: Kincaid.
Problems: (1) Death by blows to the head in a locked room.
(2) Tracks in the snow which suddenly stop.

1798. "The High House" *short story* in Mystery Book Magazine, Spring 1948
Detective: Kincaid.
Problem: Death by falling from a roof unoccupied by anyone but the victim.

1799. ✓ "The Other Side" *short story* in "The Art of the Impossible" U.K.: Xanadu, 1990; "Murder Impossible" U.S.: Carroll, 1990
Detectives: Kincaid and Svetozar Vok.
Problem: Death by shooting in a room under constant observation and in which the victim was apparently alone.

Teed, J. H.

1800. ✓ "The Da Vinci Disappearance" *short story* in "Amazing Stories from the World of Crime" U.K.: Hamlyn, 1983
Detective: Jake von Ballin.
Problem: Disappearance of a Da Vinci cartoon from a watched and guarded gallery.

Teilhet, Darwin L.

1801. MURDER IN THE AIR *novel* U.S.: Morrow, 1931
Detective: Peter Blue.
Problem: Disappearance of a man from an airborne aircraft.

1802. ✓ THE TALKING SPARROW MURDERS *novel* U.K.: Gollancz, 1934; U.S.: Morrow, 1934

Detectives: William Tatson, plant engineer (unofficial detective), and Herr Kresch (official detective).
Problem: Just before he is shot, an old man says that a sparrow has just spoken to him.

1803. THE TICKING TERROR MURDERS *novel* U.S.: Doubleday, 1935; U.K.: Methuen, 1936
Detective: Baron Franz Maximilian Karagoz von Kaz, ex-Austrian police official.
Problem: Death by stabbing in a magician's cabinet under constant observation.

Templeton, Jesse (George Goodchild, q.v.)

1804. Chapter One of "Inch of the C.I.D." *short story* U.K.: Ward, 1932
Detective: Inspector John Inch.
Problem: Death by carbon-monoxide poisoning in a locked bedroom.
Note: The book was later republished under the George Goodchild name.

Terris, E. Wilmot

1805. ✓ THE MYSTERY OF THE PURPLE CLOAK *novel* U.K.: Modern, c. 1939
Detective: C. Wryte, solutionist.
Problem: Death from unknown means of a man in a room on his own.

Thayer, Lee

1806. THE GLASS KNIFE *novel* U.K.: Hurst, (1932); U.S.: Sears, 1932
Detective: Peter Clancy.
Problem: Death by stabbing in a locked room.

1807. THE KEY *novel* U.K.: Hurst, (1924); U.S.: Doubleday, 1924
Detective: Clancy.
Problem: Death by stabbing in a locked tower.

1808. ✓ MURDER STALKS THE CIRCLE *novel* U.S.: Dodd, 1947; U.K.: Hurst, 1949
Detective: Clancy.
Problem: Death by poisoning in a locked wing of a house.

1809. THE MYSTERY OF THE THIRTEENTH FLOOR *novel* U.K.: Hurst, (1919); U.S.: Century, 1919
Detective: Clancy.
Problem: Death by stabbing in an office under surveillance.

1810. Q.E.D. *novel* U.S.: Doubleday, 1922; U.K. (as "The Puzzle"): Hurst, (1923)
Detective: Clancy.
Problem: Death by throat cutting/neck breaking in snow unmarked but for the victim's own footprints.

Thomas, Alan

1811. THE DEATH OF LAURENCE VINING *novel* U.K.: Benn, 1929; U.S.: Lippincott, 1929
Detective: Inspector Widgeon.
Problem: Death by stabbing in a locked lift.

1812. ✓ THE TREMAYNE CASE *novel* U.K.: Benn, 1929; U.S.: Lippincott, 1930
Detective: Jimmy Thurston.
Problem: Death by stabbing in a taxi containing only the victim and an innocent driver.

Thompson, Leonard

1813. "Close Shave" *short story* in EQMM, May 1946; EQMM "Overseas Edition for the Armed Forces" May 1946; EQMM (Australia) January 1948
Detective: William S. Gray, lawyer.
Problem: Death by shooting in a closed bathroom containing the victim and one innocent witness.

1814. "Squeeze Play" *short story* in EQMM, January 1946; EQMM "Overseas Edition for the Armed Forces" January 1946; EQMM (Australia) November 1947; "Twentieth Century Detectives" U.S.: World, 1948
Detective: Gray.
Problem: Death by shooting in an open but guarded room.

Thomson, Basil

1815. "The Vanishing of Mrs. Fraser" *short story* in "Mr. Pepper, Investigator" U.K.: Castle, 1925; "Great Short Stories of Detection, Mystery and Horror" U.K.: Gollancz, 1932; "Second Omnibus of Crime" U.S.: Coward, 1932
Detective: Mr. Pepper.
Problem: Disappearance of a woman from a hotel that afterwards denied that she or her daughter had ever been there.

Thorndike, Russell

1816. ✓ Episode from "The Further Adventures of Doctor Syn" *(short story)* U.K.: Rich, 1936

Detective: Doctor Syn.
Problem: Escape by flying of the figure of the notorious criminal "The Scarecrow" from a locked tower room with a barred window.

Thorne, Anthony

1817. ✓ SO LONG AT THE FAIR *novel* U.K.: Heinemann, 1947; U.S.: Random, 1947
Detectives: Victoria Barton and George Jones.
Problem: Disappearance of a hotel room and its occupant.

Timins, Douglas

1818. THE PHANTOM TRAIN *novel* U.K.: Hutchinson, (1926)
Detective: Philip Raines Cartwright.
Problem: Appearance and disappearance of an unscheduled train from a stretch of track.

Tiner, John Hudson

1819. ✓ "The Preacher and the Locked Shed" *short story* in EQMM, December 1990
Detective: The Preacher.
Problem: Theft of equipment from a shed locked with a padlock to which there was only one key.

Tomlinson, Gerald

1820. ✓ "The Glass House" *short story* in Ed McBain's 87th Precinct Mystery Magazine, May 1975; AHMM, Oct. 1, 1980
Detective: Kidd Reno.
Problem: Disappearance of a man seen to enter a glass-bottle manufacturing plant that was then thoroughly searched by the police.

Toussaint-Samat, Jean

1821. SHOES THAT HAD WALKED TWICE *novel* U.S.: Lippincott, 1933
Detective: M. Jacquot.
Problem: Death by blunt instrument in a locked room.

Towne, Stuart (Clayton Rawson, q.v.)

1822. "The Claws of Satan" *novelette* in Red Star Mystery Magazine, October 1940; "Death from Nowhere" U.S.: Wiegers, c. 1950; Canada: "The Magical Mysteries of Don Diavolo", Battered Silicon Dispatch Box, 2004
Detective: Don Diavalo, magician.
Problem: Disappearance of a man from a guarded upper-storey room, leaving a chair propped up against the inside of the door.

1823. "Death from the Past" *novelette* in (as "Ghost of the Undead") Red Star Mystery Magazine, June 1940; "Death Out of Thin Air" U.S.: Coward, 1941, and U.K.: Cassell, 1947; "The Magical Mysteries of Don Diavolo"
Detective: Don Diavalo.
Problem: Various disappearances and in particular a death in a locked upper-storey room with the only means of exit a window letting on to a sheer wall outside.

1824. "Death from the Unseen" *novelette* in (as "Death Out of Thin Air") Red Star Mystery Magazine, August 1940; "Death Out of Thin Air"; "The Magical Mysteries of Don Diavolo"; "Big Book of Locked-Room Mysteries", Black Lizard, 2014
Detective: Don Diavalo.
Problem: Death by shooting within a locked office.

1825. "The Enchanted Dagger" *novelette* in Red Star Mystery Magazine, December 1940; "Death from Nowhere"; "The Magical Mysteries of Don Diavolo"
Detective: Don Diavalo.
Problem: Death by stabbing in and disappearances from guarded rooms.

Toye, Stanley P.

1826. ✓ THE LAUGHING CAT *novel* U.K.: Melrose, 1950
Detectives: Anthony Read and Jacqueline Norris, cipher solvers.
Problem: Death by shooting in a locked room.

Tracy, Louis

1827. THE PASSING OF CHARLES LANSON *novel* U.S.: Clode, 1924- **U.K.:** Hodder, 1925
Detective: Charles Francois Furneaux.
Problem: Death by stabbing in a locked house.

Travis, Falcon

1828. ✓ "The Locked Room" *short story* in "Super Sleuth!" U.K.: Hodder, 1982/83
Detective: Inspector Swift.
Problem: Death by shooting in a locked library.

Treat, Lawrence

1829. ✓ "Into Thin Air" *problem story* in "Cluedo Armchair Detective" U.K.: Kindersley, 1983
Detective: The reader.

Problem: Disappearance of a diamond from a guarded exhibition room.

1830. ✓ "Peacock's Poser" *problem story* in "Cluedo Armchair Detective"
Detective: The reader.
Problem: Death by shooting in a locked room.

Tree, Gregory

1831. A SHROUD FOR GRANDMAMA *novel* U.K.: Gollancz, 1951; U.S. (as by Douglas Ashe): Scribner, 1951; (as "The Longstreet Legacy") U.S.: Paperback Library, 1970
Detectives: Inspector Stephen Eliot and Arthur Crump.
Problem: Death by induced "natural causes" in a room where the dust lay undisturbed but for a circle of prints around the body.

Tree, Herbert Beerbohm

1832. "The Mystery of Howard Romaine" *short story* in "Nothing Matters and Other Stories" U.K.: Cassell, 1917; U.S.: Houghton, 1917
Detective: None.
Problem: Disappearance of a coffin and a body from a locked room.

Trevor, A. C.

1833. DEATH HAUNTS THE LOUNGE *novel* U.K.: Harrap, 1936
Detective: Superintendent Roach.
Problem: Death by shooting in a lounge under constant observation.

Trevor, Ralph

1834. BEHIND THE GREEN MASK *novel* U.K.: Wright, 1940
Detective: Inspector Lockett.
Problem: Death by induced heart attack in a locked room.

t'Serstevens, Albert

1835. "The Captain's Cup" *short story* in Argosy, Oct. 1, 1938
Problem: The discovery of a ship abandoned by its crew in circumstances reminiscent of the "Marie Celeste."

Tucker, Wilson

1836. ✓ TO THE TOMBAUGH STATION *novel* U.S.: Ace, 1960
Detective: Kate Bristol.
Problem: Death due to lack of air pressure in a spacecraft in which the pilot was alone.

Turner, John V. (see also Brady, Nicholas)

1837. DEATH MUST HAVE LAUGHED *novel* U.K.: Putnam, 1932, and Bles, 1934; U.S. (as "First Round Murder"): Holt, 1932
Detective: Amos Petrie.
Problem: Boxer who was knocked out was found to have been poisoned.

U

Upfield, Arthur

1838. AN AUTHOR BITES THE DUST *novel* Australia and U.K.: Angus, 1948; U.S.: Doubleday, 1948
Detective: Napoleon Bonaparte.
Problem: Death by poisoning in a locked room.

1839. WINGS OVER THE DIAMANTINA *novel* Australia: Angus, 1936; U.K. (as "The Winged Mystery"): J. Hamilton, 1937; U.S. (as "Wings Above the Claypan"): Doubleday, 1943
Detective: Bonaparte.
Problem: Discovery of a parked monoplane on a sandy dry lake with no footprints to explain the absence of the pilot.

Upward, Allen

1840. THE VENETIAN KEY *novel* U.K.: Faber, 1927; U.S.: Lippincott, 1927
Detective: Sir Frank Tarleton, medical adviser to the Home Office.
Problem: Death by shooting in a locked strong room.

V

Vachell, Horace Annesley

1841. "The D'Avenant Mystery" *short story* in "Quinney's Adventures" U.K.: Murray, 1924; U.S.: Doran, 1924
Detective: Joe Quinney, antique dealer.
Problem: Death by poisoning in a locked room.

Vaile, William N.

1842. THE MYSTERY OF THE GOLCONDA *novel* U.S.: Doubleday, 1925; U.K.: Cassell, 1927
Detective: Judge Dunaway.
Problem: Death by shooting in a locked room.

Van de Water, Frederick F.

1843. HIDDEN WAYS *novel* U.S.: Bobbs, 1935; U.K.: Jenkins, 1937
Detective: David Mallory.
Problem: Death by stabbing in a room in a hotel, the only exit from which is constantly guarded.

Van Dine, S. S.

1844. THE CANARY MURDER CASE *novel* U.K.: Benn, 1927; U.S.: Scribners, 1927
Detective: Philo Vance.
Problem: Death by strangulation in a locked apartment.

1845. THE DRAGON MURDER CASE *novel* U.S.: Scribners, 1933; U.K.: Cassell, 1934
Detective: Vance.
Problem: Disappearance of a man from a pool into which he had dived while under constant observation.

1846. THE KENNEL MURDER CASE *novel* U.K.: Cassell, 1933; U.S.: Scribners, 1933
Detective: Vance.
Problem: Death by shooting in a locked bedroom.

Van Greenaway, Peter

1847. ✓ DOPPELGANGER *novel* U.K.: Gollancz, 1975
Detectives: Inspector Cherry and Sergeant Duff.
Problem: Disappearance of a man seen to go into an inner study.

Van Gulik, Robert

1848. ✓ THE RED PAVILION *novel* U.K.: Heinemann, 1964; U.S.: Scribners, 1968
Detective: Judge Dee.
Problems: (1) Death by cutting of the jugular vein in a locked room.
(2) Death by unknown means in the same locked room.

1849. ✓ "The Chinese Gold Murders" *novelette* in "The Chinese Gold Murders" U.K.: Joseph, 1959; U.S.: Harper, 1961
Detective: Judge Dee.
Problem: Death by poisoning in a locked library.

1850. "The Chinese Maze Murders" *novelette* in "The Chinese Maze Murders" U.K.: Joseph, 1962; in "The Haunted Monastery and The Chinese Maze Murders" U.S.: Dover, 1977
Detective: Judge Dee.
Problem: Death by stabbing in a locked room.

Verner, Gerald (see also Stuart, Donald) (John Robert Stuart Pringle)

1851. THE CLUE OF THE GREEN CANDLE *novel* U.K.: Wright, 1938
Detectives: Trevor Lowe and Inspector Shadgold.
Problem: Death by poisoning in a bedroom that no one but the victim had entered.

1852. THE CROOKED CIRCLE *novel* U.K.: Wright, 1935; U.S.: Macaulay, 1937
Detective: Superintendent Robert Budd.
Problem: Death by shooting in a locked room.

1853. THE LAST WARNING *novel* U.K.: Wright, 1962
Detective: Budd.
Problem: Death by shooting in a locked room.

1854. THE ROYAL FLUSH MURDERS *novel* U.K.: Wright, 1948
Detective: Budd.
Problem: Death by shooting in a room under guard.

1855. TERROR TOWER *novel* U.K.: Wright, 1935
Detective: Trevor Lowe.
Problem: Death by poisoning in a locked room.

1856. THEY WALK IN DARKNESS *novel* U.K.: Wright, 1947
Detectives: Peter Chard and Inspector Donaldson.
Problem: Death by poison in a cottage surrounded by snow unmarked but for the prints of the victim.

1857. "The Beard of The Prophet" *short story* in "Mr. Budd Again" U.K.: Wright, 1939
Detective: Superintendent Budd.
Problem: Death by blunt instrument in a room under police guard.

1858. ✓ "Red Snow" *short story* in "Mr. Whipple Explains" U.K.: Wright, 1936
Detective: Augustus Whipple.
Problem: For details see "The Clue of the Crimson Snow" as by Donald Stuart (Item 1777).

Verron, Robert

1859. ✓ THE CURSE OF CRAIG'S END *novel* U.K.: Wright, 1953
Detective: Inspector Brummel.
Problem: Disappearance of two men from a haunted tower.
Vickers, Roy (see also Durham, David)

1860. MURDER OF A SNOB *novel* U.K.: Jenkins, 1949; U.S.: British Book Center, 1958

Detective: Colonel Crisp, Chief Constable.
Problem: Death by blunt instrument in a locked room.

Vincent-Holytown, G.

1861. ✓ "The Man Who Vanished" *short story* in Pearson's Weekly, April 27, 1901
Detective: None.
Problem: Disappearance of a man from within a coal mine.

Virden, Katharine

1862. THE CROOKED EYE *novel* U.K.: Chapman, 1930; U.S.: Doubleday, 1930
Detective: Tom Clayton.
Problem: Death by blunt instrument in a room under observation.

Vivian, E. Charles

1863. ✓ ACCESSORY AFTER *novel* U.K.: Ward, 1934
Detective: Inspector Head.
Problem: Disappearance of a murderer whose footprints in the snow lead to a gate and then completely disappear.

1864. "Locked In" *short story* in "My Best Mystery Story" U.K.: Faber, 1939
Detective: Head.
Problem: Death by shooting in a locked room.
Note: The same author's novel "The Impossible Crime" is no such thing.

Von Elsner, Don

1865. YOU CAN'T DO BUSINESS WITH MURDER *novel* U.S.: Signet, 1962
Detective: Col. David Danning.
Comment: Another specimen of blurb-writing inaccuracy. The blurb suggests that there is an impossible-vanishing scene and there is also a murder in an elevator; they do not, however, seem to add up to an impossible crime.

W

Wade, Henry

1866. ✓ THE HANGING CAPTAIN *novel* U.K.: Constable, 1932; U.S.: Harcourt, 1933
Detective: Superintendent Dawle.

Problem: Death by hanging in a locked study.

Wainwright, John

1867. ✓ HIGH-CLASS KILL *novel* U.K.: Macmillan, 1973
Detective: Assistant Chief Constable Sullivan.
Problem: Death by falling from a flat roof, the access to which was barred by a locked door. The only key was found on the corpse.

Wallace, Carlton

1868. DEATH OF A LIBERTINE *novel* U.K.: Long, 1936
Detective: Ex-Superintendent Bendilow.
Problem: Death by shooting in a room under surveillance.

Wallace, Edgar

1869. BIG FOOT *novel* U.K.: Long, 1927
Detective: Superintendent Minter.
Problem: Death by shooting in a locked room.

1870. THE CLUE OF THE NEW PIN *novel* U.K.: Hodder, (1923); U.S.: Small, 1923
Detectives: Tab Holland, newspaperman, and Inspector Carver.
Problem: Death by shooting in a locked room.

1871. THE CLUE OF THE TWISTED CANDLE *novel* U.S.: Small, 1916; U.K.: Newnes, (1918)
Detective: T. X. Meredith, assistant commissioner of police.
Problem: Death by shooting in a locked room.

1872. THE CRIMSON CIRCLE *novel* U.K.: Hodder, (1922); U.S.: Doubleday, 1929
Detective: Inspector Parr.
Problem: Death by poison gas in a locked room.

1873. THE FOUR JUST MEN *novel* U.K.: Tallis, 1905; U.S.: Small, 1920
Detective: Superintendent Falmouth.
Problem: Death in a locked room.

1874. ✓ A KING BY NIGHT *novel* U.K.: Long, 1925; U.S.: Doubleday, 1926
Detective: Selby Lowe.
Problem: Death by stabbing of a man standing on his own outside a door.

1875. THE TERRIBLE PEOPLE *novel* U.K.: Hodder, (1927); U.S.: Doubleday, 1926; originally (as "The Gallows Hand") in The People, 1925-26

Detective: Inspector Arnold "Betcher" Long.
Problem: Death by shooting in a locked room.

1876. TERROR KEEP *novel* U.K.: Hodder, (1927); U.S.: Doubleday, 1927
Detective: Mr. J. G. Reeder.
Problems: (1) Entrance of an intruder into a locked and bolted room, and his subsequent disappearance from the room.
(2) Death by stabbing in a locked room.

1877. THE THREE JUST MEN *novel* U.K.: Hodder, (1926); U.S.: Doubleday, 1929
Detectives: The Three Just Men.
Problem: Death by poisoning of a man under constant observation and unapproached by any other person.

1878. ✓ WHITE FACE *novel* U.K.: Hodder, 1930; U.S.: Doubleday, 1931
Detectives: Chief Inspector Mason and Sergeant Elk.
Problem: Death by stabbing, under constant watch, by apparently invisible agent.

1879. ✓ "Case for Angel, Esquire" *short story* in Ideas, March 24, 1909; (as "The Impossible Theft") in "The Sooper and Others" U.K.: Dent, 1984
Detective: Christopher Angle ("Angel, Esquire")
Problem: Theft of bank notes from a man in a side street when both exits were under watch.

1880. "Dr. Fifer's Patient" *short story* in "Sergeant Sir Peter" U.K.: Chapman, 1932, Newnes, 1933, and U.S.: Doubleday, 1933; also in "Sergeant Dunn C.I.D." U.K.: Digit, 1962
Detective: Sergeant Sir Peter Dunn.
Problem: Death by poisoning in a locked bathroom.

1881. ✓ "Hailey's Comet, the Cowboy and Lord Dorrington" *short story* in The Weekly Tale-Teller, May 21, 1910; "The Death Room" U.K.: Kimber, 1986
Detective: None
Problem: Three men apparently transported in a trice across continents by Hailey's Comet.

1882. "The Lone House Mystery" *short story* in "The Lone House Mystery" U.K.: Collins, 1929; serialized in Detective Story Magazine September 28, October 5, October 12 1929
Detective: Superintendent Minter.

Problem: A girl locked in a room of a house where the man with the key is stabbed to death. Footprints and locked room, but apparently no impossible crime.

1883. ✓ "Lord Exenham Creates a Sensation" *short story* in The Strand Magazine, February 1918; "The Death Room"
Detective: Superintendent Branbury.
Problem: A thumbprint found at the scene of a crime proved to be identical to that of the long-deceased son of a noted fingerprint expert.

1884. ✓ "The Missing Romney" *short story* in Weekly News, Dec. 27, 1919; "Four Square Jane" U.K.: Readers Library, 1929; as "The Stolen Romney" in 101 Years' Entertainment, U.S. Little Brown, 1941; "The Art of the Impossible" U.K.: Xanadu, 1990; "Murder Impossible" U.S.: Carroll, 1990
Detective: Chief Superintendent Peter Dawes.
Problem: Theft of a valuable picture from a heavily guarded art collection.

Wallace, Robert

1885. ✓ SEVEN MEN ARE MURDERED *novel* U.S.: Fiction League, 1930
Detective: Sergeant Doyle.
Problems: (1) Death by shooting with a gun not to be found in the murder room.
(2) Death by poison by apparently invisible means.

1886. THE VAMPIRE MURDERS *novel* U.S.: Regency, 1965; originally in The Phantom, 1940
Detective: The Phantom.
Problem: Death by throat laceration in a locked room.

Walling, R.A.J.

1887. MURDER AT THE KEYHOLE *novel* U.K.: Methuen, 1929; U.S.: Morrow, 1929
Detective: Professor Laxton.
Problem: Death by shooting in a locked room before seven witnesses, and subsequent disappearance of the murder weapon.

Wallmann, Jeffrey M.

1888. "Now You See Her" *short story* in MSMM, March 1971; "The Art of the Impossible" U.K.: Xanadu, 1990; "Murder Impossible" U.S.: Carroll, 1990
Detective: Hal Devlin.

Problem: Disappearance of a woman from an apartment under constant surveillance.

Walsh, J. M.

1889. THE HAIRPIN MYSTERY *novel* U.K.: J. Hamilton, 1926
Detective: Inspector Gore.
Problem: Disappearance of a man from a locked room.

1890. THE HAND OF DOOM *novel* U.K.: J. Hamilton, (1926)
Detective: Inspector Quaile.
Problem: Death and near death by poison gas in a locked room.

Walsh, J. M., and Audry Baldwin

1891. "The Death of Eli Brent" *short story* in "The Weekend Crime Book" U.K.: J. Hamilton, (1929)
Detective: Inspector Dale.
Problem: Death by shooting in a locked room.

1892. "Gassed" *short story* in "The Weekend Crime Book"
Detective: An unnamed police detective.
Problem: Death by gassing in a locked room.

Ward, A. Sarsfield (see also Rohmer, Sax)

1893. ✓ "The Death of Cyrus Pettigrew" *short story* in London Magazine, March 1909; (as by Sax Rohmer) in "The Art of the Impossible" U.K.: Xanadu, 1990; "Murder Impossible" U.S.: Carroll, 1990
Detective: Dr. Saxham.
Problem: Death by poisoning in a locked, noncorridor railway compartment.

1894. ✓ "The Green Spider" *short story* in Pearson's Magazine, October 1904
Detective: Harborne.
Problem: Disappearance of a body from a locked top-floor university laboratory and the appearance in it of a monstrous green spider thought to have made off with the victim.

1895. ✓ "The Mysterious Mummy" *short story* in Pearson's Weekly Xmas Xtra, 1903
Detective: None.
Problem: Theft of the fabulous Rienzi Vase from a museum guarded with a policeman in every room.

Warren, C. Delves

1896. "Mr. Kerr—Financier" *short story* in "Some Cases of Sherwood Lang, Detective" U.K.: Drane, (1924)

Detective: Sherwood Lang.
Problem: Death by stabbing in a locked house.

Waugh, Douglas S.

1897. ✓ "Vanishing Act" *short story* in The Seminole American, November-December 1989
Detective: Dr. Bligh, college professor and master magician.
Problem: Disappearance of diamonds from a locked room under constant surveillance.

Webster, F.A.M.

1898. ✓ "The Secret of the Engineer's Son" *short story* in The Blue Magazine; "Old Ebbie Returns" U.K.: Chapman, 1925
Detective: Old Ebbie Entwistle.
Problem: Death in a locked room by throat cutting of a man and a boy.

1899. ✓ "The Secret of the Singing Skull" *short story* in The Blue Magazine; "Old Ebbie Returns"
Detective: Entwistle.
Problem: Death by poison in a locked room.

Weir, Hugh C.

1900. "The Bullet from Nowhere" *short story* in "Miss Madelyn Mack, Detective" U.S.: Page 1914
Detective: Miss Madelyn Mack.
Problem: Death by shooting in a locked room.

1901. ✓ "The Man with Nine Lives" *short story* in "Miss Madelyn Mack, Detective"; "Crime on Her Mind" U.S.: Pantheon 1975; U.K.: Joseph, 1976
Detective: Mack.
Problem: Death by unknown means in a locked room.

Wellman, Manly Wade

1902. FIND MY KILLER *novel* U.S.: Farrar, 1947; U.K.: Low, 1948
Detective: Jackson Yates, private eye.
Problem: Death by shooting in a locked room.

1903. ✓ "A Knife Between Brothers" *short story* in EQMM, February 1947; "Ellery Queen's The Golden 13", World Publishing Company, 1970; "Masterpieces of Mystery: Detective Directory: Part One" U.S.: Davis, 1977; "Big Book of Locked-Room Mysteries", Black Lizard, 2014
Detective: David Return, Indian-agency policeman.
Problem: Death by stabbing in a room guarded at its one exit

and with one slightly open window through which a killer could neither have reached through nor thrown a knife.

1904. "Murder Among Magicians" *short story* in Popular Detective, December 1939; "Sleight of Crime" U.S.: Regnery, 1977
Detective: Inspector Grinstead.
Problem: Death by strangulation in a locked closet.

Wells, Carolyn

1905. ANYBODY BUT ANNE *novel* U.K. and U.S.: Lippincott, 1914; U.K.: Thomson, 1929 (Red Letter Novel No. 224)
Detective: Fleming Stone.
Problem: Death by stabbing in a locked room.

1906. ✓ THE BEAUTIFUL DERELICT *novel* U.K. and U.S.: Lippincott, 1935
Detective: Stone.
Problems: (1) Death by blunt instrument aboard a yacht shared with one other murdered person who had not committed the crime.
(2) Death by stabbing in a locked room.

1907. THE BLACK NIGHT MURDERS *novel* U.S.: Lippincott, 1941
Detective: Stone.
Problem: Death by poisoning in a room under constant observation.

1908. THE BROKEN O *novel* U.K. and U.S.: Lippincott, 1933
Detective: Stone.
Problem: Death by poison in a locked room.

1909. A CHAIN OF EVIDENCE *novel* U.S.: Lippincott, 1912
Detective: Stone.
Problem: Death by stabbing in a locked apartment with a chain inside the door.

1910. CRIME INCARNATE *novel* U.S.: Lippincott, 1940
Detective: Stone.
Problem: Two violent deaths in a locked room.

1911. CRIME TEARS ON *novel* U.S.: Lippincott, 1939
Detective: Stone.
Problem: Death by stabbing in a locked room.

1912. THE DAUGHTER OF THE HOUSE *novel* U.K. and U.S.: Lippincott, 1925
Detective: Stone.
Problem: Death by stabbing in a locked room.

1913. THE DIAMOND PIN *novel* U.K. and U.S.: Lippincott, 1919
Detective: Stone.
Problem: Death by bludgeoning in a locked room.

1914. FACE CARDS *novel* U.K. and U.S.: Putnam, 1925
Detective: Tony Barron.
Problem: Death by poisoning in a locked room.

1915. FEATHERS LEFT AROUND *novel* U.K. and U.S.: Lippincott, 1923
Detective: Fleming Stone.
Problem: Death by poisoning in a locked room.

1916. THE FOURTEENTH KEY *novel* U.K. and U.S.: Putnam, 1924
Detective: Lorimer Lane.
Problem: Disappearance of a man from a house under observation.

1917. ✓ GILT EDGED GUILT *novel* U.S.: Lippincott, 1938
Detective: Fleming Stone.
Problem: Death by stabbing in a locked bedroom.

1918. HORROR HOUSE *novel* U.K. and U.S.: Lippincott, 1931
Detective: Stone.
Problem: Death by poisoning in a locked bedroom.

1919. THE KILLER *novel* U.S.: Lippincott, 1938
Detective: Stone.
Problem: Death by poisoning in a locked room.

1920. THE MAN WHO FELL THROUGH THE EARTH *novel* U.S.: Doran, 1919; U.K.: Harrap, 1924
Detective: Pennington Wise.
Problem: Disappearance of two fighting men from a locked office.

1921. THE MOSS MYSTERY *novel* U.S.: Garden City, 1924
Detective: Owen Prall.
Problem: Death by gassing in a locked room.

1922. THE MYSTERY GIRL *novel* U.K. and U.S.: Lippincott, 1922
Detective: Fleming Stone.
Problem: Death by stabbing in a locked study.

1923. RASPBERRY JAM *novel* U.K. and U.S.: Lippincott, 1920
Detective: Stone.
Problem: Death by poison in a locked suite of rooms.

1924. THE ROOM WITH THE TASSELS *novel* U.S.: Doran, 1918
Detective: Pennington Wise.

Problems: (1) Deaths by invisible means of two people at a predestined time.
(2) The ability of a "ghost" to penetrate locked rooms.

1925. THE SIXTH COMMANDMENT *novel* U.S.: Doran, 1927
Detective: Christopher Cox.
Problem: Death by poisoning in a locked room.

1926. THE SKELETON AT THE FEAST *novel* U.S.: Doubleday, 1931
Detective: Kenneth Carlisle.
Problem: Death by shooting in a locked room.

1927. SPOOKY HOLLOW *novel* U.K. and U.S.: Lippincott, 1923
Detective: Fleming Stone.
Problem: Death by stabbing in a locked room.

1928. THE TANNAHILL TANGLE *novel* U.K. and U.S.: Lippincott, 1928
Detective: Stone.
Problem: Death by shooting in a locked library.

1929. THE VANISHING OF BETTY VARIAN *novel* U.S.: Doran, 1922; U.K.: Collins, 1924
Detective: Pennington Wise.
Problem: Disappearance of a girl from a house under constant observation.

1930. THE WHITE ALLEY *novel* U.K. and U.S.: Lippincott, 1915
Detective: Fleming Stone.
Problem: Death by stabbing in a locked house protected by a burglar alarm.

1931. THE WOODEN INDIAN *novel* U.K. and U.S.: Lippincott, 1935
Detective: Fleming Stone.
Problem: Death by shooting with an arrow in an impenetrable room.

West, John

1932. "The Vanishing Passenger" *short story* in The Mysterious Traveler, June 1952
Detective: Jonathan Duke.
Problem: Disappearance of a male passenger murder suspect from an express train.

Westlake, Donald E. (see also Coe, Tucker)

1933. "The Secret of the Locked Room" *short story* in "A Travesty" in "Enough" U.K.: Evans, 1977
Detective: Carey Thorpe, film critic.

Problem: Death by strangulation in a locked room.

Weyman, Stanley J.

1934. ✓ "The Man of Monceaux" *short story* in "The Memoirs of a Minister of France" U.K.: Cassell, 1895; U.S.: Longman, 1895
Detective: None.
Problem: Disappearance of a man from a turret room, with an unbarred window but a sheer drop of fifty feet, while the room was closely guarded.

Wheatley, Dennis

1935. THE MALINSAY MASSACRE *crime dossier novel* U.K.: Hutchinson, (1938)
Detective: Colin Raeburn.
Problem: Death by gassing in a locked room.

Wheeler, H. E.

1936. NO CRIME IS PERFECT *novel* U.K.: Jenkins, 1935
Detective: Kendal Graydon.
Problem: Death by poisoning in a locked laboratory.

Wheelock, Dorothy

1937. ✓ DEAD GIVEAWAY *novel* U.S.: Phoenix, 1942
Detective: Mehatibel (Hetty) Bellamy, sob-sister reporter
Problem: Death from the bends in a New York apartment.

Whetstone, Raymond

1938. ✓ "Death Is Invisible" *short story* in Red Star Mystery Magazine, Vol. 1, No. 1, June 1940
Detective: Larry Brent.
Problem: Deaths by tearing out of the throat in an area of ground where only the victims' footprints could be found.

Whipple, Kenneth

1939. THE MURDERS AT LOON LAKE *novel* U.S.: King, 1933
Detective: Clifton Brentwood.
Problem: Death by stabbing in a locked room.

Whitaker, Arthur

1940. "The Case of the Man Who Was Wanted" *short story* in Cosmopolitan, August 1948; The Sunday Despatch, Jan. 2, 9, 16, 1949; U.K. (as "The Adventure of the Sheffield Banker") "The Further Adventures of Sherlock Holmes" Penguin, 1985
Detective: Sherlock Holmes.
Problem: Disappearance of a man from a group of cabins under observation.

White, Ethel Lina

1941. SHE FADED INTO AIR *novel* U.K.: Collins, 1941; U.S.: Harper, 1941
Detective: Alan Foam.
Problem: Disappearance of a woman from a house under observation.

1942. THE WHEEL SPINS *novel* U.K.: Collins, 1936, and U.S.: Harper, 1936; U.S. (as "The Lady Vanishes"): Paperback Library, 1966
Detective: Iris Carr.
Problem: Disappearance of a woman from a transcontinental express.

White, Fred M.

1943. ✓ THE CARDINAL MOTH *novel* U.K.: Ward, 1905; Street, 19??
Detective: Inspector Townsend.
Problem: Death by strangulation in a conservatory with its only entrance under constant guard.

1944. WHO KILLED JAMES TRENT? *novel* in Pearson's Weekly, April 13 to Aug. 8, 1901
Detective: Jasper Carr, rising young novelist.
Problem: Death by stabbing in a room under guard.

White, Stewart Edward, and Samuel Hopkins Adams

1945. THE MYSTERY *novel* U.S.: McClure, 1907; U.K.: Hodder, 1907
Detective: Ralph Slade, free-lance adventurer.
Problem: Disappearance of various crews from the "Laughing Lass," a ship with the qualities of the "Marie Celeste."

White, T. H.

1946. DARKNESS AT PEMBERLEY *novel* U.K.: Gollancz, 1932; U.S.: Dover, 1978
Detective: Inspector Buller.
Problem: Victim shot in his locked lounge.

Whitechurch, Victor L.

1947. ✓ "The Mystery of the Corridor Express" *short story* in Pearson's Weekly, April 22,1899; "The Chronicles of Humphrey Judd" U.K.: Ferret, 1990; "Blood on the Tracks"; British Library, 2018
Detective: Humphrey Judd.
Problem: Death by hanging in a railway compartment under constant surveillance.

1948. ✓ "Sir Gilbert Murrell's Picture" *short story* in "Thrilling

Stories of the Railway" U.K.: Pearson, 1912; EQMM, May 1947; "Crime on the Lines" U.K.: Paul, 1975; U.K. (as "Stories of the Railway"): Routledge, 1977; U.S.: "Realm of the Impossible", Locked Room International, 2017

Detective: Thorpe Hazell.

Problem: Disappearance from a stretch of railway track of a wagon containing a valuable picture.

Whitten, Leslie H.

1949. MOON OF THE WOLF *novel* U.S.: Doubleday, 1967; U.K. (as "Death of a Nurse"): Hale, 1968

Comment: On the same lines as the earlier "Progeny of the Adder"—see Item 1950—but set just before the second World War. Here the killer may or may not be a werewolf. Excellent but not quite as good as the first book.

1950. PROGENY OF THE ADDER *novel* U.S.: Doubleday, 1965; U.K.: Hodder, 1966

Comment: Chillingly effective combination of police procedural and horror story. Deliberately understated story of the search for a killer who may or may not be a vampire and may or may not be endowed with superhuman powers.

Wicks, Frederick

1951. GOLDEN LIVES: THE STORY OF A WOMAN'S COURAGE *novel* U.K.: Blackwood, 1891; U.S. (as "A Woman's Courage"): Remington, 1892

Detectives: Chudleigh & Co.

Problem: Disappearance of two figures from a street under constant observation and with no apparent bolt holes.

Wiener, L. E.

1952. "The Disappearing Monster" *short story* in The Detective Magazine, April 13, 1923

Detective: Herrig of Scotland Yard.

Problem: The disappearance of a slip coach containing a heavy artillery gun.

Wilde, Percival

1953. ✓ "The Pillar of Fire" *short story* in "Rogues in Clover" U.S.: Appleton, 1929; "Great Short Stories of Detection, Mystery and Horror: Part III" U.K.: Gollancz, 1939

Detective: Bill Parmelee, cardsharp.

Problem: Cheating at cards by a man wearing no more than a pair of bathing trunks.

Wilkinson, Ellen

1954. ✓ THE DIVISION BELL MYSTERY *novel* U.K.: Harrap, 1932; U.S.: Garland, 1976

Detectives: Robert West, M.P., and Donald Shaw.

Problem: Death by shooting in a room (in the Houses of Parliament) that was under constant observation.

Williams, Henry Smith

1955. ✓ THE WITNESS OF THE SUN *novel* U.S.: Doubleday, 1920

Detective: Jack Henley.

Problem: Death by shooting in a room under constant observation.

Williams, Sidney

1956. THE BODY IN THE BLUE ROOM *novel* U.S.: Penn, 1922; U.K.: Hurst, 1924

Detective: Dr. Ben Morrison.

Problem: Death by stabbing in a locked bedroom.

Williams, Valentine

1957. THE YELLOW STREAK *novel* U.K.: Jenkins, 1922; U.S.: Houghton, 1922

Detectives: Mary Trevert and Robin Greve.

Problem: Death by shooting in a locked library.

Willis, Ted

1958. ✓ DEATH MAY SURPRISE US *novel* U.K.: Macmillan, 1974; U.S. (as "Westminster One"): Putnam, 1975

Detective: Commander John Knowles.

Problem: Disappearance of the Prime Minister and his wife from a caravan under observation and which was then blown to smithereens.

Wills, Cecil M.

1959. ✓ THE CASE OF THE R. E. PIPE *novel* U.K.: Hodder, 1940

Detectives: Chief Inspector Boscobell and Roger Ellerdine.

Problem: Death by unknown means when no one was present with the victim.

1960. DEATH AT THE PELICAN *novel* U.K.: Heritage, 1934

Detectives: Inspector Kettle and Sergeant Boscobell.

Problem: Death by shooting in a locked room.

Wilson, Alexander

1961. ✓ "Sentiment and Suicide" *short story* in "Wallace of the Secret

Service" U.K.: Jenkins, 1933
Detective: Sir Leonard Wallace.
Problem: Death by shooting in a locked laboratory.

Wilson, Anthony C.

1962. "The Mystery of Moulton's Farm" *short story* in "Norman Bones Detective" U.K.: Methuen, 1949
Detectives: Norman and Henry Bones.
Problem: Appearance of "devil's hoofprints" tied in with the disappearance of a man.

Wilson, Christopher

1963. FOR A WOMAN'S HONOUR *novel* U.K.: Paul, (1911)
Detective: Inspector Oswald.
Problem: Death by shooting in a locked room.

Wilson, David

1964. ✓ THE CORPSE MAKER *novel* U.S.: Award, 1974
Detective: Marshall Sam McCloud.
Problem: Disappearance of a girl's body from the guarded gallery of a high-storey apartment.

Wilson, P. W.

1965. ✓ THE OLD MILL *novel* U.S.: Rinehart, 1946; U.K.: Boardman, 1948
Detective: Sir Julian Morthoe.
Problem: Death by unknown means of a man whose body was found by the roadside.

Winn, Patrick

1966. ✓ INVISIBLE EVIDENCE *novel* U.K.: Hale, 1963
Detective: Lee Seddon.
Problem: Death by electrocution where the supply had been switched off and there appeared to be no way in which anyone could have got near enough to switch it back on while the victim worked on an attached cable.

Winslow, Horatio, and Leslie Quirk

1967. INTO THIN AIR *novel* U.K.: Gollancz, 1928; U.S.: Doubleday 1929
Detectives: Dr. Klotz and the Grand Galeoto.
Problem: Numerous appearances and disappearances of people and things in graveyards and at séances, etc.

Winsor, G. McLeod

1968. THE MYSTERIOUS DISAPPEARANCES *novel* U.K.: Faber, 1926;

U.S. (as "Vanishing Men"): Morrow, 1927
Detective: Inspector Gilmour.
Problem: Various disappearances of people in confined spaces.

Withers, E. L.

1969. DIMINISHING RETURNS *novel* U.S.: Rinehart, 1960; U.K.: Harrap, 1961
Detectives: Lieutenant Michaels and Mr. Wetherby.
Problem: Deaths of all but one of a group of people. The survivor is innocent.

Witting, Clifford

1970. CATT OUT OF THE BAG *novel* U.K.: Hodder, 1939
Detective: Inspector Charlton.
Problem: Disappearance of a man from a carol-singing party.

Wodehouse, P. G.

1971. "The Education of Detective Oakes" *short story* in Pearson's Magazine, December 1914; (as "Death at the Excelsior") in "The Uncollected Wodehouse" U.S.: Seabury, 1976; EQMM, May 1978; "The Best of Ellery Queen #2" U.K.: Hale, 1984; "Big Book of Locked-Room Mysteries", Black Lizard, 2014
Detectives: Paul Snyder and Elliot Oakes.
Problem: Death by snake poison in a locked room.

1972. "The Harmonica Mystery" *short story* in All-Story Cavalier Weekly Mar 13 1915; Detective Fiction Weekly October 13 1928; The Saint Detective Magazine June 1955; The Saint Detective Magazine (UK) October 1955; "Argosy Special Commemorative Issue 1976"; original appearance in Argosy (U.S.) not located
Comment: The same story as Item 1971 but somewhat abbreviated and set in Long Island, U.S.A., instead of England.
Skupin Comment: Adey mentions not locating the original Argosy appearance. This is likely because All-Story Cavalier Weekly changed names twice and became Argosy.

Wodhams, Jack

1973. ✓ "Big Time Operator" *short story* in Analog, December 1970; "Tantalizing Locked Room Mysteries" U.S.: Walker, 1982
Detective: None.
Problem: Disappearance of various people from a sealed time machine.

Wolson, Morton

1974. "The Glass Room" *short story* in EQMM, September 1957 EQMM (UK) September 1957; EQMM (Australia) November 1957
Detective: Inspector Anthony J. Quinn.
Problem: Death by shooting in a phone booth under observation and with the door closed.

Woodiwiss, John C.

1975. THE EBONY TORSO *novel* U.K.: Gifford, 1939
Detective: Inspector Hopton.
Problem: Death by strangulation in a locked room.

Woolrich, Cornell (see also Irish, William)

1976. ✓ "Murder at the Automat" *short story* in Dime Detective Magazine, August 1937; "Tantalizing Locked Room Mysteries" U.S.: Walker, 1982
Detective: Nelson.
Problem: Death by poison from a wrapped sandwich bought in an automat and apparently handled by no one but the victim.

1977. ✓ "The Room with Something Wrong" *novelette* in Detective Fiction Weekly, June 4, 1938 (as "Mystery in Room 913"); "Somebody on the Phone" U.S.: Lippincott, 1950, and U.K.: Hutchinson, 1951 (as by William Irish); "Death Locked In" U.S.: IPL, 1987
Detective: Striker, hotel detective.
Problem: Defenestration from a ninth-floor hotel window of a room locked on the inside.

1978. ✓ "The Screaming Laugh" *short story* in Clues Detective, November 1938; "Night Webs" U.S.: Harper, 1971; U.K.: Gollancz, 1973
Detective: Al Traynor.
Problem: Death from a burst blood vessel induced by invisible agency.

Wren, Lassiter, and Randle McKay

1979. "Mr. Brown's Perfect Crime" *short puzzle story* in "The Third Baffle Book" U.S.: Doubleday, 1930
Detective: None.
Problem: Entry made through a door on which the chain lock remained secure.

Wylie, Philip

1980. CORPSES AT INDIAN STONES *novel* U.S.: Farrar, 1943
Detective: Agamemnon Telemachus Plum, archaeologist.
Problem: Death by stabbing in a locked room.

1981. ✓ "It Couldn't Be Murder" *short story* in The Saint Mystery Magazine (U.S.), January 1954 The Saint Detective Magazine (Australia) November 1954; The Saint Detective Magazine (UK) January 1955
Detective: Jerry Jenks, illustrator.
Problem: Deaths by unknown means causing the victims to suddenly drop dead.

Wynne, Anthony

1982. THE BLUE VESUVIUS *novel* U.K.: Hutchinson, (1930); U.S.: Lippincott, 1931
Detective: Dr. Eustace Hailey.
Problem: Death by stabbing in a locked room.

1983. THE CASE OF THE GOLD COINS *novel* U.K.: Hutchinson, (1933); U.S.: Lippincott, 1934
Detective: Hailey.
Problem: Death by stabbing on unmarked sand.

1984. THE CASE OF THE GREEN KNIFE *novel* U.K.: Hutchinson, (1932); U.S. (as "The Green Knife"): Lippincott, 1932
Detective: Hailey.
Problem: Deaths (three) by stabbing in a locked room.

1985. THE CASE OF THE RED-HAIRED GIRL *novel* U.K.: Hutchinson, (1932); U.S. (as "The Cotswold Case"): Lippincott, 1933
Detective: Hailey.
Problem: Death by shooting in a locked room.

1986. DEATH OF A BANKER *novel* U.K.: Hutchinson, (1934); U.S.: Lippincott, 1934
Detective: Hailey.
Problem: Death by stabbing of a lone horse rider in plain view of spectators.

1987. DEATH OF A GOLFER *novel* U.K.: Hutchinson, (1937); U.S.: Lippincott, 1934; (as "Murder in the Morning") U.S.: Detective Novel Classic, 194??
Detective: Hailey.
Problem: Death by stabbing of a golfer who had just teed off, with no one seemingly near enough to strike the blow.

1988. DEATH OF A KING *novel* U.K.: Hutchinson, (1938); U.S. (as "Murder Calls Dr. Hailey"): Lippincott, 1938
Detective: Hailey.
Problem: Death by stabbing in a locked room in front of an innocent witness.

1989. DEATH OF A SHADOW *novel* U.K.: Hutchinson, 1950
Detective: Hailey.
Problem: Death by stabbing on unmarked sand on a beach.

1990. DOOR NAILS NEVER DIE *novel* U.K.: Hutchinson, (1939); U.S.: Lippincott, 1939
Detective: Hailey.
Problem: Death by stabbing of a man who had been on his own after opening a heavy gate that his wound would have prevented him from opening.

1991. EMERGENCY EXIT *novel* U.K.: Hutchinson, (1941); U.S.: Messner, 1944
Detective: Hailey.
Problem: Death by stabbing in a private, sealed air-raid shelter surrounded by unmarked snow aside from the victim's footprints.

1992. THE HOLBEIN MYSTERY *novel* U.K.: Hutchinson, (1935); U.S. (as "The Red Lady"): Lippincott, 1935
Detective: Hailey.
Problem: Death by stabbing of a man standing on his own in front of the picture called "the red lady."

1993. ✓ THE HORSEMAN OF DEATH *novel* U.K.: Hutchinson, 1927; U.S.: Lippincott, 1928
Detective: Hailey.
Problem: Death by blunt instrument in a tower room in which the victim was alone and the disappearance of the whip that he was carrying.

1994. THE HOUSE ON THE HARD *novel* U.K.: Hutchinson, (1940)
Detective: Hailey.
Problem: Death by stabbing of the sole occupant of a boat on an otherwise empty stretch of water.

1995. ✓ THE LOVING CUP *novel* U.K.: Hutchinson, 1933; U.S. (as "Death Out of the Night"): Lippincott, 1933
Detective: Hailey.
Problem: Murder by blunt instrument in a room under constant

observation.

1996. ✓ MURDER IN A CHURCH *novel* U.K.: Hutchinson, 1942
Detective: Hailey.
Problems: (1) Disappearance of a killer and weapon after a fatal shooting in a church that was then searched from top to bottom. (2) Disappearance of a man from the same church while all exits were guarded.

1997. MURDER IN THIN AIR *novel* U.K.: Hutchinson, (1936); U.S.: Lippincott, 1936
Detective: Hailey.
Problem: Death by stabbing and shooting of the solo pilot of an aircraft.

1998. MURDER OF A LADY *novel* U.K.: Hutchinson, 1931; U.S. (as "The Silver Scale Mystery"): Lippincott, 1931
Detective: Hailey.
Problems: (1) Death by stabbing in a locked room.
(2) Death by blunt instrument in a locked room.

1999. ✓ THE MYSTERY OF THE ASHES *novel* U.K.: Hutchinson, 1927; U.S.: Lippincott, 1927
Detective: Hailey.
Problem: Disappearances (2) of murderer and victim from a locked house.

2000. ✓ RED SCAR *novel* U.K.: Hutchinson, 1928; U.S.: Lippincott, 1928
Detective: Hailey.
Problem: Disappearance of a body and reappearance of it the next day in a car where there was no hiding place for the body and insufficient time to make the transfer.

2001. THE ROOM WITH THE IRON SHUTTERS *novel* U.K.: Hutchinson, (1929); U.S.: Lippincott, 1929
Detective: Hailey.
Problem: Death by stabbing in a locked study.

2002. THE TOLL-HOUSE MYSTERY *novel* U.K.: Hutchinson, (1934); U.S.: Lippincott, 1935
Detective: Hailey.
Problem: Death by stabbing of the solo driver of a locked car in unmarked snow.

2003. "Footsteps" *short story* in Flynn's January 9 1926; "Sinners Go Secretly" U.K.: Hutchinson, (1927), and U.S.: Lippincott, 1928;

"Challenge to the Reader" U.S.: Stokes, 1938
Detective: Hailey.
Problem: The hearing of ghostly footsteps in an old castle.

2004. "The Gold of Tso-Fu" *short story* in Flynn's February 13 1926; "Sinners Go Secretly"; "Fifty Famous Detectives of Fiction" U.K.: Odhams, 1938
Detective: Hailey.
Problem: Death by shooting in a room under observation.

Y

Yaffe, James

2005. "The Comic Opera Murders" *short story* in EQMM, February 1946; EQMM "Overseas Edition for the Armed Forces" February 1946; EQMM (Australia) May 1948
Detective: Paul Dawn.
Problem: Disappearance of an elderly man from a locked dressing room under observation in which only a younger injured man is found.

2006. "Cul de Sac" *short story* in EQMM, March 1945 EQMM "Overseas Edition for the Armed Forces" March 1945
Detective: Dawn.
Problem: Disappearance of a valuable document from a blind alley under observation.

2007. "Department of Impossible Crimes" *short story* in EQMM, July 1943; "Best Stories from Ellery Queen's Mystery Magazine" U.S.: Detective Book Club, 1944; EQMM (Australia) August 1947; "Ellery Queen's Anthology #44", Davis, 1982; "Big Book of Locked-Room Mysteries", Black Lizard, 2014
Detective: Dawn.
Problem: Death by stabbing in a closed lift between floors and unoccupied but for the victim.

2008. "Mr. Kiroshubi's Ashes" *short story* in EQMM, March 1944; EQMM (Australia) September 1947
Detective: Dawn.
Problem: Death by shooting in a locked railway-carriage compartment.

2009. "The Problem of the Emperor's Mushrooms" *short story* in

EQMM, September 1945; "To the Queen's Taste" U.S.: Little, 1946, and U.K.: Faber, 1949; EQMM "Overseas Edition for the Armed Forces" September 1945; EQMM (Australia) December 1947; "All But Impossible!" U.S.: Ticknor, 1981
Detective: Dawn.
Problem: Death by poisoning from eating mushrooms that had proved harmless to the emperor's professional taster.

2010. "The Seventh Drink" *short story* in EQMM, September 1944; EQMM "Overseas Edition for the Armed Forces" September 1944; EQMM (Australia) October 1947
Detective: Dawn.
Problem: Death by poisoning from a glass of water from which the victim had taken six previous, harmless, drinks.

Z

Zangwill, Israel

2011. THE BIG BOW MYSTERY *short novel* U.K.: Henry, 1892, and U.S.: Rand, 1895; "The Grey Wig" U.K: Heinemann, 1903; "The Locked Room Reader" U.S. Random, 1968; "8 Keys to Murder" U.S.: Dell, 1970
Detective: George Goodman.
Problem: Death by throat cutting in a locked bedroom.

Zangwill, Louis ("Z.Z.")

2012. A NINETEENTH CENTURY MIRACLE *novel* U.K.: Chatto, 1897
Detective: Mr. Warlock-Jones.
Problem: A drowned corpse falls through the skylight of a studio in London moments after the living man had been swept off a channel packet. Also see Item 1219.

Zochert, Donald

2013. ✓ MURDER IN THE HELLFIRE CLUB *novel* U.S.: Holt, 1978
Detective: Ben Franklin.
Problem: Death by unknown means in a locked room.

Addendum

Carr, John Dickson

2014. ✓ "The Devil in the Summer-House" *play* in "Fell and Foul Play" U.S. IPL, 1991

Detective: Dr. Gideon Fell.

Problem: As per the other version of this play (see Item 350).

Comment: Typically, Carr has a different murderer in this version and there are subtle distinctions in the clueing.

2015. ✓ "The Dim Queen" *short story* in The Haverfordian, May 1926; "Fell and Foul Play"

Detective: None.

Problem: Nonimpossible.

Comment: Carr's earliest fiction. A story set in immediately post-Napoleonic Spain and concerning a strange duel and a sad fate—with a twist in the tail.

2016. ✓ "Who Killed Matthew Corbin?" *radio play* broadcast BBC Home Service December 27, 1939, in "Fell and Foul Play"

Detective: Dr. Fell.

Problem: Nonimpossible. Which of four people in a London House shot to death Matthew Corbin.

Comment: Lovely radio drama and lots of clever and obvious (once you know) clues.

Rohmer, Sax

2017. ✓ THE DRUMS OF FU MANCHU *novel* U.K.: Cassell, 1939; U.S.: Doubleday, 1939

Detective: Nayland Smith.

Problem: Death by poisoning in a locked room.

Smith, Mitchell

2018. ✓ STONE CITY *novel* U.K.: Collins, 1990; U.S.: Simon, 1990

Detective: Charles Bauman, incarcerated college professor.

Problem: Death by throat cutting of inmates in locked prison cells.

Skupin Comment: This terrific novel also has a detailed and workable proposed method of escaping from the maximum security prison depicted in the novel. Perhaps this is one of Professor S.F.X Van Dusen's "two other ways out" from "The Problem of Cell 13"!

Wilhelm, Kate

2019. ✓ SMART HOUSE *novel* U.K.: Gollancz, 1989; U.S.: St. Martin's, 1989

Detectives: Charlie Meiklejohn and Constance Leidl.
Problem: Death by suffocation in a lift and by drowning in a jacuzzi in a private room when entrance to both lift and room was controlled and monitored by computer, and was apparently impossible.

Analysis of Solutions

MAJOR DISCUSSIONS on the subject of locked-room murders are to be found in Carr's *The Hollow Man (The Three Coffins),* Rawson's *Death from a Top Hat,* and Holmes's *Nine Times Nine.* There appear to be some twenty different ways in which that locked room can be breached:

1. Accident.
2. Suicide.
3. Remote control—poison, gas, or impelled to do so with his own hands.
4. Mechanical and other devices.
5. Animal.
6. Outside agency made to look like inside agency—e.g., dagger fired through window.
7. The victim was killed earlier but made to appear alive later.
8. Presumed dead but not killed till later—e.g., by the first person to enter the room.
9. The victim was wounded outside but died inside.
10. Turning key, bolt, catch, etc., from outside with pliers, string, etc.
11. Unhinging and rehinging door or windows.
12. Taking out and replacing window pane.
13. Acrobatic manoeuvre.
14. Door locked or wedged on outside. Key replaced or bolt thrown after re-entrance.
15. Door locked on the outside. Key returned before re-entrance.
16. Other methods of gimmicking doors, windows, etc.
17. Secret passages, sliding panels, etc.
18. The murderer was still in the room when entrance was forced.
19. Alibi provided while the murder was committed in an apparently guarded area.
20. Other impersonation stunts.

In most cases I have given a brief description of the solution(s) of the puzzle(s). In one or two, however, I have given merely a cross-reference to the above schedule to indicate the means by which the author solved the impossible crime.

Solutions

1. The killer took the door off its hinges, turned the lock, inserted it in the catch, then screwed the hinges on again.
2. (1) Struck by a tear-gas capsule fired from below.
   (2) Swung in through an apparently inaccessible window.
3. The victim had been stung by a deadly scorpion that was then removed by one of the first people on the scene after the victim collapsed.
4. Hollow wall through which "messages" are spoken.
5. Introduction of distillate of victim's allergy concentrate into victim's bloodstream.
6. She had escaped in a trunk with the connivance of a removal man.
7. This murderer had time to get away before the victim's neighbours, all of advanced years, had time to reach the murder room.

   A tale involving the supernatural, but the impossible element is extremely peripheral.
8. The affair had been carefully staged by the victim and his murderer. The latter had been one of the two people to burst open the locked door and had then, after the other witness had gone to fetch help, actually killed the victim who up to that point, as part of the game, had only been feigning death. The mortal wounds by the "rat" were, of course, inflicted by the killer.
9. The victim was killed by a shot from a catapult (slingshot) fired by someone from over the top of the shower stall partition.

   Not really a locked-room puzzle and not a great deal of detection, but very well written and therefore quite enjoyable.
10. The killer got out of the window by means of a rope.
11. Minor relevance; murderer wore victim's shoes and carried him there, then waded downstream after putting shoes back on victim. The perfect example of the impossible-crime story not played up as one. In fact, Chapter 1 reveals all the murderer's movements, but not his identity. Quite good.
12. The room is decorated with life-size statuary, one of which has been replaced by a nude female spy who is listening to and

passing on the information divulged during the meetings.

13. The victim was poisoned by a lipstick sent to her through the post.

14. There was a secret entrance into the kitchen from the building behind.

15. The window was open and, although proved to be unreachable from below, had been reached from above by means of a scaling ladder.

16. Another person had masqueraded as Father Savrola and had indeed been one of the witnesses as to his presence.

    A pleasant book that just about qualifies for entry in this bibliography.

17. The prints were hand prints of a demented juggler who stabbed his victims. An excellent period piece, doubly interesting when compared with the novelised version—see Item 19.

18. The murderer had tied the knife to a bundle of fish bones that had been taken away by a cat.

19. The prints were hand prints made by a demented juggler who stabbed his victims; novelised version of Item 17 and very enjoyable reading. At the end the author throws in the appearance of a prehistoric bird, which is the only major departure from the short-story version.

20. The killer, a contortionist, flushed himself down the commodious toilet!

    Highly enjoyable, an outrageous lampoon (probably *the* most outrageous lampoon ever) with loads of devious in jokes for the cognoscenti. Befz indeed!

21. The shot was fired from a second weapon, a derringer, which was then whisked out of sight by means of an elasticated cord.

22. (1) Replacement of key.
    (2) The catch was off the door, which was then wedged.

    A most promising debut that has the added merit of referring to locked-room stories by other writers, a feature that always endears a book to me.

23. The victim was stabbed through a keyhole as she listened at it.

24. The blow was struck by a mechanical device designed to protect the chapel's valuables. Some play is also made around a locked-room situation, but it proves to be irrelevant.

25. Minor relevance; a secret passage behind a sliding door.

26. Foucault's pendulum device set up to dislodge the monument.

27. The poison was smeared on one edge of the blade of a carving knife used to carve a joint, and this one side affected only the first slice of meat, which was given to the victim.

28. The victim was killed earlier but made to appear alive later.

29. Escaped through the window. The second—or third—American locked- room mystery, featuring an eccentric detective and a pseudo-confession. Remarkably easy reading for so early a book.

30. The victim fell onto a balcony below from whence his body was removed.

31. The train was operated for arms-running purposes, and its ghostliness deliberately manufactured to deter investigators.

Novelisation of a very successful play whose author, Arnold Ridley, was amazingly at over eighty starring in *Dad's Army,* a successful BBC television series.

32. There was a secret exit through a hollow pedestal in the room, and it was also possible for the bars of the window to be moved up and down.

33. The victim's "cries for help" were fabricated by means of a radio and an electric transcription.

34. The bolt was drawn across from outside the door by use of a magnet.

35. The victim was impelled to do so by means of single frames inserted into films that he was shown. The frames, seen subconsciously but not consciously, contained messages that he should kill himself.

Written by a famous American TV star; the same idea was used later by Helen McCloy.

36. In one instance the victim had been killed earlier than had originally been thought the case. The other solutions, however, all depend upon the victims being hypnotised into doing things or believing that they had done them.

An utterly preposterous book in which the impossible-crime situations are explained away in a most outrageous manner. The whole thing is entirely forgettable and has to be read to be believed, if not remembered.

37. The gas fire was alight, but the gas was turned off outside the room and then turned back on.

38. The vanisher was an acrobat who pulled himself over the wall.

39. The body had been moved by a policeman into another policeman's area because he thought it a nonviolent death and did not want to be troubled with it officially. Afterwards, he was afraid to speak up.

40. The husband had come into some money—a football-pools win—and had seized the opportunity for his wife and himself to disentangle themselves from the clutches of their family by hopping over the back fence.

41. The owner gave the fur coat to a second party, who took it out in a suitcase. The solutions to this and Item 40 are not strictly fair.

42. The items had been placed in a hole in the wail over which a sticker had been pasted. (The murder victim was a bill poster.)

43. The yacht's chef had poisoned all the people on board and thrown their bodies into the sea. He was observed doing so by the yacht owner's faithful pet baboon, which consequently killed him and threw him overboard. It then hid in a secret place above a wardrobe.

44. The fer-de-lance left by the killer responded to the temperature rise and killed after the victim had relocked the door.

    An unremarkable singleton in which the locked-room murder occurs but is not brought to the forefront as a problem itself. Some South American interest.

45. A small tablet of cyanide-salt crystals was stuck to the back of a bulb which, when lit by remote control, grew hot and deposited the tablet into a container of prussic acid beneath, thus creating lethal cyanide gas.

46. The bolt on the inside of the connecting door had been manoeuvred across from outside by means of a toothpick that had been positioned to stop the knob or the bolt from falling into position and a piece of wire by which the bolt was drawn into position from outside.

47. The gold was siphoned off through a dummy electric-wire conduit.

    The only Infallible Godahl story to qualify, though several others come near. Imaginative and delightful.

48. A lump of cyanide had been hidden beneath the floorboards and gave off its deadly gas each time a fire was lit in the furnace.

49. The box of jewels was placed outside the ship, then held on by ship's gravity until destination reached when the centrifugal force of rotation flung them away from the ship.

50. Posed as a locked-room problem but it's really all to do with spring locks and isn't a genuine locked-room problem at all.

    A very disappointing work from an author who could do much better —e.g., *The Resources of Mycroft Holmes.* The plot is poor, the dialogue is worse, the characterisation is awful.

51. The victim was stabbed elsewhere, locked himself in, and died in the bathroom.

    In this desperately, poorly produced, written, and illustrated story, the word *limited* (150 copies) will take on a new meaning.

52. The killer exited through a skylight and bolted the window after he left by "a curious little plan" that he promised to show the narrator—but never did!

    A most unlikely author to pen a locked-room tale and, given that no solution was provided, quite effective.

53. The noise was made by electric sirens operated by a group of moonshiners.

54. The opening of the door released a spring, a floorboard slid back, and a long arm shot out with stunning force and struck the would-be unlocker.

55. He hid within the crinoline skirts of a female accomplice.

56. The victim had committed suicide, and the gun's kick had thrown it some distance from him.

57. The victim had shot himself with a real gun under the impression that he was handling a toy one.

58. The poodle had hidden it under a loose tile in the room.

59. The killer had left via the window.

60. The owl was introduced into the house via a secret passage.

61. He had been shot earlier and the noise of a shot produced later by a balloon, heated by an electric fire, exploding.

62. The door was locked from the outside by means of knitting needle passed through the key and string running from the needle under the door.

63. A button on the mantlepiece fired the gun when it was pressed. Primitive attempt to create a locked-room problem and solve it. The room is not properly locked, and there are some terrible red herrings.

64. Poison was put on spikes that were outside the bedroom window. The victims were induced to lean out, scratched themselves, and then in agony shot themselves or fractured their own skulls!

Preposterous, and no challenge for a super-detective.

65. The killer relied on a rigged-up contraption. No other details available.
66. They were hidden in a decanter of wine.
67. The killer exited by cutting a hole in the door panel through which he locked and bolted the door, then carefully replaced the section he had removed. This section was smashed with the rest of the door panel when the room was broken into.
68. The hinge pins of the door had been knocked out from the inside, enabling the door to be opened far enough to get at the bolt and lock.
69. The dust had been sprayed on with a fruit-tree sprayer.
70. The picture was hidden under a freshly papered wall.
71. He had made his getaway on stilts.
72. The poison was contained in a hollow spoon from which medicine was administered.
73. The ruby had been hidden in a decanter of port.
74. The killer stayed inside the locked room after the murder and made good his escape after the door had been opened with a duplicate key produced by an accomplice.
75. The booby trap tied in with a farm implement; primitive.
76. The victim was carried out unconscious to the murder spot by the killer wearing the victim's shoes. After killing him the murderer replaced the shoes and exited via a ladder into a tree. He had previously pushed the ladder into position from the other side of the tree, and after the murder this was the same way he escaped, pulling the ladder after him.
77. The tank had been stolen earlier and replaced by a plywood replica that was burnt after it was removed.
78. Secret exit beneath an old desk; unfair to the reader.
79. Sliding panel; more unfairness to the reader.
80. A booby trap fixed up to be activated by movement of a roller blind.

Fairly primitive and the very last Dixon Hawke story.

81. The diamonds were dropped into a carafe of water; a very old-fashioned device.

82. A pencil run through the end of the key and string attached to the pencil.

83. The vault in the room had a false back to it.

84. Brilliant variation on No. 6: Detective shot victim dead while shooting off the door's lock.

One of the most memorable of all the locked room stories; a perfect blend of urbane humor, witty characterisation, finely etched plotting, and the most original solution for years. What more can one say? Why, oh why, did U.S. publishers overlook this, the best of the Shaffers's work?

85. The victim was killed by poison administered before the surveillance began. The corpse was then stabbed on the following morning after the surveillance had ceased, with a needle, and this more obvious injury was thought to be the cause of death.

86. No. 11; hinge pins removed and replaced.

87. The murder was committed earlier than at first believed. The killers had propped up the inner lock with a piece of ice that was later dislodged, the door locking with an audible snap that was assumed to be the act of the victim inside.

88. The victim was deposited in the library by a man who then exited via the French windows, closing them by holding the catch up with his knife and letting it drop as he pulled them to behind him.

Surprisingly well written, even if the author doesn't quite solve all the problems he sets.

89. The victim went to bed with the gas radiator on, but it was later switched off by the killer at a connection outside under the sidewalk and then switched back on again.

90. The telephone had in fact fallen on its side after it had been used, and the first person to enter the room had tidily set it upright.

91. The poison was contained in the gum on the back of a stamp sent to the victim.

Entertaining writing about the gentleman adventurer and his supporting crew. A pity that the solution is such old hat.

92. A double hired as part of a plot to discredit a great man.

Not a whodunit, as the plot is revealed right from the word go. This is Armstrong's usual practice, and a pity as she writes so well.

93. The killer swung over the top of the high electrified fence by using the branches of trees.

An excellent and original Holmes pastiche and an impossible-crime story rather better than a brief precis can indicate.

94. The shot had been fired through the window by a man on a ladder that was loosely secured by the rope and that he pushed away from the building to which it was secured in order to get in the correct position for the shot.

95. The roof was lifted up from outside by jacks.

A real delight: witty, ingenious, unique.

96. The victim was wrapped in a frozen bed sheet that was pushed onto the ice-covered surface of the snow. Because of the weight distribution it made no mark as it slid into a snowdrift.

A truly ingenious story, topnotch in every respect.

97. The roof was lifted up from outside by jacks.

Unsigned juvenile version of Item 95; less gruesome but equally enjoyable.

98. The killer had left a window off the latch but looking as though it was latched. He pretended that it was locked and helped to smash it in and force an entrance.

99. The victim had been shot before entering the summer house.

100. The murderer had let himself in with the victim's keys, killed, and left the keys with the victim. An accomplice took his place and let other witnesses continue to see the murderer's cigarette glowing.

101. The victim was stabbed outside the room, entered it, and locked the door behind himself. The victim then shot himself by means of a rigged desk-set in which the gun was cocked by pressing back the pen.

102. He was the victim of a new sonic weapon that could destroy from a distance.

103. The person who had administered the poison was still in the room when the door was broken in.

104. Exit was achieved via a secret panel.

This and Item 103 were published as true adventures, but there is little evidence to corroborate this.

105. A blaster was given to the robot who crossed open countryside and delivered it to the murderer, who had by this time crossed

the checkpoints into the restricted area. Superior science-fiction novel with unusual impossible situation.

106. The arm of a robot was used. Another excellent science-fiction detective novel with an impossible-crime situation to fit the setting.

107. Escape through the fourth dimension of time.

One of a trio of stories that used much the same rather intriguing theme. See Items 467 and 575.

108. The killer locked the door on the inside and then, supported by some stout twine, stepped out of the window and made his way along to the next room.

109. (1) The killer wore stilts.
(2) The bullets had been fired previously from the gun and were later fired fatally from a crossbow.

110. The gas was turned off at the main but the gas-jet was left open. It was later turned on again at main. Highly unoriginal locked-room solution, though one of the most practicable.

111. The murderer was already in the bathroom when the barricade was erected. He killed the victim and exited; the barricade was not replaced.

112. Poison was inserted in a tap (faucet) that the victim turned on in order to get a drink of water, thereby poisoning herself.

113. The print was that of a toe. The meat of this story could have been encapsulated into a short story. The rest is just a filler.

The idea behind the solution is a clever one and was repeated by Stuart Palmer in his short story "Fingerprints Never Lie," though Ellery Queen congratulated Palmer as the innovator.

114. The double had been masquerading at the command of the detective chief to confuse the criminal elements.

Included here because of the bizarre nature of the crime. The solution is perhaps inevitable, but the book is generally well written.

115. The lighting fixture of the room could be manipulated from the floor above to make a small tubular gap through which the shot was fired.

116. The owner had in fact forgotten to lock the safe! A grim true story where the apparently impossible element was eventually very simply explained.

117. After locking the door from the outside, the killer tossed the key over the transom back into the room.

118. Not impossible crime.

119. Parts of a bed could be so manipulated from outside that the occupier could be pinioned, suspended head down, and almost stifled; apoplexy was the intended result.

A remarkable plagiarism of the famous earlier story by Wilkie Collins. See also Joseph Conrad (Item 515) for another variation on the same theme.

120. The victims were given a poisoned drink.

Very disappointing, and the murderer commits suicide. As my correspondent for this so rightly says, “And I don’t blame him.”

121. The victim was dropped from a helicopter.

122. The girl had been stabbed before she got into the seat.

123. The victim, while in the bath, was tricked into handling a copper spider through which an electric current was passed.

124. The victim was tricked into opening the small hatch in the door (used for placing shoes in to be cleaned) and was injected through it by a hypodermic syringe containing cyanide solution.

125. The victim, who was play-acting, was killed by the first person to enter the room.

An enjoyable book. The solution is not too startling, but Mr. Dormer, the “cat napper,” is a more interesting character than so many other detectives. Barber's only detective novel.

126. Killed earlier by one of the guarding witnesses, who then threw his voice to imitate the victim.

127. Another person had been present, had committed the murder, and then locked the exit door after he re-entered subsequent to the discovery of the body.

The game of Clue (Cluedo) features in this novel. The suspects all bear similar names to the characters in the game and are indeed engaged in playing the game when the book opens. A good idea, but the author doesn’t really do anything much with it.

128. (1) The door key was left inside on the floor near the door, but the door was locked from the outside with a second key.

(2) The body was lifted out through a wide, old-fashioned chimney.

129. The knife was projected through the letter box of the locked door by means of a pair of braces (suspenders) secured to the walls.

130. The fatal shot was fired from outside the sanded area, and the gun was then thrown next to the body. Powder burns on gloves and helmet worn by the victim had been put on earlier.

131. After killing, the murderer stepped into an incinerator and incinerated himself.

132. The vanisher had been playing a double role and became his own valet. An explanation of the James Phillimore problem.

133. The body, still "alive" but in a state of suspended animation, was hidden in a false laboratory bench.

134. The door was locked on the outside, and the key thrust back under the door.

135. The killer left a bullet on top of a blazing log to explode after he had killed, exited, and locked the door behind him. Thus he made it appear that the murder took place later than it actually did. He returned the key to the murder room at a later time.

A very muddled affair.

136. The victim had staged the whole affair himself and had rigged the murder weapon to fire when the door was opened. Due to a miscalculation, the shot was fatal.

137. A slip lever was operated to release the coach, which was then diverted onto a loop off the main track.

138. Gun booby trap behind a picture.

139. The door was locked from the outside and the key returned inside by means of twine running through the door panel.

140. There was a series of secret passages between the room and a nearby room, and one of them opened out into the bedroom.

Typical Victorian melange: lunatics, ineffectual police, misunderstood hero, Indian background—utter tosh.

141. The victim had ingested the poison while sealing the provided, but doctored, detachable pages in a mystery book. He had intended to enter the publisher's competition by sending in the page with his solution of the mystery—but became embroiled in a murder mystery peculiarly his own.

142. The victim was stabbed under the pretense of rearranging a lap robe.

Disappointing after a bright beginning. The book is, in terms of plot, somewhat cliché ridden, and the blurb was reaching when it referred to “a shipboard equivalent of a locked room murder.”

143. One of the fake spikes had been switched for a real one by the props man, a former Nazi, who then switched them again afterwards.

Typical breezy fare from Bellem. A well-posed impossible crime with the solution falling somewhat short of the problem.

144. (1) The victims were shot from outside through a small window held open by a rod of glass made of special Prince Rupert's drops. This particular type of glass when fractured dissolves completely into tiny fragments that are virtually invisible. Therefore after the fatal shot a second was fired to smash the rod into nothingness, and allowing the window to close with no indications that it had previously been open.

(2) The victim tripped over a trip cord and fell down some stairs. She was bludgeoned to death by the first person to reach her.

A real surprise from Phoenix. Reasonably well written, interesting, a clever locked-room gimmick, and plenty of other twists along the way. Quite undeserving of the obscurity in which it languishes.

145. The shot was fired from a further weapon, a derringer, which was then whisked out of sight by means of an elasticated cord.

Literary references and name droppings abound in this entertaining little tale by an author whose pseudonyms are as cunning and as numerous as his plots.

146. The killer, a midget, was still in the room hidden in a leather hatbox when the door was broken down.

147. The statue had been taken up to heaven and was eventually brought down by an Indian using the famous rope trick.

A charming and amusing fantasy and, inevitably perhaps, a locked- room solution somewhat out of the ordinary.

148. The man who had stood guard had lied and had in fact let out the second man, who had committed the murder.

A disappointing solution but a rattling good yarn full of monumentally evil Orientals, devilishly cunning methods of execution, damsels in distress, etc.

149. Conifer is a colossal snob and expands to a degree commensurate to the company he finds himself in. When,

through a series of mishaps, he wakes to find himself ill in a poor ward of a workhouse infirmary, it is all too much for him and he shrinks away to absolutely nothing— leaving just his pyjamas behind!

Clearly not a rational explanation, but such a diverting and amusing irrational one that I couldn't resist including it.

150. The star deliberately disguised herself and took passage on a ship under an assumed name.

151. A detonator was fitted into one of the clubs. The damaged club was replaced by the murderer, who was the first man on the scene.

152. The peer had been killed at an earlier point in his tour. The killer then assumed his identity until a convenient time when he could become himself again.

153. The lawyer had deliberately disguised himself at his office for a number of years, then threw off the disguise after he had absconded with funds.

154. A secret entrance into the room that was revealed when a safe was made to swing out from its normal position.

155. The safe in the room had a secret exit built into its back.

Herrivell appeared in nine novels written along classical lines but rather lacking in credibility. He was then abandoned and replaced by the rougher and tougher Dick Marlow and Glen Gibson.

156. The victim was strangled by a trained chimpanzee who entered and exited via a dumb-waiter serving hatch.

157. The victim was struck by an icicle dart containing poison. The book contains an introduction by Len Harvey, a famous British boxer of the thirties.

158. A hypodermic syringe in the form of a chair button. The author's last book, and his worst.

159. A sharp pull on a lattice window after closure brought down a heavy handle.

A good debut by a writer who was later to write one or two classic detective stories. From a quality point of view one of Berkeley's middle-order offerings.

160. Various solutions, including a hidden tunnel and a mishmash of stage- managed effects.

161. A door hidden in the wall. Illustrated with scenes from the

photoplay of a Universal Production.

162. (1) The sword and cabinet were stolen, and replaced by an identical but empty cabinet.
(2) The jailed man was impersonated by his disciple.
(3) The missing man did not enter the cave; again, he was impersonated by a disciple who then abandoned the impersonation and became himself before exiting.

163. One man played two parts—of the supposed victim and of a witness.

164. The murderer used a combination of methods: specially constructed "devil's feet" to walk on and the victim's own shoes, the victim having been killed elsewhere.

Dreadful attempt at an English dialect but otherwise probably Berrow's best effort.

165. The killer imitated the victim's voice after he had murdered him. Occult forces play a part in this story.

166. The deaths were engineered by a person dressed as a werewolf, who had designs on the inheritance of one of his would-be victims.

167. No. 17, a secret entrance.

168. (1) The man had used a different entrance. The other party who had professed to have been unable to see him was an accomplice.
(2) The lift was rigged to appear to go up two floors when it fact it did not, and room was changed while lift was in progress.
(3) Insertion of a false piece of brickwork (on a frame) in the entrance to the street.

The outlandish nature of the solutions speak for themselves. The author's ideas for problems are fine, but the solutions don't live up to them—and the writing is stilted and uneven.

169. A current, controlled from outside, was passed into a towel rail that the victim grasped.

170. The victim was killed by the first person to enter the room after the alarm had been falsely given by an accomplice.

171. (1) Shot with a silencer. A false shot was fired later.
(2) The gun was attached to an expander and then whisked away.
(3) The gun was concealed in a Bible. It exploded when the book was opened.

An extraordinarily complex work that makes far from easy reading. The solutions are quite ingenious but lose a lot in the telling. A combination of the worst and best elements of the thirties; all rather preposterous.

172. The killer had taken in with him a key-cutting machine with which he had cut a duplicate after committing the murder.

173. The scapegoat was hypnotised into letting out the murderer, locking up, and taking the blame. The author never quite comes to grips with the locked-room problem.

174. The trick was effected with pencil and string.

175. Slow-acting gelatin-covered poison capsule swallowed earlier in the day.

176. The victim was wounded outside and after entering the office caused the bullet to move by reaching up to fix a window.

177. The killer brought and left a block of frozen nitroglycerin that exploded as the fishmonger attempted to break it with his hammer.

178. (1) Mirror effect, then the mirror—made of special substance—was dissolved into liquid by intense heat.
(2) A poison pin exploded by sonic waves.

Not a bad little book. The solutions to the two impossible problems are of a highly technical nature but sound as though, at a stretch, they might work. Typical of Fearn's output, under a variety of pen names.

179. He had been transmitted by a new invention, a matter transferrer.

A disappointing end, rationally speaking, to an interesting series of detective novels.

180. A needle was fired into the brain by a gun concealed in a drinks flask.

181. The victim had been wounded earlier and died of his wounds after locking himself in the room.

182. The victim had suffered a head injury one week before and was killed by its belated effects.

183. Gas taps turned on before murderer left the room, but while the gas meter was empty. The victim then locked the door and the murderer placed a coin in the outside meter.

184. The killer had leprosy.

185. The victim was killed after the apartment was broken into by the police, and not earlier, as had been thought.

186. The victim committed suicide with a very light pistol, and afterward a pigeon flew away with it. A very slight affair with

a highly improbable solution.

187. The man had been kidnapped and was taken out through a skylight, the entire frame of which had been unscrewed and lifted out.

188. (1) The killer was a gorilla who literally took to the trees and left his scent on the ground.
(2) The figure was projected by means of steam and a magic lantern.

189. The gun was fired by using a water bottle as a burning glass with which to ignite the fatal charge.

190. The murderer, who was in the next compartment, caused the victim to put his head out of the window and struck him with a paperweight.

191. The diamonds were still in the case, which could be made to look empty by means of a trick switch.

192. One of the witnesses lied and had taken the man out by a supposedly locked exit.

Despite the letdown on the impossible-crime problem, the book was a generally enjoyable, pacey first novel.

193. (1) The crime had already been committed: Shot fired by dying victim and weapon secreted by murderer on entering.
(2) As (1) except that the second shot was deliberately fired by the murderer.

The seeds of a good idea, but it doesn't quite come off; a good example of the problems with works in translation.

194. Impersonation of the victims in order that the servant could sell property in the victims' name and depart with the proceeds.

195. The lock was booby-trapped so that a small flintlock gun fired if the wrong key was used in the lock.

196. A booby trap hidden in an easy chair.

197. The killer left the house via a secret exit in the vault.

198. (1) The exit was made via a secret panel into a neighbouring nightclub.
(2) The figure was a mannikin.

199. The wrong key was on the inside of the door while the door was locked on the outside with the right key.

A good story and clever—though not unique—solution. Enough good material for a short story but rather padded for a novel.

200. The vanisher dressed a life-size balloon in his clothes and then deflated it and withdrew the deflated balloon.

201. The killer escaped by means of a time machine.

202. Murder by a disembodied extraterrestrial being.

203. The victim cut his own throat and then disposed of the blade down a razor-blade-disposal slot.

204. Key hung loosely in the inside while the door was locked on the outside with a duplicate. The author's only book.

205. There was a secret room off the locked room in which the murderer had been imprisoned for twenty years by the murdered man, her husband.

Very effective *Grand Guignol* from a scarce collection of historical mystery stories that Queen apparently didn't know about.

206. The videotape had been angled to record a mirror image of the shooting, thus making it appear that the victim was shot from an impossible angle. In fact, he was shot from outside the barred window, fell onto a tarpaulin that was then pulled along from outside, thus reorienting the body.

207. It was taken by a trained monkey.

208. The murderer used his own key to exit. The trickery lay in leaving the victim's key in plain view, thus suggesting that his was the one that mattered. Marginal.

209. The killer had removed the nails that secured a library window on the outside and then replaced them and nailed the window shut again after killing and using the window to exit.

210. The gas was lightable due to a filed-down tap that always allowed a little gas to flow and an automatic gas lighter. The water came not from the taps but was forced up the pipes into the bath from below.

211. Electrocution by means of a kite with a wire attached to a window handle.

Marginal. Impossible-crime situation set up but not used.

212. (1) The murderer had approached the lodge on tiptoe when she visited to murder and then covered the tracks with her footprints when she "discovered" the body the next morning.

(2) After the murder, the murderer had covered the floor evenly with dust by means of a vacuum-cleaner reverse switch and then walked backwards out of the room in the victim's slippers,

afterward throwing them back toward the body.

213. A severed head in a suit of armour gave an alibi for the killer who murdered and then substituted himself in another set of armour.

Delightful, witty novel involving a battle for honours between the two detectives. The solution is also a delight.

214. The murderer, dressed as a policeman, hid behind the door and joined the real policemen after they had broken in.

215. A false explosion created by a paper bag being burst. Thus the murderer gained the opportunity of being in a position to fire the fatal shot.

A nice complex little story with one particularly delectable clue concerning a bag of apples.

216. The sheik had been stabbed as he entered the limousine, and what had been glimpsed inside had been the reflection of the witness's own cab driver.

217. The shot was fired from an ancient matchlock concealed behind the woodwork and activated by means of a burning glass.

218. The gun was electrically wired to fire from offstage when a button was pressed.

219. (1) Secret passage from a storage bin.
(2) Climbed through a window onto a convenient ladder.
(3) An accomplice covered the footprints by which the "vanisher" had left the beach.

220. The killer had escaped through a window and then climbed up to the next floor by means of a makeshift rope lowered by a confederate.

221. The killer had disguised himself as one of the passengers—an accomplice—whose place he took during the vital period.

222. The killer entered the house disguised as an elephant, and escaped down a secret tunnel that he later nailed shut, after the house had been broken into.

A delightful parody of the master. The solution is a bit disappointing in locked-room terms—"disappointing" was the author's own word on the matter—but the pastiche is good and the dialogue rings particularly true.

223. The catcher had previously gone through the tunnel and left his mask and other equipment halfway through the tunnel for the vanisher to don and thus enter the dressing room in disguise.

224. It was only erased from maps by a vengeful oilman.

An entertaining pastiche of Ed Hoch's Sam Hawthorne series.

225. The victim accidentally threw a live cartridge into a live electric-light socket (twenties style). The metal base of the cartridge melted, and it was fired as if from a revolver.

226. The victim had been strangled earlier and dropped from a helicopter.

227. The victim had been killed by a person still in the room; i.e., his invalid sister.

228. A secret stairway and panel.

229. A previously undiscovered secret passage.

230. The victim had been hypnotised into stabbing himself.

A book with little to recommend it. Neatly posed impossible crime but a solution scarcely up to the standard of a pre-World War I boy's story.

231. The victim had his hands on the window handles as he was shot and closed the window as he fell backwards.

232. The murderer had amputated the leg with an axe prior to death and took it back to the trap. He then went for help along the tracks already made.

233. The murderer climbed out of a large chimney in the room and then lit the fire in the hearth from above.

234. The blunt instrument was in fact a pool ball in a sock. After the attack the ball was rolled away out of the area and ended up in a crowded closet.

235. The disappearance had occurred earlier than had been thought. The boy had made the room seem occupied by using an outside fuse-box switch to start and stop a model railway within the room.

236. The mask had been smuggled out in the pouch of a stuffed kangaroo, taken out for cleaning.

237. The envelope was steamed open at the opposite end to where it was sealed and taped.

238. Gas was fed through a pipe that was pushed through a small hole in the bedroom. The gas tap of the empty meter in the room was turned on in an attempt to maintain the fiction of suicide.

A story in which the reader is shown the murder attempt, step by step, as it happens.

239. None given! The detective merely remarks at the end that tricks were played (in an attempt to frighten someone away) and the "body was used as a gimmick."

Utter twaddle.

240. There was a secret exit via a revolving wardrobe.

241. The cavalier was suspended above the snow in a basket on a wire and appeared to walk on the snow when the basket was moved. The kidnap victim was in the phantom's pay, and having been lifted by the phantom, they made good their escape as the lights were put out onto the roof and took the wires and basket, etc., with them.

242. There was a secret exit from the library. This story features Blake's popular adversary, Waldo the Wonder-Man.

243. The victim, already dead, was lowered down from the storey above by the murderer's accomplice.

244. A duplicate key was used to lock the door from outside after the murder. The other key was left near the lock where it would be assumed to have fallen when the door was broken through.

245. (1) Death was due to an electric shock caused by the static electrified metallic side of a lamp shade. (2) The victim was hypnotized and told to swim out to a nonexistent raft.

246. Before the paint had completely dried, a mischievous nephew had sprayed the barn with octylduoacelefrtosulfodyne, a chemical with the property of turning organic paints to their complementary colour.

I have no idea whether such a chemical, with such a property, exists.

247. The paper had first been examined by the light of a red lantern, and the pink marks didn't reveal themselves.

Same gimmick as "Miracle on Vine Street" (Item 257).

248. Ernie had accidentally pulled over the silo while trying to straighten a section, and when he subsequently pulled it upright again hadn't noticed that the animals had strayed onto the ground it covered.

249. The haystack trail was in fact made by a circus elephant that was stealing hay from the stack.

250. After some ammonia was accidentally tipped into the water well, the windmill touched against high-tension wires and the combination of all three elements caused a kind of giant

refrigerator.

251. The farmer's young son was playing a prank by releasing different numbers of sheep each night through a loose board in the back of the shed and causing them to be counted twice.

252. It wasn't the scarecrow but his sleepwalking owner checking up, subconsciously, on some valuable bonds accidentally left in his old coat currently donned by the scarecrow. In his sleep the owner had moved the scarecrow to a more central point in the field in order to provide the bonds with better protection.

253. The duck was an inflated rubber one that was burst in a second by a missile from a slingshot.

254. Extra eggs were being added by a neighboring farmer who had seen the light after years of dishonesty and was seeking to make amends.

255. The tractor had in fact been there before the snow fell and had had the snow cleaned off it. The owner thought that he had seen it in his barn at the critical time, but that was another, similar vehicle.

256. The victim, a cardiac case, had deliberately run into the middle of the field in order to exert and kill himself. On his back was his accomplice, a dwarf, who then donned the shoes of the suicide's enemy, walked backwards in the tracks already made, and thus implicated the enemy.

257. The prints, which were actually a dog's, had been put on before the paper was affixed to the ceiling and had not been detected because the paperhangers were working by lantern light, and the lantern was a red one.

258. A ventilator above the corpse was removed, leaving a small hole through which an armadillo, rolled into a ball, was lowered. It proceeded to deface the dead man. Ingenious and apparently fair.

259. The murderers got past the guard to the victim by impersonating a horse.

260. Escape was effected by going hand over hand on a rope fixed at two points above the snow level.

261. Train was diverted onto a minor line and into a private yard. Tunnel on main line was destroyed at both ends to create a diversion.

262. Use of sewers.

Fairly weak tale, saved by the presence of the larger-than-life figure of Sir Bruton Kaines.

263. It was not Coryell's wife who disappeared but a substitute who simply stepped out of the back door.

264. Prussic acid was secreted in a hole in the victim's false teeth and a substance used to block the hole that would melt with the heat of the mouth. The teeth concerned were then removed by the killer posing as a doctor apparently coming to the rescue.

The setting for this quite inventive little drama is Simla in Northern India.

265. (1) The victim was killed by one of the first persons to enter the room.

(2), (3), and (4): Various acrobatic manoeuvres involving ropes and windows.

A classic parody of the golden-age detective novel. Delightful caricatures of three famous detectives, and the introduction of one of the very few successful comic sleuths.

266. The victim was thrown from the balcony. The door was then locked from the outside and the key replaced near the victim's body.

Even-paced, evenly written story about nondescript schoolmaster 'tec. Solution satisfying if unoriginal.

267. The murderer had escaped by climbing up the chimney.

268. No impossibility here although advertisements for this book suggest otherwise.

269. (1) From the stove that heated the studio was a pipe to the outside. On the outside of the pipe was a metal plate that could be removed to facilitate cleaning of the pipes. This plate was exactly level with the inside feeding hatch of the stove, so that when the flap of the hatch was hanging down and the plate removed, there was an open space through which a fatal shot was fired from outside. The murder weapon was catapulted into the room by a specially made apparatus, and the murderer put the stove-hatch flaps into place again when the room had been broken into.

(2) A number of the fencing posts had been cleverly sawn through, and they could be quickly and temporarily removed to allow a vehicle to pass through into woodland on the other side.

270. The old man's body had been removed from the house by the connivance of one of the other inmates who had then simply

locked up again.

271. The killer escaped through a window that he later fastened from the inside.

272. Sun's rays directed through a magnifying glass outside the window to explode the powder in the gun's pan.

273. The poison was contained on a pin concealed in the victim's morning newspaper.

274. The hut had a second door at the rear. Much is made of the problem, little of the solution.

275. The victim had been poisoned by cyanide gas given off when he used a piece of chalk impregnated with cyanide.

276. The room was sealed by a still-living relative, presumed dead, who used it as a hideout reached through a trap door.

277. The murderer threw the knife through a small, open cat window.

278. Electrocuted by outside agency passing a current into the bath tap.

279. Wood had been cut away from around the hasp of the inside of the door. The cut-away wood was refixed with cement and the door closed from outside so that the wood fell into place. When the cement had dried, the door would withstand pressure from outside.

280. The murder weapon was an angular medieval knife that had been thrown, boomerang-wise, from around a corner by the victim's twin brother from Australia.

One of the best pastiches of short-story length that I have come across.

281. A secret exit through a closet.

282. (1) Two of the victims had been killed earlier than supposed and had been impersonated by others. The dead organs of the third had been filled with various substances—e.g., pepsin—to advance decay.

(2) The attacker in the space above the ceiling let down the light fixture and inflicted the wound with a fishing rod with steel claws attached, then withdrew it and pulled back the light fixture.

283. Secret panel and passage.

284. (1) Killed by hydrocyanic acid sprayed from a perfume atomiser.

(2) The escape was made via a secret panel.

(3) Too numerous to mention. Read the book!

Very typical of its period. Abounding with bizarre situations, it proved a perfect vehicle for a Universal picture in 1929.

285. Hijacking. As an ex-stewardess, the author deals well with the in-flight situation. The plot is not particularly brilliant, but then the scope is inevitably limited by the plot.

286. See Item 904.

287. The bludgeoning occurred when the victim slammed his head against a lamp during convulsions brought on by a combination of sweat- blocking medication and the deliberate cutting off of the air-conditioning system.

288. The bullet fired through a transom.

289. The door was locked on the outside with one key while a duplicate with thread attached hung loose on the inside. This was pulled into position after the key on the outside had been removed.

290. The film star's place had been taken by a substitute who, having entered the star's room, changed out of her disguise and exited as herself.

291. The door had a double lock requiring two turns of the key. Murderer turned key once only to demonstrate to watchers that the door was locked.

292. Not impossible crime.

293. The poisoning was by accident and the house was not fully locked.

Often incorrectly cited as one of Carr's locked-room mysteries, but not strictly legitimate.

294. Not impossible crime.

295. Not impossible crime.

296. It was an identical room in a clean state and in another house in which the murder had taken place.

297. (1) The vanisher had not exited through the bricked-up door. She had exited through one directly opposite to it, and the witness had seen a reflection of this through a mirror.

(2) The body was transferred first of all to a funeral urn in the crypt and later, after witnesses had searched the coffin, out of the crypt, before the urn was searched. A strange book in which the author offers an alternative supernatural solution.

298. The stabbing was carried out by a man completely cloaked in black, using a blackened sword.

299. (1) A block of dry ice was left in the room, evaporated and formed carbonic-acid gas, and forced the occupant to jump from the window to escape suffocation.
(2) The bolt was pulled into position from outside by means of a fishing rod and line.

300. The vanisher swung himself onto the roof of the train.

301. (1) (False) The victim was killed by an expertly thrown jagged leaden ball of metal on a fishing line.
(2) The victim was killed by a legless man who drew him down to his level—behind the bushes—and left no footprints.

302. The killer rigged up a line between two points and a heavy weight on that line that could be made to shoot down at speed and at a calculated angle and strike the victim. The line and weight could later be hauled up and away.

303. The victim had climbed out of her window onto a ledge on which there were iron brackets that moved when touched and administered an electric shock.

304. The wrong key was left in the lock on the inside of the room, and the door was locked from the outside with the right key. The wrong key was then pushed onto the floor inside the room, drawn out under the door, and then, by sleight of hand, the right key was substituted.

305. Not impossible crime.

306. One of the witnesses had so arranged matters by wearing dark clothes, placing the furniture in particular positions, and using a dummy hand and a hidden panel, that he could exit unseen, commit the crime, and take up his original position again.

307. The victim was stabbed with a knitting needle.

308. Not impossible crime.

309. Not impossible crime.

310. Not impossible crime.

311. The fatal bullet was fired from an air-gun resembling a knotted walking stick that was not at once identified as a deadly weapon.

312. Not impossible crime.

313. The victim had been killed earlier, and one of the witnesses fired and pocketed the gun used on the second occasion.

314. An unwitting accomplice played the part of the victim. Dr. Fell's first novel-length adventure.

315. The victim was wounded with a thin-bladed weapon and did not

realise he was seriously hurt. He died later.

316. (1) The victim was wounded outside, adopted a disguise, and by a trick with mirrors let himself into his own room. Once inside he overexerted himself and died of his wound.
(2) The victim was shot in another location, took the gun, and walked through the snow, then fired the weapon before dying.
One of the all-time classics; quite ingenious; breathtaking. It contains the famous locked-room essay.

317. The victim himself closed and locked the windows after he had been shot.

318. The shot was fired through a window that was then smashed to conceal the bullet hole, and the body was moved by the assailant to make it appear that the bullet had come from a different direction.

319. Poisoning by nitrobenzene used on flowers near the balcony's edge. This produced an intoxicating effect on the victim.

320. An accomplice of the killer impersonated the victim, entered the room, and immediately exited. He was not seen because he was protected by the projection of another room.

321. (1) The limousine was actually being driven by a midget who sat beneath the figure of the dead chauffeur.
(2) A secret room, rather unusually, above the room where the appearances and disappearances were taking place.

322. The victim had been killed elsewhere by falling on the shaft and was carried into the tower afterwards.

323. The gun was worked by an electromagnetic force.

324. Not impossible crime.

325. The poison pellet was flicked into the drink by someone sitting some distance away from it.

326. The victim was killed by the bolt being dropped on her from the box above when she was tricked into leaning out from her own box. The killer then fired the crossbow later—without bolt—to make it appear that that was when the shot was fired.

327. The seat of the carriage contained a secret hiding place beneath it.

328. One of the observers had committed the murder in a moment while the other's back was turned.

329. The poison was in the soda siphon used with the brandy.

330. A rope was rigged up between two poles at either end of the

court, and the victim, whose throat was encircled in the middle of the court, was strangled by vigorous pulling at an end.

331. The conservatory door was left open by an accomplice.

Despite a dust-jacket blurb that suggests the contrary, this is not really an impossible-crime novel.

332. The coffin was moved by underground streams that flowed spasmodically. The problem follows a famous real-life inexplicable circumstance in Barbados.

333. A witness was tricked into thinking that the bullet hole was made later than it was and some time after the poisoning had occurred. In fact, it had been made immediately after the victim was poisoned, and the window catch had been closed by means of a piece of thread that passed through the bullet hole.

334. The murderer sealed the fire escape and entered the suite via a linen- closet window.

335. Not impossible crime.

336. The murder had been committed earlier and elsewhere. The body was carried to the beach-hut by someone whose footprints were not in question.

337. He made his exit disguised as a milkman.

338. The gas tap was opened very slightly before the victim came into the room, locked it, and closed the window. The gas then built up over a number of hours.

339. The poison was injected by pressure in the cup's handles. The later drinker was aware of this and knew how to handle the cup.

340. John Wilkes Booth.

341. The circle broke when the victim was heard to cry in agony. In fact, the murderer had made the noise and then stabbed the victim between the time of making the noise and switching on the light.

342. The victim was lassoed from another balcony and pulled over the ledge.

343. The cabin number was switched by the missing passenger, who was in fact a ship's officer.

344. She was struck on the head, partly recovered, and went to a Turkish bath. There she collapsed and was carried back to the murder spot by a third party.

345. Not impossible crime.

346. Not impossible crime.

347. The phone stood on a desk, underneath which was a tiny microphone that picked up all the caller was saying. In the phone itself was a low- power radio receiving unit that allowed someone to reply.

348. The knife was dropped from several floors above the victim as he bent to pick up a wallet.

349. The vanishers had assumed the disguises of a Father Christmas and a little-girl customer.

350. The victim was shot from outside and evidence planted afterwards to make it appear that he died by his own hand. Also see Item 2014.

351. The victim was lured to a lonely house with a grim past and made to believe in a visitation by a suicide victim.

Based on Ambrose Bierce's "The Suitable Surroundings."

352. The killer entered via a secret door and murdered the victim with chloroform over an ointment to prevent marks.

353. The victim stabbed himself with a glass knife that he then wiped clean and dropped into a pitcher of water.

A story with a truly gruesome denouement.

354. The victim had been accidentally electrocuted in his bath. His servant had then dressed him and placed him in the empty flat.

355. The victim, who was dying of a terminal illness, stabbed himself and deliberately arranged matters, by handcuffing himself, etc., to make it appear that he had been killed by a third party.

356. The deed was done while the observer's face was momentarily covered by the barber's towel.

357. The murder was committed by the person who broke open the door and fired through his cloak with a gun equipped with a silencer.

358. The will was hidden as kindling paper in the fire grate.

359. Short-story version of Item 606.

360. The trajectory of the bullet had been incorrectly calculated because the raised arms of the victim had not been taken into account.

361. (1) Exited through a trick window.

(2) The girl was murdered and dismembered in the cottage and her remains were carried out in three picnic hampers.

Considered by myself and many other critics to be the best short story of impossible crime.

362. The victim was strangled with a long whip over the victim's silk scarf.

363. The victim had been knocked out by a Mickey Finn in a soda siphon. He was then struck with a blunt instrument by one of the first two persons to enter the room.

364. A Mickey Finn in a soda siphon that produced unconsciousness and nose bleeding, following by an assault with a blunt instrument by the murderer after the door had been forced.

365. The dead man was an impostor engaged by the young man's younger brother so that when the impostor died, the younger brother would inherit.

This works very well both as a mystery story and a very spooky short story, not unreminiscent of L. P. Hartley's "Someone from Down Under."

366. A German agent had laid an invisible fuse of dead leaves soaked in oil around the margin of the surrounding woodland. If this was lit—and naturally it wasn't!—it would have picked out the factory perfectly.

367. The victim had been killed before the train started, by a man who strangled him through the partly open window.

368. The victim was not shot from within the gallery but was stabbed with an arrow by someone lurking in the doorway when the lights went out.

369. The bullet had been fired earlier at a rifle range and later retrieved with rifling marks intact. It was then fired from a different murder weapon but was first wrapped in dry moss to keep the original rifling marks intact.

370. (1) The vanisher adopted the disguise as another member of the party, by arrangement, and merely mingled with the others as the second man when the door was unlocked.

(2) The switch in the first puzzle had enabled the other man who had a key to the locked house to go and commit the murder, and yet have an apparently iron-clad alibi.

A magnificent story in which all the pieces dovetail perfectly. And this Carr's first employment of one of his regular detectives!

371. She had put on an apron, picked up a tray of crockery, and assumed the identity of a waitress.

372. The victims were stabbed by a mechanism in a pair of

binoculars that were then dropped from the tower window through which they were being used.

This story, rewritten, appears as “The Wrong Problem” (Item 380).

373. The victim opened a window and was shot from outside. The other guns had been deliberately involved to cause confusion over the question of who had fired the shots and from what angles.

374. The poison was in an ice cube taken with a drink.

375. When they returned, via a series of passages, they were taken to a second, identical room that looked out on a different side of the house.

376. Not impossible crime.

377. Not impossible crime.

378. The poison was in ice cubes placed in drinks. Note: This is a fake problem and solution.

379. Wilson’s racket was to provide doubles for famous people at boring functions. This is what had been seen and why the suit of clothes had been left there.

380. A pair of binoculars with a hidden-dagger mechanism. Also see Item 372.

381. The killer was one of the wounded men who placed the gun in a holster around a trained falcon’s neck, and the bird then flew off with the weapon.

382. A heart attack caused by a blood clot caused by close-range use of short waves in the hard radio frequencies.

383. Solution impossible to determine.

384. The woman had adopted the guise of a washerwoman and was not recognised.

385. The plans had been secreted in the folds of an umbrella by one thief and that umbrella then switched for another by a second thief.

A surprisingly sophisticated little tale, the sophistication being that the second thief picked up the wrong umbrella and thus left the plans inside the original one in the office.

386. The victim was killed in a scuffle, and the other person, who was wearing a head-to-toe red outfit, ran into the printing room and flattened herself against the back of one of the printing machines. The lights over the machine were red and turned into

the centre of the room, so that when she got behind them she just dissolved.

Joe Commings used a similar trick many years later.

387. The professor had been carrying out a scientific experiment and was sucked, temporarily, into the ether.

388. The story of the unhelpful staff was made up by the hotel manager to obtain publicity by comparing the bad treatment of the imaginary staff with the excellent treatment, cuisine, etc., of the real hotel.

389. The killer swung over to the window on a wire, took out a pane of glass, and after the murder put the pane back with fresh putty and swung back on the wire.

390. Part of the windmill tower had been made to revolve, so that the exit lay over the cliffs, and the victims simply stepped out and fell to their deaths.

An undeservedly obscure novel with lots of atmosphere. A tale of adventure rather than a detective novel, but very well written—a little in the Stevenson mould.

391. (1) The bell ringing was a recording, started by a timing mechanism, and the victim had in fact been killed earlier.

(2) The bullets assumed to have been the fatal ones and fired from the locked-up gun had been fired earlier and substituted by the killer for the genuinely fatal bullets fired from another weapon.

Better fare than average from an author not normally associated with impossible crimes. Good, lively writing.

392. (1) The killer had taken a pane of glass out of a window and then replaced it using tacks from the outside.

(2) The killer took the dead man's recorded fingerprints, photographed them, and then used the negative and some thin unvulcanised rubber to produce prints that he cemented to the appropriate fingers of a pair of gloves.

393. The bar of the door was fixed to the door with candle grease, and after the door was closed a blazing fire in the room melted the grease, which allowed the bar to drop.

394. The stabbing had been done by the last visitor, who had kept up a one-sided conversation that had fooled the guard into thinking that the victim was still alive.

395. (1) Sleight of hand assisted by a black sleeve against a black

coverlet.

(2) The knife was fired by remote control and was activated by the victim's walking through rays just as for a burglar alarm.

396. The victim was stabbed by the first person to enter the room after the door had been broken in.

397. The killer made himself invisible by the use of Professor Bingo's snuff.

A locked-room fantasy that proves that the author was much more at home in the world of the private eye. Originally published in the obscure magazine *Go.*

398. The victim had been shot, and the exit hole of the bullet had been used as the entry point of the umbrella shaft.

399. (1) (False) The victim arranged for the death weapon to be pulled out of the window by an attached weight after the shot was fired.

(2) (True) The victim was impersonated by the Saint after he had killed him. The Yale lock operated as he left.

400. A pencil through the head of the key and attached to a piece of string running outside.

401. The victim was shown a toy gun designed to draw moving film through its barrel, but this was then switched for a real gun with which he shot himself.

402. The victim had been killed by a visiting frogman.

403. (1) The victim was killed by a midget who got in through an apparently impossible entrance.

(2) The victim was pulled out of high-storey window by man hanging from above.

404. The murderer, with breathing apparatus, was hidden inside a safe in the gallery. He made his exit from the gallery when the guard made his very brief round.

405. The murderer was still in the cabin when the door was forced and simply joined the other witnesses from the bathroom where he had been hiding. A nice touch was that someone had been impersonating him outside the cabin just before the door was broken in.

406. The killing had been done slightly earlier, and the door was in fact not locked when first stated to be so, but was then locked with a duplicate key from the inside by the person who claimed that the key would not unlock it.

407. The victim was drugged and then stabbed by the first person to approach him after the cabin door was broken down.
408. He had been trapped and crushed behind the steel plate in his experimental folding bed. Horrible denouement revealed in the most matter- of-fact way. *Not* a locked-room death but could well have been.
409. The "victim" was a magician who was practising his escapology routine.
410. Trap door from the floor above.
411. Stabbed with an arrow by the last person in the room.
412. It was a ruse by a clerk to prove to his employer that he had never noticed his facial features.
413. The lid of the tomb is rigged to close on the head of one of the defilers when the body inside is touched. A nice bit of misdirection.
414. The corpse was dressed up and thrown out on the snow by the murderer. Excellent atmosphere and a cleverly woven plot.
415. Secret passage. Very good atmosphere and the locked-room solution is really no letdown.
416. One millionaire was not killed. He and his accomplice had cooked up the third murder while each of them killed one of the other millionaires.
417. Hammer had been dropped on the victim from a great height.
418. Ice had been deliberately broken at a point in the pond where the murderer had known that there was a deep submerged well—into which the victim fell.
419. The killer posed as a postman, was unnoticed as he entered, and carried the victim out in a sack.
420. The three figures were reflections in a mirror that had been slid across to allow the victim to be stabbed with a spear from within an adjoining room.
421. As the victim peered out of his window he was lassoed from above and pulled out of the window. A brilliant exposition.
422. Swordstick thrust through the trellis work of a summer house.
423. The witness had confused killer and victim. The victim had been killed and thrown from the pier while the killer, who was not the man everybody talked about, exited in the normal way.
424. The hand caught had in fact been that of the catcher, who had then grabbed the suspected thief.

425. Attacks were by light razor touch, gas, and a boomerang.
426. The body was that of the vanished man, but the head had been smuggled in and belonged to a recently executed criminal. The head belonging to the body was recovered later.
427. The murderer had paddled in from the seaward side, pulled over the victim with a net, and stabbed him with a geological-hammer point.
428. One of the guards stole the fish and then masqueraded as an Eastern mystic.
429. The coin, which was a counterfeit of base metal, had been lifted from above by means of a magnet.
430. He was killed by being thrown onto a bank of earth from a high window.
431. The diamonds were shot out in small quantities from a blunderbuss owned by the foremost of the guardians.
432. His throat was cut while he was being shaved, and the body was then placed in a potato sack and disposed of.
433. (1) The man disguised himself as a scarecrow.
(2) A third detective who had looked into the room through the opposite window had shot his two colleagues. There had been no one in the room.
434. The victim was drugged, then stabbed by the first person to enter the room.
435. The alleged victim made the prints himself to trick a policeman into shooting dead a relation whom he supposed to be the invisible man.
436. The victim had put his neck into a snare deliberately prepared. His death was caused when the killer pulled on his legs from behind.
437. Swinging door jamb.

One of the most disappointing books encountered. The characters are ridiculous and the plot hackneyed, as is the locked-room method, which Le Fanu did so much better nearly a century before. A prime candidate for the "worst locked-room mystery" award.
438. The murderer swung a weight down from the balcony above.
439. The murderer had a duplicate key.
440. The contents of the murder room were arranged so that they would fall over when manipulated from outside and a sound like

a dying man was manufactured with a deflating balloon.

This book couldn't show more clearly the difference in approach between Christie and Carr to the locked-room problem. With Christie's book, the locked-room situation emerges as such only in the closing pages and is solved with aplomb by the suave Belgian. A very satisfactory book.

441. The victim was killed by a heavy weight suspended from above outside a window. The position of the body was changed by the first person to enter the room—the murderer.
442. One of the victims staged his own death, killed off the remaining victims, and finally engineered his own suicide to look like the original murder.
443. The murderer left by using a duplicate key and arranged a fire cracker up the chimney that went off later and was assumed to be the fatal shot.
444. The man was playing two parts and merely assumed his other role.
445. The victim had locked the door herself, and the killing bottle was exchanged for a harmless one by the murderer after the door had been broken in.
446. A sharp blow on the French windows after closure brought down the inside catch.
447. The victim was induced to put his head out of the window and was shot from the adjoining room. The killer later entered the murder room and closed the window.
448. The murderer impersonated the victim to make her appear dead before she actually was.
449. The victim had accidentally fallen and knocked himself out. He was then stabbed by the first person to reach him.
450. Suicide made to look like murder by someone who wished to throw blame on people who had ill-treated the suicide.
451. The murderer impersonated a maid who had quite legitimately entered the murder area.
452. The victim was made to seem alive by means of ventriloquism.
453. The real diamond had been replaced by a glass imitation that was smashed on the floor together with a wine glass.
454. The vanisher had exited, dressed as a plumber.
455. Shot with an automatic bolt setter, a machine that fires nails.

Good example of the modern detective novel. The

impossible problem is neatly worked out, and the solution is a very feasible one.

456. The signal flares were in fact contact-starshells that were being fired into the air from a house outside the ring of troops. The rifle was silenced, the starshells exploded above the hill and fell, thus giving the impression that they were being fired from the hill.

457. The gun was a very small antique hand gun that, after use, had been secreted in a bore hole.

458. Escape was made by means of steel rods, smuggled in, which were used to reach across to a nearby house.

459. A key was used to lock the door on the outside while the booby trap was kept in place by means of a wire running through the gap between door and architrave.

460. After entrance had been made, the murderer exited by means of a fire escape.

Practically a nonstarter. The discerning reader will spot the locked- room situation, but the solution is a letdown.

461. Heart attack brought on by mild electric shock engineered from outside.

Above-average golden-age novel. Well written, with the inevitable padding, genuinely interesting, and well researched. The ending is a highly original and practicable locked-room-murder method.

462. It is proved that the killer could have escaped through the only unlatched window to the adjoining house by use of a plank lying across iron spikes inserted into the holes left in the house wall where a balcony, now removed, had been. In fact, this is a false solution, as the murder had been committed by an apparently trustworthy witness who had simply locked the second of the two doors after he had escaped through it.

463. A booby trap had been rigged up in the bathroom cabinet to fire when it was opened.

464. The villain of the piece achieved these strange and apparently incredible acts, including pulling the victims out of upper-storey rooms, by being able to climb up vertical walls with the help of discs of india rubber attached to his wrists and knees.

465. The murderer was a policeman and mingled with the investigating officers when they entered.

466. He had crossed on the back of a cow.

467. The pentacle had been made by an accidental spillage of ink. Further ink was spilt to break the pentacle. The demon's fellow-demon-help- mate was then trapped by a clever angel!

One of a trio of stories with much the same theme—see also Items 107 and 575. Cogswell had originally suggested the combination of devil deal and locked-room mystery—and produced the best story of the three.

468. The victim was killed earlier but it was made to seem later by a shot timed to be fired by use of an alarm clock. The key was returned to the lock by the killer after re-entrance.

469. A blunderbuss was rigged up to explode when the victim answered the telephone.

470. The key was replaced in the lock after the entrance had been forced.

471. The "ghost" was wearing a black cloak, so that when he turned around he seemed to disappear. He then ran up some stairs, shinned up a rope, and made good his escape.

472. One of the first persons to enter the room after the discovery had bolted the door through which he (the murderer) had originally exited.

473. After dispatching his victim, the murderer loosened the internal bolt mechanism so that it would later seem to have been forced, closed the door behind him (it opened outwards), and put a concealed wedge under it to stop it being pulled open.

474. The suspect had locked himself in, made a small hole in the wall near a light fixture, and threw out the key, then repaired the wall inside with quick-drying cement and plaster.

475. The killer removed a window pane, reached in, closed the window, and then replaced the pane.

476. Canopy on top of four-poster bed came down by means of a ratchet and smothered the sleeping victim.

A very early, very famous story that qualifies for inclusion here. It was also the subject/victim of a number of later plagiarisms. See, in particular, Items 119 and 515.

477. The figure was in fact a mask and gloves hung on the knocker of a black door that was opened inwards and appeared to admit a robed figure.

478. The victim had faked death by pinching the doctor's

stethoscope tube.

479. What appeared to be a shadowy figure within the cell was in fact a man-sized silhouette thrown up by the killer holding a small cardboard figure in front of his flashlight lens.

Typical Commings ingenuity.

480. The murderer had survived in a pocket of air in the sunken ship, swam out and stabbed the diver, and then swam to the other side of the rescue vessel.

481. The murderer wore an all-red costume—and cloaked his face—and killed the victim while the camera rolled automatically. He then filtered out all the red on the film so that his dash across the white walls would be obliterated from the film.

482. (1) The actor went into the rigging by means of a rope and pulley. He remained there until he died.

(2) The illusion of the magician disappearing from his cabinet was worked by a backdrop that was in fact a mirror. The murderer used the same device to reach the victim and afterwards to escape.

483. The murderer hid the slim, deadly instrument by secreting it in the gullet of his victim.

484. (1) The man was not in the room. It was his reflection seen on the glass entrance door.

(2) The man was knocked unconscious and rolled up in a movie screen.

485. Each woman was wearing a dress impregnated with formaldehyde and absorbed the poison into her system.

Here the author draws on his knowledge of the seventeenth century when the use of poisoned skirts was well known.

486. Dry ice entered the room by means of a champagne bucket. This later evaporated and formed deadly carbon dioxide.

487. The prints were made by the toes of one of the witnesses, a former circus artiste able to use feet like hands. She had slipped out of her shoes and left the other witnesses touching them empty.

488. (1) The coins were carried out each day in the hollow handle of a broom.

(2) The murder occurred earlier than the shot that was heard. The shot was produced by mean of an iodine-and-ammonia-soaked paper ignited in the victim's pipe.

489. The weapon was tied on to the front of a car; an excellent and ingenious offering.

490. See Item 484.

491. Struck across the throat with a steel-tipped bull whip.

Typically ingenious handling by Commings and good atmosphere.

492. One victim had accidentally killed himself; a second was killed by another person wearing a baseball-catcher's mask. The footprints to and from the mausoleum had been made by a boy wearing a man's overshoes, while the writing in the dust inside the mausoleum had been made by the boy when he took advantage of a few moments when the lights were out.

493. Both murderer and victim got into position by using the chandelier as the axis for a pulley.

494. (1) The stabbing was done with a sliver of glass from a window broken in the room.

(2) The key used to open the door was made of crystal glass and did not register on the fluoroscope. The key was swallowed before entry into the room, regurgitated, then swallowed again.

495. See Item 505.

496. See Item 505.

497. The victim was killed by a man in the well house with him and dressed as a policeman. When the door was broken down, the impostor mingled with the other real policemen.

498. Killed by a guard and the body disposed of down a laundry chute.

Good picture painted of Banner—but not quite a top-line Commings mystery.

499. The messages were written in chalk on the blades of the fan that cooled the rooms and could not be seen while the fan was working.

500. The pool's ladders had been removed and the water lowered to a level high enough to drown but not high enough to enable the victim to get out of the pool. When she became exhausted, she drowned.

501. The murderer killed the victim in the room, piled furniture up inside the middle of the room, placed a jack on top of the furniture, and raised the whole room by its ceiling. He then propped up the room by placing stools under each of two of its

sides, took away the jack, replaced the furniture, left the room again, and pulled away the two stools.

502. The second "man" was a dummy that the real man donned to exit.

503. The capsule was stuck to the 300-pound marker on a set of bathroom scales and would only come to light when someone of equal weight (Senator Banner!) stood on it.

504. The killer was wearing an all-black outfit, including veil, and the murders occurred at night.

Banner in his usual good form and finding a solution that Carr has used at least once.

505. (1) The bullet was lodged in a heater that discharged it when it became hot.

(2) The cards were carried out in the rolls of abdominal fat of a gross man wearing trunks only.

The usual ingenuity, but the locked-room solution would require a great deal of luck.

506. The killer had walked barefoot to the scarecrow, removed its shoes, walked back in the shoes over the original footprints, then pitched the shoes back to where they had originally been.

507. The murderer slid along some overhead insulated electricity wires.

508. One victim shot the other, then killed himself, with a gun he had stashed away in a floating decoy duck. The gun, tied to a line and sinker, was then pulled overboard.

509. (1) A trick with slightly warped mirrors that did not reflect anyone standing in front of them.

(2) A beach umbrella pushed slightly through spy hole, opened out, and knocked against the mirrors.

Not quite top-line Commings but, as always, good atmosphere and unusual plotting.

510. The murder was committed by a pistol—with silencer fitted—three minutes before the shots recorded on a tape were played. The gun had meantime been switched to a sealed envelope.

What an opening gimmick! The solution could never hope to live up to the uniqueness of the problem, but it doesn't do at all a bad job in trying.

511. (1)The footsteps had been going down to the basement, not up as the witness had thought.

(2) The diamond was a fake made of glass that also shattered in the explosion.

512. The child was removed through the cabinet's false back door, chloroformed, and kidnapped.

Unhappy mixture of soft pornography and mystery fiction.

513. The aerodrome buildings, which were used in a fiendish plan to decoy planes, were lowered by mechanical means to below ground level.

One of a series of air-mystery stories by this author.

514. Complicated business with thread and sealing wax or possibly pliers.

Usual sound though uninspired stuff from this author—but why am I always put off by the surnames he gives his characters?

515. The canopy on top of the bed was lowered to smother the victim.

Amazingly, a third use of the basic plot line previously employed in Items 119 and 476.

516. The poison had been introduced by way of a fork with a false prong filled with poison.

517. Access was gained via a secret staircase that could be lowered and raised from the studio to the floor below.

518. The killer strapped little bamboo stilts to her toes and "tippy-tip- tipped" over the mud in them.

519. The fly was a fisherman's fly cast from outside by an expert fisherman.

520. The conflagration was caused by the action of rubidium in the presence of water. The rubidium was comet dust that was showered on the Earth every so many years when the tail of the Leonides passed close to it.

521. The blow was struck by means of compressed liquid air in a brazen cylinder with a barrel to it in which was a spicule of frozen water, an icicle like a barb. The attacker was hiding in a tree that he had gained by means of stilts.

522. The water was fresh, the outflow from the Rio Grande, which surges directly in the Gulf for over 100 miles.

523. The murderer was one of a pair of Siamese twins inextricably conjoined. The execution would have meant the inevitable death of his innocent twin, hence the quashing of the sentence.

524. The bullet had originally been fired in a duel 200 years before and had lodged in a tree. Two hundred years later a piece of the

tree was placed on the fire in a house and the bullet in it was shot out when the marsh gas in the wood was ignited.

525. (1) The horse and rider were brought down by means of a South American-style bolo.

(2) The manifestations were produced by means of the latest experimental cinematographical equipment.

526. The killer closed the French window by arranging that a mild slam dropped the hook over the appropriate eyelet.

527. The bolt of the door was shot from outside by means of an electromagnet.

528. The wraithlike figure hid in a large flower box with a false soil-and- flora covering. The levitation was hoaxed by a second wraithlike figure being on call in the other block.

Neat, intricate, and successful. But why the pseudonym?

529. Same story as Item 528.

530. The woman shot herself and the recoil took the gun through the partly open window. The second bullet was one that the gun had fired previously but failed to eject due to an imperfect powder charge.

531. Metallic springs worn on the heels enabling large spaces to be cleared.

The only story I've yet encountered featuring the mythical creature Spring-Heeled Jack, the flying man, endowed with the ability to clear great heights and spaces.

532. The victim was shot earlier with a gun bearing a silencer, from a courtyard, through a room in which two men were listening to opera, across an outdoor passageway hallway, and through another window to the victim's forehead. Later the murderer closed the room's window, faked some evidence, and left the gun in the room. Finally he fired a blank from a different gun to change the apparent time of the murder.

533. (1) The stock of toys had been moved in temporarily and was then moved out again.

(2) The victim was knocked unconscious by the last person in the room and her mouth and nose were blocked to cause death. The murderer then entered first and tied a cord around the victim's neck to simulate strangling.

534. The unconscious victim was roped to a lift mechanism that hung him when the lift was operated.

535. The driver had been killed earlier by the station master, who had taken up his own post after driving the engine into the station.

536. The victim was wounded outside and died inside. A neat secondary clue concerning a palindrome.

537. The victim swallowed a letter sent to him that was impregnated with poison—believing it to be morphine, to which he was addicted.

538. The porthole was pushed open from outside and then pulled shut again by means of a rubber suction cap.

539. (1) The open gas pipe was plugged up, then the plug was withdrawn by cord from outside the door.
(2) The murderer was in the room when the door was broken in.
The usual workmanlike Crofts opus; quite readable but lacking in atmosphere.

540. The window was removed and then replaced with fresh putty, etc.
Looks good and starts well, but tails off badly. The murderer's identity is never much of a secret, and the locked-room explanation is highly unoriginal.

541. False finger plates on the door, which could be taken off to allow access to the locks and bolts.

542. They were shot by arrows made of ice.

543. A test tube of poison was fired at the victim by means of an air gun.

544. (1) As the victims entered the pool, they trod on drawing pins smeared with curare. They pulled out the pins but died nevertheless, and their deaths were attributed to drowning following cramp.
(2) The figure was a man on stilts who pulled himself onto an upper balcony and so avoided his pursuers.

545. The jewels had not been stolen. They had fallen into a false compartment within the safe.

546. The killer removed the plate around the doorknob, reached through, turned the lock, then restored the plate.

547. The fingerprints of the vanisher were false and were created by rubbing the surplus ink off his fingers after the first fingerprint had been taken, and thus reversing the ridges and valleys for the second fingerprinting. Therefore no one had left the house and thus the lack of footprints.

548. The pieces were smuggled out in a number of local tradesmen's small vans.

549. The door was not in fact locked but was made to appear so by the man who smashed in one of its panels and fiddled with the key and bolts inside the door.

550. The door was wedged. The murderer appeared to break it open and draw the bolts from inside.

551. Gas was fed into the room through a pipe pushed through the transom.

552. The killer found a key that had fallen from someone else's pocket. The poorest solution of all.

553. The victim had been stabbed outside the room, escaped from the killer, locked herself in the room, and then collapsed and died.

554. The message was contained in a telephoned bet made to the betting- office owner.

555. The thief had fished them out through the transom with a rod and line.

556. The killer had a duplicate key.

557. (1) (a) Murderer shinned up a rope outside the room's window, (b) Key pushed under door.
(2) Blood extracted by means of a syringe with hollow needle and pump.

Plenty of shocks in this one to keep the bloodthirsty reader happy. Moves along quite well, though not all the solutions are very clearly stated, and the human-vampire idea sounds extremely unlikely—though the vampire idea itself is good. Surprising that so few authors have allied the impossible crime to the vampire theme.

558. She had eloped over the wall with her lover.

559. The victim was stabbed by one of the players on the pretence of going over to pour him a drink. The fingerprints came from a glove made from the skin of a human hand and burned later in the fireplace.

560. The unconscious victim was locked into a cabin and a large, sharp knife wedged between two pillows right at the victim's throat. The seas were rough and the motion of the boat caused the knife to move backwards and forwards and slowly cut the throat while the victim was alone.

561. The victim, in a drunken stupor, was killed by the first person

to approach him after the door was unlocked by our heroine.

562. The key to another door also fitted the locked door, and was used to lock it.

563. The two fatal shots were silent, while a coincidental shot fired in a nearby room was the one heard.

564. The house was demountable and was simply moved away after our hero left. The idea was to discredit him and have him committed to a lunatic asylum—but it would have been so much easier to have quietly bumped him off. Pretty poor stuff.

565. The body was removed via a fireplace that swung back into the flat next door.

566. The victim was made to collapse by a drugged cigarette and was stabbed by the first person on the scene.

567. The key had been returned to the room under the door.

568. The victims were killed when their body heat released a Borgia-type poison gas from metal objects with which they had been in contact.

No attempt is made to identify the mysterious poison. "How they treated the metal is a lost secret," says our hero, so all in all somewhat of a disappointment.

569. The car was concealed inside an overwide, unwieldy caravan.

570. The money was taken out of the envelopes before they were posted.

571. The train was lowered into a subterranean kingdom run by a master criminal.

572. The killer had wired up a zip gun hidden in a chandelier to fire when the victim switched off the light.

573. The victim had been killed by poison, and the first person into the room had created the illusion of death by stabbing by plunging a knife into the dead body and smearing on his own blood.

Quite a neat and original locked-room solution at the end of a book that suffers from thirties wordiness.

574. The Spider descended onto the outer balconies by rope ladder from the floor above and entered by the window. The detective is a cad and gets killed; rather unusual for so early a book.

575. Teleported by the devil. The victim then escaped from his apparent obligation by a combination of legal trickery and insanity.

One of a trio; see also Items 107 and 467.

576. The girl was kidnapped, raped, and locked up, but later escaped.
This is a fictional treatment of the well-known Elizabeth Canning case.

577. The murderer entered and exited via a broken window. After the murder the murderer was the first person to enter the room, out of sight but within earshot of others, and broke a second pane of glass to make it sound as though she had to break in.

578. The killer, an African pygmy, was hidden in a coal basket when the entrance was forced.

579. The murderer had constructed a door within a door with its own separate lock and used this to exit from the murder room.

580. The body had been moved from a nearby building by the use of a cable that ran from the building to a tall tree. It was pulled along the cable in midair until, at a central point, a securing sheep-shank knot was pulled free, loosing the body to fall to the ground below.

581. Burglars had broken in and witnessed the murder. They then left by the same window with the body and proceeded to blackmail the killers.

582. The window was wedged on the outside after the murderer exited.

583. (1) On the first occasion there had been no such thief, and various witnesses, including the elevator boy, had lied.
(2) On the second occasion it was the elevator boy in disguise. Once in the elevator he had abandoned the disguise and pretended that he had been threatened by a third party.

584. The man was lifted from above into a tree and the "tracks" were made by his killer.

585. The victims were strangled by a hybrid creeper.

586. The man played two parts, the vanisher and the observer, and merely switched roles.

587. The train had been diverted onto a spur where a scrap-metal firm was in being. It was "hidden" among other engines destined for breaking, and its number was altered.

588. A secret entrance to an underground chamber where there were grisly doings over a number of years.

589. The key was dropped on the floor of the room after the door had been broken in.

590. (1) The murder was committed by a trained monkey.

(2) A booby-trapped telephone.

The impossible murders are two from a batch of six performed by a "series killer," who himself has only a short time to live. The solutions are somewhat incredible, and the book rises to no great heights in any aspect.

591. The victim died of fright caused by the long-range hypnotic power of her husband.

592. The victim had been given the poison earlier by means of a capsule in a cup of coffee (!). When it later dissolved, the poison acted.

593. The poison had been put into a dental filling and plugged with soluble cement. When the cement came out, so did the poison.

594. The fatal wound had apparently been inflicted earlier than had been supposed and before the group in the room had gathered there.

A complicated affair and, in the way of these round-robins, one feels that the writer of the final and explanatory chapter (the ingenious Ronald Knox) has an unholy mess to clear up. I think the solution I have given is the one he propounds. The other various hands were Hugh Walpole, Agatha Christie, Dorothy L. Sayers, Anthony Berkeley, and E. C. Bentley. A distinguished company.

595. The bullet had passed quite by chance through a slit in the shutter.

596. The killer, an undersized woman, had gained entrance through a small hole underground leading to a stream and a system of caves.

597. The victim was killed earlier but a tape-recording was used to make it appear that the killing took place later.

The master of the unusual setting produces here a locked-room mystery set in a private zoo where the only witness is an ape who can communicate with man. Excellent.

598. Not impossible crime.

599. (1) The chest was not made of iron, but was a light folding model made of cardboard.

(2) The cardboard chest had been burnt in the fire grate, and the diamonds, like coal, lay in the ashes.

600. The murder took place before the observation began, and the

murderer later impersonated the victim to make it appear that he was still alive.

601. The lead surrounds of a glass panel of the window were melted with a blowtorch, and the panel was lifted up to allow the catch of the window to be lifted.

602. The vanisher masqueraded as one of her own servants.

603. Not really a gimmick—simply that a drunken caretaker locked a door and forgot that he had done so.

A very enjoyable book indeed, although the impossible crime itself is not truly impossible. H.M., as usual, in top form. *Skupin Comment: Adey doesn't address the real impossibility, which is that there appears to have been no way to administer the poison. It had been frozen into ice cubes.*

604. Not impossible crime.

605. Not impossible crime.

606. The man who jumped in removed his clothes in the water, swam underwater, then came up impersonating another man who had left the pool unobserved.

607. Gummed paper was drawn into position by the use of a vacuum cleaner on the outside.

This book was written as the result of a challenge issued by Clayton Rawson—who came up with a different solution to the same problem! Excellent in every way.

608. Doorknob removed from outside and arrow shot through the aperture.

Probably the best locked-room mystery ever written. It has H.M., tense courtroom scenes, and an ingenious solution—in fact, all the John Dickson Carr magic.

609. Not impossible crime.

610. Murderer deliberately soaked his fingers in the blood, then dried them off. Thus, when he afterwards, again deliberately, made the prints, they were exactly opposite to what they should have been as the blood was in the inner ridges of the fingers and not, as it should have been, on the outer ridges.

611. The bodies had been buried in bunkers on golf courses and thus gave no sign of being disturbed.

612. The widow, observed by a drugged girl in the room, was in fact her own reflection. Her face had been painted while she was drugged and was afterwards cleaned by someone else under the

guise of bathing it.

613. Shot with a rock-salt (dissolvable) bullet of the same diameter as the knife that was thought to have done the deed.

This excellent, eerie novel introduces the number one, in my book, locked-room solver, H.M. A first-class debut with plenty of atmosphere.

614. The victims were electrocuted in their baths and afterwards removed elsewhere from them and dressed by their killers.

615. Presented with a flask poisoned with curare that killed him via a wound caused by a lanced gum. The flask was then removed by the murderer.

Nicely worked-in red herring about a room that kills and a treasure guarded by a poison booby trap. Good average Carr.

616. The rubber knife was switched with a real knife by remote means of lazy tongs.

Very good middle-period Carr, with lots of skilfully laid false trails. I could never understand why the later paperback edition was called *Cross of Murder*

617. The victims had falsified the first set of footprints to make it appear that they had jumped from the leap. Later, when the tide had come in, they went over the same route again and did jump. They were killed as they were making their planned escape in a rock cave, and their bodies were thrown back into the sea.

618. The victim had been struck just above the ankles with a cricket bat held by a boy who had wormed his way across the flat roof on his stomach and was therefore invisible to those below.

619. (1) Shot once through a slightly open window, then the gun was thrown through a window into the murder room where it exploded on impact with the floor and struck again.

(2) An apparent stabbing was in fact a wound by a knife thrown from a distance—which enabled the murderer to establish an alibi.

A very capable work and closely plotted. The author, in presenting a quite feasible solution, gives page references for the earlier clues.

620. The murderer pretended to be the victim, fell apparently murdered down one flight of stairs, and then pushed the real victim's body, already dead, from behind a screen down the second flight.

Superbly handled piece with masquerading master criminals and master sleuths, H.M. and supporting company, a really clever impossible crime, and an isolated castle where most of the action takes place. First-rate Carr.

621. The murder was made to look as if it occurred later than it really did. The body was then carried through the snow that was not at that point thick enough to show that the maker of the tracks was carrying extra weight.

622. The victim fell downstairs and accidentally cut and burnt herself. The witness said that he saw someone with her because he did not wish to bring her injuries—that he had seen—to his companions' attention and thus effect her salvation.

623. The room had been changed to simulate another room in a deliberate attempt to effect a confidence trick. It had then been changed back again after the hero had blundered in and been knocked out.

624. The performance had been given by a substitute, and the victim was killed earlier.

625. A fishing rod had been used through one of the windows to pull back and later push back the bolt on the door.

626. The death was a fake setup to enable a struggling financier to make a discreet exit when his murdered body was washed out to sea.

627. The murderer had used an innocent party's shoes and walked on his hands inside the shoes. His own shoe had caught the hedge and made one print.

628. The money was hidden in a dummy central-heating radiator.

629. The trick was worked with mirrors and had been deliberately set up to play a joke on the observer.

630. His brother had arranged for his double, a dying man, to kill him prior to his own death, but the double baulked at the task. Ends with a supernatural killing.

631. Not impossible crime.

632. The victim was stabbed with a glass knife later concealed in a jug of water.

633. The victim had been tricked into bending over to pick up a wallet and was killed by a knife dropped from above, unseen in the glistening falling rain.

634. A device that exploded on descent and then dropped into the lift

shaft.

A little on the heavy-handed side and a very complicated murder device indeed!

635. The victim, already dying, locked the door himself after the murderer had exited.

636. One door was locked from the inside and the bolt was thrown on the other by the killer when an entrance was forced through the locked door.

637. The killer had committed the murder earlier, then went back, removed a door panel, gained access through it, arranged the locking and blocking of the door, and finally left via the panel, which he secured with small wooden wedges, and later retrieved them after the door had been broken in.

638. Other keys were held.

A book that treats strangely with many facets of the fictional field of detection, mystery, and the occult. Liking or disliking it will depend on one's allegiance to the original forms of the same fiction.

639. The door had a Yale-type spring lock that operated when the killer made his exit.

640. There was a trick door that was opened by means of andirons being moved.

641. The cases were false demountable ones containing bladders full of water that were emptied into the washbasin.

642. The dust was evenly distributed, after the body had been dumped, by means of a pipe attached to a pump with an equalising chamber.

643. The victim was scratched through the ventilator by a poisoned arrow tip.

644. No one had been murdered. The "murderer" had, in fact, fired his shots at a mirror that was reflecting a figure from outside the room. (This solution given in the issue of Oct. 22, 1898.)

645. The killer had had a duplicate key cut.

646. The thief was a trained rat and his exit a drain.

647. The murderer was let into the cabin by an accomplice who had hidden in the cabin's generator pit.

Unusual publication and quite pleasantly written, although the locked-room explanation is unconvincing.

648. A small hole was bored a few inches above the lock, and the

key was manipulated by means of a piece of thread.

The full text of this story has not been studied.

649. The man had been rendered unconscious and abducted by a giant talking ape who had then placed the emerald in the gutter, having no particular interest in it.

An oddity and scarcely an impossible crime, though to some extent set up like one. An interesting variation on the ape theme—see also Poe and Leroux—and an element of fantasy.

650. The victims were frightened by a monster breed of Cuban spider.

651. The victims were shot from outside the window that was then broken in the act of entry.

652. The fear was caused by the introduction of a deadly snake into the room.

653. The ship was taken over by a half-caste who organised the black crew members and killed the white ones. The ship was abandoned once it reached the African coast.

654. The victim had committed suicide with a gun to which string and a weight were attached, which whisked it away after the shot was fired.

A locked-room type of trick, but not in this instance truly an impossible situation.

655. The train was driven into a deep, disused mine.

656. The old man had faked his broken hip and climbed through the window. After he had been killed, his murderer broke the victim's hip.

657. The car's speed had taken it over a surrounding ditch onto hard turf that did not bear its tracks.

658. One of the men killed the other and then himself.

Interesting variation. The problem was to discover which of the dead men had killed both of them. All tied up with insurance, of course.

659. The victim was stabbed through the open window before the train started, and the killer impersonated the victim's voice to make him seem alive later on.

660. The body had been lodged against some stones on the roof. They gradually gave way and caused the body to slip through and over the edge.

661. There was a secret entrance to the box.

662. A second key had been made.

663. A miniature radio receiver had been rigged up as a fuse to an explosive planted in the tower. The plane happened to be on the same waveband and was accidentally operated by the receiver. After the plane crashed, the receiver acted to set off the explosive.

664. (1) The killer wore—Indian style—a covering of feathers on his feet.
(2) The car was left-hand drive and could be driven at speed by a driver who kept his eye on the near-side white line.

665. The killer had climbed out through a window after locking the door. He then arranged a record to play and emit screams to make it seem as though the victim was still alive.
A very badly titled story, as this killer was monumentally stupid and made it patently obvious that it was murder and that he had done it.

666. There was a small hole in the window through which an arrow passed. The window was then knocked out and the small hole disappeared.
More than just an excellent essay on the locked-room theme. This is a really first-rate detective novel from a writer better known in the science-fiction field. The British edition has a most interesting dust- wrapper design.

667. The crooks had a painting made of the front of the safe and attached this to a frame that they then stretched in front of the real one. This is what was seen by the outside viewers while the real safe was broken into behind it.

668. He killed a guard, mutilated both his own face and that of the guard, and took his place.

669. The girl was murdered in the bungalow, cut up, and eaten by the killer.

670. The door was locked on the outside with a duplicate key, and the key on the inside was not dislodged.

671. The diamond was hidden in a specially manufactured light bulb.

672. The diamonds, placed in a metal cylinder, were hidden up the chimney from whence they left the house by virtue of a hydrogen-filled balloon.

673. The tapestries were returned to the room before the guard was arranged and covered in a substance that is a derivative of iodine of nitrogen. Once this had hardened, it was painted to match the

wallpaper and was thus camouflaged. The highly inflammable covering was later burnt off by remote control to reveal the missing tapestry.

674. After a great deal of byplay with alibis and witnesses, the killer proves to have made his entry past one of the guards who had fallen asleep.

Very disappointing.

675. The poison was in tooth fillings, and the murderer was the dentist.

Marginal.

676. The door had a spring lock that closed automatically behind the killer.

677. The person who broke in a panel of the door already had the key in the hand which he thrust through to unlock the door from the inside.

678. A window tested by witnesses was in fact stiff but not locked. It was accidentally locked when a witness was testing it.

679. The victim had been attacked by piranha fish.

680. The victim was killed by a small metal bolt, fired from a crossbow, that passed right through the body.

681. The killer fired a stick from a crossbow through the hatch of the observatory.

682. The murder had taken place earlier than at first supposed, and the murderer had then impersonated the victim for the benefit of the last visitor.

I wasn't entirely satisfied with the answer to the impossible crime, and an earlier apparent impossibility was also explained away by means of gymnastic ability. However, I did enjoy this tale, set in a small West Indian island, and the dry and often witty observation.

683. Externally operated mechanical device that operates locks, etc.

The most interesting aspect here is the production of the book itself. Larger than standard size, beautifully produced, and profusely illustrated, it purports to be a collector's item with a story of Poe-like quality to match. Alas, the story, which involves two bodies in a locked room, is a disappointment, and the locked-room element, tantalisingly posed, is all a bit of a cheat and never properly explained. The detectives, Inspector Cassidy included, are guilty of some really horrible gaffes, while Bobby Weathersby is an incredibly stupid “Watson.”

684. The concentrated rays of the sun fired a gun within the room.

685. The fatal projectile was shot out by someone playing a flute.

686. A gun had been so fixed with wire in the log woodwork of the door that it fired when anyone attempted to slide home the bolt.

687. The murderer hid in the folds of a curtain until the room was full of people and then joined them.

688. The child was removed from the train during one of its stops.

Marginal, and included only because of its similarity to the “Vanishing Lady” theme (see Item 1942).

689. The killer blew up a balloon and put it into the open fireplace. The hot air took it up the flue so that the opening was blocked and carbon- monoxide fumes pervaded the room and killed the victim after he had locked the door following the departure of his murderer.

Ingenious, if unlikely, solution. Characters and situations not without interest but the lack of humour makes it heavy going.

690. (1) The victim had been chloroformed and dumped overboard through a baggage door.

(2) A poisoned cigarette. The killer used a dart shot from a tobacco pipe/blow pipe to divert suspicion.

A mystery from the publisher whose books Bill Pronzini discussed so entertainingly in *The Armchair Detective* (April 1977) and in *Gun in Cheek* (Coward, 1982) and a typical example of its sensational, if unoriginal, outpourings.

691. The producer had been killed and his body hidden inside a fake statue that formed part of the set.

692. (1) A cat had got into the room in which the deceased sat in a rocking chair, and had set the chair rocking.

(2) The vanisher had slipped into an alcove.

(3) The maid was in fact a man dressed as a maid. He went into the study, discarded the disguise, and came out as the man he really was.

693. Two of the rooms in a suite of three adjacent were capable of being moved across within the frame of the whole suite, rather like a conjuror’s magic box. The victim had entered one room, and it had then been moved over to become the room next to it.

694. (1) A suicide note, believed to be forged and thus generating the murder theory, proved to be genuine, while the victim’s other

supposed writings were false.

(2) At first it was thought that he had exited while disguised as an iceman, but later his body was discovered on the roof of the cupola.

695. (1) While the rest of the crew and ship's members and guests were drugged, the criminal removed the gold bit by bit and hid it in three 10-gallon kegs in one of the lifeboats. He then drugged himself and also put about a story of another ship that had come alongside.

(2) It was a dummy that had been thrown overboard, not the drugged man.

An excellent story, surely long overdue for anthologising.

696. The actress had fainted and been caught up in the curtain. She had remained caught up in it when it was raised and had suffocated there.

697/ The poison, in liquid form, had been thrown in through an unglazed, barred window into a filter by a man skilled in the game of cottabos.

698. A booby trap, fitted into a safe, fired the fatal shot.

Contains the absolutely unforgettable phrase: "This has me beat to a custard."

699. The thief had a key to the room and was filmed by the camera, but a second intruder found the hidden camera and exchanged the incriminating film for a blank one.

700. String was passed through the end of the key and turned from outside.

A familiarity with stockbroking terminology will help with a book that almost tries to pack in too much for clarity's sake. Nevertheless quite meritorious.

701. The victim had been killed by a giant chimpanzee that had entered and exited via a window.

702. The murder was committed by the first person to the enter the room.

703. (1) The victim was shot through a sliding panel.

(2) The waxed seals were opened and afterwards reclosed by means of a heated knife.

704. Exactly the same as in Item 707.

705. The jewels were removed from the wearer's head by the use of a whip with a snapper attached.

706. The waxed seals were opened and afterwards reclosed by means of a heated knife.

A reworking in hard covers of Item 703, "The Crystal Cell."

707. The jury were poisoned by odourless poisoned gas introduced into the room by means of a glass phial placed in the keyhole and broken when the key was pushed in and turned. The keyhole cover prevented the gas from blowing back into the corridor when the key was extracted.

708. Gas-filled balloons dressed in witch's garb attached to a magnetised broomstick that was radio controlled.

709. The killer used a suppressor (silencer) on his rifle from a distance, plus a primitive infrared night sight.

710. Same as Item 708, plus a siren on the broomstick to produce the laughter.

711. (1) Piranha fish (what else?) that, after the killings, are "called" from the pool via a concealed pipe.

(2) Reflections in the rippling water of overhead Chinese lanterns.

712. The killer was a one-armed man whose disability had forced him to become skilled in the use of his feet, and it was with them that he had strangled the unconscious victim.

A story which, like a number of others in the same volume, flirts with the impossible crime.

713. The needle had been fired through the partly open taxi window from a compressed-air weapon in the form of a walking stick.

714. The victim had consumed the poison before retiring to his bedroom. It was not soluble in water but proved to be so in whisky.

715. A hidden passage.

716. The victim had been killed elsewhere and dropped from a glider.

717. The window of the room had a stained-glass panel with a picture of the man murdered centuries before set in it. At this particular time of the year, and no other, the sun's rays struck the panel and projected the image into the locked room.

For a reworking, see Item 719.

718. A science-fictional solution: Reducing the metal to atomic form and then transferring it in its changed state.

719. (1) A poisonous root gave off fumes when the lamp was lit. The solution is the same as and has a reference to Conan Doyle's

nonimpossible story, "The Adventure of the Devil's Foot."
(2) The window of the room had a stained-glass panel with a picture of the man murdered centuries before set in it. At this particular time of the year, and no other, the sun's rays struck the panel and projected the image into the locked room.

720. A mechanism beneath the round house was used to turn it around so that when the victims left the room, they plunged into an abyss.

721. The killer had a duplicate key.

722. The killer went through a window and jumped down into a pickup truck parked below, the back of which was loaded up with old mattresses.

723. One of the men shot the other, then himself; he arranged the gun to look as though it had been fired by the other victim.

724. The murder weapon was concealed in a box camera with which the victim thought she was having her photograph taken.

725. The deceased woman's brother had constructed two lamps, the glasses of which acted as reproducers of outside noises such as wind whistles.

726. The victim died on his own of poison administered before the door was locked. The first person to enter stabbed the corpse to make it seem that that was how he had been killed.

727. The girl hid in one post-office van and then, before it was searched, moved to another that had already been searched.

728. Both men had been drenched with nitroglycerine at an earlier stage of the game, its absorption causing their deaths.

729. The chief guardian of the jewels himself stole them and then placed the blame on a hapless guardsman whom he had wounded in taking the jewels.

Not, strictly speaking, an impossible crime, but certainly one of the cleverest, most terrible crime stories that I have been privileged to read.

730. The door had been bolted from the outside by reaching through a flap in the door used by the family dog.

731. The window of the room had been opened by levering between the junction of the two sashes. The victim was then stabbed by a knife held in a long prop pushed through the bars of the window. After the prop was withdrawn, a loop of wire was passed around the knob on the window catch, the sashes were

drawn together, the catch closed with the wire, and the wire finally pulled out.

732. The victim was shot from a yacht on the bay with a rifle using both scope and a device called a Steadicam.

733. One of the first people on the scene had retrieved the object and hidden it in the lawn mower's petrol tank

734. The killer bolted the French windows after the door had been broken in.

735. The victim licked the seal on an envelope that had been dosed with aconite.

736. The bus made a stop in the fog outside a two-storey shop where the real dead body was housed. The substitution was then made between the live and dead bodies, each dressed alike.

737. The key was returned to the victim's pocket after the entrance had been forced.

738. The man was kidnapped by villains who had a passkey; depressingly simple.

739. The victim switched off the alarm and admitted his killer. After the murder, the killer left the house and reset the alarm switch by means of a slip knot of string passed through the keyhole.

740. The poison was on a lace handkerchief given to the victim. The application of toilet water to the handkerchief caused the poison to act, and the fumes were inhaled by the victim.

741. The killer escaped onto the roof and shinned down a rope.

742. All the cabins in the camp were identical, and the deception was achieved by switching round the cabin names.

743. (1) The poison was activated from inside the speaking tube of a dictaphone machine as soon as the machine was used.
(2) The victim poisoned himself with poison from a cup that he then just had the strength to throw into a nearby fire.

744. The key was replaced by the first person entering the room after the door was forced.
An excellent novel.

745. A complex but quite feasible combination involving delayed time switches, panes removed from windows, window catches opened and closed with coins. Ingenious.

746. The houseboat got by one of the bridges whilst disguised as a coastal tanker and was then hidden behind the facade of a derelict house on an island.

747. The plane that the witness had seen from a balloon was a model of the real aircraft that was not recognised as being a model because the witness had no reference point to indicate its true size.

748. The sealed room had been entered through a supposedly locked communicating door. The key to the communicating door was found in the safe when the room was unsealed but was in fact palmed there after the unsealing by one of the officials taking part.

Set in Istanbul.

749. The diver had been killed earlier than originally supposed, the miscalculation as to time of death stemming from the speed with which air is breathed at a depth of seventy feet under water.

750. An electrical current was conveyed from the adjoining flat by means of a magnet on the end of a rod to which a wire was attached that ran to the electrical supply in the first flat.

751. The room had been disguised as a broom cupboard and partly blocked off; the man had been kidnapped.

752. The murderer said that the door was locked—but it was not. It was then broken down. The last murder in a series and the only impossible one.

An average Foster novel.

753. (1) The carpet had been treated with a mixture of hydroquinine and sulfite that after exposure to air produced a reddish-brown stain in the shape of footprints.

(2) The killer planted beneath the sand a series of wooden-sole shoes specially treated to give way and then be utterly destroyed. When they gave way, it created the impression that foot marks were being made.

754. The gold Buddha was disguised with a coat of bronze leaf, and one of the bronze Buddhas was hidden within the hollow center of another.

755. During a temporary, contrived blackout, the magician's place was taken by an accomplice. He was later released from the coffin by the magician before it was submerged in water.

The author is better known as Hank Janson, writer of numerous exotic and erotic thrillers.

756. Not impossible crime.

757. There was a trap in the ceiling through which a bulb containing

poison had been introduced.

758. The key was turned by means of a string attached to a match stick through the head of the key. When the string was pulled, the match turned the key.

759. The dagger was fired in through the open window by means of a compressed-air rifle.

760. The landing lights on the genuine landing strip were doused by German infiltrators who then lit up an alternative landing strip nearby controlled by them. Groan!

761. Simply a ruse by the millionaire to ensnare the three investigators.

A charlatan entry; a spin-off from an American TV series, *The Most Deadly Game,* which also seems not to have made the grade.

762. The murder had been done with a harpoon gun fired from an upper window as the victim bent over to pick up a £5 note.

763. The key was pushed back under the door.

764. A pencil was pushed through the end of the key and a string attached to the pencil. The string was then pulled from outside the door. It turned the key via the pencil, then detached itself. Both pencil and string were retrieved under the door.

765. The victim had locked himself in, eaten part of a deadly mushroom, and bashed his head as he fell.

766. A secret exit through the bathroom wall.

767. The bolt was drawn from outside by means of wire poked through the keyhole.

768. A glass vessel was placed over the victims' mouths and a stopcock turned at the other end of the vessel, thus creating a vacuum. The puncture mark indicated where, after death, the vacuum was broken to enable the deadly apparatus to be removed.

769. The vision was manufactured by staging the scene in a room below the crystal and relaying the picture by means of a series of mirrors to a pipe in the leg of the table on which the crystal stood.

770. The illusion was created by a man wearing clothes covered in phosphorus whose reflection was seen in a sliding mirror that was afterwards withdrawn into a recess.

771. The victim had stopped for petrol and on a pitch-black night had

then turned his car in entirely the wrong direction.

Written as the answer to his wife's "Grinning God" (Item 781). She proposed the problem, he disposed of it with the aid of Professor van Dusen.

772. The child was picked up by an orangutan.

773. A midget, hidden in a suitcase brought in by an accomplice to the laboratory's anteroom, slipped in and stole the radium while the accomplice distracted the guard's attention.

774. The necklace was taken from the boat in many small packages by a number of homing pigeons.

775. The car proved to be two high-powered motorcycles being ridden close to one another.

776. The prisoner used a disused drainpipe that began in his cell as a means of communication with the outside world, and through it obtained various supplies, including acid and a wig. He cut through the bars of his cell with the acid, caused the outside arc lights to malfunction, and then, wearing his disguise, exited as an electrician.

777. The thief was an artist who had been allowed access to the gallery to make a copy of another picture. He had removed the valuable canvas from its frame and had made his copy of the other picture on top of that.

778. One of the women had unlocked the safe in her sleep, and the diamond had been pecked loose and swallowed by a pet cockatoo.

779. A lighted gas jet within the room was blown out from outside the room by simply blowing into one of the outside gas pipes.

780. The man climbed onto an outside ledge, climbed along it, and then in by another window letting into another room.

781. This is the story that proposed the problem solved in Item 771.

782. The victim killed himself when he ignited a piece of whipcord that ran in turn to an elastic band that held the trigger of a crossbow. This released a knife laid in the groove cut in the stock where the bolt would normally go.

A slim, rare wartime paperback.

783. The thief's pet monkey had got in through the door's ventilator and exited with the necklace.

784. A sliding panel and fixed gun that could be operated from another room.

785. The killer was a trapeze artist wearing a birdman costume who swung across to the tower on a long rope from a conveniently, if improbably, placed nearby apartment building.

786. The power was supplied via a dynamo hidden under a small windmill that provided power when the wind blew strongly.

787. The dart was shot through a small hole in the wall from an adjoining room. The automaton and the possibility of a person inside it were blinds.

788. The condemned man was hidden in a secret narrow recess at the side of the switchboard (and we don't mean G.P.O. style!) and was later smuggled out of the adjacent autopsy room under cover of another corpse.

Pretty feeble.

789. Not impossible crime.

790. (1) The chest was hidden inside a slightly larger chest.
(2) The diamonds were removed by carrier pigeon.

791. The killer was on horseback.

792. The last man in the room, other than the victim, left one shutter unlocked to enable the murderer to enter. Then as the first man in the room after the murder, he simply locked the shutter again.

793. Sword thrust through keyhole.

A not entirely happy hybrid of sword-and-sorcery, magic, and science. The locked-room situation does a little to dull the pain.

794. The victim, who was already injured following a fall, was shot by the first person to approach him.

795. The victim was struck in the back by a heavy lamp that swung down on a chain when the victim set off a booby trap by lighting the gas lamp.

796. A piece of wood was placed under the heavy bar on the rear door, and string attached to the piece of wood. When the string was pulled from outside, the piece of wood fell away, the bar fell, and the door was locked.

For the record, this was the third Lord Darcy short story, the earlier two being the nonimpossible "The Eyes Have It" *(Analog,* January 1964) and "A Case of Identity" *(Analog,* September 1964).

797. The death was by natural causes, and the documents were hidden in a tunnel concealed behind a dummy wine rack in the

cellar.

798. The last person to enter the room had drugged the victim, tied a noose around his neck, and secured the rope. He then had lodged the drugged body on a high beam and left the room. Then later he had, with the aid of a long spear, pushed through a partly opened window and dislodged the body of the victim from the beam, and in falling he was hanged.

799. The gun was arranged to go off when a cord was pulled in the course of a treasure hunt.

800. The killer placed the key inside the door through the panel he had just splintered to gain access.

801. The murderer, apparently locked in his room, escaped by means of a hidden trap door, lured the victims to a room where the lower part was unlit, and thereby hid a trap in the floor. As they fell through it, a noose was placed over their heads.

802. Not impossible crime.

803. The victim had been killed earlier, and his body had been placed at the foot of the tower. His impersonator had then gone onto the balcony, locked the door, and let himself down from the balcony by means of a rope that he afterwards released.

804. The killer had locked a window behind him by use of a knife on the catch securing the window sashes.

805. The vanisher had at first hidden in the trestles of a large table and later escaped using an exit flap in the cellar.

806. There was a secret exit gained by removal of panels and sidings on both the inner and outer walls of the vault.

807. A secret entrance under the carpeted floor of the room.

808. The broadcast was done by the actress's double.

809. The victim was killed by the lid of the old Victorian bath in which he was sitting, which fell on him when he picked up a rigged loofah (!).

810. The victim's own body was held in position against the door as the murderer eased through it in such a way that as it fell it moved the bolt across.

811. The murderer impersonated the victim.

A delightful first novel set in a cathedral close. The author was to do as well again, but certainly no better.

812. The victim had been suffocated elsewhere and his body put into the tunnel from above.

813. The woman was in fact a man in disguise who then took off his disguise and left the pub dressed as a sailor.

814. The murderer obtained a duplicate key to the apartment and entered it. He knocked out the owner when she arrived, unscrewed and reversed the lock plates. She was left to die in the soundproof room, after which the killer then reversed the lock plates back to their original position.

815. A gun was rigged up with wire so that it would fire when the wire was accidentally touched as the victim reached to switch off the night lamp.

816. The victim was killed when a light bulb containing a measure of ether and hydrocyanic acid exploded in his face as it was switched on.

The same gimmick as the author used many years earlier in Item 1324. Then I questioned its practicability, but the author, a distinguished chemist, has confirmed that he has carried out a successful experiment that proves the method (though presumably not with the same test conditions as in the book!)

817. The killer rigged the room so that a halon fire extinguisher went off while the victim was in the room. He was smoking a cigar, and the halon thus became converted into deadly cyanide.

818. The murderer was carrying a steel band hidden in his belt.

819. The victim played a practical joke and pretended to be stabbed. He was then really stabbed by the first person to enter the car.

820. Delayed-action poison capsule.

821. The poison was in the salt used on the egg.

822. An earlier version of Item 819.

823. The fingerprints were put on the victim by someone wearing gloves on the tips of which were rubber strips that were in fact stamps of the dead man's fingerprints.

824. The victim was using a walking stick into the head of which had been introduced radium needles that gave off deadly rays into the victim's body.

825. The picture was actually painted by another artist who had been there.

Nice idea but perhaps inevitably a mundane solution.

826. The genuine picture had been switched for a copy on which blood was smeared. The villain was a solicitor against whom, naturally enough, nothing could be proved.

827. The door was locked by means of a pair of pliers.

828. A string was looped over the bolt and passed through the keyhole. The bolt was then pulled home by leverage on the two ends of the string. Afterwards, the string was loosened at one end and was pulled through the keyhole.

829. The murderer exited via a window and slid down a convenient drainpipe.

830. The murderer had slid down the cable, killed his victim, and then managed to get away again by the cable.

831. The door was locked from the outside, and the murderer then went and locked herself away in another room of the house that, inexplicably, the police failed to search.

832. The victim had licked the piece of gummed paper at the end of a spool of photographic film, and this had contained the poison.

833. It was so arranged that, when a certain book was removed by the victim from the shelves, a knife fell from above on his unprotected head.

834. The thief had disconnected the electric wire that operated the room alarm, removed a picture, then rejoined the wire, thus setting off the alarm and sealing off the rest of the collection.

835. The apparently impregnable room was breached through a contrivance from the outside using a steel spike to unlock a ventilator that, with a section of the wall, fell down as a hinge with the spike still intact and speared the sleeping victim.

A rather more detailed than average mechanical-device solution. Incidentally, the butler did it!

836. A radiator that contained a gun/booby trap.

837. The house had not disappeared; the road-name sign had been switched so that those searching were looking in the wrong road.

838. The numbers and indicators on the fourteenth floor and in the lift had been altered. The interior of the room itself, on the fourteenth floor, had been changed around to deceive the dupe when he returned.

There is an excellent "Alice in Wonderland" quality about the first part of this story.

839. One window was a trick one. The window was wired, but in fact it was the whole frame that opened.

840. By "communion" and by "telement."

The book must be read to understand the solution. A most

unusual science-fiction novel; hard but rewarding reading.

841. No solution.

This short spoof, contained in an obscure magazine published in Borneo, involves many other detectives of the period: Dr. Fortune, Dr. Thorndyke and Polton, Lord Peter Wimsey, Bulldog Drummond, Hercule Poirot, Joseph Rouletabille, Col. Anthony Gethryn, Madame Storey, and Inspector French. All are killed off, with the exception of Fortune and Philo Vance, who was "not available."

842. The pistol was ignited from outside the library by an agent of HATE (Humanitarian Alliance for Total Espionage) using a heat-beam weapon.

843. The jewels had been stolen by a trained white rat whose hideaway was a footstool with a false compartment.

One of a series of "Mr. Fordham's Strange Cases" in *The Ludgate Magazine,* but not, it seems, collected in volume form.

844. The killer hid in a closet in the room and later escaped into an adjoining room and so arranged matters that the door locked itself when the adjoining room had been safely reached.

845. The murder occurred earlier than had at first been thought. A starting gun fired for a boat race just happened to coincide with the finding of the corpse and the resultant screams. In addition, one of the witnesses lied under threat.

846. The victim had shot himself, but a second person had then made it appear like murder by locking the door on the inside and climbing out through the transom.

847. The victim was shot while standing on his head.

First-rate humorous treatment of the subject with a series of ingenious twists at the end.

848. Not impossible crime.

849. The victims were killed by a weight hidden in the ceiling of the library and released by a mechanical device that was operated elsewhere.

850. Bullets made of ice fired from outside the restricted area.

851. Shorn of all its complications, what it boils down to is that she escaped on horseback dressed as a man.

852. The door was locked from the outside, and the key was returned by the person who broke down the door (the policeman).

Not really a fully fledged locked-room mystery, but the

author does nonetheless appear to give a nod, even the briefest, towards the impossible-crime tradition.

853. The victim sat in a chair in the arm of which was a hidden spring that activated a needle that killed the seated victim.

854. After the murder, the killer left the room, locked the door, and passed the key back into the room under the door via a thread that ran from the door though a steel eye within the room and back through the keyhole. The key, once inside, was released via a slip knot, and the thread withdrawn.

855. The fatal punctures had been made by a device attached to a fishing line and cast by the murderer.

856. The bullet was enclosed in a hollow arrow. The bullet was fired when the arrow made contact with the outside wall of the murder room.

Very far-fetched idea with at least one basic flaw in the solution.

857. Webs spun across the magnifying lens of a telescope by a pet Venusian spider caused brain damage to the victim when he looked through it; the strangulation marks were made by the victim.

858. An electric-light bulb in which the inner element had been changed for one that gave off a lethal poison.

859. The victim was hit by a poison-tipped gramophone needle projected by an elastic band and afterwards retrieved by use of a magnet.

Well, what do you expect from a kids' album!

860. The bus was hidden under a stairway with a secret opening.

861. The key in one of the doors was turned in such a way that only a touch was needed to snap the lock. This was done from outside though a window by means of a long thin rod with a hook on the end.

862. The pavilion door had an automatic Yale device that made it unopen- able from inside or outside without a key. The murderer dragged the victim's body over to the door, used the key to open the door, which he then wedged while he moved the body back to the centre of the room.

863. Someone had a duplicate key.

Included here mainly because its title would lead most people to expect better from it.

864. The vanisher had walked out onto the ice wearing galoshes, had then removed them, and walked backwards in his own (smaller) shoes.

865. The victim had been lassoed from a tree above, pulled up, and swung out over the hedgerows.

866. A piece of string, affixed by a drawing pin to a table in the murder room, was passed through the head of the key. The key was passed out through a small peephole, normally shuttered on the inside, and the door locked with it. The string, which had of course also passed, with the key, through the peephole, was then drawn taut and the key slid down it onto the table in the room. The string was then jerked free and pulled out through the peephole, which was then closed from the outside by a sharp blow.

867. The man was walking in shoes with long spikes in them pointing downwards. Thus the heels and soles of the shoes did not touch the snow.

868. The victims were killed by poisoned prongs shot from a catapult projector and then retrieved by means of attached black thread.

869. The pilot was hidden in the front cockpit, and an accomplice made sure that the innocent witness did not get to see him.

870. The victim was impersonated by the killer when a visitor came, and later the killer locked the door with a skeleton key.

871. The warehouse had a secret door that opened onto a secret passage.

872. Entry and exit were made via a secret door in a cupboard that led to the building next door.

873. The young man was in fact a transvestite who, after escaping, assumed his other identity as a young woman tenant of one of the upper-storey apartments.

874. Secret panel; very weak.

875. Underground passage; fairly weak.

876. The victim was shot with an air pistol attached to a spinning wheel that could be operated remotely.

Very far-fetched, and there is a loophole in that the victim was also stabbed while the lights were out and could presumably also have been shot by the person who entered and exited.

877. The first two victims were electrocuted by a device set to protect

a precious stone, and the third was poisoned by a murderer who entered via a secret passage.

878. The watchman had been bitten by a deadly snake concealed in the safe. The money had been taken by the manager who had reported the matter.

879. The poison was introduced on the wings of a moth that flew into the room and was activated when it flew over the heat from a lamp. The victim let it out of the room, closed the window, and then died.

880. The statue's place was taken by a live model for a critical period while the real statue was taken through a door apparently screwed shut but where the retaining screws had been cut through.

881. The killer posed as the statue and wore a rubber glove. Since no explanation is provided for the locked-door element, it is logical to suppose that he or she held the pose after the door was opened and later made good his or her escape.

882. The formula was removed by someone thought to be above suspicion.

Set up as a locked-room situation but not really pursued.

883. The poison came from a "pellet of hyoscene in the mouth of a syphon."

884. The victim was shot through an arrow slit with a poisoned shaft made of ice.

885. The diamonds were hidden in the smuggler's stateroom, which the smuggler booked for a later outward journey. He then recovered the jewels and passed them to his wife, who had come to see him off.

886. The vanisher had somersaulted into a ravine.

887. (1) The saccharin was hidden in glass tubes concealed in hard-boiled eggs.

(2) The match was held in a black-gloved hand against a black background.

888. Escape had been made via a balloon and a skylight.

889. The fatal wound was inflicted by a South American snake.

890. The killer locked the door with a stolen key and then with the aid of an accomplice climbed into another train that was moving alongside.

891. The switch was made when a midget, masquerading as a baby,

was held up by an accomplice.

892. The victim licked his fingers as he turned the pages of a notebook, and the pages were impregnated with poison.

893. A gramophone produced the laughter, while the death was produced by electrocution from a death trap.

894. The thief used a stolen key and seal ring.

895. There was a secret passage.

896. Poison was placed in an alcohol lamp.

Could this be the same story as "The Mystery of the Rose of Fire"?

897. (1) The poison was administered by a boomerang covered with a "native poison, Woorali."

(2) Secret passage.

Wild and woolly, even by Hanshew's standards.

898. The death room contained a sliding panel that communicated with a false-backed wardrobe in the adjoining room.

899. A secret passage through a roll-top desk.

900. The bells were being rung through the agency of a small black monkey.

901. The whole setup, including the dwarf itself, was a fake. The breath (in a mirror) was steam manufactured by placing a piece of cloth, soaked in water and then squeezed, inside the dummy dwarf's mouth. The perspiration was manufactured by a light spray of water on an area that had been previously lightly wiped over with oil.

902. Secret panel; primitive.

903. A false wall, previously erected, could be swung into place to hide the corridor and alter the look of the entire area.

904. The murder occurred earlier, and the door was locked from the outside. The killer then transmitted, via a wireless and a concealed loudspeaker, the sounds that were heard in the cabin when the murder occurred.

905. After the room had been seen by witnesses, the villain of the piece erected a new false blank wall, entirely covering the old wall and door and thereby changing the aspect and making it unrecognisable.

906. The victim had committed suicide, and the gun had been removed by the first person to enter the room.

907. (1) The victim had sucked a poisoned mint.

(2) The victim had been sent a catalogue with the pages stuck together. He had moistened his fingers to open the pages and thus transferred the poison from the page ends to his mouth.

908. The victim had committed suicide, and the gun had been removed by the first person to enter the room.

An earlier version of Item 906.

909. The shooting took place in a darkened hall of mirrors, and he was in fact using his left hand to fire at a different target, but appeared through various mirror images to be using his right hand to fire at the two men.

910. The fatal dart was on the end of an umbrella ferrule that was plunged into the victim's heart by an expert swordsman while all eyes were on the screen.

911. The victim, bending to retrieve an object from the snow, was struck a fatal blow by a large, sharp icicle falling from the eaves of a nearby building, thawed by the sun.

912. In the adjoining room the killer changed the barrel of the gun that had just fired the shot and that could tie it in with the bullet for another barrel that would not match. He hid the original barrel in a flower vase.

913. Hidden recess in which the vanisher stayed until the coast was clear.

914. The murderer exited via a sliding panel and a secret passage.

915. The monkeys had killed him.

A book of the film book. I never saw the film, but the book is quite gripping. The fate of the two scientists who go to investigate is predictable but quite well handled. A mixture of fantasy and mystery fiction.

916. The vanisher slipped behind a wicket gate, donned a heavy coat and a hat, and stepped back into the courtyard as a coachman.

917. The door was locked from outside after the murder was committed, and the keyhole was blocked to seem like the key was still inside. A fake shot was then caused by pulling a thread running through the keyhole and various trappings were removed and the key replaced in the lock by the murderer after the door had been broken in.

918. The victim was smoking and the murderer used the lighted tip of the cigarette as a guide.

919. The key was placed under the body by one of the first people to

break into the room.

920. The killer entered the house hidden in a mummy case and made his escape after the killing when the front door of the house was left open.

921. The murderer was concealed in a hidden inner room in the murder room.

922. The trick was worked by fooling the security cameras with a false wall to the laboratory.

An odd book from the opening moments when, set in England, the detective munches on a "jelly-laiden muffin," via the impossible crime with the complex explanation I have entirely failed to encapsulate above and a second science-fictional explanation I really didn't understand, through to demonic possession and artificially created life.

923. The door was locked by an innocent party who then exited by means of a window. His movements were noted and presumed to have been those of the victim.

924. The vanisher changed clothes in ten seconds with a sandwich-board man and hid under that guise.

925. The victim had been scratched by a dart before entering and locking the bathroom door. The fact that the bathroom window was partly open doesn't invalidate the locked-room setup.

926. The bolt was drawn home by use of a piece of wire pushed through the keyhole.

927. A hole had been bored in the door just above the inner bolt. A thin piece of steel with a hinge was passed through the hole and engaged with the bolt. Then a flick of the wrist could lock the door from outside, and the hole was later stopped up with putty.

928. The door was locked on the outside and the key was replaced by the person who broke in the door.

929. The victim was killed by a paper knife shot from above by a crossbow.

930. The murderer hid in a mummy case until the initial investigation was over.

931. A gun had been set in position aimed at the victim and was activated by means of a whistle emitting a supersonic sound that operated a tiny motor to pull the trigger.

932. After the murder was committed and the murderers had gone, a small boy locked the door and shot the bolts on the inside and

escaped through the transom.

933. The house was built around the corpse.

934. None given as to method. The point is that the narrator—Inspector Thorne—is a little mad and committed the last murder, if not the earlier ones, himself. Shades of "The Hands of Mr. Ottermole"!

935. The victim was poisoned and her body carried out under a mackintosh.

A good, original setting, but the problem and its resolution do not live up to the synopsis at the front of the book.

936. The prisoner was released by a guard. It is noteworthy that the guard's name was Lucifer Addison.

937. The door to the room had a sliding panel, and the shot was fired through it.

938. The killer had freed one hand by a little twitching, and substituted the forefinger of one hand for the little finger of the other.

939. The victim was stabbed outside and locked himself in before dying.

940. The victim had been bitten by a deadly snake that had entered through a mousehole and exited via a broken radiator.

A story and solution that owe more than a little to Conan Doyle.

941. A window pane was taken out and then put back again after the murderer had stepped through the aperture onto a veranda.

942. The gun was rigged up to fire when a revolving chair was used and a connecting wire, of magnesium, was destroyed.

This may well be the first example of the use of a self-destruct mechanism.

943. The murderer had climbed in from outside.

Probably the first locked-room spoof.

944. A lighted brazier was lowered down the chimney, the top of which was then blocked by a wet blanket.

945. The rational and incorrect solution provided part way through the story is that the lift operator screened the action from the other occupants and conned them into believing that it had happened as he described. The real explanation is that it was a ghostly re-enactment of a killing many years before.

946. The lock of the window had been loosened so that it was

ineffective. The killer took steps to ensure that the window needed to be opened almost as soon as the body was found.

947. The murderer "borrowed" the keys, opened the door, and stabbed the victim!

948. The first death had been an accident by means of a real lightning bolt. The later deaths were contrived by means of bare electric wires on the surface of water, etc.

949. What he heard was a recording of the previous year's parade.

950. The apartment name and lock had been changed to allow a drug deal within to be carried out, while the girl had been deliberately decoyed away.

951. The policeman had switched two accident reports that had occurred in the same area and within a short time of one another in order to cover up for someone implicated in the earlier accident.

952. The victim had been strangled earlier and put in his car, which the murderer then shunted along with the car behind until they got into a traffic jam.

953. Each man had removed his suit and made his exit in shirtsleeves. In the police-station instance a badge and gun were worn under the suit to foster the illusion that the man was just another policeman.

954. The original padlock was filed off and replaced by one externally identical. The keyhole of the new padlock was jammed with wax and a match stick, as the original had been, and the keys, which only fitted the original, could therefore not be used.

955. The wounds were inflicted by the razor-sharp propeller blades of a remote-controlled model plane.

956. The maker of the tracks—and murderer—made them by walking on the points of his ballet shoes.

957. The victim had set up a booby trap by means of a pouch of water that would touch the gun's trigger when the water expanded due to the intense cold. Owing to a rapid fall in the temperature, the expansion took place more rapidly than expected and killed the would-be murderer.

958. The shaft of the trident had been pushed through the wire mesh of a partly opened window before the killer left the room. He was then able to stab the victim from outside by holding that

part of the shaft that projected outside.

959. The shot was fired by a zip gun masquerading as an automatic pencil.

960. The victim's throat was cut through an upper-floor window by a man standing outside and using a pruning hook.

961. She had never actually entered the room and simply closed the door from the outside. The noises from inside were made by a tape recorder.

962. The victim faked death in the locked room and, after the connivance of a doctor, later committed suicide while en route in the ambulance.

The story was adapted for use in the *Macmillan and Wife* TV series.

963. What the witnesses really saw on the screen was a videotaped bolting and shooting that had occurred earlier. The killer pushed the bolt across after the door had been smashed in.

964. The murderer broke the window, then hid behind the door and joined the throng that crowded into the room. He later killed the victim and threw him from the broken window.

Another story adapted for *Macmillan and Wife.*

965. An automatic window was in operation as the shot was fired and closed completely after the victim was shot.

966. The victim simulated his own wounding and was then killed by the first person to reach him.

967. (1) The diamonds had been removed earlier so that the thief was carrying nothing when he was collared.

(2) The diamonds were hidden in a coffee tin, the bottom of which had been partly opened to let a little coffee out and replace it with the diamonds.

968. The negatives were taped to the blades of an electric fan in use.

969. They had been dropped into lighted candles and had sunk at once into the opaque molten wax.

970. The escapee was a much younger impostor who had used a rope to scale the wall.

971. The master criminal jammed the door's latch bolt when his food was brought to him. When the door was closed, it did not lock properly and enabled him to escape.

972. The abandoned bike had been left there by an accomplice while the vanisher had cycled off the road on the second bike in a

different direction.

973. The victim was already dead and in the haystack when someone masquerading as him had been seen finishing off the tarpaulin tying.

974. The man who entered the car was the driver in disguise. He then abandoned his disguise and clambered over into the driver's seat.

975. The victims were shot before they entered the common by a doorman blowing his whistle to call cabs.

976. The physically incapable witness impersonated the victim and locked the door after the real killer had made good his escape.

977. The screws holding the bolt receiver to the door frame had been loosened so that the door could be opened and closed again. After closure, the door would appear still to be bolted.

978. The body was buried in the ground in a cylinder, and then a slightly larger cylinder, which the witnesses had examined, was lowered on top of it and fitted together so well that when they were later uncovered it was though that there was only one cylinder.

979. The glass chosen by the victim was intended for another person, who introduced the poison capsule before the water was poured into it.

980. The horse and buggy had turned off before reaching the bridge and the tracks had been obliterated by cattle. False tracks had been laid to the bridge by a man pushing a pair of wheels and wearing blocks on his feet with horseshoes nailed to them.

981. The victim stabbed himself before entering the room and inserted an already-fired bullet into the wound. Once in the room he created the sound of an explosion by treading on a child's explosive cap.

982. The cutting had been done with a razor that was attached to a balloon that was then allowed to float up to the top of the barn's high roof.

983. The cyanide was in a piece of hard candy that the victim was already munching.

984. The seal was intact and the switch was made, dynamite stick for firecracker, after the package had been opened.

985. The shot was fired from outside through an exhaust fan and with a single-barrelled shotgun, not the double-barrelled shotgun

found in the store, thought to be the murder weapon and too big to fire through the fan.

986. Two of the four people had already been murdered before the boat sailed, and the other two had, by imitating laughter and wearing their clothes, made it appear that they all embarked. The two killers then slipped overboard on the side away from the shore.

987. The woman had deliberately thrown herself off the bridge so that a body already in the creek farther on would be believed to be hers.

988. (1) The victim had died of a heart attack, and the bullet had been fired into him after death by the doctor performing the autopsy. He had fired the bullet through a thin board held against the chest to slow down the bullet and prevent its exit through the back, and had disguised the entrance hole with putty as make-up.

(2) The gypsy wagons had departed before the surveillance began. What the watchers had seen were skilfully designed cardboard silhouettes against the campfire glow.

Ed was rather reaching in this one.

989. The killer wore over his hood a cloak made of crepe paper and covered with flash powder. The watchers were blinded by the flash, which destroyed the cloak and gave the killer time to get rid of the hood.

990. The earlier victims had died as the result of poisonous sap emanating from poles, made of oleander wood, supporting the tepee. The last victim died as the result of oleander fed to him in his food.

Neat story in which both Ben Snow and the good Doctor feature.

991. The killer had cycled to the lodge entrance and had ridden along the track made by a water-carrying pipe.

992. The trapeze artists were each dressed in a different color. Two of them fell into the safety net, but only one climbed back up again. However, by skilful use of coloured spotlights as he climbed, it appeared to different parts of the audience that two different-coloured costumes had adorned the one who climbed back up.

993. The red-haired boy had been abducted a few minutes previously.

The boy on the swing was a dark-haired substitute wearing a red wig. He disappeared by removing the wig and becoming someone else.

994. The victim's throat was cut by a fishing line enforced with steel wire that was drawn taut across the victim's throat from outside.

995. The victim robbed the safe in the caboose, handed the goods out through a small barred window to an accomplice who then stabbed him. The window had a snap catch that closed it.

996. The murderer escaped via the window. String ran from the window catch to the door, and when the door, which opened outwards, was pulled open, the string turned the latch and locked the window.

997. The trunk had been filled with ice to take the place of the books and to simulate their weight. A small hole had been bored in the trunk, and when the ice had melted the water had escaped through the hole, leaving nothing.

998. The victim was not in fact dead when the first witness reached him, but was feigning death. He was later strangled by the murderer.

999. Both incidents occurred when gasoline-filled balloons were accidentally ignited.

1000. One of the occupants was engaged in painting a wall and simply held the envelope against the wall and then painted over it.

1001. The victim was killed away from the farmhouse and was transported back into the compound via a delivery van, and thence into the house itself by the driver/killer while the one witness (Dr. H.) was busy with the dog.

1002. The killer had disguised herself as a statue and escaped detection immediately after the murder was discovered. She then replaced the statue at the first possible opportunity.

1003. The murder had taken place earlier and the victim's body lodged against the guard rail in such a way that, by means of attached fishing line, it could be made to topple over the rail from the ground by someone pulling the other end of the line.

1004. The poison was injected into the bottle through the seal and the cork with a hypodermic syringe.

1005. The killer reached the cabin roof via specially enforced aerial cables and got in through a skylight.

1006. The attack was made by the woman's brother, who was wearing his sister's clothes and had shaved off his beard.

1007. The killer was in the cabin when the lock was forced, and when she appeared it was assumed that she had done so from outside the cabin.

1008. The murder had occurred earlier, and the killer had created the illusion that the victim was still alive by reactivating a radio in the murder room by means of a replaced fuse elsewhere and by having the telephone in the studio ring only once as if the victim had answered it.

1009. The victim mortally wounded himself and then put the knife inside the inviolable ballot box.

One of the most satisfying of the Hawthorne stories.

1010. It was someone impersonating the victim who had entered the room. That person had then left it via a secret space under the floorboards.

1011. The poison had been introduced via a pair of hypodermic needles with which the victim, who was asleep, was injected by the person who, under the very nose of Holmes, was apparently trying to wake him.

1012. The sorceress was in fact a diver engaged in nefarious underwater activities.

1013. The victim was killed by a poisoned dart shot from an air rifle.

1014. They were smuggled out in the thief's watch.

1015. A disk had been sewn into the victim's coat, which emitted electronic sounds exactly like footsteps when a remote-control box was operated. Ingenious use of new technology.

1016. The sapphire had been hidden in a trumpet case placed in a locker.

1017. Someone had been immersing the statue in water every evening, then leaving it overnight in the deep freeze so that some of the water froze on. When it was secretly replaced in the church each morning, the water on the statue would slowly thaw out.

1018. The blueprints had been hidden behind wallpaper that had just been pasted up.

1019. The object of value was the dust on the floor, evidence of a crime committed.

1020. The vanisher had fastened the rear seat belt before entering the car and had closed the door from outside before the car started and while the driver was distracted by the front-seat passenger.

This same passenger then provided by ventriloquism the voice of the absent rear-seat passenger.

1021. (1) The removal of the furniture had taken place earlier and what the witness saw was an impression created by placing a blown-up photograph of the room in the doorway.

(2) The wheel, which had been used in illegal gambling establishments, disappeared out of sight at the touch of a button.

(3) The card remained in the person's hands, but the invisible ink on it disappeared after a time and created the impression that the card had disappeared.

An excellent example of one of Hoch's more complicated and adroit pieces of business.

1022. When the detective, illicitly, broke into the murder room, the murderer hid in a closet behind a full-length tapestry.

1023. The witness lied when she said that he did not descend. Unusual problem neatly handled.

1024. While on the river, the crew changed the boat's livery and its name and came back under a different identity.

1025. The girl had taken an overdose of drugs before entering the Ferris- wheel car, had collapsed, and was lying on the floor of it out of sight when it came round.

1026. The knife had been projected by means of a booby trap made from a skeet-shooting trap, and the story about the 200-year-old disappearance had been fabricated by the murderer.

1027. The victim, a nervous old woman, was given a highly inflammable garment and set fire to it herself accidentally.

1028. The victim was wearing a device containing a hypodermic needle full of cyanide. He thought it contained an antidote to a nervous complaint and injected himself in a moment of stress. The doctor who had deliberately misled him removed the device while examining the body.

1029. The girl had been thrown live down into a secret passage and had later made her escape.

1030. Pins were removed from hinges in the doors and were replaced after the murder had been committed.

A somewhat unusual item to find in one of the later hardboiled magazines.

1031. The specially constructed bullion room had a false wall built by the carpenter in their pay. Over the course of the voyage the thieves moved the gold little by little from the bullion room to the cargo hold, and substituted the lead.

1032. The murderer, a half-crazed stowaway, was hidden above the water tanks and stabbed the victim through a ventilator hatch.

1033. Some of the noises were made, ventriloquially, by the villain.

One of the fairly rare breed of stories in which a rational explanation is provided but a few loose ends are left that the detective attributes to other forces.

1034. Death was caused by the bed in which the victim slept. The bed was capable of being shut up like a book, and thus crushing any occupant to death, when a peg on the floor below was removed that passed through a beam and a strut that went upwards from the lower floor and supported the heavy hinged mattress of the bed.

According to a footnote to the story, such a bed actually existed. Holiday Inns, please note!

1035. A booby trap built into a gate post of the chancel gateway.

1036. The accused eventually admitted that there was a secret passage leading out of the apartments and this he had used to convey the victim home.

Currently believed to be the earliest locked-room story, this entertaining, if discursive, tale uses the gimmick in a far from classic manner, but it is nevertheless central to the plot and the resolution. Available over the years in various editions of Hoffman's stories.

1037. The prisoner, a skilled carpenter, had made a key out of wood. He kept it hidden inside the handle of a stick that he had because of a deliberately injured foot.

1038. The key was returned to the lock after the door was broken in.

1039. The killer was still in the room when the witnesses entered. He had made the victim seem alive after his death by sitting in his chair—on top of the corpse—and moving his leg, which was the only part of his anatomy that could be seen from outside the room.

1040. The killer was made to appear in the room after he had left by virtue of a paper model that was then drawn out through a small hole in the wall.

A quite unique solution in a book that is well above average. Chapter 14 contains probably the third-best discussion of locked-room solutions.

1041. The victim was double-jointed and stabbed himself, but more violently than he intended, thus killing himself.

1042. At the denouement no mention is made of the locked-room aspect of the murder, out of a series of four or five. I am therefore left with the detective's theorising at the time of the discovery of the body: The key was turned in the lock from the outside by the use of a pair of tweezers.

1043. The victim was killed by a booby trap that could be remotely controlled by the operation of a telegraph instrument.

1044. The car was driven by a second person lying on the floor of the car and operating the clutch and steering gear by means of attached wires.

1045. The wound had been caused over a long period by radium placed in the hat band of the victim's hat.

1046. The victim strangled himself while under the influence of poisoned cigarettes.

1047. The victim strangled himself while under the influence of poisoned cigarettes. An earlier version of Item 1046.

1048. Not terribly clear, but it appears that the body was left there by someone who then departed, walking on his hands.

A typical Horler muddle/melange. But a tip of the hat to anyone who, in a mere eighty pages, can introduce human bodies drained of blood, a crazed professor, an ape man, and a vampire tree!

1049. Not impossible crime.

1050. String was attached to a knitting needle thrust through the key handle.

One of a series of crime problems illustrated at each step with a photograph. The solution is doubly convincing because of a photograph showing how the trick could be worked.

1051. The pistol, which belonged to the detective and had been lying near him, had been set off by a jackdaw attracted to its glinting barrel.

1052. The key on the inside of the door had been turned from the outside by means of a pair of small, strong tweezers.

1053. The victim was not dead but had suffered an epileptic fit. The strangulation marks had in fact been put on her by her chiropractor.

1054. The main gas valve for the house was turned off, then the valve in the bedroom was opened. The main gas valve was then turned on again after the victim had retired and locked herself in.

1055. The gun was rigged up with a pulley and string to be fired by the suicide.

1056. A dagger was made from a plastic ashtray that, after it had been used, reverted on application of hot water (in a teapot) to its original shape.

1057. The chalice had been stolen earlier, and it was another cup that one of the witnesses had seen being replaced in a cabinet and assumed was the chalice. Another witness who would have recognised the real chalice only saw the thief putting something back in the cabinet and assumed that it must be the chalice.

1058. The killer presumably exited through a sash window.

In this his last novel, published posthumously, Hume doesn't actually provide a specific explanation for the locked room. He further complicates matters by having someone look through a keyhole—to view the corpse—which is later stated to have a key in it! A very old-fashioned novel, as the publisher is quite ready to admit, but the dialogue and action hold up surprisingly well even if the plot creaks. *Hansom Cab* tends to come in for fashionably harsh criticism these days, but I always found it to be one of the more readable of the Victorian mystery novels.

1059. The standard holding up the jewels was shot away by an expert marksman, and the valuables fell from the pagoda to those waiting below.

1060. The chauffeur had lied when he said no stops had been made. The car had in fact been driven up to an identical house, and the foreign secretary had been attacked and kidnapped once inside it. The car had resumed the journey to his own house.

1061. None given! The text states quite emphatically that "entry was forbidden by an inside bolt," but later nothing is made of this fact, and I can find no explanation for this circumstance at all.

1062. The killer got in by a window and exited through a side door, after he had taken steps to entice away someone who was preventing him from leaving by way of the door.

A very good detective novel, even if the resolution of the locked-room problem is rather disappointing.

1063. A false door had been made in the back of the specie room by burning through with an oxy-hydrogen flame and slipping a false plate inside.

1064. The room contained gold and jewels and was booby trapped to kill the first person who entered.

Not strictly an impossible crime, but a very early use of a sealed-room situation. The author died in 1862, which places the story chronologically at the beginning of this history.

1065. There was a secret exit via a door masquerading as bookshelves.

Disappointing solution but otherwise a typically urbane and enjoyable Innes.

1066. The metal of the gun contracted in the extreme cold and released the trigger.

This book, a leisurely tale, is not quite in the top Innes bracket, although it contains some of the delightful touches. Typically Innes, it does not pose a locked-room—or impossible-crime—problem in the traditional way, although it could easily have done so.

1067. The real horse had been replaced (before the journey started and the box was locked) by a dummy horse-shaped balloon secured by a deliberately fraying rope. When the rope eventually broke, the "horse" drifted out of the box.

1068. The killer had first removed the body, then later walked back to the death site in the victim's shoes. The body was lowered to him from a helicopter, by which means he also exited.

An obvious spoof.

1069. The bride, an heiress, had been kidnapped and was to be killed. All the people involved had been paid for their silence so that the bridegroom would be thought to be out of his head.

1070. The bed on which the victim slept was hooked from outside with a fishing line and moved to face a different direction. The victim was then woken by a very strong light being shone at him, and, thinking that he was moving towards the bathroom to switch off the light, stepped through the window to his doom.

1071. The shot was fired through a hole made by temporarily moving a knot from the wooden window frame.

1072. The victim was killed by a knife thrown by a dwarf hidden behind a statue of Pompey.

1073. Entrance to the building was gained by swinging across telegraph wires, a sleep-producing gas was fired at the guard, one key was already held, and the second was obtained from the drunken holder on the floor below who woke up when it was being replaced and was shot. The guard above was still asleep and therefore heard nothing.

Whew!

1074. The strips sealing the inside of the door were in fact broken when they were put in place as the killer realised that they would be and could appear broken once the door had been forced.

1075. After the victim's body was deposited on the floor, the dust was evenly sprayed over the footprints by means of a small industrial sprayer normally used for spraying trees.

1076. The disappearances were staged by means of a series of black-gauze screens that were let down, the locked room was hocused by means of windows with concealed spring actions and dummy latches, the levitation arranged by means of sandals with telescopic heels—though the detective sergeant suggests that it may have been a genuine levitation— and the cat talked via a ventriloquist.

See Jacques Pendower's *Out of This World* (Item 1414) for a rewrite of the same story.

1077. The killer exited through the false back of a wardrobe.

1078. When the lights were switched off, one of the watchers passed the money up the chimney to a waiting confederate, a South American Indian.

This has the lot: an old house with secret rooms, a gang of desperadoes, a "particularly deadly form of poison, the composition of which is a closely guarded secret of certain Amazon Valley natives." There's also a spectral hand that appears in impossible circumstances, and for which no doubt an equally unlikely explanation is provided.

1079. The murderer had his own key!

A cheat of a story, which centres round a deadly poison invented by Buddhist monks!

1080. The key on the inside was turned from the outside by use of a pencil and string, and was then pushed out of the lock and pulled back under the door after a section of cork flooring had been taken up and carefully replaced.

1081. A pencil pushed through the end of the key and turned from outside by means of a string attached to the pencil.

The illustrations on the dust wrapper and in the text of the book show a needle, not a pencil.

1082. The door had a trick lock and bolt that could remain in place even when the door was opened.

1083. The victim stabbed himself with a pointed rod of carbon-dioxide ice.

1084. (1) A very small gun was attached to the end of a gastroscope that was lowered into the victim's stomach, and the gun was then fired.

(2) The victim's drink was spiked with a substance that changed, under ultraviolet light, to a fast-acting poison.

(3) Remote-controlled electronic snakes fitted with tiny hypodermics.

A great pudding-mix of a novel, choc-a-block with ideas, good and bad. Among the good is a really excellent idea for a new impossible crime, the internal wound without the corresponding external signs— and an explanation just as ingenious.

1085. The knife was thrown from a trapeze and entered the room above the height of the wall.

1086. The key was slid back under the door after the killer had locked it on the outside.

1087. The door was locked on the outside and the key returned via a piece of wire that ran down through the port hole.

1088. The key had been returned to the room after the door was locked by means of a pulley and line that ran under the door.

1089. (1) The bolt was pulled home by means of a piece of string that ran through the keyhole.

(2) The door was self-locking and was merely pulled to by the killer after the crime was committed.

1090. The capsule was left in a planter for the victim to pick up.

Advertised as an impossible-crime story, but barely qualifies.

1091. The victim was struck by lightning.

1092. (1) The money had been removed on the previous day, and the teller concerned pretended that the disappearance had not occurred until the following day.

(2) The victim killed himself with a poisoned needle that he had

in his sleeve.

(3) The jewellery tray contained a deep bottom, and a false empty top was deftly placed over the original jewellery-filled one.

(4) The victim partly opened the rear door of the room and was shot before he could remove the burglar-chain, barricades, etc. After he had been killed, the door was pulled to from the outside.

(5) A mirror image of the tiara was made to disappear, and in the confusion the real one was passed to an accomplice.

A little primitive but containing a lot of good ideas, including doors mysteriously opening and footprints of the mysterious enemy equally mysteriously appearing—as well as those described in greater detail.

1093. The victim had poisoned himself under the mistaken impression that he was taking an aphrodisiac.

Brilliant parody of John Dickson Carr.

1094. (1) The door was locked from outside and the key returned inside by pushing it through a narrow gap at the edge of the door and sliding it down a thread pinned inside the strong room. The pin and thread were then removed.

(2) The victim killed himself out of fear.

The first solution was rather clever, the second rather weak.

1095. The key was turned in the lock by pliers from the outside. The key was then pushed out of the lock into the murder room.

A nice, well-plotted little story that, for once, has not suffered in translation. The detective's hobby is "bilboquet," a French game played with a ball on a string and a staff.

1096. The victim had been rendered unconscious by a switch made in his habitual morphine injection and was stabbed by the first person to enter the locked room.

1097. The door was locked from the outside after leaving a brass-topped staple in the keyhole that looked from the outside like the key. This was pushed through from the outside onto a piece of paper already holding the real door key, and the paper was then drawn back under the door carrying a key that had apparently been pushed out of the keyhole.

1098. The door was locked on the outside after the killer had left the wrong key (but similar in design) inside the room.

1099. He was poisoned by eardrops that penetrated his perforated ear drum.

1100. The victim was killed by shots fired through the ceiling of the room below. The killer was the first to enter the room when the door was broken down and covered the marks on the floor with a rug.

1101. The victim was mortally wounded outside, tried to protect himself by locking the door behind him, and then died inside.

1102. The killer had a duplicate key.

1103. The owner, who claimed to be innocent, was lying.

1104. One of the persons who were supposed to have had the room under observation had entered it, knocked out the victim, and then held under his nose and mouth an ice bucket containing club soda just taken out of the refrigerator.

1105. The man remained hidden in a secret compartment behind a large bureau.

Pure John Dickson Carr.

1106. The victim had been hit by a metal rod painted to look like striped candy.

1107. The piano had been dismantled and lowered out of the window via a ladder by three neighbours who could no longer stand the singing of the piano's owner. A gem of a story.

1108. The bullet was in fact fired from a booby-trapped drawer inside the room. The bullet broke the glass window on its way out and misled the detectives initially into thinking that the killer had stood on the balcony outside.

1109. The murder scene was projected by a mini-projector and made to appear to the witness, who was viewing it through what she thought to be a spy hole, as though it was really happening as she saw it.

1110. The victim had killed himself and at the same time contrived to remove the weapon from the room by means of a rubber inner tube that catapulted it through a trap door in the ceiling.

1111. The note was removed by its owner who made the complaint and devised this test to check the efficiency of the police.

1112. The vanisher bent down to clean out the plug hole of the shower and thus disappeared from view. Later in the pandemonium he was able to dress and slip out unobserved.

1113. The jewels were hidden in one of the binocular tubes of a microscope. Anyone looking through the microscope would not realise that only one tube was really working.

1114. The messages were passed in the form of different coloured liquids down a sink waste pipe.

1115. (1) Killed by a midget operating from a helicopter.
(2) Killed by a midget operating from a tightrope.

1116. The truck had passed through one of the checkpoints, disguised as a different truck by means of revolving panels on its body.

1117. The victim had died of an elipeptiform seizure. Various pieces of evidence that substantiated other theories had been made by the victim himself.

A companion volume to Item 1115.

1118. The victim committed suicide but was impelled to do so by a dream.

Not the greatest locked-room story ever written, but a typically bizarre Keeler finale.

1119. A fern pot concealed a gun that could be operated from outside the room by twisting two wires together to complete a circuit.

The part of the story that contains the locked-room murder was written by Hazel Goodwin Keeler.

1120. Not impossible crime.

1121. Exit was made via the self-locking garage door.

A poor, muddled sort of business.

1122. The victim had been killed earlier with a gun, fitted with a silencer, by the last person to leave, who then pretended to order the victim to bolt the door. A device, afterwards disposed of like the silencer down an internal ash chute, then operated to fake a second shot, and the killer was one of those to break in the apparently bolted door, in fact only locked by a spring lock.

1123. The victims were knocked unconscious, loosely tied to a post with their feet over a railing and outside the window and a weight hanging down outside the building. When they recovered consciousness, as soon as they freed themselves from the binding twine, they plummeted to their deaths—while the killer had established an alibi elsewhere.

1124. A booby-trapped gun was set to fire when a pet dog carried out his habit of passing through a particular spot in the balcony's ornamental hedge.

1125. The killer had disconnected the alarm system that worked by means of an electromagnet. He hid while the guard checked the suite, then left and reconnected the alarm.

1126. A clockwork device that simultaneously locked the room and poisoned the atmosphere.

1127. The killer wore stilts.

1128. The flat owner had committed the crime earlier and established an alibi —i.e., that he was on the phone when the doorbell rang—by making a connection between the wires of the bell (inside the flat) with the spike of a ski stick.

1129. The killers, former acrobats, had got in and out by use of a rope up the tower wall and their natural athletic prowess.

1130. The key was returned to the room from outside by means of a double loop of cord jerked in through a partly opened window.

1131. Most of the passengers were kidnapped before takeoff and confined in the air terminal's underground boiler room. The plane then took off, flew out a short distance, and then returned as a different flight with bogus passengers.

1132. The little girl had accomplished the apparently superhuman feat by means of a trick culled from a book entitled *Ten Thousand Things a Young Boy Can Do.* The trick involved sticking the needle down the centre of a soft cork.

1133. The victim was shot from the floor above through a small hole in the ceiling.

This book was a British vanity-publishing venture. Considering that the author probably paid to have the book published, it's not at all bad.

1134. The deceased had drunk whiskey containing a radioactive isotope before he entered the locked room. The whiskey had been considered harmless because the murderer had already partaken of it, but he had taken care to immunise himself before drinking.

1135. A trap door was nailed down with a nail that was old and rusty. It had, however, been so nailed only after the murder.

1136. The victims drank coffee to which had been added an acid that, though harmless in itself, formed a deadly poison when sugar was added.

1137. The killer had gone down in the lift after the witness had left it and had then returned it to the terrace level by use of a demountable fishing rod pressed against the up button.

1138. The witness was distracted from watching the codex. The codex was then removed by the guard who had been outside.

An excellent atmospheric story, despite the rather ordinary-sounding solution to the impossible-crime problem.

1139. A wheelbarrow had been converted into a guillotine and a quicklime pit lay beneath a pile of debris.

A little weaker than the other Mr. Tarrant stories but still very effective.

1140. A knife was thrown by someone outside the confined area.

Not quite as "impossible" as several of the other Mr. Tarrant stories.

1141. The murderer was hiding in a specially devised hole under the floorboards.

Very good.

1142. (1) A gimmicked stair that threw an echo down behind a running person.

(2) A gimmicked window designed to reflect the moon's rays from a particular angle.

An excellent story packed with ingenuity.

1143. A pair of giant amphibious wolf-spiders inhabited the boat, and emerged each time the boat's motor became hot.

Well staged and handled with genuine horror.

1144. The harp remained in the room but in the form of a model ship. The longest Tarrant story and an excellent one.

1145. The actress played two parts so that it was quite easy for her to drop one part (herself) and disappear.

A little essay on the locked room, with Tarrant and his companions providing several alternative solutions apart from the correct one. Lacks the spontaneity of the earlier Tarrant stories.

1146. Electrocution by means of a flex attached to the screws in the floor.

1147. The alarm sounded only when a metal object—such as shoe nails— touched the floor. The killer wore slippers and arranged the body on a Slowly leaking pneumatic cushion that would cause it to fall on the floor long after he had left and sound the alarm by means of the metal dagger with which the murder had been committed.

1148. Mainly with the help of hidden passages, secret passages, and the like.

1149. The poisoned knife was dropped through a small hole drilled in the ceiling by the killer, who was on the beams above the ceiling.

1150. He had heaved overboard the body of one of his victims and taken his place beneath the sheet that had been covering it.

1151. The poison was contained on the flap of an envelope licked by the victim.

1152. The killer hid in a space under a table across the front of which was hung a canvas painted to represent the space under the table unoccupied.

1153. The gas was pumped through a tube that had been forced into a compartment from a nearby one along the route taken by the communication cord.

1154. The victim was stabbed by a stork from a nearby zoo.

1155. (1) Gas piped through a window from the bedroom on the floor above.

(2) The victim had committed suicide.

(3) The victim had accidentally left a gas tap on and so died. A third party later switched off the tap and locked the bedroom door, then later helped to break down that door and replaced the key through the broken door panel.

Complex and ingenious. Solutions (1) and (2) were incorrect; (3) was correct.

1156. The escape was made in the garb of a railway official.

1157. The victim was drugged while in bed and then the bed was pulled forty feet upwards in the air by means of ropes already attached. The victim suffered from acrophobia and therefore remained on the bed until he died of starvation. The bed was then let down again and the ropes drawn up and away.

1158. The fatal revolver was held loosely in place with wires. A piece of soft iron was fitted to the trigger, and this was pulled back when the electric light was switched on and was connected to an electromagnet.

1159. Victim created an alibi in order to give himself the opportunity to kill— but was himself killed.

Ingeniously complex variation on No. 19; a perfectly legitimate locked-room puzzle that is impossible to encapsulate and must be read for full appreciation.

1160. The ruby had been plucked from its holder by a dog trained to leap over the specially wired and protected area. The ruby was then hidden in a cup of coffee that never left the hand of the thief.

1161. The victim was being poisoned by a faulty central-heating system and, in rising with desperate suddenness to escape it, struck his head on the painted base of a chandelier.

1162. (1) The wooden bar on the inside of the door was dropped into place from the outside by means of a rod or a stout cord.
(2) A thin, sharp wire was placed around the victim's neck, and when he ran away onto the newly varnished floor, he cut his own throat.
(3) Not explained. Lord Darcy "still investigating."

1163. A key, found on the body and presumed to be the locked-room key, is not the key of the room.

A neat locked-room situation set in a good, solid golden-age detective novel. Recommended for golden-age readers.

1164. The killer had scaled the cliff with the help of a monster lizard to which a rope was tied before it climbed the cliff and then became the brace the killer needed to be able to follow it up.

1165. The killer was in the locked library with the other two men. He was got up to look exactly like the victim and confused the witness by masquerading as him in this large and somewhat cluttered room. After the killing he simply moved around the room from one place of refuge to another, and eventually slipped out when the door was opened.

A pleasant surprise. Expecting very little from this book, I found the atmosphere appropriate, the action fast if often incredible, the writing good—given the use of expressions such as "toddle off"—and the impossible crime very well presented even if the explanation tends to stretch credulity.

1166. The room could be entered only by a secret doorway that could be operated only by a person of a precisely particular weight.

Villainous hunchbacks, incompetent police, drug-crazed victims—the lot—except for an original or convincing solution to the impossible- crime problem.

1167. The victim was poisoned when he licked and sealed an envelope just before the séance started.

1168. The murderer was hidden in the room when it was broken into and simply joined those who had gained entrance.

1169. The victims were attacked by blood-sucking bats that emerged from holes in decorative carvings in the ceiling.

1170. The killing occurred later than had been thought, masked by the sound of some offstage shots fired in accordance with the script.

1171. (1) The fatal capsule was consumed outside the locked room but acted inside it once the gelatin covering had dissolved. Harmful capsules were then substituted by harmless ones by means of a pruning pole through a hole in the ceiling.

(2) The box was never put there in the first place, merely the outer covering.

Latimer is a very underrated author with a real flair for snappy dialogue.

1172. The door was locked on the outside with a key that was replaced by the killer after the door had been broken down.

1173. The killer was lifted up to the window by an accomplice; he then opened the window and dropped the body out.

1174. A poisoned burr was contained in a telegram opened by the victim.

1175. The victim was struck by a meteorite.

1176. The owner was duped into calling in a top policeman to organise the security, but he and his team were in fact criminals.

1177. The theft was effected by the owner of the tapestries who drugged his own guards.

1178. The man had made the tracks as he exited, walking backwards.

1179. He had dressed himself in the clothes of a scarecrow and lay without moving in plain view of those searching for him.

1180. The thief had gained entrance via a hinged pane in a window by inserting an instrument through a cleft in the pane and pressing down upon the ring that then opened the pane.

1181. The victim had been fatally wounded before entering the cabin.

1182. The killer obscured his own exiting footprints when he later re-entered.

1183. The poison gas was fed in through a gas fire in the study.

1184. The solution could be a second door, an open window, or simply the removal and replacement of the original seal—take your pick.

Ghostwritten by Craig Rice.

1185. The victim unlocked the door and admitted his killer.

Set up as a locked-room mystery but in fact a nonqualifier. An interesting study and an early example of the type of story in which the character who appears to be an investigator proves to be the murderer.

1186. The murderer entered through a dummy-hinged window.

The third (and most successful) working of a device originally used by the author in the very first locked-room-murder tale. See also Items 1188 and 1189.

1187. Shorter version of Item 1185.

1188. As for Item 1186. The second version of the first locked-room mystery story.

1189. As for Item 1186. The very first locked-room tale, used later in Items 1188 and 1186.

1190. Shorter version of Item 1185.

1191. His pyjamas doubled as a track suit and enabled him to get away unnoticed.

1192. (1) The identity of Mr. Diabolo was assumed by wearing bright paper covers on clothes. When these were quickly destroyed, another identity was taken.

(2) The key was returned to the dead body after entrance was forced.

Almost a classic, and would have been had the detectives been a little more interesting and the book rather longer.

1193. The key was turned in the lock from the outside with a pair of pliers.

1194. The victims had all handled the envenomed pages of an ancient tome originally owned by the Borgia family. Attacks also occurred via the medium of poisoned rings, poisoned nails on banisters, etc., etc.

One of Lequeux's hidden-treasure yarns and far more readable today than most of his pure espionage thrillers.

1195. The key was turned in the lock from the outside with a pair of pliers.

1196. The victim, posing as the owner of the laboratory, entered by use of duplicate keys and was caught inside and killed by the real owner.

Very disappointing. The narrator is an imbecilic motor-garage owner who stumbles blindly about throughout the whole affair. Nothing here to change my views on Lequeux.

1197. The victim was shot by a "humane killer" used by a monkey trained to climb into the room and steal and kill.

1198. The library had a secret underfloor entrance.

1199. Solution difficult to ascertain despite careful reading. It seems to be a combination of solutions 5 and 13 in that the perpetrator was probably an ape employed by a band of fiendish brothers—but I'm not absolutely sure.

The book was originally advertised under the title of "The Mysterious Mr. Noel" but appeared as *Balaoo*.

1200. Not impossible crime.

1201. (1) The victim had been attacked in her room, but the assailant left without killing her. She later locked herself in, and then accidentally fell, sustaining a wound after hitting her head on a piece of furniture.

(2) The man being chased removed a disguise and became one of the chasers.

1202. The body was that of one of the people who were thought to have been accounted for. His place was taken by someone in disguise who had secreted himself in the quarters before the watch was kept.

1203. The woman to whom it had been given to place in the box had slipped it into the pocket of one of the people who had given it to her, and replaced it with another envelope she had up her sleeve (literally).

1204. The victim, who had been drugged, was stabbed by the first person to enter the room.

1205. The killer had locked the door from the outside in the normal way and then from the outside inserted backwards into the lock a key with the handle removed and protuberances filed down, so that from the outside it appeared that the key was still in the inside of the locked door. When the door was broken open, he simply substituted the real key.

First of a short-lived series about Langtry and by no means the worst of its kind, with the added attraction of a variation on the locked-room theme that appears to be original.

1206. A booby-trapped telephone operated by the sound of a voice.

1207. The murderer swung down by means of a rope attached to a chimney, removed a pane of glass from the window, and, after the murder, replaced the pane with fresh putty.

1208. The blow was struck by a weight on the end of a rope attached to a huge catapult. After the deed, the weight (and rope) went back to the catapult via the window that it had broken to get in.

1209. The victim had been accidentally caught by the grappling hook of an overhead flying machine.

1210. The suitcase containing the jewel was switched for another by means " of a device that took the original suitcase under the floor.

1211. She had been shot earlier, after which her companion had dived overboard and was seen to be far from the canoe when the explosion was heard that he'd rigged by using a blasting cap and fuse.

1212. The door was not in fact locked at all but was only said to be so by the killer, who then, with help, broke it down.

An excellently written book.

1213. The instrument was tied on the end of a rope and used like a bolo.

An unusual little tale that starts with a black snow storm and a naked man claiming to be a visitor from another planet. Quite well handled throughout.

1214. The vital organs were from a chimpanzee, and the substitutions, etc., were effected by the physician at the morgue, who had waited for a corpse to be brought in that resembled the alter ego he had been busy establishing.

1215. The victim had been projected there—and so killed—by means of a giant catapult.

1216. The bolt had been pulled across from the outside by means of thread in the form of a slip knot that was then released.

Perfectly reasonable private-eye yarn from an author who, for reasons not known to me, does not seem to command the attention of a lot of his peers. His detective is, incidentally, stone deaf, but that is worked in quite neatly.

1217. A poison ring worn by the victim was accidentally activated while bolting the door.

1218. The track on which the train ran was built on thixotropic cement specially designed to liquefy if a train was driven over it at other than a prescribed speed. The train, with its invading force, was simply swallowed up by the cement.

1219. After being washed overboard, the man was picked up by a balloon that deposited him almost twenty-four hours later over land. As the international dateline had been crossed, it appeared that the two events had happened simultaneously.

One hundred copies of this story were issued with the first one hundred copies sold of the first edition of this bibliography. The plot was, of course, suggested by Louis Zangwill's *A Nineteenth Century Miracle* (Item 2012), but I consider that this version provides an altogether more ingenious solution.

1220. Not impossible crime.

1221. The room was hidden behind the false wall of a closet, which could be opened by means of a windlass. It had originally been used as a room in which runaway slaves could hide.

1222. Jiggery-pokery with a phonograph and a radio.

1223. The ball had been carried there by a fire walker whose hands, like his feet, were impervious to the intense heat of the ball.

1224. The killer caused a temporary short circuit by the use of drops of whiskey and water from a dropper, made his escape, then seconds later when the liquid evaporated, the electricity and the automatic bolt operated again and locked the room.

1225. The victim was "stabbed" by a knife thrown by his accomplice.

One of a series of parodies in EQMM published under a number of names, each one an anagram of the author parodied. Here, Conway Lonstar = Clayton Rawson, while Maitre Glenthier = The Great Merlini.

1226. The killer let himself down from the upper storey by means of a rope already fixed in place.

1227. (1) The killer ran a wire through the keyhole of the studio's skylight, lassoed the victim, and strangled him.

(2) The window was closed from outside with a powerful electromagnet.

(3) The door self locked as it closed.

(4) Again the good old electromagnet to close the bolt in the elevator's trap door.

1228. A wet handkerchief belonging to the victim was, unknown to him, attached to the positive terminal on the transformer, and when he bent to retrieve it, he received a massive and fatal shock.

1229. The gun had been fashioned out of a bone that, after the shooting, was removed by the family dog.

1230. The locked room was prefabricated and built around the body.

1231. The criminal hid in the room dressed as a guard, knocked out a real guard, broke open the safe and removed the rubies, hid the rubies on the real guard's person, shot him dead, and then mingled with the other guards as they came bursting in. He was searched on the way out, even though he was taken for a guard, and planned to retrieve the rubies from the corpse, which was not searched, after it had been removed from the building.

1232. An identical van had been stolen some months before and was switched for the bullion-laden van when the express slowed while climbing a hill and then slowed again because of a signal at the foot of the hill as it descended the other side.

1233. The murderer had his own key.

1234. The killer had crossed from an adjoining house by putting a plank from one window to the other.

1235. The bolt inside had already broken, and the door opened outward. A wedge of wood was keeping the door shut.

An 87th Precinct novel with the impossible crime neatly, if not particularly originally, handled.

1236. The victim had been poisoned by thermol, which produced the extreme body-heat effect.

1237. The intruder entered by means of the rubbish chute, from which he himself had slipped the catch during a visit to the flat.

1238. The victim was killed by the last man to leave the room.

Very effective use made of a background of the macabre.

1239. The victim was affected by a film into which had been introduced interpolated frames particularly frightening to the victim.

1240. The doppelganger was the woman's nephew in female garb.

This book, possibly the author's best, contains both a rational solution and one based on fantasy.

1241. Short-story version of Item 1240.

1242. A line ran from the trigger of the gun down the side of the skirting board and into the cellar below. The murderer pulled on the line when he heard his victim in the cloakroom above.

1243. The killer slipped out of the room unseen and the door locked behind him.

1244. (1) The master criminal set up mirrors to create the illusion that he was entering the vault, when in fact he was not.

(2) The entrance was effected before the snow fell and through a false section of wall that opened into an old, wide chimney.

1245. The knife was thrown from a distance through a slit curtain at the back of the set.

1246. The victim cut her own throat and the razor fell through a crack in the floorboards. Four people within the house could have done it but in fact played no part at all and therefore did not spoil the locked-house aspect of the story.

1247. The bolt was drawn from outside by means of twine and beeswax.

1248. The gun was attached to a yew shoot that carried it away from the suicide.

The author in fact did not put this situation to an impossible-crime use—but could have done.

1249. The killer had entered via a window that he had reached by means of a rope let down from the floor above.

1250. The sack with the gold was switched for another sack containing less valuable coin when the borrower was called back to give a receipt.

1251. (1) The first wound had been delivered in the heat of the moment by someone whom the victim forgave and did not wish to give away. The second and fatal wound was given by the first person to enter the room. (2) The killer got to the victim by means of a secret passage that connected adjoining rooms. After the deed, the killer attempted to close the secret entrance forever by the use of quick-drying cement.

1252. He had been struck by a meteorite.

This story found in an unusual Scottish paperback containing stories set in America.

1253. Platinum wire ran from outside the room to metal fittings within. The victim touched water and the fittings at the same time.

1254. The gas was ejected from a hollowed-out jade tortoise and having done its work was expelled by use of bellows.

As bad as they come. Candidate for worst story of the decade, it could only have come from a vanity-publishing house.

1255. The killer descended from the floor above by a wire ladder, committed the murder, and then went back up the ladder.

1256. In order to insert the spare key to open the door to get to the victim, witnesses pushed out from the inside of the keyhole what they believed was the original key, which was still inside the lock. However, they found not only the key inside but a coin, and it was the coin that had been blocking the keyhole.

Original variation on a fairly-well-worn locked-room device. Quite an enjoyable novel with its cast initially on a remote Scottish island cut off from the mainland by storm. Well written and with nice humorous touches.

1257. A thread on the head of a bolt was drawn from outside the room.

An early example of a case investigated by an eccentric detective. The author is one of the lesser-known lights in the early period of detective fiction but produced some credible books. Fascinating reference is made to an early untranslated story by the French writer Armand Silvestre, called "Le Verrou" ("The Bolt"), which provided the murderer with the means of locking the door.

1258. A section of the apartment could be moved upwards into the flat above, and this is the method by which the vanishers disappeared.

1259. The house was dismantleable, could be entered by removing a section, and was completely removed in sections.

1260. The rear window of the brougham had been tampered with to allow a man standing on the rear axle to reach through and render the woman inside insensible. She was then removed from the vehicle when it had to stop at a gate, the door having been muffled to hide the noise.

1261. The murderer lowered himself out of a window by means of a rope that he then detached.

1262. (1) The victim was propelled through the window by a trap that operated on a weight-and-counterpoise system.

(2) The victim was struck by a stone that came through a window and had been propelled from a sling.

1263. The killer was still in the room when the door was forced, and mingled with the surging crowd.

A minor classic.

1264. The door was closed by means of a piece of dental floss looped round the inner knob and running outside the door. When pulled from outside, it locked the door, then released itself and was pulled through.

1265. Use of projection equipment.

One of the bad Markhams.

1266. (1) No one was outside the window. The effect was created by a silhouette hung down from an upper window.

(2) A booby trap was rigged to fire a gun from inside a desk when a trip wire was activated.

1267. The victims were struck by a heavy and ancient arm of iron that was operated by a spring, remotely controlled.

1268. The whole front of the cabin came apart, as with a doll's house. The breaks were carefully concealed with a weatherstrip when in the closed position.

One of the good Markhams.

1269. A practical joke that went wrong.

Included here because of the "Marie Celeste"-like quality of the opening. The rest of the book, including the solution, fails to live up to the bright beginning.

1270. The exit was made with the help of a trick door, the whole frame of which could be moved.

1271. The murder had been committed earlier than had been supposed by a gimmick whereby the wireless was turned on from a distance but it was supposed that only the victim could have turned it on and must therefore have still been alive.

1272. The victim was killed offstage and brought in under cover of a hobbyhorse outfit.

1273. The gas was on and lit in the room when the murderer blew down the lead-in pipe outside, caused an airlock, and extinguished the flame.

1274. The killer left via a window, the shutter of the room below, and the water spout of the adjacent building.

1275. The vanisher had walked up both walls using his hands and the soles of his feet, just as a climber will walk up a cliff chimney. One of the guards, a policeman, then walked underneath him, and in the dark failed to notice him.

Well-constructed tale.

1276. The victim was stabbed through a black backdrop by a knife held in the end of a long black rod.

1277. The victim had been shot there from a circus cannon.

1278. The killer left through the window and climbed up a knotted rope thrown over the roof of the house and secured to the bumper of his car on the other side.

Problem stated on page 16, solved on page 17. Fast work, Mr. Hughes!

1279. Exit was effected via a column with a hidden door.

1280. Not impossible crime.

1281. The fatal wound had been caused, not by a gun, but by a horn-tipped arrow that had then passed on into a nearby fire and been utterly consumed. There was therefore no gun to find.

1282. The villain had on a parachute, crawled out of the rear platform of the last car and allowed the onward rush of the train to fill the parachute, drag him off the platform, and be saved from certain death by the effect of the parachute itself.

The detective describes the escape as "daring." I'm sure that we can all think of other descriptive phrases.

1283. One of the children was abnormally strong, having in conception been the object of a vengeful scientist's experiments.

1284. The victim was made to appear alive after his death by means of a record that was removed when the entry was forced.

The butler did it!

1285. The murderer pricked the victim's hand with a poisoned needle as he handed something to him, then after his death he put poison in his glass and smeared a little on his lips to make it seem that this was the cause of his death.

1286. The murderer was a man hideously deformed as the result of a fire.

1287. Exit was made via a window; rather a letdown.

1288. The victim was wearing an undervest that had been impregnated with a corrosive substance that after a time caused an extreme burning sensation—so much so that he jumped into the water.

1289. The killer had unlocked the door, entered, killed his victim, exited, and then pretended that the door was locked. All this while his companion was rushing round to the French windows that he found open but with no signs of an assailant.

A poor, muddled affair, even by Masterman's standards. Dick Stuart, from whom I bought my copy, left in it a set of notes he had made about the book, and I can only echo his comments: "A hopeless mixture of detection story and thriller." Dick's comments, if in sufficient quantity about sufficient books, would make a super book.

1290. The key was turned in the lock from outside by means of pincers.

1291. The victim spoke into a microphone that was modified to emit a knockout gas at the sound of his voice. He was then stabbed with a dart bearing a lethal poison by the first person to reach his prostrate body.

1292. Arsenic was introduced into coffee from outside the room, then taken in by the victim, who locked the door. The only incriminating evidence was thrown out by the victim through the ventilator.

1293. A sliding panel revealing a secret passage.

A disappointing locked-room solution but a very interesting historical detective novel.

1294. The murderer wore a tartan kilt and blended in with the scenery.

1295. A body was seen to fall from the window of the locked turret room. It was that of a drugged servant whose body was replaced by that of another victim stabbed earlier.

1296. The woman's figure, last seen on the diving board, was in fact a hologram created the day before by holographic process.

1297. The fatal wound had been inflicted much earlier, and of the two later shots one had missed the mark entirely.

A borderline entry.

1298. The pianist was playing a special arrangement of a Brahms piece, containing dissonances that had the effect of shattering some aspirins just swallowed by the victim, thus killing him.

The biggest farrago of nonsense I've read in a long time.

1299. Gas was emitted from a book when it was opened.

No locked-room murder, but there could so easily have been. The author gives a detailed two-page description showing how the opening of this particular book, attached by a chain to the bookcase, gave off a deadly gas.

1300. The occupant wore a wig under which on his bald head the ghastly face had been painted.

1301. The victim was being poisoned by carbon-monoxide gas emanating from a false palm plant in a pot.

1302. The voice came from a man in a diving outfit when he came briefly to the surface from his submarine boat.

1303. The voice came from a makeshift speaking tube fashioned from the feed to a fountain spray.

1304. The poison, hydrobromide of hyoscene, was introduced by a small spike so positioned in the victims' boots as to inject the victim when the boots were worn.

1305. The victim was placed in a tank containing liquid air, died instantly, was frozen solid in forty minutes, and was then powdered into mortar by a stone-breaking machine.

1306. The gold had been melted down and cast into one of the balls that was incorporated into the pawnbroker's sign.

1307. The floor of the room was made to revolve at rapid speeds by connection to a mill wheel, and this caused the occupants of the room to suffer enormous congestion of the brain due to centrifugal force!

1308. The men were overcome by a natural escape of the deadly carbonic- acid gas.

1309. The safe had been locked with the wrong key, one which in fact had not properly locked it at all, and thus had been left to the mercy of the thief.

1310. The suffocation was attempted by means of the lowering onto the victim of the canopy of a four-poster and entrance to the room gained by a secret passage at the back of a tapestry.

1311. The victims had been killed, removed, and devoured by a giant snake that lived on the rock (book version).

Solutions suggested by competitors in the magazine involved the snake, crows and hawks, balloons, and even indigestion on the part of Bell. However, the author's solution was ingenious—a kite operated by a villainous mechanician.

1312. The coffin contained magnetic iron ore that controlled the metal door.

1313. A container of cyanide was placed in the air-ducting system, which carried it into the cell.

1314. The killer was a mad scientist who had invented a machine capable of transmitting matter. He simply transmitted his own hands to the victim's throat and thus throttled him.

Not really a relevant entry to this study as the solution is science fictional.

1315. An impersonation/publicity stunt. The male secretary, who said that he'd left the author in the study, and the author himself were one and the same person. The dismembered hand, identified by the secretary as being his employer's, had been purloined from the mortuary!

1316. The victim had been killed elsewhere, and the study was later arranged to look as though a bomb had exploded in it.

An ingenious problem, but the solution does not live up to it.

1317. The killer exited via a rope from a window.
1318. The corpse was in fact only in an induced trance, from which she was roused, and made her escape via the window.
1319. The bars had been smeared with a newly invented solution that over a period gave them a leadlike coating and made it appear that the gold had been stolen and lead substituted.
1320. They were taken by the Boneless Wonder, a circus performer, who hid in a trunk thought to be too small to hold a man, and therefore not searched.
1321. It was written in vanishing ink.
1322. The victim had been shot from a diabolically rigged camera placed on a rack above the victim.
1323. The thief removed several tiles from the roof, pushed through the gap a hollow bamboo cane, to the end of which was attached a bladder. This was pushed onto the decanter, inflated from above, and the cane and decanter lifted through the hole in the roof.
1324. The murderer drilled a hole through the base of a light bulb, dropped in a deadly mixture of ether and hydrocyanic acid, and then resealed it. When the victim switched on the lamp in which the bulb was fitted, it burst and the deadly vapour emerged and did its work.

A surprisingly good attempt to fuse together the classic detection novel with the American gangster thriller—or at least in its British version. Excellent solution also, if it's practicable.

1325. The ship had been taken over by a gang of criminals who had murdered the honest crew members, faked the loss of the ship, and converted it while at sea into what appeared to be another vessel.
1326. Poisoned by a booby-trapped packet of cigarettes that operated when pressed.

A modern vanity-press publication.

1327. The key was slid under the door and the bolt was helped home by the jarrings and knockings on the door.
1328. The escapee hid under the bed in the cell. When the Colonel of the guard, who was in his pay, gave the alarm and led the guard elsewhere, he slipped into the guard room, put on a greatcoat, and made good his escape.

It would be difficult to think of a less likely title for a

Sherlock Holmes tale.

1329. A false door jamb that operated as the door was opened, and allowed the killer to escape.

Note: The spine of the book shows the publisher as Stanley Paul, who took Greening over.

1330. The poison had been on the gum of an envelope he had licked.

1331. The poison, extracted from black-widow spiders, was contained in a capsule designed to melt at body heat under a protective bandage, and poisoned the victim when it did melt. The doctors mistakenly diagnosed it as peritonitis.

1332. Not impossible crime.

1333. The killer's invisibility was effected by means of electrically controlled mirrors in the theatre.

1334. A glass vessel containing poison gas that was inside the room was broken by the notes of a time signal broadcast by the radio.

See also Item 1339.

1335. The victim was killed with a thin, sharp strip of metal stuck to the sole of the foot of one of the other swimmers.

1336. The car was driven by remote control.

1337. Hidden exit through the dummy drawers of a desk.

1338. The thief had entered via a transom made of a special glass that could be bent out of the frame when hot—and was.

1339. A radio time signal triggered off a tube of poison concealed in a dictionary.

See also Item 1334.

1340. The poison was introduced via a cylinder pushed from the next compartment into the pipe holding the communication chain.

1341. The victim was killed by one of the other two occupants, who smuggled in the murder weapon, a strip of thick celluloid with a razorlike edge, attached to the sole of his bare foot with flesh-coloured adhesive.

1342. A dictaphone was rigged to shoot a mouthful of hydrocyanic acid into the victim's mouth when he pressed the start button.

1343. The journey had been done in a car into which the killer had been assisted by his victim. The mileometer reading did not reveal the fact because the journey back had been in reverse gear and thus it did not register on the instrument.

1344. A minute splinter of wood had been wedged upright on the surfboard, and this had been coated with curare. When this pierced the victim's chest, he died.

1345. The noise was made by her nephew to cover up the fact that he was breaking into, over a period, the premises next door.

A very similar plot line was used in Item 1332.

1346. A key was left on the inside of the door, which was locked on the outside with a key filed down at the nose. The tape was pulled into position by suction from a carpet sweeper.

1347. Not impossible crime.

1348. The man guarding the codes was hypnotised by the villain into handing them over and then into forgetting what had happened.

1349. The murderer was the apparently incapable witness, who had killed while under hypnotic influence.

1350. The victim's piano was rigged so that an air rifle would fire a dagger when a particular note was struck.

1351. The poison was contained in and projected from the fangs in a lion's head carved in a chair in the room.

1352. A second bookseller had absentmindedly left the key where the killer could make use of it.

This five-page parody was published as a Christmas card by two enterprising American booksellers.

1353. The murderer was hiding in the room when the entrance was forced.

1354. The victim was feigning death with the help of drugs and made his escape after the door was broken in.

1355. Sliding panels to adjoining rooms.

1356. The killer locked the museum from the outside, reached through a window and replaced the keys on their hook by means of a stick, and then slammed the window shut so that the latch inside fell into place.

1357. The victim was killed with a specially made weapon that fitted inside a camera lens.

1358. The final wall of the locked room was built after the body had been placed inside the smaller, newly constructed room.

A bright debut but the solution is not the original one that the blurb promises.

1359. The daggers were fired from a spring gun through a hole in a mounted elephant's head.

1360. The bolt was drawn across from outside by means of a piece of cord attached to it and passed through to the outside.

Quite a reasonable golden-age novel suffering a little, however, from the heavy-handedness of the period. The impossible crime is handled better than the characterisation and the personal relationships.

1361. The victim pierced his hand on a poisoned spike while acting out a spurious keep-fit programme played by the murderer.

1362. The killer hid in a closet and made his escape dressed as a policeman with the aid of a crooked police confederate.

1363. The victim put the noose around his own neck for histrionic effect, but, as he was heavily under the influence of drugs, couldn't prevent himself from asphyxiating.

1364. The victim was stabbed by one of the half-inch strips of steel that acted as a support in his girdle. The strip had been filed to razor edge.

Well, that's about it. No point reading any more locked-room stories after this monumentally preposterous endeavour.

1365. The killer exited via the transom window.

Not much mystery here, as the accompanying drawing for the story shows the killer making his acrobatic exit.

1366. The heart attack was brought about by turning up the heat in the hot house to a very high temperature.

1367. The key was returned after the door was broken in.

1368. The killer exited by the use of a low-inertia machine.

If you want to know more, you'll have to read the story. Transmission of such technical data is definitely not my forte.

1369. The beam was fired from inside the complex and reflected back from a mirror on the outside made of frozen water that later evaporated When the sun came up.

1370. The killer had fixed the knobs on the gas cooker so as to prevent it being turned off, had removed all matches from the room to prevent it being lit, and had arranged matters from the outside that neither the door nor the window could be opened from the inside.

1371. The deaths were engineered by a malevolent kindlewitch, in the first instance by taking possession of the victim and compelling him to commit suicide, and in the second by means of an animal—a falcon, as I understand it—which was in her power.

I hope that I have this right. Though clearly literate, just not my sort of book at all.

1372. There was a secret exit into a passage through the back of a wardrobe.

A curious item written, disconcertingly, in the second person. E.g., " 'I'll be all right, honey,' you said. You locked the door behind her."

1373. The author may know it, I certainly didn't, and neither, it seems, did Mr. Kilgarvan. A second locked-room murder in the same room also went unexplained.

1374. The end of the key stem was turned with pliers from outside the room.

1375. The victim was shot from outside, after which the gun and spent cartridges were pushed into the room through the ventilator slot.

1376. The burglar threw something out of the window to create a noise so that it seemed that someone had left via the window, and then slipped away and hid in a broom cupboard before exiting later by more conventional means.

1377. The key was replaced inside the lock by the person who broke in the glass panel of the door.

1378. The victim had been struck down with a block of ice that had then melted.

A clever story from a volume that should have been elevated to Queen's Quorum status.

1379. They had been hit by a napalm-bearing model plane.

1380. They were being kidnapped by a psychopathic janitor and imprisoned in the building's basement.

1381. The old man had exited, via a secret panel, to a private suite of rooms in the depths of the club.

1382. He had been bound and gagged and stowed in one of the supposedly locked and empty offices in the block.

Set up as an impossible crime but not in fact so.

1383. A trip wire was set over which the victim fell onto spikes planted in the river. He was later pulled back onto the bank and the paraphernalia removed.

1384. The murder had been committed earlier than at first supposed, and the murderer had assumed the identity of the victim.

1385. The victim died elsewhere and was taken to the murder site where by use of a rake some panes were broken and a large hole made beneath which the body was laid.

The author writes well enough, but I wish that this was not

in the first person and that I found the locked-room solution rather more convincing.

1386. The victim had not, as had been thought, deliberately swallowed the key but had been forced to swallow it by the killer, who had then shot him, put the gun in the box, and closed and thereby locked it.

1387. (1) The shed was lifted by a crane and turned so that the door could be used. Afterwards, it was replaced as it had previously been.

(2) The cellar trap door had originally had the bolt upwards, but the position was changed when the shed and its base and the trap door below it were moved.

The genuine article, but with solutions so complicated that I'm not at all sure I entirely understood or have correctly explained it.

1388. The car was switched onto a siding and then submerged in a flooded sand pit.

A story that ought to make a spectacular film, but too disjoined to make a good book.

1389. The murder was committed by the narrator while in a kind of trauma- induced trance; a somewhat unusual ending.

1390. The victim was thrown from the window by an acrobat who had swung down on a rope from an upper storey.

1391. The murderer used a remote-control model plane to fly in through an open window of the apartment, shoot the victim, eject the weapon, and thus simulate suicide.

1392. The victim sustained a serious wound outside the room, entered it, locked himself in, and died there.

1393. There was another key, and the chain was a trick one where two links could be parted.

Nothing brilliant in locked rooms but an exceptionally good psychological thriller with lots of atmosphere, some chilling scenes, and a neat denouement.

1394. There was a secret exit reached by removing a floorboard.

1395. A pane of glass in one of the leaded windows has been fixed to enable easy removal and replacement. Through this the fatal shot was fired.

1396. The woman who died was not the meal consumer. It was an impersonation stunt.

1397. The door was locked by a midget, who exited via the transom.

1398. The killer had broken the door in earlier, then set it up again so that he could smash it for a second time with witnesses present.

1399. A knife was held against the door's spring lock while it was pulled to. The knife was then removed and the latch clicked shut.

1400. The bolt on the door had been moved into position by means of a magnet.

Hardly a novel locked-room solution but nevertheless an extremely enjoyable first mystery with a very interesting milieu.

1401. Two-way locking device that locked on one side but not on the other; a disappointing solution.

1402. The body had been taken into the courtyard via a low-level grating in the wall.

1403. She had gained entrance via a passage leading between two wells, one inside and one outside the harem.

1404. The would-be assassin's plot had been followed throughout by his wife's servant, an ex-serviceman trained to kill with his hands.

1405. The murder was committed with a second identical ruler, and the fingerprinted one left in its place.

1406. The plane had been landed by a third party, and the body, which had been carried there on the plane, was deposited near it before the pilot made off.

1407. The victim choked himself one handed.

1408. The locked room seems to be a figment of the blurb writer's imagination as the killer had simply unlocked a door earlier to allow easy passage in and out of the murder room. It was supposed to be locked, but it wasn't.

Otherwise a fresh and enjoyable novel that fades somewhat at the end.

1409. Giant octopus in attendance.

1410. No solution given. The point of the story is that, in this way, Ubique established an alibi while he committed the murder.

1411. (1) The midget had never gone on the island. His place had been taken by a boy before he reached it.

(2) One boy escaped via a fire-drake that ran down a rope from the castle to the mainland.

(3) Another boy went hand-over-hand by the rope.

(4) The third boy escaped across the moat disguised as a

crocodile.

(5) The fourth boy hid under a woman's velvet farthingale.

(6) The final boy wore short stilts and disguised himself as one of the guards.

1412. Under cover of a smoke screen she removed a veil, slipped on a wig, and transformed herself into another and different female assistant.

1413. The stabbing had in fact taken place earlier than had first been thought.

1414. The locked windows had dummy latches that had been specially but uselessly sealed, as the windows could be opened by concealed springs. Convincing explanations are also provided for the other magician's tricks worked by a fake medium.

1415. The killer hid behind the door as it was opened, and was dressed in the same garb as one of the breakers-in, who was his accomplice. Substitution was possible for a few moments to enable the murderer to escape.

1416. The length of carpet, when pulled from outside the sealed room's door, pulled into position a knife raised vertically in a block of wax and on the second pull knocked the victim onto her back on the knife.

A fine example of the work of a forgotten author of the latter part of the golden age. Easy to read with its amusing characters, love interest, and the diabolical Heath Robinson (or, in the U.S., Rube Goldberg) murder device.

1417. The bus had been loaded onto a large trailer truck.

An expanded version of Item 1418.

1418. The bus had been loaded onto a large trailer truck.

1419. One disappearance was simply a magician's trick with mirrors and plate glass; the other never happened. It was reported to help substantiate the existence of the invisibility ray gun.

1420. No solution given.

Ellery Queen, quite correctly, calls this the sealed-room murder to end all sealed-room murders. It's all about a playwright who works out but then forgets a perfect locked-room method. He tries to trace the only person to whom he had divulged the forgotten secret—with terrible results.

1421. They had been electrocuted by high-voltage equipment in the X-ray room and their bodies removed to the garden subsequently.

1422. Firecrackers were exploded in the room to make it appear that shots had been fired. In fact, the fatal shot was fired later by a gun equipped with a silencer.

1423. The so-called victim had in fact exited with the rescue team, and the body was that of someone else shot elsewhere.

1424. The last person to leave the tomb before it was locked had secretly left false indications that desecration had taken place. Some time later he and a shortsighted witness had opened the tomb and seen the false signs. While the witness went to fetch help, the thief secreted the gold and valuables inside a large oil jar that stood, with others, inside the tomb.

1425. The spy was in fact in the room when the door was broken open, but he had assumed the identity of the man who had pursued him into the room.

1426. The killer approached his victim in an air balloon.

1427. (1) The effect was achieved by the skilful use of makeup.
(2) They were caused by a little-known microbe common to certain Hindu provinces.

Merely a sampling of the many odd and imperfectly explained events in a rather preposterous book. Douglas Green's review in *The Poisoned Pen* deals admirably with this deservedly obscure book.

1428. The victim was shot through a window screen with a pistol that fired a lethal liquid gas.

Considered by Bill Pronzini, with irrefutable justification, as one of the alternative-classic shorts.

1429. The box contained a Mirror of Truth that is designed optically to reflect only those facial lines that the distortion called personality creates. The victims, seeing themselves thus for the first time, died of shock.

1430. The woman had in fact entered the next room and had been incorrectly stated* by the witness to have entered and screamed from her own room.

1431. The thieves/drivers/vanishers had developed the power to teleport themselves over short distances.

1432. The victim had been impaled and carried off on the horns of a bull.

1433. Wire in a bed's mattress was sensitive to heat and ejected a highly poisonous substance when rested upon.

1434. A dagger on a string.

Awful! Enough to put anyone off locked-room mysteries—and Phillpotts—for life.

1435. He exited from the tower of the Treasure House by unscrewing a bar from a window and then screwing it back in place again.

1436. The chapel was unlocked with a duplicate key, and the coffin was pulled open from outside by means of a rubber sucker.

Set in his native Devon, this is probably Phillpotts's best impossible- crime story, dealing with the miraculous movement of the corpse of a man who had a Poe-like fear of being buried alive.

1437. The gold had been moved into a secret compartment built in the space between the bulkheads.

1438. The shot was fired from a booby trap fitted within the saddle.

1439. Not impossible crime.

1440. She had hidden in the innards of a large couch (and had ignored a secret passage!)

1441. (1) The victim was stabbed by someone who approached him swimming underwater.

(2) The knife was extracted by means of a block and tackle.

(3) A line was looped under the victim's armpits and was attached at the other end to a captive shark. When the shark was released, it raced off and dragged the victim overboard.

1442. The knife, which had a skewerlike blade, had been fitted into a cartridge case and fired from a rifle.

1443. (1) Exit was made via a secret panel, and the "dead man" was in fact his younger brother.

(2) An optical illusion caused by sunlight reflecting shadows on unusually thick mist.

An example of a late Gothic-style story in which passages and panels abound and are the explanation for pretty well all the apparent impossibilities found in them. A tenuous connection to Le Fanu can be noted but virtually none at all to Poe's Dupin.

1444. The victim accidentally killed himself whilst trying to re-enact a murder he had witnessed.

1445. The murderer was admitted and let out by one of the innocent parties.

Yuch!

1446. The murderer escaped through a window apparently nailed down but in fact not so because the nails in it were broken.

1447. The killer took the key away with him. Virtually a nonstarter!

1448. The bolt was drawn across by string attached to its head and passed under the door frame. The highly sprung lock was shot from outside by a sharp blow.

1449. The victim was dehydrated, stuffed through the cell bars, and then, once back inside, rehydrated. A hardcore pastiche and very enjoyable.

1450. The killer had put a chimpanzee into the room. It had swung on the ball and thus caused it to rise a little higher and so hit the helpless victim.

1451. Poison gas in a spare tyre that killed when a little was let out because the tyre was overinflated.

1452. Mosquitoes were introduced into the suspect's room at night, and when recaptured, the blood in their stomachs could only have come from the victim and thereby proved his blood type.

1453. The ruby had been wrapped in a large piece of chewed gum that had been thrown at—and had stuck to—the wall of the adjoining building.

1454. The brass bolt contained a small iron piece that was moved magnetically from outside.

One of the best of the Porges stories. It has a very good piece of clueing showing how the murderer kept coffee hot in the murder room and so established an alibi.

1455. The cash was hidden in a false section of a telegraph pole.

1456. As the victim lay drunk on his bed, the murderer, through the transom, used a fishing rod to put on his face a rag soaked in carbon tetrachloride. This combined with alcohol to form phosgene and killed him.

1457. The victim's neck had been crushed by a pair of bronze hands from a cherub welded onto a hydraulic jack.

1458. Most of the prints were made by a spongy fabric shot from a bow but retractable by means of a woollen thread.

1459. The fires were started by incendiary bombs tied to bats.

1460. The killer did not climb the peak but took the photographs from a suitably elevated position by means of a camera on a kite.

1461. The victim's body was pushed through the hole like a ship into a bottle.

1462. The horse collar was linked to a small electrical charge, which immediately heated a metal plate in the victim's head and killed him.

1463. It was catapulted there from a young sapling.

The magazine couldn't make up its mind whether to use the title shown here or "The Impassable Gulf," which appeared at the head of the story and on the index page!

1464. The jewel was smuggled out hidden in the fur of a pet cat that exited via a cat hatch.

1465. The diamond had been substituted for the lead in a cartridge and fired into an adjoining building.

1466. The body was hidden in a hot-water tank from which all internal pipes had been removed.

1467. The small pistol that did the shooting was itself shot out of the murder area by means of a rifle (like a grenade thrower).

Quite well worked out; it sounds feasible.

1468. The Body had been hidden inside a disused electric pole at the property.

1469. The arrow was slung by hand with the aid of a string tied to the arrow.

Good.

1470. Sent out in a model aircraft.

Average fare.

1471. The victim was poisoned by cyanide injected into an outside water pipe that fed a tap in the cell.

1472. The poison pellet had been propelled into his mouth by means of a peashooter aimed by a deadly enemy.

1473. An ebony cane shot by a crossbow and retrieved by a pet dog.

A very cleverly handled story; one of Porges's best.

1474. Murder committed with the hollow shell of the concrete block, which was then filled with more concrete.

1475. The victim had shot himself, but then his brother, wishing to throw suspicion on the maker of the footprints, had hooked the gun out of the area with rod and line.

1476. The gas was in a balloon that was moved across to the hotel-room window by means of a wire and a magnet that attached itself to the wire mesh protecting the window. The killer then burst the balloon, and the released gas was sucked into the room via the air-cooler grill.

1477. The diamond was hidden in a light bulb, lit by a smaller bulb inside it.

1478. The gun was buried in the concrete base of a plant holder, using quick drying cement.

1479. An iron missile carrying a deadly electric charge was fired from a crossbow operated from the roof of an adjacent and equally high building.

1480. The chain had been thrown into a vat of molten lead and had dissolved in it.

1481. The thief had placed the picture between two flags sewn together and run them up the mast.

1482. The bomb was buried in the grounds near the building. Detonating wires were attached to the larvae of the cicada. The insects' cycle would call for them to move from their position after seventeen years, at which point the bomb would thereby be detonated.

1483. The thief had found a piece of tinsel string, had fashioned a form of slingshot, and whisked the bag of jewels and the string onto the rooftop. Subsequently a jackdaw, attracted by the string, had removed it, with the bag of jewels, to its nest.

1484. The gun was at the bottom of a frozen birdbath, supercooled instantly into ice by the action of the missile on the water.

1485. The killer had run a lead off the telephone wire in the basement to the nearby sewer pipe. When he telephoned from elsewhere, the strong current caused by the ringing passed through the sewer pipe and electrocuted the victim.

1486. The killer had loosed out carbon dioxide from a lot of fire extinguishers, and this had lain in the hollow where the family lived and killed them.

1487. The murder weapon—a derringer—was placed in the mouth of the victim and later retrieved.

A clever idea, well used.

1488. A rock on the end of a piece of rope swung from a balcony opposite, with a flagpole as its axis.

Quite good.

1489. The body was concealed on top of the rock under a false lid to the rock.

Neat, but no attempt to create atmosphere.

1490. Water dripping from a tap at a determined rate was the time fuse that started a chain reaction—after six weeks—that led to the fire.

1491. The assassin interfered with the house's water supply from outside so that when the victim brushed his teeth he would have been poisoned.

1492. The disability was caused by bombarding the victim with X-rays from the floor above.

1493. The platinum dust was taken out in honey consumed by bees owned by the thief.

1494. The key was turned from outside by means of string. The murderer drank the water in which he drowned his victim.

1495. The victim set off the gun himself by means of a fishing rod and a filed- down trigger. The gun's recoil carried it backwards and out through a window slit into the sea below.

1496. The sun focussed on and exploded the percussion cap of a gun standing on a rack.

1497. The engine was run through the tunnel and switched into one of the sheds. The tunnel was blown as a blind.

1498. The gold had been stolen by the miser's daughter, who lived with him.

A disappointment from a locked-room point of view but some nice occult misdirection.

1499. The victim was struck on the head by a heavy chest that he accidentally pulled down on top of himself.

Advertised as a novel, *The Nameless Thing* is in fact a collection of short stories within a central theme. The lead story is the locked-room one, not so ingeniously explained as some of Post's other works. The central theme—i.e., the "Nameless Thing"—is "fate."

1500. The knife had been slipped into the pocket of one of the people searching.

1501. She had hidden behind a seat when the bus reached the school and had slipped away once the bus had got back to the depot.

Mundane solution to a nice story.

1502. The theft was carried out by three midget human reproductions who hid inside another piece of luggage on the rocket. The midgets gained strength by losing size and were able to withstand the rocket journey, which would have killed a normal man.

Neat science-fictional answer, but by no means the best of the SF entries.

1503. The woman exited via a window, to the catch of which a string/fuse was attached. She then lit the end of the fuse and established an alibi for when, shortly afterwards, the fuse finished burning with an explosion and closed the catch on the window.

1504. After the killing, the murderer locked the door and then forced it open from the outside. He then closed it again after putting the key on the inside of the door, and later in the presence of witnesses appeared to break the door open from the outside.

This author's best locked-room novel to date and probably his best Nameless novel as well. Excellent in all respects.

1505. (1) The victim bolted the door himself shortly before he died.
(2) The murderer so arranged matters that after he left the shed and closed the door behind him, he was able to pull a twine that brought down a step ladder on which the victim's body was balanced. The victim's right index finger was wedged in the head of the door key, and as the body fell from the ladder it had the effect of turning the key.

1506. (1) See the explanation to the same author's "Thin Air" (Item 1520).
(2) See the explanation to the same author's "A Killing in Xanadu" (Item 1513).
(3) See the explanation to the same author's "A Nice Easy Job" (Item 1514).

1507. The murder had been committed earlier, after which the gun and documents had been pushed into the building's lift shaft via the gap between the lift and the floor. The shot had been fabricated later by the bursting of a paper bag.

1508. The gun was hidden in a ship in a bottle. The end of the bottle was cut off and then replaced.

1509. The victim's place was taken by a large man-sized silk balloon that burst as the drop occurred. The remnants were secreted by one of the guards.

1510. The items concerned were removed, unwittingly, in a hollow cane used by the store owner, who switched off the surveillance system in his role as last person to leave.

1511. The murder had been committed earlier, and the shot heard while the lion house was under observation was from a tape recording.

1512. The man had hidden by burrowing into soft mud under the beached boat of one of the people searching for him.

1513. The killer exited through a wide dormer-style window split into vertical halves. He used a thin strip of film to hold the locking bar until he had closed the windows, then withdrew the film, thus allowing the bar to fall into the bracket and the window to be locked.

1514. The theft had taken place earlier, and the thief placed a suction clamp on the outside of the window, jerked the bar of the clamp so that the window broke and the shards fell outwards.

1515. The victim was knocked through the window by his dog, whom he had regularly mistreated.

1516. A drawer in a desk was booby trapped to project a home-made missile when it was pulled open.

1517. The bullet was fired from a home-made zip gun that the other person present, an ex-showground performer, afterwards ate.

1518. The criminal broke in through a door secured by a spring lock and a chain lock. The spring lock was opened by a small tool or credit card, and he snipped through the chain of the chain lock, then once inside removed the original chain lock and replaced it with an exact duplicate. He then left via another door with dead bolts that could be opened from the inside and closed behind him.

1519. Before the door was opened the killer had sliced off the bottom of a bottle containing a ship, hidden the gun inside the ship, and glued the bottom of the bottle back on again.

1520. The victim was killed later and left the car as it was moving slowly before coming to a complete stop. He set up a cigarette end to ignite a match to make it look as though the car was still occupied.

1521. The victim had been killed outside and then carried in through a window. The window was protected on the inside by a padlocked gate and on the outside by a shutter. The killer opened the shutter and the window, which he had left unlocked, and then reached through and unlocked the padlocked gate. On his way out again, he was able to lock the gate but not the window. However, this was not immediately noticeable.

1522. The murderer, staying in the adjoining room, had drilled a hole through the wall at the point in the closet where the rod holding the hangers fitted. He had tapped the rod and drawn it into his own room, thus leaving an aperture through which to shoot. After the killing, he had replaced the rod and withdrawn the tap.

1523. The cash was hidden inside a false tape roll of an adding machine.

1524. The man was a policeman in uniform over which he wore a breakaway costume. When he rapidly discarded the costume and a false beard, he again became the policeman.

1525. The victim was hypnotised into thinking he was eating when in fact he was not.

Nice little story despite a somewhat way-out solution.

1526. The killer had what might be termed a split personality, though that is not the medical term. Thus the guilty personality did the killing and left the innocent one to take the rap.

A most remarkable short novel from a professor of philosophy. The blurb points out that Ellery Queen might well have turned the book into a locked-room mystery, but Mr. Puccetti does very well indeed to provide a most unusual solution and a most able and gripping book. Also recommended to those who like courtroom scenes.

1527. The stabbing was done with the sharpened end of a cripple's crutch.

1528. The gun had been hidden in the mouth of a performing horse.

1529. The bolt was shot by means of the weight of the victim's body. For a full explanation, it is necessary to refer to the book itself. A second door was in fact unlocked, but for reasons given in the book could not be used by the murderer.

1530. The victim cut her own throat and her pet bird carried the murder weapon out through the barred window.

1531. The knife had been removed by a pet raven.

1532. The gun was concealed in a bottle of brandy, which was carried out by one of the witnesses.

1533. The victim had carried the killer over the mud on his shoulders and been strangled by him after he had unlocked the cave entrance. The killer had then exited via the rear cave window into a lake below.

This particular play has never been available in written form, a fact much bewailed by Francis M. Nevins, Jr., in his excellent study of Queen, *Royal Bloodline* (Bowling Green, 1974). High time it was available.

1534. The murderer had a second key.
1535. The victim's coat had been smeared with phosphorescent paint.
1536. The diamonds were not stolen by the occupant but by the next person to enter, who falsely reported that they were already stolen.
1537. The murderer swung across from an adjoining window by means of a window cleaner's strap and stabbed the victim through the window of the room.
1538. The electricity was turned off by the man who made tracks by wearing two right shoes.
1539. The theft was executed after the period of display by the attorney who was supposed to be safeguarding it. After the display, he examined the doll, pronounced it a fake, and in the confusion switched the real doll for a fake.
1540. The vanisher hid in a roll-top desk and later attempted to exit disguised as a young telegraph messenger.
1541. The vanisher escaped through a window onto a ledge and into the adjoining office. He then assumed a disguise, re-entered the room from which he had escaped, and locked the window.
1542. The murder was committed by the guard.

A dying-message story with the locked-room element being very minor.

1543. The house had not moved its position at all, but some of the occupants of the house next door thought that it had because they had, without their knowledge, been secretly moved to an identical house that had no house next door.
1544. The bills had been slipped into one of the searchers' pockets.
1545. A stationmaster at one end of the tracked area had lied when he said that the train had passed him into the area. It had in fact been stopped at an earlier point.
1546. The poison was introduced by the victim's doctor on the end of a thermometer.
1547. The victim was induced to open his multilocked door by the murderer posing as a fireman—with an axe—and resorting to the gambit of a dummy fire in the outer hall.
1548. The room, with locked door, had been created after the victim's death by erecting a further dividing wall in the larger room

where the murder occurred.

The product of another author employing the Queen house name, it is competently written and well plotted. The ending, however, is too glib.

1549. A secret hiding place made by means of dummy panels and mirrors.

1550. Not impossible crime.

1551. The murderer escaped through the French windows that were then closed by a witness, who did so without consciously realising that he had done so.

1552. The French windows had a catch that locked automatically when pulled to from the outside.

1553. There was a minute gap at the bottom of one of the windows, and it was through this that the bullet was fired.

1554. He escaped via a secret passage.

I suspect that this early and well-known Gothic novel is one of many such to feature this kind of mysterious disappearance and attendant secret-passage explanation. I have neither the time nor the inclination to probe further.

1555. The victim had swallowed a keratin-coated capsule, and the coating was later slowly dissolved by a double whisky.

1556. She died from poison injected into her by the cat.

1557. The killer was still in the room, hid behind the door, and joined the crowd who rushed in when the door was opened.

1558. The companion had bisected the sandwich with a knife smeared with poison on one side only of the blade. He gave the victim the half affected by the poisoned blade.

1559. The poison was in the ice cubes used in the drinks.

1560. The catch on the communicating door was left balanced in such a way that as the door was pulled to, the catch dropped into the relevant slot.

1561. A ball made of onion-skin-thin glass was filled with hydrogen-arsenide and then tossed into the room or car occupied by the victims. When the ball broke, the gas was released and put the victims temporarily to sleep.

1562. The victim died earlier than had at first been supposed, and her voice, heard from outside and thus establishing an alibi for the killer, was on a gramophone record. A second suspect also left the building, leaving a locked door behind him, and Professor

Stubbs dealt briefly with the ways in which he could have achieved this—tweezers and twine, etc.

1563. He was impersonated by the killer.

1564. The house had been reduced to rubble by a machine that destroyed wood, metal, and glass, but left all other materials intact.

1565. The victim was stabbed by an arrow through the cabin's logs, and his wig, of which no one had known, was withdrawn with the arrow.

1566. When the victim grabbed both the microphone and its stand, he completed an electrical circuit and received a massive shock.

1567. The victim was poisoned by cyanide released from a temporary tooth filling.

Bill Deeck, who bravely read this book, was sorry he did and remarks, with admirable restraint, "a poor thriller, rather than a mystery."

1568. (1) (a) The bolt was slid across after the front door was smashed in.

(2) (b) Voices heard from a gimmicked radio. The victim was killed earlier.

(3) An exchange was made with the taxi driver.

An excellent, if involved, debut by one of the few specialist locked- room authors. Chapter 13 contains the second-best essay on the methods of effecting a locked-room murder; the best is in Carr's *Hollow Man*.

1569. (1) The footprints were put on the ceiling by an acrobat.

(2) The gun was thrown and exploded on impact with the ground.

The close plotting well repays leisurely reading. The whole book gives an impression of impossibility, although in fact the true impossible problems are small.

1570. Merlini unlocked the electrically controlled door with a picklock but did not open the door. Then when the current was switched off while the guards entered the cell to put out a fire deliberately started inside it, Merlini was able to open the door about half an inch so that when the current was reactivated it did not affect that door.

1571. The unarmed witness had shot the victim and then swallowed the weapon that fired the shot.

1572. The murderer was hiding behind the door and put in an appearance after the entrance had been forced.

1573. The door was not locked but merely said to be locked by the murderer. The tape had been ripped by the murderer when he had exited earlier but was made to seem intact by a fake tearing noise he made as the door was later burst open.

1574. The diamonds were in a pack of cards in constant use by the suspect, who had in other respects been thoroughly searched.

1575. The victim was killed, the phone placed in his hands, and a lead weight placed on the phone cradle. A call was put through on the phone, and after two rings the lead weight was pulled off the cradle by means of an attached fishing line. The bell thus stopped ringing, and it appeared to those outside that the victim had answered the phone.

1576. The nude man was the murderer and had shot the victim by means of a cartridge, a two-inch length of brass pipe, and a soldering iron.

1577. The victim squatted down in the booth and an accomplice looked in and pretended that he had vanished. Then, while the observer made his way through the crowds toward them, the accomplice moved along to the next booth, which was empty, and the observer did not realise that the booths had been switched.

1578. A sealed sugar packet had been slit and poison inserted. This was then left by the assailant when he took another sugar packet for himself.

1579. The killer had learned that the victim had a great fear of spiders and arranged for one to be in his inkwell, thus giving him a heart attack.

They don't come any more preposterous.

1580. The murderer helped to break down the door and replaced the key after the entrance had been forced.

1581. A parcel was placed in the room and exploded the moment the wrapper was broken, injecting the victim with flying slivers of poisoned glass.

1582. The fatal bullet had been fired through a tube located in the barrel of a cannon and operated by remote control when a trigger device was pulled by one of the musket-bearing execution squad

1583. The killer unscrewed the outside knob of the door and tied the inside knob with its connecting rod to the strangulation cloth. He fastened some strong wire to the connecting rod, threaded it through the hole in the latch, went outside, shut the door, pulled the knob and connecting rod into place, and reconnected the outside knob. The victim was strangled when the door was pulled open.

1584. The victim had been killed earlier than thought, and the screams of the missing man had been prerecorded and played back after the diving bell had submerged.

1585. The man was killed within the room and hidden in a secret receptacle covered with wallpaper. His killer then escaped by a window that he locked from outside by means of a patent device (described in detail in the book).

Typical vanity-press publication.

1586. The innocent party locked the doors before she discovered that the murder had been committed

1587. Not impossible crime.

1588. The victim was poisoned when she touched a counterfeit bell push and activated a small reservoir of deadly poison connected to a hollow needle.

1589. The killer had attached a ladder to the rope floor from the lower level, jumped onto the ladder, thus causing the victim on the rope floor to fall on it, scaled the ladder, reached through the rope floor, and stabbed him.

1590. The killer wore a completely black outfit and similarly covered his face so that he merged in totally with the background and could not be seen.

1591. During a period of darkness on stage, the killer climbed up a belt that stretched from his own waist to that of the victim.

Again, good byplay between the detective and his wife, but a solution I found quite impossible to swallow—in terms of probability, if not feasibility.

1592. Not impossible crime.

1593. The killer used a fire door, but the main gimmick was getting past the doorman. This he achieved by covering up the light which was reflected each time the connecting door was opened and normally alerted the doorman.

1594. A complicated affair well suited to the complex safety system in the townhouse, involving hydraulic elevators, fail-safe release switches, et al. Impossible to encapsulate.

A witty and unusual treatment.

1595. The victim was induced to inject himself with a fatal dose of strychnine under the impression that it was an antidote to a drug that he thought he had been given by a visitor who had left the dispensary some minutes before.

1596. An ice cube shot from a catapult.

Good, solid, reasonably literate rendering, with a clever variation on an old theme, and it all ends, in true Priestley fashion, securely tied. I can see why Priestley had his fans, even though I could never become one myself.

1597. The victim had admitted the killer who, after the deed, went out by the door, which locked behind him.

1598. The killer had entered by means of a duplicate key.

1599. Steam was fed from a kettle into a hose attached to the outside end of a pipe that led inside to a burning fire in a grate within the house. This produced the relevant poison gas.

1600. The case had been opened by its owner, who had expected to see his bull fiddle in it.

A very obvious solution—but what a delightful locked-room situation!

1601. The victim, who had the peculiar habit of eating grapes from the wallpaper design, was poisoned by someone who knew of the habit and put cyanide on the wallpaper in the room.

1602. The victim was persuaded to hang himself on the understanding that the rope would break and he would thus get into the prison hospital. It didn't.

1603. A pigeon had been trained to turn on the gas tap.

1604. The killer removed and replaced the window pane, making the new putty look old by smearing it with soot.

The blurb states that Edgar Allan Poe could not have invented a better way into that locked room. For me, the chief interest lies in the author's name. The paperback edition shows "R. T. Rich" on the cover the boards edition "A. T. Rich" there. The title page bears "R. x Rich." My vote, however, goes to "Arthur T. Rich," the fullest name given, which is shown on the publisher's list at the back of the boards edition.

1605. Arsene gas was frozen solid in a cellophane container that ruptured when the gas warmed to room temperature.

1606. The victim was shot by a poisoned dart fired through a skylight. An accomplice was then lowered down through the skylight and strung up the victim.

A promising start to this book, but it falls apart and the locked-room solution is woefully weak.

1607. The house concerned had old doors with locks with identical keys. The key to another room had been used to open the bedroom.

1608. The killer used a remote-control gramophone that played through the speaker of a radio in the victim's room. By switching on the gramophone, it appeared that the victim was still alive and had switched on her radio, whereas, in fact, she was already dead.

1609. The killer removed the slats holding in a window pane, stepped out onto the balcony, bolted the door from the inside, and then replaced the pane.

The author, true to his usual style, adds a twist at the end that throws the whole locked-room issue wide open.

1610. The pearls, which were imitation, were dropped into a water glass that in fact contained acid—and dissolved.

1611. The victim's body was swung pendulumlike from a window and then, at the full arc, was dropped so that the body fell beneath the window next to that from which it was dropped.

1612. The killer knew the victim was allergic to rabbits and introduced one into the sack before the trick commenced. The resulting rabbit hairs caused an asthmatic attack during the course of the trick, and such a bad one that the victim was physically unable to carry out the rest of the manoeuvres—and drowned.

1613. Although the window of the room was solidly barred, the whole window frame itself could be opened inwards on a hinge, and this is the way the vanisher disappeared.

All part of an insurance swindle, incidentally, and a neat and enjoyable little tale.

1614. The victim was killed much earlier and elsewhere. His murderer then impersonated him within the sealed studio and was the first man to enter the studio after the alarm was given.

1615. Not impossible crime.

1616. The arm had come through a grill in the wall and was then withdrawn.

1617. One of the victims had been hypnotised and induced to lock all the doors and gas both herself and the other victim.

1618. The killer waited until the victim was locked in her room asleep with the gas fire on. He then switched off the gas supply at the mains and immediately switched it back on again.

1619. The victim was killed elsewhere and carried to the murder room by his twin brother and an accomplice.

Included in this volume as one of the earliest examples of the locked- room situation being used, not as a "locked room—how did the murderer escape?" problem, which indeed it is not, but as the strengthening of the idea of suicide by the victim. The book itself is a typical Victorian mystery but is not as long-winded as so many of them tend to be.

1620. The poison gas was fed in under the door.

1621. Not impossible crime.

1622. The various witnesses had been anaesthetised, and the crimes, escapes, etc., had been committed while they were in that state.

1623. He exited to the floor below by means of a "collapsible metal grappling hook, to the shank of which was affixed a slender and very stout silken cord."

1624. The victim had been killed by poison gas released from a trained falcon. A timing device then caused the conflagration that hid the fact that the victim was not the cabin occupier, who had in fact exited by normal means and locked the cabin door behind him.

1625. Poison was squirted from a pump gun, formed a vapour, and poisoned anything with which it came into contact.

1626. The stabbing was done by an already present diabolical floating machine that afterwards burnt itself out.

1627. The bullets were made of a chemical that evaporates when exposed to air. They were coated with inflammable paint that burned off when the gun was discharged.

1628. A secret button let down the back of the trunk. From there the vanisher went through a trap door.

1629. The person who locked the door after the shooting had taken place exited by dropping out of a rear bedroom window.

1630. The victim admitted the killer into the room and was stabbed to death by him. A powerful heat source was then applied to the body, which then smouldered for hours until totally consumed.

A weak and unconvincing finish to an otherwise enjoyable book.

1631. One of the classic tours de force of all time. A magnificent maze of clues and murders, laid out in a uniquely eccentric manner. The pursuit and disappearance of Corkscrew the maniacal hitchhiker, who seemingly hewed down victim after victim, is the theme of the book. The explanation, given little by little, is impossible to describe fully here and is dazzlingly brilliant. Impossible to put down.

1632. After the first victim was killed, the murderer left the apartment, which the second victim then entered, locking the door behind her. After the door was broken in to gain entry, the killer murdered the second victim before she could reveal her part in the sequence of events.

Wonderfully devious stuff from a master of misdirection.

1633. Someone hid in the hut before the body was placed there, stole a key from the body, unlocked the hut, and removed the body.

1634. The killer, half man, half beast, exited through a window.

1635. The poison had been administered by a red ant enticed by a scent on an envelope delivered to the victim.

One of a number of episodes comprising the first Fu Manchu novel.

1636. The murderer, a dwarf, was hidden in a box apparently too small to contain anyone.

1637. The monkey was used as a stepping stone by the criminal, who also supported himself with two stout sticks until he got to firmer ground.

Nothing if not imaginative.

1638. While the attention of the others was distracted, one of the inmates threw the diamond through a small, square ventilator over the door to a waiting accomplice.

1639. The statue had been removed earlier, and its place taken by the original living model, who was later helped to escape through a skylight.

1640. The poison was administered by a hidden needle in a harp if the instrument was picked up in a certain way.

1641. The victim was shot from outside through the window. This was then closed by an accomplice who exited via a dumb waiter.

1642. The vanisher was in the room when it was broken in and joined the other searchers. He had been impersonating the man whom they had expected to find.

1643. The disappearing player had been wearing a special outfit that was easily ripped off and secreted by the opposing players, who were in on the whole deal. This revealed a second outfit in the opposing team's colours, and thus the disappearing player was able to walk away from the heap unrecognised.

A novel based on a TV script.

1644. A gun was rigged up that fired when the victim answered the phone.

1645. (1) Scratched by a cat with poison on its claws.
(2) A booby trap that fired a gun when a drawer was opened.

1646. The victim was killed earlier by a blow struck with a hammerlike weapon, but with a long sharp spike. In the point of the spike was a cup into which a bullet was fitted, which could be left in the fatal wound. The shot heard later was made by a leaden capsule filled with gunpowder attached to a slow-burning fuse.

1647. The victim had committed suicide with a gun attached by elastic to a stout piece of wood hidden up the room's chimney.

1648. The victim was shot through a grill in the ceiling.

1649. The attack never took place, and was therefore simulated by one of the two occupants to cast suspicion on the other. There was therefore no intruder.

1650. The victim was not, in fact, dead. He had merely overslept.

A spoof play acted out at the Edgar Allan Poe Awards Dinner of 1949 with John Dickson Carr as St. John and Lawrence G. Blochman as Trout.

1651. The bolt on the door was shot from the outside by means of string tied around the knob on the bolt. The string was afterwards pulled clear.

1652. Entrance made through a transom.

The impossible crime is only a subplot in a book, set slightly in the future against the background of a developing European war, that maintains a fast pace throughout without ever losing its literacy or its ability to surprise.

1653. (1) The victim was shot through the keyhole of the door of the room.

(2) The vanisher escaped through a trap door in the ceiling of the room that let him into a buried coffin.

A most enjoyable romp. With voodoo priests, zombies, a series killer eliminating one by one the heirs to a Haitian estate, the whole thing moves at a frantic pace, sets up and eventually explains all manner of weird problems, and, great literature though it isn't, is a book entirely redolent of its period and pedigree, and one I enjoyed immensely.

1654. (1) The drum was being beaten by a foot pedal to which a length of twine was attached, thus enabling the beating to take place by remote control.

(2) The body of the woman was hidden inside the drum.

1655. The platinum was still there, dissolved in a teapot full of solvent.

1656. Special poisoned powder on the coal, activated when lit.

Plenty of action in this very correctly named "thriller" of the most sensational variety. It involves a master criminal called Yellow Face.

1657. The murderer had unscrewed the fingerplate from the outside of the door, bored a small hole in the door through to the inside bolt into which a small hole had also been bored. After the murder had been set up, the murderer left by the door and after unscrewing the fingerplate pulled the bolt into position from outside.

1658. She was in a trance during which he went outside, was knocked insensible by a hansom, and was rushed off to hospital.

1659. The witness/murderer lied when he said that he had not opened the lift gates with his key.

1660. The victim was killed by his passenger, who then borrowed a bicycle from a conveniently passing friend and rode out of the tunnel.

A book that promises far more than it provides.

1661. The victim was shot with a gun with a silencer, then an unsilenced shot was fired with a gun set up with a candle-and-string firing device.

1662. The victim was killed by a stiletto fired from a spring gun and retrieved by means of a strong fish line attached to it.

Typical early-thirties pulp-magazine concoction of strange characters, impersonations, bizarre murders, and characters with names like the detective's, not forgetting Peter Unger, Dr. Spinelli, and the redoubtable Boomalacka Browne.

1663. The killer fed chilled compressed liquid air through the piping instead of water.

1664. The rape was carried out by an incubus that eventually proved to have a female host rather than the anticipated male one.

1665. Not impossible crime.

1666. Poisoned gas was fed into the room through a pipe that led to some candle holders.

1667. Not impossible crime.

1668. The bullets had been extracted from the pistols prior to firing, a fact of which the firer was not aware and did not become aware of due to the firing action peculiar to, and the lack of chambers on, a horse- pistol.

1669. The killer had abnormal eyesight and could see in conditions in which people would not normally be able to see.

1670. It was in fact the cabinet that had been substituted by another—empty —one.

1671. The witness had been hypnotised by music.

1672. The killer locked the door from the outside with a piece of wire.

An episode from an unrecorded collection of short stories in which the antiheroines start as professional cardsharps and cracksmen, take morphine, but finally end up on the right side of the law.

1673. (1) A door thought to be locked was not.

(2) No solution provided. The police verdict was suicide, but the author's strong intimation was that it was murder. She couldn't presumably think of a way to get out of the locked room.

1674. Carbon monoxide was fed into the room via a speaking tube and the victim kept awake—and therefore more vulnerable—by a phantom hand that slid down from an outside wire.

1675. A large metal mass was put into motion when a hidden panel was activated.

1676. The victim was about to close the window as he was shot. He convulsively threw up his arms and thereby closed the window.

1677. The room had been struck by lightning and the metal fused and magnetised; it had thus found its way into the hollow of a large bell.

1678. (1) The canvas was destroyed inside the gallery.

(2) The man seen on the other side of the fence was not the same man who had been seen previously.

(3) The black maria was waylaid on the blind side of a humpback bridge.

1679. A large quantity of liquid nitrogen was poured into the room through a slightly open window. The liquid evaporated into a lethal gas that was in turn dispersed when the room was broken into.

1680. The glass bottom of the coffin was momentarily replaced by a plastic one, which bent to allow the magician's vanishing girl assistant to fall through, and as the gap opened the killer shot the magician from below.

1681. The witness had in fact been looking through the keyhole into a small black box containing the described scene in miniature perspective.

1682. The poison had been introduced into the bottle by means of a hollow corkscrew, and the victim had then, before drinking it, locked himself in.

1683. The thieves leant a ladder up against the garden wall, climbed up it, and fished the peaches off with a net.

1684. The murder had been committed earlier than at first supposed, and the murderer had impersonated the victim's voice. Also, access to the house was found to be possible by removing a pane of glass where the leading was loose.

1685. The blade was released by a jerk on a cord attached to the knife hilt. The jerk was administered by the descent of the lift-

1686. The victim was shot by a bullet fired from an impromptu zip gun—the tube of the apartment door's peephole, from which the lens had been removed.

1687. The jewellery had been stolen earlier and was not in the bag, which was in fact made of cardboard that the thief tore to pieces in the alley and scattered among a lot of other paper and cardboard debris.

1688. The murderer arrived and escaped by balloon.

1689. The escape was made via a secret underground passage.

1690. The resurrected man was the corpse's twin brother.

1691. The killer climbed out of a window and down a ladder.

1692. There was a trick door frame that could be opened like the door itself.

1693. The victim was wounded elsewhere and locked himself in.
1694. The house was an old-fashioned caravan.
1695. The key was replaced after the door was broken in.
1696. The theft was executed by a dwarf who was lowered down on a rope hanging outside the room's window.
1697. The room was in a house littered with secret passages, secret exits and entrances, and it was through one of them that the woman made her escape.
1698. The thief got aboard the luggage van in the false compartment of a coffin. En route he broke open the bullion container and substituted lead for the gold. The gold was carried out in the private luggage— belonging to the thief—that had previously contained the lead.
1699. The cracksman remained in the mint under cover of an arranged conflagration, later rifled the gold, carried it up through the system of flues and chimneys of the mint, and rolled out the gold coin through a canvas chute to a building opposite to which it was also attached
1700. When the lid of the casket was closed, the diamond became attached to and concealed by a large emerald that formed part of the decoration of the casket.
1701. The bullet had been fired at an earlier date from the victim's own gun and thus bore the weapon's rifling marks. It was then fired, fatally, from another's shotgun.
1702. The rapist swung out on a rope and made his way across a frozen, snow-covered pond on skates, leaving no discernible track.

The original Dickens characters romp in this erotic Christmas fare, and *The Pickwick Papers* will probably never be the same.

1703. The victim was poisoned with a hypodermic syringe used by a trained monkey.
1704. (1) The bearded man was also the clean-shaven man, the chin being false and disposed of in a stove.

(2) The body was secreted in a trick wardrobe within the apartment and thus escaped detection.

(3) The sealed door had no effect as the casing was not fixed.

Partly set in New Zealand and at 566 action-packed pages quite a read. Courtroom scenes, cyphers, at least one more possibly impossible disappearance, and extremely detailed explanation of all aspects of the mystery make this a long but quite engrossing novel.

1705. The murder was committed elsewhere, and the body was transported into the room tied by slip knots on to the underneath of the supper trolley. The knots were released, and the body dropped noiselessly on a rug.

An anonymous review in the "Crooks in Books" column of the February 1955 issue of the *London Mystery Magazine* described this book as "gorgeously styled, searingly witty, bafflingly insoluble, the whole book is one long, outrageous tour de force, sent to the reader not only to tax his brains but to try his sense of the artificial." I couldn't agree more but feel that I must point out that in all subsequent issues of the magazine the reviews were signed Anthony Shaffer!

1706. The murderer, an ex-ballet dancer, walked on his points along the white tape that divides the service boxes and threw the body from there.

1707. The assassin had escaped up a large chimney by so arranging matters that staples that blocked the aperture could be pulled aside to afford egress.

1708. The child had been killed, and when the building was searched, her body was hidden inside a bed-davenport.

1709. An accidental shot fired by a neighbour's child.

One of a series of middle-rank police procedurals. The sealed-area element is well set up, but the solution is rather a letdown.

1710. The keys had been turned in the locks from outside.

1711. The victim was using the handle of his own hunting knife to ease a cartridge into the magazine of his rifle when the cartridge exploded and forced the knife back into its owner.

1712. The victim fired a bullet into his own heart region, walked into the guarded house, and then massaged the bullet into its fatal position in the heart.

A brief, brilliant exposition by the master of another form of crime fiction.

1713. The victim was induced to kill himself by means of autosuggestion.

1714. The victim, a young man, was killed by an infernal machine rigged to explode when his rescuing father unlocked the door of the room in which he had been imprisoned.

An unusual and ingenious use of the locked-room theme.

1715. The assailant had entered and left by a false door in the back of a clothes cupboard.

1716. The door latched itself as it closed after the victim fell.

I usually finish a book that I start, but this one was an exception. Bad with few bright spots.

1717. The gun was fired inside the room by means of a fishing line and brass ring operated from outside it.

1718. An electromagnetically controlled weight that fell on the victim when she switched off the light.

Clever and quite convincing.

1719. The murderer swung himself down from above.

A mountaineering story, the solution of which should appeal to the climbing fraternity.

1720. The killer had left via a secret passage.

The trick in the story, and the violation of one of Monsignor Knox's commandments, is that there are two secret passages, and the first discovered doesn't lead to the murder room.

1721. The victim had been pushed from the car by a man who had then parachuted out.

1722. (1) The victim was never in the lavatory.

(2) An arrangement with a mirror made of papier-màché with a silver plastic film.

Avery good novel. Probably the best offering of 1974 and much better than the short story—see Item 1724—that won the author a competition.

1723. (1) The victim was stifled with an inflatable balloon cushion pushed and held through a lavatory window too small to admit even the smallest person. After insertion through the window it was inflated to suffocate the victim, and later withdrawn after deflation

(2) The victim was outside the house with all the suspects inside. She put her head through a tiny door and the murderer struck with a blunt instrument, and later moved the body to a different location to make it appear that, based on the established time of death, none of the supects could have committed the crime.

(3) The third murder is less clearly constructed, but notably depends on the victim being, unknown to everyone at the scene,

blind.

1724. The detective was set to watch the wrong locked door into which the false victim entered. The door belonged to the apartment on the floor below that in which the murder occurred.

Winner of the 1972 Cape/The Times detective-short-story competition. Success well merited.

1725. A science-fiction spoof in which the author irreverently examines the various forms through the medium of a quick review of Worth's old cases.

1726. The gun was rigged up to fire when a piece of taut wire that held the trigger was snapped. The snapping was effected by a high musical note sung outside the room.

1727. The key on the inside of the door was turned on the outside by a pair of pliers.

1728. The victim wedged the weapon in the back of a chair and then walked backwards into it.

1729. He had been struck by a meteorite.

1730. A secret passage leading from the chimney to the roof.

1731. The poison was shot into the sleeping victim's open mouth by a toy water pistol through the bars of the window.

1732. The killer had the ability to swallow and regurgitate the knife with which he did the killing.

1733. The gifts were hidden in the room before the little boy locked it. One of them was a giant teddy bear that contained a midget who took out all the presents and was later substituted by a normal teddy bear.

Charming short-short yarn in a book of puzzles combining mystery stories and crossword puzzles.

1734. The killers had a duplicate key.

Almost a nonstarter as a locked-room murder, but otherwise an entertaining and well-constructed novel with just an occasional unconvincing piece of dialogue.

1735. (1) A duplicate key was used and the bolt thrown by the murderer's accomplice.

(2) The victim was killed outside the locked room, thus providing an alibi for the killer. The victim was then replaced in the locked room.

Very much the locked-room fan's locked-room novel, and written by one of the foremost locked-room students of all time.

A much neglected book with two complex but ingenious impossible murders and a host of locked-room lore, mainly in Chapter 5. An essential item for any locked-room collection.

1736. The murderer was one of the sentries.

1737. When Phillimore stepped back into his house, he was cudgelled to death, carted away via the back door, and buried in concrete. Sherlock Holmes is present but fails to solve.

1738. The vanisher had made himself invisible—a trick he learnt in the East —and stepped out as soon as the door was unlocked.

1739. The victim has been accidentally snagged by the grapnel of a passing air balloon and thus been lifted up. Subsequently the material on his coat tore and let him fall.

1740. The killer exited via a dumbwaiter into a room hidden behind a row of mirrors. He eventually made good his escape from the roof by means of ropes and harness down the outside of the building.

1741. A bomb had been placed within the victim's body during surgery and was exploded by remote control.

1742. A booby trap had been set so that a gun hidden in a scarecrow's arm fired when a nearby spade was pulled from the earth.

1743. The cubes were made of ginger ale and when they melted became the ginger ale in the glass.

Revamped two years later for Dr. Haledjian to solve—see Item 1744.

1744. The cubes were made of frozen ginger ale. When they melted, the ginger ale was found.

1745. During initiation ceremonies a secret implantation was made under the tribal mark on the forehead. When tapped, it released a deadly poison.

1746. The key was turned from outside by means of a "squeeze," a type of steel tube used by professional cracksmen.

1747. The victim was poisoned and shot herself to avoid unnecessary pain.

1748. They were taken away in a yacht so moored near the house that they did not realise that they were aboard.

1749. The murderer had rented the neighbouring apartment and had a secret corridor constructed between it and his own, the entrance being behind a mirror.

1750. One woman had been killed and her body strapped under the bed between the mattress and the loose sacking. The other woman was the murderer whose own gloved hand it was that had appeared to pull her back into the room. She then locked herself in a wardrobe and turned the key from inside with a set of long-nosed pliers.

1751. The victim had been killed before the guard was set, but was thought to be alive and elsewhere at the time because of the substitution of a wax dummy that was seen in another room.

1752. A special second tank had been temporarily installed that was gauged to feed in a small supply of poison when the tap was used in the normal way.

A strange book of fiendish plots, secret societies, séances, and a host of other typically thirties devices. Moves along at a pace, however, and Sprigg certainly knew how to write.

1753. The victim was killed by poison injected by a watch he was wearing.

1754. The thief cut into the compartment from the one next to it.

1755. There was a slight hiatus between the taxi arriving and the door being opened. It was then that the crime was committed.

How could such a perceptive and literate critic write such bad books?

1756. The victim was wounded outside but died after he had entered the room and locked the door.

1757. The house contained a hidden staircase that led to a maze of cellars used by a gang of counterfeiters.

1758. The killer bored a hole through the wall that joined the victim's flat to the next one and discharged into it a puff of poison gas from a pistol.

1759. Not impossible crime.

1760. They had shot one another, and the wounded man had flung his gun from the room.

1761. The murderer killed the victim, exited from the lift, and then from two floors above pressed the button to summon the lift.

1762. The arsenic was a compound that the murderer had been mixing in with wood scraps that he'd given the victim to burn on her open fire.

1763. One key was left inside the room while the door was locked from outside with a duplicate.

1764. The murderer was perched on the top of the ceiling fan and made his escape after the room had been broken in.

1765. The killer had entered and exited from the floor above by means of a rope ladder.

An earlier false solution was provided: The bolt had been drawn into place from the outside by means of a pin and piece of string and reference made to an earlier (presumably unrecorded) case of Bigelow's.

1766. Two of the witnesses had lied about the situation in the room when they had left. In other words, the victim had died earlier than originally believed.

The second (of two) mysteries set in the Rome of Cesar Borgia, well written with only a couple of lapses into the modern vernacular. The book does not, however, live up to the locked-room-murder blurb given it by the publisher.

1767. Entry was gained after the victim was drugged and a cat induced by catnip to dislodge the bolt. After the deed the murderer stayed in the stable in a dark corner and joined the others after they had broken in.

1768. The shot was fired in through an open window, and the victim, who was seated in a swivel chair, ended up in a position that made a shot from the window seem impossible. In any event, the window was pushed to from outside and locked automatically.

1769. Not impossible crime.

1770. The gas was produced by a car engine and fed through a rubber pipe that led to a hole in the iron window frame of the room.

1771. At the end of the book there are several false solutions, including the logical one of suicide. Apparently, however, the murder was done by one of the locked-in occupants and we are not informed as to how he got out of and back into his own locked room.

Nicely written but an unconvincing solution. In a later book, *The Meriwether Mystery* (Doubleday, 1932), the author stated in respect of *Footprints* that she had received thirty-two letters "that had inquired how the character she named as guilty could have fired the shot from behind a locked bedroom door far down the hall." She still didn't give an explanation.

1772. Her mother had died overnight of bubonic plague, and the conspiracy of silence was contrived to ensure that no word of the plague got out.

1773. The door was opened and locked with a locksmith's key.

1774. While looking over the edge, she had been struck hard by a stone thrown by the murderer, an ardent cricketer.

1775. The victim was shot through a hole in the ceiling.

1776. The poison was administered by the doctor who had already pronounced the victim dead after the room was broken into.

See also Item 1855 for another version of the same.

1777. The victim opened the window when it was hit from outside by a piece of coal on a string. When he leant out and looked up, he was shot from the floor above with a silenced pistol. A firecracker was later set off that was taken to be the fatal shot.

1778. The murderer used an exit while the person watching was distracted by the murderer's accomplice.

1779. The key was replaced after the room had been broken into.

1780. The killer removed a pane of glass, made his entrance, and replaced the pane after killing.

1781. The child was lifted up bodily by an adult and carried out of the ring.

1782. The document was taped to the back of the unsuspecting man who carried out the search of the room.

1783. An oxygen cylinder had been replaced by a nitrogen cylinder.

1784. The killer left an unvarnished track open from the corner of the room to the door, strangled his victim in the corner, then walked backwards along the track out of the room, pulling behind him a squeegee mop covered with varnish that painted in the gap more quickly than any brush could have done.

1785. The killer exited via a secret passage.

1786. The key was thrown down by the murderer after the door had been broken down.

1787. Not impossible crime.

1788. The victim was killed by a gun that had been made from a compressed- air cylinder and fitted with a timing device.

1789. The medium held lead in one hand when he placed it on his neighbour's. He was thus able to withdraw that hand and yet by the weight of the lead convince his neighbour that the hand was still there.

1790. A pencil through the end of the key and a string from the pencil going under the door.

1791. The shot had been fired through a knot hole, after which the knot had been replaced and secured with glue.

1792. The killer was the Punch and Judy man and changed his incriminating clothes in the privacy of his closed Punch and Judy stand.

1793. The pearls had been swallowed by one of the guests, a former professional sword swallower.

1794. Shot with a poison dart through a ventilator grill.

A one-page spoof composed by the author to point ridicule at one of his pet hates, the locked-room murder. The other victim of the article is the American hard-boiled story. Symons states *inter alia* that locked rooms should be banned and that what he really wants is realism. Naturally, I must emphatically disagree, but bearing in mind that two of Symons's own short stories qualify for this bibliography, I wonder whether he can yet be converted.

1795. The victim locked the door after the murderer had exited.

1796. (1) Substitution of bodies.

(2) A key was hung loosely in the lock on the inside while a second key was used to lock the door from the outside. The inside bolt was already loosened on the inside.

The only author to successfully emulate Carr. He is in fact a very satisfactory mixture of Carr and Rawson, combining Carr's flair for atmosphere and the bizarre with Rawson's magical tricks. Probably the best new writer of the forties.

1797. (1) A thread was tied to a mirror and pulled from outside to create the illusion that a window was being broken by the escaping murderer.

(2) The track maker used a pole to vault away from one end of the track. He then "discovered" the track and obliterated his own marks leading to it.

No precis of mine can do justice to the complicated and brilliant plots woven into the book.

1798. The murder had been committed earlier and the body left deliberately balanced so that it could be pulled down by an attached thread.

1799. The shot was fired from the adjoining room through a hole made when light fixtures were briefly and temporarily removed.

1800. The cartoon had been secreted in a rolled-up roller blind.

1801. The vanisher assumed a disguise and became the plane's copilot.

1802. The words from the sparrow in fact emanated from a nearby grating above a sewer in which the victim's son was trapped.

1803. As the victim was being winched through the false bottom of the cabinet and her chest was level with the floor of the stage, she was stabbed through a ventilator hole in the cabinet by a hat pin fitted to the killer's shoe. The book contains a detailed diagram of the operation.

1804. The deadly gas had been blown up a speaking tube that ended in the bedroom.

1805. The victim was killed by means of a poisonous gas injected within a telephone receiver and released, fatally, when the victim lifted the receiver from the hook.

Bits of deduction in this book tend to remain with you. For instance:

"Tiepin of a certain secret society," added Wryte. "Top joint of little finger on left hand missing. He had peculiar eyes—one grey and one nearly green. His right shoe was much more creased than the other."

"What's that mean?"

"He has an artificial leg," replied Wryte.

Sherlock Holmes, eat your heart out!

1806. The key was returned into the room through a broken window pane.

1807. A bat flew in and dislodged the dagger from its position on the wall. It fell and transfixed the victim.

1808. The murderer broke in by waiting for a locked door to come open when two heavy freights passed each other nearby and consequently the house shook and the locked door came open. He subsequently got out by bolting one exit from the inside and going out by using the catch on the other door.

Distinctly borderline but has been referred to as a locked-room mystery.

1809. The victim was killed by a knife thrown from a dressing-room door.

Disappointing and unconvincing,

1810. The victim's injuries were caused by a taut wire stretched between two trees.

1811. The victim was knocked unconscious and his place in the lift taken by another person who pretended to have been stabbed. The real body was substituted and stabbed after an independent witness had helped to find the fake body in the lift and then been despatched to fetch help.

1812. The victim was killed earlier and carried to the taxi while the driver was loading the luggage. The victim was then impersonated by the killer, who stepped out of the other side of the taxi while the driver was once again distracted.

1813. The victim had been shot from the cellar beneath through a hole in the pipe leading from the wash bowl.

1814. The victim was shot from outside thorough the crack in the open door.

1815. The woman had contracted bubonic plague, and the denial of her existence was part of a plot to stop the knowledge getting out.

1816. The Scarecrow removed his outer apparel—i.e., his disguise—stitched the jacket to the breeches and the cloak, mask, and hat, and forced the whole item through the bars, emitting a terrible shriek as he did so. He then tied himself up and was discovered so when the door was opened.

1817. The occupant had contracted the plague and been removed to a hospital where he could be nursed. The hotel had closed the room, covered the doorway during the night, and pretended that the room did not exist.

Novel of a really excellent film with delightful music and lovely performances from Jean Simmons and Dirk Bogarde.

1818. The train was one specially built by a wily oriental to ferry gold that he'd secretly excavated.

A detective adventure of the most rollicking and unusual variety. The same writer roved in other works into the realms of the fantastic. An author's note at the front of the book makes the point that the draft of the novel was completed in 1921, five years before the famous play "The Ghost Train"—see Item 31—was produced in London.

1819. On the previous occasion that the padlock had been removed, another had been substituted before it was put back and closed. The thief had the key to the substitute padlock and used it to open the shed. He had also secreted the original padlock, still in the open position, which he finally put back into position and closed.

Neat and logical.

1820. The vanisher donned a disguise that he was carrying in a toolbox and assumed an identity already established for him as one of the work force.

1821. The killer locked the door after exiting and then threw the key back into the room through a fanlight.

1822. The murderer exited as a window cleaner who went unremarked by the witness, and the chair was left against the door by means of a lace that was pulled through the keyhole and then removed.

1823. The murderer, a mountaineering expert, climbed in and out of the room from the next storey.

1824. The killer, a midget, was hiding in a filing cabinet.

1825. The witnesses were drugged and in that state were convinced that they had not seen the killing done or the exit made.

1826. The victim was shot in the eye from outside the room as he peered through a secret spyhole in the door, the cover of which fell back into place after he was shot.

1827. The murderer had escaped into a hidden turret room, where he died.

Rather weak ending.

1828. The only key had been returned to the dead man's top pocket via a double line of thread running from his button hole via an open fanlight to a point just outside the library.

1829. While one of the visitors created a diversion, the diamond was hidden in an overhead chandelier.

1830. A nut had been removed from the back of the door leaving a hole big enough through which to pass a wire and push home the bolt.

1831. The dust was laid on the floor by bringing it down from the ceiling by using a heavy roller on the floor above. The person who put the body down made the tracks deliberately to hide the fact that the dust did not fall beneath an overhead chandelier. He reached the position under the chandelier with the body and afterwards exited again by means of a rope attached to the chandelier itself.

1832. The victim in the coffin was not dead and extricated himself from the room by means of the chain of a crane used in the building of an adjacent house.

1833. A wall cupboard in the room had a secret exit built into its back.

1834. A heart attack was deliberately caused by a figure who stood outside the locked French windows in a hideous green mask.

1835. All the crew except one were engaged in a swimming match around the boat when the last man also fell in. Since none of them had any means of getting back into the boat, they all drowned.

1836. A technician had made a minor adjustment that caused the pilot to be thrown against the two flushing levers that jointly operated the air- pressure system.

1837. Hydrocyanic acid smeared on the boxer's gum shields.

Nice, leisurely paced golden-age novel, with an interesting detective.

1838. A second key was used to open the Yale-type lock.

1839. The pilot had switched off the engine, bailed out, and the plane landed itself.

1840. Small metal darts had been fired into the victim at an earlier time and had gradually worked their way to the heart, causing death while the victim happened to be in the locked room.

1841. The murderer had hidden a poisoned needle inside the mouth of a blue porcelain god. The victim felt inside the mouth and was thereby poisoned.

Joe Quinney featured in a series of short-story collections, describing his adventures in the antique field. Despite the fact that many of the stories were criminous, Ellery Queen lists none of them in *The Detective Short Story*.

1842. The victim lodged a hair-triggered pistol in the partly open window and hit the trigger with a shot from his own pistol. The resultant return shot killed him at the same time as the gun fell out of the window and the window closed.

1843. The killer escaped by getting into the elevator and climbing down the cables. Virtually impossible.

1844. The door was bolted from outside by means of string attached to tweezers fixed over the bolt-handle. After pulling the string to operate the bolt, a quick jerk released the tweezers from the bolt-handle. There is an excellent diagram to illustrate the point.

1845. The murderer was under the water in a diving suit and with grapnel. With this he grabbed the victim as he dived and kept him under water until he drowned. Later he exited with the body and walked across a plank laid down especially to avoid leaving incriminating footprints.

1846. The door was closed from outside by means of string passed through the keyhole around pins and around the head of the bolt. An excellent diagram in the book explains the method in full detail.

1847. There was a secret exit behind some panelling.

1848. (1) The key was put back in the lock by the first person to enter after the room was broken into.
(2) The victim was half strangled through a barred window and then succumbed to a heart attack.

1849. The poison was contained in wax pills inserted in the ceiling directly above the place where water was boiled for tea making. The steam melted the wax and the poison fell into the boiling water with which the fatal drink was made.

1850. The fatal knife was projected from a booby-trapped hollow writing brush that operated when the brush was being heated.

1851. The candle was made of a substance that, when burnt off, gave off a poisonous gas.
Not, in fact, a locked-room problem, but it could so easily have been.

1852. The victim was shot through a hole in the ceiling normally covered by a moveable plaster rose from which the flex sprang supporting a light above the victim's desk.
Another version of Item 1775.

1853. The shot was fired from above through a hole in the ceiling that had been hidden by the central rose from which the lighting flex hung.

1854. The victim was killed earlier by a gun with a silencer. The later explosion, while the room was under guard, was made by a fireworks-type device.

1855. The victim was alive when the door was unlocked, was pronounced dead by the doctor, who then administered the poison.

1856. The killer, a former circus artist, had exited without leaving tracks by a tightrope-walking act across a rope and wire fence.

1857. The victim was killed by a weight on the end of a wire that swung in and out again, pendulum-wise, through an open window back to the nearby tree to which it was attached.

1858. For details see "The Clue of the Crimson Snow" as by Donald

Stuart (Item 1777).

1859. The first man lay in wait for the second, killed him, and secreted his body in a hidden passage. He was in turn then attacked by a third man. The haunted tower didn't really feature.

As bad as they come.

1860. The key was turned from the outside by the use of a pair of pliers.

1861. He was incinerated in an underground furnace.

1862. The killer exited through a rear window and was seen by his brother, who did not give him away.

A very poor specimen.

1863. The killer had climbed a tree, gone out on a bough, and lowered himself down onto the ground at a different point.

1864. The room's door had in it a sliding panel that, when operated, allowed the key inside to be turned from the outside.

1865. Not impossible crime.

1866. The murderer had exited via a window that he had pushed shut. He had intended to latch it from the inside after the body was discovered but was prevented from doing so by a witness.

1867. The key was switched by the killer, who was the first to reach the body.

1868. The victim had been shot earlier, but an explosion was caused in the room some time later by combining fulminate of mercury with nitric acid.

1869. There are a couple of dummy solutions, but it seems that the killer used a spring-lock door in order to escape.

1870. After locking the door on the outside the key was returned to the room via thread that ran through the keyhole to a pin attached lightly to a centrally positioned table. The pin and thread were afterwards removed by pulling.

1871. By means of ductile candles the killer arranged that the door latch would fall and the telephone come from its hook after he left the room.

1872. Bubbles containing the poison gas were blown through a grating and released the gas on bursting.

1873. Booby-trapped electrified telephone.

1874. He had in fact simply collapsed and was stabbed by the person into whose arms he fell.

1875. A booby-trapped telephone.

1876. (1) A trick panel in the door that opened at the touch of a spring.

(2) A secret passageway.

1877. He was poisoned by an ice dart fired through a cigarette holder.

1878. The victim collapsed from a heart attack and was stabbed by the first person to reach him.

1879. The notes were carried away attached to the leg of a carrier pigeon.

1880. The victim was killed by cyanide introduced into his toothpaste.

1881. The three men were confidence tricksters who used this ploy to come to the attention of a great student of bizarre phenomena and thus gain admission to and rob his house.

1882. Not impossible crime.

1883. The fingerprint belonged to the expert's daughter, member of a gang of thieves. Her father had deliberately confused it with his dead son's to ensure that she was freed from arrest.

1884. While an accomplice created a diversion, master criminal Four Square Jane cut the picture from its frame and hid it in a rolled-up window blind.

1885. (1) The gun was hidden behind a baseboard.

(2) The victim was stabbed with a hypodermic needle while attention was distracted by some shooting.

1886. The victims were killed by a shaped, pronged extending rod pushed through the keyhole or a false knot hole.

1887. The murder weapon was fired in the room and then hidden in a little desk.

1888. She had been murdered and dismembered by her husband, and placed bit by bit in a self-clean oven that had then been switched to its maximum temperature of nearly 900 degrees. The slight residue finally left in the oven had been cleaned up with a vacuum cleaner that had then been reversed, blowing its contents out through the window.

1889. The voice heard inside the room was a recording.

1890. A small glass bomb containing poison gas was shot through the open window, broke, and released its contents.

My copy is a reprint that refers to the first edition as 1926. The British Library gives 1927 as the date of publication.

1891. The key on the inside of the lock was turned from outside by pliers.

1892. A gas light inside the room was extinguished by turning a meter tap outside the room. The tap was then turned again to let gas into the room.

1893. The victim was killed by a venomous spider that was whirled in through the open carriage window on a black silk line, then out again.

1894. The body was not dead and had staged the whole business, including the spider by magic lantern. He left the top floor lab by means of a plank that took him to a nearby building.

1895. The thief disguised himself by shucking off his rather conspicuous street clothes, to reveal a bandaged mummylike appearance that he completed and then slipped into an empty mummy case. Eventually after decoying the police he stole the vase, chloroformed a policeman, and later exited while dressed in his clothes.

Full of ingenious moves, this may well be the famous author's first published story and perhaps the first to feature a thief who steals to demonstrate bad security and then returns the stolen item for a fee.

1896. The killer descended into the room via the panelled ceiling above.

Absolutely awful. The author failed to divulge until well into the story that there were occupied rooms above that of the deceased!

1897. The diamonds were hidden in a hollowed-out doorstop that one of the police detectives had kicked out into the hallway as soon as they entered.

1898. The man had cut the boy's throat, then his own, and projected the knife by means of elastic through a window pane, which it slightly broke, to be embedded in a tree outside.

1899. The victim was poisoned by phosgene gas introduced into the bed chamber by means of an electric mechanism.

1900. A device that exploded on contact with a note of a piano.

Average fare, although a fairly early example.

1901. The victim was killed by smothering fumes produced by a devilish pipe that he had been given to smoke.

1902. The key was returned to the lock after the door had been broken in.

1903. The killer had stabbed the victim through the window with a knife attached to a bamboo pole. The knife had stayed stuck in the victim while the pole was removed and broken up.

1904. The closet contained a hidden sliding panel.
1905. A secret exit behind a sliding panel.
1906. (1) The victim was struck by a heavy bar, rigged to operate when anyone tried to start the auxiliary motor.
(2) The murderer got in by descending on a chandelier that could be operated like a dumb waiter.
1907. The poison was introduced into a whisky bottle before the observation started, and switched for one containing uncontaminated whisky after the body was discovered.
1908. The murderer inserted into the heart of the victim a tiny glass bulb containing a poisonous gas that insidiously killed the surrounding tissues until death occurred suddenly, one or two days later.
1909. The killer had a key that unlocked the door, and he sprung open the chain by a sharp jerk from outside.
1910. A secret passage beneath the floor.
1911. The door had on it a spring bolt that could be opened by the murderer to permit exit and would then automatically lock.
1912. There was a secret entrance into the room through a chimney.
Apart from the disappointing solution, this novel also contains that most forbidden of fruits—twins.
1913. The victim tripped, fell, and struck her head on a fender.
1914. The victim licked a postage stamp coated with poison.
1915. The victim was killed by means of a poisoned toothpick, for which a harmless one was substituted when the door was broken in.
1916. The man who had entered had been in disguise. He later vanished by taking off that disguise.
1917. Entrance was gained by means of a secret panel in the wall.
1918. The poison had been smeared inside the spigot of a soda siphon that the victim used in the privacy of his own room.
Typical Carolyn Wells fare: four murders—two of them rather nasty —a quite unbelievable murderer, and a house party attended, as usual, by that most ominous of guests, Fleming Stone.
1919. A hidden extra door frame with concealed hinges and lock.
1920. One man exited by one door as the witness entered by another, while the second exited by means of a secret elevator.
1921. Through a hole in the gas tap a thread was run that passed out

of the room through a hole in the wall. The tap was thus turned from outside the room.

1922. The deceased stabbed himself with an icicle that afterwards melted.

1923. The rooms had been entered by a human fly who scaled an outside, apparently unclimbable, wall.

1924. (1) One of the victims consumed poisoned tea while the second was scratched, by a sharp pointed instrument dipped in poison, by the killer, who was pretending to comfort her.
(2) Either a duplicate key or by turning the key from the outside by means of narrow pliers.

1925. The victim was poisoned by a drink she had intended for someone else. She herself locked the room after the switch had been made.

1926. The door was locked from outside with a duplicate key. The bolts were drawn across by means of a thread that ran from outside under the door.

1927. The drugged victim was stabbed by the first person to enter the room after the door had been broken down.

1928. The key was replaced after a door panel had been broken in from outside.

1929. She was abducted via a secret subterranean passage.

1930. The killer got into the house by means of a shaft that ran between the chimney and the external wall.

1931. The killer got into the room through a trap door that let into a large grilled cabinet in the room. He fired the arrow through the grill and hoped to pin the blame on a weird wooden Indian.

1932. He had assumed a disguise as a female.

1933. The killer was still in the room when the door was broken in. She was hidden above a false ceiling.
A complete story in itself, within a short novel. Two other stories, "The Footprints in the Snow" and "The Chainlock Mystery," have minor impossible-crime connotations.

1934. An accomplice flew a kite with a knotted rope attached to it up to the window. This was tied with a slip knot to the inside of the cell, the escapee slid down the rope to freedom, and then disengaged the rope.

1935. The poison gas was pumped into the room through the wash basin, and later sucked back again with a reverse-action pump.

The third Wheatley "Crime Dossier."

1936. The poison gas was introduced into the laboratory through a small hole under a wall sink.

1937. The victim was chloroformed (in his drink), was put into a diving suit and helmet, compressed air pumped in, and later the suit was removed.

1938. The victims' throats were torn by sharp steel barbs attached to a rod and line operated from a distance by a fisherman of uncanny ability.

1939. The key was slipped under the door after it had been locked on the outside.

1940. The vanisher had assumed a second identity and taken up a second prearranged cabin.

Thought at first to be a lost Conan Doyle Holmes story, it had in fact been given to Doyle by the true author.

1941. The attention of the main witness was diverted momentarily while the vanishing girl slipped into a waiting car, and her place was taken by a second girl in disguise.

1942. The victim had been rendered unconscious and was then imprisoned in the heavy bandaging of an invalid.

1943. The victim became entangled in a rope from which he was trying to steal a rare orchid, and increased humidity caused by a steam jet caused the rope to contract and strangle him.

1944. The stabbing was achieved by a knife thrown from outside by a highly skilled Zingari.

1945. On board the ship was a chest that contained a secret nuclear-type power source. When the chest was opened it caused those on board to suffer burning from which the only escape was to jump overboard.

1946. The victim was made to appear alive later than supposed, via a trick with a gramophone. The arm of the gramophone was propped up on a tripod made of ice resting on the record. From the catch on the gramophone ran a piece of string, the end of which protruded very slightly through the door's keyhole. One of the witnesses then pulled this string, released the catch, and as the tripod was propelled from the moving record, the arm fell and the record started to play. The string was then pulled through the keyhole by the witness, who by the presence of the other witness, had established an unimpeachable alibi.

A superb combination of thriller and detective novel, with perhaps the cleverest, most cold-blooded villain ever created.

1947. The murder was committed by someone dressed as and mistaken for a railway guard.

1948. As the train was moving, the thieves arranged matters so that the other wagons around the one containing the picture were joined by one rope while the wagon was joined to the next one by another rope but was otherwise entirely separate. Then they cut free the wagon with the picture, switched it to another line, and used the other rope to join the remaining wagons together again.

As the detective remarks, "The cleverest thing I've heard of," but very difficult for me to explain succinctly.

1949. Not impossible crime.

1950. Not impossible crime.

1951. The men had vanished through a section of wall that was carried on an iron framework and that opened inwards to those who knew the secret.

1952. The coach had been deliberately and carefully derailed and run off into a river.

1953. His opponents' cards were being signalled to him by a confederate by means of movements of his cigarette.

1954. The first stroke of the division bell released an electrical contact that pulled the trigger on a gun hidden in the room's grating.

1955. The victim was killed by a shot from a long-range anti-aircraft gun, electronically controlled. Ugh!

1956. The killer exited via a window and a trellis.

1957. The killer had exited via a window that he had then closed behind him.

1958. The victims were abducted through a trap door in the floor of the caravan.

1959. The victim's death was caused by the introduction into his bloodstream of a concentrated culture of bacteria through the medium of a needle rigged in his pipe.

1960. The door was locked from outside with a master key that did not disturb the ordinary door key in position in the lock on the inside.

1961. The keys had been abstracted and returned via the ventilator.

1962. The vanisher had fixed onto his shoes a pair of reversible wooden hooves.

One of a series of books about the boy detectives whose adventures were first heard—with great pleasure in my case—on the radio.

1963. The killer had a duplicate key that had not been known to exist.

1964. The girl was under the influence of a drug that made her appear dead. She got away from the balcony via a ledge that ran to another balcony.

1965. The victim stepped into the porch at the front of the mill, which then became perfectly sealed and all the air was drawn out.

1966. The switch was reactivated by means of a thin nylon fishing line attached to it.

1967. A variety of solutions, including luminous cloth and sleight of hand.

Sheer golden-age delight with impossible situations galore, outrageous characters, a marvelous detective, Dr. Klotz, excellent solutions, and a fine denouement. A singleton when one would so much have liked a series.

1968. The criminal responsible for the disappearances tied to each person a belt made of antigravitational matter and thus shot them off into space.

1969. Three fake deaths; two of those "killed" were the murderers.

The poor man's *Ten Little Niggers*, it fails throughout to grip and has a feeble ending.

1970. The victim was knocked on the head and his body weighted and dropped down the well. The impossible-crime element is elusory.

1971. The victim was scratched by a cat whose claws had been smeared with snake poison.

1972. Same story as Item 1971.

1973. The time machine had a trap door that dropped its time travellers into a very deep mine shaft.

Ingenious and highly unusual story, on its own worth the price of the anthology in which it is most readily available.

1974. The victim opened the door to speak to the killer, who screamed out at the same time as she shot him. She then closed the door with her foot and continued screaming as she took steps to hide the weapon.

1975. A real letdown. After setting up a locked-room murder complete with wounds caused by devil's claws and even a devil's footprint on a snow-covered sill, we discover that a witness was mistaken about the door being locked, and that the real solution was that the murderer simply closed the spring-locked door from the outside after the murder was committed.

1976. The sandwich had been bought earlier, poison introduced, and then put back into the system by the first purchaser in time for the victim to take it.

Excellent, grisly piece typical of Woolrich at his best.

1977. The bed in which the victims were sleeping was dragged over to an open window by means of a skilfully operated rod and line operated by the killer in an adjacent bedroom. He then shone a very bright light into the victims' eyes, and they, not realizing the position, stepped out into oblivion.

1978. The victim had literally been tickled to death.

1979. The chain was snapped open by means of an elastic band and a thumb tack, and replaced after entry had been made.

1980. The knife was thrown in through a small window and clasped by the victim.

1981. The victims were killed with poisoned glass bullets that were shot into their open mouths when they spoke or yawned.

1982. The killer impersonated the victim's voice after he had died, and hid behind furniture when the room was entered until he could make his escape.

1983. The victim had been wounded earlier elsewhere and was swept onto the dunes by water from a mill pond. When he finally fell, the dagger already in his back was forced home fatally.

1984. The victims were stabbed through the gap between door and jamb as the door was forced open.

1985. The victim was fatally wounded in a struggle, helped his assailant to escape, then locked the window after him.

1986. The victim had been killed earlier and his place on horseback taken by the killer. The killer had then, when in view of the spectators, ridden to where the body lay concealed, slipped out of the saddle, hung on to the side of the horse, and removed the covering from the body as they rode past. To the spectators it looked as though it was the victim who had fallen from the saddle to the ground.

1987. The golfer's original collapse was caused by a blow from a ball.

The stabbing was carried out by someone who was pretending to revive him.

1988. The murderer had stabbed the victim through a curtain and later escaped into his private suite, locking the door behind her. Her black raiment prevented her from being observed in the murder room.

1989. The victim had been stabbed by a swimmer who came and went by water.

1990. The victim had received his wound earlier and fell against the gate, which was later opened by an accidental blow from a horse's hoof.

1991. The victim was murdered earlier and his body later carried down to the shelter by the killer, wearing the victim's galoshes. The killer then hid on top of the shelter and later exited by the footboards laid down after the victim had been discovered.

1992. The killer had fixed a dummy stage knife to the victim's back and also poisoned him. When he collapsed, he rushed to the victim and stabbed him with the real knife.

1993. The victim had accidentally activated the mechanism that opened a section of wall that revealed a hidden tunnel. The barrier swung around on a pivot, struck and killed him, and his whip was carried round by the revolving wall into the tunnel.

1994. The victim was killed before the boat was pushed out to sea by the murderer.

1995. The victim was killed by a mechanical device built into an Italian chair.

1996. (1) The killer shot from the pulpit, then after the killing climbed to the belfry and went out onto the roof.

(2) The killer locked the belfry door from the outside, cut a length of rope from the flagstaff, hung it from a fastening, and thereby slipped to the ground and made his escape.

1997. As the pilot was taxiing to take off, a second person had jumped aboard and shot and stabbed him. The killer had then taken the aircraft up and parachuted out prior to its descent and crash.

1998. The victims were leaning out of the window when an ice block was dropped from above. It splintered and a shard of ice caused a fatal wound, although the victim was able to close the window. In the second case, a second block scored a direct hit on the head of the victim.

1999. There was a secret passage.

2000. The body originally seen was a live one. The dead body found next day in the car was freshly killed.

2001. The victim was killed by the first person to examine him after the room was broken into.

2002. There was in fact a passenger who stabbed the driver, then swung himself onto the tollgate as the car careered on and crashed, jamming all doors.

2003. The noise was recorded and the recording operated when a switch, set in a floorboard, was stepped upon.

2004. The victim was stabbed by a spring knife operated at the touch of a button on a golden statue.

2005. The younger man had played both roles and had injured himself to allay suspicion.

2006. The document had been tied to a balloon that floated up and out of the alley.

In a subsequent issue of EQMM, Ellery Queen apologised for the fact that both he and the author had been unaware that the balloon, filled with human breath, would not have risen. It would have had to have been filled with a gas lighter than air.

2007. The victim had fainted and was stabbed by the first person to enter the lift.

2008. The killer, a small boy, was still in the room when the door was broken down. The boy was hidden in the unmade bed.

2009. The emperor was not poisoned by the mushrooms but by the feather stuck down his throat to make him sick when he had been convinced that he had been poisoned.

2010. The poison pill was in the drink in a cube of ice with a soap stopper, which released the poison when it melted.

2011. The victim was killed by the first person to enter the room.

There are several innovations in this novel. There are discussions by the characters about various means by which a locked-room crime could be carried out—a harbinger of Dr. Fell's famous dissertation. The "Bow" of the title refers to a district in London.

2012. Deception—the victim had never been on board the vessel.

An extremely unusual item and the author's only detective novel. The impossible problem is quite unique, and the solution no worse than one would expect. Warlock-Jones in no way resembles the illustrious detective whose name his own resembles. Also see Item 1219.

2013. The victim was electrocuted when he reached for a water basin attached to which was a wire running down and through the wall to the room next door where it was connected to a group of charged leyden jars.

2014. See Item 350.

2015. Not impossible crime.

2016. Not impossible crime.

2017. The victim had picked up and spoken into a phone, thereby shattering a small, hollow glass bead concealed in it, so releasing a deadly poison.

2018. 1. The killer had the ability to manoeuvre himself into very small spaces and was able to move within the ventilation ducts of the prison. He then pushed a rod with a razor attached through the ventilator grills and cut the victims' throats.

I have not yet had the opportunity to read this book but am reliably informed that it is first rate and a welcome addition to the genre. Soon to be filmed with Dustin Hoffman.

2019. There was a secret override hand control that was used to gain entry.

Anthologies

YOU MIGHT be excused for thinking that the earliest locked-room anthology was Leslie Charteris's 1945 paperback, *The Saint's Choice of Impossible Crime.* However, track this elusive volume down, as I did, and you will discover that the contents are science fiction—and very good examples, it has to be said—and for impossible read incapable of rational solution.

The world had to wait another twenty-three years for the first impossible-crime anthology, but it was well worth waiting for. *The Locked Room Reader* (1968) ran to an impressive 464 pages (still the second largest page count), contained a mouth-watering selection of stories—including a complete Henry Kane novel and a previously unpublished Anthony Boucher short—and was edited by one of the most perceptive and knowledgeable of editors, Hans Stefan Santesson, most of whose dozen anthologies covered science fiction or fantasy. For the later paperback reprinting, this weighty tome was split into two: *8 Doors to Death* and *8 Keys to Murder.*

Surprisingly, another thirteen years passed before the next offering, Edward D. Hoch's *All But Impossible!* (1981). Ed is perhaps uniquely qualified to edit such a collection in view of his own voluminous writings, many of which—even back in 1981—have featured impossible crime. It shows to good effect in Ed's anthology with another excellent menu and a typically fascinating Hoch introduction in which is revealed the result of a poll of locked-room favourites by seventeen enthusiasts not unacquainted with bizarre stories.

The following year, 1982, brought *Tantalizing Locked Room Mysteries,* jointly edited by Isaac Asimov, Charles G. Waugh, and Martin Harry Greenberg. Again a commendable level of little-known tales, some real gems (take Jack Wodham's "Big Time Operator," originally published in a science-fiction magazine), and an introduction in which Asimov reveals the name of his favourite mystery writer.

In 1986 came *Locked Room Puzzles,* Volume 3 in a well-planned series of paperback novella collections. Inevitably the shortest of the anthologies under consideration, it should not be overlooked, and its eclectic contents speak well for the scholarship of editors Greenberg and Bill Pronzini.

Nineteen eighty-seven saw the publication of what is so far the fattest impossible-crime anthology. *Death Locked In* was edited by

Douglas Greene and me, with a work ratio of something like nine to one in Doug's favour. Doug, who also wrote the introduction, has in the last decade achieved wide recognition as an eminent scholar on many aspects of mystery fiction and on John Dickson Carr in particular. He went to great pains to produce a balanced collection with plenty of variety both in the authors and the types of problems solved. The 553 pages covered a massive time span—Le Fanu in 1838 to Pronzini in 1979—with many early stories by half-forgotten names and more than the odd surprise in the authors' roster.

To 1990 and the last, to date, of the anthologies. *The Art of the Impossible* (or *Murder Impossible,* to which the U.S. publisher perversely insisted it should be changed) was a collaborative effort between Jack Adrian and me. Jack is someone who, for his comparatively tender years, knows far more about popular fiction than he has a right to know. Our combined knowledge produced a volume in which familiar stories were far outweighed by the unfamiliar, and the discriminating reader could expect, we hoped, to be deceived and delighted more than occasionally.

To complete the picture, a mention of two other anthologies, not devoted to impossible crime as such but with definite leanings in that direction: Otto Penzler's *Whodunit? Houdini?* (1976), "Thirteen tales of magic, murder, mystery," and the less well-known yet equally worthwhile *Sleight of Crime* (1977), "Fifteen classic tales of murder, mayhem and magic," edited by Cedric E. Clute, Jr., and Nicholas Lewin. Seek them out. They will repay you.

The Locked Room Reader, edited by Hans Stefan Santesson (U.S.: Random, 1968)

Introduction
"The Locked Room" by John Dickson Carr
"The Dauphin's Doll" by Ellery Queen
"Nothing Is Impossible" by Clayton Rawson
"His Heart Could Break" by Craig Rice
"The Oracle of the Dog" by G. K. Chesterton
"When a Felon Needs a Friend" by Morris Hershman
"The Doomdorf Mystery" by Melville Davisson Post
"The Big Bow Mystery" by Israel Zangwill
"The Man Who Read John Dickson Carr" by William Brittain
"The Long Way Down" by Edward D. Hoch

"Time Trammel" by Miriam Allen deFord
"Reprieve" by Lawrence G. Blochman
"The Smoke-Filled Locked Room" by Anthony Boucher
"Bones for Davy Jones" by Joseph Commings
"The Fine Italian Hand" by Thomas Flanagan
"The Narrowing Lust" by Henry Kane

8 Keys to Murder: Tales front The Locked Room Reader (U.S.: Dell, *1970)*
Introduction
"The Locked Room" by John Dickson Carr
"The Dauphin's Doll" by Ellery Queen
"Nothing Is Impossible" by Clayton Rawson
"His Heart Could Break" by Craig Rice
"The Oracle of the Dog" by G. K. Chesterton
"When a Felon Needs a Friend" by Morris Hershman
"The Doomdorf Mystery" by Melville Davisson Post
"The Big Bow Mystery" by Israel Zangwill

8 Doors to Death: More Tales from The Locked Room Reader (U.S.: *Dell, 1970)*
Introduction
"The Man Who Read John Dickson Carr" by William Brittain
"The Long Way Down" by Edward D. Hoch
"Time Trammel" by Miriam Allen deFord
"Reprieve" by Lawrence G. Blochman
"The Smoke-Filled Locked Room" by Anthony Boucher
"Bones for Davy Jones" by Joseph Commings
"The Fine Italian Hand" by Thomas Flanagan
"The Narrowing Lust" by Henry Kane

Tantalizing Locked Room Murders, edited by Isaac Asimov, Charles G. Waugh, and Martin Harry Greenberg (U.S.: Walker, 1982)
Introduction: "No One Done It" by Isaac Asimov
"The Murders in the Rue Morgue" by Edgar Allan Poe
"The Adventure of the Speckled Band" by Arthur Conan Doyle
"The Problem of Cell 13" by Jacques Futrelle
"The Light at Three O'Clock" by MacKinlay Kantor
"The Exact Opposite" by Erie Stanley Gardner

"The Blind Spot" by Barry Perowne
"The 51st Sealed Room" by Robert Arthur
"The Bird House" by William March
"Big lime Operator" by Jack Wodhams
"The Leopold Locked Room" by Edward D. Hoch
"Vanishing Act" by Bill Pronzini and Michael Kurland

All But Impossible! edited by Edward D. Hoch (U.S.: Ticknor, 1981)
Introduction
"The Shadow of the Goat" by John Dickson Carr
"The Little House at Croix-Rousse" by Georges Simenon
"The Problem of the Emperor's Mushrooms" by James Yaffe
"From Another World" by Clayton Rawson
"Through a Glass, Darkly" by Helen McCloy
"Snowball in July" by Ellery Queen
"The Newtonian Egg" by Peter Godfrey
"The Triple-Lock'd Room" by Lillian de la Torre
"The Brazen Locked Room" by Isaac Asimov
"The Martian Crown Jewels" by Poul Anderson
"The Day the Children Vanished" by Hugh Pentecost
"As If by Magic" by Julian Symons
"The Impossible Theft" by John F. Suter
"Mr. Strang Takes a Field Trip" by William Brittain
"No One Likes to be Played for a Sucker" by Michael Collins
"The Arrowmont Prison Riddle" by Bill Pronzini
"Box in a Box" by Jack Ritchie
"The Number 12 Jinx" by Jon L. Breen
"The Magician's Wife" by J. F. Peirce
"The Problem of the Covered Bridge" by Edward D. Hoch

Locked Room Puzzles, edited by Martin H. Greenberg and Bill Pronzini (U.S.: Academy, 1986)
"The Third Bullet" by John Dickson Carr
"Booktaker" by Bill Pronzini
"From Another World" by Clayton Rawson
"Day of the Wizard" by Edward D. Hoch

Death Locked In, edited by Douglas G. Greene and Robert C. S. Adey (U.S.: IPL, 1987)

Introduction
"The First Locked Room" by Lillian de la Torre
"Passage in the Secret History of an Irish Countess" by Joseph Sheridan Le Fanu
"I Can Find My Way Out" by Ngaio Marsh
"The Suicide of Kiaros" by L. Frank Baum
"The Spherical Ghoul" by Fredric Brown
"Out of His Head" by Thomas Bailey Aldrich
"Murder by Proxy" by M. McDonnell Bodkin
"Out of This World" by Peter Godfrey
"The Mystery of the Hotel de L'Orme" by M.M.B.
"The Magic Bullet" by Edward D. Hoch
"A Terribly Strange Bed" by Wilkie Collins
"The Room with Something Wrong" by Cornell Woolrich
"Invisible Hands" by John Dickson Carr
"The X Street Murders" by Joseph Commings
"The Mystery of Room No. 11" by Nicholas Carter
"The Man Who Disappeared" by L. T. Meade and Robert Eustace
"The Invisible Man" by G. K. Chesterton
"The Adventure of the Man Who Could Double the Size of Diamonds" by Ellery Queen
"The Mystery of the Lost Special" by A. Conan Doyle
"Off the Face of the Earth" by Clayton Rawson
"The Grinning God" by May Futrelle
"The House That Was" by Jacques Futrelle
"Thin Air" by Bill Pronzini
"Elsewhen" by Anthony Boucher

The Art of the Impossible, edited by Jack Adrian and Robert Adey (U.K.: Xanadu, 1990; as *Murder Impossible* U.S.: Carroll, 1990)
Introduction
"The House in Goblin Wood" by John Dickson Carr
"The Other Side" by Hake Talbot
"The Courtyard of the Fly" by Vincent Cornier
"Coffee Break" by Arthur Porges
"Bullion!" by W. Hope Hodgson
"Proof of Guilt" by Bill Pronzini
"An Absence of Air" by Jacques Futrelle
"The Impossible Theft" by John F. Suter

"It's a Dog's Life" by John Lutz
"The Death of Cyrus Pettigrew" by Sax Rohmer
"Ghost in the Gallery" by Joseph Commings
"The Missing Romney" by Edgar Wallace
"The House of Screams" by Gerald Findler
"The Impossible Murder" by Edward D. Hoch
"A Nineteenth Century Debacle" by George Locke
"A Razor in Fleet Street" by John Dickson Carr
"Dinner at Garibaldi's" by Leonard Pruyn
"The Hanging Rope" by Joel Townsley Rogers
"Now You See Her" by Jeffrey Wallmann
"The Blind Spot" by Barry Perowne
"Chapter the Last: Merriman Explains" by Alex Atkinson

Foreign-Language Books

THIS BIBLIOGRAPHY deals almost entirely with books written in, or translated into, the English language. There are, however, many more novels and short stories of impossible crime that were published in other languages and that have never been translated into English. My own knowledge of the subject is regrettably sketchy, and my ability to translate is restricted to schoolboy French. That I am able to offer a greatly enlarged French listing in this section is entirely due to the help and encouragement of the French scholar and enthusiast Roland Lacourbe, who together with his wife, Danièle, has shown remarkable patience and fortitude in answering my questions.

The list of items not translated into English now reads as follows:

Finland

Mika Waltari: *Kuka Murhasi Rouva Skrofin?* (1939) (Who Murdered Madame Skrof?). Issued in France in 1939 as *Qui a Tué Madame Skrof?*

France

Bill Blondy: *Chambres Closes* (1955) (Locked Rooms)

Pierre Boileau: *La Pierre Qui Tremble* (1934) (The Rock That Trembled)

Le Repos de Bacchus (1938) (The Sleep of Bacchus)

Six Crimes Sans Assassin (1939) (Six Murders and No Murderer). It should be noted that this book was advertised in 1949 by Sampson Low among its "recent and forthcoming detective stories." However, the publishers themselves disappeared about that time and all efforts to trace a proof—if such a stage had been reached—or a draft of the translation, or the translator, one Eric Sutton, have proved entirely unrewarding.

L'Assassin Vient les Mains Vides (1945) (The Murderer Comes with Empty Hands). Published only as a serial in the newspaper *France-Soir*.

Noré Brunei: *Le Crime Impossible* (1945) (The Impossible Crime)

Eugène Chavette: *La Chambre du Crime* (1875) (The Room of the Crime)

Antoine Chollier: *Dossier No.* 7 (1946) (File No. 7)

Stéphan Corbière: *La Plaie en Triangle* (1930) (The Triangular Wound)

Maurice-Bernard Endrebe: *La Vielle Dame Sans Merci* (1952) (The Old Woman Without Mercy)

Elvire a La Tour Monte (1956) (Elvire Climbs the Tower)

Mona Gloria: *L'Enigme de la Chambre Close* (1938) (The Puzzle of the Locked Room)

Paul Halter: *La Quatrième Porte* (1987) (The Fourth Door)

Le Brouillard Rouge (1988) (The Red Mist)

La Mort Vous Invite (1988) (Death Invites You)

La Mort Derrière les Rideaux (1989) (Death Behind the Curtain)

La Chambre du Fou (1990) (Madman's Room)

La Tète du Tigre{\99\) (The Head of the Tiger)

Michel Herbert and Eugène Wyl:

La Maison Interdite (1932) (The Confused House)

Le Crime Derrière la Porte (1934) (The Crime Behind the Door)

L'Homme Qui Disparut (1937) (The Man Who Vanished)

Marcel F. Lanteaume: *La Treizième Balle* (1942) (The Thirteenth Bullet)

Orage sur la Grande Semaine (1944) (Storm on the Big Weekend)

Trompe L'Oeil (1945)

Paul Mystère: *Terreur sur le Manoir* (1945) (Terror at the Manor)

Thomas Narcejac: *La Mort Est du Voyage* (1948) (Death Is on Board)

Fernand Peyre: *La Chambre 27* (Room 27)

René Réouven: *Les Humeurs Fatales* (1968) (The Deadly Humours)

Pierre Salva: *Des Clients pour L'Enfer* (1979) (Some Customers for Hell)

Jean-Toussaint Samat: *L'Horrible Mort de Miss Gildchrist* (1932) (The Horrible Death of Miss Gildchrist)

Roch de Santa-Maria: *Pendu Trop Court* (1942) (Hung by Too Little)

Armand Silvestre: "Le Verrou" (The Bolt). A short story in a volume or magazine yet to be traced.

Stanislas-André Steeman: *L'Infaillable Silas Lord* (1936) (The Infallible Silas Lord)

Louis True: *Cadavre en Premiere Classe* (1949) (First Class Corpse)

Pierre Very: *Les Quatre Vipères* (1940) (The Four Vipers)

Noel Vindry: *La Maison Qui Tue* (1932) (The House That Killed)

Le Piège aux Diamants (1933) (The Diamond Trap)

Le Fantome de Midi (1934) (The Phantom at Twelve O'Clock)

La Bète Hurlante (1934) (The Howling Beast)

Le Collier de Sang (1934) (The Necklace of Blood)

Le Cri des Mouettes (1934) (The Seagulls' Cry)
Le Double Alibi (1934) (Double Alibi)
Masques Noirs (1935) (Black Masks)
A Travers les Murailles (1937) (Across the Ramparts)
Les Verres Noirs (1938) (The Black Glasses)

Roland Lacourbe is also responsible for a series of fine, meaty impossible-crime anthologies that have been published in recent years:

Les Meilleures Histoires de Chambres Closes (Minerve, 1985) (The Best Locked Room Stories)
Vingt Mystères de Chambres Closes (Terrain Vague Losfeld, 1988, with a preface by Claude Chabrol) (20 Locked Room Mysteries)
Le Magiciens du Crime (Minerve, 1990) (The Magicians of Crime)
And, coming soon—
Les Detectives de L'Impossible (scheduled for 1991) (The Detectives of the Impossible)
Chambres Rouges (scheduled for 1992) (Red Rooms)

Even more exciting, 1991 should at last see the publication of Roland's superb critical work:

99 Chambres Closes + 33 Autres Curiosités (99 Locked Rooms and 33 Other Curiosities)

in which he describes and reviews those books, other than by Carr, which he has found particularly rewarding. British and American publishers should note the fact that many of these books have never been translated into English.

And if Carr is missing, quite deliberately, from *99 Locked Rooms,* M. Lacourbe more than makes amends by beginning this year on a publishing project of vital importance to French-speaking mystery fans: the whole of the maestro's work, much of it for the first time in French, in a long series of volumes.

Germany

"Sir John Retcliffe": *Nena Sahib* (1858)

Sweden

Jean Bolinder: *Hogsta Ratt* (1970) (Supreme Justice)
Och Sedan Nar Oksa Du Ar Dod (1971) (And Later, When You Are Dead)

Ulf Durling: *Gamal Ost* (1971). Translated into French as "Pour un Bout de Fromage" (1973) (For a Bit of Cheese)

Jan Ekstrom: *Alkistan* (1967) (The Eel Cage)

Elddansen (1970) (The Fire Dance)

"Dnr 94,028.72—Mord" (Diary-Number 94,028.72—Murder). A short story that can be found in *Upp I Rok* (1973) (Into Thin Air), an anthology of considerable merit, edited by Jan Broberg. The same editor has an earlier volume to his credit, *Mord i Slutna Rum* (1967) (Murder in Locked Rooms), and a more recent one (Nothing Is Impossible) scheduled for publication in 1984.

Robert C.S. Adey

Whether as Robert, Robert C.S., or just plain Bob, Robert Adey was an active mystery fan for many years and was recognized for his outstanding contributions to the field by being designated Fan Guest of Honor at the 1990 World Mystery Convention in London, England. In addition to collecting and commenting on locked-room stories and novels, Adey co-edited of two anthologies dedicated to impossible crimes: *Death Locked In* with Douglas G. Greene (International Polygonics, 1987) and *Murder Impossible* (Carroll & Graf, 1991) with Jack Adrian.

Brian Skupin

Brian Skupin is Consulting Editor for Locked Room International, and co-publisher of Mystery Scene Magazine, for which he has won the Mystery Writers of America Ellery Queen Award, the Poirot Award from Malice Domestic, and the Anthony award from Bouchercon.

Lightning Source UK Ltd.
Milton Keynes UK
UKHW011818061218
333594UK00019B/951/P

9 781720 746508